THE COMPLETE SHORT STORIES OF
DE MAUPASSANT

SHORT STORIES OF DE MAUPASSANT

Including *The Necklace, A Passion, The Piece of String, Babette,* and *The Wedding Night.*

THE BOOK LEAGUE OF AMERICA

New York

1941
BLUE RIBBON BOOKS
14 WEST 49TH STREET, NEW YORK, N. Y.

CL
PRINTED IN THE UNITED STATES OF AMERICA

CONTENTS

	PAGE
BALL-OF-FAT	1
THE NECKLACE	27
THE PIECE OF STRING	34
THE STORY OF A FARM GIRL	38
IN THE MOONLIGHT	51
MADAME TELLIER'S EXCURSION	54
LOVE	71
MADEMOISELLE FIFI	75
MONSIEUR PARENT	83
USELESS BEAUTY	108
AN AFFAIR OF STATE	120
BABETTE	127
A COCK CROWED	131
LILIE LALA	134
A VAGABOND	138
THE MOUNTEBANKS	146
UGLY	149
THE DEBT	151
A NORMANDY JOKE	155
THE FATHER	158
THE ARTIST	164
FALSE ALARM	167
THAT PIG OF A MORIN	171
MISS HARRIET	179
THE HOLE	193
THE INN	198
A FAMILY	206
BELLFLOWER	210
IN THE WOOD	213
THE MARQUIS DE FUMEROL	217
SAVED	222
THE SIGNAL	226
THE DEVIL	230

CONTENTS

	PAGE
THE VENUS OF BRANIZA	235
THE RABBIT	237
LA MORILLONNE	242
EPIPHANY	245
SIMON'S PAPA	253
WAITER, A BOCK!	259
THE SEQUEL TO A DIVORCE	264
THE CLOWN	268
THE MAD WOMAN	271
MADEMOISELLE	273
A BAD ERROR	276
THE PORT	280
CHÂLI	287
JEROBOAM	294
VIRTUE IN THE BALLET	297
THE DOUBLE PINS	300
HOW HE GOT THE LEGION OF HONOR	304
A CRISIS	308
GRAVEYARD SIRENS	313
GROWING OLD	318
A FRENCH ENOCH ARDEN	321
JULIE ROMAIN	325
AN UNREASONABLE WOMAN	331
ROSALIE PRUDENT	334
HIPPOLYTE'S CLAIM	337
BENOIST	340
FECUNDITY	344
A WAY TO WEALTH	350
AM I INSANE?	354
FORBIDDEN FRUIT	356
THE CHARM DISPELLED	361
MADAME PARISSE	364
MAKING A CONVERT	369
A LITTLE WALK	374
A WIFE'S CONFESSION	378
A DEAD WOMAN'S SECRET	381
LOVE'S AWAKENING	384

CONTENTS

	PAGE
BED No. 29	388
MARROCA	396
A PHILOSOPHER	402
A MISTAKE	406
FLORENTINE	410
CONSIDERATION	414
WOMAN'S WILES	418
MOONLIGHT	422
DOUBTFUL HAPPINESS	425
HUMILIATION	429
THE WEDDING NIGHT	433
THE NONCOMMISSIONED OFFICER	438
IN THE COURTROOM	443
A PECULIAR CASE	446
A PRACTICAL JOKE	450
A STRANGE FANCY	453
AFTER DEATH	457
ON CATS	462
ROOM No. 11	466
ONE PHASE OF LOVE	470
GOOD REASONS	475
A FAIR EXCHANGE	478
THE TOBACCO SHOP	484
A POOR GIRL	489
THE SUBSTITUTE	493
A PASSION	496

BALL-OF-FAT

For many days now the fag end of the army had been straggling through the town. They were not troops but a disbanded horde. The beards of the men were long and filthy, their uniforms in tatters, and they advanced at an easy pace without flag or regiment. All seemed worn out and back broken, incapable of a thought or a resolution, marching by habit solely and falling from fatigue as soon as they stopped. In short, they were a mobilized, pacific people, bending under the weight of the gun; some little squads on the alert, easy to take alarm and prompt in enthusiasm, ready to attack or to flee; and in the midst of them some red breeches, the remains of a division broken up in a great battle; some somber artillerymen in line with these varied kinds of foot soldiers, and sometimes the brilliant helmet of a dragoon on foot who followed with difficulty the shortest march of the lines.

Some legions of free shooters, under the heroic names of Avengers of the Defeat, Citizens of the Tomb, Partakers of Death, passed in their turn with the air of bandits.

Their leaders were former cloth or grain merchants, ex-merchants in tallow or soap, warriors of circumstance, elected officers on account of their escutcheons and the length of their mustaches, covered with arms and with braid, speaking in constrained voices, discussing plans of campaign and pretending to carry agonized France alone on their swaggering shoulders but sometimes fearing their own soldiers, prison birds, that were often brave at first and later proved to be plunderers and debauchees.

It was said that the Prussians were going to enter Rouen.

The National Guard who for two months had been carefully reconnoitering in the neighboring woods, shooting sometimes their own sentinels and ready for a combat whenever a little wolf stirred in the thicket, had now returned to their firesides. Their arms, their uniforms, all the murderous accouterments with which they had lately struck fear into the national heart for three leagues in every direction, had suddenly disappeared.

The last French soldiers finally came across the Seine to reach the Audemer bridge through Saint-Sever and Bourg-Achard; and marching behind, on foot, between two officers of ordnance, the general, in despair, unable to do anything with these incongruous tatters, himself lost in the breaking up of a people accustomed to conquer, and disastrously beaten in spite of his legendary bravery.

A profound calm, a frightful, silent expectancy had spread over the city. Many of the heavy citizens, emasculated by commerce, anxiously awaited the conquerors, trembling lest their roasting spits or kitchen knives be considered arms.

All life seemed stopped; shops were closed, the streets dumb. Sometimes an inhabitant, intimated by this silence, moved rapidly along next the walls. The agony of waiting made them wish the enemy would come.

In the afternoon of the day which followed the departure of the French troops some uhlans, coming from one knows not where, crossed the town with celerity. Then a little later a black mass descended the side of St Catherine, while two other invading bands appeared by the way of Darnetal and Bois-Guillaume. The advance guard of the three bodies joined one another at the same moment in Hôtel de Ville square, and by all the neighboring streets the German army continued to arrive, spreading out its battalions, making the pavement resound under their hard, rhythmic step.

Some orders of the commander, in a foreign, guttural voice, reached the houses which seemed dead and deserted, while behind closed shutters eyes were watching these victorious men, masters of the city, of fortunes, of lives, through the "rights of war." The inhabitants, shut up in their rooms, were visited with the kind of excitement that a cataclysm or some fatal upheaval of the earth brings to us, against which all force is useless. For the same sensation is produced each time that the established order of things is overturned, when security no longer exists and all that protect the laws of man and of nature find themselves at the mercy of unreasoning, ferocious brutality. The trembling of the earth crushing the houses and burying an entire people; a river overflowing its banks and carrying in its course the drowned peasants, carcasses of beeves and girders snatched from roofs, or a glorious army massacring those trying to defend themselves, leading other prisoners, pillaging in the name of the sword and thanking God to the sound of the cannon; all are alike frightful scourges which disconnect all belief in eternal justice, all the confidence that we have in the protection of Heaven and the reason of man.

Some detachments rapped at each door, then disappeared into the houses. It was occupation after invasion. Then the duty commences for the conquered to show themselves gracious toward the conquerors.

After some time, as soon as the first terror disappears, a new calm is established. In many families the Prussian officer eats at the table. He is sometimes well bred and, through politeness, pities France and speaks of his repugnance in taking part in this affair. One is grateful to him for this sentiment; then, one may be, someday or other, in need of his protection. By treating him well one has, perhaps, a less number of men to feed. And why should we wound anyone on whom we are entirely dependent? To act thus would be less bravery than temerity. And temerity is no longer a fault of the commoner of Rouen as it was at the time of the heroic defense when their city became famous. Finally each told himself that the highest judgment of French urbanity required that they be allowed to be polite to the strange soldier in the house, provided they did not show themselves familiar with him in public. Outside they would not make themselves known to each other, but at home they could chat freely, and the German might remain longer each evening warming his feet at their hearthstones.

The town even took on, little by little, its ordinary aspect. The French scarcely went out, but the Prussian soldiers grumbled in the streets. In short, the officers of the Blue Hussars, who dragged with arrogance their great weapons of death up and down the pavement, seemed to have no more grievous scorn for the simple citizens than the officers or the sportsmen who, the year before, drank in the same cafés.

There was, nevertheless, something in the air, something subtle and unknown, a strange, intolerable atmosphere like a penetrating odor, the odor of invasion. It filled the dwellings and the public places, changed the taste of the food, gave the impression of being on a journey, far away among barbarous and dangerous tribes.

The conquerors exacted money, much money. The inhabitants always paid and they were rich enough to do it. But the richer a trading Norman becomes the more he suffers at every outlay, at each part of his fortune that he sees pass from his hands into those of another.

Therefore, two or three leagues below the town, following the course of the river toward Croisset, Dieppedalle or Biessard, mariners and fishermen often picked up the swollen corpse of a German in uniform from the bottom of the river, killed by the blow of a knife, the head crushed with a stone, or perhaps thrown into the water by a push from the high bridge. The slime of the river bed buried these obscure vengeances, savage but legitimate, unknown heroisms, mute attacks more perilous than the battles of broad day and without the echoing sound of glory.

For hatred of the foreigner always arouses some intrepid ones who are ready to die for an idea.

Finally, as soon as the invaders had brought the town quite under subjection with their inflexible discipline, without having been guilty of any of the horrors for which they were famous along their triumphal line of march, people began to take courage, and the need of trade put new heart into the commerce of the country. Some had large interests at Havre, which the French army occupied, and they wished to try and reach this port by going to Dieppe by land and there embarking.

They used their influence with the German soldiers with whom they had an acquaintance, and finally an authorization of departure was obtained from the general in chief.

Then, a large diligence with four horses having been engaged for this journey, and ten persons having engaged seats in it, it was resolved to set out on Tuesday morning before daylight, in order to escape observation.

For some time before, the frost had been hardening the earth, and on Monday, toward three o'clock, great black clouds coming from the north brought the snow which fell without interruption during the evening and all night.

At half-past four in the morning the travelers met in the courtyard of Hôtel Normandie, where they were to take the carriage.

They were still full of sleep and shivering with cold under their wraps.

They could only see each other dimly in the obscure light, and the accumulation of heavy winter garments made them all resemble fat curates in long cassocks. Only two of the men were acquainted; a third accosted them and they chatted: "I'm going to take my wife," said one. "I too," said another. "And I," said the third. The first added: "We shall not return to Rouen, and if the Prussians approach Havre, we shall go over to England." All had the same projects, being of the same mind.

As yet the horses were not harnessed. A little lantern, carried by a stable-boy, went out one door from time to time, to immediately appear at another. The feet of the horses striking the floor could be heard, although deadened by the straw and litter, and the voice of a man talking to the beasts, sometimes swearing, came from the end of the building. A light tinkling of bells announced that they were taking down the harness; this murmur soon became a clear and continuous rhythm by the movement of the animal, stopping sometimes, then breaking into a brusque shake which was accompanied by the dull stamp of a sabot upon the hard earth.

The door suddenly closed. All noise ceased. The frozen citizens were silent; they remained immovable and stiff.

A curtain of uninterrupted white flakes constantly sparkled in its descent to the ground. It effaced forms and powdered everything with a downy moss. And nothing could be heard in the great silence. The town was calm and buried under the wintry frost as this fall of snow, unnamable and floating, a sensation rather than a sound (trembling atoms which only seem to fill all space), came to cover the earth.

The man reappeared with his lantern, pulling at the end of a rope a sad horse which would not come willingly. He placed him against the pole, fastened the traces, walked about a long time adjusting the harness, for he had the use of but one hand, the other carrying the lantern. As he went for the second horse he noticed the travelers, motionless, already white with snow, and said to them: "Why not get into the carriage? You will be under cover at least."

They had evidently not thought of it, and they hastened to do so. The three men installed their wives at the back and then followed them. Then the other forms, undecided and veiled, took in their turn the last places without exchanging a word.

The floor was covered with straw, in which the feet ensconced themselves. The ladies at the back having brought little copper foot stoves, with a carbon fire, lighted them and for some time, in low voices, enumerated the advantages of the appliances, repeating things that they had known for a long time.

Finally the carriage was harnessed with six horses instead of four, because the traveling was very bad, and a voice called out:

"Is everybody aboard?"

And a voice within answered: "Yes."

They were off. The carriage moved slowly, slowly for a little way. The wheels were imbedded in the snow; the whole body groaned with heavy cracking sounds; the horses glistened, puffed and smoked; and the great whip of the driver snapped without ceasing, hovering about on all sides, knotting and unrolling itself like a thin serpent, lashing brusquely some horse on the rebound, which then put forth its most violent effort.

Now the day was imperceptibly dawning. The light flakes, which one of the travelers, a Rouenese by birth, said looked like a shower of cotton, no longer fell. A faint light filtered through the great dull clouds, which rendered more brilliant the white of the fields, where appeared a line of great trees clothed in whiteness or a chimney with a cap of snow.

In the carriage each looked at the others curiously in the sad light of this dawn.

At the back, in the best places, M. Loiseau, wholesale merchant of wine, of Grand-Pont Street, and Mme Loiseau were sleeping opposite each other. Loiseau had bought out his former patron, who failed in business, and made his fortune. He sold bad wine at a good price to small retailers in the country and passed among his friends and acquaintances as a knavish wag, a true Norman full of deceit and joviality.

His reputation as a sharper was so well established that one evening at the residence of the prefect, M. Tournel, author of some fables and songs, of keen, satirical mind, a local celebrity, having proposed to some ladies, who seemed to be getting a little sleepy, that they make up a game of "Loiseau tricks," the joke traversed the rooms of the prefect, reached those of the town and then, in the months to come, made many a face in the province expand with laughter.

Loiseau was especially known for his love of farce of every kind, for his jokes, good and bad; and no one could ever talk with him without thinking: "He is invaluable, this Loiseau." Of tall figure, his balloon-shaped front was surmounted by a ruddy face surrounded by gray whiskers.

His wife, large, strong and resolute, with a quick, decisive manner, was the order and arithmetic of this house of commerce, while he was the life of it through his joyous activity.

Beside them M. Carré-Lamadon held himself with great dignity, as if belonging to a superior caste; a considerable man in cottons, proprietor of three mills, officer of the Legion of Honor and member of the General Council. He had remained, during the Empire, chief of the friendly opposition, famous for making the emperor pay more dear for rallying to the cause than if he had combated it with blunted arms, according to his own story. Mme Carré-Lamadon, much younger than her husband, was the consolation of officers of good family sent to Rouen in garrison. She sat opposite her husband, very dainty, petite and pretty, wrapped closely in furs and looking with sad eyes at the interior of the carriage.

Her neighbors, the Count and Countess Hubert de Breville, bore the name of one of the most ancient and noble families of Normandy. The count, an old gentleman of good figure, accentuated by the artifices of his toilette his resemblance to King Henry IV, who, following a glorious legend of the family, had impregnated one of the De Breville ladies, whose husband, for this reason, was made a count and governor of the province.

A colleague of M. Carré-Lamadon in the General Council, Count Hubert represented the Orléans party in the department.

The story of his marriage with the daughter of a little captain of a privateer had always remained a mystery. But as the countess had a grand air, received better than anyone and passed for having been loved by the son of Louis Philippe, all the nobility did her honor, and her salon remained the first in the country, the only one which preserved the old gallantry and to which the entree was difficult. The fortune of the Brevilles amounted, it was said, to five hundred thousand francs in income, all in good securities.

These six persons formed the foundation of the carriage company, the society side, serene and strong, honest, established people, who had both religion and principles.

By a strange chance all the women were upon the same seat, and the countess had for neighbors two sisters who picked at long strings of beads and muttered some "Paters" and "Aves." One was old and as pitted with smallpox as if she had received a broadside of grapeshot full in the face. The other, very sad, had a pretty face and a disease of the lungs, which, added to their devoted faith, illumined them and made them appear like martyrs.

Opposite these two devotees were a man and a woman who attracted the notice of all. The man, well known, was Cornudet the democrat, the terror of respectable people. For twenty years he had soaked his great red beard in the bocks of all the democratic cafés. He had consumed with his friends and confreres a rather pretty fortune left him by his father, an old confectioner, and he awaited the establishing of the Republic with impatience, that he might have the position he merited by his great expenditures. On the fourth of September, by some joke perhaps, he believed himself elected prefect, but when he went to assume the duties the clerks of the office were masters of the place and refused to recognize him, obliging him to retreat. Rather a good bachelor on the whole, inoffensive and serviceable, he had busied himself, with incomparable ardor, in organizing the defense against the Prussians. He had dug holes in all the plains, cut down young trees from the neighboring forests, sown snares over all routes and, at the approach of the enemy, took himself quickly back to the town. He now thought he could be of more use in Havre, where more entrenchments would be necessary.

The woman, one of those called a coquette, was celebrated for her *embonpoint*, which had given her the nick-name of "Ball-of-Fat." Small, round and fat as lard, with puffy fingers choked at the phalanges like chaplets of short sausages, with a stretched and shining skin, an enormous bosom which shook under her dress, she was, nevertheless, pleasing and sought after on account of a certain freshness and breeziness of disposition. Her face was a round apple, a peony bud ready to pop into bloom, and inside that opened two great black eyes shaded with thick brows that cast a shadow within; and below, a charming mouth, humid for kissing, furnished with shining, microscopic baby teeth. She was, it was said, full of admirable qualities.

As soon as she was recognized a whisper went around among the honest women, and the words "prostitute" and "public shame" were whispered so loud that she raised her head. Then she threw at her neighbors such a provoking, courageous look that a great silence reigned, and everybody looked down except Loiseau, who watched her with an exhilarated air.

And immediately conversation began among the three ladies, whom the presence of this girl had suddenly rendered friendly, almost intimate. It seemed to them they should bring their married dignity into union in opposition to that sold without shame; for legal love always takes on a tone of contempt for its free confrere.

The three men, also drawn together by an instinct of preservation at the sight of Cornudet, talked money with a certain high tone of disdain for the poor. Count Hubert talked of the havoc which the Prussians had caused, the losses which resulted from being robbed of cattle and from destroyed crops, with the assurance of a great lord, ten times millionaire, whom these ravages would scarcely cramp for a year. M. Carré-Lamadon, largely experienced in the cotton industry, had had need of sending six hundred thousand francs to England, as a trifle in reserve if it should be needed. As for Loiseau, he had arranged with the French administration to sell them all the wines that remained in his cellars, on account of which the State owed him a formidable sum which he counted on collecting at Havre.

And all three threw toward each other swift and amicable glances.

Although in different conditions, they felt themselves to be brothers through money, that grand freemasonry of those who possess it and make the gold rattle by putting their hands in their trousers' pockets.

The carriage went so slowly that at ten o'clock in the morning they had not gone four leagues. The men had got down three times to climb hills on foot. They began to be disturbed because they should be now taking breakfast at Tôtes, and they despaired now of reaching there before night. Each one had begun to watch for an inn along the route, when the carriage foundered in a snowdrift and it took two hours to extricate it.

Growing appetites troubled their minds; and no eating house, no wine-shop showed itself, the approach of the Prussians and the passage of the troops having frightened away all these industries.

The gentlemen ran to the farms along the way for provisions, but they did not even find bread, for the defiant peasant had concealed his stores for fear of being pillaged by the soldiers who, having nothing to put between their teeth, took by force whatever they discovered.

Toward one o'clock in the afternoon Loiseau announced that there was a decided hollow in his stomach. Everybody suffered with him, and the violent need of eating, ever increasing, had killed conversation.

From time to time someone yawned; another immediately imitated him; and each, in his turn, in accordance with his character, his knowledge of life and his social position, opened his mouth with carelessness or modesty, placing his hand quickly before the yawning hole from whence issued a vapor.

Ball-of-Fat, after many attempts, bent down as if seeking something under her skirts. She hesitated a second, looked at her neighbors, then sat up again tranquilly. The faces were pale and drawn. Loiseau affirmed that he would give a thousand francs for a small ham. His wife made a gesture as if in protest, but she kept quiet. She was always troubled when anyone spoke of squandering money and could not comprehend any pleasantry on the subject. "The fact is," said the count, "I cannot understand why I did not think to bring some provisions with me." Each reproached himself in the same way.

However, Cornudet had a flask full of rum. He offered it; it was refused coldly. Loiseau alone accepted two swallows and then passed back the flask saying, by way of thanks: "It is good all the same; it is warming and checks the appetite." The alcohol put him in good humor, and he proposed that they do as they did on the little ship in the song, eat the fattest of the passengers. This indirect allusion to Ball-of-Fat choked the well-bred people. They said nothing. Cornudet alone laughed. The two good sisters had ceased to mumble their rosaries and, with their hands enfolded in their great sleeves, held themselves immovable, obstinately lowering their eyes, without doubt offering to Heaven the suffering it had brought upon them.

Finally at three o'clock, when they found themselves in the midst of an interminable plain, without a single village in sight, Ball-of-Fat, bending down quickly, drew from under the seat a large basket covered with a white napkin.

At first she brought out a little china plate and a silver cup, then a large dish in which there were two whole chickens, cut up and imbedded in their own jelly. And one could still see in the basket other good things, some *pâtés*, fruits and sweetmeats, provisions for three days if they should not see the kitchen of an inn. Four necks of bottles were seen among the packages of food. She took a wing of a chicken and began to eat it delicately with one of those biscuits called "Regence" in Normandy.

All looks were turned in her direction. Then the odor spread, enlarging the nostrils and making the mouth water, besides causing a painful contraction of the jaw behind the ears. The scorn of the women for this girl became ferocious, as if they had a desire to kill her and throw her out of the carriage into the snow, her silver cup, her basket, provisions and all.

But Loiseau with his eyes devoured the dish of chicken. He said: "Fortunately Madame had more precaution than we. There are some people who know how to think ahead always."

She turned toward him, saying: "If you would like some of it, sir? It is hard to go without breakfast so long."

He saluted her and replied: "Faith, I frankly cannot refuse; I can stand it no longer. Everything goes in time of war, does it not, madame?" And then, casting a comprehensive glance around, he added: "In moments like this, one can but be pleased to find people who are obliging."

He had a newspaper which he spread out on his knees that no spot might come to his pantaloons, and upon the point of a knife that he always carried in his pocket he took up a leg all glistening with jelly, put it between his teeth and masticated it with a satisfaction so evident that there ran through the carriage a great sigh of distress.

Then Ball-of-Fat, in a sweet and humble voice, proposed that the two sisters partake of her collation. They both accepted instantly and, without raising their eyes, began to eat very quickly, after stammering their thanks. Cornudet no longer refused the offers of his neighbor, and they formed with the sisters a sort of table, by spreading out some newspapers upon their knees.

The mouths opened and shut without ceasing; they masticated, swallowed, gulping ferociously. Loiseau in his corner was working hard and, in a low voice, was trying to induce his wife to follow his example. She resisted for a long time; then, when a drawn sensation ran through her body, she yielded. Her husband, rounding his phrase, asked their "charming companion" if he might be allowed to offer a little piece to Mme Loiseau.

She replied: "Why, yes, certainly, sir," with an amiable smile as she passed the dish.

An embarrassing thing confronted them when they opened the first bottle of Bordeaux: they had but one cup. Each passed it after having tasted. Cornudet alone, for politeness without doubt, placed his lips at the spot left humid by his fair neighbor.

Then, surrounded by people eating, suffocated by the odors of the food, the Count and Countess de Breville, as well as Mme and M. Carré-Lamadon, were suffering that odious torment which has preserved the name of Tantalus. Suddenly the young wife of the manufacturer gave forth such a sigh that all heads were turned in her direction; she was as white as the snow without; her eyes closed, her head drooped; she had lost consciousness. Her husband, much excited, implored the help of everybody. Each lost his head completely, until the elder of the two sisters, holding the head of the sufferer, slipped Ball-of-Fat's cup between her lips and forced her to swallow a few drops of wine. The pretty little lady revived, opened her eyes, smiled and declared in a dying voice that she felt very well now. But, in order that the attack might not return, the sister urged her to drink a full glass of Bordeaux and added: "It is just hunger, nothing more."

Then Ball-of-Fat, blushing and embarrassed, looked at the four travelers who had fasted and stammered: "Goodness knows! if I dared to offer anything to these gentlemen and ladies, I would——" Then she was silent, as if fearing an insult. Loiseau took up the word: "Ah! certainly in times like these all the world are brothers and ought to aid each other. Come, ladies, without ceremony; why the devil not accept? We do not know whether we shall even find a house where we can pass the night. At the pace we are going now, we shall not reach Tôtes before noon tomorrow."

They still hesitated, no one daring to assume the responsibility of a "Yes." The count decided the question. He turned toward the fat, intimidated girl and, taking on a grand air of condescension, he said to her:

"We accept with gratitude, madame."

It is the first step that counts. The Rubicon passed, one lends himself to the occasion squarely. The basket was stripped. It still contained a *pâté de foie gras*, a *pâté* of larks, a piece of smoked tongue, some preserved pears, a loaf of hard bread, some wafers and a full cup of pickled gherkins and onions, of which crudities Ball-of-Fat, like all women, was extremely fond.

They could not eat this girl's provisions without speaking to her. And so they chatted, with reserve at first; then, as she carried herself well, with more abandon. The ladies De Breville and Carré-Lamadon, who were acquainted with all the ins and outs of good breeding, were gracious with a certain delicacy. The countess, especially, showed that amiable condescension of very noble ladies who do not fear being spoiled by contact with anyone and was charming. But the great Mme Loiseau, who had the soul of a plebian, remained crabbed, saying little and eating much.

The conversation was about the war, naturally. They related the horrible deeds of the Prussians, the brave acts of the French; and all of them, although running away, did homage to those who stayed behind. Then personal stories began to be told, and Ball-of-Fat related, with sincere emotion and in the heated words that such girls sometimes use in expressing their natural feelings, how she had left Rouen:

"I believed at first that I could remain," she said. "I had my house full of provisions, and I preferred to feed a few soldiers rather than expatriate myself, to go I knew not where. But as soon as I saw them, those Prussians, that was too much for me! They made my blood boil with anger, and I wept for very shame all day long. Oh! if I were only a man! I watched them from my windows, the great porkers with their pointed helmets, and my maid held my hands to keep me from throwing the furniture down upon them. Then one of them came to lodge at my house; I sprang at his throat the first thing; they are no more difficult to strangle than other people. And I should have put an end to that one then and there had they not pulled me away by the hair. After that it was necessary to keep out of sight. And finally, when I found an opportunity, I left town and—here I am!"

They congratulated her. She grew in the estimation of her companions, who had not shown themselves so hot-brained, and Cornudet, while listening to her, took on the approving, benevolent smile of an apostle, as a priest would if he heard a devotee praise God, for the long-bearded democrats have a monopoly of patriotism, as the men in cassocks have of religion. In his turn he spoke in a doctrinal tone, with the emphasis of a proclamation such as we see pasted on the walls about town, and finished by a bit of eloquence whereby he gave that "scamp of a Badinguet" a good lashing.

Then Ball-of-Fat was angry, for she was a Bonapartist. She grew redder than a cherry and, stammering with indignation, said:

"I would like to have seen you in his place, you other people. Then everything would have been quite right; oh yes! It is you who have betrayed this man! One would never have had to leave France if it had been governed by blackguards like you!"

Cornudet, undisturbed, preserved a disdainful, superior smile, but all felt that the high note had been struck, until the count, not without some difficulty, calmed the exasperated girl and proclaimed with a manner of authority that all sincere opinions should be respected. But the countess and the manufacturer's wife, who had in their souls an unreasonable hatred for the people that favor a republic and the same instinctive tenderness that all women have for a decorative, despotic government, felt themselves drawn, in spite of themselves, toward this prostitute so full of dignity, whose sentiments so strongly resembled their own.

The basket was empty. By ten o'clock they had easily exhausted the contents and regretted that there was not more. Conversation continued for some time, but a little more coldly since they had finished eating.

The night fell; the darkness little by little became profound, and the cold, felt more during digestion, made Ball-of-Fat shiver in spite of her plumpness. Then Mme de Breville offered her the little foot stove, in which the fuel had been renewed many times since morning; she accepted it immediately, for her feet were becoming numb with cold. The ladies Carré-Lamadon and Loiseau gave theirs to the two religious sisters.

The driver had lighted his lanterns. They shone out with a lively glimmer, showing a cloud of foam beyond, the sweat of the horses; and, on both sides of the way, the snow seemed to roll itself along under the moving reflection of the lights.

Inside the carriage one could distinguish nothing. But a sudden movement seemed to be made between Ball-of-Fat and Cornudet; and Loiseau, whose eye penetrated the shadow, believed that he saw the big-bearded man start back quickly as if he had received a swift, noiseless blow.

Then some twinkling points of fire appeared in the distance along the road. It was Tôtes. They had traveled eleven hours, which, with the two hours given to resting and feeding the horses, made thirteen. They entered the town and stopped before the Hotel of Commerce.

The carriage door opened! A well-known sound gave the travelers a start; it was the scabbard of a sword hitting the ground. Immediately a German voice was heard in the darkness.

Although the diligence was not moving, no one offered to alight, fearing someone might be waiting to murder them as they stepped out. Then the conductor appeared, holding in his hand one of the lanterns which lighted the carriage to its depth and showed the two rows of frightened faces whose mouths were open and whose eyes were wide with surprise and fear.

Outside, beside the driver, in plain sight stood a German officer, an excessively tall young man, thin and blond, squeezed into his uniform like a girl in a corset and wearing on his head a flat oilcloth cap which made him resemble the porter of an English hotel. His enormous mustache, of long straight hairs, growing gradually thin at each side and terminating in a single blond thread so fine that one could not perceive where it ended, seemed to weigh heavily on the corners of his mouth and, drawing down the cheeks, left a decided wrinkle about the lips.

In Alsatian French he invited the travelers to come in, saying in a suave tone: "Will you descend, gentlemen and ladies?"

The two good sisters were the first to obey, with the docility of saints accustomed ever to submission. The count and countess then appeared, followed by the manufacturer and his wife; then Loiseau, pushing ahead of him his larger half. The last named, as he set foot on the earth, said to the officer:

"Good evening, sir," more as a measure of prudence than politeness. The officer, insolent as all powerful people usually are, looked at him without a word.

Ball-of-Fat and Cornudet, although nearest the door, were the last to descend, grave and haughty before the enemy. The fat girl tried to control herself and be calm. The democrat waved a tragic hand, and his long beard seemed to tremble a little and grow redder. They wished to preserve their dignity, comprehending that in such meetings as these they represented in some degree their great country; and somewhat disgusted with the docility of her companions, the fat girl tried to show more pride than her neighbors, the honest women, and as she felt that someone should set an example she continued her attitude of resistance assumed at the beginning of the journey.

They entered the vast kitchen of the inn, and the German, having demanded their traveling papers signed by the general in chief (in which the name, the description and profession of each traveler was mentioned) and having examined them all critically, comparing the people and their signatures, said: "It is quite right," and went out.

Then they breathed. They were still hungry and supper was ordered. A half-hour was necessary to prepare it, and while two servants were attending to this they went to their rooms. They found them along a corridor which terminated in a large glazed door.

Finally they sat down at table, when the proprietor of the inn himself appeared. He was a former horse merchant, a large, asthmatic man with a constant wheezing and rattling in his throat. His father had left him the name of Follenvie. He asked:

"Is Miss Elizabeth Rousset here?"

Ball-of-Fat started as she answered: "It is I."

"The Prussian officer wishes to speak with you immediately."

"With me?"

"Yes, that is, if you are Miss Elizabeth Rousset."

She was disturbed and, reflecting for an instant, declared flatly:

"That is my name, but I shall not go."

A stir was felt around her; each discussed and tried to think of the cause of this order. The count approached her, saying:

"You are wrong, madame, for your refusal may lead to considerable difficulty, not only for yourself but for all your companions. It is never worth while to resist those in power. This request cannot assuredly bring any danger; it is, without doubt, about some forgotten formality."

Everybody agreed with him, asking, begging, beseeching her to go, and at last they convinced her that it was best; they all feared the complications that might result from disobedience. She finally said:

"It is for you that I do this, you understand."

The countess took her by the hand, saying: "And we are grateful to you for it."

She went out. They waited before sitting down at table.

Each one regretted not having been sent for in the place of this violent, irascible girl and mentally prepared some platitudes in case they should be called in their turn.

But at the end of ten minutes she reappeared, out of breath, red to suffocation and exasperated. She stammered: "Oh! the rascal; the rascal!"

All gathered around to learn something, but she said nothing; and when the count insisted she responded with great dignity: "No, it does not concern you; I can say nothing."

Then they all seated themselves around a high soup tureen whence came the odor of cabbage. In spite of alarm the supper was gay. The cider was good; the beverage Loiseau and the good sisters took as a means of economy. The others called for wine; Cornudet demanded beer. He had a special fashion of uncorking the bottle, making froth on the liquid, carefully filling the glass and then holding it before the light to better appreciate the color. When he drank, his great beard, which still kept some of the foam of his beloved beverage, seemed to tremble with tenderness; his eyes were squinted, in order not to lose sight of his tipple, and he had the unique air of fulfilling the function for which he was born. One would say that there was in his mind a meeting, like that of affinities, between the two great passions that occupied his life—Pale Ale and Revolutions; and assuredly he could not taste the one without thinking of the other.

M. and Mme Follenvie dined at the end of the table. The man, rattling like a cracked locomotive, had too much trouble in breathing to talk while eating, but his wife was never silent. She told all her impressions at the arrival of the Prussians, what they did, what they said, reviling them because they cost her some money and because she had two sons in the army. She addressed herself especially to the countess, flattered by being able to talk with a lady of quality.

When she lowered her voice to say some delicate thing her husband would interrupt, from time to time, with: "You had better keep silent, Madame Follenvie." But she paid no attention, continuing in this fashion:

"Yes, madame, those people there not only eat our potatoes and pork but our pork and potatoes. And it must not be believed that they are at all proper —oh no! Such filthy things they do, saving the respect I owe to you! And if you could see them exercise for hours in the day! They are all there in the field, marching ahead, then marching back, turning here and turning there. They might be cultivating the land or at least working on the roads of their own country! But no, madame, these military men are profitable to no one. Poor people have to feed them or perhaps be murdered! I am only an old woman without education, it is true, but when I see some endangering their constitutions by raging from morning to night I say: 'When there are so many people found to be useless, how unnecessary it is for others to take so much trouble to be nuisances!' Truly, is it not an abomination to kill people, whether they be Prussian or English or Polish or French? If one man revenges himself upon another who has done him some injury, it is wicked and he is punished; but when they exterminate our boys as if they were game, with guns, they give decorations, indeed, to the one who destroys the most! Now, you see, I can never understand that, never!"

Cornudet raised his voice: "War is a barbarity when one attacks a peaceable neighbor but a sacred duty when one defends his country."

The old woman lowered her head.

"Yes, when one defends himself it is another thing; but why not make it a duty to kill all the kings who make these wars for their pleasure?"

Cornudet's eyes flashed. "Bravo, my countrywoman!" said he.

M. Carré-Lamadon reflected profoundly. Although he was prejudiced as a captain of industry, the good sense of this peasant woman made him think of the opulence that would be brought into the country were the idle and consequently mischievous hands, and the troops which were now maintained in unproductiveness, employed in some great industrial work that it would require centuries to achieve.

Loiseau, leaving his place, went to speak with the innkeeper in a low tone of voice. The great man laughed, shook and squeaked, his corpulence quivered with joy at the jokes of his neighbor, and he bought of him six cases of wine for spring, after the Prussians had gone.

As soon as supper was finished, as they were worn out with fatigue, they retired.

However, Loiseau, who had observed things, after getting his wife to bed glued his eye and then his ear to a hole in the wall to try and discover what are known as "the mysteries of the corridor."

At the end of about an hour he heard a groping and, looking quickly, he perceived Ball-of-Fat, who appeared still more plump in a blue cashmere negligee trimmed with white lace. She had a candle in her hand and was directing her steps toward the great door at the end of the corridor. But a door at the side opened, and when she returned at the end of some minutes Cornudet, in his suspenders, followed her. They spoke low, then they stopped. Ball-of-Fat seemed to be defending the entrance to her room with energy. Loiseau, unfortunately, could not hear all their words, but finally, as they raised their voices, he was able to catch a few. Cornudet insisted with vivacity. He said:

"Come, now, you are a silly woman; what harm can be done?"

She had an indignant air in responding: "No, my dear, there are moments when such things are out of place. Here it would be a shame."

He doubtless did not comprehend and asked why. Then she cried out, raising her voice still more:

"Why? You do not see why? When there are Prussians in the house, in the very next room, perhaps?"

He was silent. This patriotic shame of the harlot, who would not suffer his caress so near the enemy, must have awakened the latent dignity in his heart, for after simply kissing her he went back to his own door with a bound.

Loiseau, much excited, left the aperture, cut a caper in his room, put on his pajamas, turned back the clothes that covered the bony carcass of his companion, whom he awakened with a kiss, murmuring: "Do you love me, dearie?"

Then all the house was still. And immediately there arose somewhere, from an uncertain quarter which might be the cellar but was quite as likely to be the garret, a powerful snoring, monotonous and regular, a heavy, prolonged sound, like a great kettle under pressure. M. Follenvie was asleep.

As they had decided that they would set out at eight o'clock the next morning, they all collected in the kitchen. But the carriage, the roof of which was covered with snow, stood undisturbed in the courtyard, without horses and without a conductor. They sought him in vain in the stables, in the hay and in the coach house. Then they resolved to scour the town and started out. They found themselves in a square, with a church at one end and some low houses on either side, where they perceived some Prussian soldiers. The first one they saw was paring potatoes. The second, further off, was cleaning the hairdresser's shop. Another, bearded to the eyes, was tending a troublesome brat, cradling it and trying to appease it; and the great peasant women, whose husbands were "away in the army," indicated by signs to their obedient conquerors the work they wished to have done: cutting wood, cooking the soup, grinding the coffee or what not. One of them even washed the linen of his hostess, an impotent old grandmother.

The count, astonished, asked questions of the beadle who came out of the rectory. The old man responded:

"Oh! those men are not wicked; they are not the Prussians we hear about. They are from far off, I know not where; and they have left wives and children in their country; it is not amusing to them, this war, I can tell you! I am sure they also weep for their homes and that it makes as much sorrow among them as it does among us. Here, now, there is not so much unhappiness for the moment, because the soldiers do no harm and they work as if they were in their own homes. You see, sir, among poor people it is necessary that they aid one another. These are the great traits which war develops."

Cornudet, indignant at the cordial relations between the conquerors and the conquered, preferred to shut himself up in the inn. Loiseau had a joke for the occasion: "They will repeople the land."

M. Carré-Lamadon had a serious word: "They try to make amends."

But they did not find the driver. Finally they discovered him in a café of the village, sitting at table fraternally with the officer of ordnance. The count called out to him:

"Were you not ordered to be ready at eight o'clock?"

"Well, yes, but another order has been given me since."

"By whom?"

"Faith! the Prussian commander."

"What was it?"

"Not to harness at all."

"Why?"

"I know nothing about it. Go and ask him. They tell me not to harness, and I don't harness. That's all."

"Did he give you the order himself?"

"No sir, the innkeeper gave the order for him."

"When was that?"

"Last evening, as I was going to bed."

The three men returned, much disturbed. They asked for M. Follenvie, but the servant answered that that gentleman, because of his asthma, never rose before ten o'clock. And he had given strict orders not to be wakened before that, except in case of fire.

They wished to see the officer, but that was absolutely impossible since, while he lodged at the inn, M. Follenvie alone was authorized to speak to him upon civil affairs. So they waited. The women went up to their rooms again, and occupied themselves with futile tasks.

Cornudet installed himself near the great chimney in the kitchen, where there was a good fire burning. He ordered one of the little tables to be brought from the café, then a can of beer; he then drew out his pipe, which plays among democrats a part almost equal to his own, because in serving Cornudet it was serving its country. It was a superb pipe, an admirably colored meerschaum, as black as the teeth of its master, but perfumed, curved, glistening, easy to the hand, completing his physiognomy. And he remained motionless, his eyes as much fixed upon the flame of the fire as upon his favorite tipple and its frothy crown; and each time that he drank he passed his long thin fingers through his scanty gray hair with an air of satisfaction, after which he sucked in his mustache fringed with foam.

Loiseau, under the pretext of stretching his legs, went to place some wine among the retailers of the country. The count and the manufacturer began to talk politics. They could foresee the future of France. One of them believed in an Orléans, the other in some unknown savior for the country, a hero who would reveal himself when all were in despair: a Guesclin or a Joan of Arc, perhaps, or would it be another Napoleon First? Ah! if the Prince Imperial were not so young!

Cornudet listened to them and smiled like one who holds the word of destiny. His pipe perfumed the kitchen.

As ten o'clock struck M. Follenvie appeared. They asked him hurried questions, but he could only repeat two or three times, without variation, these words:

"The officer said to me: Monsieur Follenvie, you see to it that the carriage is not harnessed for those travelers tomorrow. I do not wish them to leave without my order. That is sufficient."

Then they wished to see the officer. The count sent him his card, on which M. Carré-Lamadon wrote his name and all his titles. The Prussian sent back word that he would meet the two gentlemen after he had breakfasted, that is to say, about one o'clock.

The ladies reappeared and ate a little something, despite their disquiet. Ball-of-Fat seemed ill and prodigiously troubled.

They were finishing their coffee when the word came that the officer was ready to meet the gentlemen. Loiseau joined them; but when they tried to enlist Cornudet, to give more solemnity to their proceedings, he declared proudly that he would have nothing to do with the Germans, and he betook himself to his chimney corner and ordered another liter of beer.

The three men mounted the staircase and were introduced to the best room of the inn, where the officer received them, stretched out in an armchair, his feet on the mantelpiece, smoking a long porcelain pipe and enveloped in a flamboyant dressing gown, appropriated, without doubt, from some dwelling belonging to a common citizen of bad taste. He did not rise nor greet them in any way, not even looking at them. It was a magnificent display of natural blackguardism transformed into the military victor.

At the expiration of some moments he asked: "What is it you wish?"

The count became spokesman: "We desire to go on our way, sir."

"No."

"May I ask the cause of this refusal?"

"Because I do not wish it."

"But I would respectfully observe to you, sir, that your general in chief gave us permission to go to Dieppe, and I know of nothing we have done to merit your severity."

"I do not wish it—that is all; you can go."

All three, having bowed, retired.

The afternoon was lamentable. They could not understand this caprice of the German, and the most singular ideas would come into their heads to trouble them. Everybody stayed in the kitchen and discussed the situation endlessly, imagining all sorts of unlikely things. Perhaps they would be retained as hostages—but to what end?—or taken prisoners—or rather a considerable ransom might be demanded. At this thought a panic prevailed. The richest were the most frightened, already seeing themselves constrained to pay for their lives with sacks of gold poured into the hands of this insolent soldier. They racked their brains to think of some acceptable falsehoods to conceal their riches and make them pass themselves off for poor people, very poor people. Loiseau took off the chain to his watch and hid it away in his pocket. The falling night increased their apprehensions. The lamp was lighted, and as there was still two hours before dinner, Mme Loiseau proposed a game of thirty-one. It would be a diversion. They accepted. Cornudet himself, having smoked out his pipe, took part for politeness.

The count shuffled the cards, dealt, and Ball-of-Fat had thirty-one at the outset; and immediately the interest was great enough to appease the fear that haunted their minds. Then Cornudet perceived that the house of Loiseau was given to tricks.

As they were going to the dinner table, M. Follenvie again appeared and in wheezing, rattling voice announced:

"The Prussian officer orders me to ask Miss Elizabeth Rousset if she has yet changed her mind."

Ball-of-Fat remained standing and was pale; then, suddenly becoming crimson, such a stifling anger took possession of her that she could not speak. But finally she flashed out: "You may say to the dirty beast, that idiot, that carrion of a Prussian, that I shall never change it; you understand, never, never, never!"

The great innkeeper went out. Then Ball-of-Fat was immediately surrounded, questioned and solicited by all to disclose the mystery of his visit. She resisted at first, but soon, becoming exasperated, she said: "What does he want? You really want to know what he wants? He wants to sleep with me."

Everybody was choked for words, and indignation was rife. Cornudet broke his glass, so violently did he bring his fist down upon the table. There was a clamor of censure against this ignoble soldier, a blast of anger, a union of all for resistance, as if a demand had been made on each one of the party for the sacrifice exacted of her. The count declared with disgust that those people conducted themselves after the fashion of the ancient barbarians. The women, especially, showed to Ball-of-Fat a most energetic and tender commiseration. The good sisters, who only showed themselves at mealtime, lowered their heads and said nothing.

They all dined, nevertheless, when the first furore had abated. But there was little conversation; they were thinking.

The ladies retired early, and the men, all smoking, organized a game at cards to which M. Follenvie was invited, as they intended to put a few casual questions to him on the subject of conquering the resistance of this officer. But he thought of nothing but the cards and, without listening or answering, would keep repeating: "To the game, sirs, to the game." His attention was so taken that he even forgot to expectorate, which must have put him some points to the good with the organ in his breast. His whistling lungs ran the whole asthmatic scale, from deep, profound tones to the sharp rustiness of a young cock essaying to crow.

He even refused to retire when his wife, who had fallen asleep previously, came to look for him. She went away alone, for she was an "early bird," always up with the sun, while her husband was a "night owl," always ready to pass the night with his friends. He cried out to her: "Leave my creamed chicken before the fire!" and then went on with his game. When they saw that they could get nothing from him they declared that it was time to stop, and each sought his bed.

They all rose rather early the next day, with an undefined hope of getting away, which desire the terror of passing another day in that horrible inn greatly increased.

Alas! the horses remained in the stable and the driver was invisible. For want of better employment they went out and walked around the carriage.

The breakfast was very doleful, and it became apparent that a coldness had arisen toward Ball-of-Fat and that the night, which brings counsel, had slightly modified their judgments. They almost wished now that the Prussian had secretly found this girl, in order to give her companions a pleasant surprise in the morning. What could be more simple? Besides, who would know anything about it? She could save appearances by telling the officer that she took pity on their distress. To her it would make so little difference!

No one had avowed these thoughts yet.

In the afternoon, as they were almost perishing from ennui, the count proposed that they take a walk around the village. Each wrapped up warmly and the little party set out, with the exception of Cornudet who preferred to remain near the fire, and the good sisters, who passed their time in the church or at the curate's.

The cold, growing more intense every day, cruelly pinched their noses and ears; their feet became so numb that each step was torture; and when they came to a field it seemed to them frightfully sad under this limitless white, so that everybody returned immediately, with hearts hard pressed and souls congealed.

The four women walked ahead, the three gentlemen followed just behind. Loiseau, who understood the situation, asked suddenly if they thought that girl there was going to keep them long in such a place as this. The count, always courteous, said that they could not exact from a woman a sacrifice so hard, unless it should come of her own will. M. Carré-Lamadon remarked that if the French made their return through Dieppe, as they were likely to, a battle would surely take place at Tôtes. This reflection made the two others anxious.

"If we could only get away on foot," said Loiseau.

The count shrugged his shoulders. "How can we think of it in this snow and with our wives?" he said. "And then we should be pursued and caught in ten minutes and led back prisoners at the mercy of these soldiers."

It was true, and they were silent.

The ladies talked of their clothes, but a certain constraint seemed to disunite them. Suddenly at the end of the street the officer appeared. His tall wasplike figure in uniform was outlined upon the horizon formed by the snow, and he was marching with knees apart, a gait particularly military, which is affected that they may not spot their carefully blackened boots.

He bowed in passing near the ladies and looked disdainfully at the men, who preserved their dignity by not seeing him, except Loiseau, who made a motion toward raising his hat.

Ball-of-Fat reddened to the ears, and the three married women resented the great humiliation of being thus met by this soldier in the company of this girl whom he had treated so cavalierly.

But they spoke of him, of his figure and his face. Mme Carré-Lamadon, who had known many officers and considered herself a connoisseur of them, found this one not at all bad; she regretted even that he was not French, because he would make such a pretty hussar, one all the women would rave over.

Again in the house, no one knew what to do. Some sharp words, even, were said about things very insignificant. The dinner was silent, and almost immediately after it each one went to his room to kill time in sleep.

They descended the next morning with weary faces and exasperated hearts. The women scarcely spoke to Ball-of-Fat.

A bell began to ring. It was for a baptism. The fat girl had a child being brought up among the peasants of Yvetot. She had not seen it for a year or thought of it; but now the idea of a child being baptized threw into her heart a sudden and violent tenderness for her own, and she strongly wished to be present at the ceremony.

As soon as she was gone everybody looked at each other, then pulled their chairs together, for they thought that finally something should be decided upon. Loiseau had an inspiration: it was to hold Ball-of-Fat alone and let the others go.

M. Follenvie was charged with the commission but he returned almost immediately, for the German, who understood human nature, had put him out. He pretended that he would retain everybody so long as his desire was not satisfied.

Then the commonplace nature of Mme Loiseau burst out with:

"Well, we are not going to stay here to die of old age. Since it is the trade of this creature to accommodate herself to all kinds, I fail to see how she has the right to refuse one more than another. I can tell you she has received all she could find in Rouen, even the coachmen! Yes, madame, the prefect's coachman! I know him very well, for he bought his wine at our house. And to think that today we should be drawn into this embarrassment by this affected woman, this minx! For my part, I find that this officer conducts himself very well. He has perhaps suffered privations for a long time, and doubtless he would have preferred us three; but no, he is contented with common property. He respects married women. And we must remember too that he is master. He has only to say 'I wish,' and he could take us by force with his soldiers."

The two women had a cold shiver. Pretty Mme Carré-Lamadon's eyes grew brilliant and she became a little pale, as if she saw herself already taken by force by the officer.

The men met and discussed the situation. Loiseau, furious, was for delivering "the wretch" bound hand and foot to the enemy. But the count, descended through three generations of ambassadors and endowed with the temperament of a diplomatist, was the advocate of ingenuity.

"It is best to decide upon something," said he. Then they conspired.

The women kept together, the tone of their voices was lowered, each gave advice and the discussion was general. Everything was very harmonious. The ladies, especially, found delicate shades and charming subtleties of expression for saying the most unusual things. A stranger would have understood nothing, so great was the precaution of language observed. But the light edge of modesty with which every woman of the world is barbed only covers the surface; they blossom out in a scandalous adventure of this kind, being deeply amused and feeling themselves in their element, mixing love with sensuality as a greedy cook prepares supper for his master.

Even gaiety returned, so funny did the whole story seem to them at last. The count found some of the jokes a little off color, but they were so well told that he was forced to smile. In his turn Loiseau came out with some still bolder tales, and yet nobody was wounded. The brutal thought expressed by his wife dominated all minds: "Since it is her trade, why should she refuse this one more than another?" The genteel Mme Carré-Lamadon seemed to think that in her place she would refuse this one less than some others.

They prepared the blockade at length, as if they were about to surround a fortress. Each took some role to play, some arguments he would bring to bear, some maneuvers that he would endeavor to put into execution. They decided on the plan of attack, the ruse to employ, the surprise of assault that should force this living citadel to receive the enemy in her room.

Cornudet remained apart from the rest and was a stranger to the whole affair.

So entirely were their minds distracted that they did not hear Ball-of-Fat enter. The count uttered a light "Ssh!" which turned all eyes in her direction. There she was. The abrupt silence and a certain embarrassment hindered them from speaking to her at first. The countess, more accustomed to the duplicity of society than the others, finally inquired:

"Was it very amusing, that baptism?"

The fat girl, filled with emotion, told them all about it: the faces, the attitudes and even the appearance of the church. She added: "It is good to pray sometimes."

And up to the time for luncheon these ladies continued to be amiable toward her in order to increase her docility and her confidence in their counsel. At the table they commenced the approach. This was in the shape of a vague conversation upon devotion. They cited ancient examples: Judith and Holophernes, then, without reason, Lucrece and Sextus, and Cleopatra obliging all the generals of the enemy to pass by her couch and reducing them in servility to slaves. Then they brought out a fantastic story, hatched in the imagination of these ignorant millionaires, where the women of Rome went to Capua for the purpose of lulling Hannibal to sleep in their arms and his lieutenants and phalanxes of mercenaries as well. They cited all the women who have been taken by conquering armies, making a battlefield of their bodies, making them also a weapon and a means of success; and all those hideous and detestable beings who have conquered by their heroic caresses and sacrificed their chastity to vengeance or a beloved cause. They even spoke in veiled terms of that great English family which allowed one of its women to be inoculated with a horrible and contagious disease in order to transmit it to Bonaparte, who was miraculously saved by a sudden illness at the hour of the fatal rendezvous.

And all this was related in an agreeable, temperate fashion, except as it was enlivened by the enthusiasm deemed proper to excite emulation.

One might finally have believed that the sole duty of woman here below was a sacrifice of her person and a continual abandonment to soldierly caprices.

The two good sisters seemed not to hear, lost as they were in profound thought. Ball-of-Fat said nothing.

During the whole afternoon they let her reflect. But in the place of calling her "Madame," as they had up to this time, they simply called her "Mademoiselle" without knowing exactly why, as if they had a desire to put her down a degree in their esteem, which she had taken by storm, and make her feel her shameful situation.

The moment supper was served M. Follenvie appeared with his old phrase: "The Prussian officer orders me to ask if Miss Elizabeth Rousset has yet changed her mind."

Ball-of-Fat responded dryly: "No sir."

But at dinner the coalition weakened. Loiseau made three unhappy remarks. Each one beat his wits for new examples but found nothing; then the countess, without premeditation, perhaps feeling some vague need of rendering homage to religion, asked the elder of the good sisters to tell them some great deeds in the lives of the saints. It appeared that many of their acts would have been considered crimes in our eyes, but the Church gave absolution of them readily, since they were done for the glory of God or for the good of all. It was a powerful argument; the countess made the most of it.

Thus it may be by one of those tacit understandings, or the veiled complacency in which anyone who wears the ecclesiastical garb excels, it may be simply from the effect of a happy unintelligence, a helpful stupidity, but in fact the religious sister lent a formidable support to the conspiracy. They had thought her timid, but she showed herself courageous, verbose, even violent. She was not troubled by the chatter of the casuist; her doctrine seemed a bar of iron; her faith never hesitated; her conscience had no scruples. She found the sacrifice of Abraham perfectly simple, for she would immediately kill father or mother on an order from on high. And nothing, in her opinion, could displease the Lord if the intention was laudable. The countess put to use the authority of her unwitting accomplice and added to it the edifying paraphrase and axiom of Jesuit morals: "The need justifies the means."

Then she asked her: "Then, my sister, do you think that God accepts intentions and pardons the deed when the motive is pure?"

"Who could doubt it, madame? An action blamable in itself often becomes meritorious by the thought it springs from."

And they continued thus, unraveling the will of God, foreseeing his decisions, making themselves interested in things that, in truth, they would never think of noticing. All this was guarded, skillful, discreet. But each word of the saintly sister in a cap helped to break down the resistance of the unworthy courtesan. Then the conversation changed a little, the woman of the chaplet speaking of the houses of her order, of her Superior, of herself, of her dainty neighbor, the dear sister Saint Nicephore. They had been called to the hospitals of Havre to care for the hundreds of soldiers stricken with smallpox. They depicted these miserable creatures, giving details of the malady. And while they were stopped, en route, by the caprice of this Prussian officer, a great number of Frenchmen might die whom perhaps they could have saved! It was a specialty with her, caring for soldiers. She had been in Crimea, in Italy, in Austria, and in telling of her campaigns she revealed herself as one of those religious aids to drums and trumpets who seem made to follow camps, pick up the wounded in the thick of battle and, better than an officer, subdue with a word great bands of undisciplined recruits. A true good sister of the rataplan, whose ravaged face, marked with innumerable scars, appeared the image of the devastation of war.

No one could speak after her, so excellent seemed the effect of her words.

As soon as the repast was ended they quickly went up to their rooms, with the purpose of not coming down the next day until late in the morning.

The luncheon was quiet. They had given the grain of seed time to germinate and bear fruit. The countess proposed that they take a walk in the afternoon. The count, being agreeably inclined, gave an arm to Ball-of-Fat and walked behind the others with her. He talked to her in a familiar, paternal tone, a little disdainful, after the manner of men having girls in their employ, calling her "my dear child," from the height of his social position, of his undisputed honor. He reached the vital part of the question at once:

"Then you prefer to leave us here, exposed to the violences which follow a defeat, rather than consent to a favor which you have so often given in your life?"

Ball-of-Fat answered nothing.

Then he tried to reach her through gentleness, reason, and then the sentiments. He knew how to remain "the count," even while showing himself gallant or complimentary or very amiable if it became necessary. He exalted the service that she would render them and spoke of his appreciation, then suddenly became gaily familiar and said:

"And you know, my dear, it would be something for him to boast of that he had known a pretty girl; something it is difficult to find in his country."

Ball-of-Fat did not answer but joined the rest of the party. As soon as they entered the house she went to her room and did not appear again. The disquiet was extreme. What were they to do? If she continued to resist, what an embarrassment!

The dinner hour struck. They waited in vain. M. Follenvie finally entered and said that Miss Rousset was indisposed and would not be at the table. Everybody pricked up his ears. The count went to the innkeeper and said in a low voice:

"Is he in there?"

"Yes."

For convenience he said nothing to his companions but made a slight sign with his head. Immediately a great sigh of relief went up from every breast and a light appeared in their faces. Loiseau cried out:

"Holy Christopher! I pay for the champagne, if there is any to be found in the establishment." And Mme Loiseau was pained to see the proprietor return with four quart bottles in his hands.

Each one had suddenly become communicative and buoyant. A wanton joy filled their hearts. The count suddenly perceived that Mme Carré-Lamadon was charming, the manufacturer paid compliments to the countess. The conversation was lively, gay, full of touches.

Suddenly Loiseau, with anxious face and hand upraised, called out: "Silence!" Everybody was silent, surprised, already frightened. Then he listened intently and said: "S-s-sh!" his two eyes and his hands raised toward the ceiling, listening, and then continuing in his natural voice: "All right! All goes well!"

They failed to comprehend at first, but soon all laughed. At the end of a quarter of an hour he began the same farce again, renewing it occasionally during the whole afternoon. And he pretended to call to someone in the story above, giving him advice in a double meaning, drawn from the fountainhead—the mind of a commercial traveler. For some moments he would assume a sad air, breathing in a whisper: "Poor girl!" Then he would murmur between his teeth, with an appearance of rage: "Ugh! That scamp of a Prussian." Sometimes, at a moment when no more was thought about it, he would say in an affected voice, many times over: "Enough! enough!" and add, as if speaking to himself: "If we could only see her again; it isn't necessary that he should kill her, the wretch!"

Although these jokes were in deplorable taste they amused all and wounded no one, for indignation, like other things, depends upon its surroundings, and the atmosphere which had been gradually created around them was charged with sensual thoughts.

At the dessert the women themselves made some delicate and discreet allusions. Their eyes glistened; they had drunk much. The count, who preserved even in his flights his grand appearance of gravity, made a comparison, much relished, upon the subject of those wintering at the Pole, and the joy of shipwrecked sailors who saw an opening toward the south.

Loiseau suddenly arose, a glass of champagne in his hand, and said: "I drink to our deliverance." Everybody was on his feet; they shouted in agreement. Even the two good sisters consented to touch their lips to the froth of the wine which they had never before tasted. They declared that it tasted like charged lemonade, only much nicer.

Loiseau resumed: "It is unfortunate that we have no piano, for we might make up a quadrille."

Cornudet had not said a word nor made a gesture; he appeared plunged in very grave thoughts and made sometimes a furious motion, so that his great beard seemed to wish to free itself. Finally, toward midnight, as they were separating, Loiseau, who was staggering, touched him suddenly on the stomach and said to him in a stammer: "You are not very funny this evening; you have said nothing, citizen!" Then Cornudet raised his head brusquely and, casting a brilliant, terrible glance around the company, said: "I tell you all that you have been guilty of infamy!" He rose, went to the door and again repeated: "Infamy, I say!" and disappeared.

This made a coldness at first. Loiseau, interlocutor, was stupefied; but he recovered immediately and laughed heartily as he said: "He is very green, my friends. He is very green." And then, as they did not comprehend, he told them about the "mysteries of the corridor." Then there was a return of gaiety. The women behaved like lunatics. The count and M. Carré-Lamadon wept from the force of their laughter. They could not believe it.

"How is that? Are you sure?"

"I tell you I saw it."

"And she refused——"

"Yes, because the Prussian officer was in the next room."

"Impossible!"

"I swear it!"

The count was stifled with laughter. The industrial gentleman held his sides with both hands. Loiseau continued:

"And now you understand why he saw nothing funny this evening! No, nothing at all!" And the three started out half ill, suffocated.

They separated. But Mme Loiseau, who was of a spiteful nature, remarked to her husband as they were getting into bed that "that grisette" of a little Carré-Lamadon was yellow with envy all the evening. "You know," she continued, "how some women will take to a uniform, whether it be French or Prussian. It is all the same to them. Oh, what a pity!"

And all night, in the darkness of the corridor, there were to be heard light noises like whisperings and walking in bare feet and imperceptible creakings. They did not go to sleep until late, that is sure, for there were threads of light shining under the doors for a long time. The champagne had its effect; they say it troubles sleep.

The next day a clear winter's sun made the snow very brilliant. The diligence, already harnessed, waited before the door while an army of white pigeons, in their thick plumage, with rose-colored eyes with a black spot in the center, walked up and down gravely among the legs of the six horses, seeking their livelihood in the manure there scattered.

The driver, enveloped in his sheepskin, had a lighted pipe under the seat, and all the travelers, radiant, were rapidly packing some provisions for the rest of the journey. They were only waiting for Ball-of-Fat. Finally she appeared.

She seemed a little troubled, ashamed. And she advanced timidly toward her companions, who all, with one motion, turned as if they had not seen her. The count, with dignity, took the arm of his wife and removed her from this impure contact.

The fat girl stopped, half stupefied; then, plucking up courage, she approached the manufacturer's wife with "Good morning, madame," humbly murmured. The lady made a slight bow of the head which she accompanied with a look of outraged virtue. Everybody seemed busy and kept themselves as far from her as if she had had some infectious disease in her skirts. Then they hurried into the carriage, where she came last, alone, and where she took the place she had occupied during the first part of the journey.

They seemed not to see her or know her; although Mme Loiseau, looking at her from afar, said to her husband in a half tone: "Happily, I don't have to sit beside her."

The heavy carriage began to move, and the remainder of the journey commenced. No one spoke at first. Ball-of-Fat dared not raise her eyes. She felt indignant toward all her neighbors and at the same time humiliated at having yielded to the foul kisses of this Prussian into whose arms they had hypocritically thrown her.

Then the countess, turning toward Mme Carré-Lamadon, broke the difficult silence:

"I believe you know Madame d'Etrelles?"

"Yes, she is one of my friends."

"What a charming woman!"

"Delightful! A very gentle nature and well educated besides; then she is an artist to the tips of her fingers, sings beautifully and draws to perfection."

The manufacturer chatted with the count, and in the midst of the rattling of the glass an occasional word escaped such as "coupon—premium—limit—expiration."

Loiseau, who had pilfered the old pack of cards from the inn, greasy through five years of contact with tables badly cleaned, began a game of bezique with his wife.

The good sisters took from their belt the long rosary which hung there, made together the sign of the cross and suddenly began to move their lips in a lively murmur, as if they were going through the whole of the "Oremus." And from time to time they kissed a medal, made the sign anew, then recommenced their muttering, which was rapid and continued.

Cornudet sat motionless, thinking.

At the end of three hours on the way, Loiseau put up the cards and said: "I am hungry."

His wife drew out a package from whence she brought a piece of cold veal. She cut it evenly in thin pieces and they both began to eat.

"Suppose we do the same," said the countess.

They consented to it and she undid the provisions prepared for the two couples. It was in one of those dishes whose lid is decorated with a china hare to signify that a *pâté* of hare is inside, a succulent dish of pork, where white rivers of lard cross the brown flesh of the game, mixed with some other viands hashed fine. A beautiful square of Gruyère cheese, wrapped in a piece of newspaper, preserved the imprint "divers things" upon the unctuous plate.

The two good sisters unrolled a big sausage which smelled of garlic, and Cornudet plunged his two hands into the vast pockets of his overcoat at the same time and drew out four hard eggs and a piece of bread. He removed the shells and threw them in the straw under his feet; then he began to eat the eggs, letting fall on his vast beard some bits of clear yellow which looked like stars caught there.

Ball-of-Fat, in the haste and distraction of her rising, had not thought of anything; and she looked at them exasperated, suffocating with rage at all of them eating so placidly. A tumultuous anger swept over her at first, and she opened her mouth to cry out at them, to hurl at them a flood of injury which mounted to her lips; but she could not speak, her exasperation strangled her.

No one looked at her or thought of her. She felt herself drowned in the scorn of these honest scoundrels who had first sacrificed her and then rejected her, like some improper or useless article. She thought of her great basketful of good things they had greedily devoured, of her two chickens shining with jelly, of her *pâtés*, her pears and the four bottles of Bordeaux; and her fury suddenly falling, as a cord drawn too tightly breaks, she felt ready to weep. She made terrible efforts to prevent it, making ugly faces, swallowing her sobs as children do; but the tears came and glistened in the corners of her eyes, and then two great drops, detaching themselves from the rest, rolled slowly down like little streams of water that filter through rock and, falling regularly, rebounded upon her breast. She sits erect, her eyes fixed, her face rigid and pale, hoping that no one will notice her.

But the countess perceives her and tells her husband by a sign. He shrugs his shoulders, as much as to say:

"What would you have me do? It is not my fault."

Mme Loiseau indulged in a mute laugh of triumph and murmured:

"She weeps for shame."

The two good sisters began to pray again, after having wrapped in a paper the remainder of their sausage.

Then Cornudet, who was digesting his eggs, extended his legs to the seat opposite, crossed them, folded his arms, smiled like a man who is watching a good farce and began to whistle the "Marseillaise."

All faces grew dark. The popular song assuredly did not please his neighbors. They became nervous and agitated, having an appearance of wishing to howl, like dogs when they hear a barbarous organ. He perceived this but did not stop. Sometimes he would hum the words:

> "Sacred love of country
> Help, sustain th' avenging arm;
> Liberty, sweet Liberty,
> Ever fight, with no alarm."

They traveled fast, the snow being harder. But as far as Dieppe, during the long sad hours of the journey, across the jolts in the road, through the falling night, in the profound darkness of the carriage, he continued his vengeful, monotonous whistling with a ferocious obstinacy, constraining his neighbors to follow the song from one end to the other and to recall the words that belonged to each measure.

And Ball-of-Fat wept continually, and sometimes a sob, which she was not able to restrain, echoed between the two rows of people in the shadows.

THE NECKLACE

SHE WAS one of those pretty, charming young ladies, born, as if through an error of destiny, into a family of clerks. She had no dowry, no hopes, no means of becoming known, appreciated, loved and married by a man either rich or distinguished; and she allowed herself to marry a petty clerk in the office of the Board of Education.

She was simple, not being able to adorn herself, but she was unhappy, as one out of her class; for women belong to no caste, no race, their grace, their beauty and their charm serving them in the place of birth and family. Their inborn finesse, their instinctive elegance, their suppleness of wit, are their only aristocracy, making some daughters of the people the equal of great ladies.

She suffered incessantly, feeling herself born for all delicacies and luxuries. She suffered from the poverty of her apartment, the shabby walls, the worn chairs and the faded stuffs. All these things, which another woman of her station would not have noticed, tortured and angered her. The sight of the little Breton, who made this humble home, awoke in her sad regrets and desperate dreams. She thought of quiet antechambers with their oriental hangings lighted by high bronze torches and of the two great footmen in short trousers who sleep in the large armchairs, made sleepy by the heavy air from the heating apparatus. She thought of large drawing rooms hung in old silks, of graceful pieces of furniture carrying bric-a-brac of inestimable value and of the little perfumed coquettish apartments made for five o'clock chats with most intimate friends, men known and sought after, whose attention all women envied and desired.

When she seated herself for dinner before the round table, where the tablecloth had been used three days, opposite her husband who uncovered the tureen with a delighted air, saying: "Oh! the good potpie! I know nothing better than that," she would think of the elegant dinners, of the shining silver, of the tapestries peopling the walls with ancient personages and rare birds in the midst of fairy forests; she thought of the exquisite food served on marvelous dishes, of the whispered gallantries, listened to with the smile of the Sphinx while eating the rose-colored flesh of the trout or a chicken's wing.

She had neither frocks nor jewels, nothing. And she loved only those things. She felt that she was made for them. She had such a desire to please, to be sought after, to be clever and courted.

She had a rich friend, a schoolmate at the convent, whom she did not like to visit; she suffered so much when she returned. And she wept for whole days from chagrin, from regret, from despair and disappointment.

. . . .

One evening her husband returned, elated, bearing in his hand a large envelope.

"Here," he said, "here is something for you."

She quickly tore open the wrapper and drew out a printed card on which were inscribed these words:

The Minister of Public Instruction and Madame George Ramponneau ask the honor of M. and Mme Loisel's company Monday evening, January 18, at the Minister's residence.

Instead of being delighted, as her husband had hoped, she threw the invitation spitefully upon the table, murmuring:

"What do you suppose I want with that?"

"But, my dearie, I thought it would make you happy. You never go out, and this is an occasion, and a fine one! I had a great deal of trouble to get it. Everybody wishes one, and it is very select; not many are given to employees. You will see the whole official world there."

She looked at him with an irritated eye and declared impatiently:

"What do you suppose I have to wear to such a thing as that?"

He had not thought of that; he stammered:

"Why, the dress you wear when we go to the theater. It seems very pretty to me."

He was silent, stupefied, in dismay, at the sight of his wife weeping. Two great tears fell slowly from the corners of her eyes toward the corners of her mouth; he stammered:

"What is the matter? What is the matter?"

By a violent effort she had controlled her vexation and responded in a calm voice, wiping her moist cheeks:

"Nothing. Only I have no dress and consequently I cannot go to this affair. Give your card to some colleague whose wife is better fitted out than I."

He was grieved but answered:

"Let us see, Matilda. How much would a suitable costume cost, something that would serve for other occasions, something very simple?"

She reflected for some seconds, making estimates and thinking of a sum that she could ask for without bringing with it an immediate refusal and a frightened exclamation from the economical clerk.

Finally she said in a hesitating voice:

"I cannot tell exactly, but it seems to me that four hundred francs ought to cover it."

He turned a little pale, for he had saved just this sum to buy a gun that he might be able to join some hunting parties the next summer, on the plains at Nanterre, with some friends who went to shoot larks up there on Sunday. Nevertheless, he answered:

"Very well. I will give you four hundred francs. But try to have a pretty dress."

. . . . . .

The day of the ball approached, and Mme Loisel seemed sad, disturbed, anxious. Nevertheless, her dress was nearly ready. Her husband said to her one evening:

"What is the matter with you? You have acted strangely for two or three days."

And she responded: "I am vexed not to have a jewel, not one stone, nothing to adorn myself with. I shall have such a poverty-laden look. I would prefer not to go to this party."

He replied: "You can wear some natural flowers. At this season they look very chic. For ten francs you can have two or three magnificent roses."

She was not convinced. "No," she replied, "there is nothing more humiliating than to have a shabby air in the midst of rich women."

Then her husband cried out: "How stupid we are! Go and find your friend Madame Forestier and ask her to lend you her jewels. You are well enough acquainted with her to do this."

She uttered a cry of joy. "It is true!" she said. "I had not thought of that."

The next day she took herself to her friend's house and related her story of distress. Mme Forestier went to her closet with the glass doors, took out a large jewel case, brought it, opened it and said: "Choose, my dear."

She saw at first some bracelets, then a collar of pearls, then a Venetian cross of gold and jewels and of admirable workmanship. She tried the jewels before the glass, hesitated, but could neither decide to take them nor leave them. Then she asked:

"Have you nothing more?"

"Why, yes. Look for yourself. I do not know what will please you."

Suddenly she discovered in a black satin box a superb necklace of diamonds, and her heart beat fast with an immoderate desire. Her hands trembled as she took them up. She placed them about her throat, against her dress, and remained in ecstasy before them. Then she asked in a hesitating voice full of anxiety:

"Could you lend me this? Only this?"

"Why, yes, certainly."

She fell upon the neck of her friend, embraced her with passion, then went away with her treasure.

. . . .

The day of the ball arrived. Mme Loisel was a great success. She was the prettiest of all, elegant, gracious, smiling and full of joy. All the men noticed her, asked her name and wanted to be presented. All the members of the Cabinet wished to waltz with her. The minister of education paid her some attention.

She danced with enthusiasm, with passion, intoxicated with pleasure, thinking of nothing, in the triumph of her beauty, in the glory of her success, in a kind of cloud of happiness that came of all this homage and all this admiration, of all these awakened desires and this victory so complete and sweet to the heart of woman.

She went home toward four o'clock in the morning. Her husband had been half asleep in one of the little salons since midnight, with three other gentlemen whose wives were enjoying themselves very much.

He threw around her shoulders the wraps they had carried for the coming home, modest garments of everyday wear, whose poverty clashed with the elegance of the ball costume. She felt this and wished to hurry away in order not to be noticed by the other women who were wrapping themselves in rich furs.

Loisel detained her. "Wait," said he. "You will catch cold out there. I am going to call a cab."

But she would not listen and descended the steps rapidly. When they were in the street they found no carriage, and they began to seek for one, hailing the coachmen whom they saw at a distance.

THE NECKLACE

They walked along toward the Seine, hopeless and shivering. Finally they found on the dock one of those old nocturnal coupés that one sees in Paris after nightfall, as if they were ashamed of their misery by day.

It took them as far as their door in Martyr Street, and they went wearily up to their apartment. It was all over for her. And on his part he remembered that he would have to be at the office by ten o'clock.

She removed the wraps from her shoulders before the glass for a final view of herself in her glory. Suddenly she uttered a cry. Her necklace was not around her neck.

Her husband, already half undressed, asked: "What is the matter?"

She turned toward him excitedly:

"I have—I have—I no longer have Madame Forestier's necklace."

He arose in dismay: "What! How is that? It is not possible."

And they looked in the folds of the dress, in the folds of the mantle, in the pockets, everywhere. They could not find it.

He asked: "You are sure you still had it when we left the house?"

"Yes, I felt it in the vestibule as we came out."

"But if you had lost it in the street we should have heard it fall. It must be in the cab."

"Yes. It is probable. Did you take the number?"

"No. And you, did you notice what it was?"

"No."

They looked at each other, utterly cast down. Finally Loisel dressed himself again.

"I am going," said he, "over the track where we went on foot, to see if I can find it."

And he went. She remained in her evening gown, not having the force to go to bed, stretched upon a chair, without ambition or thoughts.

Toward seven o'clock her husband returned. He had found nothing.

He went to the police and to the cab offices and put an advertisement in the newspapers, offering a reward; he did everything that afforded them a suspicion of hope.

She waited all day in a state of bewilderment before this frightful disaster. Loisel returned at evening, with his face harrowed and pale, and had discovered nothing.

"It will be necessary," said he, "to write to your friend that you have broken the clasp of the necklace and that you will have it repaired. That will give us time to turn around."

She wrote as he dictated.

. . . .

At the end of a week they had lost all hope. And Loisel, older by five years, declared:

"We must take measures to replace this jewel."

The next day they took the box which had inclosed it to the jeweler whose name was on the inside. He consulted his books.

"It is not I, madame," said he, "who sold this necklace; I only furnished the casket."

Then they went from jeweler to jeweler, seeking a necklace like the other one, consulting their memories, and ill, both of them, with chagrin and anxiety.

In a shop of the Palais-Royal they found a chaplet of diamonds which seemed to them exactly like the one they had lost. It was valued at forty thousand francs. They could get it for thirty-six thousand.

They begged the jeweler not to sell it for three days. And they made an arrangement by which they might return it for thirty-four thousand francs if they found the other one before the end of February.

Loisel possessed eighteen thousand francs which his father had left him. He borrowed the rest.

He borrowed it, asking for a thousand francs of one, five hundred of another, five louis of this one and three louis of that one. He gave notes, made ruinous promises, took money of usurers and the whole race of lenders. He compromised his whole existence, in fact, risked his signature without even knowing whether he could make it good or not, and, harassed by anxiety for the future, by the black misery which surrounded him and by the prospect of all physical privations and moral torture, he went to get the new necklace, depositing on the merchant's counter thirty-six thousand francs.

When Mme Loisel took back the jewels to Mme Forestier the latter said to her in a frigid tone:

"You should have returned them to me sooner, for I might have needed them."

She did open the jewel box as her friend feared she would. If she should perceive the substitution what would she think? What should she say? Would she take her for a robber?

· · · · · · ·

Mme Loisel now knew the horrible life of necessity. She did her part, however, completely, heroically. It was necessary to pay this frightful debt. She would pay it. They sent away the maid; they changed their lodgings; they rented some rooms under a mansard roof.

She learned the heavy cares of a household, the odious work of a kitchen. She washed the dishes, using her rosy nails upon the greasy pots and the bottoms of the stewpans. She washed the soiled linen, the chemises and dishcloths, which she hung on the line to dry; she took down the refuse to the street each morning and brought up the water, stopping at each landing to breathe. And, clothed like a woman of the people, she went to the grocer's, the butcher's and the fruiterer's with her basket on her arm, shopping, haggling to the last sou her miserable money.

Every month it was necessary to renew some notes, thus obtaining time, and to pay others.

The husband worked evenings, putting the books of some merchants in order, and nights he often did copying at five sous a page.

And this life lasted for ten years.

At the end of ten years they had restored all, all, with interest of the usurer, and accumulated interest, besides.

Mme Loisel seemed old now. She had become a strong, hard woman, the crude woman of the poor household. Her hair badly dressed, her skirts awry, her hands red, she spoke in a loud tone and washed the floors in large pails of water. But sometimes, when her husband was at the office, she would seat herself before the window and think of that evening party of former times, of that ball where she was so beautiful and so flattered.

How would it have been if she had not lost that necklace? Who knows? Who knows? How singular is life and how full of changes! How small a thing will ruin or save one!

. . . .

One Sunday, as she was taking a walk in the Champs Elysées to rid herself of the cares of the week, she suddenly perceived a woman walking with a child. It was Mme Forestier, still young, still pretty, still attractive. Mme Loisel was affected. Should she speak to her? Yes, certainly. And now that she had paid, she would tell her all. Why not?

She approached her. "Good morning, Jeanne."

Her friend did not recognize her and was astonished to be so familiarly addressed by this common personage. She stammered:

"But, madame—I do not know—— You must be mistaken."

"No, I am Matilda Loisel."

Her friend uttered a cry of astonishment: "Oh! my poor Matilda! How you have changed."

"Yes, I have had some hard days since I saw you, and some miserable ones—and all because of you."

"Because of me? How is that?"

"You recall the diamond necklace that you loaned me to wear to the minister's ball?"

"Yes, very well."

"Well, I lost it."

"How is that, since you returned it to me?"

"I returned another to you exactly like it. And it has taken us ten years to pay for it. You can understand that it was not easy for us who have nothing. But it is finished, and I am decently content."

Mme Forestier stopped short. She said:

"You say that you bought a diamond necklace to replace mine?"

"Yes. You did not perceive it then? They were just alike."

And she smiled with a proud and simple joy. Mme Forestier was touched and took both her hands as she replied:

"Oh, my poor Matilda! Mine were false. They were not worth over five hundred francs!"

THE PIECE OF STRING

Along all the roads around Goderville the peasants and their wives were coming toward the burgh because it was market day. The men were proceeding with slow steps, the whole body bent forward at each movement of their long twisted legs; deformed by their hard work, by the weight on the plow which, at the same time, raised the left shoulder and swerved the figure, by the reaping of the wheat which made the knees spread to make a firm "purchase," by all the slow and painful labors of the country. Their blouses, blue, "stiff-starched," shining as if varnished, ornamented with a little design in white at the neck and wrists, puffed about their bony bodies, seemed like balloons ready to carry them off. From each of them a head, two arms and two feet protruded.

Some led a cow or a calf by a cord, and their wives, walking behind the animal, whipped its haunches with a leafy branch to hasten its progress. They carried large baskets on their arms from which, in some cases, chickens and, in others, ducks thrust out their heads. And they walked with a quicker, livelier step than their husbands. Their spare straight figures were wrapped in a scanty little shawl pinned over their flat bosoms, and their heads were enveloped in a white cloth glued to the hair and surmounted by a cap.

Then a wagon passed at the jerky trot of a nag, shaking strangely, two men seated side by side and a woman in the bottom of the vehicle, the latter holding onto the sides to lessen the hard jolts.

In the public square of Goderville there was a crowd, a throng of human beings and animals mixed together. The horns of the cattle, the tall hats, with long nap, of the rich peasant and the headgear of the peasant women rose above the surface of the assembly. And the clamorous, shrill, screaming voices made a continuous and savage din which sometimes was dominated by the robust lungs of some countryman's laugh or the long lowing of a cow tied to the wall of a house.

All that smacked of the stable, the dairy and the dirt heap, hay and sweat, giving forth that unpleasant odor, human and animal, peculiar to the people of the field.

Maître Hauchecome of Breaute had just arrived at Goderville, and he was directing his steps toward the public square when he perceived upon the ground a little piece of string. Maître Hauchecome, economical like a true Norman, thought that everything useful ought to be picked up, and he bent painfully, for he suffered from rheumatism. He took the bit of thin cord from the ground and began to roll it carefully when he noticed Maître Malandain, the harness maker, on the threshold of his door, looking at him. They had heretofore had business together on the subject of a halter, and they were on bad terms, both being good haters. Maître Hauchecome was seized with a sort of shame to be seen thus by his enemy, picking a bit of string out of the dirt. He concealed his "find" quickly under his blouse, then in his trousers' pocket; then he pretended to be still looking on the ground for something which he did not find, and he went toward the market, his head forward, bent double by his pains.

He was soon lost in the noisy and slowly moving crowd which was busy with interminable bargainings. The peasants milked, went and came, perplexed, always in fear of being cheated, not daring to decide, watching the vender's eye, ever trying to find the trick in the man and the flaw in the beast.

The women, having placed their great baskets at their feet, had taken out the poultry which lay upon the ground, tied together by the feet, with terrified eyes and scarlet crests.

They heard offers, stated their prices with a dry air and impassive face, or perhaps, suddenly deciding on some proposed reduction, shouted to the customer who was slowly going away: "All right, Maître Authirne, I'll give it to you for that."

Then little by little the square was deserted, and the Angelus ringing at noon, those who had stayed too long scattered to their shops.

At Jourdain's the great room was full of people eating, as the big court was full of vehicles of all kinds, carts, gigs, wagons, dumpcarts, yellow with dirt, mended and patched, raising their shafts to the sky like two arms or perhaps with their shafts in the ground and their backs in the air.

Just opposite the diners seated at the table the immense fireplace, filled with bright flames, cast a lively heat on the backs of the row on the right. Three spits were turning on which were chickens, pigeons and legs of mutton, and an appetizing odor of roast beef and gravy dripping over the nicely browned skin rose from the hearth, increased the jovialness and made everybody's mouth water.

All the aristocracy of the plow ate there at Maître Jourdain's, tavern keeper and horse dealer, a rascal who had money.

The dishes were passed and emptied, as were the jugs of yellow cider. Everyone told his affairs, his purchases and sales. They discussed the crops. The weather was favorable for the green things but not for the wheat.

Suddenly the drum beat in the court before the house. Everybody rose, except a few indifferent persons, and ran to the door or to the windows, their mouths still full and napkins in their hands.

After the public crier had ceased his drumbeating he called out in a jerky voice, speaking his phrases irregularly:

"It is hereby made known to the inhabitants of Goderville, and in general to all persons present at the market, that there was lost this morning on the road to Benzeville, between nine and ten o'clock, a black leather pocketbook containing five hundred francs and some business papers. The finder is requested to return same with all haste to the mayor's office or to Maître Fortune Houlbreque of Manneville; there will be twenty francs reward."

Then the man went away. The heavy roll of the drum and the crier's voice were again heard at a distance.

Then they began to talk of this event, discussing the chances that Maître Houlbreque had of finding or not finding his pocketbook.

And the meal concluded. They were finishing their coffee when a chief of the gendarmes appeared upon the threshold.

He inquired:

"Is Maître Hauchecome of Breaute here?"

Maître Hauchecome, seated at the other end of the table, replied:

"Here I am."

And the officer resumed:

"Maître Hauchecome, will you have the goodness to accompany me to the mayor's office? The mayor would like to talk to you."

The peasant, surprised and disturbed, swallowed at a draught his tiny glass of brandy, rose and, even more bent than in the morning, for the first steps after each rest were specially difficult, set out, repeating: "Here I am, here I am."

The mayor was awaiting him, seated on an armchair. He was the notary of the vicinity, a stout, serious man with pompous phrases.

"Maître Hauchecome," said he, "you were seen this morning to pick up, on the road to Benzeville, the pocketbook lost by Maître Houlbreque of Manneville."

The countryman, astounded, looked at the mayor, already terrified by this suspicion resting on him without his knowing why.

"Me? Me? Me pick up the pocketbook?"

"Yes, you yourself."

"Word of honor, I never heard of it."

"But you were seen."

"I was seen, me? Who says he saw me?"

"Monsieur Malandain, the harness maker."

The old man remembered, understood and flushed with anger.

"Ah, he saw me, the clodhopper, he saw me pick up this string here, M'sieu the Mayor." And rummaging in his pocket, he drew out the little piece of string.

But the mayor, incredulous, shook his head.

"You will not make me believe, Maître Hauchecome, that Monsieur Malandain, who is a man worthy of credence, mistook this cord for a pocketbook."

The peasant, furious, lifted his hand, spat at one side to attest his honor, repeating:

"It is nevertheless the truth of the good God, the sacred truth, M'sieu the Mayor. I repeat it on my soul and my salvation."

The mayor resumed:

"After picking up the object you stood like a stilt, looking a long while in the mud to see if any piece of money had fallen out."

The good old man choked with indignation and fear.

"How anyone can tell—how anyone can tell—such lies to take away an honest man's reputation! How can anyone——"

There was no use in his protesting; nobody believed him. He was confronted with Monsieur Malandain, who repeated and maintained his affirmation. They abused each other for an hour. At his own request Maître Hauchecome was searched; nothing was found on him.

Finally the mayor, very much perplexed, discharged him with the warning that he would consult the public prosecutor and ask for further orders.

The news had spread. As he left the mayor's office the old man was surrounded and questioned with a serious or bantering curiosity in which there was no indignation. He began to tell the story of the string. No one believed him. They laughed at him.

He went along, stopping his friends, beginning endlessly his statement and his protestations, showing his pockets turned inside out to prove that he had nothing.

They said:

"Old rascal, get out!"

And he grew angry, becoming exasperated, hot and distressed at not being believed, not knowing what to do and always repeating himself.

Night came. He must depart. He started on his way with three neighbors to whom he pointed out the place where he had picked up the bit of string, and all along the road he spoke of his adventure.

In the evening he took a turn in the village of Breaute in order to tell it to everybody. He only met with incredulity.

It made him ill at night.

The next day about one o'clock in the afternoon Marius Paumelle, a hired man in the employ of Maître Breton, husbandman at Ymanville, returned the pocketbook and its contents to Maître Houlbreque of Manneville.

This man claimed to have found the object in the road, but not knowing how to read, he had carried it to the house and given it to his employer.

The news spread through the neighborhood. Maître Hauchecome was informed of it. He immediately went the circuit and began to recount his story completed by the happy climax. He was in triumph.

"What grieved me so much was not the thing itself as the lying. There is nothing so shameful as to be placed under a cloud on account of a lie."

He talked of his adventure all day long; he told it on the highway to people who were passing by, in the wineshop to people who were drinking there and to persons coming out of church the following Sunday. He stopped strangers to tell them about it. He was calm now, and yet something disturbed him without his knowing exactly what it was. People had the air of joking while they listened. They did not seem convinced. He seemed to feel that remarks were being made behind his back.

On Tuesday of the next week he went to the market at Goderville, urged solely by the necessity he felt of discussing the case.

Malandain, standing at his door, began to laugh on seeing him pass. Why?

He approached a farmer from Crequetot who did not let him finish and, giving him a thump in the stomach, said to his face:

"You big rascal."

Then he turned his back on him.

Maître Hauchecome was confused; why was he called a big rascal?

When he was seated at the table in Jourdain's tavern he commenced to explain "the affair."

A horse dealer from Monvilliers called to him:

"Come, come, old sharper, that's an old trick; I know all about your piece of string!"

Hauchecome stammered:

"But since the pocketbook was found."

But the other man replied:

"Shut up, papa, there is one that finds and there is one that reports. At any rate you are mixed with it."

The peasant stood choking. He understood. They accused him of having had the pocketbook returned by a confederate, by an accomplice.

He tried to protest. All the table began to laugh.

He could not finish his dinner and went away in the midst of jeers.

He went home ashamed and indignant, choking with anger and confusion, the more dejected that he was capable, with his Norman cunning, of doing what they had accused him of and ever boasting of it as of a good turn. His innocence to him, in a confused way, was impossible to prove, as his sharpness was known. And he was stricken to the heart by the injustice of the suspicion.

Then he began to recount the adventures again, prolonging his history every day, adding each time new reasons, more energetic protestations, more solemn oaths which he imagined and prepared in his hours of solitude, his whole mind given up to the story of the string. He was believed so much the less as his defense was more complicated and his arguing more subtile.

"Those are lying excuses," they said behind his back.

He felt it, consumed his heart over it and wore himself out with useless efforts. He wasted away before their very eyes.

The wags now made him tell about the string to amuse them, as they make a soldier who has been on a campaign tell about his battles. His mind, touched to the depth, began to weaken.

Toward the end of December he took to his bed.

He died in the first days of January, and in the delirium of his death struggles he kept claiming his innocence, reiterating:

"A piece of string, a piece of string—look—here it is, M'sieu the Mayor."

THE STORY OF A FARM GIRL

As THE WEATHER was very fine the people on the farm had dined more quickly than usual and had returned to the fields.

The female servant, Rose, remained alone in the large kitchen, where the fire on the hearth was dying out under the large boiler of hot water. From time to time she took some water out of it and slowly washed her plates and dishes, stopping occasionally to look at the two streaks of light which the sun threw onto the long table through the window and which showed the defects in the glass.

Three venturesome hens were picking up the crumbs under the chairs, while the smell of the poultry yard and the warmth from the cow stall came in through the half-open door, and a cock was heard crowing in the distance.

When she had finished her work, wiped down the table, dusted the mantelpiece and put the plates onto the high dresser, close to the wooden clock with its enormous pendulum, she drew a long breath, as she felt rather oppressed without knowing exactly why. She looked at the black clay walls, the rafters that were blackened with smoke, from which spiders' webs were hanging amid pickled herrings and strings of onions, and then she sat down, rather overcome by the stale emanations from the floor, on which so many things had been spilled. With these was mingled the smell of the pans of milk, which were set out to raise the cream in the adjoining dairy.

She wanted to sew, as usual, but she did not feel strong enough for it, and so she went to get a mouthful of fresh air at the door, which seemed to do her good.

The fowls were lying on the smoking dunghill; some of them were scratching with one claw in search of worms, while the cock stood up proudly among them. Now and then he selected one of them and walked round her with a slight cluck of amorous invitation. The hen got up in a careless way as she received his attentions, supported herself on her legs and spread out her wings; then she shook her feathers to shake out the dust and stretched herself out on the dunghill again, while he crowed in sign of triumph, and the cocks in all the neighboring farmyards replied to him, as if they were uttering amorous challenges from farm to farm.

The girl looked at them without thinking; then she raised her eyes and was almost dazzled at the sight of the apple trees in blossom, which looked almost like powdered heads. Just then a colt, full of life and friskiness, galloped past her. Twice he jumped over the ditches and then stopped suddenly, as if surprised at being alone.

She also felt inclined to run; she felt inclined to move and to stretch her limbs and to repose in the warm, breathless air. She took a few undecided steps and closed her eyes, for she was seized with a feeling of animal comfort; then she went to look for the eggs in the hen loft. There were thirteen of them, which she took in and put into the storeroom, but the smell from the kitchen disgusted her again, and she went out to sit on the grass for a time.

The farmyard, which was surrounded by trees, seemed to be asleep. The tall grass, among which the tall yellow dandelions rose up like streaks of yellow light, was of a vivid green, the fresh spring green. The apple trees threw their shade all round them, and the thatched houses, on which the blue and yellow iris flowers with their swordlike leaves grew, smoked as if the moisture of the stables and barns was coming through the straw.

The girl went to the shed where the carts and traps were kept. Close to it, in a ditch, there was a large patch of violets whose scent was perceptible all round, while beyond it could be seen the open country, where the corn was growing, with clumps of trees in the distance and groups of laborers here and there, who looked as small as dolls, and white horses like toys, who were pulling a child's cart, driven by a man as tall as one's finger.

She took up a bundle of straw, threw it into the ditch and sat down upon it; then, not feeling comfortable, she undid it, spread it out and lay down upon it at full length on her back, with both arms under her head and her limbs stretched out.

Gradually her eyes closed, and she was falling into a state of delightful languor. She was, in fact, almost asleep, when she felt two hands on her bosom, and then she sprang up at a bound. It was Jacques, one of the farm laborers, a tall fellow from Picardy, who had been making love to her for a long time. He had been looking after the sheep and, seeing her lying down in the shade, he had come stealthily, holding his breath, with glistening eyes and bits of straw in his hair.

He tried to kiss her, but she gave him a smack in the face, for she was as strong as he, and he was shrewd enough to beg her pardon, so they sat down side by side and talked amicably. They spoke about the favorable weather, of their master, who was a good fellow, then of their neighbors, of all the people in the country round, of themselves, of their village, of their youthful days, of their recollections, of their relatives whom they had not seen for a long time and might not see again. She grew sad, as she thought of it, while he, with one fixed idea in his head, rubbed against her with a kind of shiver, overcome by desire.

"I have not seen my mother for a long time," she said. "It is very hard to be separated like that." And she directed her looks into the distance, toward the village in the north, which she had left.

Suddenly, however, he seized her by the neck and kissed her again, but she struck him so violently in the face with her clenched fist that his nose began to bleed, and he got up and laid his head against the stem of a tree. When she saw that she was sorry and, going up to him, she said:

"Have I hurt you?"

He, however, only laughed. "No, it was a mere nothing," though she had hit him right on the middle of the nose. "What a devil!" he said, and he looked at her with admiration, for she had inspired him with a feeling of respect and of a very different kind of admiration, which was the beginning of real love for that tall, strong wench.

When the bleeding had stopped he proposed a walk, as he was afraid of his neighbor's heavy hand, if they remained side by side like that much longer, but she took his arm of her own accord in the avenue, as if they had been out for an evening walk, and said: "It is not nice of you to despise me like that, Jacques."

He protested, however. No, he did not despise her. He was in love with her; that was all.

"So you really want to marry me?" she asked.

He hesitated and then looked at her aside, while she looked straight ahead of her. She had fat red cheeks, a full, protuberant bust under her muslin dress, thick red lips, and her neck, which was almost bare, was covered with small beads of perspiration. He felt a fresh access of desire and, putting his lips to her ear, he murmured: "Yes, of course I do."

Then she threw her arms round his neck and kissed for such a long time that they both of them lost their breath. From that moment the eternal story of love began between them. They plagued one another in corners; they met in the moonlight under a haystack and gave each other bruises on the legs with their heavy nailed boots. By degrees, however, Jacques seemed to grow tired of her: he avoided her, scarcely spoke to her and did not try any longer to meet her alone, which made her sad and anxious, especially when she found that she was pregnant.

At first she was in a state of consternation; then she got angry, and her rage increased every day, because she could not meet him, as he avoided her most carefully. At last, one night when everyone in the farmhouse was asleep, she went out noiselessly in her petticoat, with bare feet, crossed the yard and opened the door of the stable where Jacques was lying in a large box of straw over his horses. He pretended to snore when he heard her coming, but she knelt down by his side and shook him until he sat up.

"What do you want?" he then asked of her. And she, with clenched teeth and trembling with anger, replied:

"I want—I want you to marry me, as you promised."

But he only laughed and replied: "Oh, if a man were to marry all the girls with whom he has made a slip, he would have more than enough to do."

Then she seized him by the throat, threw him on to his back, so that he could not disengage himself from her, and, half strangling him, she shouted into his face: "I am *enceinte*, do you hear? I am *enceinte!*"

He gasped for breath, as he was nearly choked, and so they remained, both of them, motionless and without speaking, in the dark silence which was only broken by the noise that a horse made as he pulled the hay out of the manger and then slowly chewed it.

When Jacques found that she was the stronger he stammered out: "Very well, I will marry you, as that is the case."

But she did not believe his promises. "It must be at once," she said. "You must have the banns put up."

"At once," he replied.

"Swear solemnly that you will."

He hesitated for a few moments and then said: "I swear it, by heaven."

Then she released her grasp and went away without another word.

She had no chance of speaking to him for several days, and as the stable was now always locked at night, she was afraid to make any noise, for fear of creating a scandal. One day, however, she saw another man come in at dinnertime, and so she said: "Has Jacques left?"

"Yes," the man replied; "I have got his place."

This made her tremble so violently that she could not take the saucepan off the fire, and later, when they were all at work, she went up into her room and cried, burying her head in her bolster so that she might not be heard.

During the day, however, she tried to obtain some information without exciting any suspicions, but she was so overwhelmed by the thoughts of her misfortune that she fancied that all the people whom she asked laughed maliciously. All she learned, however, was that he had left the neighborhood altogether.

II

Then a cloud of constant misery began for her. She worked mechanically, without thinking of what she was doing, with one fixed idea in her head: "Suppose people were to know."

This continual feeling made her so incapable of reasoning that she did not even try to think of any means of avoiding the disgrace that she knew must ensue, which was irreparable and drawing nearer every day and which was as sure as death itself. She got up every morning long before the others and persistently tried to look at her figure in a piece of broken looking glass at which she did her hair, as she was very anxious to know whether anybody would notice a change in her, and during the day she stopped working every few minutes to look at herself from top to toe, to see whether the size of her abdomen did not make her apron look too short.

The months went on. She scarcely spoke now, and when she was asked a question she did not appear to understand. She had a frightened look, with haggard eyes and trembling hands, which made her master say to her occasionally: "My poor girl, how stupid you have grown lately."

In church she hid behind a pillar and no longer ventured to go to confession. She feared to face the priest, to whom she attributed a superhuman power which enabled him to read people's consciences, and at mealtimes the looks of her fellow servants almost made her faint with mental agony. She was always fancying that she had been found out by the cowherd, a precocious and cunning little lad, whose bright eyes seemed always to be watching her.

One morning the postman brought her a letter, and as she had never received one in her life before, she was so upset by it that she was obliged to sit down. Perhaps it was from him? But as she could not read, she sat anxious and trembling with that piece of paper covered with ink in her hand; after a time, however, she put it into her pocket, as she did not venture to confide her secret to anyone. She often stopped in her work to look at the lines, written at regular intervals and terminating in a signature, imagining vaguely that she would suddenly discover their meaning. At last, as she felt half mad with impatience and anxiety, she went to the schoolmaster, who told her to sit down and read the letter to her, as follows:

"My Dear Daughter: *I write to tell you that I am very ill. Our neighbor, Monsieur Dentu, begs you to come, if you can,*
"*For your affectionate mother,*
"Cesaire Dentu,
"*Deputy Mayor.*"

She did not say a word and went away, but as soon as she was alone her legs gave way, and she fell down by the roadside and remained there till night.

When she got back she told the farmer her trouble. He allowed her to go home for as long as she wanted, promised to have her work done by a charwoman and to take her back when she returned.

Her mother died soon after she got there, and the next day Rose gave birth to a seven months' child, a miserable little skeleton, thin enough to make anybody shudder. It seemed to be suffering continually, to judge from the painful manner in which it moved its poor little limbs, which were as thin as a crab's legs, but it lived, for all that. She said that she was married but that she could not saddle herself with the child, so she left it with some neighbors who promised to take great care of it, and she went back to the farm.

But then in her heart, which had been wounded so long, there arose something like brightness, an unknown love for that frail little creature which she had left behind her, but there was fresh suffering in that very love, suffering which she felt every hour and every minute, because she was parted from the child. What pained her most, however, was a mad longing to kiss it, to press it in her arms, to feel the warmth of its little body against her skin. She could not sleep at night; she thought of it the whole day long, and in the evening, when her work was done, she used to sit in front of the fire and look at it intently, like people do whose thoughts are far away.

They began to talk about her and to tease her about her lover. They asked her whether he was tall, handsome and rich. When was the wedding to be, and the christening? And often she ran away to cry by herself, for these questions seemed to hurt her, like the prick of a pin, and in order to forget their jokes she began to work still more energetically and, still thinking of her child, she sought for the means of saving up money for it and determined to work so that her master would be obliged to raise her wages.

Then by degrees she almost monopolized the work and persuaded him to get rid of one servant girl who had become useless since she had taken to working like two; she economized in the bread, oil and candles, in the corn which they gave to the fowls too extravagantly and in the fodder for the horses and cattle, which was rather wasted. She was as miserly about her master's money as if it had been her own, and by dint of making good bargains, of getting high prices for all their produce and by baffling the peasants' tricks when they offered anything for sale, he at last intrusted her with buying and selling everything, with the direction of all the laborers and with the quantity of provisions necessary for the household, so that in a short time she became indispensable to him. She kept such a strict eye on everything about her, that under her direction the farm prospered wonderfully, and for five miles round people talked of "Master Vallin's servant," and the farmer himself said everywhere: "That girl is worth more than her weight in gold."

But time passed by, and her wages remained the same. Her hard work was accepted as something that was due from every good servant and as a mere token of her good will, and she began to think rather bitterly that if the farmer could put fifty or a hundred crowns extra into the bank every month, thanks to her, she was still earning only her two hundred francs a year, neither more nor less, and so she made up her mind to ask for an increase of wages. She went to see the schoolmaster three times about it, but when she got there she spoke about something else. She felt a kind of modesty in asking for money, as if it were something disgraceful, but at last one day, when the farmer was having breakfast by himself in the kitchen, she said to him with some embarrassment that she wished to speak to him particularly. He raised his head in surprise, with both his hands on the table, holding his knife, with its point in the air, in one, and a piece of bread in the other. He looked fixedly at the girl, who felt uncomfortable under his gaze but asked for a week's holiday, so that she might get away, as she was not very well. He acceded to her request immediately and then added in some embarrassment himself:

"When you come back I shall have something to say to you myself."

III

The child was nearly eight months old, and she did not know it again. It had grown rosy and chubby all over, like a little bundle of living fat. She threw herself onto it as if it had been some prey and kissed it so violently that it began to scream with terror, and then she began to cry herself, because it did not know her and stretched out its arms to its nurse as soon as it saw her. But the next day it began to get used to her and laughed when it saw her, and she took it into the fields and ran about excitedly with it and sat down under the shade of the trees, and then, for the first time in her life, she opened her heart to somebody and told the infant her troubles, how hard her work was, her anxieties and her hopes, and she quite tired the child with the violence of her caresses.

She took the greatest pleasure in handling it, in washing and dressing it, for it seemed to her that all this was the confirmation of her maternity, and she would look at it, almost feeling surprised that it was hers, and she used to say to herself in a low voice as she danced it in her arms: "It is my baby; it is my baby."

She cried all the way home as she returned to the farm and had scarcely got in, before her master called her into his room. She went in, feeling astonished and nervous, without knowing why.

"Sit down there," he said.

She sat down, and for some moments they remained side by side in some embarrassment, with their arms hanging at their sides, as if they did not know what to do with them and looking each other in the face, after the manner of peasants.

The farmer, a stout, jovial, obstinate man of forty-five, who had lost two wives, evidently felt embarrassed, which was very unusual with him. But at last he made up his mind and began to speak vaguely, hesitating a little and looking out of the window as he talked.

"How is it, Rose," he said, "that you have never thought of settling in life?"

She grew as pale as death and, seeing that she gave him no answer, he went on:
"You are a good, steady, active and economical girl, and a wife like you would make a man's fortune."

She did not move but looked frightened; she did not even try to comprehend his meaning, for her thoughts were in a whirl, as if at the approach of some great danger; so after waiting for a few seconds he went on:
"You see, a farm without a mistress can never succeed, even with a servant like you are."

Then he stopped, for he did not know what else to say, and Rose looked at him with the air of a person who thinks that he is face to face with a murderer and ready to flee at the slightest movement he may make, but after waiting for about five minutes he asked her:

"Well, will it suit you?"

"Will what suit me, master?"

And he said quickly: "Why, to marry me, by Jove!"

She jumped up but fell back onto her chair as if she had been struck, and there she remained, motionless, like a person who is overwhelmed by some great misfortune. But at last the farmer grew impatient and said: "Come, what more do you want?"

She looked at him almost in terror; then suddenly the tears came into her eyes, and she said twice in a choking voice: "I cannot; I cannot!"

"Why not?" he asked. "Come, don't be silly; I will give you until tomorrow to think it over."

And he hurried out of the room, very glad to have finished a matter which had troubled him a good deal. He had no doubt that she would the next morning accept a proposal which she could never have expected and which would be a capital bargain for him, as he thus bound a woman to himself who would certainly bring him more than if she had the best dowry in the district.

Neither could there be any scruples about an unequal match between them, for in the country everyone is very nearly equal. The farmer works just like his laborers do; the latter frequently become masters in their turn, and the female servants constantly become the mistresses of the establishment, without making any change in their life or habits.

Rose did not go to bed that night. She threw herself, dressed as she was, onto her bed, and she had not even strength to cry left in her; she was so thoroughly astonished. She remained quite inert, scarcely knowing that she had a body and without being at all able to collect her thoughts, though at moments she remembered a part of that which had happened, and then she was frightened at the idea of what might happen. Her terror increased, and every time the great kitchen clock struck the hour she broke into a perspiration from grief. She lost her head and had a nightmare; her candle went out, and then she began to imagine that someone had thrown a spell over her, as country people so often fancy, and she felt a mad inclination to run away, to escape and flee before her misfortune, as a ship scuds before the wind.

An owl hooted, and she shivered, sat up, put her hands to her face, into her hair and all over her body, and then she went downstairs, as if she were walking in her sleep. When she got into the yard she stooped down so as not to be seen by any prowling scamp, for the moon which was setting shed a bright light over the fields. Instead of opening the gate she scrambled over the fence, and as soon as she was outside she started off. She went on straight before her with a quick, elastic trot, and from time to time she unconsciously uttered a piercing cry. Her long shadow accompanied her, and now and then some night bird flew over her head, while the dogs in the farmyards barked as they heard her pass. One even jumped over the ditch, followed her and tried to bite her, but she turned round at it and gave such a terrible yell that the frightened animal ran back and cowered in silence in its kennel.

The stars grew dim, and the birds began to twitter; day was breaking. The girl was worn out and panting, and when the sun rose in the purple sky she stopped, for her swollen feet refused to go any farther. But she saw a pond in the distance, a large pond whose stagnant water looked like blood under the reflection of this new day, and she limped on with short steps and with her hand on her heart, in order to dip both her feet in it.

She sat down on a tuft of grass, took off her sabots which were full of dust, pulled off her stockings and plunged her legs into the still water, from which bubbles were rising here and there.

A feeling of delicious coolness pervaded her from head to foot, and suddenly, while she was looking fixedly at the deep pool, she was seized with giddiness and with a mad longing to throw herself into it. All her sufferings would be over in there; over forever. She no longer thought of her child; she only wanted peace, complete rest, and to sleep forever, and she got up with raised arms and took two steps forward. She was in the water up to her thighs and she was just about to throw herself in, when sharp, pricking pains in her ankles made her jump back. She uttered a cry of despair, for from her knees to the tips of her feet long black leeches were sucking in her lifeblood and were swelling as they adhered to her flesh. She did not dare to touch them and screamed with horror, so that her cries of despair attracted a peasant who was driving along at some distance to the spot. He pulled off the leeches one by one, applied herbs to the wounds and drove the girl to her master's farm in his gig.

She was in bed for a fortnight, and as she was sitting outside the door on the first morning that she got up the farmer suddenly came and planted himself before her.

"Well," he said, "I suppose the affair is settled, isn't it?"

She did not reply at first, and then, as he remained standing and looking at her intently with his piercing eyes, she said with difficulty: "No, master, I cannot."

But he immediately flew into a rage. "You cannot, girl; you cannot? I should just like to know the reason why?"

She began to cry and repeated: "I cannot."

He looked at her and then exclaimed angrily: "Then I suppose you have a lover?"

"Perhaps that is it," she replied, trembling with shame.

The man got as red as a poppy and stammered out in a rage: "Ah! So you confess it, you slut! And pray, who is the fellow? Some penniless, half-starved ragamuffin, without a roof to his head, I suppose? Who is it, I say?"

And as she gave him no answer he continued: "Ah! So you will not tell me. Then I will tell you; it is Jean Bauda!"

"No, not he," she exclaimed.

"Then it is Pierre Martin?"

"Oh no, master."

And he angrily mentioned all the young fellows in the neighborhood, while she denied that he had hit upon the right one and every moment wiped her eyes with the corner of her blue apron. But he still tried to find it out with his brutish obstinacy and, as it were, scratched her heart to discover her secret as a terrier scratches at a hole to try and get at the animal which he scents in it. Suddenly, however, the man shouted: "By George! It is Jacques, the man who was here last year. They used to say that you were always talking together and that you thought about getting married."

Rose was choking and she grew scarlet, while her tears suddenly stopped and dried upon her cheeks, like drops of water on hot iron, and she exclaimed: "No, it is not he; it is not he!"

"Is that really a fact?" asked the cunning farmer who partly guessed the truth, and she replied hastily:

"I will swear it; I will swear it to you." She tried to think of something by which to swear, as she did not dare to invoke sacred things.

But he interrupted her: "At any rate, he used to follow you into every corner and devoured you with his eyes at mealtimes. Did you ever give him your promise, eh?"

This time she looked her master straight in the face. "No, never, never; I will solemnly swear to you that if he were to come today and ask me to marry him I would have nothing to do with him."

She spoke with such an air of sincerity that the farmer hesitated, and then he continued, as if speaking to himself: "What then? You have not *had a misfortune*, as they call it, or it would have been known, and as it has no consequences, no girl would refuse her master on that account. There must be something at the bottom of it, however."

She could say nothing; she had not the strength to speak, and he asked her again: "You will not?"

"I cannot, master," she said with a sigh, and he turned on his heel.

She thought she had got rid of him altogether and spent the rest of the day almost tranquilly, but as worn out as if she, instead of the old white horse, had been turning the threshing machine all day. She went to bed as soon as she could and fell asleep immediately. In the middle of the night, however, two hands touching the bed woke her. She trembled with fear, but she immediately recognized the farmer's voice when he said to her: "Don't be frightened, Rose, I have come to speak to you."

She was surprised at first, but when he tried to take liberties with her she understood what he wanted and began to tremble violently. She felt quite alone in the darkness, still heavy from sleep and quite unprotected, by the side of the man who stood near her. She certainly did not consent but resisted carelessly, herself struggling against that instinct which is always strong in simple natures and very imperfectly protected by the undecided will of an exhausted body. She turned her head now toward the wall and now toward the room, in order to avoid the attentions which the farmer tried to press on her, and her body writhed under the coverlet, weakened as she was by the fatigue of the struggle, while he became brutal, intoxicated by desire.

They lived together as man and wife, and one morning he said to her: "I have put up our banns, and we will get married next month."

She did not reply, for what could she say? She did not resist, for what could she do?

IV

She married him. She felt as if she were in a pit with inaccessible edges, from which she could never get out, and all kinds of misfortunes remained hanging over her head, like huge rocks, which would fall on the first occasion. Her husband gave her the impression of a man from whom she had stolen and who would find it out someday or other. And then she thought of her child who was the cause of her misfortunes but was also the cause of all her happiness on earth. She went to see him twice a year and she came back more unhappy each time.

But she gradually grew accustomed to her life; her fears were allayed; her heart was at rest, and she lived with an easier mind, although still with some vague fear floating in her mind. So years went on, and the child was six. She was almost happy now, when suddenly the farmer's temper grew very bad.

For two or three years he seemed to have been nursing some secret anxiety, to be troubled by some care, some mental disturbance, which was gradually increasing. He remained at table a long time after dinner, with his head in his hands, sad and devoured by sorrow. He always spoke hastily, sometimes even brutally, and it even seemed as if he bore a grudge against his wife, for at times he answered her roughly, almost angrily.

One day, when a neighbor's boy came for some eggs and she spoke rather crossly to him, for she was very busy, her husband suddenly came in and said to her in his unpleasant voice: "If that were your own child you would not treat him so."

She was hurt and did not reply, and then she went back into the house with all her grief awakened afresh. At dinner the farmer neither spoke to her nor looked at her and seemed to hate her, to despise her, to know something about the affair at last. In consequence she lost her head and did not venture to remain alone with him after the meal was over but left the room and hastened to the church.

It was getting dusk; the narrow nave was in total darkness, but she heard footsteps in the choir, for the sacristan was preparing the tabernacle lamp for the night. That spot of trembling light which was lost in the darkness of the arches looked to Rose like her last hope, and with her eyes fixed on it she fell on her knees. The chain rattled as the little lamps swung up into the air, and almost immediately the small bell rang out the Angelus through the increasing mist. She went up to him as he was going out.

"Is Monsieur le Curé at home?" she asked.

"Of course he is; this is his dinnertime."

She trembled as she rang the bell of the parsonage. The priest was just sitting down to dinner, and he made her sit down also. "Yes, yes, I know all about it; your husband has mentioned the matter to me that brings you here."

The poor woman nearly fainted, and the priest continued: "What do you want, my child?" And he hastily swallowed several spoonfuls of soup, some of which dropped on to his greasy cassock. But Rose did not venture to say anything more but got up to go, while the priest said: "Courage."

So she went out and returned to the farm, without knowing what she was doing. The farmer was waiting for her, as the laborers had gone away during her absence, and she fell heavily at his feet and, shedding a flood of tears, she said to him: "What have you got against me?"

He began to shout and to swear: "What have I got against you? That I have no children, by God! When a man takes a wife he does not want to be left alone with her until the end of his days. That is what I have against you. When a cow has no calves she is not worth anything, and when a woman has no children she is also not worth anything."

She began to cry and said: "It is not my fault! It is not my fault!"

He grew rather more gentle when he heard that and added: "I do not say that it is, but it is very annoying, all the same."

V

From that day forward she had only one thought—to have a child, another child. She confided her wish to everybody, and in consequence of this, a neighbor told her of an infallible method. This was to make her husband a glass of water with a pinch of ashes in it every evening. The farmer consented to try it but without success, so they said to each other: "Perhaps there are some secret ways?" And they tried to find out. They were told of a shepherd who lived ten leagues off, and so Vallin one day drove off to consult him. The shepherd gave him a loaf on which he had made some marks; it was kneaded up with herbs, and both of them were to eat a piece of it before and after their mutual caresses, but they ate the whole loaf without obtaining any results from it.

Next a schoolmaster unveiled mysteries and processes of love which were unknown in the country but infallible, so he declared, but none of them had the desired effect. Then the priest advised them to make a pilgrimage to the shrine at Fécamp. Rose went with the crowd and prostrated herself in the abbey and, mingling her prayers with the coarse wishes of the peasants around her, she prayed that she might be fruitful a second time, but it was in vain, and then she thought that she was being punished for her first fault and she was seized by terrible grief. She was wasting away with sorrow; her husband was growing old prematurely, and was wearing himself out in useless hopes.

Then war broke out between them; he called her names and beat her. They quarreled all day long, and when they were in bed together at night he flung insults and obscenities at her, panting with rage, until one night, not being able to think of any means of making her suffer more, he ordered her to get up and go and stand out of doors in the rain until daylight. As she did not obey him he seized her by the neck and began to strike her in the face with his fists, but she said nothing and did not move. In his exasperation he knelt on her, and with clenched teeth and mad with rage began to beat her. Then in her despair she rebelled and, flinging him against the wall with a furious gesture, she sat up and in an altered voice she hissed: "I have had a child; I have had one! I had it by Jacques; you know Jacques well. He promised to marry me, but he left this neighborhood without keeping his word."

The man was thunderstruck and could hardly speak, but at last he stammered out: "What are you saying? What are you saying?"

Then she began to sob, and amid her tears she said: "That was the reason why I did not want to marry you. I could not tell you, for you would have left me without any bread for my child. You have never had any children, so you cannot understand; you cannot understand!"

He said again, mechanically, with increasing surprise: "You have a child? You have a child?"

"You won me by force, as I suppose you know. I did not want to marry you," she said, still sobbing.

Then he got up, lighted the candle and began to walk up and down, with his arms behind him. She was cowering on the bed and crying, and suddenly he stopped in front of her and said: "Then it is my fault that you have no children?"

She gave him no answer, and he began to walk up and down again, and then, stopping again, he continued: "How old is your child?"

"Just six," she whispered.

"Why did you not tell me about it?" he asked.

"How could I?" she replied with a sigh.

He remained standing, motionless. "Come, get up," he said.

She got up with some difficulty, and then when she was standing on the floor he suddenly began to laugh with his hearty laugh of his good days, and, seeing how surprised she was, he added: "Very well, we will go and fetch the child, as you and I can have none together."

She was so scared that if she had the strength she would assuredly have run away, but the farmer rubbed his hands and said: "I wanted to adopt one, and now we have found one. I asked the curé about an orphan some time ago."

Then, still laughing, he kissed his weeping and agitated wife on both cheeks and shouted out, as if she could not hear him: "Come along, Mother, we will go and see whether there is any soup left; I should not mind a plateful."

She put on her petticoat, and they went downstairs; and while she was kneeling in front of the fireplace and lighting the fire under the saucepan, he continued to walk up and down the kitchen with long strides and said: "Well, I am really glad at this; I am not saying it for form's sake, but I am glad; I am really very glad."

IN THE MOONLIGHT

WELL MERITED was the name "soldier of God" by the Abbé Marignan. He was a tall, thin priest, fanatical to a degree, but just and of an exalted soul. All his beliefs were fixed, with never a waver. He thought that he understood God thoroughly, that he penetrated His designs, His wishes, His intentions.

Striding up and down the garden walk of his little country parsonage, sometimes a question arose in his mind: "Why did God make that?" Then in his thoughts, putting himself in God's place, he searched obstinately and nearly always was satisfied that he found the reason. He was not the man to murmur in transports of pious humility, "O Lord, thy ways are past finding out!" What he said was: "I am the servant of God; I ought to know the reason of what he does or to divine it if I do not."

Everything in nature seemed to him created with an absolute and admirable logic. The "wherefore" and the "because" were always balanced. The dawns were made to rejoice you on waking, the days to ripen the harvests, the rains to water them, the evenings to prepare for sleeping and the nights dark for sleep.

The four seasons corresponded perfectly to all the needs of agriculture, and to him the suspicion could never have come that nature has no intention and that all which lives has accustomed itself, on the contrary, to the hard conditions of different periods, of climates and of matter.

But he hated women; he hated them unconsciously and despised them by instinct. He often repeated the words of Christ, "Woman, what have I to do with thee?" and he would add, "One would almost say that God himself was ill pleased with that particular work of his hands." Woman for him was indeed the "child twelve times unclean" of whom the poet speaks. She was the temptress who had ensnared the first man and who still continued her damnable work; she was the being who is feeble, dangerous, mysteriously troublous. And even more than her poisonous beauty he hated her loving soul.

He had often felt women's tenderness attack him, and though he knew himself to be unassailable he grew exasperated at this need of loving which quivers continually in their hearts.

To his mind God had only created woman to tempt man and to test him. Man should not approach her without those precautions for defense which he would take, and the fears he would cherish, near an ambush. Woman, indeed, was just like a trap, with her arms extended and her lips open toward a man.

He had toleration only for nuns, rendered harmless by their vow; but he treated them harshly notwithstanding, because, ever at the bottom of their chained-up hearts, their chastened hearts, he perceived the eternal tenderness that constantly went out even to him although he was a priest.

He had a niece who lived with her mother in a little house near by. He was bent on making her a sister of charity. She was pretty and harebrained and a great tease. When the abbé sermonized she laughed; when he was angry at her she kissed him vehemently, pressing him to her heart while he would seek involuntarily to free himself from her embrace. Notwithstanding, it made him taste a certain sweet joy, awaking deep within him that sensation of fatherhood which slumbers in every man.

Often he talked to her of God, of his God, walking beside her along the footpaths through the fields. She hardly listened but looked at the sky, the grass, the flowers, with a joy of living which could be seen in her eyes. Sometimes she rushed forward to catch some flying creature and, bringing it back, would cry: "Look, my uncle, how pretty it is; I should like to kiss it." And this necessity to "kiss flies" or sweet flowers worried, irritated and revolted the priest who saw, even in that, the ineradicable tenderness which ever springs in the hearts of women.

One day the sacristan's wife, who kept house for the Abbé Marignan, told him very cautiously that his niece had a lover!

He experienced a dreadful emotion, and he stood choking, with the soap all over his face, in the act of shaving.

When he found himself able to think and speak once more he cried: "It is not true; you are lying, Melanie!"

But the peasant woman put her hand on her heart. "May our Lord judge me if I am lying, Monsieur le Curé. I tell you she goes to him every evening as soon as your sister is in bed. They meet each other beside the river. You have only to go there between ten o'clock and midnight and see for yourself."

He ceased scratching his chin and commenced to pace the room quickly, as he always did in his hours of gravest thought. When he tried to begin his shaving again he cut himself three times from nose to ear.

All day long he remained silent, swollen with anger and with rage. To his priestly zeal against the mighty power of love was added the moral indignation of a father, of a teacher, of a keeper of souls, who has been deceived, robbed, played with by a child. He felt the egotistical sorrow that parents feel when their daughter announces that she has chosen a husband without them and in spite of their advice.

After his dinner he tried to read a little, but he could not attune himself to it and he grew angrier and angrier. When it struck ten he took his cane, a formidable oaken club which he always carried when he had to go out at night to visit the sick. Smilingly he regarded the enormous cudgel, holding it in his solid, countryman's fist and cutting threatening circles with it in the air. Then suddenly he raised it and, grinding his teeth, he brought it down upon a chair, the back of which, split in two, fell heavily to the ground.

He opened his door to go out, but he stopped upon the threshold, surprised by such a splendor of moonlight as you seldom see.

Endowed as he was with an exalted spirit, such a spirit as must have belonged to those dreamer-poets, the Fathers of the Church, he felt himself suddenly softened and moved by the grand and serene beauty of the pale-faced night.

In his little garden, bathed in the soft brilliance, his fruit trees, all arow, were outlining in shadow upon the walk their slender limbs of wood scarce clothed with green; while the giant honeysuckle climbing on the house wall exhaled delicious sugared breaths which hovered through the warm clear night like a perfumed soul.

He began to breathe deep, drinking the air as drunkards drink their wine and walking slowly, ravished, surprised and almost oblivious of his niece.

As he stepped into the open country he stopped to contemplate the whole plain, inundated by this caressing radiance and drowned in the tender and languishing charm of the serene night. In chorus the frogs threw into space their short metallic notes, and with the seduction of the moonlight distant nightingales mingled that fitful music of theirs which brings no thoughts but dreams, a light and vibrant melody which seems attuned to kisses.

The abbé continued his walk, his courage failing, he knew not why. He felt, as it were, enfeebled and suddenly exhausted; he had a great desire to sit down, to pause right there and praise God in all His works.

Below him, following the bends of the little river, wound a great line of poplars. On and about the banks, wrapping all the tortuous watercourse in a kind of light, transparent wadding, hung suspended a fine mist, a white vapor, which the moon rays crossed and silvered and caused to gleam.

The priest paused yet again, penetrated to the depths of his soul by a strong and growing emotion. And a doubt, a vague uneasiness, seized on him; he felt that one of those questions he sometimes put to himself was now being born.

Why had God done this? Since the night is destined for sleep, for unconsciousness, for repose, for forgetfulness of everything, why, then, make it more charming than the day, sweeter than dawns and sunsets? And this slow, seductive star, more poetical than the sun and so discreet that it seems designed to light up things too delicate, too mysterious for the great luminary—why had it come to brighten all the shades? Why did not the sweetest of all songsters go to rest like the others? Why set himself to singing in the vaguely troubling dark? Why this half veil over the world? Why these quiverings of the heart, this emotion of the soul, this languor of the body? Why this display of seductions which mankind never sees, since night brings sleep? For whom was this sublime spectacle intended, this flood of poetry poured from heaven to earth? The abbé did not understand it at all.

But then, down there along the edge of the pasture, appeared two shadows walking side by side under the arched roof of the trees all soaked in glittering mist.

The man was the taller and had his arm about his mistress's neck; from time to time he kissed her on the forehead. They animated the lifeless landscape which enveloped them, a divine frame made, as it were, expressly for them. They seemed, these two, a single being, the being for whom this calm and silent night was destined; and they approached the priest like a living answer, the answer vouchsafed by his Master to his question.

He stood stock-still, overwhelmed and with a beating heart. He likened it to some Bible story such as the loves of Ruth and Boaz, the accomplishment of the will of the Lord in one of those great scenes talked of in Holy Writ. Through his head ran the versicles of the *Song of Songs,* the ardent cries, the calls of the body, all the passionate poetry of that poem which burns with tenderness and love. And he said to himself, "God perhaps has made such nights as this to clothe with his ideals the loves of men."

He withdrew before the couple, who went on arm in arm. It was really his niece, and now he asked himself if he had not been about to disobey God. For does not God indeed permit love, since He surrounds it visibly with splendor such as this?

And he fled in amaze, almost ashamed, as if he had penetrated into a temple where he had no right to enter.

MADAME TELLIER'S EXCURSION

MEN WENT there every evening at about eleven o'clock, just as they went to the café. Six or eight of them used to meet there, always the same set—not fast men, but respectable tradesmen and young men in government or some other employ—and they used to drink their chartreuse and tease the girls, or else they would talk seriously with Madame, whom everybody respected, and then would go home at twelve o'clock. The younger men would sometimes stay the night.

It was a small, comfortable house at the corner of a street behind St Etienne's Church. From the windows one could see the docks, full of ships which were being unloaded, and on the hill the old gray chapel, dedicated to the Virgin.

Madame, who came of a respectable family of peasant proprietors in the department of the Eure, had taken up her profession, just as she would have become a milliner or dressmaker. The prejudice against prostitution, which is so violent and deeply rooted in large towns, does not exist in the country places in Normandy. The peasant simply says: "It is a paying business," and sends his daughter to keep a harem of fast girls, just as he would send her to keep a girls' school.

She had inherited the house from an old uncle to whom it had belonged. Monsieur and Madame, who had formerly been innkeepers near Yvetot, had immediately sold their house, as they thought that the business at Fécamp was more profitable. They arrived one fine morning to assume the direction of the enterprise, which was declining on account of the absence of a head. They were good enough people in their way and soon made themselves liked by their staff and their neighbors.

Monsieur died of apoplexy two years later, for as his new profession kept him in idleness and without exercise, he had grown excessively stout, and his health had suffered. Since Madame had been a widow, all the frequenters of the establishment had wanted her, but people said that personally she was quite virtuous, and even the girls in the house could not discover anything against her. She was tall, stout and affable, and her complexion, which had become pale in the dimness of her house, the shutters of which were scarcely ever opened, shone as if it had been varnished. She had a fringe of curly false hair, which gave her a juvenile look, which in turn contrasted strongly with her matronly figure. She was always smiling and cheerful and was fond of a joke, but there was a shade of reserve about her which her new occupation had not quite made her lose. Coarse words always shocked her, and when any young fellow who had been badly brought up called her establishment by its right name, she was angry and disgusted.

In a word, she had a refined mind, and although she treated her women as friends, yet she very frequently used to say that she and they were not made of the same stuff.

Sometimes during the week she would hire a carriage and take some of her girls into the country, where they used to enjoy themselves on the grass by the side of the little river. They behaved like a lot of girls let out from a school and used to run races and play childish games. They would have a cold dinner on the grass and drink cider and go home at night with a delicious feeling of fatigue and in the carriage kiss Madame as a kind mother who was full of goodness and complaisance.

The house had two entrances. At the corner there was a sort of low café, which sailors and the lower orders frequented at night, and she had two girls whose special duty it was to attend to that part of the business. With the assistance of the waiter, whose name was Frederic and who was a short, light-haired, beardless fellow, as strong as a horse, they set the half bottles of wine and the jugs of beer on the shaky marble tables and then, sitting astride on the customers' knees, would urge them to drink.

The three other girls (there were only five in all) formed a kind of aristocracy and were reserved for the company on the first floor, unless they were wanted downstairs and there was nobody on the first floor. The salon of Jupiter, where the tradesmen used to meet, was papered in blue and embellished with a large drawing representing Leda stretched out under the swan. That room was reached by a winding staircase which ended at a narrow door opening on to the street, and above it all night long a little lamp burned behind wire bars, such as one still sees in some towns at the foot of the shrine of some saint.

The house, which was old and damp, rather smelled of mildew. At times there was an odor of eau de cologne in the passages, or a half-open door downstairs allowed the noise of the common men sitting and drinking downstairs to reach the first floor, much to the disgust of the gentlemen who were there. Madame, who was quite familiar with those of her customers with whom she was on friendly terms, did not leave the salon. She took much interest in what was going on in the town, and they regularly told her all the news. Her serious conversation was a change from the ceaseless chatter of the three women; it was a rest from the doubtful jokes of those stout individuals who every evening indulged in the commonplace amusement of drinking a glass of liquor in company with girls of easy virtue.

The names of the girls on the first floor were Fernande, Raphaelle and Rosa the Jade. As the staff was limited, Madame had endeavored that each member of it should be a pattern, an epitome of each feminine type, so that every customer might find as nearly as possible the realization of his ideal. Fernande represented the handsome blonde; she was very tall, rather fat and lazy, a country girl who could not get rid of her freckles and whose short, light, almost colorless, towlike hair, which was like combed-out flax, barely covered her head.

Raphaelle, who came from Marseilles, played the indispensable part of the handsome Jewess. She was thin, with high cheekbones covered with rouge, and her black hair, which was always covered with pomatum, curled onto her forehead. Her eyes would have been handsome if the right one had not had a speck in it. Her Roman nose came down over a square jaw, where two false upper teeth contrasted strangely with the bad color of the rest.

Rosa the Jade was a little roll of fat, nearly all stomach, with very short legs. From morning till night she sang songs which were alternately indecent or sentimental in a harsh voice, told silly, interminable tales and only stopped talking in order to eat, or left off eating in order to talk. She was never still, was as active as a squirrel, in spite of her fat and her short legs, and her laugh, which was a torrent of shrill cries, resounded here and there, ceaselessly, in a bedroom, in the loft, in the café, everywhere, and always about nothing.

The two women on the ground floor were Louise, who was nicknamed "la Cocotte,"[1] and Flora, whom they called "Balançière,"[2] because she limped a little. The former always dressed as Liberty with a tricolored sash, and the other as a Spanish woman with a string of copper coins, which jingled at every step she took, in her carroty hair. Both looked like cooks dressed up for the carnival and were like all other women of the lower orders, neither uglier nor better looking than they usually are. In fact, they looked just like servants at an inn and were generally called the "Two Pumps."

A jealous peace, very rarely disturbed, reigned among these five women, thanks to Madame's conciliatory wisdom and to her constant good humor; and the establishment, which was the only one of the kind in the little town, was very much frequented. Madame had succeeded in giving it such a respectable appearance; she was so amiable and obliging to everybody; her good heart was so well known, that she was treated with a certain amount of consideration. The regular customers spent money on her and were delighted when she was especially friendly toward them. When they met during the day they would say: "This evening, you know where," just as men say: "At the café after dinner." In a word, Madame Tellier's house was somewhere to go to, and her customers very rarely missed their daily meetings there.

[1] Slang for a lady of easy virtue.
[2] Swing, or seesaw.

One evening toward the end of May the first arrival, M. Poulin, who was a timber merchant and had been mayor, found the door shut. The little lantern behind the grating was not alight; there was not a sound in the house; everything seemed dead. He knocked gently at first, and then more loudly, but nobody answered the door. Then he went slowly up the street, and when he got to the market place he met M. Duvert, the gunmaker, who was going to the same place, so they went back together but did not meet with any better success. But suddenly they heard a loud noise close to them, and on going round the corner of the house they saw a number of English and French sailors who were hammering at the closed shutters of the café with their fists.

The two tradesmen immediately made their escape, for fear of being compromised, but a low *pst* stopped them; it was M. Tournevau, the fish curer, who had recognized them and was trying to attract their attention. They told him what had happened, and he was all the more vexed at it, as he, a married man and father of a family, only went there on Saturdays—*securitatis causa*, as he said, alluding to a measure of sanitary policy which his friend Dr Borde had advised him to observe. That was his regular evening, and now he would be deprived of it for the whole week.

The three men went as far as the quay together, and on the way they met young M. Phillippe, the banker's son, who frequented the place regularly, and M. Pinipesse, the collector. They all returned to the Rue aux Juifs together to make a last attempt. But the exasperated sailors were besieging the house, throwing stones at the shutters and shouting, and the five first-floor customers went away as quickly as possible and walked aimlessly about the streets.

Presently they met M. Dupuis, the insurance agent, and then M. Vassi, the judge of the tribunal of commerce, and they all took a long walk, going to the pier first of all. There they sat down in a row on the granite parapet and watched the rising tide, and when the promenaders had sat there for some time, M. Tournevau said: "This is not very amusing!"

"Decidedly not," M. Pinipesse replied, and they started off to walk again.

After going through the street on the top of the hill they returned over the wooden bridge which crosses the Retenue, passed close to the railway and came out again onto the market place, when suddenly a quarrel arose between M. Pinipesse and M. Tournevau about an edible fungus which one of them declared he had found in the neighborhood.

As they were out of temper already from annoyance, they would very probably have come to blows if the others had not interfered. M. Pinipesse went off furious, and soon another altercation arose between the ex-mayor, M. Poulin and M. Dupuis, the insurance agent, on the subject of the tax collector's salary and the profits which he might make. Insulting remarks were freely passing between them when a torrent of formidable cries were heard, and the body of sailors, who were tired of waiting so long outside a closed house, came into the square. They were walking arm in arm, two and two, and formed a long procession and were shouting furiously. The landsmen went and hid themselves under a gateway, and the yelling crew disappeared in the direction of the abbey. For a long time they still heard the noise which diminished like a storm in the distance, and then silence was restored. M. Poulin and M. Dupuis, who were enraged with each other, went in different directions without wishing each other good-by.

The other four set off again and instinctively went in the direction of Mme Tellier's establishment which was still closed, silent, impenetrable. A quiet, but obstinate drunken man was knocking at the door of the café; then he stopped and called Frederic, the waiter, in a low voice, but finding that he got no answer, he sat down on the doorstep and awaited the course of events.

The others were just going to retire when the noisy band of sailors reappeared at the end of the street. The French sailors were shouting the "Marseillaise," and the Englishmen, "Rule Britannia." There was a general lurching against the wall, and then the drunken brutes went on their way toward the quay, where a fight broke out between the two nations in the course of which an Englishman had his arm broken and a Frenchman his nose split.

The drunken man who had stopped outside the door was crying by this time, as drunken men and children cry when they are vexed, and the others went away. By degrees calm was restored in the noisy town; here and there at moments the distant sound of voices could be heard, only to die away in the distance.

One man was still wandering about, M. Tournevau, the fish curer, who was vexed at having to wait until the next Saturday. He hoped for something to turn up; he did not know what, but he was exasperated at the police for thus allowing an establishment of such public utility, which they had under their control, to be thus closed.

He went back to it, examined the walls and tried to find out the reason. On the shutter he saw a notice stuck up, so he struck a wax vesta and read the following in a large, uneven hand: "Closed on account of the confirmation."

Then he went away, as he saw it was useless to remain, and left the drunken man lying on the pavement, fast asleep, outside the inhospitable door.

The next day all the regular customers, one after the other, found some reason for going through the Rue aux Juifs with a bundle of papers under their arm, to keep them in countenance, and with a furtive glance they all read that mysterious notice:

CLOSED ON ACCOUNT OF THE
CONFIRMATION

II

Madame had a brother who was a carpenter in their native place, Virville, in the department of Eure. When Madame had still kept the inn at Yvetot she had stood godmother to that brother's daughter, who had received the name of Constance, Constance Rivet, she herself being a Rivet on her father's side. The carpenter, who knew that his sister was in a good position, did not lose sight of her, although they did not meet often, as they were both kept at home by their occupations and lived a long way from each other. But when the girl was twelve years old and about to be confirmed, he seized the opportunity to write to his sister and ask her to come and be present at the ceremony. Their old parents were dead, and as Madame could not well refuse, she accepted the invitation. Her brother, whose name was Joseph, hoped that by dint of showing his sister attentions she might be induced to make her will in the girl's favor, as she had no children of her own.

His sister's occupation did not trouble his scruples in the least, and, besides, nobody knew anything about it at Virville. When they spoke of her they only said: "Madame Tellier is living at Fécamp," which might mean that she was living on her own private income. It was quite twenty leagues from Fécamp to Virville, and for a peasant twenty leagues on land are more than is crossing the ocean to an educated person. The people at Virville had never been farther than Rouen, and nothing attracted the people from Fécamp to a village of five hundred houses in the middle of a plain and situated in another department. At any rate, nothing was known about her business.

But the confirmation was coming on, and Madame was in great embarrassment. She had no undermistress and did not at all dare to leave her house, even for a day. She feared the rivalries between the girls upstairs and those downstairs would certainly break out; that Frederic would get drunk, for when he was in that state he would knock anybody down for a mere word. At last, however, she made up her mind to take them all with her with the exception of the man, to whom she gave a holiday until the next day but one.

When she asked her brother he made no objection but undertook to put them all up for a night. So on Saturday morning the eight o'clock express carried off Madame and her companions in a second-class carriage. As far as Beuzeille they were alone and chattered like magpies, but at that station a couple got in. The man, an aged peasant dressed in a blue blouse with a folding collar, wide sleeves, tight at the wrist and ornamented with white embroidery, wore an old high hat with long nap. He held an enormous green umbrella in one hand and a large basket in the other, from which the heads of three frightened ducks protruded. The woman, who sat stiffly in her rustic finery, had a face like a fowl and a nose that was as pointed as a bill. She sat down opposite her husband and did not stir as she was startled at finding herself in such smart company.

There was certainly an array of striking colors in the carriage. Madame was dressed in blue silk from head to foot and had over her dress a dazzling red shawl of imitation French cashmere. Fernande was panting in a Scottish-plaid dress whose bodice, which her companions had laced as tight as they could, had forced up her falling bosom into a double dome that was continually heaving up and down and which seemed liquid beneath the material. Raphaelle, with a bonnet covered with feathers so that it looked like a nestful of birds, had on a lilac dress with gold spots on it; there was something oriental about it that suited her Jewish face. Rosa the Jade had on a pink petticoat with large flounces and looked like a very fat child, an obese dwarf, while the Two Pumps looked as if they had cut their dresses out of old flowered curtains, dating from the Restoration.

Perceiving that they were no longer alone in the compartment, the ladies put on staid looks and began to talk of subjects which might give the others a high opinion of them. But at Bolbec a gentleman with light whiskers, with a gold chain and wearing two or three rings, got in and put several parcels wrapped in oilcloth into the net over his head. He looked inclined for a joke and a good-natured fellow.

"Are you ladies changing your quarters?" he asked. The question embarrassed them all considerably. Madame, however, quickly recovered her composure and said sharply, to avenge the honor of her corps:

"I think you might try and be polite!"

He excused himself and said: "I beg your pardon; I ought to have said your nunnery."

As Madame could not think of a retort, or perhaps as she thought herself justified sufficiently, she gave him a dignified bow and pinched in her lips.

Then the gentleman, who was sitting between Rosa the Jade and the old peasant, began to wink knowingly at the ducks, whose heads were sticking out of the basket. When he felt that he had fixed the attention of his public he began to tickle them under their bills and spoke funnily to them, to make the company smile.

"We have left our little pond, qu-ack! qu-ack! to make the acquaintance of the little spit, qu-ack! qu-ack!"

The unfortunate creatures turned their necks away to avoid his caresses and made desperate efforts to get out of their wicker prison and then suddenly, all at once, uttered the most lamentable quacks of distress. The women exploded with laughter. They leaned forward and pushed each other so as to see better; they were very much interested in the ducks, and the gentleman redoubled his airs, his wit and his teasing.

Rosa joined in and, leaning over her neighbor's legs, she kissed the three animals on the head. Immediately all the girls wanted to kiss them in turn, and the gentleman took them onto his knees, made them jump up and down and pinched them. The two peasants, who were even in greater consternation than their poultry, rolled their eyes as if they were possessed, without venturing to move, and their old wrinkled faces had not a smile or a movement.

Then the gentleman, who was a commercial traveler, offered the ladies braces by way of a joke and, taking up one of his packages, he opened it. It was a trick, for the parcel contained garters. There were blue silk, pink silk, red silk, violet silk, mauve silk garters, and the buckles were made of two gilt metal Cupids embracing each other. The girls uttered exclamations of delight and looked at them with that gravity which is natural to a woman when she is hankering after a bargain. They consulted one another by their looks or in a whisper and replied in the same manner, and Madame was longingly handling a pair of orange garters that were broader and more imposing than the rest, really fit for the mistress of such an establishment.

"Come, my kittens," he said, "you must try them on."

There was a torrent of exclamations, and they squeezed their petticoats between their legs, as if they thought he was going to ravish them, but he quietly waited his time and said: "Well, if you will not I shall pack them up again."

And he added cunningly: "I offer any pair they like to those who will try them on."

But they would not and sat up very straight and looked dignified.

But the Two Pumps looked so distressed that he renewed the offer to them. Flora especially hesitated, and he pressed her:

"Come, my dear, a little courage! Just look at that lilac pair; it will suit your dress admirably."

That decided her and, pulling up her dress, she showed a thick leg, fit for a milkmaid, in a badly fitting coarse stocking. The commercial traveler stooped down and fastened the garter below the knee first of all and then above it, and he tickled the girl gently, which made her scream and jump. When he had done he gave her the lilac pair and asked: "Who next?"

"I! I!" they all shouted at once, and he began on Rosa the Jade, who uncovered a shapeless, round thing without any ankle, a regular "sausage of a leg," as Raphaelle used to say.

The commercial traveler complimented Fernande and grew quite enthusiastic over her powerful columns.

The thin tibias of the handsome Jewess met with less flattery, and Louise Cocotte, by way of a joke, put her petticoats over the man's head, so that Madame was obliged to interfere to check such unseemly behavior.

Lastly Madame herself put out her leg, a handsome, muscular Norman leg, and in his surprise and pleasure the commercial traveler gallantly took off his hat to salute that master calf, like a true French cavalier.

The two peasants, who were speechless from surprise, looked askance out of the corners of their eyes. They looked so exactly like fowls that the man with the light whiskers, when he sat up, said, "Co—co—ri—co" under their very noses, and that gave rise to another storm of amusement.

The old people got out at Motteville with their basket, their ducks and their umbrella, and they heard the woman say to her husband as they went away:

"They are sluts who are off to that cursed place, Paris."

The funny commercial traveler himself got out at Rouen, after behaving so coarsely that Madame was obliged sharply to put him into his right place. She added as a moral: "This will teach us not to talk to the firstcomer."

At Oissel they changed trains, and at a little station farther on M. Joseph Rivet was waiting for them with a large cart and a number of chairs in it, which was drawn by a white horse.

The carpenter politely kissed all the ladies and then helped them into his conveyance.

Three of them sat on three chairs at the back, Raphaelle, Madame and her brother on the three chairs in front, and Rosa, who had no seat, settled herself as comfortably as she could on tall Fernande's knees, and then they set off.

But the horse's jerky trot shook the cart so terribly that the chairs began to dance, throwing the travelers into the air, to the right and to the left, as if they had been dancing puppets. This made them make horrible grimaces and screams, which, however, were cut short by another jolt of the cart.

They clung to the sides of the vehicle; their bonnets fell onto their backs, their noses on their shoulders, and the white horse trotted on, stretching out his head and holding out his tail quite straight, a little hairless rat's tail, with which he whisked his buttocks from time to time.

Joseph Rivet, with one leg on the shafts and the other bent under him, held the reins with elbows high and kept uttering a kind of chuckling sound which made the horse prick up its ears and go faster.

The green country extended on either side of the road, and here and there the colza in flower presented a waving expanse of yellow, from which there arose a strong, wholesome, sweet and penetrating smell which the wind carried to some distance.

The cornflowers showed their little blue heads among the rye, and the women wanted to pick them, but M. Rivet refused to stop.

Then sometimes a whole field appeared to be covered with blood, so thickly were the poppies growing, and the cart, which looked as if it were filled with flowers of more brilliant hue, drove on through the fields colored with wild flowers, to disappear behind the trees of a farm, then to reappear and go on again through the yellow or green standing crops studded with red or blue.

One o'clock struck as they drove up to the carpenter's door. They were tired out and very hungry, as they had eaten nothing since they left home. Madame Rivet ran out and made them alight, one after another, kissing them as soon as they were on the ground. She seemed as if she would never tire of kissing her sister-in-law, whom she apparently wanted to monopolize. They had lunch in the workshop, which had been cleared out for the next day's dinner.

A capital omelet, followed by boiled chitterlings and washed down by good sharp cider, made them all feel comfortable.

Rivet had taken a glass so that he might hobnob with them, and his wife cooked, waited on them, brought in the dishes, took them out and asked all of them in a whisper whether they had everything they wanted. A number of boards standing against the walls and heaps of shavings that had been swept into the corners gave out the smell of planed wood, of carpentering, that resinous odor which penetrates the lungs.

They wanted to see the little girl, but she had gone to church and would not be back until evening, so they all went out for a stroll in the country.

It was a small village through which the high road passed. Ten or a dozen houses on either side of the single street had for tenants the butcher, the grocer, the carpenter, the innkeeper, the shoemaker and the baker and others.

The church was at the end of the street. It was surrounded by a small churchyard, and four enormous lime trees which stood just outside the porch shaded it completely. It was built of flint, in no particular style, and had a slated steeple. When you got past it you were in the open country again, which was broken here and there by clumps of trees which hid some homestead.

Rivet had given his arm to his sister out of politeness, although he was in his working clothes, and was walking with her majestically. His wife, who was overwhelmed by Raphaelle's gold-striped dress, was walking between her and Fernande, and rotund Rosa was trotting behind with Louise Cocotte and Flora, the seesaw, who was limping along, quite tired out.

The inhabitants came to their doors; the children left off playing, and a window curtain would be raised so as to show a muslin cap, while an old woman with a crutch, who was almost blind, crossed herself as if it were a religious procession. They all looked for a long time after those handsome ladies from the town who had come so far to be present at the confirmation of Joseph Rivet's little girl, and the carpenter rose very much in the public estimation.

As they passed the church they heard some children singing; little shrill voices were singing a hymn, but Madame would not let them go in for fear of disturbing the little cherubs.

After a walk, during which Joseph Rivet enumerated the principal landed proprietors, spoke about the yield of the land and the productiveness of the cows and sheep, he took his flock of women home and installed them in his house, and as it was very small, he had put them into the rooms two and two.

Just for once Rivet would sleep in the workshop on the shavings; his wife was going to share her bed with her sister-in-law, and Fernande and Raphaelle were to sleep together in the next room. Louise and Flora were put into the kitchen, where they had a mattress on the floor, and Rosa had a little dark cupboard at the top of the stairs to herself, close to the loft, where the candidate for confirmation was to sleep.

When the girl came in she was overwhelmed with kisses; all the women wished to caress her with that need of tender expansion, that habit of professional wheedling which had made them kiss the ducks in the railway carriage.

They took her onto their laps, stroked her soft, light hair and pressed her in their arms with vehement and spontaneous outbursts of affection, and the child, who was very good natured and docile, bore it all patiently.

As the day had been a fatiguing one for everybody, they all went to bed soon after dinner. The whole village was wrapped in that perfect stillness of the country, which is almost like a religious silence, and the girls, who were accustomed to the noisy evenings of their establishment, felt rather impressed by the perfect repose of the sleeping village. They shivered, not with cold, but with those little shivers of solitude which come over uneasy and troubled hearts.

As soon as they were in bed, two and two together, they clasped each other in their arms, as if to protect themselves against this feeling of the calm and profound slumber of the earth. But Rosa the Jade, who was alone in her little dark cupboard, felt a vague and painful emotion come over her.

She was tossing about in bed, unable to get to sleep, when she heard the faints sobs of a crying child close to her head through the partition. She was frightened and called out and was answered by a weak voice, broken by sobs. It was the little girl who, being used to sleeping in her mother's room, was frightened in her small attic.

Rosa was delighted, got up softly so as not to awaken anyone and went and fetched the child. She took her into her warm bed, kissed her and pressed her to her bosom, caressed her, lavished exaggerated manifestations of tenderness on her and at last grew calmer herself and went to sleep. And till morning the candidate for confirmation slept with her head on Rosa's naked bosom.

At five o'clock the little church bell ringing the Angelus woke these women up, who as a rule slept the whole morning long.

The peasants were up already, and the women went busily from house to house, carefully bringing short, starched muslin dresses in bandboxes, or very long wax tapers with a bow of silk fringed with gold in the middle and with dents in the wax for the fingers.

The sun was already high in the blue sky which still had a rosy tint toward the horizon, like a faint trace of dawn, remaining. Families of fowls were walking about the hen houses, and here and there a black cock with a glistening breast raised his head, crowned by his red comb, flapped his wings and uttered his shrill crow, which the other cocks repeated.

Vehicles of all sorts came from neighboring parishes and discharged tall Norman women in dark dresses, with neck handkerchiefs crossed over the bosom and fastened with silver brooches, a hundred years old.

The men had put on blouses over their new frock coats or over their old dress coats of green cloth, the tails of which hung down below their blouses. When the horses were in the stable there was a double line of rustic conveyances along the road: carts, cabriolets, tilburies, charabancs, traps of every shape and age, resting on their shafts or pointing them in the air.

The carpenter's house was as busy as a beehive. The ladies, in dressing jackets and petticoats, with their long, thin, light hair which looked as if it were faded and worn by dyeing, were busy dressing the child, who was standing motionless on a table while Madame Tellier was directing the movements of her battalion. They washed her, did her hair, dressed her, and with the help of a number of pins they arranged the folds of her dress and took in the waist, which was too large.

Then when she was ready she was told to sit down and not to move, and the women hurried off to get ready themselves.

The church bell began to ring again, and its tinkle was lost in the air, like a feeble voice which is soon drowned in space. The candidates came out of the houses and went toward the parochial building which contained the school and the mansion house. This stood quite at one end of the village, while the church was situated at the other.

The parents, in their very best clothes, followed their children with awkward looks and with the clumsy movements of bodies that are always bent at work.

The little girls disappeared in a cloud of muslin which looked like whipped cream, while the lads, who looked like embryo waiters in a café and whose heads shone with pomatum, walked with their legs apart, so as not to get any dust or dirt onto their black trousers.

It was something for the family to be proud of; a large number of relatives from distant parts surrounded the child, and consequently the carpenter's triumph was complete.

Mme Tellier's regiment, with its mistress as its head, followed Constance; her father gave his arm to his sister; her mother walked by the side of Raphaelle, Fernande with Rosa, and the Two Pumps together. Thus they walked majestically through the village, like a general's staff in full uniform, while the effect on the village was startling.

At the school the girls arranged themselves under the Sister of Mercy and the boys under the schoolmaster, and they started off, singing a hymn as they went. The boys led the way in two files between the two rows of vehicles, from which the horses had been taken out, and the girls followed in the same order. As all the people in the village had given the town ladies the precedence out of politeness, they came immediately behind the girls and lengthened the double line of the procession still more, three on the right and three on the left, while their dresses were as striking as a bouquet of fireworks.

When they went into the church the congregation grew quite excited. They pressed against each other; they turned round; they jostled one another in order to see. Some of the devout ones almost spoke aloud, so astonished were they at the sight of these ladies, whose dresses were trimmed more elaborately than the priest's chasuble.

The mayor offered them his pew, the first one on the right, close to the choir, and Mme Tellier sat there with her sister-in-law; Fernande and Raphaelle, Rosa the Jade and the Two Pumps occupied the second seat, in company with the carpenter.

The choir was full of kneeling children, the girls on one side and the boys on the other, and the long wax tapers which they held looked like lances, pointing in all directions. Three men were standing in front of the lectern, singing as loud as they could.

They prolonged the syllables of the sonorous Latin indefinitely, holding on to the amens with interminable *a—as*, which the serpent of the organ kept up in the monotonous, long-drawn-out notes, emitted by the deep-throated pipes.

A child's shrill voice took up the reply, and from time to time a priest sitting in a stall and wearing a biretta got up, muttered something and sat down again. The three singers continued, with their eyes fixed on the big book of plain song lying open before them on the outstretched wings of an eagle mounted on a pivot.

Then silence ensued. The service went on, and toward the end of it Rosa, with her head in both her hands, suddenly thought of her mother and her village church on a similar occasion. She almost fancied that that day had returned when she was so small and almost hidden in her white dress, and she began to cry.

First of all she wept silently; the tears dropped slowly from her eyes, but her emotion increased with her recollections, and she began to sob. She took out her pocket handkerchief, wiped her eyes and held it to her mouth so as not to scream, but it was useless.

A sort of rattle escaped her throat, and she was answered by two other profound, heartbreaking sobs; for her two neighbors, Louise and Flora, who were kneeling near her, overcome by similar recollections, were sobbing by her side. There was a flood of tears, and as weeping is contagious, Madame soon found that her eyes were wet and on turning to her sister-in-law she saw that all the occupants of the pew were crying.

Soon throughout the church here and there a wife, a mother, a sister, seized by the strange sympathy of poignant emotion and agitated by the grief of those handsome ladies on their knees who were shaken by their sobs, was moistening her cambric pocket handkerchief and pressing her beating heart with her left hand.

Just as the sparks from an engine will set fire to dry grass, so the tears of Rosa and of her companions infected the whole congregation in a moment. Men, women, old men and lads in new blouses were soon sobbing; something superhuman seemed to be hovering over their heads—a spirit, the powerful breath of an invisible and all-powerful being.

Suddenly a species of madness seemed to pervade the church, the noise of a crowd in a state of frenzy, a tempest of sobs and of stifled cries. It passed over the people like gusts of wind which bow the trees in a forest, and the priest, overcome by emotion, stammered out incoherent prayers, those inarticulate prayers of the soul when it soars toward heaven.

The people behind him gradually grew calmer. The cantors, in all the dignity of their white surplices, went on in somewhat uncertain voices, and the organ itself seemed hoarse, as if the instrument had been weeping. The priest, however, raised his hand as a sign for them to be still and went to the chancel steps. All were silent immediately.

After a few remarks on what had just taken place, which he attributed to a miracle, he continued, turning to the seats where the carpenter's guests were sitting:

"I especially thank you, my dear sisters, who have come from such a distance and whose presence among us, whose evident faith and ardent piety have set such a salutary example to all. You have edified my parish; your emotion has warmed all hearts; without you this day would not, perhaps, have had this really divine character. It is sufficient at times that there should be one chosen to keep in the flock, to make the whole flock blessed."

His voice failed him again from emotion, and he said no more but concluded the service.

They all left the church as quickly as possible; the children themselves were restless, tired with such a prolonged tension of the mind. Besides, the elders were hungry, and one after another left the churchyard to see about dinner.

There was a crowd outside, a noisy crowd, a babel of loud voices in which the shrill Norman accent was discernible. The villagers formed two ranks, and when the children appeared each family seized their own.

The whole houseful of women caught hold of Constance, surrounded her and kissed her, and Rosa was especially demonstrative. At last she took hold of one hand, while Mme Tellier held the other, and Raphaelle and Fernande held up her long muslin petticoat so that it might not drag in the dust. Louise and Flora brought up the rear with Mme Rivet, and the child, who was very silent and thoughtful, set off home in the midst of this guard of honor.

The dinner was served in the workshop on long boards supported by trestles, and through the open door they could see all the enjoyment that was going on. Everywhere people were feasting; through every window could be seen tables surrounded by people in their Sunday clothes. There was merriment in every house—men sitting in their shirt sleeves, drinking cider, glass after glass.

In the carpenter's house the gaiety took on somewhat of an air of reserve, the consequence of the emotion of the girls in the morning. Rivet was the only one who was in good cue, and he was drinking to excess. Mme Tellier was looking at the clock every moment, for in order not to lose two days following they ought to take the 3:55 train, which would bring them to Fécamp by dark.

The carpenter tried very hard to distract her attention so as to keep his guests until the next day. But he did not succeed, for she never joked when there was business to be done, and as soon as they had had their coffee she ordered her girls to make haste and get ready. Then, turning to her brother, she said:

"You must have the horse put in immediately," and she herself went to complete her preparations.

When she came down again her sister-in-law was waiting to speak to her about the child, and a long conversation took place in which, however, nothing was settled. The carpenter's wife finessed and pretended to be very much moved, and Mme Tellier, who was holding the girl on her knees, would not pledge herself to anything definite but merely gave vague promises: she would not forget her; there was plenty of time, and then, they were sure to meet again.

But the conveyance did not come to the door, and the women did not come downstairs. Upstairs they even heard loud laughter, falls, little screams and much clapping of hands, and so while the carpenter's wife went to the stable to see whether the cart was ready Madame went upstairs.

Rivet, who was very drunk and half undressed, was vainly trying to kiss Rosa, who was choking with laughter. The Two Pumps were holding him by the arms and trying to calm him, as they were shocked at such a scene after that morning's ceremony, but Raphaelle and Fernande were urging him on, writhing and holding their sides with laughter, and they uttered shrill cries at every useless attempt that the drunken fellow made.

The man was furious; his face was red; his dress disordered, and he was trying to shake off the two women who were clinging to him while he was pulling Rosa's bodice with all his might and ejaculating: "Won't you, you slut?"

But Madame, who was very indignant, went up to her brother, seized him by the shoulders and threw him out of the room with such violence that he fell against a wall in the passage, and a minute afterward they heard him pumping water onto his head in the yard. When he came back with the cart he was already quite calmed down.

They seated themselves in the same way as they had done the day before, and the little white horse started off with his quick, dancing trot. Under the hot sun their fun, which had been checked during dinner, broke out again. The girls now were amused at the jolts which the wagon gave, pushed their neighbors' chairs and burst out laughing every moment, for they were in the vein for it after Rivet's vain attempt.

There was a haze over the country; the roads were glaring and dazzled their eyes. The wheels raised up two trails of dust which followed the cart for a long time along the highroad, and presently Fernande, who was fond of music, asked Rosa to sing something. She boldly struck up the "*Gros Curé de Meudon,*" but Madame made her stop immediately, as she thought it a song which was very unsuitable for such a day, and added:

"Sing us something of Béranger's."

After a moment's hesitation Rosa began Béranger's song, "The Grandmother," in her worn-out voice, and all the girls, and even Madame herself, joined in the chorus:

> "*How I regret*
> *My dimpled arms,*
> *My well-made legs,*
> *And my vanished charms!*"

"That is first-rate," Rivet declared, carried away by the rhythm. They shouted the refrain to every verse, while Rivet beat time on the shafts with his foot and on the horse's back with the reins. The animal himself, carried away by the rhythm, broke into a wild gallop and threw all the women in a heap, one on top of the other, in the bottom of the conveyance.

They got up, laughing as if they were crazy, and the song went on, shouted at the top of their voices, beneath the burning sky and among the ripening grain, to the rapid gallop of the little horse who set off every time the refrain was sung and galloped a hundred yards, to their great delight. Occasionally a stone breaker by the roadside sat up and looked at the wild and shouting female load through his wire spectacles.

When they got out at the station the carpenter said:

"I am sorry you are going; we might have had some fun together."

But Madame replied very sensibly: "Everything has its right time, and we cannot always be enjoying ourselves."

And then he had a sudden inspiration: "Look here, I will come and see you at Fécamp next month." And he gave a knowing look with his bright and roguish eyes.

"Come," Madame said, "you must be sensible; you may come if you like, but you are not to be up to any of your tricks."

He did not reply, and as they heard the whistle of the train he immediately began to kiss them all. When it came to Rosa's turn he tried to get to her mouth which she, however, smiling with her lips closed, turned away from him each time by a rapid movement of her head to one side. He held her in his arms, but he could not attain his object as his large whip, which he was holding in his hand and waving behind the girl's back in desperation, interfered with his efforts.

"Passengers for Rouen, take your seats, please!" a guard cried, and they got in. There was a slight whistle, followed by a loud one from the engine, which noisily puffed out its first jet of steam while the wheels began to turn a little with visible effort. Rivet left the station and went to the gate by the side of the line to get another look at Rosa, and as the carriage full of human merchandise passed him he began to crack his whip and to jump, singing at the top of his voice:

> "How I regret
> My dimpled arms,
> My well-made legs,
> And my vanished charms!"

And then he watched a white pocket handkerchief which somebody was waving as it disappeared in the distance.

III

They slept the peaceful sleep of quiet consciences until they got to Rouen. When they returned to the house, refreshed and rested, Madame could not help saying:

"It was all very well, but I was already longing to get home."

They hurried over their supper, and then, when they had put on their usual light evening costumes, waited for their usual customers. The little colored lamp outside the door told the passers-by that the flock had returned to the fold, and in a moment the news spread; nobody knew how or by whom.

M. Philippe, the banker's son, even carried his audacity so far as to send a special messenger to M. Tournevau, who was in the bosom of his family.

The fish curer used every Sunday to have several cousins to dinner, and they were having coffee, when a man came in with a letter in his hand. M. Tournevau was much excited; he opened the envelope and grew pale; it only contained these words in pencil:

The cargo of fish has been found; the ship has come into port; good business for you. Come immediately.

He felt in his pockets, gave the messenger twopence and, suddenly blushing to his ears, he said: "I must go out." He handed his wife the laconic and mysterious note, rang the bell, and when the servant came in he asked her to bring him his hat and overcoat immediately. As soon as he was in the street he began to run, and the way seemed to him to be twice as long as usual, in consequence of his impatience.

Mme Tellier's establishment had put on quite a holiday look. On the ground floor a number of sailors were making a deafening noise, and Louise and Flora drank with one and the other so as to merit their name of the Two Pumps more than ever. They were being called for everywhere at once; already they were not quite sober enough for their business, and the night bid fair to be a very jolly one.

The upstairs room was full by nine o'clock. M. Vassi, the judge of the tribunal of commerce, Madame's usual platonic wooer, was talking to her in a corner in a low voice, and they were both smiling, as if they were about to come to an understanding.

M. Poulin, the ex-mayor, was holding Rosa on his knees, and she, with her nose close to his, was running her hands through the old gentleman's white whiskers.

Tall Fernande, who was lying on the sofa, had both her feet on M. Pinipesse the tax collector's stomach and her back on young M. Philippe's waistcoat; her right arm was round his neck, and she held a cigarette in her left.

Raphaelle appeared to be discussing matters with M. Depuis, the insurance agent, and she finished by saying: "Yes, my dear, I will."

Just then the door opened suddenly, and M. Tournevau came in. He was greeted with enthusiastic cries of: "Long live Tournevau!" And Raphaelle, who was twirling around, went and threw herself into his arms. He seized her in a vigorous embrace, and without saying a word, lifting her up as if she had been a feather, he carried her through the room.

Rosa was chatting to the ex-mayor, kissing him every moment and pulling both his whiskers at the same time in order to keep his head straight.

Fernande and Madame remained with the four men, and M. Philippe exclaimed: "I will pay for some champagne; get three bottles, Madame Tellier." And Fernande gave him a hug and whispered to him: "Play us a waltz, will you?" So he rose and sat down at the old piano in the corner and managed to get a hoarse waltz out of the entrails of the instrument.

The tall girl put her arms round the tax collector, Madame asked M. Vassi to take her in his arms, and the two couples turned round, kissing as they danced. M. Vassi, who had formerly danced in good society, waltzed with such elegance that Madame was quite captivated.

Frederic brought the champagne; the first cork popped, and M. Philippe played the introduction to a quadrille, through which the four dancers walked in society fashion, decorously, with propriety of deportment, with bows and curtsies, and then they began to drink.

M. Philippe next struck up a lively polka, and M. Tournevau started off with the handsome Jewess whom he held up in the air without letting her feet touch the ground. M. Pinipesse and M. Vassi had started off with renewed vigor, and from time to time one or other couple would stop to toss off a long glass of sparkling wine. The dance was threatening to become never ending, when Rosa opened the door.

"I want to dance," she exclaimed. And she caught hold of M. Dupuis, who was sitting idle on the couch, and the dance began again.

But the bottles were empty. "I will pay for one," M. Tournevau said.

"So will I," M. Vassi declared.

"And I will do the same," M. Dupuis remarked.

Then all began to clap their hands, and it soon became a regular ball. From time to time Louise and Flora ran upstairs quickly, had a few turns while their customers downstairs grew impatient, and then they returned regretfully to the café. At midnight they were still dancing.

Madame shut her eyes to what was going on, and she had long private talks in corners with M. Vassi, as if to settle the last details of something that had already been agreed upon.

At last at one o'clock the two married men, M. Tournevau and M. Pinipesse, declared that they were going home and wanted to pay. Nothing was charged for except the champagne, and that only cost six francs a bottle instead of ten, which was the usual price, and when they expressed their surprise at such generosity Madame, who was beaming, said to them:

"We don't have a holiday every day."

LOVE

THREE PAGES FROM A SPORTSMAN'S BOOK

I HAVE JUST READ among the general news in one of the papers a drama of passion. He killed her and then he killed himself, so he must have loved her. What matters He or She? Their love alone matters to me, and it does not interest me because it moves me or astonishes me or because it softens me or makes me think, but because it recalls to my mind a remembrance of my youth, a strange recollection of a hunting adventure where Love appeared to me, as the Cross appeared to the early Christians, in the midst of the heavens.

I was born with all the instincts and the senses of primitive man, tempered by the arguments and the restraints of a civilized being. I am passionately fond of shooting, yet the sight of the wounded animal, of the blood on its feathers and on my hands, affects my heart so as almost to make it stop.

That year the cold weather set in suddenly toward the end of autumn, and I was invited by one of my cousins, Karl de Rauville, to go with him and shoot ducks on the marshes at daybreak.

My cousin was a jolly fellow of forty with red hair, very stout and bearded, a country gentleman, an amiable semibrute of a happy disposition and endowed with that Gallic wit which makes even mediocrity agreeable. He lived in a house, half farmhouse, half château, situated in a broad valley through which a river ran. The hills right and left were covered with woods, old manorial woods where magnificent trees still remained and where the rarest feathered game in that part of France was to be found. Eagles were shot there occasionally, and birds of passage, such as rarely venture into our overpopulated part of the country, invariably lighted amid these giant oaks as if they knew or recognized some little corner of a primeval forest which had remained there to serve them as a shelter during their short nocturnal halt.

In the valley there were large meadows watered by trenches and separated by hedges; then, further on, the river, which up to that point had been kept between banks, expanded into a vast marsh. That marsh was the best shooting ground I ever saw. It was my cousin's chief care, and he kept it as a preserve. Through the rushes that covered it, and made it rustling and rough, narrow passages had been cut, through which the flat-bottomed boats, impelled and steered by poles, passed along silently over dead water, brushing up against the reeds and making the swift fish take refuge in the weeds and the wild fowl, with their pointed black heads, dive suddenly.

I am passionately fond of the water: of the sea, though it is too vast, too full of movement, impossible to hold; of the rivers which are so beautiful but which pass on and flee away; and above all of the marshes, where the whole unknown existence of aquatic animals palpitates. The marsh is an entire world in itself on the world of earth—a different world which has its own life, its settled inhabitants and its passing travelers, its voices, its noises and above all its mystery. Nothing is more impressive, nothing more disquieting, more terrifying occasionally, than a fen. Why should a vague terror hang over these low plains covered with water? Is it the low rustling of the rushes, the strange will-o'-the-wisp lights, the silence which prevails on calm nights, the still mists which hang over the surface like a shroud; or is it the almost inaudible splashing, so slight and so gentle, yet sometimes more terrifying than the cannons of men or the thunders of the skies, which make these marshes resemble countries one has dreamed of, terrible countries holding an unknown and dangerous secret?

No, something else belongs to it—another mystery, perhaps the mystery of the creation itself! For was it not in stagnant and muddy water, amid the heavy humidity of moist land under the heat of the sun, that the first germ of life pulsated and expanded to the day?

I arrived at my cousin's in the evening. It was freezing hard enough to split the stones.

During dinner, in the large room whose sideboards, walls and ceiling were covered with stuffed birds with wings extended or perched on branches to which they were nailed—hawks, herons, owls, nightjars, buzzards, tercels, vultures, falcons—my cousin, who, dressed in a sealskin jacket, himself resembled some strange animal from a cold country, told me what preparations he had made for that same night.

We were to start at half-past three in the morning so as to arrive at the place which he had chosen for our watching place at about half-past four. On that spot a hut had been built of lumps of ice so as to shelter us somewhat from the trying wind which precedes daybreak, a wind so cold as to tear the flesh like a saw, cut it like the blade of a knife, prick it like a poisoned sting, twist it like a pair of pincers and burn it like fire.

My cousin rubbed his hands. "I have never known such a frost," he said; "it is already twelve degrees below zero at six o'clock in the evening."

I threw myself onto my bed immediately after we had finished our meal and went to sleep by the light of a bright fire burning in the grate.

At three o'clock he woke me. In my turn I put on a sheepskin and found my cousin Karl covered with a bearskin. After having each swallowed two cups of scalding coffee, followed by glasses of liqueur brandy, we started, accompanied by a gamekeeper and our dogs, Plongeon and Pierrot.

From the first moment that I got outside I felt chilled to the very marrow. It was one of those nights on which the earth seems dead with cold. The frozen air becomes resisting and palpable, such pain does it cause; no breath of wind moves it, it is fixed and motionless; it bites you, pierces through you, dries you, kills the trees, the plants, the insects, the small birds themselves, who fall from the branches onto the hard ground and become stiff themselves under the grip of the cold.

The moon, which was in her last quarter and was inclining all to one side, seemed fainting in the midst of space, so weak that she was unable to wane, forced to stay up yonder, seized and paralyzed by the severity of the weather. She shed a cold mournful light over the world, that dying and wan light which she gives us every month at the end of her period.

Karl and I walked side by side, our backs bent, our hands in our pockets and our guns under our arms. Our boots, which were wrapped in wool so that we might be able to walk without slipping on the frozen river, made no sound, and I looked at the white vapor which our dogs' breath made.

We were soon on the edge of the marsh and entered one of the lanes of dry rushes which ran through the low forest.

Our elbows, which touched the long ribbonlike leaves, left a slight noise behind us, and I was seized, as I had never been before, by the powerful and singular emotion which marshes cause in me. This one was dead, dead from cold, since we were walking on it in the middle of its population of dried rushes.

Suddenly, at the turn of one of the lanes, I perceived the ice hut which had been constructed to shelter us. I went in, and as we had nearly an hour to wait before the wandering birds would awake I rolled myself up in my rug in order to try and get warm. Then, lying on my back, I began to look at the misshapen moon, which had four horns through the vaguely transparent walls of this polar house. But the frost of the frozen marshes, the cold of these walls, the cold from the firmament penetrated me so terribly that I began to cough. My cousin Karl became uneasy.

"No matter if we do not kill much today," he said. "I do not want you to catch cold; we will light a fire." And he told the gamekeeper to cut some rushes.

We made a pile in the middle of our hut, which had a hole in the middle of the roof to let out the smoke, and when the red flames rose up to the clear crystal blocks they began to melt, gently, imperceptibly, as if they were sweating. Karl, who had remained outside, called out to me: "Come and look here!" I went out of the hut and remained struck with astonishment. Our hut, in the shape of a cone, looked like an enormous diamond with a heart of fire which had been suddenly planted there in the midst of the frozen water of the marsh. And inside we saw two fantastic forms, those of our dogs, who were warming themselves at the fire.

But a peculiar cry, a lost, a wandering cry, passed over our heads, and the light from our hearth showed us the wild birds. Nothing moves one so much as the first clamor of a life which one does not see, which passes through the somber air so quickly and so far off, just before the first streak of a winter's day appears on the horizon. It seems to me, at this glacial hour of dawn, as if that passing cry which is carried away by the wings of a bird is the sigh of a soul from the world!

"Put out the fire," said Karl; "it is getting daylight."

The sky was, in fact, beginning to grow pale, and the flights of ducks made long rapid streaks which were soon obliterated on the sky.

A stream of light burst out into the night; Karl had fired, and the two dogs ran forward.

And then nearly every minute now he, now I, aimed rapidly as soon as the shadow of a flying flock appeared above the rushes. And Pierrot and Plongeon, out of breath but happy, retrieved the bleeding birds whose eyes still, occasionally, looked at us.

The sun had risen, and it was a bright day with a blue sky, and we were thinking of taking our departure, when two birds with extended necks and outstretched wings glided rapidly over our heads. I fired, and one of them fell almost at my feet. It was a teal with a silver breast, and then, in the blue space above me, I heard a voice, the voice of a bird. It was a short, repeated, heart-rending lament; and the bird, the little animal that had been spared, began to turn round in the blue sky over our heads, looking at its dead companion which I was holding in my hand.

Karl was on his knees, his gun to his shoulder, watching it eagerly until it should be within shot. "You have killed the duck," he said, "and the drake will not fly away."

He certainly did not fly away; he circled over our heads continually and continued his cries. Never have any groans of suffering pained me so much as that desolate appeal, as that lamentable reproach of this poor bird which was lost in space.

Occasionally he took flight under the menace of the gun which followed his movements and seemed ready to continue his flight alone, but as he could not make up his mind to this he returned to find his mate.

"Leave her on the ground," Karl said to me; "he will come within shot by and by." And he did indeed come near us, careless of danger, infatuated by his animal love, by his affection for his mate which I had just killed.

Karl fired, and it was as if somebody had cut the string which held the bird suspended. I saw something black descend, and I heard the noise of a fall among the rushes. And Pierrot brought it to me.

I put them—they were already cold—into the same gamebag, and I returned to Paris the same evening.

MADEMOISELLE FIFI

THE Major Graf[1] von Farlsberg, the Prussian commandant, was reading his newspaper, lying back in a great armchair, with his booted feet on the beautiful marble fireplace, where his spurs had made two holes which grew deeper every day during the three months that he had been in the château of Urville.

A cup of coffee was smoking on a small inlaid table which was stained with liquors, burnt by cigars, notched by the penknife of the victorious officer who occasionally would stop while sharpening a pencil to jot down figures or to make a drawing on it, just as it took his fancy.

When he had read his letters and the German newspapers which his baggagemaster had brought him he got up, and after throwing three or four enormous pieces of green wood onto the fire—for these gentlemen were gradually cutting down the park in order to keep themselves warm—he went to the window. The rain was descending in torrents, a regular Normandy rain, which looked as if it were being poured out by some furious hand, a slanting rain, which was as thick as a curtain and which formed a kind of wall with oblique stripes and which deluged everything, a regular rain, such as one frequently experiences in the neighborhood of Rouen, which is the watering pot of France.

For a long time the officer looked at the sodden turf and at the swollen Andelle beyond it, which was overflowing its banks, and he was drumming a waltz from the Rhine on the windowpanes with his fingers, when a noise made him turn round; it was his second in command, Captain Baron von Kelweinstein.

The major was a giant with broad shoulders and a long, fair beard, which hung like a cloth onto his chest. His whole solemn person suggested the idea of a military peacock, a peacock who was carrying his tail spread out onto his breast. He had cold, gentle blue eyes and the scar from a sword cut which he had received in the war with Austria; he was said to be an honorable man as well as a brave officer.

The captain, a short, red-faced man who was tightly girthed in at the waist, had his red hair cropped quite close to his head and in certain lights

[1] Count.

almost looked as if he had been rubbed over with phosphorous. He had lost two front teeth one night, though he could not quite remember how. This defect made him speak so that he could not always be understood, and he had a bald patch on the top of his head, which made him look rather like a monk with a fringe of curly, bright golden hair round the circle of bare skin.

The commandant shook hands with him and drank his cup of coffee (the sixth that morning) at a draught, while he listened to his subordinate's report of what had occurred; and then they both went to the window and declared that it was a very unpleasant outlook. The major, who was a quiet man with a wife at home, could accommodate himself to everything, but the captain, who was rather fast, being in the habit of frequenting low resorts and much given to women, was mad at having been shut up for three months in the compulsory chastity of that wretched hole.

There was a knock at the door, and when the commandant said, "Come in," one of their automatic soldiers appeared and by his mere presence announced that breakfast was ready. In the dining room they met three other officers of lower rank: a lieutenant, Otto von Grossling, and two sublieutenants, Fritz Scheunebarg and Count von Eyrick, a very short, fair-haired man, who was proud and brutal toward men, harsh toward prisoners and very violent.

Since he had been in France his comrades had called him nothing but "Mademoiselle Fifi." They had given him that nickname on account of his dandified style and small waist, which looked as if he wore stays, from his pale face, on which his budding mustache scarcely showed, and on account of the habit he had acquired of employing the French expression, *fi, fi donc,* which he pronounced with a slight whistle when he wished to express his sovereign contempt for persons or things.

The dining room of the château was a magnificent long room whose fine old mirrors, now cracked by pistol bullets, and Flemish tapestry, now cut to ribbons and hanging in rags in places from sword cuts, told too well what Mademoiselle Fifi's occupation was during his spare time.

There were three family portraits on the walls: a steel-clad knight, a cardinal and a judge, who were all smoking long porcelain pipes which had been inserted into holes in the canvas, while a lady in a long pointed waist proudly exhibited an enormous pair of mustaches drawn with a piece of charcoal.

The officers ate their breakfast almost in silence in that mutilated room which looked dull in the rain and melancholy under its vanquished appearance, although its old oak floor had become as solid as the stone floor of a public house.

When they had finished eating and were smoking and drinking, they began, as usual, to talk about the dull life they were leading. The bottle of brandy and of liquors passed from hand to hand, and all sat back in their chairs, taking repeated sips from their glasses and scarcely removing the long bent stems, which terminated in china bowls painted in a manner to delight a Hottentot, from their mouths.

As soon as their glasses were empty they filled them again with a gesture of resigned weariness, but Mademoiselle Fifi emptied his every minute, and a soldier immediately gave him another. They were enveloped in a cloud of strong tobacco smoke; they seemed to be sunk in a state of drowsy, stupid intoxication, in that dull state of drunkenness of men who have nothing to do, when suddenly the baron sat up and said: "By heavens! This cannot go on; we must think of something to do." And on hearing this, Lieutenant Otto and Sublieutenant Fritz, who pre-eminently possessed the grave, heavy German countenance, said: "What, Captain?"

He thought for a few moments and then replied: "What? Well, we must get up some entertainment if the commandant will allow us."

"What sort of an entertainment, Captain?" the major asked, taking his pipe out of his mouth.

"I will arrange all that, Commandant," the baron said. "I will send *Le Devoir* to Rouen, who will bring us some ladies. I know where they can be found. We will have supper here, as all the materials are at hand, and at least we shall have a jolly evening."

Graf von Farlsberg shrugged his shoulders with a smile: "You must surely be mad, my friend."

But all the other officers got up, surrounded their chief and said: "Let Captain have his own way, Commandant; it is terribly dull here."

And the major ended by yielding. "Very well," he replied, and the baron immediately sent for *Le Devoir*.

The latter was an old corporal who had never been seen to smile, but who carried out all orders of his superiors to the letter, no matter what they might be. He stood there with an impassive face while he received the baron's instructions and then went out; five minutes later a large wagon belonging to the military train, covered with a miller's tilt, galloped off as fast as four horses could take it under the pouring rain, and the officers all seemed to awaken from their lethargy; their looks brightened, and they began to talk.

Although it was raining as hard as ever, the major declared that it was not so dull, and Lieutenant von Grossling said with conviction that the sky was clearing up, while Mademoiselle Fifi did not seem to be able to keep in his place. He got up and sat down again, and his bright eyes seemed to be looking for something to destroy. Suddenly, looking at the lady with the mustaches, the young fellow pulled out his revolver and said: "You shall not see it." And without leaving his seat he aimed and with two successive bullets cut out both the eyes of the portrait.

"Let us make a mine!" he then exclaimed, and the conversation was suddenly interrupted, as if they had found some fresh and powerful subject of interest. The mine was his invention, his method of destruction and his favorite amusement.

When he left the château the lawful owner, Count Fernand d'Amoys d'Urville, had not had time to carry away or to hide anything except the plate, which had been stowed away in a hole made in one of the walls so that, as he was very rich and had good taste, the large drawing room, which opened into the dining room, had looked like the gallery in a museum before his precipitate flight.

Expensive oil paintings, water colors and drawings hung upon the walls, while on the tables, on the hanging shelves and in elegant glass cupboards there were a thousand knickknacks: small vases, statuettes, groups in Dresden china, grotesque Chinese figures, old ivory and Venetian glass, which filled the large room with their precious and fantastical array.

Scarcely anything was left now; not that the things had been stolen, for the major would not have allowed that, but Mademoiselle Fifi *would have a mine,* and on that occasion all the officers thoroughly enjoyed themselves for five minutes. The little marquis went into the drawing room to get what he wanted, and he brought back a small, delicate china teapot, which he filled with gunpowder, and carefully introduced a piece of German tinder into it, through the spout. Then he lighted it and took this infernal machine into the next room, but he came back immediately and shut the door. The Germans all stood expectantly, their faces full of childish, smiling curiosity, and as soon as the explosion had shaken the château they all rushed in at once.

Mademoiselle Fifi, who got in first, clapped his hands in delight at the sight of a terra-cotta Venus, whose head had been blown off, and each picked up pieces of porcelain and wondered at the strange shape of the fragments, while the major was looking with a paternal eye at the large drawing room which had been wrecked in such a Neronic fashion and which was strewn with the fragments of works of art. He went out first and said, with a smile: "He managed that very well!"

But there was such a cloud of smoke in the dining room mingled with the tobacco smoke that they could not breathe, so the commandant opened the window, and all the officers, who had gone into the room for a glass of cognac, went up to it.

The moist air blew into the room and brought a sort of spray with it which powdered their beards. They looked at the tall trees which were dripping with the rain, at the broad valley which was covered with mist and at the church spire in the distance which rose up like a gray point in the beating rain.

The bells had not rung since their arrival. That was the only resistance which the invaders had met with in the neighborhood. The parish priest had not refused to take in and to feed the Prussian soldiers; he had several times even drunk a bottle of beer or claret with the hostile commandant, who often employed him as a benevolent intermediary, but it was no use to ask him for a single stroke of the bells; he would sooner have allowed himself to be shot. That was his way of protesting against the invasion, a peaceful and silent protest, the only one, he said, which was suitable to a priest who was a man of mildness and not of blood; and everyone for twenty-five miles round praised Abbé Chantavoine's firmness and heroism in venturing to proclaim the public mourning by the obstinate silence of his church bells.

The whole village grew enthusiastic over his resistance and was ready to back up their pastor and to risk anything, as they looked upon that silent protest as the safeguard of the national honor. It seemed to the peasants that thus they had deserved better of their country than Belfort and Strassburg, that they had set an equally valuable example and that the name of their little village would become immortalized by that, but with that exception, they refused their Prussian conquerors nothing.

The commandant and his officers laughed among themselves at that inoffensive courage, and as the people in the whole country round showed themselves obliging and compliant toward them, they willingly tolerated their silent patriotism. Only little Count Wilhelm would have liked to have forced them to ring the bells. He was very angry at his superior's politic compliance with the priest's scruples, and every day he begged the commandant to allow him to sound "dingdong, dingdong" just once, only just once, just by way of a joke. And he asked it like a wheedling woman, in the tender voice of some mistress who wishes to obtain something, but the commandant would not yield, and to console *herself* Mademoiselle Fifi made a *mine* in the château.

The five men stood there together for some minutes, inhaling the moist air, and at last Sublieutenant Fritz said with a laugh: "The ladies will certainly not have fine weather for their drive." Then they separated, each to his own duties, while the captain had plenty to do in seeing about the dinner.

When they met again as it was growing dark, they began to laugh at seeing each other as dandified and smart as on the day of a grand review. The commandant's hair did not look as gray as it did in the morning, and the captain had shaved—had only kept his mustache on, which made him look as if he had a streak of fire under his nose.

In spite of the rain they left the window open, and one of them went to listen from time to time. At a quarter past six the baron said he heard a rumbling in the distance. They all rushed down, and soon the wagon drove up at a gallop with its four horses, splashed up to their backs, steaming and panting. Five women got out at the bottom of the steps, five handsome girls whom a comrade of the captain, to whom *Le Devoir* had taken his card, had selected with care.

They had not required much pressing, as they were sure of being well treated, for they had got to know the Prussians in the three months during which they had had to do with them. So they resigned themselves to the men as they did to the state of affairs. "It is part of our business, so it must be done," they said as they drove along, no doubt to allay some slight, secret scruples of conscience.

They went into the dining room immediately, which looked still more dismal in its dilapidated state when it was lighted up, while the table, covered with choice dishes, the beautiful china and glass and the plate, which had been found in the hole in the wall, where its owner had hidden it, gave to the place the look of a bandits' resort, where they were supping after committing a robbery. The captain was radiant; he took hold of the women as if he were familiar with them, appraising them, kissing them, valuing them for what they were worth as *ladies of pleasure,* and when the three young men wanted to appropriate one each he opposed them authoritatively, reserving to himself the right to apportion them justly, according to their several ranks, so as not to wound the hierarchy. Therefore, so as to avoid all discussion, jarring and suspicion of partiality, he placed them all in a line according to height and addressing the tallest, he said in a voice of command:

"What is your name?"

"Pamela," she replied, raising her voice.

Then he said: "Number one, called Pamela, is adjudged to the commandant."

Then, having kissed Blondina, the second, as a sign of proprietorship, he proffered stout Amanda to Lieutenant Otto, Eva, "the Tomato," to Sub-lieutenant Fritz, and Rachel, the shortest of them all, a very young, dark girl, with eyes as black as ink, a Jewess, whose snub nose confirmed by exception the rule which allots hooked noses to all her race, to the youngest officer, frail Count Wilhelm von Eyrick.

They were all pretty and plump, without any distinctive features, and all were very much alike in look and person from their daily dissipation and the life common to houses of public accommodation.

The three younger men wished to carry off their women immediately, under the pretext of finding them brushes and soap, but the captain wisely opposed this, for he said they were quite fit to sit down to dinner and that those who went up would wish for a change when they came down, and so would disturb the other couples, and his experience in such matters carried the day. There were only many kisses, expectant kisses.

Suddenly Rachel choked and began to cough until the tears came into her eyes, while smoke came through her nostrils. Under pretense of kissing her the count had blown a whiff of tobacco into her mouth. She did not fly into a rage and did not say a word, but she looked at her possessor with latent hatred in her dark eyes.

They sat down to dinner. The commandant seemed delighted; he made Pamela sit on his right and Blondina on his left and said as he unfolded his table napkin: "That was a delightful idea of yours, Captain."

Lieutenants Otto and Fritz, who were as polite as if they had been with fashionable ladies, rather intimidated their neighbors, but Baron von Kelweinstein gave the reins to all his vicious propensities, beamed, made doubtful remarks and seemed on fire with his crown of red hair. He paid them compliments in French from the other side of the Rhine and sputtered out gallant remarks, only fit for a low pothouse, from between his two broken teeth.

They did not understand him, however, and their intelligence did not seem to be awakened until he uttered nasty words and broad expressions which were mangled by his accent. Then all began to laugh at once, like mad women, and fell against each other, repeating the words which the baron then began to say all wrong, in order that he might have the pleasure of hearing them say doubtful things. They gave him as much of that stuff as he wanted, for they were drunk after the first bottle of wine and, becoming themselves once more and opening the door to their usual habits, they kissed the mustaches on the right and left of them, pinched their arms, uttered furious cries, drank out of every glass and sang French couplets and bits of German songs which they had picked up in their daily intercourse with the enemy.

Soon the men themselves, intoxicated by that which was displayed to their sight and touch, grew very amorous, shouted and broke the plates and dishes, while the soldiers behind them waited on them stolidly. The commandant was the only one who put any restraint upon himself.

Mademoiselle Fifi had taken Rachel onto his knees and, getting excited, at one moment kissed the little black curls on her neck, inhaling the pleasant warmth of her body and all the savor of her person through the slight space there was between her dress and her skin, and at another pinched her furiously through the material and made her scream, for he was seized with a species of ferocity and tormented by his desire to hurt her. He often held her close to him, as if to make her part of himself, and put his lips in a long kiss on the Jewess's rosy mouth until she lost her breath, and at last he bit her until a stream of blood ran down her chin and onto her bodice.

For the second time she looked him full in the face, and as she bathed the wound she said: "You will have to pay for that!"

But he merely laughed a hard laugh and said: "I will pay."

At dessert champagne was served, and the commandant rose, and in the same voice in which he would have drunk to the health of the Empress Augusta he drank: "To our ladies!" Then a series of toasts began, toasts worthy of the lowest soldiers and of drunkards, mingled with filthy jokes which were made still more brutal by their ignorance of the language. They got up, one after the other, trying to say something witty, forcing themselves to be funny, and the women, who were so drunk that they almost fell off their chairs, with vacant looks and clammy tongues applauded madly each time.

The captain, who no doubt wished to impart an appearance of gallantry to the orgy, raised his glass again and said: "To our victories over hearts!" Thereupon Lieutenant Otto, who was a species of bear from the Black Forest, jumped up, inflamed and saturated with drink and seized by an access of alcoholic patriotism, cried: "To our victories over France!"

Drunk as they were, the women were silent, and Rachel turned round with a shudder and said: "Look here, I know some Frenchmen in whose presence you would not dare to say that." But the little count, still holding her on his knees, began to laugh, for the wine had made him very merry, and said: "Ha! ha! ha! I have never met any of them myself. As soon as we show ourselves they run away!"

The girl, who was in a terrible rage, shouted into his face: "You are lying, you dirty scoundrel!"

For a moment he looked at her steadily, with his bright eyes upon her, as he had looked at the portrait before he destroyed it with revolver bullets, and then he began to laugh: "Ah yes, talk about them, my dear! Should we be here now if they were brave?" Then, getting excited, he exclaimed: "We are the masters! France belongs to us!" She jumped off his knees with a bound and threw herself into her chair, while he rose, held out his glass over the table and repeated: "France and the French, the woods, the fields and the houses of France belong to us!"

The others, who were quite drunk and who were suddenly seized by military enthusiasm, the enthusiasm of brutes, seized their glasses and, shouting, "Long live Prussia!" emptied them at a draught.

The girls did not protest, for they were reduced to silence and were afraid. Even Rachel did not say a word, as she had no reply to make, and then the little count put his champagne glass, which had just been refilled, onto the head of the Jewess and exclaimed: "All the women in France belong to us also!"

At that she got up so quickly that the glass upset, spilling the amber-colored wine onto her black hair, as if to baptize her, and broke into a hundred fragments as it fell onto the floor. With trembling lips she defied the looks of the officer, who was still laughing, and she stammered out in a voice choked with rage: "That—that—that—is not true—for you shall certainly not have any French women."

He sat down again, so as to laugh at his ease and, trying effectually to speak in the Parisian accent, he said: "That is good, very good! Then what did you come here for, my dear?"

She was thunderstruck and made no reply for a moment, for in her agitation she did not understand him at first, but as soon as she grasped his meaning she said to him indignantly and vehemently: "I! I am not a woman; I am only a strumpet, and that is all that Prussians want."

Almost before she had finished he slapped her full in her face, but as he was raising his hand again, as if he would strike her, she, almost mad with passion, took up a small dessert knife from the table and stabbed him right in the neck, just above the breastbone. Something that he was going to say was cut short in his throat, and he sat there with his mouth half open and a terrible look in his eyes.

All the officers shouted in horror and leaped up tumultuously, but, throwing her chair between Lieutenant Otto's legs, who fell down at full length, she ran to the window, opened it before they could seize her and jumped out into the night and pouring rain.

In two minutes Mademoiselle Fifi was dead. Fritz and Otto drew their swords and wanted to kill the women, who threw themselves at their feet and clung to their knees. With some difficulty the major stopped the slaughter and had the four terrified girls locked up in a room under the care of two soldiers. Then he organized the pursuit of the fugitive as carefully as if he were about to engage in a skirmish, feeling quite sure that she would be caught.

The table, which had been cleared immediately, now served as a bed on which to lay Fifi out, and the four officers made for the window, rigid and sobered, with the stern faces of soldiers on duty, and tried to pierce through the darkness of the night, amid the steady torrent of rain. Suddenly a shot was heard and then another a long way off, and for four hours they heard from time to time near or distant reports and rallying cries, strange words uttered as a call in guttural voices.

In the morning they all returned. Two soldiers had been killed and three others wounded by their comrades in the ardor of that chase and in the confusion of such a nocturnal pursuit, but they had not caught Rachel.

Then the inhabitants of the district were terrorized; the houses were turned topsy-turvy; the country was scoured and beaten up over and over again, but the Jewess did not seem to have left a single trace of her passage behind her.

When the general was told of it he gave orders to hush up the affair so as not to set a bad example to the army, but he severely censured the commandant, who in turn punished his inferiors. The general had said: "One does not go to war in order to amuse oneself and to caress prostitutes." And Graf von Farlsberg, in his exasperation, made up his mind to have his revenge on the district, but as he required a pretext for showing severity, he sent for the priest and ordered him to have the bell tolled at the funeral of Count von Eyrick.

Contrary to all expectation, the priest showed himself humble and most respectful, and when Mademoiselle Fifi's body left the Château d'Urville on its way to the cemetery, carried by soldiers, preceded, surrounded and followed by soldiers, who marched with loaded rifles, for the first time the bell sounded its funereal knell in a lively manner, as if a friendly hand were caressing it. At night it sounded again, and the next day and every day; it rang as much as anyone could desire. Sometimes even it would start at night and sound gently through the darkness, seized by strange joy, awakened; one could not tell why. All the peasants in the neighborhood declared that it was bewitched, and nobody except the priest and the sacristan would now go near the church tower, and they went because a poor girl was living there in grief and solitude, secretly nourished by those two men.

She remained there until the German troops departed, and then one evening the priest borrowed the baker's cart and himself drove his prisoner to Rouen. When they got there he embraced her, and she quickly went back on foot to the establishment from which she had come, where the proprietress, who thought that she was dead, was very glad to see her.

A short time afterward a patriot who had no prejudices, who liked her because of her bold deed and who afterward loved her for herself, married her and made a lady of her.

MONSIEUR PARENT

LITTLE GEORGE was piling hills of sand in one of the walks. He scooped the sand up with both his hands, made it into a pyramid and then put a chestnut leaf on the top, and his father, sitting on an iron chair, was looking at him with concentrated and affectionate attention, seeing nobody else in the small public garden, which was full of people. All along the circular road other children were busy in the same manner or were indulging in other childish games, while nursemaids were strolling two and two with their bright cap ribbons floating behind them and carrying something wrapped up in lace in their arms. Here and there little girls in short petticoats and bare legs were talking seriously together while resting from trundling their hoops.

The sun was just disappearing behind the roofs of the Rue Saint-Lazare but still shed its rays obliquely on that little overdressed crowd. The chestnut trees were lighted up with its yellow rays, and the three fountains before the lofty porch of the church shone like molten silver.

M. Parent looked at his boy sitting there in the dusk; he followed his slightest movements with affection in his glance; but accidentally looking up at the church clock, he saw that he was five minutes late, so he got up, took the child by the arm and shook his sand-covered dress, wiped his hands and led him in the direction of the Rue Blanche. He walked quickly, so as not to get in after his wife, but as the child could not keep up the pace he took him up and carried him, though it made him pant when he had to walk up the steep street. Parent was a man of forty, turning gray already, rather stout. He had married, a few years previously, a young woman whom he dearly loved but who now treated him with the severity and authority of an all-powerful despot. She found fault with him continually for everything that he did or did not do, reproached him bitterly for his slightest acts, his habits, his simple pleasures, his tastes, his movements and walk and for having a round stomach and a placid voice.

He still loved her, however, but above all he loved the boy she had borne him, and George, who was now three, had become the greatest joy, in fact the preoccupation, of his heart. He himself had a modest private fortune and lived without doing anything on his twenty thousand francs[1] a year, and his wife, who had been quite portionless, was constantly angry at her husband's inactivity.

At last he reached his house, put down the child, wiped his forehead and walked upstairs. When he got to the second floor he rang. An old servant who had brought him up, one of those mistress-servants who are the tyrants of families, opened the door to him, and he asked her anxiously: "Has Madame come in yet?"

The servant shrugged her shoulders. "When have you ever known Madame to come home at half-past six, monsieur?"

And he replied with some embarrassment: "Very well; all the better; it will give me time to change my things, for I am very hot."

The servant looked at him with angry and contemptuous pity and grumbled: "Oh! I can see that well enough, you are covered with perspiration, monsieur. I suppose you walked quickly and carried the child, and only to have to wait until half-past seven, perhaps, for Madame. I have made up my

---

[1] About $4000.

mind not to have it ready at that time but shall get it for eight o'clock, and if you have to wait, I cannot help it; roast meat ought not to be burnt!"

M. Parent, however, pretended not to hear and only said: "All right! all right. You must wash George's hands, for he has been making sand pits. I will go and change my clothes; tell the maid to give the child a good washing."

And he went into his own room, and as soon as he got in he locked the door, so as to be alone, quite alone. He was so used now to being abused and badly treated that he never thought himself safe except when he was locked in. He no longer ventured even to think, reflect and reason with himself unless he had secured himself against her looks and insinuations by locking himself in. Having thrown himself into a chair, in order to rest for a few minutes before he put on clean linen, he remembered that Julie was beginning to be a fresh danger in the house. She hated his wife—that was quite plain; but she hated still more his friend Paul Limousin, who had continued to be the familiar and intimate friend of the house after having been the inseparable companion of his bachelor days, which is very rare. It was Limousin who acted as a buffer between his wife and himself and who defended him ardently and even severely against her undeserved reproaches, against crying scenes and against all the daily miseries of his existence.

But now for six months Julie had constantly been saying things against her mistress. She would repeat twenty times a day: "If I were you, monsieur, I should not allow myself to be led by the nose like that. Well, well! But there—everyone according to his nature." And one day she had even ventured to be insolent to Henriette, who, however, merely said to her husband at night: "You know, the next time she speaks to me like that I shall turn her out of doors." But she, who feared nothing, seemed to be afraid of the old servant, and Parent attributed her mildness to her consideration for the old domestic who had brought him up and who had closed his mother's eyes. Now, however, Henriette's patience was exhausted; matters could not go on like that much longer, and he was frightened at the idea of what was going to happen. What could he do? To get rid of Julie seemed to him to be such a formidable undertaking that he hardly ventured to think of it; but it was just as impossible to uphold her against his wife, and before another month could pass the situation between the two would become unbearable. He remained sitting there with his arms hanging down, vaguely trying to discover some means to set matters straight, but without success, and he said to himself: "It is lucky that I have George; without him I should be very miserable."

Then he thought he would consult Limousin, but the recollection of the hatred that existed between his friend and the servant made him fear lest the former should advise him to turn her away, and again he was lost in doubt and sad uncertainty. Just then the clock struck seven, and he started up. Seven o'clock, and he had not even changed his clothes! Then, nervous and breathless, he undressed, put on a clean shirt and hastily finished his toilette as if he had been expected in the next room for some event of extreme importance; then he went into the drawing room, happy at having nothing to fear. He glanced at the newspaper, went and looked out of the window and then sat down on a sofa again. The door opened and the boy came in, washed, brushed and smiling, and Parent took him up in his arms and kissed him passionately; then he tossed him into the air and held him up to the ceiling but soon sat down again, as he was tired with all his efforts, and taking George onto his knee, he made him "ride a cockhorse." The child laughed and clapped his hands and shouted with pleasure, as his father did, laughing until his big stomach shook, for it amused him almost more than it did the child.

Parent loved the boy with all the heart of a weak, resigned, ill-used man. He loved with mad bursts of affection, with caresses and with all the bashful tenderness which was hidden in him and which had never found an outlet, even at the early period of his married life, for his wife had always shown herself cold and reserved. Just then, however, Julie came to the door, with a pale face and glistening eyes, and said in a voice which trembled with exasperation: "It is half-past seven, monsieur." Parent gave an uneasy and resigned look at the clock and replied: "Yes, it certainly is half-past seven."

"Well, my dinner is quite ready now."

Seeing the storm which was coming, he tried to turn it aside. "But did you not tell me when I came in that it would not be ready before eight?"

"Eight! What are you thinking about? You surely do not mean to let the child dine at eight o'clock? It would ruin his stomach. Just suppose that he only had his mother to look after him! She cares a great deal about her child. Oh yes, we will speak about her; she is a mother. What a pity it is that there should be any mothers like her!"

Parent thought it was time to cut short a threatened scene, and so he said: "Julie, I will not allow you to speak like that of your mistress. You understand me, do you not? Do not forget it for the future."

The old servant, who was nearly choked with surprise, turned round and went out, slamming the door so violently after her that the lusters on the chandelier rattled and for some seconds it sounded as if a number of little invisible bells were ringing in the drawing room.

George, who was surprised at first, began to clap his hands merrily, and blowing out his cheeks, he gave a great *boom* with all the strength of his lungs, to imitate the noise of the door banging. Then his father began telling him stories, but his mind was so preoccupied that he continually lost the thread of his story, and the child, who could not understand him, opened his eyes wide in astonishment.

Parent never took his eyes off the clock; he thought he could see the hands move, and he would have liked to have stopped them until his wife's return. He was not vexed with her for being late, but he was frightened, frightened of her and Julie, frightened at the thought of all that might happen. Ten minutes more would suffice to bring about an irreparable catastrophe, words and acts of violence that he did not dare to picture to himself. The mere idea of a quarrel, of loud voices, of insults flying through the air like bullets, of two women standing face to face, looking at each other and flinging abuse at each other, made his heart beat and his tongue feel as parched as if he had been walking in the sun. He felt as limp as a rag, so limp that he no longer had the strength to lift up the child and dance him on his knee.

Eight o'clock struck; the door opened once more and Julie came in again. She had lost her look of exasperation, but now she put on an air of cold and determined resolution which was still more formidable.

"Monsieur," she said, "I served your mother until the day of her death, and I have attended to you from your birth until now, and I think it may be said that I am devoted to the family."

She waited for a reply, and Parent stammered:

"Why, yes, certainly, my good Julie."

She continued: "You know quite well that I have never done anything for the sake of money but always for your sake, that I have never deceived you nor lied to you, that you have never had to find fault with me."

"Certainly, my good Julie."

"Very well then, monsieur, it cannot go on any longer like this. I have said nothing and left you in your ignorance, out of respect and liking for you, but it is too much, and everyone in the neighborhood is laughing at you. Everybody knows about it, and so I must tell you also, although I do not like to repeat it. The reason why Madame comes in at any time she chooses is that she is doing abominable things."

He seemed stupefied, unable to understand, and could only stammer out: "Hold your tongue, you know I have forbidden you——" But she interrupted him with irresistible resolution.

"No, monsieur, I must tell you everything now. For a long time Madame has been doing wrong with Monsieur Limousin; I have seen them kiss scores of times behind the doors. Ah! you may be sure that if Monsieur Limousin had been rich, Madame would never have married Monsieur Parent. If you remember how the marriage was brought about, you would understand the matter from beginning to end."

Parent had risen and stammered out, deadly pale: "Hold your tongue—hold your tongue or——"

She went on, however: "No, I mean to tell you everything. She married you from interest, and she deceived you from the very first day. It was all settled between them beforehand. You need only reflect for a few moments to understand it; and then she was not satisfied with having married you, as she did not love you, she has made your life miserable, so miserable that it has almost broken my heart when I have seen it."

He walked up and down the room with his hands clenched, repeating: "Hold your tongue—hold your tongue," for he could find nothing else to say; the old servant, however, would not yield; she seemed resolved on everything, but George, who had been at first astonished and then frightened at those angry voices, began to utter shrill screams. He hid behind his father and roared, with his face puckered up and his mouth open.

His son's screams exasperated Parent and filled him with rage and courage. He rushed at Julie with both arms raised, ready to strike her, and exclaiming:

"Ah! you wretch! you will send the child out of his senses." He was almost touching her when she said:

"Monsieur, you may beat me if you like, me who reared you, but that will not prevent your wife from deceiving you or alter the fact that your child is not yours!"

He stopped suddenly and let his arms fall, and he remained standing opposite to her, so overwhelmed that he could understand nothing more, and she added: "You need only look at the child to know who is its father! He is the very image of Monsieur Limousin; you need only look at his eyes and forehead; why, a blind man could not be mistaken in him!"

But he had taken her by the shoulders and was now shaking her with all his might while he ejaculated: "Viper! viper! Go out the room, viper! Go out, or I shall kill you! Go out! Go out!"

And with a desperate effort he threw her into the next room. She fell on the table which was laid for dinner, breaking the glasses. Then, getting up, she put it between her master and herself, and while he was pursuing her, in order to take hold of her again, she flung terrible words at him: "You need only go out this evening after dinner and come in again immediately and you will see—you will see whether I have been lying! Just try it—and you will see." She had reached the kitchen door and escaped, but he ran after her, up the backstairs to her bedroom into which she had locked herself, and knocking at the door, he said: "You will leave my house this very instant."

"You may be certain of that, monsieur," was her reply. "In an hour's time I shall not be here any longer."

He then went slowly downstairs again, holding onto the banister so as not to fall, and went back to the drawing room where little George was sitting on the floor crying; he fell into a chair and looked at the child with dull eyes. He understood nothing, he knew nothing more; he felt dazed, stupefied, mad, as if he had just fallen on his head, and he scarcely even remembered the dreadful things the servant had told him. Then by degrees his reason grew clearer, like muddy water settling, and the abominable revelation began to work in his heart.

Julie had spoken so clearly, with so much force, assurance and sincerity, that he did not doubt her good faith, but he persisted in not believing her penetration. She might have been deceived, blinded by her devotion to him, carried away by unconscious hatred for Henriette. However, in measure as he tried to reassure and to convince himself, a thousand small facts recurred to his recollection: his wife's words, Limousin's looks, a number of unobserved, almost unseen trifles, her going out late, their simultaneous absence; and even some almost insignificant but strange gestures, which he could not understand, now assumed an extreme importance for him and established a connivance between them. Everything that had happened since his engagement surged through his overexcited brain in his misery, and he doggedly went through his five years of married life, trying to recollect every detail month by month, day by day, and every disquieting circumstance that he remembered stung him to the quick like a wasp's sting.

He was not thinking of George any more, who was quiet now and on the carpet, but seeing that no notice was being taken of him, the boy began to cry. Then his father ran up to him, took him into his arms and covered him with kisses. His child remained to him at any rate! What did the rest matter? He held him in his arms and pressed his lips onto his light hair and, relieved and composed, he whispered: "George—my little George—my dear little George!" But he suddenly remembered what Julie had said. Yes! she had said that he was Limousin's child. Oh, it could not be possible, surely! He could not believe it, could not doubt, even for a moment, that George was his own child. It was one of those low scandals which spring from servants' brains! And he repeated: "George—my dear little George." The youngster was quiet again now that his father was fondling him.

Parent felt the warmth of the little chest penetrate to his through their clothes, and it filled him with love, courage and happiness; that gentle heat soothed him, fortified him and saved him. Then he put the small curly head away from him a little and looked at it affectionately, still repeating: "George! Oh, my little George!" But suddenly he thought: "Suppose he were to resemble Limousin after all!"

There was something strange working within him, a fierce feeling, a poignant and violent sensation of cold in his whole body, in all his limbs, as if his bones had suddenly been turned to ice. Oh! if the child were to resemble Limousin—and he continued to look at George, who was laughing now. He looked at him with haggard, troubled eyes and tried to discover whether there was any likeness in his forehead, in his nose, mouth or cheeks. His thoughts wandered like they do when a person is going mad, and his child's face changed in his eyes and assumed a strange look and unlikely resemblances.

Julie had said: "A blind man could not be mistaken in him." There must, therefore, be something striking, an undeniable likeness. But what? The forehead? Yes, perhaps; Limousin's forehead, however, was narrower. The mouth, then? But Limousin wore a beard, and how could anyone verify the likeness between the plump chin of the child and the hairy chin of that man?

Parent thought: "I cannot see anything now, I am too much upset; I could not recognize anything at present. I must wait; I must look at him well tomorrow morning, when I am getting up." And immediately afterward he said to himself: "But if he is like me, I shall be saved! saved!" And he crossed the drawing room in two strides to examine the child's face by the side of his own in the looking glass. He had George on his arm so that their faces might be close together, and he spoke out loud almost without knowing. "Yes—we have the same nose—the same nose perhaps, but that is not sure—and the same look. But no, he has blue eyes. Then—good heavens! I shall go mad. I cannot see anything more—I am going mad!"

He went away from the glass to the other end of the drawing room and, putting the child into an easy chair, he fell into another and began to cry. He sobbed so violently that George, who was frightened at hearing him, immediately began to scream. The hall bell rang, and Parent gave a bound as if a bullet had gone through him.

"There she is," he said. "What shall I do?" And he ran and locked himself up in his room, so at any rate to have time to bathe his eyes. But in a few moments another ring at the bell made him jump again, and then he remembered that Julie had left without the housemaid knowing it, and so nobody would go to open the door. What was he to do? He went himself, and suddenly he felt brave, resolute, ready for dissimulation and the struggle. The terrible blow had matured him in a few moments, and then he wished to know the truth, he wished it with the rage of a timid man, with the tenacity of an easygoing man who has been exasperated.

But nevertheless he trembled! Was it fear? Yes. Perhaps he was still frightened of her? Does one know how much excited cowardice there often is in boldness? He went to the door with furtive steps and stopped to listen; his heart beat furiously, and he heard nothing but the noise of that dull throbbing in his chest and of George's shrill voice, who was still crying in the drawing room. Suddenly, however, the noise of the bell over his head startled him like an explosion; then he seized the lock, turned the key and, opening the door, saw his wife and Limousin standing before him on the steps.

With an air of astonishment which also betrayed a little irritation she said: "So *you* open the door now? Where is Julie?" His throat felt tight and his breathing was labored, and he tried to reply without being able to utter a word, so she continued:

"Are you dumb? I asked you where Julie is."

And then he managed to say: "She—she—has—gone."

Whereupon his wife began to get angry. "What do you mean by *gone?* Where has she gone? Why?"

By degrees he regained his coolness, and he felt rising in him an immense hatred for that insolent woman who was standing before him. "Yes, she has gone altogether. I sent her away."

"You have sent away Julie? Why, you must be mad."

"Yes, I sent her away because she was insolent—and because, because she was ill-using the child."

"Julie?"

"Yes, Julie."

"What was she insolent about?"

"About you."

"About me?"

"Yes, because the dinner was burnt and you did not come in."

"And she said?"

"She said offensive things about you which I ought not—which I could **not** listen to."

"What did she say?"

"It is no good repeating them."

"I want to hear them."

"She said it was unfortunate for a man like me to be married to a woman like you, unpunctual, careless, disorderly, a bad mother and a bad wife."

The young woman had gone into the anteroom followed by Limousin, who did not say a word at this unexpected position of things. She shut the door quickly, threw her cloak onto a chair and, going straight up to her husband, she stammered out:

"You say—you say—that I am——"

He was very pale and calm and replied:

"I say nothing, my dear. I am simply repeating what Julie said to me, as you wanted to know what it was, and I wish you to remark that I turned her off just on account of what she said."

She trembled with a violent longing to tear out his beard and scratch his face. In his voice and manner she felt that he was asserting his position as master, although she had nothing to say by way of reply, and she tried to assume the offensive by saying something unpleasant.

"I suppose you have had dinner?" she asked.

"No, I waited for you."

She shrugged her shoulders impatiently. "It is very stupid of you to wait after half-past seven," she said. "You might have guessed that I was detained, that I had a good many things to do, visits and shopping."

And then suddenly she felt that she wanted to explain how she had spent her time, and she told him in abrupt, haughty words that, having to buy some furniture in a shop a long distance off, very far off, in the Rue de Rennes, she had met Limousin at past seven o'clock on the Boulevard Saint-Germain and that then she had gone with him to have something to eat in a restaurant, as she did not like to go to one by herself although she was faint with hunger. That was how she had dinner, with Limousin, if it could be called dining, for they had only had some soup and half a fowl, as they were in a great hurry to get back, and Parent replied simply:

"Well, you were quite right. I am not finding fault with you."

Then Limousin, who had not spoken till then and who had been half hidden behind Henriette, came forward and put out his hand, saying: "Are you very well?"

Parent took his hand and, shaking it gently, replied: "Yes, I am very well."

But the young woman had felt a reproach in her husband's last words: "Finding fault! Why do you speak of finding fault? One might think that you meant to imply something."

"Not at all," he replied by way of excuse. "I simply meant that I was not at all anxious although you were late and that I did not find fault with you for it."

She, however, took the high hand and tried to find a pretext for a quarrel.

"Although I was late? One might really think that it was one o'clock in the morning and that I spent my nights away from home."

"Certainly not, my dear. I said *late* because I could find no other word. You said you would be back at half-past six, and you returned at half-past eight. That was surely being late! I understand it perfectly well. I am not at all surprised even. But—but—I can hardly use any other word."

"But you pronounce them as if I had been out all night."

"Oh no; oh no!"

She saw that he would yield on every point, and she was going into her own room when at last she noticed that George was screaming, and then she asked with some feeling: "Whatever is the matter with the child?"

"I told you that Julie had been rather unkind to him."

"What has the wretch been doing to him?"

"Oh! Nothing much. She gave him a push, and he fell down."

She wanted to see her child and ran into the dining room but stopped short at the sight of the table covered with spilt wine, with broken decanters and glasses and overturned saltcellars. "Who did all that mischief?" she asked.

"It was Julie who——"

But she interrupted him furiously: "That is too much, really; Julie speaks of me as if I were a shameless woman, beats my child, breaks my plates and dishes, turns my house upside down, and it appears that you think it all quite natural."

"Certainly not, as I have got rid of her."

"Really!—you have got rid of her! But you ought to have given her in charge. In such cases one ought to call in the commissary of police!"

"But, my dear—I really could not—there was no reason. It would have been very difficult."

She shrugged her shoulders disdainfully. "There, you will never be anything but a poor wretched fellow, a man without a will, without any firmness or energy. Ah! she must have said some nice things to you, your Julie, to make you turn her off like that. I should like to have been here for a minute, only for a minute." Then she opened the drawing-room door and ran to George, took him into her arms and kissed him and said: "Georgie, what is it, my darling, my pretty one, my treasure?" But as she was fondling him he did not speak, and she repeated: "What is the matter with you?" And he, having seen with his child's eyes that something was wrong, replied, "Julie beat Papa."

Henriette turned toward her husband in stupefaction at first, but then an irresistible desire to laugh shone in her eyes, passed like a slight shiver over her delicate cheeks, made her upper lip curl and her nostrils dilate, and at last a clear, bright burst of mirth came from her lips, a torrent of gaiety which was lively and sonorous as the song of a bird. With little mischievous exclamations which issued from between her white teeth and hurt Parent as much as a bite would have done, she laughed: "Ha!—ha!—ha!—ha! she beat—she beat—my husband—ha!—ha!—ha! How funny! Do you hear, Limousin? Julie has beaten—has beaten—my—husband. Oh dear—oh dear—how very funny!"

But Parent protested: "No—no—it is not true, it is not true. It was I, on the contrary, who threw her into the dining room so violently that she knocked the table over. The child did not see clearly; I beat her!"

"Here, my darling," Henriette said to her boy; "did Julie beat Papa?"

"Yes, it was Julie," he replied. But then, suddenly turning to another idea, she said: "But the child has had no dinner? You have had nothing to eat, my pet?"

"No, Mamma."

Then she again turned furiously on her husband. "Why, you must be mad, utterly mad! It is half-past eight, and George has had no dinner!"

He excused himself as best he could, for he had nearly lost his wits by the overwhelming scene and the explanation and felt crushed by this ruin of his life.

"But, my dear, we were waiting for you, as I did not wish to dine without you. As you come home late every day, I expected you every moment."

She threw her bonnet, which she had kept on till then, into an easy chair, and in an angry voice she said: "It is really intolerable to have to do with people who can understand nothing, who can divine nothing and do nothing by themselves. So I suppose if I were to come in at twelve o'clock at night, the child would have had nothing to eat? Just as if you could not have understood that, as it was after half-past seven, I was prevented from coming home, that I had met with some hindrance!"

Parent trembled, for he felt that his anger was getting the upper hand, but Limousin interposed and, turning toward the young woman, he said: "My dear friend, you are altogether unjust. Parent could not guess that you would come here so late, as you never do so, and then how could you expect him to get over the difficulty all by himself after having sent away Julie?"

But Henriette was very angry and replied: "Well, at any rate, he must get over the difficulty himself, for I will not help him. Let him settle it!" And she went into her own room, quite forgetting that her child had not had anything to eat.

Then Limousin immediately set to work to help his friend. He picked up the broken glasses which strewed the table and took them out; he replaced the plates and knives and forks and put the child into his high chair while Parent went to look for the lady's maid to wait at table. She came in in great astonishment, as she had heard nothing in George's room, where she had been working. She soon, however, brought in the soup, a burnt leg of mutton and mashed potatoes.

Parent sat by the side of the child, very much upset and distressed at all that had happened. He gave the boy his dinner and endeavored to eat something himself, but he could only swallow with an effort, as if his throat had been paralyzed. By degrees he was seized by an insane desire to look at Limousin, who was sitting opposite to him and making bread pellets, to see whether George was like him. He did not venture to raise his eyes for some time; at last, however, he made up his mind to do so and gave a quick, sharp look at the face which he knew so well. He almost fancied that he had never looked at it carefully, since it looked so different to what he had anticipated. From time to time he scanned him, trying to find a likeness in the smallest lines of his face, in the slightest features, and then he looked at his son, under the pretext of feeding him.

Two words were sounding in his ears: "His father! his father! his father!" They buzzed in his temples at every beat of his heart. Yes, that man, that tranquil man who was sitting on the other side of the table, was, perhaps, the father of his son, of George, of his little George. Parent left off eating; he could not manage any more; a terrible pain, one of those attacks of pain which make men scream, roll on the ground and bite the furniture, was tearing at his entrails, and he felt inclined to take a knife and plunge it into his stomach. It would ease him and save him, and all would be over.

For how could he live now? Could he get up in the morning, join in the meals, go out into the streets, go to bed at night and sleep with that idea dominating him: "Limousin is little George's father!" No, he would not have the strength to walk a step, to dress himself, to think of anything, to speak to anybody! Every day, every hour, every moment, he would be trying to know, to guess, to discover this terrible secret. And the little boy—his dear little boy—he could not look at him any more without enduring the terrible pains of that doubt, of being tortured by it to the very marrow of his bones. He would be obliged to live there, to remain in that house, near a child whom he might love and yet hate! Yes, he should certainly end by hating him. What torture! Oh! If he were sure that Limousin was George's father, he might, perhaps, grow calm, become accustomed to his misfortunte and his pain; but ignorance was intolerable.

Not to know—to be always trying to find out, to be continually suffering, to kiss the child every moment, another man's child, to take him out for walks, to carry him, to caress him, to love him and to think continually: "Perhaps he is not my child?" Wouldn't it be better not to see him, to abandon him—to lose him in the streets or to go away, far away, himself, so far away that he should never hear anything more spoken about, never!

He started when he heard the door open. His wife came. "I am hungry," she said; "are not you also, Limousin?"

He hesitated a little and then said: "Yes, I am, upon my word." And she had the leg of mutton brought in again, while Parent asked himself: "Have they had dinner? Or are they late because they have had a lovers' meeting?"

They both ate with a very good appetite. Henriette was very calm but laughed and joked, and her husband watched her furtively. She had on a pink dressing gown trimmed with white lace, and her fair head, her white neck and her plump hands stood out from that coquettish and perfumed dress as from a sea shell edged with foam. What had she been doing all day with that man? Parent could see them kissing and stammering out words of ardent love! How was it that he could not manage to know everything, to guess the whole truth by looking at them, sitting side by side, opposite to him?

What fun they must be making of him if he had been their dupe since the first day. Was it possible to make a fool of a man, of a worthy man, because his father had left him a little money? Why could one not see these things in people's souls? How was it that nothing revealed to upright souls the deceit of infamous hearts? How was it that voices had the same sound for adoring as for lying—why was a false, deceptive look the same as a sincere one? And he watched them, waiting to catch a gesture, a word, an intonation. Then suddenly he thought: "I will surprise them this evening," and he said: "My dear, as I have dismissed Julie I will see about getting another this very day, and I shall go out immediately to procure one by tomorrow morning, so I may not be in until late."

"Very well," she replied, "go; I shall not stir from here. Limousin will keep me company. We will wait for you." And then, turning to the maid, she said: "You had better put George to bed, and then you can clear away and go up to your own room."

Parent had got up; he was unsteady on his legs, dazed and giddy, and saying: "I shall see you again later on," he went out, holding onto the wall, for the floor seemed to roll like a ship. George had been carried out by his nurse, while Henriette and Limousin went into the drawing room.

As soon as the door was shut he said: "You must be mad, surely, to torment your husband as you do." She immediately turned on him. "Ah! Do you know that I think the habit you have got into lately of looking upon Parent as a martyr is very unpleasant."

Limousin threw himself into an easy chair and crossed his legs. "I am not setting him up as a martyr in the least, but I think that, situated as we are, it is ridiculous to defy this man as you do from morning till night."

She took a cigarette from the mantelpiece, lighted it and replied: "But I do not defy him, quite the contrary; only he irritates me by his stupidity, and I treat him as he deserves."

Limousin continued impatiently: "What you are doing is very foolish! However, all women are alike. Look here: Parent is an excellent, kind fellow, stupidly confiding and good, who never interferes with us, who does not suspect us for a moment, who leaves us quite free and undisturbed whenever we like, and you do all you can to put him into a rage and to spoil our life."

She turned to him. "I say, you worry me. You are a coward like all other men are! You are frightened of that poor creature!" He immediately jumped up and said furiously: "I should like to know what he does and why you are so set against him? Does he make you unhappy? Does he beat you? Does he deceive you and go with another woman? No, it is really too bad to make him suffer merely because he is too kind and to hate him merely because you are unfaithful to him."

She went up to Limousin and, looking him full in the face, she said: "And you reproach me with deceiving him? You? You? What a filthy heart you must have."

He felt rather ashamed and tried to defend himself. "I am not reproaching you, my dear; I am only asking you to treat your husband gently, because we both of us require him to trust us. I think that you ought to see that."

They were close together—he, tall, dark, with long whiskers and the rather vulgar manners of a good-looking man who is very well satisfied with himself; she, small, fair and pink, a little Parisian, half shopkeeper, half one of those girls of easy virtue, born in a shop, brought up at its door to entice customers by her looks and married accidentally, in consequence, to a simple, unsophisticated man who saw her outside the door every morning when he went out and every evening when he came home.

"But do you not understand, you great booby," she said, "that I hate him just because he married me, because he bought me, in fact, because everything that he says and does, everything that he thinks, reacts on my nerves? He exasperates me every moment by his stupidity, which you call kindness—by his dullness, which you call his confidence, and then, above all, because he is my husband, instead of you! I feel him between us although he does not interfere with us much. And then? And then? No, after all, it is too idiotic of him not to guess anything! I wish he would at any rate be a little jealous. There are moments when I feel inclined to say to him, 'Don't you see, you stupid fool, that Paul is my lover?'"

Limousin began to laugh. "Meanwhile it would be a good thing if you were to keep quiet and not disturb our life."

"Oh! I shall not disturb it, you may be sure! There is nothing to fear with such a fool. But it is quite incomprehensible that you cannot understand how hateful he is to me, how he irritates me. You always seem to like him, and you shake hands with him cordially. Men are very surprising at times."

"One must know how to dissimulate, my dear."

"It is no question of dissimulation but of feeling. One might think that when you men deceive another you like him all the more on that account, while we women hate a man from the moment that we have betrayed him."

"I do not see why I should hate an excellent fellow because I love his wife."

"You do not see it? You do not see it? You, all of you, are wanting in that fineness of feeling! However, that is one of those things which one feels and which one cannot express. And then, moreover, one ought not. No, you would not understand, it is quite useless! You men have no delicacy of feeling."

And smiling with the gentle contempt of a debauched woman, she put both her hands onto his shoulders and held up her lips to him, and he stooped down and clasped her closely in his arms, and their lips met. And as they stood in front of the mirror another couple exactly like them embraced behind the clock.

They had heard nothing—neither the noise of the key nor the creaking of the door, but suddenly Henriette, with a loud cry, pushed Limousin away with both her arms, and they saw Parent, who was looking at them, livid with rage, without his shoes on and his hat over his forehead. He looked at them, one after the other, with a quick glance of his eyes without moving his head. He seemed possessed, and then, without saying a word, he threw himself on Limousin, seized him as if he were going to strangle him and flung him into the opposite corner of the room so violently that the lover lost his balance and, clutching at the air with his hands, banged his head against the wall.

But when Henriette saw that her husband was going to murder her lover she threw herself onto Parent, seized him by the neck and, digging her ten delicate and rosy fingers into his neck, she squeezed him so tightly, with all the vigor of a desperate woman, that the blood spurted out under her nails, and she bit his shoulder as if she wished to tear it with her teeth. Parent, half strangled and choked, loosened his hold on Limousin in order to shake off his wife, who was hanging onto his neck, and putting his arms around her waist, he flung her also to the other end of the drawing room.

Then, as his passion was short lived, like that of most good-tempered men, and as his strength was soon exhausted, he remained standing between the two, panting, worn out, not knowing what to do next. His brute fury had expended itself in that effort like the froth of a bottle of champagne, and his unwonted energy ended in a want of breath. As soon as he could speak, however, he said: "Go away—both of you—immediately—go away!"

Limousin remained motionless in his corner against the wall, too startled to understand anything as yet, too frightened to move a finger; while Henriette, with her hands resting on a small round table, her head bent forward with her hair hanging down, the bodice of her dress unfastened and bosom bare, waited like a wild animal which is about to spring. Parent went on in a stronger voice: "Go away immediately. Get out of the house!"

His wife, however, seeing that he had got over his first exasperation, grew bolder, drew herself up, took two steps toward him and, grown almost insolent already, she said: "Have you lost your head? What is the matter with you? What is the meaning of this unjustifiable violence?" But he turned toward her, and raising his fist to strike her, he stammered out: "Oh! Oh! this is too much —too much! I heard everything! Everything! Do you understand? Everything! you wretch—you wretch; you are two wretches! Get out of the house—both of you! Immediately—or I shall kill you! Leave the house!"

She saw that it was all over and that he knew everything, that she could not prove her innocence and that she must comply; but all her impudence had returned to her, and her hatred for the man, which was aroused now, drove her to audacity, making her feel the need of bravado and of defying him. So she said in a clear voice: "Come, Limousin, as he is going to turn me out of doors, I will go to your lodgings with you."

But Limousin did not move, and Parent, in a fresh access of rage, cried out: "Go, will you!—go, you wretches!—or else!—or else!" And he seized a chair and whirled it over his head.

Then Henriette walked quickly across the room, took her lover by the arm, dragged him from the wall, to which he appeared fixed, and led him toward the door, saying: "Do come, my friend. You see that the man is mad. Do come!"

As she went out she turned round to her husband, trying to think of something that she could do, something that she could invent to wound him to the heart as she left the house. An idea struck her, one of those venomous, deadly ideas in which all a woman's perfidy shows itself, and she said resolutely: "I am going to take my child with me."

Parent was stupefied and stammered: "Your—your child? You dare to talk of your child? You venture—you venture to ask for your child after after—— Oh! oh! that is too much! Go, you horrid wretch! Go!" She went up to him again, almost smiling, avenged already, and defying him, standing close to him and face to face, she said: "I want my child, and you have no right to keep him, because he is not yours. Do you understand? He is not yours—he is Limousin's."

And Parent cried out in bewilderment: "You lie—you lie—you wretch!"

But she continued: "You fool! Everybody knows it except you. I tell you, this is his father. You need only look at him to see it."

Parent staggered back from her, and then he suddenly turned round, took a candle and rushed into the next room. Almost immediately, however, he returned, carrying little George wrapped up in his bedclothes, and the child, who had been suddenly awakened, was crying from fright. Parent threw him into his wife's arms and then, without saying anything more, he pushed her roughly out toward the stairs, where Limousin was waiting from motives of prudence.

Then he shut the door again, double-locked it and bolted it, and he had scarcely got into the drawing room when he fell full length on the floor.

II

Parent lived alone, quite alone. During the five weeks that followed their separation the feeling of surprise at his new life prevented him from thinking much. He had resumed his bachelor life, his habits of lounging about, and he took his meals at a restaurant as he had done formerly. As he had wished to avoid any scandal he made his wife an allowance, which was settled by their lawyers. By degrees, however, the thoughts of the child began to haunt him. Often when he was at home alone at night he suddenly thought he heard George calling out "Papa," and his heart would begin to beat. One night he got up quickly and opened the door to see whether, by chance, the child might have returned, like dogs or pigeons do. Why should a child have less instinct than an animal?

After finding that he was mistaken he went and sat down in his armchair again and thought of the boy. Finally he thought of him for hours and whole days. It was not only a moral but still more a physical obsession, a nervous longing to kiss him, to hold and fondle him, to take him onto his knees and dance him. He felt the child's little arms around his neck, the little mouth pressing a kiss on his beard, the soft hair tickling his cheeks, and the remembrance of all those childish ways made him suffer like the desire for some loved woman who has run away. Twenty or a hundred times a day he asked himself the question whether he was or was not George's father, and at night, especially, he indulged in interminable speculations on the point and almost before he was in bed. Every night he recommenced the same series of despairing arguments.

After his wife's departure he had at first not felt the slightest doubt; certainly the child was Limousin's; but by degrees he began to waver. Henriette's words could not be of any value. She had merely braved him and tried to drive him to desperation, and calmly weighing the pros and cons, there seemed to be every chance that she had lied, though perhaps only Limousin could tell the truth. But how was he to find it out, how could he question him or persuade him to confess the real facts?

Sometimes Parent would get up in the middle of the night fully determined to go and see Limousin and to beg him, to offer him anything he wanted, to put an end to this intolerable misery. Then he would go back to bed in despair, reflecting that her lover would, no doubt, also lie. He would, in fact, be sure to lie, in order to avoid losing the child, if he were really his father. What could he, Parent, do then? Absolutely nothing!

And he began to feel sorry that he had thus suddenly brought about the crisis, that he had not taken time for reflection, that he had not waited and dissimulated for a month or two, so as to find out for himself. He ought to have pretended to suspect nothing and have allowed them to betray themselves at their leisure. It would have been enough for him to see the other kiss the child, to guess and to understand. A friend does not kiss a child as a father does. He should have watched them behind the doors. Why had he not thought of that? If Limousin, when left alone with George, had not at once taken him up, clasped him in his arms and kissed him passionately, if he had looked on indifferently while he was playing, without taking any notice of him, no doubt or hesitation could have been possible; in that case he would not have been the father, he would not have thought that he was, would not have felt that he was. Thus Parent would have kept the child while he got rid of the mother, and he would have been happy, perfectly happy.

He tossed about in bed, hot and unhappy, trying to recollect Limousin's ways with the child. But he could not remember anything suspicious, not a gesture, not a look, neither word nor caress. And then the child's mother took very little notice of him; if she had him by her lover she would, no doubt, have loved him more.

They had, therefore, separated him from his son out of vengeance, from cruelty, to punish him for having surprised them, and he made up his mind to go the next morning and obtain the magistrate's assistance to gain possession of George, but almost as soon as he had formed that resolution he felt assured of the contrary. From the moment that Limousin had been Henriette's lover, her adored lover, she would certainly have given herself up to him from the very first with that ardor of self-abandonment which belongs to women who love. The cold reserve which she had always shown in her intimate relations with him, Parent, was surely also an obstacle to her bearing him a son.

In that case he would be claiming, he would take with him, constantly keep and look after the child of another man. He would not be able to look at him, kiss him, hear him say "Papa" without being struck and tortured by the thought, "He is not my child." He was going to condemn himself to that torture and that wretched life every moment! No, it would be better to live alone, to grow old alone and to die alone.

And every day and every night these dreadful doubts and sufferings, which nothing could calm or end, would recommence. Especially did he dread the darkness of the evening, the melancholy feeling of the twilight. A flood of sorrow would invade his heart, a torrent of despair, which threatened to overwhelm him and drive him mad. He was as frightened of his own thoughts as men are of criminals, and he fled before them as one does from wild beasts. Above all things he feared his empty, dark, horrible dwelling and the deserted streets in which, here and there, a gas lamp flickers, where the isolated foot passenger whom one hears in the distance seems to be a night prowler and makes one walk faster or slower, according to whether he is coming toward you or following you.

And in spite of himself and by instinct Parent went in the direction of the broad, well-lighted, populous streets. The light and the crowd attracted him, occupied his mind and distracted his thoughts, and when he was tired walking aimlessly about among the moving crowd, when he saw the foot passengers becoming more scarce and the pavements less crowded, the fear of solitude and silence drove him into some large café full of drinkers and of light. He went there as a moth comes to a candle; he used to sit down at one of the little round tables and ask for a bock,[2] which he used to drink slowly, feeling uneasy every time that a customer got up to go. He would have liked to take him by the arm, hold him back and beg him to stay a little longer, so much did he dread the time when the waiter would come up to him and say angrily: "Come, monsieur, it is closing time!"

Every evening he would stop till the very last. He saw them carry in the tables, turn out the gas jets one by one, except his and that at the counter. He looked unhappily at the cashier counting the money and locking it up in the drawer, and then he went, being usually pushed out by the waiters, who murmured: "Another one who has too much! One would think he had no place to sleep in."

And each night as soon as he was alone in the dark street he began to think of George again and to rack his brains in trying to discover whether or not he was this child's father.

He thus got into the habit of going to the beerhouses, where the continual elbowing of the drinkers brings you in contact with a familiar and silent public, where the clouds of tobacco smoke lull disquietude while the heavy beer dulls the mind and calms the heart. He almost lived there. He was scarcely up before he went there to find people to occupy his looks and his thoughts, and soon, as he became too listless to move, he took his meals there. About twelve o'clock he used to rap on the marble table, and the waiter would quickly bring a plate, a glass, a table napkin and his lunch, when he had ordered it. When he had finished he would slowly drink his cup of black coffee with his eyes fixed on the decanter of brandy, which would soon procure him an hour or two of forgetfulness. First of all he would dip his lips into the cognac, as if to get the flavor of it with the tip of his tongue. Then he would throw his head back and pour it into his mouth, drop by drop, and turn the strong liquor over on his palate, his gums and the mucous membrane of his cheeks; then he would swallow it slowly, to feel it going down his throat and into his stomach.

Thus after every meal he, during more than an hour, sipped three or four small glasses of brandy which stupefied him by degrees; then, having drunk it, he used to raise himself up on the seat covered with red velvet, pull his trousers up and his waistcoat down, so as to cover the linen which appeared between the two, draw down his shirt cuffs and take up the newspapers

---

[2] Glass of Bavarian beer.

again, which he had already read in the morning, and read them all through again from beginning to end. Between four and five o'clock he would go for a walk on the boulevards, to get a little fresh air, as he used to say, and then come back to the seat which had been reserved for him and ask for his absinthe. He used to talk to the regular customers whose acquaintance he had made. They discussed the news of the day and political events, and that carried him on till dinnertime, and he spent the evening as he had the afternoon, until it was time to close.

It was a terrible moment for him when he was obliged to go out into the dark and into the empty room full of dreadful recollections, of horrible thoughts and of mental agony. He no longer saw any of his old friends, none of his relations, nobody who might remind him of his past life. But as his apartments were a hell to him he took a room in a large hotel, a good room on the ground floor, so as to see the passers-by. He was no longer alone in that great building; he felt people swarming round him, he heard voices in the adjoining rooms, and when his former sufferings revived at the sight of his bed, which was turned back, and of his solitary fireplace he went out into the wide passages and walked up and down them like a sentinel, before all the closed doors, and looked sadly at the shoes standing in couples outside each, women's little boots by the side of men's thick ones, and he thought that no doubt all these people were happy and were sleeping sweetly side by side or in each other's arms in their warm beds.

Five years passed thus; five miserable years with no other events except from time to time a passing love affair. But one day when he was taking his usual walk between the Madeleine and the Rue Drouot he suddenly saw a lady whose bearing struck him. A tall gentleman and a child were with her, and all three were walking in front of him. He asked himself where he had seen them before, when suddenly he recognized a movement of her hand; it was his wife, his wife with Limousin and his child, his little George.

His heart beat as if it would suffocate him, but he did not stop, for he wished to see them, and he followed them. They looked like a family of the better middle class. Henriette was leaning on Paul's arm and speaking to him in a low voice and looking at him sideways occasionally. Parent saw her side face and recognized its graceful outlines, the movements of her lips, her smile and her caressing looks, but the child chiefly took up his attention. How tall and strong he was! Parent could not see his face but only his long fair curls. That tall boy with bare legs, who was walking by his mother's side like a little man, was George.

He saw them suddenly, all three, as they stopped in front of a shop. Limousin had grown very gray, had aged and was thinner; his wife, on the contrary, was as young looking as ever and had grown stouter; George he would not have recognized, he was so different to what he had been formerly.

They went on again, and Parent followed them, then walked on quickly, passed them and then turned round so as to meet them face to face. As he passed the child he felt a mad longing to take him into his arms and run off with him, and he knocked against him, accidentally as it were. The boy turned round and looked at the clumsy man angrily, and Parent went off hastily, struck and hurt by the look. He slunk off like a thief, seized by a horrible fear lest he should have been seen and recognized by his wife and her lover, and he went to his café without stopping, fell breathless into his chair, and that evening he drank three absinthes.

For four months he felt the pain of that meeting in his heart. Every night he saw the three again, happy and tranquil, father, mother and child walking on the boulevard before going in to dinner, and that new vision effaced the old one. It was another matter, another hallucination now, and also a fresh pain. Little George, his little George, the child he had so much loved and so often kissed formerly, disappeared in the far distance and he saw a new one, like a brother of the first, a little boy with bare legs who did not know him! He suffered terribly at that thought. The child's love was dead; there was no bond between them; the child would not have held out his arms when he saw him. He had even looked at him angrily.

Then by degrees he grew calmer, his mental torture diminished, the image that had appeared to his eyes and which haunted his nights became more indistinct and less frequent. He began once more to live like everybody else, like all those idle people who drink beer off marble-topped tables and wear out the seats of their trousers on the threadbare velvet of the couches.

He grew old amid the smoke from pipes, lost his hair under the gas lights, looked upon his weekly bath, on his fortnightly visit to the barber's to have his hair cut and on the purchase of a new coat or hat as an event. When he got to his café after buying a new hat he used to look at himself in the glass for a long time before sitting down and would take it off and put it on again several times following and at last ask his friend, the lady at the bar, who watched him with interest, whether she thought it suited him.

Two or three times a year he went to the theater, and in the summer he sometimes spent his evenings at one of the open-air concerts in the Champs Elysées. He brought back from them some airs which ran in his head for several weeks and which he even hummed, beating time with his foot, while he was drinking his beer; and so the years followed each other, slow, monotonous and long because they were quite uneventful.

He did not feel them glide past him. He went on toward death without fear or agitation, sitting at a table in a café, and only the great glass against which he rested his head, which was every day becoming balder, reflected the ravages of time which flies and devours men, poor men.

He only very rarely now thought of the terrible drama which had wrecked his life, for twenty years had passed since that terrible evening; but the life he had led since then had worn him out, and the landlord of his café would often say to him: "You ought to pull yourself together a little, Monsieur Parent; you should get some fresh air and go into the country! I assure you that you have changed very much within the last few months." And when his customer had gone out he used to say to the barmaid: "That poor Monsieur Parent is booked for another world; it is no good never to go out of Paris. Advise him to go out of town for a day occasionally, he has confidence in you. It is nice weather and will do him good." And she, full of pity and good will for such a regular customer, said to Parent every day: "Come, monsieur, make up your mind to get a little fresh air; it is so charming in the country when the weather is fine. Oh! if I could, I would spend my life there."

And she told him her dreams, the simple and poetical dreams of all the poor girls who are shut up from one year's end to the other in a shop and who see the noisy life of the streets go by while they think of the calm and pleasant life in the country, under the bright sun shining on the meadows, of deep woods and clear rivers, of cows lying in the grass and of all the different flowers, blue, red, yellow, purple, lilac, pink and white, which are so pretty, so fresh, so sweet, all the wild flowers which one picks as one walks.

She liked to speak to him frequently of her continual, unrealized and unrealizable longing, and he, an old man without hope, was fond of listening to her and used to go and sit near the counter to talk to Mademoiselle Zoé and to discuss the country with her. Then by degrees he was seized by a vague desire to go just once and see whether it was really so pleasant there, as she said, outside the walls of the great city, and so one morning he said to her: "Do you know where one can get a good lunch in the neighborhood of Paris?"

"Go to the Terrace at Saint-Germain."

He had been there formerly, just after he had got engaged, and so he made up his mind to go there again, and he chose a Sunday, without any special reason but merely because people generally do go out on Sundays even when they have nothing to do all the week. So one Sunday morning he went to Saint-Germain. It was at the beginning of July, on a very bright and hot day. Sitting by the door of the railway carriage, he watched the trees and the strangely built little houses in the outskirts of Paris fly past. He felt low spirited and vexed at having yielded to that new longing and at having broken through his usual habits. The view, which was continually changing and always the same, wearied him. He was thirsty; he would have liked to get out at every station and sit down in the café which he saw outside and drink a bock or two and then take the first train back to Paris. And then the journey seemed very long to him. He used to remain sitting for whole days as long as he had the same motionless objects before his eyes, but he found it very trying and fatiguing to remain sitting while he was being whirled along and to see the whole country fly by while he himself was motionless.

However, he found the Seine interesting every time he crossed it. Under the bridge at Chatou he saw some skiffs going at great pace under the vigorous strokes of the bare-armed oarsmen, and he thought: "There are some fellows who are certainly enjoying themselves!" And then the train entered the tunnel just before you get to the station at Saint-Germain and soon stopped at the arrival platform, where Parent got out and walked slowly, for he already felt tired, toward the Terrace with his hands behind his back, and when he got to the iron balustrade he stopped to look at the distant horizon.

The vast plain spread out before him like the sea, green and studded with large villages, almost as populous as towns. White roads crossed it, and it was well wooded in places; the ponds at Vesinet glistened like plates of silver, and the distant ridges of Sannois and Argenteuil were covered with light bluish mist so that they could scarcely be distinguished. The sun bathed the whole landscape in its full warm light, and the Seine, which twined like an endless serpent through the plain, flowed round the villages and along the slopes. Parent inhaled the warm breeze which seemed to make his heart young again, to enliven his spirits and to vivify his blood, and said to himself: "It is very nice here."

Then he went on a few steps and stopped again to look about him, and the utter misery of his existence seemed to be brought out into full relief by the intense light which inundated the country. He saw his twenty years of café life, dull, monotonous, heartbreaking. He might have traveled like others did, have gone among foreigners, to unknown countries beyond the sea, have interested himself somewhat in everything which other men are passionately devoted to, in arts and sciences; he might have enjoyed life in a thousand forms, that mysterious life which is either charming or painful, constantly changing, always inexplicable and strange.

Now, however, it was too late. He would go on drinking bock after bock until he died, without any family, without friends, without hope, without any curiosity about anything, and he was seized with a feeling of misery and a wish to run away, to hide himself in Paris, in his café and his befuddlement! All the thoughts, all the dreams, all the desires which are dormant in the sloth of the stagnating hearts had reawakened, brought to life by those rays of sunlight on the plain.

He felt that if he were to remain there any longer he should lose his head, and so he made haste to get to the Pavilion Henri IV for lunch, to try and forget his troubles under the influence of wine and alcohol and at any rate to have someone to speak to.

He took a small table in one of the arbors, from which one can see all the surrounding country, ordered his lunch and asked to be served at once. Then some more people arrived and sat down at tables near him, and he felt more comfortable; he was no longer alone. Three persons were lunching near him, and he looked at them two or three times without seeing them clearly, as one looks at total strangers. But suddenly a woman's voice sent a shiver through him which seemed to penetrate to his very marrow. "George," it had said, "will you carve the chicken?" Another voice replied: "Yes, Mamma."

Parent looked up, and he understood, he guessed immediately who those people were! He should certainly not have known them again. His wife had grown quite white and very stout, an old, serious, respectable lady, and she held her head forward as she ate, for fear of spotting her dress, although she had a table napkin tucked under her chin. George had become a man; he had a slight beard, that unequal and almost colorless beard which fringes the cheeks of youths. He wore a high hat, a white waistcoat and a monocle—because it looked dandified, no doubt. Parent looked at him in astonishment! Was that George, his son? No, he did not know that young man; there could be nothing in common between them. Limousin had his back to him and was eating with his shoulders rather bent.

Well, all three of them seemed happy and satisfied; they came and dined in the country at well-known restaurants. They had had a calm and pleasant existence, a family existence in a warm and comfortable house, filled with all those trifles which make life agreeable, with affection, with all those tender words which people exchange continually when they love each other. They had lived thus, thanks to him, Parent, on his money, after having deceived him, robbed him, ruined him! They had condemned him, the innocent, the simple-minded, the jovial man, to all the miseries of solitude, to that abominable life which he had led between the pavement and the counter, to every moral torture and every physical misery! They had made him a useless being who was lost and wretched among other people, a poor old man without any pleasures or anything to look forward to and who hoped for nothing from anyone. For him the world was empty because he loved nothing in the world. He might go among other nations or go about the streets, go into all the houses in Paris, open every room, but he would not find the beloved face, the face of wife or child, that he was in search of, which smiles when it sees you, behind any door. And that idea worked upon him more than any other, the idea of a door which one opens to see and to embrace somebody behind it.

And that was the fault of those three wretches! The fault of that worthless woman, of that infamous friend and of that tall light-haired lad who put on insolent airs. Now he felt as angry with the child as he did with the other two. Was he not Limousin's son? Would Limousin have kept him and loved him otherwise? Would not Limousin very quickly have got rid of the mother and of the child if he had not felt sure that it was his, certainly his? Does anybody bring up other people's children? And now they were there, quite close to him, those three who had made him suffer so much.

Parent looked at them, irritated and excited at the recollection of all his sufferings and of his despair, and was especially exasperated at their placid and satisfied looks. He felt inclined to kill them, to throw his siphon of seltzer water at them, to split open Limousin's head which he every moment bent over his plate and raised up again immediately. And they continued to live like that, without cares or anxiety of any kind. No! no! That was really too much, after all! He would avenge himself; he would have his revenge now, on the spot, as he had them under his hand. But how? He tried to think of some means; he pictured such dreadful things as one reads of in the newspapers occasionally but could not hit on anything practical. And he went on drinking to excite himself, to give himself courage not to allow such an occasion to escape him, as he should certainly not meet with it again.

Suddenly an idea struck him, a terrible idea, and he left off drinking to mature it. A smile rose to his lips, and he murmured: "I have got them, I have got them. We will see, we will see."

A waiter asked him: "What would you like now, monsieur?"

"Nothing. Coffee and cognac. The best." And he looked at them as he sipped his brandy. There were too many people in the restaurant for what he wanted to do, so he would wait and follow them, for they would be sure to walk on the terrace or in the forest. When they had got a little distance off he would join them, and then he would have his revenge, yes, he would have his revenge! It was certainly not too soon, after twenty-three years of suffering. Ah! They little guessed what was to happen to them.

They finished their luncheon slowly, and they talked in perfect security. Parent could not hear what they were saying, but he saw their calm movements, and his wife's face, especially, exasperated him. She had assumed a haughty air, the air of a stout, devout woman, of an irreproachably devout woman, sheathed in principles, iron clad in virtue. Then they paid the bill and got up, and then he saw Limousin. He might have been taken for a retired diplomatist, for he looked a man of great importance with his soft white whiskers, the tips of which fell onto the facings of his coat.

They went out. George was smoking a cigar and had his hat on one side, and Parent followed them. First of all they went up and down the terrace and calmly admired the landscape, like people who have well satisfied their hunger, and then they went into the forest, and Parent rubbed his hands and followed them at a distance, hiding himself so as not to excite their suspicion too soon. They walked slowly, enjoying the fresh green foliage and the warm air. Henriette was holding Limousin's arm and walked upright at his side like a wife who is contented and proud of herself. George was cutting off the leaves with his stick and occasionally jumped over the ditches by the roadside like a fiery young horse ready to gallop off through the trees.

Parent came up to them by degrees, panting rather from excitement and fatigue, for he never walked now. He soon came up to them, but he was seized by fear, an inexplicable fear, and he passed them so as to turn round and meet them face to face. He walked on, his heart beating, for he knew that they were just behind him now, and he said to himself: "Come, now is the time. Courage! courage! Now is the moment!"

He turned around. They were all three sitting on the grass, at the foot of a huge tree, and were still talking. He made up his mind and came back rapidly, and then, stopping in front of them in the middle of the road, he said abruptly, in a voice broken by emotion: "It is I! Here I am! I suppose you did not expect me?" They all three looked at him carefully, for they thought that he was mad, and he continued: "One might think that you did not know me again. Just look at me! I am Parent, Henri Parent. You did not expect me, eh? You thought it was all over and that you would never see me again. Ah! But here I am once more, you see, and now we will have an explanation."

Henriette was terrified and hid her face in her hands, murmuring: "Oh! Good heavens!" And seeing this stranger who seemed to be threatening his mother, George sprang up, ready to seize him by the collar, while Limousin, who was thunderstruck, looked at this specter in horror, who, after panting for a few moments, continued: "So now we will have an explanation; the proper moment for it has come! Ah! you deceived me, you condemned me to the life of a convict, and you thought that I should never catch you!"

But the young man took him by the shoulders and pushed him back: "Are you mad?" he asked. "What do you want? Go on your way immediately, or I shall give you a thrashing!" But Parent replied: "What do I want? I want to tell you who these people are." George, however, was in a rage and shook him, was even going to strike him, but the other said: "Just let me go. I am your father. There, look whether they recognize me now, the wretches!" And the alarmed young man removed his hands and turned to his mother, while Parent, as soon as he was released, went toward her.

"Well," he said, "tell him who I am, you! Tell him that my name is Henri Parent, that I am his father because his name is George Parent, because you are my wife, because you are all three living on my money, on the allowance of ten thousand francs[3] which I have made you since I drove you out of my house. Will you tell him also why I drove you out? Because I surprised you with this beggar, this wretch, your lover! Tell him what I was, an honorable man whom you married for my money and whom you deceived from the very first day. Tell him who you are and who I am."

He stammered and panted for breath in his rage, and the woman exclaimed in a heartrending voice: "Paul, Paul, stop him; make him be quiet; do not let him say this before my son!"

Limousin had also got up, and he said in a quite low voice: "Hold your tongue! Do understand what you are doing!"

But Parent continued furiously: "I quite know what I am doing, and that is not all. There is one thing that I will know, something that has tormented me for twenty years."

And then turning to George, who was leaning against a tree in consternation, he said: "Listen to me. When she left my house she thought it was not enough to have deceived me but she also wanted to drive me to despair. You were my only consolation, and she took you with her, swearing that I was not your father but that he was your father! Was she lying! I do not know, and I have been asking myself the question for the last twenty years."

He went close up to her, tragic and terrible, and pulling away her hands with which she had covered her face, he continued: "Well, I call upon you now to tell me which of us two is the father of this young man; he or I, your husband or your lover. Come! Come! tell us." Limousin rushed at him, but Parent pushed him back, and sneering in his fury, he said: "Ah! you are brave now! You are braver than you were the day you ran out of doors because I was going to half murder you. Very well! If she will not reply, tell me yourself. You ought to know as well as she. Tell me, are you this young fellow's father? Come! Come! Tell me!"

Then he turned to his wife again. "If you will not tell me, at any rate tell your son. He is a man now, and he has the right to know who is his father. I do not know, and I never did know, never, never! I cannot tell you, my boy." He seemed to be losing his senses; his voice grew shrill, and he worked his arms about as if he had an epileptic attack. "Come! Give me an answer.

[3]About $2000.

She does not know. I will make a bet that she does not know. No—she does not know, by Jove! She used to go to bed with both of us! Ha! ha! ha! Nobody knows—nobody. How can one know such things? You will not know either, my boy; you will not know any more than I do—never. Look here. Ask her—you will find that she does not know. I do not know either. You can choose—yes, you can choose—him or me. Choose. Good evening. It is all over. If she makes up her mind to tell you, come and let me know, will you? I am living at the Hôtel des Continents. I should be glad to know. Good evening; I hope you will enjoy yourselves very much."

And he went away, gesticulating and talking to himself under the tall trees, into the empty cool air which was full of the smell of the sap. He did not turn round to look at them but went straight on, walking under the stimulus of his rage, under a storm of passion, with that one fixed idea in his mind, and presently he found himself outside the station. A train was about to start, and he got in. During the journey his anger calmed down; he regained his senses and returned to Paris, astonished at his own boldness and feeling as full of aches and fatigue as if he had broken some bones, but nevertheless he went to have a bock at his café.

When she saw him come in Mademoiselle Zoé was surprised and said: "What! Back already? Are you tired?"

"I am tired—very tired. You know, when one is not used to going out—but I have done with it. I shall not go into the country again. I had better have stopped here. For the future I shall not stir out again."

But she could not persuade him to tell her about his little excursion although she wanted very much to hear all about it, and for the first time in his life he got thoroughly drunk that night and had to be carried home.

USELESS BEAUTY

A VERY ELEGANT VICTORIA with two beautiful black horses was drawn up in front of the mansion. It was a day in the latter end of June, about half-past five in the afternoon, and the sun shone warm and bright into the large courtyard.

The Countess de Mascaret came down just as her husband, who was coming home, appeared in the carriage entrance. He stopped for a few moments to look at his wife and grew rather pale. She was very beautiful, graceful and distinguished looking with her long oval face, her complexion like gilt ivory, her large gray eyes and her black hair, and she got into her carriage without looking at him, without even seeming to have noticed him, with such a particularly highbred air that the furious jealousy by which he had been devoured for so long again gnawed at his heart. He went up to her and said: "You are going for a drive?"

She merely replied disdainfully: "You see I am!"

"In the Bois de Boulogne?"

"Most probably."

"May I come with you?"

"The carriage belongs to you."

Without being surprised at the tone of voice in which she answered him, he got in and sat down by his wife's side and said: "Bois de Boulogne." The footman jumped up by the coachman's side, and the horses, as usual, pawed the ground and shook their heads until they were in the street. Husband and wife sat side by side without speaking. He was thinking how to begin a conversation, but she maintained such an obstinately hard look that he did not venture to make the attempt. At last, however, he cunningly, accidentally as it were, touched the countess's gloved hand with his own, but she drew her arm away with a movement which was so expressive of disgust that he remained thoughtful in spite of his usual authoritative and despotic character. "Gabrielle!" he said at last.

"What do you want?"

"I think you are looking adorable."

She did not reply but remained lying back in the carriage, looking like an irritated queen. By that time they were driving up the Champs Elysées, toward the Arc de Triomphe. That immense monument at the end of the long avenue raised its colossal arch against the red sky, and the sun seemed to be sinking onto it, showering fiery dust on it from the sky.

The stream of carriages, with the sun reflecting from the bright, plated harness and the shining lamps, were like a double current flowing, one toward the town and one toward the wood, and the Count de Mascaret continued: "My dear Gabrielle!"

Then, unable to bear it any longer, she replied in an exasperated voice: "Oh, do leave me in peace, pray! I am not even at liberty to have my carriage to myself now." He, however, pretended not to hear her and continued: "You have never looked so pretty as you do today."

Her patience was decidedly at an end, and she replied with irrepressible anger: "You are wrong to notice it, for I swear to you that I will never have anything to do with you in that way again." He was stupefied and agitated and, his violent nature gaining the upper hand, he exclaimed: "What do you mean by that?" in such a manner as revealed rather the brutal master than the amorous man. But she replied in a low voice so that the servants might not hear amid the deafening noise of the wheels:

"Ah! What do I mean by that? What do I mean by that? Now I recognize you again! Do you want me to tell everything?"

"Yes."

"Everything that has been on my heart since I have been the victim of your terrible selfishness?"

He had grown red with surprise and anger, and he growled between his closed teeth: "Yes, tell me everything."

He was a tall, broad-shouldered man, with a big red beard, a handsome man, a nobleman, a man of the world, who passed as a perfect husband and an excellent father, and now for the first time since they had started she turned toward him and looked him full in the face. "Ah! You will hear some disagreeable things, but you must know that I am prepared for everything, that I fear nothing, and you less than anyone today."

He also was looking into her eyes and already was shaking with passion; then he said in a low voice: "You are mad."

"No, but I will no longer be the victim of the hateful penalty of maternity, which you have inflicted on me for eleven years! I wish to live like a woman of the world, as I have the right to do, as all women have the right to do."

He suddenly grew pale again and stammered: "I do not understand you."

"Oh yes; you understand me well enough. It is now three months since I had my last child, and as I am still very beautiful, and as, in spite of all your efforts, you cannot spoil my figure, as you just now perceived when you saw me on the outside flight of steps, you think it is time that I should become *enceinte* again."

"But you are talking nonsense!"

"No, I am not; I am thirty and I have had seven children, and we have been married eleven years, and you hope that this will go on for ten years longer, after which you will leave off being jealous."

He seized her arm and squeezed it, saying: "I will not allow you to talk to me like that for long."

"And I shall talk to you till the end, until I have finished all I have to say to you, and if you try to prevent me I shall raise my voice so that the two servants who are on the box may hear. I only allowed you to come with me for that object, for I have these witnesses, who will oblige you to listen to me and to contain yourself; so now pay attention to what I say. I have always felt an antipathy for you and I have always let you see it, for I have never lied, monsieur. You married me in spite of myself; you forced my parents, who were in embarrassed circumstances, to give me to you because you were rich, and they obliged me to marry you, in spite of my tears.

"So you bought me, and as soon as I was in your power, as soon as I had become your companion, ready to attach myself to you, to forget your coercive and threatening proceedings, in order that I might only remember that I ought to be a devoted wife and to love you as much as it might be possible for me to love you, you became jealous—you—as no man has ever been before, with the base, ignoble jealousy of a spy, which was as degrading for you as it was for me. I had not been married eight months when you suspected me of every perfidiousness, and you even told me so. What a disgrace! And as you could not prevent me from being beautiful and from pleasing people, from being called in drawing rooms and also in the newspapers one of the most beautiful women in Paris; you tried everything you could think of to keep admirers from me, and you hit upon the abominable idea of making me spend my life in a constant state of motherhood, until the time when I should disgust every man. Oh, do not deny it! I did not understand it for some time, but then I guessed it. You even boasted about it to your sister, who told me of it, for she is fond of me and was disgusted at your boorish coarseness.

"Ah! Remember our struggles, doors smashed in and locks forced! For eleven years you have condemned me to the existence of a brood mare. Then as soon as I was pregnant you grew disgusted with me, and I saw nothing of you for months and I was sent into the country to the family mansion, among fields and meadows, to bring forth my child. And when I reappeared, fresh, pretty and indestructible, still seductive and constantly surrounded by admirers, hoping that at last I should live a little like a young rich woman who belongs to society, you were seized by jealousy again, and you recommenced to persecute me with that infamous and hateful desire from which you are suffering at this moment by my side. And it is not the desire of possessing me—for I should never have refused myself to you—but it is the wish to make me unsightly.

"Besides this, that abominable and mysterious circumstance took place which I was a long time in penetrating (but I grew acute by dint of watching your thoughts and actions). You attached yourself to your children with all the security which they gave you while I bore them in my womb. You felt affection for them with all your aversion for me and in spite of your ignoble fears, which were momentarily allayed by your pleasure in seeing me a mother.

"Oh! How often have I noticed that joy in you! I have seen it in your eyes and guessed it. You loved your children as victories and not because they were of your own blood. They were victories over me, over my youth, over my beauty, over my charms, over the compliments which were paid me and over those who whispered round me, without paying them to me. And you are proud of them; you make a parade of them; you take them out for drives in your coach in the Bois de Boulogne, and you give them donkey rides at Montmorency. You take them to theatrical matinees so that you may be seen in the midst of them and that people may say: 'What a kind father!' and that it may be repeated."

He had seized her wrist with savage brutality and squeezed it so violently that she was quiet, though she nearly cried out with the pain. Then he said to her in a whisper:

"I love my children; do you hear? What you have just told me is disgraceful in a mother. But you belong to me; I am master—your master. I can exact from you what I like and when I like—and I have the law on my side."

He was trying to crush her fingers in the strong grip of his large, muscular hand, and she, livid with pain, tried in vain to free them from that vise which was crushing them; the agony made her pant, and the tears came into her eyes. "You see that I am the master and the stronger," he said. And when he somewhat loosened his grip she asked him: "Do you think that I am a religious woman?"

He was surprised and stammered: "Yes."

"Do you think that I could lie if I swore to the truth of anything to you before an altar on which Christ's body is?"

"No."

"Will you go with me to some church?"

"What for?"

"You shall see. Will you?"

"If you absolutely wish it, yes."

She raised her voice and said: "Philip!" And the coachman, bending down a little, without taking his eyes from his horses, seemed to turn his ear alone toward his mistress, who said: "Drive to St Philip-du-Roule's." And the victoria, which had reached the entrance of the Bois de Boulogne, returned to Paris.

Husband and wife did not exchange a word during the drive. When the carriage stopped before the church Countess de Mascaret jumped out and entered it, followed by the count a few yards behind her. She went without stopping as far as the choir screen and, falling on her knees at a chair, she buried her face in her hands. She prayed for a long time, and he, standing behind her, could see that she was crying. She wept noiselessly, like women do weep when they are in great and poignant grief. There was a kind of undulation in her body, which ended in a little sob, hidden and stifled by her fingers.

But Count de Mascaret thought that the situation was long drawn out, and he touched her on the shoulder. That contact recalled her to herself, as if she had been burned, and, getting up, she looked straight into his eyes.

"This is what I have to say to you. I am afraid of nothing, whatever you may do to me. You may kill me if you like. One of your children is not yours, and one only; that I swear to you before God who hears me here. That is the only revenge which was possible for me in return for all your abominable male tyrannies, in return for the penal servitude of childbearing to which you have condemned me. Who was my lover? That you will never know! You may suspect everyone, but you will never find out. I gave myself up to him without love and without pleasure, only for the sake of betraying you, and he made me a mother. Which is his child? That also you will never know. I have seven; try and find out! I intended to tell you this later, for one cannot completely avenge oneself on a man by deceiving him, unless he knows it. You have driven me to confess it today; now I have finished."

She hurried through the church toward the open door, expecting to hear behind her the quick steps of her husband whom she had defied and to be knocked to the ground by a blow of his fist, but she heard nothing and reached her carriage. She jumped into it at a bound, overwhelmed with anguish and breathless with fear; she called out to the coachman, "Home!" and the horses set off at a quick trot.

II

The Countess de Mascaret was waiting in her room for dinnertime, like a criminal sentenced to death awaits the hour of his execution. What was he going to do? Had he come home? Despotic, passionate, ready for any violence as he was, what was he meditating; what had he made up his mind to do? There was no sound in the house, and every moment she looked at the clock. Her maid had come and dressed her for the evening and had then left the room again. Eight o'clock struck; almost at the same moment there were two knocks at the door, and the butler came in and told her that dinner was ready.

"Has the count come in?"

"Yes, Madame la Comtesse; he is in the dining room."

For a moment she felt inclined to arm herself with a small revolver which she had bought some weeks before, foreseeing the tragedy which was being rehearsed in her heart. But she remembered that all the children would be there, and she took nothing except a smelling bottle. He rose somewhat ceremoniously from his chair. They exchanged a slight bow and sat down. The three boys with their tutor, Abbé Martin, were on her right, and the three girls with Miss Smith, their English governess, were on her left. The youngest child, who was only three months old, remained upstairs with his nurse.

The abbé said grace, as was usual when there was no company, for the children did not come down to dinner when there were guests present; then they began dinner. The countess, suffering from emotion which she had not at all calculated upon, remained with her eyes cast down, while the count scrutinized now the three boys and now the three girls with uncertain, unhappy looks, which traveled from one to the other. Suddenly, pushing his wineglass from him, it broke, and the wine was spilt on the tablecloth, and at the slight noise caused by this little accident the countess started up from her chair, and for the first time they looked at each other. Then almost every moment, in spite of themselves, in spite of the irritation of their nerves caused by every glance, they did not cease to exchange looks, rapid as pistol shots.

The abbé, who felt that there was some cause for embarrassment which he could not divine, tried to get up a conversation and started various subjects, but his useless efforts gave rise to no ideas and did not bring out a word. The countess, with feminine tact and obeying the instincts of a woman of the world, tried to answer him two or three times, but in vain. She could not find words in the perplexity of her mind, and her own voice almost frightened her in the silence of the large room, where nothing else was heard except the slight sound of plates and knives and forks.

Suddenly her husband said to her, bending forward: "Here, amid your children, will you swear to me that what you told me just now is true?"

The hatred which was fermenting in her veins suddenly roused her, and replying to that question with the same firmness with which she had replied to his looks, she raised both her hands, the right pointing toward the boys and the left toward the girls, and said in a firm, resolute voice and without any hesitation: "On the heads of my children, I swear that I have told you the truth."

He got up and, throwing his table napkin onto the table with an exasperated movement, turned round and flung his chair against the wall. Then he went out without another word, while she, uttering a deep sigh, as if after a first victory, went on in a calm voice: "You must not pay any attention to what your father has just said, my darlings; he was very much upset a short time ago, but he will be all right again in a few days."

Then she talked with the abbé and with Miss Smith and had tender, pretty words for all her children, those sweet, spoiling mother's ways which unlock little hearts.

When dinner was over she went into the drawing room with all her little following. She made the elder ones chatter, and when their bedtime came she kissed them for a long time and then went alone into her room.

She waited for she had no doubt that he would come, and she made up her mind then, as her children were not with her, to defend her human flesh, as she defended her life as a woman of the world; and in the pocket of her dress she put the little loaded revolver which she had bought a few weeks before. The hours went by; the hours struck, and every sound was hushed in the house. Only cabs continued to rumble through the streets, but their noise was only heard vaguely through the shuttered and curtained windows.

She waited, energetic and nervous, without any fear of him now, ready for anything and almost triumphant, for she had found means of torturing him continually during every moment of his life.

But the first gleams of dawn came in through the fringe at the bottom of her curtains without his having come into her room, and then she awoke to the fact, much to her surprise, that he was not coming. Having locked and bolted her door for greater security, she went to bed at last and remained there with her eyes open, thinking and barely understanding it all, without being able to guess what he was going to do.

When her maid brought her tea she at the same time gave her a letter from her husband. He told her that he was going to undertake a longish journey, and in a postscript he added that his lawyer would provide her with such money as she might require for her expenses.

III

It was at the opera, between two of the acts in *Robert the Devil*. In the stalls the men were standing up with their hats on, their waistcoats cut very low so as to show a large amount of white shirt front in which the gold and precious stones of their studs glistened. They were looking at the boxes crowded with ladies in low dresses, covered with diamonds and pearls, women who seemed to expand like flowers in that illuminated hothouse, where the beauty of their faces and the whiteness of their shoulders seemed to bloom for inspection in the midst of the music and of human voices.

Two friends with their backs to the orchestra were scanning those parterres of elegance, that exhibition of real or false charms, of jewels, of luxury and of pretension which showed itself off all round the Grand Theater. One of them, Roger de Salnis, said to his companion, Bernard Grandin: "Just look how beautiful Countess de Mascaret still is."

Then the elder, in turn, looked through his opera glasses at a tall lady in a box opposite, who appeared to be still very young and whose striking beauty seemed to appeal to men's eyes in every corner of the house. Her pale complexion, of an ivory tint, gave her the appearance of a statue, while a small diamond coronet glistened on her black hair like a cluster of stars.

When he had looked at her for some time Bernard Grandin replied with a jocular accent of sincere conviction: "You may well call her beautiful!"

"How old do you think she is?"

"Wait a moment. I can tell you exactly, for I have known her since she was a child, and I saw her make her debut into society when she was quite a girl. She is—she is—thirty—thirty-six."

"Impossible!"

"I am sure of it."

"She looks twenty-five."

"She has had seven children."

"It is incredible."

"And what is more, they are all seven alive, as she is a very good mother. I go to the house, which is a very quiet and pleasant one, occasionally, and she presents the phenomenon of the family in the midst of the world."

"How very strange! And have there never been any reports about her?"

"Never."

"But what about her husband? He is peculiar, is he not?"

"Yes and no. Very likely there has been a little drama between them, one of those little domestic dramas which one suspects, which one never finds out exactly, but which one guesses pretty nearly."

"What is it?"

"I do not know anything about it. Mascaret leads a very fast life now, after having been a model husband. As long as he remained a good spouse he had a shocking temper and was crabbed and easily took offense, but since he has been leading his present rackety life he has become quite indifferent, but one would guess that he has some trouble, a worm gnawing somewhere, for he has aged very much."

Thereupon the two friends talked philosophically for some minutes about the secret, unknowable troubles which differences of character or perhaps physical antipathies, which were not perceived at first, give rise to in families. Then Roger de Salnis, who was still looking at Mme de Mascaret through his opera glasses, said:

"It is almost incredible that that woman has had seven children!"

"Yes, in eleven years, after which, when she was thirty, she put a stop to her period of production in order to enter into the brilliant period of entertaining, which does not seem near coming to an end."

"Poor women!"

"Why do you pity them?"

"Why? Ah! my dear fellow, just consider! Eleven years of maternity for such a woman! What a hell! All her youth, all her beauty, every hope of success, every poetical ideal of a bright life, sacrificed to that abominable law of reproduction which turns the normal woman into a mere machine for maternity."

"What would you have? It is only nature!"

"Yes, but I say that nature is our enemy, that we must always fight against nature, for she is continually bringing us back to an animal state. You may be sure that God has not put anything on this earth that is clean, pretty, elegant or accessory to our ideal, but the human brain has done it. It is we who have introduced a little grace, beauty, unknown charm and mystery into creation by singing about it, interpreting it, by admiring it as poets, idealizing it as artists and by explaining it as learned men who make mistakes, who find ingenious reasons, some grace and beauty, some unknown charm and mystery, in the various phenomena of nature.

"God only created coarse beings, full of the germs of disease, and who, after a few years of bestial enjoyment, grow old and infirm, with all the ugliness and all the want of power of human decrepitude. He only seems to have made them in order that they may reproduce their species in a repulsive manner and then die like ephemeral insects. I said, *reproduce their species in a repulsive manner*, and I adhere to that expression. What is there, as a matter of fact, more ignoble and more repugnant than that ridiculous act of the reproduction of living beings, against which all delicate minds always have revolted and always will revolt? Since all the organs which have been invented by this economical and malicious Creator serve two purposes, why did he not choose those that were unsullied, in order to intrust them with that sacred mission, which is the noblest and the most exalted of all human functions? The mouth which nourishes the body by means of material food also diffuses abroad speech and thought. Our flesh revives itself by means of itself, and at the same time ideas are communicated by it. The sense of smell which gives the vital air to the lungs imparts all the perfumes of the world to the brain: the smell of flowers, of woods, of trees, of the sea. The ear which enables us to communicate with our fellow men, has also allowed us to invent music, to create dreams, happiness, the infinite and even physical pleasure by means of sounds!

"But one might say that the Creator wished to prohibit man from ever ennobling and idealizing his commerce with women. Nevertheless, man has found love, which is not a bad reply to that sly Deity, and he has ornamented it so much with literary poetry that woman often forgets the contact she is obliged to submit to. Those among us who are powerless to deceive themselves have invented vice and refined debauchery, which is another way of laughing at God and of paying homage, immodest homage, to beauty.

"But the normal man makes children, just a beast that is coupled with another by law.

"Look at that woman! Is it not abominable to think that such a jewel, such a pearl, born to be beautiful, admired, feted and adored, has spent eleven years of her life in providing heirs for the Count de Mascaret?"

Bernard Grandin replied with a laugh: "There is a great deal of truth in all that, but very few people would understand you."

Salnis got more and more animated. "Do you know how I picture God myself?" he said. "As an enormous creative organ unknown to us, who scatters millions of worlds into space, just as one single fish would deposit its spawn in the sea. He creates, because it is His function as God to do so, but He does not know what He is doing and is stupidly prolific in His work and is ignorant of the combinations of all kinds which are produced by His scattered germs. Human thought is a lucky little local, passing accident, which was totally unforeseen and is condemned to disappear with this earth and to recommence perhaps here or elsewhere, the same or different, with fresh combinations of eternally new beginnings. We owe it to this slight accident which has happened to His intellect that we are very uncomfortable in this world which was not made for us, which had not been prepared to receive us, to lodge and feed us or to satisfy reflecting beings, and we owe it to Him also that we have to struggle without ceasing against what are still called the designs of Providence, when we are really refined and civilized beings."

Grandin, who was listening to him attentively, as he had long known the surprising outbursts of his fancy, asked him: "Then you believe that human thought is the spontaneous product of blind, divine parturition?"

"Naturally. A fortuitous function of the nerve centers of our brain, like some unforeseen chemical action which is due to new mixtures and which also resembles a product of electricity, caused by friction or the unexpected proximity of some substance, and which, lastly, resembles the phenomena caused by the infinite and fruitful fermentations of living matter.

"But, my dear fellow, the truth of this must be evident to anyone who looks about him. If human thought, ordained by an omniscient Creator, had been intended to be what it has become, altogether different from mechanical thoughts and resignation, so exacting, inquiring, agitated, tormented, would the world which was created to receive the beings which we now are have been this unpleasant little dwelling place for poor fools, this salad plot, this rocky, wooded and spherical kitchen garden where your improvident Providence has destined us to live naked in caves or under trees, nourished on the flesh of slaughtered animals, our brethren, or on raw vegetables nourished by the sun and the rain?

"But it is sufficient to reflect for a moment, in order to understand that this world was not made for such creatures as we are. Thought, which is developed by a miracle in the nerves of the cells and our brain, powerless, ignorant and confused as it is, and as it will always remain, makes all of us who are intellectual beings eternal and wretched exiles on earth.

"Look at this earth, as God has given it to those who inhabit it. Is it not visibly and solely made, planted and covered with forests, for the sake of animals? What is there for us? Nothing. And for them? Everything. They have nothing to do but to eat or go hunting and eat each other, according to their instincts, for God never foresaw gentleness and peaceable manners; He only foresaw the death of creatures which were bent on destroying and devouring each other. Are not the quail, the pigeon and the partridge the natural prey of the hawk? The sheep, the stag and the ox that of the great flesh-eating animals, rather than meat that has been fattened to be served up to us with truffles, which have been unearthed by pigs for our special benefit?

"As to ourselves, the more civilized, intellectual and refined we are, the more we ought to conquer and subdue that animal instinct, which represents the will of God in us. And so in order to mitigate our lot as brutes, we have discovered and made everything, beginning with houses, then exquisite food, sauces, sweetmeats, pastry, drink, stuffs, clothes, ornaments, beds, mattresses, carriages, railways and innumerable machines, besides arts and sciences, writing and poetry. Every ideal comes from us as well as the amenities of life, in order to make our existence as simple reproducers, for which divine Providence solely intended us, less monotonous and less hard.

"Look at this theater. Is there not here a human world created by us, unforeseen and unknown by eternal destinies, comprehensible by our minds alone, a sensual and intellectual distraction, which has been invented solely by and for that discontented and restless little animal that we are.

"Look at that woman, Madame de Mascaret. God intended her to live in a cave naked or wrapped up in the skins of wild animals, but is she not better as she is? But speaking of her, does anyone know why and how her brute of a husband, having such a companion by his side and especially after having been boorish enough to make her a mother seven times, has suddenly left her to run after bad women?"

Grandin replied: "Oh, my dear fellow, this is probably the only reason. He found that always living with her was becoming too expensive in the end, and from reasons of domestic economy he has arrived at the same principles which you lay down as a philosopher."

Just then the curtain rose for the third act, and they turned round, took off their hats and sat down.

IV

The Count and Countess Mascaret were sitting side by side in the carriage which was taking them home from the opera, without speaking. But suddenly the husband said to his wife: "Gabrielle!"

"What do you want?"

"Don't you think that this has lasted long enough?"

"What?"

"The horrible punishment to which you have condemned me for the last six years."

"What do you want? I cannot help it."

"Then tell me which of them it is?"

"Never."

"Think that I can no longer see my children or feel them round me without having my heart burdened with this doubt. Tell me which of them it is, and I swear that I will forgive you and treat it like the others."

"I have not the right to."

"You do not see that I can no longer endure this life, this thought which is wearing me out or this question which I am constantly asking myself, this question which tortures me each time I look at them. It is driving me mad."

"Then you have suffered a great deal?" she said.

"Terribly. Should I, without that, have accepted the horror of living by your side and the still greater horror of feeling and knowing that there is one among them whom I cannot recognize and who prevents me from loving the others?"

She repeated: "Then you have really suffered very much?" And he replied in a constrained and sorrowful voice:

"Yes, for do I not tell you every day that it is intolerable torture to me? Should I have remained in that house near you and them if I did not love them? Oh! You have behaved abominably toward me. All the affection of my heart I have bestowed upon my children, and that you know. I am for them a father of the olden time, as I was for you a husband of one of the families of old, for by instinct I have remained a natural man, a man of former days. Yes, I will confess it, you have made me terribly jealous, because you are a woman of another race, of another soul, with other requirements. Oh! I shall never forget the things that you told me, but from that day I troubled myself no more about you. I did not kill you because then I should have had no means on earth of ever discovering which of our—of your—children is not mine. I have waited but I have suffered more than you would believe, for I can no longer venture to love them, except, perhaps, the two eldest; I no longer venture to look at them, to call them to me, to kiss them; I cannot take them onto my knee without asking myself: 'Can it be this one?' I have been correct in my behavior toward you for six years, and even kind and complaisant; tell me the truth, and I swear that I will do nothing unkind."

He thought, in spite of the darkness of the carriage, that he could perceive that she was moved and, feeling certain that she was going to speak at last, he said: "I beg you, I beseech you, to tell me."

"I have been more guilty than you think perhaps," she replied, "but I could no longer endure that life of continual pregnancy, and I had only one means of driving you from my bed. I lied before God, and I lied with my hand raised to my children's heads, for I have never wronged you."

He seized her arm in the darkness and, squeezing it as he had done on that terrible day of their drive in the Bois de Boulogne, he stammered: "Is that true?"

"It is true."

But he in terrible grief said with a groan: "I shall have fresh doubts that will never end! When did you lie, the last time or now? How am I to believe you at present? How can one believe a woman after that? I shall never again know what I am to think. I would rather you had said to me: 'It is Jacques,' or, 'It is Jeanne.'"

The carriage drove them into the courtyard of their mansion, and when it had drawn up in front of the steps the count got down first, as usual, and offered his wife his arm to help her up. And then as soon as they had reached the first floor he said: "May I speak to you for a few moments longer?"

And she replied: "I am quite willing."

They went into a small drawing room, while a footman in some surprise lit the wax candles. As soon as he had left the room and they were alone he continued: "How am I to know the truth? I have begged you a thousand times to speak, but you have remained dumb, impenetrable, inflexible, inexorable, and now today you tell me that you have been lying. For six years you have actually allowed me to believe such a thing! No, you are lying now; I do not know why, but out of pity for me perhaps?"

She replied in a sincere and convincing manner: "If I had not done so I should have had four more children in the last six years!"

And he exclaimed: "Can a mother speak like that?"

"Oh!" she replied. "I do not at all feel that I am the mother of children who have never been born; it is enough for me to be the mother of those that I have and to love them with all my heart. I am—we are—women who belong to the civilized world, monsieur, and we are no longer, and we refuse to be, mere females who restock the earth."

She got up, but he seized her hands. "Only one word, Gabrielle. Tell me the truth!"

"I have just told you. I have never dishonored you."

He looked her full in the face, and how beautiful she was, with her gray eyes, like the cold sky. In her dark hairdress, on that opaque night of black hair, there shone the diamond coronet, like a cluster of stars. Then he suddenly felt, felt by a kind of intuition, that this grand creature was not merely a being destined to perpetuate his race, but the strange and mysterious product of all the complicated desires which have been accumulating in us for centuries but which have been turned aside from their primitive and divine object and which have wandered after a mystic, imperfectly seen and intangible beauty. There are some women like that, women who blossom only for our dreams, adorned with every poetical attribute of civilization, with that ideal luxury, coquetry and esthetic charm which should surround the living statue who brightens our life.

Her husband remained standing before her, stupified at the tardy and obscure discovery, confusedly hitting on the cause of his former jealousy and understanding it all very imperfectly. At last he said: "I believe you, for I feel at this moment that you are not lying, and formerly I really thought that you were."

She put out her hand to him: "We are friends then?"

He took her hand and kissed it and replied: "We are friends. Thank you, Gabrielle."

Then he went out, still looking at her and surprised that she was still so beautiful and feeling a strange emotion arising in him which was, perhaps, more formidable than antique and simple love.

AN AFFAIR OF STATE

Paris had just heard of the disaster of Sedan. The Republic was proclaimed. All France was panting from a madness that lasted until the time of the commonwealth. Everybody was playing at soldier from one end of the country to the other.

Capmakers became colonels, assuming the duties of generals; revolvers and daggers were displayed on large rotund bodies enveloped in red sashes; common citizens turned warriors, commanding battalions of noisy volunteers and swearing like troopers to emphasize their importance.

The very fact of bearing arms and handling guns with a system excited a people who hitherto had only handled scales and measures and made them formidable to the first comer, without reason. They even executed a few innocent people to prove that they knew how to kill, and in roaming through virgin fields still belonging to the Prussians they shot stray dogs, cows chewing the cud in peace or sick horses put out to pasture. Each believed himself called upon to play a great role in military affairs. The cafés of the smallest villages, full of tradesmen in uniform, resembled barracks or field hospitals.

Now the town of Canneville did not yet know the exciting news of the army and the capital. It had, however, been greatly agitated for a month over an encounter between the rival political parties. The mayor, Viscount de Varnetot, a small thin man, already old, remained true to the Empire, especially since he saw rising up against him a powerful adversary in the great, sanguine form of Dr Massarel, head of the Republican party in the district, venerable chief of the Masonic lodge, president of the Society of Agriculture and the Fire Department and organizer of the rural militia designed to save the country.

In two weeks he had induced sixty-three men to volunteer in defense of their country—married men, fathers of families, prudent farmers and merchants of the town. These he drilled every morning in front of the mayor's window.

Whenever the mayor happened to appear Commander Massarel, covered with pistols, passing proudly up and down in front of his troops, would make them shout, "Long live our country!" And this, they noticed, disturbed the little viscount, who no doubt heard in it menace and defiance and perhaps some odious recollection of the great Revolution.

On the morning of the fifth of September, in uniform, his revolver on the table, the doctor gave consultation to an old peasant couple. The husband had suffered with a varicose vein for seven years but had waited until his wife had one too, so that they might go and hunt up a physician together, guided by the postman when he should come with the newspaper.

Dr Massarel opened the door, grew pale, straightened himself abruptly and, raising his arms to heaven in a gesture of exaltation, cried out with all his might, in the face of the amazed rustics:

"Long live the Republic! Long live the Republic! Long live the Republic!"
Then he dropped into his armchair weak with emotion.

When the peasant explained that this sickness commenced with a feeling as if ants were running up and down his legs the doctor exclaimed: "Hold your peace. I have spent too much time with you stupid people. The Republic is proclaimed! The Emperor is a prisoner! France is saved! Long live the Republic!" And, running to the door, he bellowed: "Celeste! Quick! Celeste!"

The frightened maid hastened in. He stuttered, so rapidly did he try to speak. "My boots, my saber—my cartridge box—and—the Spanish dagger which is on my night table. Hurry now!"

The obstinate peasant, taking advantage of the moment's silence, began again: "This seemed like some cysts that hurt me when I walked."

The exasperated physician shouted: "Hold your peace! For heaven's sake! If you had washed your feet oftener, it would not have happened." Then, seizing him by the neck, he hissed in his face: "Can you not comprehend that we are living in a republic, stupid?"

But the professional sentiment calmed him suddenly, and he let the astonished old couple out of the house, repeating all the time:

"Return tomorrow, return tomorrow, my friends; I have no more time today."

While equipping himself from head to foot he gave another series of urgent orders to the maid:

"Run to Lieutenant Picard's and to Sublieutenant Pommel's and say to them that I want them here immediately. Send Torcheboeuf to me too, with his drum. Quick now! Quick!" And when Celeste was gone he collected his thoughts and prepared to surmount the difficulties of the situation.

The three men arrived together. They were in their working clothes. The commander, who had expected to see them in uniform, had a fit of surprise.

"You know nothing, then? The Emperor has been taken prisoner. A republic is proclaimed. My position is delicate, not to say perilous."

He reflected for some minutes before the astonished faces of his subordinates and then continued:

"It is necessary to act, not to hesitate. Minutes now are worth hours at other times. Everything depends upon promptness of decision. You, Picard, go and find the curate and get him to ring the bell to bring the people together, while I get ahead of them. You, Torcheboeuf, beat the call to assemble the militia in arms, in the square, from even as far as the hamlets of Gerisaie and Salmare. You, Pommel, put on your uniform at once, that is, the jacket and cap. We, together, are going to take possession of the *mairie* and summon Monsieur de Varnetot to transfer his authority to me. Do you understand?"

"Yes."

"Act, then, and promptly. I will accompany you to your house, Pommel, since we are to work together."

Five minutes later the commander and his subaltern, armed to the teeth, appeared in the square just at the moment when the little Viscount de Varnetot, with hunting gaiters on and his rifle on his shoulder, appeared by another street, walking rapidly and followed by three guards in green jackets, each carrying a knife at his side and a gun over his shoulder.

While the doctor stopped, half stupefied, the four men entered the mayor's house and the door closed behind them.

"We are forestalled," murmured the doctor; "it will be necessary now to wait for reinforcements; nothing can be done for a quarter of an hour."

Here Lieutenant Picard appeared. "The curate refuses to obey," said he; "he has even shut himself up in the church with the beadle and the porter."

On the other side of the square, opposite the white closed front of the *mairie*, the church, mute and black, showed its great oak door with the wrought-iron trimmings.

Then, as the puzzled inhabitants put their noses out of the windows or came out upon the steps of their houses, the rolling of a drum was heard, and Torcheboeuf suddenly appeared, beating with fury the three quick strokes of the call to arms. He crossed the square with disciplined step and then disappeared on a road leading to the country.

The commander drew his sword, advanced alone to the middle distance between the two buildings where the enemy was barricaded and, waving his weapon above his head, roared at the top of his lungs: "Long live the Republic! Death to traitors!" Then he fell back where his officers were. The butcher, the baker and the apothecary, feeling a little uncertain, put up their shutters and closed their shops. The grocery alone remained open.

Meanwhile the men of the militia were arriving little by little, variously clothed but all wearing caps, the cap constituting the whole uniform of the corps. They were armed with their old rusty guns, guns that had hung on chimney pieces in kitchens for thirty years, and looked quite like a detachment of country soldiers.

When there were about thirty around him the commander explained in a few words the state of affairs. Then, turning toward his major, he said: "Now we must act."

While the inhabitants collected, talked over and discussed the matter the doctor quickly formed his plan of campaign.

"Lieutenant Picard, you advance to the windows of the mayor's house and order Monsieur de Varnetot to turn over the town hall to me in the name of the Republic."

But the lieutenant was a master mason and refused.

"You are a scamp, you are. Trying to make a target of me! Those fellows in there are good shots, you know that. No, thanks! Execute your commissions yourself!"

The commander turned red. "I order you to go in the name of discipline," said he.

"I am not spoiling my features without knowing why," the lieutenant returned.

Men of influence, in a group near by, were heard laughing. One of them called out: "You are right, Picard, it is not the proper time." The doctor, under his breath, muttered: "Cowards!" And placing his sword and his revolver in the hands of a soldier, he advanced with measured step, his eye fixed on the windows as if he expected to see a gun or a cannon pointed at him.

When he was within a few steps of the building the doors at the two extremities, affording an entrance to two schools, opened, and a flood of little creatures, boys on one side, girls on the other, poured out and began playing in the open space, chattering around the doctor like a flock of birds. He scarcely knew what to make of it.

As soon as the last were out the doors closed. The greater part of the little monkeys finally scattered, and then the commander called out in a loud voice:

"Monsieur de Varnetot?" A window in the first story opened and M. de Varnetot appeared.

The commander began: "Monsieur, you are aware of the great events which have changed the system of government. The party you represent no longer exists. The side I represent now comes into power. Under these sad but decisive circumstances I come to demand you, in the name of the Republic, to put in my hand the authority vested in you by the outgoing power."

M. de Varnetot replied: "Doctor Massarel, I am mayor of Canneville, so placed by the proper authorities, and mayor of Canneville I shall remain until the title is revoked and replaced by an order from my superiors. As mayor, I am at home in the *mairie*, and there I shall stay. Furthermore, just try to put me out." And he closed the window.

The commander returned to his troops. But before explaining anything, measuring Lieutenant Picard from head to foot, he said:

"You are a numskull, you are—a goose, the disgrace of the army. I shall degrade you."

The lieutenant replied: "I'll attend to that myself." And he went over to a group of muttering civilians.

Then the doctor hesitated. What should he do? Make an assault? Would his men obey him? And then was he surely in the right? An idea burst upon him. He ran to the telegraph office on the other side of the square and hurriedly sent three dispatches: "To the Members of the Republican Government at Paris"; "To the New Republican Prefect of the Lower Seine at Rouen"; "To the New Republican Subprefect of Dieppe."

He exposed the situation fully; told of the danger run by the commonwealth from remaining in the hands of the monarchistic mayor, offered his devout services, asked for orders and signed his name, following it up with all his titles. Then he returned to his army corps and, drawing ten francs out of his pocket, said:

"Now, my friends, go and eat and drink a little something. Only leave here a detachment of ten men, so that no one leaves the mayor's house."

Ex-Lieutenant Picard, chatting with the watchmaker, overheard this. With a sneer he remarked: "Pardon me, but if they go out, there will be an opportunity for you to go in. Otherwise I can't see how you are to get in there!"

The doctor made no reply but went away to luncheon. In the afternoon he disposed of offices all about town, having the air of knowing of an impending surprise. Many times he passed before the doors of the *mairie* and of the church without noticing anything suspicious; one could have believed the two buildings empty.

The butcher, the baker and the apothecary reopened their shops and stood gossiping on the steps. If the Emperor had been taken prisoner, there must be a traitor somewhere. They did not feel sure of the revenue of a new republic.

Night came on. Toward nine o'clock the doctor returned quietly and alone to the mayor's residence, persuaded that his adversary had retired. And as he was trying to force an entrance with a few blows of a pickax the loud voice of a guard demanded suddenly: "Who goes there?" M. Massarel beat a retreat at the top of his speed.

Another day dawned without any change in the situation. The militia in arms occupied the square. The inhabitants stood around awaiting the solution. People from neighboring villages came to look on. Finally the doctor, realizing that his reputation was at stake, resolved to settle the thing in one way or another. He had just decided that it must be something energetic when the door of the telegraph office opened and the little servant of the directress appeared, holding in her hand two papers.

She went directly to the commander and gave him one of the dispatches; then, crossing the square, intimidated by so many eyes fixed upon her, with lowered head and mincing steps, she rapped gently at the door of the barricaded house as if ignorant that a part of the army was concealed there.

The door opened slightly; the hand of a man received the message, and the girl returned, blushing and ready to weep from being stared at.

The doctor demanded with stirring voice: "A little silence, if you please." And after the populace became quiet he continued proudly:

"Here is a communication which I have received from the government." And, raising the dispatch, he read:

"*Old mayor deposed. Advise us what is most necessary. Instructions later.*
"*For the Subprefect,*
"S<small>APIN</small>, *Counselor.*"

He had triumphed. His heart was beating with joy. His hand trembled, when Picard, his old subaltern, cried out to him from the neighboring group:

"That's all right; but if the others in there won't go out, your paper hasn't a leg to stand on." The doctor grew a little pale. If they would not go out —in fact, he must go ahead now. It was not only his right but his duty. And he looked anxiously at the house of the mayoralty, hoping that he might see the door open and his adversary show himself. But the door remained closed. What was to be done? The crowd was increasing, surrounding the militia. Some laughed.

One thought, especially, tortured the doctor. If he should make an assault, he must march at the head of his men; and as with him dead all contest would cease, it would be at him and at him alone that M. de Varnetot and the three guards would aim. And their aim was good, very good! Picard had reminded him of that.

But an idea shone in upon him, and turning to Pommel, he said: "Go, quickly, and ask the apothecary to send me a napkin and a pole."

The lieutenant hurried off. The doctor was going to make a political banner, a white one, that would, perhaps, rejoice the heart of that old legitimist, the mayor.

Pommel returned with the required linen and a broom handle. With some pieces of string they improvised a standard, which Massarel seized in both hands. Again he advanced toward the house of mayoralty, bearing the standard before him. When in front of the door, he called out: "Monsieur de Varnetot!"

The door opened suddenly, and M. de Varnetot and the three guards appeared on the threshold. The doctor recoiled instinctively. Then he saluted his enemy courteously and announced, almost strangled by emotion: "I have come, sir, to communicate to you the instructions I have just received."

That gentleman, without any salutation whatever, replied: "I am going to withdraw, sir, but you must understand that it is not because of fear or in obedience to an odious government that has usurped the power." And, biting off each word, he declared: "I do not wish to have the appearance of serving the Republic for a single day. That is all."

Massarel, amazed, made no reply; and M. de Varnetot, walking off at a rapid pace, disappeared around the corner, followed closely by his escort. Then the doctor, slightly dismayed, returned to the crowd. When he was near enough to be heard he cried: "Hurrah! Hurrah! The Republic triumphs all along the line!"

But no emotion was manifested. The doctor tried again. "The people are free! You are free and independent! Do you understand? Be proud of it!"

The listless villagers looked at him with eyes unlit by glory. In his turn he looked at them, indignant at their indifference, seeking for some word that could make a grand impression, electrify this placid country and make good his mission. The inspiration came, and turning to Pommel, he said: "Lieutenant, go and get the bust of the ex-emperor, which is in the Council Hall, and bring it to me with a chair."

And soon the man reappears, carrying on his right shoulder Napoleon III in plaster and holding in his left hand a straw-bottomed chair.

Massarel met him, took the chair, placed it on the ground, put the white image upon it, fell back a few steps and called out in sonorous voice:

"Tyrant! Tyrant! Here do you fall! Fall in the dust and in the mire. An expiring country groans under your feet. Destiny has called you the Avenger. Defeat and shame cling to you. You fall conquered, a prisoner to the Prussians, and upon the ruins of the crumbling Empire the young and radiant Republic arises, picking up your broken sword."

He awaited applause. But there was no voice, no sound. The bewildered peasants remained silent. And the bust, with its pointed mustaches extending beyond the cheeks on each side, the bust, so motionless and well groomed as to be fit for a hairdresser's sign, seemed to be looking at M. Massarel with a plaster smile, a smile ineffaceable and mocking.

They remained thus face to face, Napoleon on the chair, the doctor in front of him about three steps away. Suddenly the commander grew angry.

What was to be done? What was there that would move this people and bring about a definite victory in opinion? His hand happened to rest on his hip and to come in contact there with the butt end of his revolver under his red sash. No inspiration, no further word would come. But he drew his pistol, advanced two steps and, taking aim, fired at the late monarch. The ball entered the forehead, leaving a little black hole like a spot, nothing more. There was no effect. Then he fired a second shot, which made a second hole, then a third; and then, without stopping, he emptied his revolver. The brow of Napoleon disappeared in white powder, but the eyes, the nose and the fine points of the mustaches remained intact. Then, exasperated, the doctor overturned the chair with a blow of his fist and, resting a foot on the remainder of the bust in a position of triumph, he shouted: "So let all tyrants perish!"

Still no enthusiasm was manifest, and as the spectators seemed to be in a kind of stupor from astonishment the commander called to the militiamen: "You may now go to your homes." And he went toward his own house with great strides, as if he were pursued.

His maid, when he appeared, told him that some patients had been waiting in his office for three hours. He hastened in. There were the two varicose-vein patients, who had returned at daybreak, obstinate but patient.

The old man immediately began his explanation: "This began by a feeling like ants running up and down the legs."

BABETTE

I WAS NOT very fond of inspecting that asylum for old, infirm people officially, as I was obliged to go over it in company of the superintendent, who was talkative and a statistician. But then the grandson of the foundress accompanied us and was evidently pleased at that minute inspection. He was a charming man and the owner of a large forest, where he had given me permission to shoot, and I was of course obliged to pretend to be interested in his grandmother's philanthropic work. So with a smile on my lips I endured the superintendent's interminable discourse, punctuating it here and there as best as I could by:

"Ah! Really! Very strange indeed! I should never have believed it!"

I was absolutely ignorant of the remark to which I replied thus, for my thoughts were lulled to repose by the constant humming of our loquacious guide. I was vaguely conscious that the persons and things might have appeared worthy of attention to me if I had been there alone as an idler, for in that case I should certainly have asked the superintendent: "What is this Babette whose name appears so constantly in the complaints of so many of the inmates?"

Quite a dozen men and women had spoken to us about her, now to complain of her, now to praise her, and especially the women, as soon as they saw the superintendent, cried out:

"M'sieur, Babette has again been——"

"There! That will do; that will do!" he interrupted them, his gentle voice suddenly becoming harsh.

At other times he would amicably question some old man with a happy countenance and say:

"Well, my friend! I suppose you are very happy here?"

Many replied with fervent expressions of gratitude with which Babette's name was frequently mingled. When he heard them speak so the superintendent put on an ecstatic air, looked up to heaven with clasped hands and said, slowly shaking his head: "Ah! Babette is a very precious woman, very precious!"

Yes, it would certainly interest one to know who that creature was, but not under present circumstances, and so, rather than to undergo any more of this, I made up my mind to remain in ignorance of who Babette was, for I could pretty well guess what she would be like. I pictured her to myself as a flower that had sprung up in a corner of these dull courtyards like a ray of sun shining through the sepulchral gloom of these dismal passages.

I pictured her so clearly to myself that I did not even feel any wish to know her. Yet she was dear to me because of the happy expression which they all put on when they spoke of her, and I was angry with the old women who spoke against her. One thing, certainly, puzzled me, and that was that the superintendent was among those who went into ecstasies over her, and this made me strongly disinclined to question him about her, though I had no other reason for the feeling.

But all this passed through my mind in rather a confused manner, without my taking the trouble to fix or to formulate any ideas or explanations. I continued to dream rather than to think effectively, and it is very probable that when my visit was over I should not have remembered much about it, not even with regard to Babette, if I had not been suddenly awakened by the sight of her in the flesh and been quite upset by the difference that there was between my fancy and the reality.

We had just crossed a small back yard and had gone into a very dark passage, when a door suddenly opened at the other end of it and an unexpected apparition appeared. We could indistinctly see that it was the figure of a woman. At the same moment the superintendent called out in a furious voice:

"Babette! Babette!"

He had mechanically quickened his pace and almost ran. We followed him, and he quickly opened the door through which the apparition had vanished. It led onto a staircase, and he again called out, but a burst of stifled laughter was the only reply. I looked over the balustrade and saw a woman down below who was looking at us fixedly.

She was an old woman—there could be no doubt of that from her wrinkled face and the few straggling gray locks which appeared under her cap. But one did not think of that when one saw her eyes, which were wonderfully youthful; in fact, one saw nothing but them. They were profound eyes, of a deep, almost violet blue, the eyes of a child.

Suddenly the superintendent called out to her: "You have been with *La Frieze* again!"

The old woman did not reply but shook with laughter, as she had done just before, and then she ran off, giving the superintendent a look which said as plainly as words could have done: "Do you think I care a fig for you?"

Those insulting words were clearly written in her face, and at the same time I noticed that the old woman's eyes had utterly changed, for during that short moment of bravado the childish eyes had become the eyes of a monkey, of some ferocious, obstinate baboon.

This time, in spite of my dislike to question him further, I could not help saying to him: "That is Babette, I suppose?"

"Yes," he replied, growing rather red, as if he guessed that I understood the old woman's insulting looks.

"Is she the woman who is so precious?" I added with a touch of irony, which made him grow altogether crimson.

"That is she," he said, walking on quickly so as to escape my further questions.

But I was egged on by curiosity and I made a direct appeal to our host's complaisance: "I should like to see this *Frieze*," I said. "Who is *Frieze*?"

He turned round and said: "Oh! Nothing, nothing, he is not at all interesting. What is the good of seeing him? It is not worth while."

And he ran downstairs two steps at a time. He who was usually so minute and so very careful to explain everything was now in a hurry to get finished, and our visit was cut short.

The next day I had to leave that part of the country without hearing anything more about Babette, but I came back about four months later, when the shooting season began. I had not forgotten her during that time, for nobody could ever forget her eyes, and so I was very glad to have as my traveling companion on my three hours' diligence journey from the station to my friend's house a man who talked to me about her all the time.

He was a young magistrate whom I had already met and who had much interested me by his wit, by his close manner of observing things, by his singularly refined casuistry and, above all, by the contrast between his professional severity and his tolerant philosophy.

But he never appeared so attractive to me as he did on that day when he told me the history of the mysterious Babette.

He had inquired into it and had applied all his facilities as an examining magistrate to it, for, like me, his visit to the asylum had roused his curiosity. This is what he had learned and what he told me:

When she was ten years old Babette had been violated by her own father and at thirteen had been sent to the house of correction for vagabondage and debauchery. From the time she was twenty until she was forty she had been a servant in the neighborhood, frequently changing her situations and being nearly everywhere her employer's mistress. She had ruined several families without getting any money herself and without gaining any definite position. A shopkeeper had committed suicide on her account, and a respectable young fellow had turned thief and incendiary and had finished at the hulks.

She had been married twice and had twice been left a widow, and for ten years, until she was fifty, she had been the only courtesan in the district.

"She was very pretty, I suppose?"

"No, she never was that. It seems she was short, thin, with no bust or hips, at her best, I am told, and nobody can remember that she was pretty, even when she was young."

"Then how can you explain?"

"How?" the magistrate exclaimed. "Well! What about the eyes? You could not have looked at them?"

"Yes, yes, you are right," I replied. "Those eyes explain many things, certainly. They are the eyes of an innocent child."

"Ah!" he exclaimed again enthusiastically. "Cleopatra, Diana of Poitiers, Ninon de l'Enclos, all the queens of love who were adored when they were growing old, must have had eyes like hers. A woman who has such eyes can never grow old. But if Babette lives to be a hundred she will always be loved as she has been and as she is."

"As she is! Bah! By whom, pray?"

"By all the old men in the asylum, by Jove; by all those who have preserved a fiber that can be touched, a corner of their heart that can be inflamed, or the least spark of desire left."

"Do you think so?"

"I am sure of it. And the superintendent loves her more than any of them."

"Impossible!"

"I would stake my head on it."

"Well, after all, it is possible and even probable; it is even certain. I now remember."

And I again saw the insulting, ferocious, familiar look which she had given the superintendent.

"And who is *La Frieze?*" I asked the magistrate suddenly. "I suppose you know that also?"

"He is a retired butcher who had both his legs frozen in the war of 1870 and of whom she is very fond. No doubt he is a cripple, with two wooden legs, but still a vigorous man enough, in spite of his fifty-three years. The loins of a Hercules and the face of a satyr. The superintendent is quite jealous of him!"

I thought the matter over again and it seemed very probable to me. "Does she love *La Frieze?*"

"Yes, he is the chosen lover."

When we arrived at the host's house a short time afterward we were surprised to find everybody in a terrible state of excitement. A crime had been committed in the asylum; the gendarmes were there, and our host was with them, so we instantly joined them. *La Frieze* had murdered the superintendent, and they gave us the details, which were horrible. The former butcher had hidden behind a door and, catching hold of the other, had rolled onto the ground with him and bitten him in the throat, tearing out his carotid artery, from which the blood spurted into the murderer's face.

I saw him, *La Frieze*. His fat face, which had been badly washed, was still bloodstained; he had a low forehead, square jaws, pointed ears sticking out from his head and flat nostrils, like the muzzle of some wild animal; but above all, I saw Babette.

She was smiling, and at that moment her eyes had not their monkeylike and ferocious expression; they were pleading and tender, full of the sweetest childlike candor.

"You know," my host said to me in a low voice, "that the poor woman has fallen into senile imbecility, and that is the cause of her looks, which are strange, considering the terrible sight she has seen."

"Do you think so?" the magistrate said. "You must remember that she is not yet sixty, and I do not think that it is a case of senile imbecility but that she is quite conscious of the crime that has been committed."

"Then why should she smile?"

"Because she is pleased at what she has done."

"Oh no! You are really too subtle!"

The magistrate suddenly turned to Babette and, looking at her steadily, he said:

"I suppose you know what has happened and why this crime was committed?"

She left off smiling, and her pretty, childlike eyes became abominable monkey's eyes again, and then the answer was suddenly to pull up her petticoats to show us the lower part of her limbs. Yes, the magistrate had been quite right. That old woman had been a Cleopatra, a Diana, a Ninon de l'Enclos, and the rest of her body had remained like a child's, even more than her eyes. We were thunderstruck at the sight.

"Pigs! Pigs!" *La Frieze* shouted to us. "You also want to have something to do with her!"

And I saw that actually the magistrate's face was pale and contracted and that his hands and lips trembled like those of a man caught in the act of doing wrong.

A COCK CROWED

MME BERTHA D'AVANCELLES had up till that time resisted all the prayers of her despairing adorer, Baron Joseph de Croissard. He had pursued her ardently in Paris during the winter, and now he was giving fetes and shooting parties in her honor at his château at Carville, in Normandy.

M. d'Avancelles, her husband, saw nothing and knew nothing, as usual. It was said that he lived apart from his wife on account of a physical weakness for which Mme d'Avancelles would not pardon him. He was a short, stout, bald man, with short arms, legs, neck, nose, and very ugly; while Mme d'Avancelles, on the contrary, was a tall, dark and determined young woman who laughed in her husband's face with sonorous peals while he called her openly "Mrs Housewife." She looked at the broad shoulders, strong build and fair mustaches of her titled admirer, Baron Joseph de Croissard, with a certain amount of tenderness.

She had not, however, granted him anything as yet. The baron was ruining himself for her, and there was a constant round of feting, hunting parties and new pleasures to which he invited the neighboring nobility. All day long the hounds gave tongue in the woods as they followed the fox or the wild boar, and every night dazzling fireworks mingled their burning plumes with the stars while the illuminated windows of the drawing room cast long rays of light onto the wide lawns where shadows were moving to and fro.

It was autumn, the russet-colored season of the year, and the leaves were whirling about on the grass like flights of birds. One noticed the smell of damp earth in the air, of the naked earth, like one scents the odor of the bare skin when a woman's dress falls off her after a ball.

One evening in the previous spring, during an entertainment, Mme d'Avancelles had said to M. de Croissard, who was worrying her by his importunities: "If I do succumb to you, my friend, it will not be before the fall of the leaf. I have too many things to do this summer to have any time for it." He had not forgotten that bold and amusing speech, and every day he became more pressing, every day he pushed his approaches nearer—to use a military phrase—and gained a hold on the heart of the fair, audacious woman who seemed only to be resisting for form's sake.

It was the day before a large wild-boar hunt, and in the evening Mme Bertha said to the baron with a laugh: "Baron, if you kill the brute, I shall have something to say to you." And so at dawn he was up and out, to try and discover where the solitary animal had its lair. He accompanied his huntsmen, settled the places for the relays and organized everything personally to insure his triumph. When the horns gave the signal for setting out he appeared in a closely fitting coat of scarlet and gold, with his waist drawn in tight, his chest expanded, his eyes radiant and as fresh and strong as if he had just got out of bed. They set off; the wild boar bolted through the underwood as soon as he was dislodged, followed by the hounds in full cry, while the horses set off at a gallop through the narrow side-cuts in the forest. The carriages which followed the chase at a distance drove noiselessly along the soft roads.

From mischief Mme d'Avancelles kept the baron by her side, lagging behind at a walk in an interminably long and straight drive, over which four rows of oaks hung so as to form almost an arch, while he, trembling with love and anxiety, listened with one ear to the young woman's bantering chatter and with the other to the blast of the horns and to the cry of the hounds as they receded in the distance.

"So you do not love me any longer?" she observed.

"How can you say such things?" he replied.

And she continued: "But you seem to be paying more attention to the sport than to me."

He groaned and said: "Did you not order me to kill the animal myself?" And she replied gravely: "Of course I reckon upon it. You must kill it under my eyes."

Then he trembled in his saddle, spurred his horse until it reared and, losing all patience, exclaimed: "But, by Jove, madame, that is impossible if we remain here."

Then she spoke tenderly to him, laying her hand on his arm or stroking his horse's mane, as if from abstraction, and said with a laugh: "But you must do it—or else so much the worse for you."

Just then they turned to the right into a narrow path which was overhung by trees, and suddenly, to avoid a branch which barred their way, she leaned toward him so closely that he felt her hair tickling his neck. Suddenly he threw his arms brutally round her, and putting his heavily mustached mouth to her forehead, he gave her a furious kiss.

At first she did not move and remained motionless under that mad caress; then she turned her head with a jerk, and either by accident or design her little lips met his, under their wealth of light hair, and a moment afterward, either from confusion or remorse, she struck her horse with her riding whip and went off at full gallop, and they rode on like that for some time, without exchanging a look.

The noise of the hunt came nearer; the thickets seemed to tremble, and suddenly the wild boar broke through the bushes, covered with blood and trying to shake off the hounds who had fastened onto him, and the baron, uttering a shout of triumph, exclaimed: "Let him who loves me follow me!" And he disappeared in the copse as if the wood had swallowed him up.

When she reached an open glade a few minutes later he was just getting up, covered with mud, his coat torn and his hands bloody, while the brute was lying stretched out at full length with the baron's hunting knife driven into its shoulder up to the hilt.

The quarry was cut at night by torchlight. It was a warm and dull evening, and the wan moon threw a yellow light onto the torches which made the night misty with their resinous smoke. The hounds devoured the wild boar's entrails and snarled and fought for them, while the prickers and the gentlemen, standing in a circle round the spoil, blew their horns as loud as they could. The flourish of the hunting horns resounded beyond the woods on that still night and was repeated by the echoes of the distant valleys, awakening the timid stags, rousing the yelping foxes and disturbing the little rabbits in their gambols at the edge of the rides.

The frightened night birds flew over the eager pack of hounds, while the women, who were moved by all these strangely picturesque things, leaned rather heavily on the men's arms and turned aside into the forest rides before the hounds had finished their meal. Mme d'Avancelles, feeling languid after that day of fatigue and tenderness, said to the baron: "Will you take a turn in the park, my friend?" And without replying, but trembling and nervous, he went with her, and immediately they kissed each other. They walked slowly under the almost leafless trees through which the moonbeams filtered.

and their love, their desires, their longing for a closer embrace became so vehement that they nearly yielded to it at the foot of a tree.

The horns were not sounding any longer, and the tired hounds were sleeping in the kennels. "Let us return," the young woman said, and they went back.

When they got to the château and before they went in she said in a weak voice: "I am so tired that I shall go to bed, my friend." And as he opened his arms for a last kiss she ran away, saying as a last good-by: "No—I am going to sleep. Let him who loves me follow me!"

An hour later, when the whole silent château seemed dead, the baron crept stealthily out of his room and went and scratched at her door. As she did not reply he tried to open it and found that it was not locked.

She was in a reverie, resting her arms against the window ledge. He threw himself at her knees, which he kissed madly through her dress. She said nothing but buried her delicate fingers caressingly in his hair, and suddenly, as if she had formed some great resolution, whispered with a daring look: "I shall come back; wait for me." And, stretching out her hand, she pointed with her finger to an indistinct white spot at the end of the room; it was her bed.

Then with trembling hands, and scarcely knowing what he was doing, he quickly undressed, got into the cool sheets and, stretching himself out comfortably, almost forgot his love in the pleasure he found, tired out as he was, in the contact of the linen. She did not return, however, no doubt finding amusement in making him languish. He closed his eyes with a feeling of exquisite comfort and reflected peaceably while waiting for what he so ardently longed for. But by degrees his limbs grew languid and his thoughts became indistinct and fleeting, until his fatigue gained the upper hand and he fell asleep.

He slept that unconquerable heavy sleep of the worn-out hunter, slept through until daylight. Then, as the window had remained half open, the crowing of a cock suddenly woke him. The baron opened his eyes, and feeling a woman's body against his—finding himself, much to his surprise, in a strange bed, and remembering nothing for the moment—he stammered:

"What? Where am I? What is the matter?"

Then she, who had not been asleep at all, looking at this unkempt man with red eyes and swollen lips, replied in the haughty tone of voice in which she occasionally spoke to her husband:

"It is nothing; it is only a cock crowing. Go to sleep again, monsieur, it has nothing to do with you."

LILIE LALA

"When I saw her for the first time," Louis d'Arandel said, with the look of a man who was dreaming and trying to recollect something, "I thought of some slow and yet passionate music that I once heard, though I do not remember who was the composer. It told of a fair-haired woman whose hair was so silky, so golden and so vibrating that her lover had it cut off after her death and had the strings of the magic bow of a violin made out of it, which afterward emitted such superhuman complaints and love melodies that they made its hearers love until death.

"In her eyes there lay the mystery of deep waters; one was lost in them, drowned in them like in fathomless depths, and at the corners of her mouth there lurked the despotic and merciless smile of those women who do not fear that they may be conquered, who rule over men like cruel queens, whose hearts remain as virgin as those of the strictest Carmelite nuns amid a flood of lewdness.

"I have seen her angelic head, the bands of her hair which looked like plates of gold, her tall, graceful figure, her white, slender, childish hands, in stained-glass windows in churches. She suggested pictures of the Annunciation, where the Archangel Gabriel descends with ultramarine-colored wings and Mary is sitting at her spinning wheel and spinning while uttering pious prayers, seemingly a tall sister to the white lilies that are growing beside her and the roses.

"When she went through the acacia alley she appeared on some first night in the stage box at one of the theaters, nearly always alone and apparently feeling life a great burden and angry because she could not change the eternal, dull round of human enjoyment; nobody would have believed that she went in for a fast life—that in the annals of gallantry she was catalogued under the strange name of 'Lilie Lala' and that no man could rub against her without being irretrievably caught and spending his last halfpenny on her.

"But with all that Lilie had the voice of a schoolgirl, of some little innocent creature who still uses a skipping rope and wears short dresses, and had that clear, innocent laugh which reminds people of wedding bells. Sometimes, for fun, I would kneel down before her, like before the statue of a saint, and clasping my hands as if in prayer, I used to say: '*Sancta Lilie, ora pro nobis!*'

"One evening at Biarritz, when the sky had the dull glare of intense heat and the sea was of a sinister, inky black and was swelling and rolling in enormous phosphorescent waves on the beach at Port-Vieux, Lilie, who was listless and strange and was making holes in the sand with the heels of her boots, suddenly exclaimed in one of those confidences which women sometimes bestow and for which they are sorry as soon as the story is told:

"'Ah! My dear fellow, I do not deserve to be canonized, and my life is rather a subject for a drama than a chapter from the Gospels or the *Golden Legend*. As long as I can remember anything I can remember being wrapped in lace, being carried by a woman and continually being fussed over, as are children who have been long waited for and who are consequently spoiled more than usual.

"'Those kisses were so nice that I still seem to feel their sweetness, and I shrine the remembrance of them in a little place in my heart, as one preserves some lucky talisman in a reliquary. I still seem to remember an indistinct landscape lost in the mist, outlines of trees which frightened me as they creaked and groaned in the wind and ponds on which swans were sailing. And when I look in the glass for a long time, merely for the sake of seeing myself, it seems to me as if I recognize the woman who formerly used to kiss me most frequently and speak to me in a more loving voice than anyone else did. But what happened afterward?

"'Was I carried off or sold to some strolling circus owner by a dishonest servant? I do not know; I have never been able to find out, but I remember that my whole childhood was spent in a circus which traveled from fair to fair and from place to place, with files of vans, processions of animals and noisy music.

"'I was as tiny as an insect, and they taught me difficult tricks, to dance on the tightrope and to perform on the slackrope. I was beaten as if I had been a bit of plaster, and more frequently I had a piece of dry bread to gnaw than a slice of meat. But I remember that one day I slipped under one of the vans and stole a basin of soup as my share, which one of the clowns was carefully making for his three learned dogs.

"'I had neither friends nor relations; I was employed on the dirtiest jobs, like the lowest stable help, and I was tattooed with bruises and scars. Of the whole company, however, the one who beat me the most, who was the least sparing of his thumps and who continually made me suffer, as if it gave him pleasure, was the manager and proprietor, a kind of old, vicious brute, whom everybody feared like the plague, a miser who was continually complaining of the receipts, who hid away the crown pieces in his mattress, invested his money in the funds and cut down the salaries of all as far as he could.

"'His name was Rapha Ginestous. Any other child but myself would have succumbed to such a constant martyrdom, but I grew up, and the more I grew the prettier and more desirable I became, so that when I was fifteen men were already beginning to write love letters to me and to throw bouquets to me in the arena. I felt also that all the men in the company were watching me and were coveting me as their prey; that their lustful looks rested on my pink tights and followed the graceful outlines of my body when I was posing on the rope that stretched from one end of the circus to the other or jumped through the paper hoops at full gallop.

"'They were no longer the same and spoke to me in a totally different tone of voice. They tried to come into my dressing room when I was changing my dress, and Rapha Ginestous seemed to have lost his head, and his heart throbbed audibly when he came near me. Yes, he had the audacity to propose bargains to me which covered my cheeks and forehead with blushes and which filled me with disgust, and as I felt a fierce hatred for him and detested him with all my soul and all my strength, as I wished to make him suffer the tortures which he had inflicted on me a hundredfold, I used him as the target at which I was constantly aiming.

"'Instinctively I employed every cunning perfidy, every artful coquetry, every lie, every artifice that can unset the strongest and most skeptical and place them at our mercy like submissive animals. He loved me; he really loved me, that lascivious goat who had never seen anything in a woman except a soft couch and an instrument of convenience and of forgetfulness. He loved me like old men do love, with frenzy, with degrading transports and with the prostration of his will and of his strength. I held him as in a leash and did whatever I liked with him.

" 'I was much more manageress than he was manager, and the poor wretch wasted away in vain hopes and in useless transports; he had not even touched the tips of my fingers and was reduced to bestowing his caresses on my columbine shoes, my tights and my wigs. And I cared not *that* for it, you understand! Not the slightest familiarity did I allow, and he began to grow thin and ill and became idiotic. And while he implored me and promised to marry me, with his eyes full of tears, I shouted with laughter; I reminded him of how he had beaten, abused and humiliated me and had often made me wish for death. And as soon as he left me he would swill bottles of gin and whisky and constantly got so abominably drunk that he rolled under the table and all to drown his sorrow and forget his desire.

" 'He covered me with jewels and tried everything he could to tempt me to become his wife. In spite of my inexperience in life he consulted me with regard to everything he undertook, and one evening, after I had stroked his face with my hand, I persuaded him without any difficulty to make his will, by which he left me all his savings and the circus and everything belonging to it.

" 'It was in the middle of winter, near Moscow; it snowed continually, and one almost burnt oneself at the stoves in trying to keep warm. Rapha Ginestous had had supper brought into the largest van, which was his, after the performance, and for hours we ate and drank. I was very nice toward him and filled his glass every moment; I even sat on his knee and kissed him. And all his love and the fumes of the alcohol of the wine mounted to his head and gradually made him so helplessly intoxicated that he fell from his chair, inert, as if he had been struck by lightning, without opening his eyes or saying a word.

" 'The rest of the troupe were asleep; the lights were out in all the little windows, and not a sound was to be heard, while the snow continued to fall in large flakes. So having put out the petroleum lamp, I opened the door and, taking the drunkard by the feet, as if he had been a bale of goods, I threw him out into that white shroud.

" 'The next morning the stiff and convulsed body of Rapha Ginestous was picked up, and as everybody knew his inveterate drinking habits, no one thought of instituting an inquiry or of accusing me of a crime. Thus was I avenged and gained a yearly income of nearly fifteen thousand francs.[1] What, after all, is the good of being honest and of pardoning our enemies, as the Gospel bids us?'

"And now," Louis d'Arandel said in conclusion, "suppose we go and have a cocktail or two at the casino, for I do not think that I have ever talked so much in my life before."

[1] About $3000.

A VAGABOND

For more than a month Randel had been walking, seeking for work everywhere. He had left his native place, Ville-Avary, in the department of La Manche because there was no work to be had. He was a journeyman carpenter, twenty-seven years old, a steady fellow and good workman, but for two months he, the eldest son, had been obliged to live on his family, with nothing to do but loaf in the general stoppage of work. Bread was getting scarce with them; the two sisters went out as charwomen but earned little, and he, Jacques Randel, the strongest of them all, did nothing because he had nothing to do and ate the others' bread.

Then he went and inquired at the town hall, and the mayor's secretary told him that he would find work at the labor center. So he started, well provided with papers and certificates and carrying another pair of shoes, a pair of trousers and a shirt in a blue handkerchief at the end of his stick.

He had walked almost without stopping, day and night, along interminable roads, in the sun and rain, without ever reaching that mysterious country where workmen find work. At first he had the fixed idea that he must only work at his own trade, but at every carpenter's shop where he applied he was told that they had just dismissed men on account of work being so slack, and finding himself at the end of his resources, he made up his mind to undertake any job that he might come across on the road. And so by turns he was a navvy, stableman, stone sawyer; he split wood, lopped the branches of trees, dug wells, mixed mortar, tied up fagots, tended goats on a mountain, and all for a few pence, for he only obtained two or three days' work occasionally, by offering himself at a shamefully low price in order to tempt the avarice of employers and peasants.

And now for a week he had found nothing, and he had no money left. He was eating a piece of bread, thanks to the charity of some women from whom he had begged at house doors on the road. It was getting dark, and Jacques Randel, jaded, his legs failing him, his stomach empty and with despair in his heart, was walking barefoot on the grass by the side of the road, for he was taking care of his last pair of shoes, the other pair having already ceased to exist for a long time. It was a Saturday toward the end of autumn. The heavy gray clouds were being driven rapidly among the trees, and one felt that it would rain soon. The country was deserted at that time of the evening and on the eve of Sunday. Here and there in the fields there rose up stacks of thrashed-out corn like huge yellow mushrooms, and the fields looked bare, as they had already been sown for the next year.

Randel was hungry with the hunger of some wild animal, such a hunger as drives wolves to attack men. Worn out and weakened with fatigue, he took longer strides so as not to take so many steps, and with heavy head, the blood throbbing in his temples, with red eyes and dry mouth he grasped his stick tightly in his hand with a longing to strike the first passer-by whom he should meet, and who might be going home to supper, with all his force.

He looked at the sides of the road with the image of potatoes dug up and lying on the ground before his eyes; if he had found any he would have gathered some dead wood, made a fire in the ditch and have had a capital supper off the warm, round tubers, which he would first of all have held burning hot in his cold hands. But it was too late in the year, and he would have to gnaw a raw beetroot as he had done the day before, having picked one up in a field.

For the last two days he had spoken aloud as he quickened his steps, under the influence of his thoughts. He had never done much thinking hitherto, as he had given all his mind, all his simple faculties, to his industrial requirements. But now fatigue and this desperate search for work which he could not get, refusals and rebuffs, nights spent in the open air lying on the grass, long fasting, the contempt which he knew people with a settled abode felt for a vagabond, the question which he was continually asked: "Why did you not remain at home?" distress at not being able to use his strong arms which he felt so full of vigor, the recollection of his relations who had remained at home and who also had not a halfpenny, filled him by degrees with a rage which was accumulating every day, every hour, every minute, and which now escaped his lips in spite of himself in short growling sentences.

As he stumbled over the stones which rolled beneath his bare feet he grumbled: "How wretched! how miserable! A set of hogs, to let a man die of hunger, a carpenter. A set of hogs—not twopence—not twopence. And now it is raining—a set of hogs!"

He was indignant at the injustice of fate and cast the blame on men, on all men, because Nature, that great, blind mother, is unjust, cruel and perfidious, and he repeated through his clenched teeth, "A set of hogs," as he looked at the thin gray smoke which rose from the roofs, for it was the dinner hour. And without thinking about that other injustice, which is human and which is called robbery and violence, he felt inclined to go into one of those houses to murder the inhabitants and to sit down to table in their stead.

He said to himself: "I have a right to live, and they are letting me die of hunger—and yet I only ask for work—a set of hogs!" And the pain in his limbs, the gnawing in his heart, rose to his head like terrible intoxication and gave rise to this simple thought in his brain: "I have the right to live because I breathe and because the air is the common property of everybody, and so nobody has the right to leave me without bread!"

A thick, fine, icy-cold rain was coming down, and he stopped and murmured: "How miserable! Another month of walking before I get home." He was indeed returning home then, for he saw that he should more easily find work in his native town where he was known—and he did not mind what he did—than on the highroads where everybody suspected him. As the carpentering business was not going well he would turn day laborer, be a mason's hodman, ditcher, break stones on the road. If he only earned tenpence a day, that would at any rate find him something to eat.

He tied the remains of his last pocket handkerchief round his neck to prevent the cold water from running down his back and chest, but he soon found that it was penetrating the thin material of which his clothes were made, and he glanced round him with the agonized look of a man who does not know where to hide his body and to rest his head and has no place of shelter in the whole world.

Night came on and wrapped the country in obscurity, and in the distance, in a meadow, he saw a dark spot on the grass; it was a cow, and so he got over the ditch by the roadside and went up to her without exactly knowing what he was doing. When he got close to her she raised her great head to him, and he thought: "If I only had a jug I could get a little milk." He looked at the cow, and the cow looked at him, and then suddenly, giving her a violent kick in the side, he said: "Get up!"

The animal got up slowly, letting her heavy udder hang down below her; then the man lay down on his back between the animal's legs and drank for a long time, squeezing the warm swollen teats which tasted of the cow stall with both hands, and drank as long as any milk remained in that living well. But the icy rain began to fall more heavily, and he saw no place of shelter on the whole of that bare plain. He was cold, and he looked at a light which was shining among the trees in the window of a house.

The cow had lain down again, heavily, and he sat down by her side and stroked her head, grateful for the nourishment she had given him. The animal's strong thick breath, which came out of her nostrils like two jets of steam in the evening air, blew onto the workman's face, who said: "You are not cold inside there!" He put his hands onto her chest and under her legs to find some warmth there, and then the idea struck him that he might pass the night against that large, warm stomach. So he found a comfortable place and laid his forehead against the great udder from which he had quenched his thirst just previously, and then, as he was worn out with fatigue, he fell asleep immediately.

He woke up, however, several times, with his back or his stomach half frozen, according as he put one or the other to the animal's flank. Then he turned over to warm and dry that part of his body which had remained exposed to the night air, and he soon went soundly to sleep again.

The crowing of a cock woke him; the day was breaking, it was no longer raining and the sky was bright. The cow was resting with her muzzle on the ground, and he stooped down, resting on his hands, to kiss those wide nostrils of moist flesh and said: "Good-by, my beauty, until next time. You are a nice animal! Good-by." Then he put on his shoes and went off, and for two hours he walked straight on before him, always following the same road, and then he felt so tired that he sat down on the grass. It was broad daylight by that time, and the church bells were ringing; men in blue blouses, women in white caps, some on foot, some in carts, began to pass along the road, going to the neighboring villages to spend Sunday with friends or relations.

A stout peasant came in sight, driving a score of frightened, bleating sheep in front of him whom an active dog kept together, so Randel got up and,

A VAGABOND 141

raising his cap, he said: "You do not happen to have any work for a man who is dying of hunger?" But the other, giving an angry look at the vagabond, replied: "I have no work for fellows whom I meet on the road."

And the carpenter went back and sat down by the side of the ditch again. He waited there for a long time, watching the country people pass and looking for a kind, compassionate face before he renewed his request, and finally selected a man in an overcoat, whose stomach was adorned with a gold chain. "I have been looking for work," he said, "for the last two months and cannot find any, and I have not a halfpenny in my pocket."

But the semigentleman replied: "You should have read the notice which is stuck up at the beginning of the village: 'Begging is prohibited within the boundaries of this parish.' Let me tell you that I am the mayor, and if you do not get out of here pretty quickly, I shall have you arrested."

Randel, who was getting angry, replied: "Have me arrested if you like; I should prefer it, for at any rate I should not die of hunger." And he went back and sat down by the side of his ditch again, and in about a quarter of an hour two gendarmes appeared on the road. They were walking slowly, side by side, well in sight, glittering in the sun with their shining hats, their yellow accouterments and their metal buttons, as if to frighten evildoers and to put them to flight at a distance. He knew that they were coming after him, but he did not move, for he was seized with a sudden desire to defy them, to be arrested by them and to have his revenge later.

They came on without appearing to have seen him, walking with military steps, heavily, and balancing themselves as if they were doing the goose step; and then suddenly, as they passed him, they noticed him and stopped, looking at him angrily and threateningly. The brigadier came up to him and asked: "What are you doing here?"

"I am resting," the man replied calmly.

"Where do you come from?"

"If I had to tell you all the places I have been to, it would take me more than an hour."

"Where are you going to?"

"To Ville-Avary."

"Where is that?"

"In La Manche."

"Is that where you belong to?"

"It is."

"Why did you leave it?"

"To try for work."

The brigadier turned to his gendarme and said, in the angry voice of a man who is exasperated at last by the same trick: "They all say that, these scamps. I know all about it." And then he continued: "Have you any papers?"

"Yes, I have some."

"Give them to me."

Randel took his papers out of his pocket, his certificates, those poor worn-out dirty papers which were falling to pieces, and gave them to the soldier, who spelled them through, hemming and hawing, and then, having seen that they were all in order, he gave them back to Randel with the dissatisfied look of a man whom someone cleverer than himself has tricked.

After a few moments' further reflection he asked him: "Have you any money on you?"

"No."

"None whatever?"

"None."

"Not even a sou?"

"Not even a sou!"

"How do you live then?"

"On what people give me."

"Then you beg?"

And Randel answered resolutely: "Yes, when I can."

Then the gendarme said: "I have caught you on the highroad in the act of vagabondage and begging, without any resources or trade, and so I command you to come with me."

The carpenter got up and said: "Wherever you please." And placing himself between the two soldiers, even before he had received the order to do so, he added: "Come, lock me up; that will at any rate put a roof over my head when it rains."

And they set off toward the village, whose red tiles could be seen through the leafless trees, a quarter of a league off. Service was just going to begin when they went through the village. The square was full of people who immediately formed two hedges to see the criminal, who was being followed by a crowd of excited children, pass. Male and female peasants looked at the prisoner between the two gendarmes with hatred in their eyes and a longing to throw stones at him, to tear his skin with their nails, to trample him under their feet. They asked each other whether he had committed murder or robbery. The butcher, who was an ex-spahi, declared that he was a deserter. The tobacconist thought that he recognized him as the man who had that very morning passed a bad half-franc piece off on him, and the ironmonger declared that he was the murderer of Widow Malet, for whom the police had been looking for six months.

In the hall of the municipal council, into which his custodians took him, Randel saw the mayor again, sitting on the magisterial bench with the schoolmaster by his side.

"Ah! ah!" the magistrate exclaimed, "so here you are again, my fellow. I told you I should have you locked up. Well, Brigadier, what is he charged with?"

"He is a vagabond without house or home, Monsieur le Maire, without any resources or money, so he says, who was arrested in the act of begging, but he is provided with good testimonials, and his papers are all in order."

"Show me his papers," the mayor said. He took them, read them, reread, returned them and then said: "Search him"; they searched him but found nothing, and the mayor seemed perplexed and asked the workman:

"What were you doing on the road this morning?"
"I was looking for work."
"Work? On the highroad?"
"How do you expect me to find any if I hide in the woods?"

They looked at each other with the hatred of two wild beasts which belong to different hostile species, and the magistrate continued: "I am going to have you set at liberty, but do not be brought up before me again."

To which the carpenter replied: "I would rather you locked me up; I have had enough running about the country."

But the magistrate replied severely: "Be silent." And then he said to the two gendarmes: "You will conduct this man two hundred yards from the village and let him continue his journey."

"At any rate give me something to eat," the workman said, but the other grew indignant. "It only remains for us to feed you! Ah! ah! ah! that is rather strong!"

But Randel went on firmly: "If you let me nearly die of hunger again, you will force me to commit a crime, and then so much the worse for you other fat fellows."

The mayor had risen, and he repeated: "Take him away immediately, or I shall end by getting angry."

The two gendarmes thereupon seized the carpenter by the arms and dragged him out. He allowed them to do it without resistance, passed through the village again and found himself on the highroad once more; and when the men had accompanied him two hundred yards beyond the village the brigadier said: "Now off with you, and do not let me catch you about here again, for if I do, you will know it."

Randel went off without replying or knowing where he was going. He walked on for a quarter of an hour or twenty minutes, so stupefied that he no longer thought of anything. But suddenly, as he was passing a small house where the window was half open, the smell of the soup and boiled meat stopped him suddenly in front of it, and hunger, fierce, devouring, maddening hunger, seized him and almost drove him against the walls of the house like a wild beast.

He said aloud, in a grumbling voice: "In heaven's name, they must give me some this time." And he began to knock at the door vigorously with his stick, and as nobody came he knocked louder and called out: "Hallo! you people in there, open the door!" And then, as nothing moved, he went up to the window and pushed it open with his hand, and the close warm air of the kitchen, full of the smell of hot soup, meat and cabbage, escaped into the cold outer air, and with a bound the carpenter was in the house. Two covers were laid on the table; no doubt the proprietors of the house, on going to church, had left their dinner on the fire, their nice Sunday boiled beef and vegetable soup, while there was a loaf of new bread on the chimney piece between two bottles which seemed full.

Randel seized the bread first of all and broke it with as much violence as if he were strangling a man, and then he began to eat it voraciously, swallowing great mouthfuls quickly. But almost immediately the smell of the meat attracted him to the fireplace, and having taken off the lid of the saucepan, he plunged a fork into it and brought out a large piece of beef tied with a string. Then he took more cabbage, carrots and onions until his plate was full, and having put it on the table, he sat down before it, cut the meat into four pieces and dined as if he had been at home. When he had eaten nearly all the meat, besides a quantity of vegetables, he felt thirsty and took one of the bottles off the mantelpiece.

Scarcely had he poured the liquor into his glass than he saw it was brandy. So much the better; it was warming, it would instill some fire into his veins, and that would be all right, after being so cold; and he drank some. He found it very good, certainly, for he had grown unaccustomed to it, and he poured himself out another glassful which he drank at two gulps. And then almost immediately he felt quite merry and lighthearted from the effect of the alcohol, just as if some great happiness were flowing through his system.

He continued to eat, but more slowly, dipping his bread into the soup. His skin had become burning, and especially his forehead, where the veins were throbbing. But suddenly the church bells began to ring. Mass was over, and instinct rather than fear, the instinct of prudence which guides all beings and makes them clear-sighted in danger, made the carpenter get up. He put the remains of the loaf into one pocket and the brandy bottle into the other, and he furtively went to the window and looked out into the road. It was still deserted, so he jumped out and set off walking again, but instead of following the highroad he ran across the fields toward a wood which he saw a little way off.

He felt alert, strong, lighthearted, glad of what he had done and so nimble that he sprang over the inclosures of the fields at a single bound, and as soon as he was under the trees he took the bottle out of his pocket again and began to drink once more, swallowing it down as he walked, and then his ideas began to get confused, his eyes grew dim and his legs elastic as springs, and he started singing the old popular song:

> "Oh! how nice, how nice it is,
> To pick the sweet, wild strawberries."

He was now walking on thick, damp, cool moss, and the soft carpet under his feet made him feel absurdly inclined to turn head over heels, like he used to do as a child; so he took a run, turned a somersault, got up and began over again. And between each time he began to sing again:

> "Oh! how nice, how nice it is,
> To pick the sweet, wild strawberries."

Suddenly he found himself on the edge of a sunken road, and in the road he saw a tall girl, a servant who was returning to the village with two pails of milk. He watched, stooping down and with his eyes as bright as those of a dog who scents a quail, but she saw him, raised her head and said: "Was that you singing like that?" He did not reply, however, but jumped down into the road, although it was at least six feet down, and when she saw him suddenly standing in front of her she exclaimed: "Oh dear, how you frightened me!"

But he did not hear her, for he was drunk, he was mad, excited by another requirement which was more imperative than hunger, more feverish than alcohol; by the irresistible fury of the man who has been in want of everything for two months and who is drunk, who is young, ardent and inflamed by all the appetites which nature has implanted in the flesh of vigorous men.

The girl started back from him, frightened at his face, his eyes, his half-open mouth, his outstretched hands, but he seized her by the shoulders and without a word threw her down in the road.

She let her two pails fall, and they rolled over noisily and all the milk was spilt, and then she screamed, but comprehending that it would be of no use to call for help in that lonely spot and seeing that he was not going to make an attempt on her life, she yielded without much difficulty and not very angrily either, for he was a strong, handsome young fellow and really not rough.

When she got up the thought of her overturned pails suddenly filled her with fury, and taking off one of her wooden clogs, she threw it, in her turn, at the man to break his head since he did not pay her for her milk.

But he, mistaking the reason for this sudden violent attack, somewhat sobered and frightened at what he had done, ran off as fast as he could while she threw stones at him, some of which hit him in the back.

He ran for a long time, very long, until he felt more tired than he had ever been before. His legs were so weak that they could scarcely carry him; all his ideas were confused; he lost the recollection of everything and could no longer think about anything, and so he sat down at the foot of a tree and in five minutes was fast asleep. He was soon awakened, however, by a rough shake, and on opening his eyes he saw two cocked hats of polished leather bending over him and the two gendarmes of the morning, who were holding him and binding his arms.

"I knew I should catch you again," said the brigadier jeeringly. But Randel got up without replying. The two men shook him, quite ready to ill-treat him if he made a movement, for he was their prey now; he had become a jailbird, caught by hunters of criminals who would not let him go again.

"Now, start!" the brigadier said, and they set off. It was getting evening, and the autumn twilight was settling, heavy and dark, over the land, and in half an hour they reached the village, where every door was open, for the people had heard what had happened. Peasants and peasant women and girls, excited with anger, as if every man had been robbed and every woman violated, wished to see the wretch brought back, so that they might overwhelm him with abuse. They hooted him from the first house in the village until they reached the mansion house, where the mayor was waiting for him. Eager to avenge himself on this vagabond as soon as he saw him, he cried:

"Ah! my fine fellow! Here we are!" And he rubbed his hands, more pleased than he usually was, and continued: "I said so. I said so the moment I saw him in the road." And then with increased satisfaction:

"Oh! you blackguard! Oh! you dirty blackguard! You will get your twenty years, my fine fellow!"

THE MOUNTEBANKS

COMPARDIN, the clever manager of the Eden Réunis Theater, as the theater critics invariably called him, was reckoning on a great success and had invested his last franc in the affair without thinking of the morrow or of the bad luck which had been pursuing him so inexorably for months past. For a whole week the walls, the kiosks, shop fronts and even the trees had been placarded with flaming posters, and from one end of Paris to the other carriages were to be seen which were covered with fancy sketches by Chéret, representing two strong, well-built men who looked like ancient athletes. The younger of them, who was standing with his arms folded, had the vacant smile of an itinerant mountebank, and the other, who was dressed in what was supposed to be the costume of a Mexican trapper, held a revolver in his hand. There were large-type advertisements in all the papers that the Montefiores would appear without fail at the Eden Réunis the next Monday.

Nothing else was talked about, for the puff and humbug attracted people. The Montefiores, like fashionable knickknacks, succeeded that whimsical jade, Rose Péché, who had gone off the preceding autumn between the third and fourth acts of the burlesque, *Ousca Iscar*, in order to make a study of love in company of a young fellow of seventeen who had just entered the university. The novelty and difficulty of their performance revived and agitated the curiosity of the public, for there seemed to be an implied threat of death or at any rate, of wounds and of blood in it, and it seemed as if they defied danger with absolute indifference. And that always pleases women; it holds them and masters them, and they grow pale with emotion and cruel enjoyment. Consequently all the seats in the large theater were let almost immediately and were soon taken for several days in advance. And stout Compardin, losing his glass of absinthe over a game of dominoes, was in high spirits, seeing the future through rosy glasses, and exclaimed in a loud voice: "I think I have turned up trumps, by George!"

* * *

The Countess Regina de Villégby was lying on the sofa in her boudoir, languidly fanning herself. She had only received three or four intimate friends that day, Saint Mars Montalvin, Tom Sheffield and her cousin, Mme de Rhouel, a Creole, who laughed as incessantly as a bird sings. It was growing dusk, and the distant rumbling of the carriages in the avenue of the Champs Elysées sounded like some somnolent rhythm. There was a delicate perfume of flowers; the lamps had not been brought in yet, and chatting and laughing filled the room with a confused noise.

"Would you pour out the tea?" the countess said, suddenly touching Saint

Mars's fingers, who was beginning an amorous conversation in a low voice, with her fan. And while he slowly filled the little china cup he continued: "Are the Montefiores as good as the lying newspapers make out?"

Then Tom Sheffield and the others all joined in. They had never seen anything like it, they declared; it was most exciting and made one shiver unpleasantly, as when the *espada* comes to close quarters with the infuriated brute at a bullfight.

Countess Regina listened in silence and nibbled the petals of a tea rose.

"How I should like to see them!" giddy Mme de Rhouel exclaimed.

"Unfortunately, Cousin," the countess said in the solemn tones of a preacher, "a respectable woman dare not let herself be seen in improper places."

They all agreed with her. Nevertheless, Countess de Villégby was present at the Montefiores' performance two days later, dressed all in black and wearing a thick veil, at the back of a stage box.

Mme de Villégby was as cold as a steel buckler. She had married as soon as she left the convent in which she had been educated, without any affection or even liking for her husband; the most skeptical respected her as a saint, and she had a look of virgin purity on her calm face as she went down the steps of the Madeleine on Sundays after high mass.

Countess Regina stretched herself nervously, grew pale and trembled like the strings of a violin on which an artist had been playing some wild symphony. She inhaled the nasty smell of the sawdust, as if it had been the perfume of a bouquet of unknown flowers; she clenched her hands and gazed eagerly at the two mountebanks whom the public applauded rapturously at every feat. And contemptuously and haughtily she compared those two men, who were as vigorous as wild animals that have grown up in the open air, with the rickety limbs that look so awkward in the dress of an English groom.

. . . .

Count de Villégby had gone back to the country to prepare for his election as councilor general, and the very evening that he started Regina again took the stage box at the Eden Réunis. Consumed by sensual ardor, as if by some love philter, she scribbled a few words on a piece of paper—the eternal formula that women write on such occasions.

"A carriage will be waiting for you at the stage door after the performance —*An unknown woman who adores you.*"

And then she gave it to a box opener, who handed it to the Montefiore who was the champion pistol shot.

Oh, that interminable waiting in a malodorous cab, the overwhelming emotion and the nausea of disgust, the fear, the desire of waking the coachman who was nodding on the box, of giving him her address and telling him to drive her home! But she remained with her face against the window, mechanically watching the dark passage illuminated by a gas lamp at the "actors' entrance" through which men were continually hurrying who talked in a loud voice and chewed the end of cigars which had gone out. She sat as if she were glued to the cushions and tapped impatiently on the bottom of the cab with her heels.

When the actor, who thought it was a joke, made his appearance, she could hardly utter a word, for evil pleasure is as intoxicating as adulterated liquor. So face to face with this immediate surrender and this unconstrained immodesty, he at first thought that he had to do with a streetwalker.

Regina felt various sensations and a morbid pleasure throughout her whole person. She pressed close to him and raised her veil to show how young, beautiful and desirable she was. They did not speak a word, like wrestlers before a combat. She was eager to be locked up with him, to give herself to him and, at last, to know that moral uncleanness of which she was, of course, ignorant as a chaste wife; and when they left the room in the hotel together, where they had spent hours like amorous deer, the man dragged himself along and almost groped his way like a blind man, while Regina was smiling, though she exhibited the serene candor of an unsullied virgin, like she did on Sundays after mass.

Then she took the second. He was very sentimental, and his head was full of romance. He thought the unknown woman, who merely used him as her plaything, really loved him, and he was not satisfied with furtive meetings. He questioned her, besought her, and the countess made fun of him. Then she chose the two mountebanks in turn. They did not know it, for she had forbidden them ever to talk about her to each other under the penalty of never seeing her again, and one night the younger of them said with humble tenderness as he knelt at her feet:

"How kind you are to love me and to want me! I thought that such happiness only existed in novels and that ladies of rank only made fun of poor strolling mountebanks like us!"

Regina knitted her golden brows.

"Do not be angry," he continued, "because I followed you and found out where you lived and your real name and that you are a countess and rich, very rich."

"You fool!" she exclaimed, trembling with anger. "People make you believe things as easily as they can a child!"

She had had enough of him; he knew her name and might compromise her. The count might possibly come back from the country before the elections, and then the mountebank began to love her. She no longer had any feeling, any desire for those two lovers whom a fillip from her rosy fingers could bend to her will. It was time to go on to the next chapter and to seek for fresh pleasures elsewhere.

"Listen to me," she said to the champion shot the next night, "I would rather not hide anything from you. I like your comrade; I have given myself to him and I do not want to have anything more to do with you."

"My comrade!" he repeated.

"Well, what then? The change amuses me!"

He uttered a furious cry and rushed at Regina with clenched fists. She thought he was going to kill her and closed her eyes, but he had not the courage to hurt that delicate body which he had so often covered with caresses, and in despair and hanging his head, he said hoarsely:

"Very well, we shall not meet again, since it is your wish."

The house at the Eden Réunis was as full as an overfilled basket. The violins were playing a soft and delightful waltz of Gungl's, which the reports of a revolver accentuated.

The Montefiores were standing opposite to one another, as in Chéret's picture, and about a dozen yards apart. An electric light was thrown on the younger, who was leaning against a large white target, and very slowly the other traced his living outline with bullet after bullet. He aimed with prodigious skill, and the black dots showed on the cardboard and marked the shape of his body. The applause drowned the orchestra and increased continually, when suddenly a shrill cry of horror resounded from one end of the hall to the other. The women fainted; the violins stopped, and the spectators jostled each other. At the ninth ball the younger brother had fallen to the ground, an inert mass, with a gaping wound in his forehead. His brother did not move, and there was a look of madness on his face, while the Countess de Villégby leaned on the ledge of her box and fanned herself calmly, as implacably as any cruel goddess of ancient mythology.

The next day between four and five, when she was surrounded by her usual friends in her little warm Japanese drawing room, it was strange to hear in what a languid and indifferent voice she exclaimed:

"They say that an accident happened to one of those famous clowns, the Monta—the Monte—what is the name, Tom?"

"The Montefiores, madame!"

And then they began to talk about Angèle Velours, who was going to buy the former Folies at the Hôtel Drouot before marrying Prince Storbeck.

UGLY

CERTAINLY at this blessed epoch of the equality of mediocrity, of rectangular abomination, as Edgar Allan Poe says—at this delightful period when everybody dreams of resembling everybody else, so that it has become impossible to tell the president of the Republic from a waiter—in these days which are the forerunners of that promising, blissful day when everything in this world will be of a dull, neutral uniformity, certainly at such an epoch one has the right, or rather it is one's duty, to be ugly.

Lebeau, however, assuredly exercised that right with the most cruel vigor. He fulfilled that duty with the fiercest heroism, and to make matters worse the mysterious irony of fate had caused him to be born with the name of Lebeau, while an ingenious godfather, the unconscious accomplice of the pranks of destiny, had given him the Christian name of Antinous.[1]

---

[1] A youth of extraordinary beauty, page to the Emperor Hadrian (A.D. 117-138) and the object of his extravagant affection. He was drowned in the Nile, whether by accident or in order to escape from the life he was leading is uncertain.

Even among our contemporaries, who were already on the highroad to the coming ideal of universal hideousness, Antinous Lebeau was remarkable for his ugliness; and one might have said that he positively threw zeal, too much zeal, into the matter, though he was not hideous like Mirabeau, who made people exclaim, "Oh! the beautiful monster!"

Alas! No. He was without any beauty of ugliness. He was ugly, that was all, nothing more nor less; in short, he was uglily ugly. He was not humpbacked nor knock-kneed nor potbellied; his legs were not like a pair of tongs, and his arms were neither too long nor too short, and yet there was an utter lack of uniformity about him, not only in painters' eyes but also in everybody's, for nobody could meet him in the street without turning to look after him and thinking: "Good heavens! what an object."

His hair was of no particular color, a light chestnut mixed with yellow. There was not much of it; still he was not absolutely bald but just bald enough to allow his butter-colored pate to show. Butter-colored? Hardly! The color of margarine would be more applicable, and such pale margarine!

His face was also like margarine, but of adulterated margarine, certainly. His cranium, the color of unadulterated margarine, looked almost like butter in comparison.

There was very little to say about his mouth! Less than little; the sum total was—nothing. It was a chimerical mouth.

But take it that I have said nothing about him, and let us replace this vain description by the useful formula: "Impossible to describe." But you must not forget that Antinous Lebeau was ugly, that the fact impressed everybody as soon as they saw him and that nobody remembered ever having seen an uglier person; and let us add, as the climax of his misfortune, that he thought so himself.

From this you will see that he was not a fool and not ill-natured either, but of course he was unhappy. An unhappy man thinks only of his wretchedness, and people take his nightcap for a fool's cap; while, on the other hand, goodness is only esteemed when it is cheerful. Consequently Antinous Lebeau passed for a fool and an ill-tempered fool; he was not even pitied because he was so ugly!

He had only one pleasure in life, and that was to go and roam about the darkest streets on dark nights and to hear the streetwalkers say:

"Come home with me, you handsome dark man!"

It was, alas! a furtive pleasure, and he knew that it was not true. For occasionally, when the woman was old or drunk and he profited by the invitation, as soon as the candle was lighted in the garret they no longer murmured the fallacious "handsome dark man." When they saw him the old women grew still older and the drunken women got sober. And more than one, although hardened against disgust and ready for all risks, said to him, in spite of liberal payment:

"My little man, I must say you are most confoundedly ugly."

At last, however, he renounced even that lamentable pleasure when he heard the still more lamentable words which a wretched woman could not help uttering when he went home with her:

"Well, I must have been very hungry!"

Alas! It was he who was hungry, unhappy man; hungry for something that should resemble love, were it ever so little; he longed not to live like a pariah any more, not to be exiled and proscribed by his ugliness. And the ugliest, the most repugnant woman would have appeared beautiful to him if she would only not think him ugly or, at any rate, not tell him so and not let him see that she felt horror at him on that account.

The consequence was that when he one day met a poor blear-eyed creature, with her face covered with scabs and bearing evident signs of alcoholism, with a driveling mouth and ragged and filthy petticoats, to whom he gave liberal alms for which she kissed his hand, he took her home with him, had her cleansed, dressed and taken care of, made her his servant and then his housekeeper. Next he raised her to the rank of his mistress, and finally, of course, he married her.

She was almost as ugly as he was! Almost, but certainly not quite; for she was hideous, and her hideousness had its charm and its beauty, no doubt; that something by which a woman can attract a man. And she had proved that by deceiving him, and she let him see it better still by seducing another man.

That other man was actually uglier than he was.

He was certainly uglier, a collection of every physical and moral ugliness, a companion of beggars whom she had picked up among her former vagrant associates, a jailbird, a dealer in little girls, a vagabond covered with filth, with legs like a toad's, with a mouth like a lamprey's and a death's-head in which the nose had been replaced by two holes.

"And you have wronged me with a wretch like that," the poor cuckold said. "And in my own house! And in such a manner that I might catch you in the very act! And why, why, you wretch? Why, seeing that he is uglier than I am?"

"Oh no!" she exclaimed. "You may say what you like, that I am a dirty slut and a strumpet, but do not say that he is uglier than you are."

And the unhappy man stood there, vanquished and overcome by her last words, which she uttered without understanding all the horror which he would feel at them.

"Because, you see, he has his own particular ugliness, while you are merely ugly like everybody else is."

THE DEBT

"Pst! Pst! Come with me, you handsome dark fellow. I am very nice, as you will see. Do come up. At any rate you will be able to warm yourself, for I have a capital fire at home."

But nothing enticed the foot passengers, neither being called a handsome dark fellow, which she applied quite impartially to old or fat men also, nor the promise of pleasure which was emphasized by a caressing ogle and smile, nor even the promise of a good fire, which was so attractive in the bitter December wind. And tall Fanny continued her useless walk, and the night advanced and foot passengers grew scarcer. In another hour the streets would be absolutely deserted, and unless she could manage to pick up some belated drunken man she would be obliged to return home alone.

And yet tall Fanny was a beautiful woman! With the head of a bacchante and the body of a goddess, in all the full splendor of her twenty-three years, she deserved something better than this miserable pavement, where she could not even pick up the five francs which she wanted for the requirements of the next day. But there! In this infernal Paris, in this swarming crowd of competitors who all jostled each other, courtesans, like artists, did not attain to eminence until their later years. In that they resembled precious stones, as the most valuable of them are those that have been set the oftenest.

And that was why tall Fanny, who was later to become one of the richest and most brilliant stars of Parisian gallantry, was walking about the streets on this bitter December night without a halfpenny in her pocket, in spite of the head of a bacchante and the body of a goddess and in all the full splendor of her twenty-three years.

However, it was too late now to hope to meet anybody; there was not a single foot passenger about; the street was decidedly empty, dull and lifeless. Nothing was to be heard except the whistling of sudden gusts of wind, and nothing was to be seen except the flickering gaslights, which looked like dying butterflies. Well! The only thing was to return home alone.

But suddenly tall Fanny saw a human form standing on the pavement at the next crossing. It seemed to be hesitating and uncertain which way to go. The figure, which was very small and slight, was wrapped in a long cloak which reached almost to the ground.

"Perhaps he is a hunchback," the girl said to herself. "They like tall women!" And she walked quickly toward him, from habit already saying: "*Pst! Pst!* Come home with me, you handsome dark fellow!" What luck! The man did not go away but came toward Fanny, although somewhat timidly, while she went to meet him, repeating her wheedling words so as to reassure him. She went all the quicker as she saw that he was staggering with the zigzag walk of a drunken man, and she thought to herself: "When once they sit down there is no possibility of getting these beggars up again, for they want to go to sleep just where they are. I only hope I shall get to him before he tumbles down."

Luckily she reached him just in time to catch him in her arms, but as soon as she had done so she almost let him fall in her astonishment. It was neither a drunken man nor a hunchback, but a child of twelve or thirteen in an overcoat, who was crying and who said in a weak voice: "I beg your pardon, madame, I beg your pardon. If you only knew how hungry and cold I am! I beg your pardon! Oh! I am so cold."

"Poor child!" she said, putting her arms around him and kissing him. And she carried him off with a full but happy heart, and while he continued to sob she said to him mechanically: "Don't be frightened, my little man. You will see how nice I can be! And then you can warm yourself; I have a capital fire."

But the fire was out; the room, however, was warm, and the child said as soon as they got in: "Oh! How comfortable it is here! It is a great deal better than in the streets, I can tell you! And I have been living in the streets for six days." He began to cry again and added: "I beg your pardon, madame. I have eaten nothing for two days."

Tall Fanny opened her cupboard which had glass doors. The middle shelf held all her linen, and on the upper one there was a box of Albert biscuits, a drop of brandy at the bottom of a bottle and a few small lumps of sugar in a cup. With that and some water out of a jug she concocted a sort of broth, which he swallowed ravenously, and when he had done he wished to tell his story, which he did, yawning all the time.

His grandfather (the only one of his relatives whom he had ever known), who had been a painter and decorator at Soisson, had died about a month before, but before his death he had said to him:

"When I am gone, little man, you will find a letter to my brother, who is in business in Paris, among my papers. You must take it to him, and he will be certain to take care of you. However, in any case you must go to Paris, for you have an aptitude for painting, and only there can you hope to become an artist."

When the old man was dead (he died in the hospital) the child started, dressed in an old coat of his grandfather's and with thirty francs, which was all that the old man had left behind him, in his pocket. But when he got to Paris there was nobody of the name at the address mentioned on the letter. The dead man's brother had left there six months before; nobody knew where he had gone to, and so the child was alone. For a few days he managed to exist on what he had over after paying for his journey. After he had spent his last franc he had wandered about the streets, as he had no money with which to pay for a bed, buying his bread by the halfpennyworth until for the last forty-eight hours he had been without anything, absolutely without anything.

He told her all this while he was half asleep, amid sobs and yawns, so that the girl did not venture to ask him any more questions, in spite of her curiosity, but on the contrary cut him short and undressed him while she listened and only interrupted him to kiss him and to say to him: "There, there, my poor child! You shall tell me the rest tomorrow. You cannot go on now, so go to bed and have a good sleep." And as soon as he had finished she put him to bed, where he immediately fell into a profound sleep. Then she undressed herself quickly, got into bed by his side so that she might keep him warm and went to sleep, crying to herself without exactly knowing why.

The next day they breakfasted and dined together at a common eating house on money that she had borrowed, and when it was dark she said to the child: "Wait for me here; I will come for you at closing time." She came back sooner, however, about ten o'clock. She had twelve francs which she gave him, telling him that she had *earned them,* and she continued with a laugh: "I feel that I shall make some more. I am in luck this evening, and you have brought it me. Do not be impatient, but have some milk posset while you are waiting for me."

She kissed him, and the kind girl felt real maternal happiness as she went out. An hour later, however, she was arrested by the police for having been found in a prohibited place, and off she went, food for St. Lazare.[1]

And the child, who was turned out by the proprietor at closing time and then driven from the furnished lodgings the next morning, where they told him that *tall Fanny was in jail,* began his wretched vagabond life in the streets again with only the twelve francs to depend on.

.   .   .   .

Fifteen years afterward the newspapers announced one morning that the famous Fanny Clariet, the celebrated "horizontal" whose caprices had caused a revolution in high life, that queen of frail beauties for whom three men had committed suicide and so many others had ruined themselves, that incomparable living statue who had attracted all Paris to the theater where she impersonated Venus in her transparent skin tights made of woven air and a knitted nothing, had been shut up in a lunatic asylum. She had been seized suddenly; it was an attack of general paralysis, and as her debts were enormous, when her estate had been liquidated she would have to end her days at La Salpêtrière.

"No, certainly not!" François Guerland, the painter, said to himself when he read the notice of it in the papers. "No, the great Fanny shall certainly not end like that." For it was certainly she; there could be no doubt about it. For a long time after she had shown him that act of charity which he could never forget, the child had tried to see his benefactress again. But Paris is a very mysterious place, and he himself had had many adventures before he grew up to be a man and, eventually, almost somebody! But he only found her in the distance; he had recognized her at the theater, on the stage, or as she was getting into her carriage which was fit for a princess. And how could he approach her then? Could he remind her of the time when her price was five francs? No, assuredly not, and so he had followed her, thanked her and blessed her from a distance.

But now the time had come for him to pay his debt and he paid it. Although tolerably well known as a painter with a future in store for him, he was not rich. But what did that matter? He mortgaged that future which people prophesied for him and gave himself over, hand and foot, to a picture dealer. Then he had the poor woman taken to an excellent asylum where she could have not only every care, but every necessary comfort and even luxury. Alas, however, general paralysis never forgives. Sometimes it releases its prey, like the cruel cat releases the mouse, for a brief moment, only to lay hold of it again later, more fiercely than ever. Fanny had that period of abate-

---

[1] A prison in Paris.

ment in her symptoms, and one morning the physician was able to say to the young man: "You are anxious to remove her? Very well! But you will soon have to bring her back, for the cure is only apparent, and her present state will only endure for a month at most, and then only if the patient is kept free from every excitement and excess!"

"And without that precaution?" Guerland asked him.

"Then," the doctor replied, "the final crisis will be all the nearer; that is all. But whether it would be nearer or more remote, it will not be the less fatal."

"You are sure of that?"

"Absolutely sure."

François Guerland took tall Fanny out of the asylum, installed her in splendid apartments and went to live with her there. She had grown old, bloated, with white hair and sometimes wandered in her mind, and she did not recognize in him the poor little lad on whom she had taken pity in the days gone by, nor did he remind her of the circumstances. He allowed her to believe that she was adored by a rich young man who was passionately devoted to her. He was young, ardent and caressing. Never had a mistress such a lover, and for three weeks before she relapsed into the horrors of madness, which were happily soon terminated by her death, she intoxicated herself with the ecstasy of his kisses and thus bade farewell to conscient life in an apotheosis of love.

.   .   .   .

The other day at dessert after an artists' dinner, they were speaking of François Guerland, whose last picture at the Salon had been so deservedly praised.

"Ah yes!" one of them said with a contemptuous voice and look. "That handsome fellow Guerland!"

And another, accentuating the insinuation, added boldly: "Yes, that is exactly it! That handsome, too handsome fellow Guerland, the man who allows himself to be kept by women."

A NORMANDY JOKE

THE PROCESSION came in sight in the hollow road which was shaded by the tall trees which grew on the slopes of the farm. The newly married couple came first, then the relations, then the invited guests and lastly the poor of the neighborhood, while the village urchins, who hovered about the narrow road like flies, ran in and out of the ranks or climbed up the trees to see it better.

The bridegroom was a good-looking young fellow, Jean Patu, the richest farmer in the neighborhood. Above all things he was an ardent sportsman who seemed to lose all common sense in order to satisfy that passion, who spent large sums on his dogs, his keepers, his ferrets and his guns. The bride,

Rosalie Roussel, had been courted by all the likely young fellows in the district, for they all thought her prepossessing and they knew that she would have a good dowry, but she had chosen Patu—partly, perhaps, because she liked him better than she did the others, but still more, like a careful Normandy girl, because he had more crown pieces.

When they went in at the white gateway of the husband's farm forty shots resounded without anyone seeing those who fired. The shooters were hidden in the ditches, and the noise seemed to please the men, who were sprawling about heavily in their best clothes, very much. Patu left his wife, and running up to a farm servant whom he perceived behind a tree, he seized his gun and fired a shot himself, kicking his heels about like a colt. Then they went on, beneath the apple trees heavy with fruit, through the high grass and through the herd of calves, who looked at them with their great eyes, got up slowly and remained standing with their muzzles turned toward the wedding party.

The men became serious when they came within measurable distance of the wedding dinner. Some of them, the rich ones, had on tall, shining silk hats, which seemed altogether out of place there; others had old head coverings with a long nap, which might have been taken for moleskin, while the humbler among them wore caps. All the women had on shawls, which they wore as loose wraps, holding the ends daintily under their arms. They were red, particolored, flaming shawls, and their brightness seemed to astonish the black fowls on the dung heap, the ducks on the side of the pond and the pigeons on the thatched roofs.

The extensive farm buildings awaited the party at the end of that archway of apple trees, and a sort of vapor came out of open door and windows, an almost overwhelming smell of eatables, which permeated the vast building, issuing from its openings and even from its very walls. The string of guests extended through the yard; when the foremost of them reached the house they broke the chain and dispersed, while behind they were still coming in at the open gate. The ditches were now lined with urchins and poor curious people. The shots did not cease but came from every side at once, injecting a cloud of smoke, and that powdery smell which has the same intoxicating effects as absinthe, into the atmosphere.

The women were shaking their dresses outside the door to get rid of the dust, were undoing their cap strings and folding their shawls over their arms. Then they went into the house to lay them aside altogether for the time. The table was laid in the great kitchen, which could hold a hundred persons; they sat down to dinner at two o'clock and at eight o'clock they were still eating; the men, in their shirt sleeves, with their waistcoats unbuttoned and with red faces, were swallowing the food and drink as if they were insatiable. The cider sparkled merrily, clear and golden in the large glasses, by the side of the dark, blood-colored wine; and between every dish they made the *trou*, the Normandy *trou*, with a glass of brandy which inflamed the body and put foolish notions into the head.

From time to time one of the guests, being as full as a barrel, would go out for a few moments to get a mouthful of fresh air, as they said, and then return with redoubled appetite. The farmers' wives, with scarlet faces and their corsets nearly bursting, did not like to follow their example, until one of them, feeling more uncomfortable than the others, went out. Then all the rest followed her example and came back quite ready for any fun, and the rough jokes began afresh. Broadsides of doubtful jokes were exchanged across the table, all about the wedding night, until the whole arsenal of peasant wit was exhausted. For the last hundred years the same broad jokes had served for similar occasions, and although everyone knew them, they still hit the mark and made both rows of guests roar with laughter.

At the bottom of the table four young fellows, who were neighbors, were preparing some practical jokes for the newly married couple, and they seemed to have got hold of a good one by the way they whispered and laughed. Suddenly one of them, profiting by a moment of silence, exclaimed: "The poachers will have a good time tonight with this moon! I say, Jean, you will not be looking at the moon, will you?" The bridegroom turned to him quickly and replied: "Only let them come, that's all!" But the other young fellow began to laugh and said: "I do not think you will neglect your duty for them!"

The whole table was convulsed with laughter, so that the glasses shook, but the bridegroom became furious at the thought that anybody should profit by his wedding to come and poach on his land and repeated: "I only say: just let them come!"

Then there was a flood of talk with a double meaning which made the bride blush somewhat, although she was trembling with expectation, and when they had emptied the kegs of brandy they all went to bed. The young couple went into their own room, which was on the ground floor as most rooms in farmhouses are. As it was very warm they opened the windows and closed the shutters. A small lamp in bad taste, a present from the bride's father, was burning on the chest of drawers, and the bed stood ready to receive the young people, who did not stand upon all the ceremony which is usual among refined people.

The young woman had already taken off her wreath and her dress and was in her petticoat, unlacing her boots, while Jean was finishing his cigar and looking at her out of the corners of his eyes. It was an ardent look, more sensual than tender, for he felt more desire than love for her. Suddenly, with a brusque movement, like a man who is going to set to work, he took off his coat. She had already taken off her boots and was now pulling off her stockings, then she said to him: "Go and hide yourself behind the curtains while I get into bed."

He seemed as if he were going to refuse but with a cunning look went and hid himself with the exception of his head. She laughed and tried to cover up his eyes, and they romped in an amorous and happy manner, without shame or embarrassment. At last he did as she asked him, and in a moment she unfastened her petticoat, which slipped down her legs, fell at her feet and lay on the floor in a circle. She left it there, stepped over it, naked with the exception of her floating chemise, and slipped into the bed, whose springs creaked beneath her weight. He immediately went up to her, without his shoes and in his trousers, and, stooping over his wife, sought her lips, which she hid beneath the pillow, when a shot was heard in the distance, in the direction of the forest of Râpées, as he thought.

He raised himself anxiously, and running to the window, with his heart beating, he opened the shutters. The full moon flooded the yard with yellow light, and the silhouettes of the apple trees made black shadows at his feet, while in the distance the fields gleamed, covered with the ripe corn. But as he was leaning out, listening to every sound in the still night, two bare arms were put around his neck, and his wife whispered, trying to pull him back: "Do leave them alone; it has nothing to do with you. Come to bed."

He turned round, put his arms round her and drew her toward him, feeling her warm skin through the thin material, and lifting her up in his vigorous arms, he carried her toward their couch; but just as he was laying her on the bed, which yielded beneath her weight, they heard another report, considerably nearer this time. Jean, giving way to his tumultuous rage, swore aloud: "Good God! Do you think I shall not go out and see what it is because of you? Wait, wait a few minutes!" He put on his shoes again, took down his gun, which was always hanging within reach upon the wall, and, as his wife threw herself on her knees in her terror to implore him not to go, he hastily freed himself, ran to the window and jumped into the yard.

She waited one hour, two hours, until daybreak, but her husband did not return. Then she lost her head, aroused the house, related how angry Jean was and said that he had gone after the poachers, and immediately all the male farm servants, even the boys, went in search of their master. They found him two leagues from the farm, tied hand and foot, half dead with rage, his gun broken, his trousers turned inside out, three dead hares hanging round his neck and a placard on his chest with these words:

Who goes on the chase loses his place.

And later on when he used to tell this story of his wedding night he generally added: "Ah! As far as a joke went, it was a good joke. They caught me in a snare, as if I had been a rabbit, the dirty brutes, and they shoved my head into a bag. But if I can only catch them someday, they had better look out for themselves!"

That is how they amuse themselves in Normandy on a wedding day.

THE FATHER

As HE LIVED at Batignolles and was a clerk in the Public Education Office, he took the omnibus every morning to the center of Paris, sitting opposite a girl with whom he fell in love.

She went to the shop where she was employed at the same time every day. She was a little brunette, one of those dark girls whose eyes are so dark that they look like spots and whose complexion has a look like ivory. He always saw her coming at the corner of the same street. She generally ran to catch the heavy vehicle and would spring upon the steps before the horses had quite stopped. Then getting inside rather out of breath and sitting down, she would look round her.

The first time that he saw her François Tessier felt that her face pleased him extremely. One sometimes meets a woman whom one longs to clasp madly in one's arms immediately without even knowing her. That girl answered to his inward desires, to his secret hopes, to that sort of ideal of love which one cherishes in the depths of the heart without knowing it.

He looked at her intently, in spite of himself, and she grew embarrassed at his looks and blushed. He saw it and tried to turn away his eyes, but he involuntarily fixed them upon her again every moment, although he tried to look in another direction, and in a few days they knew each other without having spoken. He gave up his place to her when the omnibus was full and got outside, though he was very sorry to do it. By this time she had gone so far as to greet him with a little smile, and although she always dropped her eyes under his looks, which she felt were too ardent, yet she did not appear offended at being looked at in such a manner.

They ended by speaking. A kind of rapid intimacy had become established between them, a daily intimacy of half an hour, which was certainly one of the most charming half-hours in his life to him. He thought of her all the rest of the time, saw her continually during the long office hours, for he was haunted and bewitched by that floating and yet tenacious recollection which the image of a beloved woman leaves in us, and it seemed to him that the entire possession of that little person would be maddening happiness to him, almost above human realization.

Every morning now she shook hands with him, and he preserved the feeling of that touch and the recollection of the gentle pressure of her little fingers until the next day. He almost fancied that he preserved the imprint of it on his skin, and he anxiously waited for this short omnibus ride all the rest of the time, while Sundays seemed to him heartbreaking days. However, there was no doubt that she loved him, for one Sunday in spring she promised to go and lunch with him at Maison-Lafitte the next day.

II

She was at the railway station first, which surprised him, but she said: "Be fore going I want to speak to you. We have twenty minutes, and that is more than I shall take for what I have to say."

She trembled as she hung on his arm and looked down, while her cheeks were pale, but she continued: "I do not want you to be deceived in me, and I shall not go there with you unless you promise, unless you swear—not to do—not to do anything that is at all improper."

She had suddenly become as red as a poppy and said no more. He did not know what to reply, for he was happy and disappointed at the same time. At the bottom of his heart he perhaps preferred that it should be so, and yet during the night he had indulged in anticipations that sent the hot blood flowing through his veins. He should love her less, certainly, if he knew that her conduct was light, but then it would be so charming, so delicious for him! And he made all a man's usual selfish calculations in love affairs.

As he did not say anything she began to speak again in an agitated voice and with tears in her eyes: "If you do not promise to respect me altogether I shall return home."

And so he squeezed her arm tenderly and replied: "I promise you shall only do what you like." She appeared relieved in mind and asked with a smile: "Do you really mean it?"

And he looked into her eyes and replied, "I swear it."

"Now you may take the tickets," she said.

During the journey they could hardly speak, as the carriage was full, and when they got to Maison-Lafitte they went toward the Seine. The sun, which shone full upon the river, upon the leaves and upon the turf, seemed to reflect in them his brightness, and they went hand in hand along the bank, looking at the shoals of little fish swimming near the bank, brimming over with happiness, as if they were raised from earth in their lightness of heart.

At last she said: "How foolish you must think me!"

"Why?" he asked.

"To come out like this all alone with you."

"Certainly not; it is quite natural."

"No, no, it is not natural for me—because I do not wish to commit a fault, and yet this is how girls fall. But if you only knew how wretched it is, every day the same thing, every day in the month and every month in the year. I live quite alone with Mamma, and as she has had a great deal of trouble, she is not very cheerful. I do the best I can and try to laugh in spite of everything, but I do not always succeed. But all the same it was wrong in me to come, though you, at any rate, will not be sorry."

By the way of an answer he kissed her ardently on the ear that was nearest him, but she started away from him with an abrupt movement and, getting suddenly angry, exclaimed: "Oh! Monsieur François, after what you swore to me!" And they went back to Maison-Lafitte.

They had lunch at the Petit-Havre, a low house buried under four enormous poplar trees by the side of the river. The air, the heat, the small bottle of white wine and the sensation of being so close together made them red and silent with a feeling of oppression, but after the coffee they regained their high spirits and, having crossed the Seine, started off along the bank toward the village of La Frette. Suddenly he asked: "What is your name?"

"Louise."

"Louise," he repeated and said nothing more.

The river, which described a long curve, bathed a row of white houses in the distance which were reflected in the water. The girl picked the daisies and made them into a great bunch, while he sang vigorously, as intoxicated as a colt that has been turned into a meadow. On their left a vine-covered slope followed the river. Suddenly François stopped motionless with astonishment: "Oh! Look there!" he said.

The vines had come to an end, and the whole slope was covered with lilac bushes in flower. It was a violet-colored wood! A kind of great carpet stretched over the earth, reaching as far as the village, more than two miles off. She also stood surprised and delighted and murmured: "Oh! How pretty!" And, crossing a meadow, they walked toward that curious low hill which every year furnishes all the lilac which is sold through Paris on the carts of the flower peddlers.

A narrow path went beneath the trees, so they took it, and when they came to a small clearing they sat down.

Swarms of flies were buzzing around them and making a continuous, gentle sound, and the sun, the bright sun of a perfectly still day, shone over the bright slopes, and from that wood of flowers a powerful aroma was borne toward them, a wave of perfume, the breath of the flowers.

A church clock struck in the distance. They embraced gently, then clasped each other close, lying on the grass without the knowledge of anything except of that kiss. She had closed her eyes and held him in her arms, pressing him to her closely without a thought, with her reason bewildered and from head to foot in passionate expectation. And she surrendered herself altogether without knowing that she had given herself to him. But she soon came to herself with the feeling of a great misfortune, and she began to cry and sob with grief, with her face buried in her hands.

He tried to console her, but she wanted to start, to return and go home immediately, and she kept saying as she walked along quickly: "Good heavens! Good heavens!"

He said to her: "Louise! Louise! Please let us stop here." But now her cheeks were red and her eyes hollow, and as soon as they got to the railway station in Paris she left him without even saying good-by.

III

When he met her in the omnibus next day she appeared to him to be changed and thinner, and she said to him: "I want to speak to you; we will get down at the boulevard."

As soon as they were on the pavement she said: "We must bid each other good-by; I cannot meet you again after what has happened."

"But why?" he asked.

"Because I cannot; I have been culpable and I will not be so again."

Then he implored her, tortured by desire, maddened by the wish of having her entirely in the absolute freedom of nights of love, but she replied firmly: "No, I cannot; I cannot."

He, however, only grew all the more excited and promised to marry her, but she said: "No," and left him.

For over a week he did not see her. He could not manage to meet her, and as he did not know her address he thought he had lost her altogether. On the ninth day, however, there was a ring at his bell, and when he opened it she was there. She threw herself into his arms and did not resist any longer, and for three months she was his mistress. He was beginning to grow tired of her, when she told him a woman's most precious secret, and then he had one idea and wish—to break with her at any price. As, however, he could not do that, not knowing how to begin or what to say, full of anxiety, he took a decisive step. One night he changed his lodgings and disappeared.

The blow was so heavy that she did not look for the man who had abandoned her but threw herself at her mother's knees, confessed her misfortune and some months after gave birth to a boy.

IV

Years passed, and François Tessier grew old without there having been any alteration in his life. He led the dull, monotonous life of bureaucrats, without hopes and without expectations. Every day he got up at the same time, went through the same streets, went through the same door, past the same porter, went into the same office, sat in the same chair and did the same work. He was alone in the world, alone during the day in the midst of his different colleagues, and alone at night in his bachelor's lodgings, and he laid by a hundred francs a month against old age.

Every Sunday he went to the Champs Elysées to watch the elegant people, the carriages and the pretty women, and the next day he used to say to one of his colleagues: "The return of the carriages from the Bois de Boulogne was very brilliant yesterday." One fine Sunday morning, however, he went into the Parc Monceau where the mothers and nurses, sitting on the sides of the walks, watched the children playing, and suddenly François Tessier started. A woman passed by holding two children by the hand: a little boy of about ten and a little girl of four. It was she.

He walked another hundred yards and then fell into a chair, choking with emotion. She had not recognized him, and so he came back, wishing to see her again. She was sitting down now, and the boy was standing by her side very quietly, while the little girl was making sand castles. It was she; it was certainly she, but she had the serious looks of a lady, was dressed simply and looked self-possessed and dignified. He looked at her from a distance, for he did not venture to go near, but the little boy raised his head, and François Tessier felt himself tremble. It was his own son; there could be no doubt of that. And as he looked at him he thought he could recognize himself as he appeared in an old photograph taken years ago. He remained hidden behind a tree, waiting for her to go, that he might follow her.

He did not sleep that night. The idea of the child especially harassed him. His son! Oh! If he could only have known, have been sure. But what could he have done? However, he went to the house where she had once lived and asked about her. He was told that a neighbor, an honorable man of strict morals, had been touched by her distress and had married her; he knew the fault she had committed and had married her and had even recognized the child, his, François Tessier's child, as his own.

He returned to the Parc Monceau every Sunday, for then he always saw her, and each time he was seized with a mad, an irresistible longing to take his son into his arms, cover him with kisses and to steal him, to carry him off.

He suffered horribly in his wretched isolation as an old bachelor with nobody to care for him, and he also suffered atrocious mental torture, torn by paternal tenderness springing from remorse, longing and jealousy and from that need of loving one's own children which nature has implanted in all. And so at last he determined to make a despairing attempt and, going up to her as she entered the park, he said, standing in the middle of the path, pale and with trembling lips: "You do not recognize me?" She raised her eyes, looked at him, uttered an exclamation of horror, of terror and, taking the two children by the hand, she rushed away, dragging them after her, while he went home and wept inconsolably.

Months passed without his seeing her again. He suffered day and night, for he was a prey to his paternal love. He would gladly have died if he could only have kissed his son; he would have committed murder, performed any task, braved any danger, ventured anything. He wrote to her, but she did not reply, and after writing her some twenty letters he saw that there was no hope of altering her determination. Then he formed the desperate resolution of writing to her husband, being quite prepared to receive a bullet from a revolver if need be. His letter only consisted of a few lines, as follows:

MONSIEUR:
You must have a perfect horror of my name, but I am so miserable, so overcome by misery, that my only hope is in you, and therefore I venture to request you to grant me an interview of only five minutes.
I have the honor, etc.

The next day he received the reply:

MONSIEUR:
I shall expect you tomorrow, Tuesday, at five o'clock.

V

As he went up the staircase François Tessier's heart beat so violently that he had to stop several times. There was a dull and violent noise in his breast, the noise as of some animal galloping; he could only breathe with difficulty and had to hold onto the banisters in order not to fall.

He rang the bell on the third floor, and when a maidservant had opened the door he asked: "Does Monsieur Flamel live here?"

"Yes, monsieur. Kindly come in."

He was shown into the drawing room; he was alone and waited, feeling bewildered, as in the midst of a catastrophe, until a door opened and a man came in. He was tall, serious and rather stout; he wore a black frock coat and pointed to a chair with his hand. François Tessier sat down and said, panting: "Monsieur—monsieur—I do not know whether you know my name—whether you know——"

M. Flamel interrupted him: "You need not tell it me, monsieur; I know it. My wife has spoken to me about you."

He spoke it in the dignified tone of voice of a good man who wishes to be severe, with the commonplace stateliness of an honorable man, and François Tessier continued: "Well, monsieur, I want to say this. I am dying of grief, of remorse, of shame, and I would like once, only once, to kiss the child."

M. Flamel rose and rang the bell, and when the servant came in he said: "Will you bring Louis here?" When she had gone out they remained face to face without speaking, having nothing more to say to one another, and waited. Then suddenly a little boy of ten rushed into the room and ran up to the man whom he believed to be his father, but he stopped when he saw a stranger, and M. Flamel kissed him and said: "Now go and kiss that gentleman, my dear." And the child went up to Tessier nicely and looked at him.

François Tessier had risen; he let his hat fall and was ready to fall himself as he looked at his son, while M. Flamel had turned away, from a feeling of delicacy, and was looking out of the window.

The child waited in surprise, but he picked up the hat and gave it to the stranger. Then François, taking the child up in his arms, began to kiss him wildly all over his face, on his eyes, his cheeks, on his mouth, on his hair, and the youngster, frightened at the shower of kisses, tried to avoid them, turned away his head and pushed away the man's face with his little hands. But suddenly François Tessier put him down, cried: "Good-by! Good-by!" and rushed out of the room as if he had been a thief.

THE ARTIST

"BAH! MONSIEUR," the old mountebank said to me; "it is a matter of exercise and habit, that is all! Of course one requires to be a little gifted that way and not to be butter-fingered, but what is chiefly necessary is patience and daily practice for long, long years."

His modesty surprised me all the more, because of all performers who are generally infatuated with their own skill he was the most wonderfully clever one I had met. Certainly I had frequently seen him, for everybody had seen him in some circus or other, or even in traveling shows, performing the trick that consists of putting a man or woman with extended arms against a wooden target and in throwing knives between their fingers and round their heads from a distance. There is nothing very extraordinary in it, after all, when one knows *the tricks of the trade* and that the knives are not the least sharp and stick into the wood at some distance from the flesh. It is the rapidity of the throws, the glitter of the blades and the curve which the handles make toward their living object which give an air of danger to an exhibition that has become commonplace and only requires very middling skill.

But here there was no trick and no deception and no dust thrown into the eyes. It was done in good earnest and in all sincerity. The knives were as sharp as razors, and the old mountebank planted them close to the flesh, exactly in the angle between the fingers. He surrounded the head with a perfect halo of knives and the neck with a collar from which nobody could have extricated himself without cutting his carotid artery; while, to increase the difficulty, the old fellow went through the performance without seeing, his whole face being covered with a close mask of thick oilcloth.

Naturally, like other great artists, he was not understood by the crowd, who confounded him with vulgar tricksters, and his mask only appeared to them a trick the more, and a very common trick into the bargain.

"He must think us very stupid," they said. "How could he possibly aim without having his eyes open?"

And they thought there must be imperceptible holes in the oilcloth, a sort of latticework concealed in the material. It was useless for him to allow the public to examine the mask for themselves before the exhibition began. It was all very well that they could not discover any trick, but they were only all the more convinced that they were being tricked. Did not the people know that they ought to be tricked?

I had recognized a great artist in the old mountebank, and I was quite sure that he was altogether incapable of any trickery. I had told him so while expressing my admiration to him, and he had been touched by my open admiration and above all by the justice I had done him. Thus we became good friends, and he explained to me, very modestly, the real trick which the crowd does not understand, the eternal trick contained in these simple words: "To be gifted by nature and to practice every day for long, long years."

He had been especially struck by the certainty which I expressed that any trickery must become impossible to him. "Yes," he said to me, "quite impossible! Impossible to a degree which you cannot imagine. If I were to tell you! But where would be the use?"

His face clouded over, and his eyes filled with tears. I did not venture to force myself into his confidence. My looks, however, were not so discreet as my silence and begged him to speak, so he responded to their mute appeal.

"After all," he said, "why should I not tell you about it? You will understand me." And he added, with a look of sudden ferocity: "She understood it, at any rate!"

"Who?" I asked.

"My strumpet of a wife," he replied. "Ah! monsieur, what an abominable creature she was—if you only knew! Yes, she understood it too well, too well, and that is why I hate her so; even more on that account than for having deceived me. For that is a natural fault, is it not, and may be pardoned? But the other thing was a crime, a horrible crime."

The woman who stood against the wooden target every night with her arms stretched out and her fingers extended, and whom the old mountebank fitted with gloves and with a halo formed of his knives, which were as sharp as razors and which he planted close to her, was his wife. She might have been a woman of forty and must have been fairly pretty, but with a perverse prettiness; she had an impudent mouth, a mouth that was at the same time sensual and bad, with the lower lip too thick for the thin, dry upper lip.

I had several times noticed that every time he planted a knife in the board she uttered a laugh, so low as scarcely to be heard, but which was very significant when one heard it, for it was a hard and very mocking laugh. I had always attributed that sort of reply to an artifice which the occasion required. It was intended, I thought, to accentuate the danger she incurred and the contempt that she felt for it, thanks to the sureness of the thrower's hands, and so I was very much surprised when the mountebank said to me:

"Have you observed her laugh, I say? Her evil laugh which makes fun of me and her cowardly laugh which defies me? Yes, cowardly, because she knows that nothing can happen to her, nothing, in spite of all she deserves, in spite of all that I ought to do to her, in spite of all that I *want* to do to her."

"What do you want to do?"

"Confound it! Cannot you guess? I want to kill her."

"To kill her, because she has——"

"Because she has deceived me? No, no, not that, I tell you again. I have forgiven her for that a long time ago, and I am too much accustomed to it! But the worst of it is that the first time I forgave her, when I told her that all the same I might someday have my revenge by cutting her throat, if I chose, without seeming to do it on purpose, as if it were an accident, mere awkwardness——"

"Oh! So you said that to her?"

"Of course I did, and I meant it. I thought I might be able to do it, for you see I had the perfect right to do so. It was so simple, so easy, so tempting! Just think! A mistake of less than half an inch, and her skin would be cut at the neck where the jugular vein is, and the jugular would be severed. My knives cut very well! And when once the jugular is cut—good-by. The blood would spurt out, and one, two, three red jets, and all would be over; she would be dead, and I should have had my revenge!"

"That is true, certainly, horribly true!"

"And without any risk to me, eh? An accident, that is all; bad luck, one of those mistakes which happen every day in our business. What could they accuse me of? Whoever would think of accusing me even? Homicide through imprudence, that would be all! They would even pity me rather than accuse me. 'My wife! My poor wife!' I should say, sobbing. 'My wife, who is so necessary to me, who is half the breadwinner, who takes part in my performance!' You must acknowledge that I should be pitied!"

"Certainly, there is not the least doubt about that."

"And you must allow that such a revenge would be a very nice revenge, the best possible revenge which I could have with assured impunity."

"Evidently that is so."

"Very well! But when I told her so, as I have told you, and more forcibly still, threatening her, as I was mad with rage and ready to do the deed that I had dreamed of on the spot, what do you think she said?"

"That you were a good fellow and would certainly not have the atrocious courage to——"

"Tut! tut! tut! I am not such a good fellow as you think. I am not frightened of blood, and that I have proved already, though it would be useless to tell you how and where. But I had no necessity to prove it to her, for she knows that I am capable of a good many things, even of crime; especially of one crime."

"And she was not frightened?"

"No. She merely replied that I could not do what I said; you understand. That I could not do it!"

"Why not?"

"Ah! monsieur, so you do not understand? Why do you not? Have I not explained to you by what constant, long, daily practice I have learned to plant my knives without seeing what I am doing?"

"Yes; well, what then?"

"Well! Cannot you understand what she has understood with such terrible results, that now my hand would no longer obey me if I wished to make a mistake as I threw?"

"Is it possible?"

"Nothing is truer, I am sorry to say. For I really have wished to have the revenge which I have dreamed of and which I thought so easy. Exasperated by that bad woman's insolence and confidence in her own safety, I have several times made up my mind to kill her and have exerted all my energy and all my skill to make my knives fly aside when I threw them to make a border round her neck. I have tried with all my might to make them deviate half an inch, just enough to cut her throat. I wanted to, and I have never succeeded, never. And always the slut's horrible laugh makes fun of me, always, always."

And with a deluge of tears, with something like a roar of unsatiated and muzzled rage, he ground his teeth as he wound up: "She knows me, the jade; she is in the secret of my work, of my patience, of my trick, routine, whatever you may call it! She lives in my innermost being and sees into it more closely than you do or than I do myself. She knows what a faultless machine I have become, the machine of which she makes fun, the machine which is too well wound up, the machine which cannot get out of order—and she knows that I *cannot* make a mistake."

FALSE ALARM

"I HAVE A PERFECT HORROR of pianos," said Frémecourt, "of those hateful boxes which fill up a drawing room and have not even the soft sound and the queer shape of the mahogany or veneered spinets to which our grandmothers sighed out exquisite, long-forgotten ballads, allowing their fingers to run over the keys, while around them there floated a delicate odor of powder and muslin, and some little abbé or other turned over the leaves, continually making mistakes as he looked at the patches close to the lips on the white skin of the player instead of at the music. I wish there were a tax upon them, or that some evening during a riot the people would make huge bonfires of them which would illuminate the whole town. They simply exasperate me and affect my nerves and make me think of the tortures those poor girls must suffer who are condemned not to stir for hours but to keep on constantly strumming away at the chromatic scales and monotonous arpeggios and to have no other object in life except to win a prize at the conservatoire.

"Their incoherent music suggests to me the sufferings of those who are ill, abandoned, wounded. It proceeds from every floor of every house; it irritates you, nearly drives you mad and makes you break out into ironical fits of laughter.

"And yet when that madcap Lâlie Spring honored me with her love—I never can refuse anything to a woman who smells of rare perfume and who has a large store of promises in her looks and who puts out her red, smiling lips immediately, as if she were going to offer you hansel money—I bought a piano so that she might strum upon it to her heart's content. I got it, however, on the hire-purchase system and paid so much a month, as *grisettes*[1] do for their furniture.

"At that time I had the apartments I had so long dreamed of: warm, elegant, light, well arranged, with two entrances and an incomparable porter's wife who had been canteen keeper in a Zouave regiment and knew everything and understood everything at a wink.

"It was the kind of apartment from which a woman has not the courage to escape so as to avoid temptation, where she becomes weak and rolls herself up on the soft eider-down cushions like a cat, where she is appeased and, in spite of herself, thinks of love at the sight of the low, wide couch, so suitable for caresses, rooms with heavy curtains which quite deaden the sound of voices and of laughter and filled with flowers that scent the air, whose smell lingers on the folds of the hangings.

"They were rooms in which a woman forgets time, where she begins by accepting a cup of tea and nibbling a sweet cake and abandons her fingers timidly and with regret to other fingers which tremble and are hot and so by degrees loses her head and succumbs.

"I do not know whether the piano brought us ill luck, but Lâlie had not even time to learn four songs before she disappeared like the wind, just as she had come—*flick-flack*, good night, good-by. Perhaps it was from spite, because she had found letters from other women on my table; perhaps to change her companion, as she was not one of those to hang onto one man and become a fixture.

[1] Workgirl, a name applied to those whose virtue is not too rigorous.

"I had not been in love with her, certainly, but yet such breakings have always some effect on a man. Some string breaks when a woman leaves you, and you think that you must start all over again and take another chance in that forbidden sport in which one risks so much, the sport that one has been through a hundred times before and which leaves you nothing to show in the end.

"Nothing is more unpleasant than to lend your apartments to a friend, to realize that someone is going to disturb the mysterious intimacy which really exists between the actual owner and his fortune and violate the soul of those past kisses which float in the air; that the room whose tints you connect with some recollection, some dream, some sweet vision, and whose colors you have tried to make harmonize with certain fair-haired, pink-skinned girls, is going to become a commonplace lodging, like the rooms in an ordinary lodginghouse, fit only for hidden crime and for evanescent love affairs.

"However, poor Stanis had begged me so urgently to do him that service; he was so very much in love with Madame de Fréjus. Among the characters in this comedy there was a brute of a husband who was terribly jealous and suspicious, one of those Othellos who have always a flea in their ear and come back unexpectedly from shooting or the club, who pick up pieces of torn paper, listen at doors, smell out meetings with the nose of a detective and seem to have been sent into the world only to be cuckolds, but who know better than most how to lay a snare and to play a nasty trick. So when I went to Venice I consented to let him have my rooms.

"I will leave you to guess whether they made up for lost time, although, after all, it is no business of yours. My journey, however, which was only to have lasted a few weeks—just long enough for me to benefit by the change of air, to rid my brain of the image of my last mistress and perhaps to find another among that strange mixture of society which one meets there, a medley of American, Slav, Viennese and Italian women, who instill a little artificial life into that old city, asleep amid the melancholy silence of the lagoons—was prolonged, and Stanis was as much at home in my rooms as he was in his own.

"Madame Piquignolles, the retired canteen keeper, took great interest in this adventure, watched over their little love affair and, as she used to say, was on guard as soon as they arrived one after the other, the marchioness covered with a thick veil and slipping in as quickly as possible, always uneasy and afraid that Monsieur de Fréjus might be following her, and Stanis with the assured and satisfied look of an amorous husband who is going to meet his little wife after having been away from home for a few days.

"Well, one day during one of those delicious moments when his beloved one, fresh from her bath and invigorated by the coolness of the water, was pressing close to her lover, reclining in his arms and smiling at him with half-closed eyes, during one of those moments when people do not speak but continue their dream, the sentinel, without even asking leave, suddenly burst into the room, for worthy Madame Piquignolles was a terrible fright.

"A few minutes before a well-dressed gentleman, followed by two others of seedy appearance but who looked very strong and fit to knock anybody down, had questioned and cross-questioned her in a rough manner and tried to turn her inside out, as she said, asking her whether Monsieur de Frémecourt lived on the first floor, without giving her any explanation. When she declared that there was nobody occupying the apartments then, as her lodger was not in France, Monsieur de Fréjus—for it could certainly be nobody but he—had burst out into an evil laugh and said: 'Very well; I shall go and fetch the police commissary of the district, and he will make you let us in!'

"And as quickly as possible while she was telling her story, now in a low and then in a shrill voice, the woman picked up the marchioness's dress, cloak, lace-edge drawers, silk petticoat and little varnished shoes, pulled her out of bed without giving her time to let her know what she was doing or to moan or to have a fit of hysterics and carried her off, as if she had been a doll, with all her pretty toggery to a large, empty cupboard in the dining room that was concealed by Flemish tapestry. 'You are a man. Try to get out of the mess,' she said to Stanis as she shut the door; 'I will be answerable for Madame.' And the enormous woman who was out of breath by hurrying upstairs as she had done, and whose kind, large red face was dripping with perspiration while her ample bosom shook beneath her loose jacket, took Madame de Fréjus onto her knees as if she had been a baby whose nurse was trying to quiet her.

"She felt the poor little culprit's heart beating as if it were going to burst, while shivers ran over her skin which was so soft and delicate that the porter's wife was afraid that she might hurt it with her coarse hands. She was struck with wonder at the cambric chemise which a gust of wind would have carried off as if it had been a pigeon's feather and by the delicate odor of that scarce flower which filled the narrow cupboard and which rose up in the darkness from that supple body which was impregnated with the warmth of the bed.

"She would have liked to be there in that profaned room and to tell them in a loud voice—with her hands upon her hips as at the time when she used to serve brandy to her comrades at Daddy l'Arbi's—that they had no common sense, that they were none of them good for much, neither the police commissary, the husband nor the subordinates, to come and torment a pretty young thing, who was having a little bit of fun, like that. It was a nice job, to get over the wall in that way, to be absent from the second call of names, especially when they were all of the same sort and were glad of five francs an hour! She had certainly done quite right to get out sometimes and to have a sweetheart, and she was a charming little thing, and that she would say if she were called before the court as a witness.

"And she took Madame de Fréjus in her arms to quiet her and repeated the same thing a dozen times, whispered pretty things to her and interrupted her occasionally to listen whether they were not searching all the nooks and corners of the apartment. 'Come, come,' she said; 'do not distress yourself. Be calm, my dear. It hurts me to hear you cry like that. There will be no mischief done; I will vouch for it.'

"The marchioness, who was nearly fainting and who was prostrate with terror, could only sob out: 'Good heavens! Good heavens!'

"She scarcely seemed to be conscious of anything; her head seemed vacant; her ears buzzed, and she felt benumbed, like one who goes to sleep in the snow.

"Ah! Only to forget everything, as her love dream was over, to go out quickly like those little rose-colored tapers at Nice on Shrove Tuesday evening.

"Oh! Not to awake any more, as the tomorrow would come in black and sad, because a whole array of barristers, ushers, solicitors and judges would be against her and disturb her usual quietude, would torment her, cover her with mud, as her delicious, amorous adventure—her first—which had been so carefully enveloped in mystery and had been kept so secret behind closed shutters and thick veils, would become an everyday episode of adultery which would get wind and be discussed from door to door. The lilac had faded, and she was obliged to bid farewell to happiness, as if to an old friend who was going far, very far away, never to return!

"Suddenly, however, she started and sat up with her neck stretched out and her eyes fixed, while the ex-canteen keeper, who was trembling with emotion, put her hands to her left ear, which was her best, like a speaking trumpet, and tried to hear the cries which succeeded each other from room to room amid a noise of opening and shutting of doors.

"'Ah! Upon my word, I am not blind. It is Monsieur de Stanis who is looking for me and making all that noise. Don't you hear: "Mme Piquignolles, Mme Piquignolles?" Saved, saved!'

"Stanis was still quite pale, and in a panting voice he cried out to them: 'Nothing serious, only that fool Frémecourt who lent me the rooms has forgotten to pay for his piano for the last five months, a hundred francs[2] a month. You understand; they came to claim it, and as we did not reply, why, they fetched the police commissary and gained entrance in the name of the law.'

"'A nice fright to give one!' Madame Piquignolles said, throwing herself onto a chair. 'Confound the nasty piano!'

"It may be useless to add that the marchioness has quite renounced *trifles*, as our forefathers used to say, and would deserve a prize for virtue if the Academy would only show itself rather more gallant toward pretty women who take crossroads in order to become virtuous.

"Emotions like that cure people of running risks of that kind!"

THAT PIG OF A MORIN

"THERE, MY FRIEND," I said to Labarbe, "you have just repeated those five words, 'That pig of a Morin.' Why on earth do I never hear Morin's name mentioned without his being called a *pig?*"

[2]$20.

Labarbe, who is a deputy, looked at me with eyes like an owl's and said: "Do you mean to say that you do not know Morin's story and yet come from La Rochelle?" I was obliged to declare that I did not know Morin's story, and then Labarbe rubbed his hands and began his recital.

"You knew Morin, did you not, and you remember his large linen draper's shop on the Quai de la Rochelle?"

"Yes, perfectly."

"All right, then. You must know that in 1862 or '63 Morin went to spend a fortnight in Paris for pleasure, or for his pleasures, but under the pretext of renewing his stock, and you also know what a fortnight in Paris means for a country shopkeeper; it makes his blood grow hot. The theater every evening, women's dresses rustling up against you and continual excitement; one goes almost mad with it. One sees nothing but dancers in tights, actresses in very low dresses, round legs, fat shoulders, all nearly within reach of one's hands, without daring or being able to touch, and one scarcely ever tastes an inferior dish. And one leaves it with heart still all in a flutter and a mind still exhilarated by a sort of longing for kisses which tickle one's lips.

"Morin was in that state when he took his ticket for La Rochelle by the eight-forty night express. And he was walking up and down the waiting room at the station when he stopped suddenly in front of a young lady who was kissing an old one. She had her veil up, and Morin murmured with delight: 'By Jove, what a pretty woman!'

"When she had said good-by to the old lady she went into the waiting room, and Morin followed her; then she went on to the platform, and Morin still followed her; then she got into an empty carriage, and he again followed her. There were very few travelers by the express; the engine whistled, and the train started. They were alone. Morin devoured her with his eyes. She appeared to be about nineteen or twenty and was fair, tall and with demure looks. She wrapped a railway rug round her legs and stretched herself on the seat to sleep.

"Morin asked himself: 'I wonder who she is?' And a thousand conjectures, a thousand projects went through his head. He said to himself: 'So many adventures are told as happening on railway journeys that this may be one that is going to present itself to me. Who knows? A piece of good luck like that happens very quickly, and perhaps I need only be a little venturesome. Was it not Danton who said: "Audacity, more audacity, and always audacity." If it was not Danton it was Mirabeau, but that does not matter. But then I have no audacity, and that is the difficulty. Oh! If one only knew, if one could only read people's minds! I will bet that every day one passes by magnificent opportunities without knowing it, though a gesture would be enough to let me know that she did not ask for anything better.'

"Then he imagined to himself combinations which led him to triumph. He pictured some chivalrous deed or merely some slight service which he rendered her, a lively, gallant conversation which ended in a declaration, which ended in—in what you think.

"But he could find no opening, had no pretext, and he waited for some fortunate circumstance with his heart ravaged and his mind topsy-turvy. The night passed, and the pretty girl still slept while Morin was meditating his own fall. The day broke and soon the first ray of sunlight appeared in the sky, a long, clear ray which shone on the face of the sleeping girl and woke her so she sat up, looked at the country, then at Morin and smiled. She smiled like a happy woman, with an engaging and bright look, and Morin trembled. Certainly that smile was intended for him; it was a discreet invitation, the signal which he was waiting for. That smile meant to say: 'How stupid, what a ninny, what a dolt, what a donkey you are to have sat there on your seat like a post all night. Just look at me, am I not charming? And you have sat like that for the whole night when you have been alone with a pretty woman, you great simpleton!'

"She was still smiling as she looked at him; she even began to laugh, and he lost his head trying to find something suitable to say, no matter what. But he could think of nothing, nothing, and then, seized with a coward's courage, he said to himself: 'So much the worse; I will risk everything,' and suddenly, without the slightest warning, he went toward her, his arms extended, his lips protruding, and, seizing her in his arms, kissed her.

"She sprang up with a bound, crying out: 'Help! help!' and screaming with terror; then she opened the carriage door and waved her arm outside; then, mad with terror, she was trying to jump out while Morin, who was almost distracted and feeling sure that she would throw herself out, held her by her skirt and stammered: 'Oh, madame! Oh, madame!'

"The train slackened speed and then stopped. Two guards rushed up at the young woman's frantic signals, and she threw herself into their arms, stammering: 'That man wanted—wanted—to—to——' And then she fainted.

"They were at Mauzé station, and the gendarme on duty arrested Morin. When the victim of his brutality had regained her consciousness she made her charge against him, and the police drew it up. The poor linen draper did not reach home till night, with a prosecution hanging over him for an outrage on morals in a public place.

II

"At that time I was editor of the *Fanal des Charentes*, and I used to meet Morin every day at the Café du Commerce. The day after his adventure he came to see me, as he did not know what to do. I did not hide my opinion from him but said to him: 'You are no better than a pig. No decent man behaves like that.'

"He cried. His wife had given him a beating, and he foresaw his trade ruined, his name dragged through the mire and dishonored, his friends outraged and taking no more notice of him. In the end he excited my pity, and I sent for my colleague Rivet, a bantering but very sensible little man, to give us his advice.

"He advised me to see the public prosecutor, who was a friend of mine, and so I sent Morin home and went to call on the magistrate. He told me that the woman who had been insulted was a young lady, Mademoiselle Henriette Bonnel, who had just received her certificate as governess in Paris and spent her holidays with her uncle and aunt, who were very respectable tradespeople in Mauzé, and what made Morin's case all the more serious was that the uncle had lodged a complaint. But the public official had consented to let the matter drop if this complaint were withdrawn, so that we must try and get him to do this.

"I went back to Morin's and found him in bed, ill with excitement and distress. His wife, a tall, rawboned woman with a beard, was abusing him continually, and she showed me into the room, shouting at me: 'So you have come to see that pig of a Morin. Well, there he is, the darling!' And she planted herself in front of the bed with her hands on her hips. I told him how matters stood, and he begged me to go and see her uncle and aunt. It was a delicate mission, but I undertook it, and the poor devil never ceased repeating: 'I assure you I did not even kiss her, no, not even that. I will take my oath to it!'

"I replied: 'It is all the same; you are nothing but a pig.' And I took a thousand francs which he gave me to employ them as I thought best, but as I did not care venturing to her uncle's house alone I begged Rivet to go with me, which he agreed to do on the condition that we went immediately, for he had some urgent business at La Rochelle that afternoon. So two hours later we rang at the door of a nice country house. A pretty girl came and opened the door to us, who was assuredly the young lady in question, and I said to Rivet in a low voice: 'Confound it! I begin to understand Morin!'

"The uncle, Monsieur Tonnelet, subscribed to the *Fanal* and was a fervent political co-religionist of ours. He received us with open arms and congratulated us and wished us joy; he was delighted at having the two editors in his house, and Rivet whispered to me: 'I think we shall be able to arrange the matter of that pig of a Morin for him.'

"The niece had left the room, and I introduced the delicate subject. I waved the specter of scandal before his eyes; I accentuated the inevitable depreciation which the young lady would suffer if such an affair got known, for nobody would believe in a simple kiss. The good man seemed undecided but could not make up his mind about anything without his wife, who would not be in until late that evening. But suddenly he uttered an exclamation of triumph: 'Look here, I have an excellent idea. I will keep you here to dine and sleep, and when my wife comes home I hope we shall be able to arrange matters.'

"Rivet resisted at first, but the wish to extricate that pig of a Morin decided him, and we accepted the invitation. So the uncle got up radiant, called his niece and proposed that we should take a stroll in his grounds, saying: 'We will leave serious matters until the morning.' Rivet and he began to talk politics, while I soon found myself lagging a little behind with the girl, who was really charming! charming! and with the greatest precaution I began to speak to her about her adventure and try to make her my ally. She did not, however, appear the least confused and listened to me like a person who was enjoying the whole thing very much.

"I said to her: 'Just think, mademoiselle, how unpleasant it will be for you. You will have to appear in court, to encounter malicious looks, to speak before everybody and to recount that unfortunate occurrence in the railway carriage in public. Do you not think, between ourselves, that it would have been much better for you to have put that dirty scoundrel back into his place without calling for assistance and merely to have changed your carriage?' She began to laugh and replied: 'What you say is quite true! But what could I do? I was frightened, and when one is frightened one does not stop to reason with oneself. As soon as I realized the situation I was very sorry that I had called out, but then it was too late. You must also remember that the idiot threw himself upon me like a madman, without saying a word and looking like a lunatic. I did not even know what he wanted of me.'

"She looked me full in the face, without being nervous or intimidated, and I said to myself: 'She is a funny sort of girl, that; I can quite see how that pig Morin came to make a mistake,' and I went on jokingly: 'Come, mademoiselle, confess that he was excusable; for, after all, a man cannot find himself opposite such a pretty girl as you are without feeling a legitimate desire to kiss her.'

"She laughed more than ever and showed her teeth and said: 'Between the desire and the act, monsieur, there is room for respect.' It was a funny expression to use, although it was not very clear, and I asked abruptly: 'Well, now, supposing I were to kiss you now, what would you do?' She stopped to look at me from head to foot and then said calmly: 'Oh! you? That is quite another matter.'

"I knew perfectly well, by Jove, that it was not the same thing at all, as everybody in the neighborhood called me 'Handsome Labarbe.' I was thirty years old in those days, but I asked her: 'And why, pray?'

"She shrugged her shoulders and replied: 'Well, because you are not so stupid as he is.' And then she added, looking at me slyly: 'Nor so ugly, either.'

"Before she could make a movement to avoid me I had implanted a hearty kiss on her cheek. She sprang aside, but it was too late, and then she said: 'Well, you are not very bashful, either! But don't do that sort of thing again.'

"I put on a humble look and said in a low voice: 'Oh! mademoiselle, as for me, if I long for one thing more than another, it is to be summoned before a magistrate on the same charge as Morin.'

"'Why?' she asked.

"Looking steadily at her, I replied: 'Because you are one of the most beautiful creatures living, because it would be an honor and a glory for me to have offered you violence and because people would have said, after seeing you: "Well, Labarbe has richly deserved what he has got, but he is a lucky fellow all the same."'

"She began to laugh heartily again and said: 'How funny you are!' And she had not finished the word *funny* before I had her in my arms and was kissing her ardently wherever I could find a place, on her forehead, on her eyes, on her lips occasionally, on her cheeks, in fact all over her head, some part of which she was obliged to leave exposed, in spite of herself, in order to defend the others. At last she managed to release herself, blushing and angry. 'You are very unmannerly, monsieur,' she said, 'and I am sorry I listened to you.'

"I took her hand in some confusion and stammered out: 'I beg your pardon, mademoiselle. I have offended you; I have acted like a brute! Do not be angry with me for what I have done. If you knew——'

"I vainly sought for some excuse, and in a few moments she said: 'There is nothing for me to know, monsieur.' But I had found something to say, and I cried: 'Mademoiselle, I love you!'

"She was really surprised and raised her eyes to look at me, and I went on: 'Yes, mademoiselle, and pray listen to me. I do not know Morin, and I do not care anything about him. It does not matter to me the least if he is committed for trial and locked up meanwhile. I saw you here last year, and I was so taken with you that the thought of you has never left me since, and it does not matter to me whether you believe me or not. I thought you adorable, and the remembrance of you took such a hold on me that I longed to see you again, and so I made use of that fool Morin as a pretext, and here I am. Circumstances have made me exceed the due limits of respect, and I can only beg you to pardon me.'

"She read the truth in my looks and was ready to smile again; then she murmured: 'You humbug!' But I raised my hand and said in a sincere voice (and I really believe that I was sincere): 'I swear to you that I am speaking the truth.' She replied quite simply: 'Really?'

"We were alone, quite alone, as Rivet and her uncle had disappeared in a side walk, and I made her a real declaration of love while I squeezed and kissed her hands, and she listened to it as to something new and agreeable, without exactly knowing how much of it she was to believe, while in the end I felt agitated and at last really myself believed what I said. I was pale, anxious and trembling, and I gently put my arm round her waist and spoke to her softly, whispering into the little curls over her ears. She seemed dead, so absorbed in thought was she.

"Then her hand touched mine, and she pressed it, and I gently circled her waist with a trembling, and gradually a firmer, grasp. She did not move now, and I touched her cheeks with my lips, and suddenly, without seeking them, mine met hers. It was a long, long kiss, and it would have lasted longer still if I had not heard a *Hum! Hum!* just behind me. She made her escape through the bushes, and I, turning round, saw Rivet coming toward me and walking in the middle of the path. He said without even smiling: 'So that is the way in which you settle the affair of that pig Morin.'

"I replied conceitedly: 'One does what one can, my dear fellow. But what about the uncle? How have you got on with him? I will answer for the niece.'

"'I have not been so fortunate with him,' he replied. Whereupon I took his arm and we went indoors.

III

"Dinner made me lose my head altogether. I sat beside her, and my hand continually met hers under the tablecloth, my foot touched hers and our looks encountered each other.

"After dinner we took a walk by moonlight, and I whispered all the tender things I could think of to her. I held her close to me, kissed her every moment, moistening my lips against hers, while her uncle and Rivet were disputing as they walked in front of us. We went in, and soon a messenger brought a telegram from her aunt, saying that she would return by the first train the next morning at seven o'clock.

"'Very well, Henriette,' her uncle said, 'go and show the gentlemen their rooms.' She showed Rivet his first, and he whispered to me: 'There was no danger of her taking us into yours first.' Then she took me to my room, and as soon as she was alone with me I took her in my arms again and tried to excite her senses and overcome her resistance, but when she felt that she was near succumbing she escaped out of the room, and I got between the sheets, very much put out and excited and feeling rather foolish, for I knew that I should not sleep much. I was wondering how I could have committed such a mistake when there was a gentle knock at my door, and on my asking who was there a low voice replied: 'I.'

"I dressed myself quickly and opened the door, and she came in. 'I forgot to ask you what you take in the morning,' she said, 'chocolate, tea or coffee?' I put my arms around her impetuously and said, devouring her with kisses: 'I will take—I will take——' But she freed herself from my arms, blew out my candle and disappeared and left me alone in the dark, furious, trying to find some matches and not able to do so. At last I got some and I went into the passage, feeling half mad, with my candlestick in my hand.

"What was I going to do? I did not stop to reason; I only wanted to find her, and I would. I went a few steps without reflecting, but then I suddenly thought to myself: 'Suppose I should go into the uncle's room, what should I say?' And I stood still, with my head a void and my heart beating.

"But in a few moments I thought of an answer: 'Of course I shall say that I was looking for Rivet's room, to speak to him about an important matter,' and I began to inspect all the doors, trying to find hers, and at last I took hold of a handle at a venture, turned it and went in. There was Henriette, sitting on her bed and looking at me in tears. So I gently turned the key, and going up to her on tiptoe, I said: 'I forgot to ask you for something to read, mademoiselle.' I will not tell you the book I read, but it is the most wonderful of romances, the most divine of poems. And when once I had turned the first page she let me turn over as many leaves as I liked, and I got through so many chapters that our candles were quite burned out.

"Then, after thanking her, I was stealthily returning to my room when a rough hand seized me and a voice—it was Rivet's—whispered in my ear: 'So you have not yet quite settled that affair of Morin's?'

"At seven o'clock the next morning she herself brought me a cup of chocolate. I have never drunk anything like it, soft, velvety, perfumed, delicious. I could scarcely take away my lips from the cup, and she had hardly left the room when Rivet came in. He seemed nervous and irritable like a man who had not slept, and he said to me crossly: 'If you go on like this, you will end by spoiling the affair of that pig of a Morin!'

"At eight o'clock the aunt arrived. Our discussion was very short, for they withdrew their complaint, and I left five hundred francs for the poor of the town. They wanted to keep us for the day, and they arranged an excursion to go and see some ruins. Henriette made signs to me to stay, behind her uncle's back, and I accepted, but Rivet was determined to go, and though I took him aside and begged and prayed him to do this for me, he appeared quite exasperated and kept saying to me: 'I have had enough of that pig of a Morin's affair, do you hear?'

"Of course I was obliged to go also, and it was one of the hardest moments of my life. I could have gone on arranging that business as long as I lived, and when we were in the railway carriage, after shaking hands with her in silence, I said to Rivet: 'You are a mere brute!' And he replied: 'My dear fellow, you were beginning to excite me confoundedly.'

"On getting to the *Fanal* office, I saw a crowd waiting for us, and as soon as they saw us they all exclaimed: 'Well, have you settled the affair of that pig of a Morin?' All La Rochelle was excited about it, and Rivet, who had got over his ill-humor on the journey, had great difficulty in keeping himself from laughing as he said: 'Yes, we have managed it, thanks to Labarbe.' And we went to Morin's.

"He was sitting in an easy chair with mustard plasters on his legs and cold bandages on his head, nearly dead with misery. He was coughing with the short cough of a dying man, without anyone knowing how he had caught it, and his wife seemed like a tigress ready to eat him. As soon as he saw us he trembled violently as to make his hands and knees shake, so I said to him immediately: 'It is all settled, you dirty scamp, but don't do such a thing again.'

"He got up choking, took my hands and kissed them as if they had belonged to a prince, cried, nearly fainted, embraced Rivet and even kissed Madame Morin, who gave him such a push as to send him staggering back into his chair. But he never got over the blow; his mind had been too much upset. In all the country round, moreover, he was called nothing but that pig of a Morin, and the epithet went through him like a sword thrust every time he heard it. When a street boy called after him: 'Pig!' he turned his head instinctively. His friends also overwhelmed him with horrible jokes and used to chaff him, whenever they were eating ham, by saying: 'It's a bit of you!' He died two years later.

"As for myself, when I was a candidate for the Chamber of Deputies in 1875 I called on the new notary at Foncerre, Monsieur Belloncle, to solicit his vote, and a tall, handsome and evidently wealthy lady received me. 'You do not know me again?' she said.

"I stammered out: 'But—no, madame.'

"'Henriette Bonnel?'

"'Ah!' And I felt myself turning pale, while she seemed perfectly at her ease and looked at me with a smile.

"As soon as she had left me alone with her husband he took both my hands, and squeezing them as if he meant to crush them, he said: 'I have been intending to go and see you for a long time, my dear sir, for my wife has very often talked to me about you. I know under what painful circumstances you made her acquaintance, and I know also how perfectly you behaved, how full of delicacy, tact and devotion you showed yourself in the affair . . .' He hesitated and then said in a lower tone, as if he had been saying something low and coarse: 'In the affair of that pig of a Morin.'"

MISS HARRIET

THERE WERE SEVEN OF US in a four-in-hand, four women and three men, one of whom was on the box seat beside the coachman. We were following at a footpace the broad highway which serpentines along the coast.

Setting out from Etretat at break of day in order to visit the ruins of Tancarville, we were still asleep, chilled by the fresh air of the morning. The women especially, who were but little accustomed to these early excursions, let their eyelids fall and rise every moment, nodding their heads or yawning, quite insensible to the glory of the dawn.

It was autumn. On both sides of the road the bare fields stretched out, yellowed by the corn and wheat stubble which covered the soil like a bristling growth of beard. The spongy earth seemed to smoke. Larks were singing high up in the air, while other birds piped in the bushes.

At length the sun rose in front of us, a bright red on the plane of the horizon, and as it ascended, growing clearer from minute to minute, the country seemed to awake, to smile, to shake and stretch itself, like a young girl who is leaving her bed in her white, airy chemise. The Count d'Etraille, who was seated on the box, cried:

"Look! Look! A hare!" And he pointed toward the left, indicating a piece of hedge. The leveret threaded its way along, almost concealed by the field, only its large ears visible. Then it swerved across a deep rut, stopped, again pursued its easy course, changed its direction, stopped anew, disturbed, spying out every danger and undecided as to the route it should take. Suddenly it began to run with great bounds from its hind legs, disappearing finally in a large patch of beetroot. All the men woke up to watch the course of the beast.

René Lemanoir then exclaimed: "We are not at all gallant this morning," and, looking at his neighbor, the little Baroness of Stérennes, who was struggling with drowsiness, he said to her in a subdued voice: "You are thinking of your husband, Baroness. Reassure yourself; he will not return before Saturday, so you have still four days."

She responded to him with a sleepy smile.

"How rude you are." Then, shaking off her torpor, she added: "Now let somebody say something that will make us all laugh. You, Monsieur Chenal, who have the reputation of possessing a larger fortune than the Duke of Richelieu, tell us a love story in which you have been mixed up, anything you like."

Léon Chenal, an old painter who had once been very handsome, very strong, who was very proud of his physique and very amiable, took his long white beard in his hand and smiled; then after a few moments' reflection he became suddenly grave.

"Ladies, it will not be an amusing tale, for I am going to relate to you the most lamentable love affair of my life, and I sincerely hope that none of my friends has ever passed through a similar experience.

I

"At that time I was twenty-five years old and was making daubs along the coast of Normandy. I call 'making daubs' that wandering about with a bag on one's back from mountain to mountain under the pretext of studying and of sketching nature. I know nothing more enjoyable than that happy-go-lucky wandering life in which you are perfectly free, without shackles of any kind, without care, without preoccupation, without thought even of tomorrow. You go in any direction you please without any guide save your fancy, without any counselor save your eyes. You pull up because a running brook seduces you or because you are attracted in front of an inn by the smell of potatoes frying. Sometimes it is the perfume of clematis which decides you in your choice, or the naïve glance of the servant at an inn. Do not despise me for my affection for these rustics. These girls have soul as well as feeling, not to mention firm cheeks and fresh lips, while their hearty and willing kisses have the flavor of wild fruit. Love always has its price, come whence it may. A heart that beats when you make your appearance, an eye that weeps when you go away, these are things so rare, so sweet, so precious, that they must never be despised.

"I have had rendezvous in ditches in which cattle repose and in barns among the straw still steaming from the heat of the day. I have recollections of canvas spread on rude and creaky benches and of hearty, fresh, free kisses, more delicate, free from affectation and sincere than the subtle attractions of charming and distinguished women.

"But what you love most amid all these varied adventures are the country, the woods, the risings of the sun, the twilight, the light of the moon. For the painter these are honeymoon trips with Nature. You are alone with her in that long and tranquil rendezvous. You go to bed in the fields amid marguerites and wild poppies and, with eyes wide open, you watch the going down of the sun and descry in the distance the little village with its pointed clock tower which sounds the hour of midnight.

"You sit down by the side of a spring which gushes out from the foot of an oak, amid a covering of fragile herbs, growing and redolent of life. You go down on your knees, bend forward and drink the cold and pellucid water, wetting your mustache and nose; you drink it with a physical pleasure, as though you were kissing the spring, lip to lip. Sometimes, when you encounter a deep hole along the course of these tiny brooks, you plunge into it, quite naked, and on your skin, from head to foot, like an icy and delicious caress, you feel the lovely and gentle quivering of the current.

"You are gay on the hills, melancholy on the verge of pools, exalted when the sun is crowned in an ocean of blood-red shadows and when it casts on the rivers its red reflection. And at night under the moon, as it passes the vault of heaven, you think of things, singular things, which would never have occurred to your mind under the brilliant light of day.

"So in wandering through the same country we are in this year I came to the little village of Benouville, on the Falaise, between Yport and Etretat. I came from Fécamp, following the coast, a high coast, perpendicular as a wall, with projecting and rugged rocks falling sheer down into the sea. I had walked since the morning on the close-clipped grass as smooth and as yielding as a carpet. Singing lustily, I walked with long strides, looking sometimes at the slow and lazy flight of a gull, with its short white wings, sailing in the blue heavens, sometimes at the green sea or at the brown sails of a fishing bark. In short, I had passed a happy day, a day of listlessness and of liberty.

"I was shown a little farmhouse where travelers were put up, a kind of inn, kept by a peasant, which stood in the center of a Norman court, surrounded by a double row of beeches.

"Quitting the Falaise, I gained the hamlet, which was hemmed in by trees, and I presented myself at the house of Mother Lecacheur.

"She was an old, wrinkled and austere rustic, who always seemed to yield to the pleasure of new customs with a kind of contempt.

"It was the month of May: the spreading apple trees covered the court with a whirling shower of blossoms which rained unceasingly both upon people and upon the grass.

"I said:

" 'Well, Madame Lecacheur, have you a room for me?'

"Astonished to find that I knew her name, she answered:

" 'That depends; everything is let, but, all the same, there will be no harm in looking.'

"In five minutes we were in perfect accord, and I deposited my bag upon the bare floor of a rustic room furnished with a bed, two chairs, a table and a washstand. The room opened into the large and smoky kitchen, where the lodgers took their meals with the people of the farm and with the farmer himself, who was a widower.

"I washed my hands, after which I went out. The old woman was fricasseeing a chicken for dinner in a large fireplace in which hung the stewpot, black with smoke.

"'You have travelers then at the present time?' I said to her.

"She answered in an offended tone of voice:

"'I have a lady, an English lady, who has attained to years of maturity. She is occupying my other room.'

"By means of an extra five sous a day I obtained the privilege of dining out in the court when the weather was fine.

"My cover was then placed in front of the door, and I commenced to gnaw with hunger the lean members of the Normandy chicken, to drink the clear cider and to munch the hunk of white bread which, though four days old, was excellent.

"Suddenly the wooden barrier which opened on to the highway was opened, and a strange person directed her steps toward the house. She was very slender, very tall, enveloped in a Scotch shawl with red borders. You would have believed that she had no arms, if you had not seen a long hand appear just above the hips holding a white tourist umbrella. The face of a mummy, surrounded with sausage rolls of plaited gray hair, which bounded at every step she took, made me think, I know not why, of a sour herring adorned with curling papers. Lowering her eyes, she passed quickly in front of me and entered the house.

"This singular apparition made me curious. She undoubtedly was my neighbor, the aged English lady of whom our hostess had spoken.

"I did not see her again that day. The next day, when I had begun to paint at the end of that beautiful valley which, you know, extends as far as Etretat, lifting my eyes suddenly, I perceived something singularly attired standing on the crest of the declivity; it looked like a pole decked out with flags. It was she. On seeing me she suddenly disappeared. I re-entered the house at midday for lunch and took my seat at the common table so as to make the acquaintance of this old and original creature. But she did not respond to my polite advances, was insensible even to my little attentions. I poured water out for her with great alacrity; I passed her the dishes with great eagerness. A slight, almost imperceptible movement of the head and an English word, murmured so low that I did not understand it, were her only acknowledgments.

"I ceased occupying myself with her, although she had disturbed my thoughts. At the end of three days I knew as much about her as did Madame Lecacheur herself.

"She was called Miss Harriet. Seeking out a secluded village in which to pass the summer, she had been attracted to Benouville some six months before and did not seem disposed to quit it. She never spoke at table, ate rapidly, reading all the while a small book treating of some Protestant propaganda. She gave a copy of it to everybody. The curé himself had received no less than four copies at the hands of an urchin to whom she had paid two sous' commission. She said sometimes to our hostess abruptly, without preparing her in the least for the declaration:

"'I love the Saviour more than all; I worship him in all creation; I adore him in all nature; I carry him always in my heart.'

"And she would immediately present the old woman with one of her brochures which were destined to convert the universe.

"In the village she was not liked. In fact, the schoolmaster had declared that she was an atheist and that a sort of reproach attached to her. The curé, who had been consulted by Madame Lecacheur, responded:

"'She is a heretic, but God does not wish the death of the sinner, and I believe her to be a person of pure morals.'

"These words 'atheist,' 'heretic,' words which no one can precisely define, threw doubts into some minds. It was asserted, however, that this Englishwoman was rich and that she had passed her life in traveling through every country in the world, because her family had thrown her off. Why had her family thrown her off? Because of her natural impiety?

"She was, in fact, one of those people of exalted principles, one of those opinionated puritans of whom England produces so many, one of those good and insupportable old women who haunt the tables d'hôte of every hotel in Europe, who spoil Italy, poison Switzerland, render the charming cities of the Mediterranean uninhabitable, carry everywhere their fantastic manias, their petrified vestal manners, their indescribable toilets and a certain odor of India rubber, which makes one believe that at night they slip themselves into a case of that material. When I meet one of these people in a hotel I act like birds which see a manikin in a field.

"This woman, however, appeared so singular that she did not displease me.

"Madame Lecacheur, hostile by instinct to everything that was not rustic, felt in her narrow soul a kind of hatred for the ecstatic extravagances of the old girl. She had found a phrase by which to describe her, I know not how, but a phrase assuredly contemptuous, which had sprung to her lips, invented, probably, by some confused and mysterious travail of soul. She said: 'That woman is a demoniac.' This phrase, as uttered by that austere and sentimental creature, seemed to me irresistibly comic. I myself never called her now anything else but 'the demoniac,' feeling a singular pleasure in pronouncing this word on seeing her.

"I would ask Mother Lecacheur: 'Well, what is our demoniac about today?' To which my rustic friend would respond with an air of having been scandalized:

"'What do you think, sir? She has picked up a toad which has had its leg battered and carried it to her room and has put it in her washstand and dressed it up like a man. If that is not profanation I should like to know what is!'

"On another occasion, when walking along the Falaise, she had bought a large fish which had just been caught, simply to throw it back into the sea again. The sailor from whom she had bought it, though paid handsomely, was greatly provoked at this act—more exasperated, indeed, than if she had put her hand into his pocket and taken his money. For a whole month he could not speak of the circumstance without getting into a fury and denouncing it as an outrage. Oh yes! She was indeed a demoniac, this Miss Harriet, and Mother Lecacheur must have had an inspiration of genius in thus christening her.

"The stableboy, who was called Sapeur because he had served in Africa in his youth, entertained other aversions. He said with a roguish air: 'She is an old hag who has lived her days.' If the poor woman had but known!

"Little kindhearted Céleste did not wait upon her willingly, but I was never able to understand why. Probably her only reason was that she was a stranger, of another race, of a different tongue and of another religion. She was in good truth a demoniac!

"She passed her time wandering about the country, adoring and searching for God in nature. I found her one evening on her knees in a cluster of bushes. Having discovered something red through the leaves, I brushed aside the branches, and Miss Harriet at once rose to her feet, confused at having been found thus, looking at me with eyes as terrible as those of a wild cat surprised in open day.

"Sometimes when I was working among the rocks I would suddenly descry her on the banks of the Falaise, standing like a semaphore signal. She gazed passionately at the vast sea glittering in the sunlight and the boundless sky empurpled with fire. Sometimes I would distinguish her at the bottom of an alley, walking quickly with her elastic English step, and I would go toward her, attracted by I know not what, simply to see her illuminated visage, her dried-up features, which seemed to glow with an ineffable, inward and profound happiness.

"Often I would encounter her in the corner of a field, sitting on the grass under the shadow of an apple tree with her little Bible lying open on her knee, while she looked meditatively into the distance.

"I could no longer tear myself away from that quiet country neighborhood, bound to it as I was by a thousand links of love for its soft and sweeping landscapes. At this farm I was out of the world, far removed from everything, but in close proximity to the soil the good, healthy, beautiful green soil. And, must I avow it, there was something besides curiosity which retained me at the residence of Mother Lecacheur. I wished to become acquainted a little with this strange Miss Harriet and to learn what passes in the solitary souls of those wandering old English dames.

II

"We became acquainted in a rather singular manner. I had just finished a study which appeared to me to display genius and power, as it must have, since it was sold for ten thousand francs fifteen years later. It was as simple, however, as that two and two make four, and had nothing to do with academic rules. The whole of the right side of my canvas represented a rock, an enormous rock covered with sea wrack, brown, yellow and red, across which the sun poured like a stream of oil. The light, without which one could see the stars concealed in the background, fell upon the stone and gilded it as if with fire. That was all. A first stupid attempt at dealing with light, with burning rays, with the sublime.

"On the left was the sea, not the blue sea, the slate-colored sea, but a sea of jade, as greenish, milky and thick as the overcast sky.

"I was so pleased with my work that I danced from sheer delight as I carried it back to the inn. I wished that the whole world could have seen it at one and the same moment. I can remember that I showed it to a cow which was browsing by the wayside, exclaiming at the same time: 'Look at that, my old beauty; you will not often see its like again.'

"When I had reached the front of the house I immediately called out to Mother Lecacheur, shouting with all my might:

"'Ohé! Ohé! My mistress, come here and look at this.'

"The rustic advanced and looked at my work with stupid eyes which distinguished nothing and did not even recognize whether the picture was the representation of an ox or a house.

"Miss Harriet came into the house and passed in rear of me just at the moment when, holding out my canvas at arm's length, I was exhibiting it to the female innkeeper. The 'demoniac' could not help but see it, for I took care to exhibit the thing in such a way that it could not escape her notice. She stopped abruptly and stood motionless, stupefied. It was her rock which was depicted, the one which she usually climbed to dream away her time, undisturbed.

"She uttered a British 'Oh,' which was at once so accentuated and so flattering that I turned round to her, smiling, and said:

"'This is my last work, mademoiselle.'

"She murmured ecstatically, comically and tenderly:

"'Oh, monsieur, you must understand what it is to have a palpitation.'

"I colored up of course and was more excited by that compliment than if it had come from a queen. I was seduced, conquered, vanquished. I could have embraced her—upon my honor.

"I took my seat at the table beside her, as I had always done. For the first time she spoke, drawling out in a loud voice:

"'Oh! I love nature so much.'

"I offered her some bread, some water, some wine. She now accepted these with the vacant smile of a mummy. I began to converse with her about the scenery.

"After the meal we rose from the table together and walked leisurely across the court; then, attracted by the fiery glow which the setting sun cast over the surface of the sea, I opened the outside gate which faced in the direction of the Falaise, and we walked on side by side, as satisfied as any two persons could be who have just learned to understand and penetrate each other's motives and feelings.

"It was a misty, relaxing evening, one of those enjoyable evenings which impart happiness to mind and body alike. All is joy; all is charm. The luscious and balmy air, loaded with the perfumes of herbs, with the perfumes of grass wrack, with the odor of the wild flowers, caresses the soul with a penetrating sweetness. We were going to the brink of the abyss which overlooked the vast sea and rolled past us at the distance of less than a hundred meters.

"We drank with open mouth and expanded chest that fresh breeze from the ocean which glides slowly over the skin, salted as it is by long contact with the waves.

"Wrapped up in her square shawl, inspired by the balmy air and with teeth firmly set, the Englishwoman gazed fixedly at the great sun ball as it descended toward the sea. Soon its rim touched the waters, just in rear of a ship which had appeared on the horizon, until by degrees it was swallowed up by the ocean. We watched it plunge, diminish and finally disappear.

"Miss Harriet contemplated with passionate regard the last glimmer of the flaming orb of day.

"She muttered: 'Oh! Love—I love——' I saw a tear start in her eye. She continued: 'I wish I were a little bird so that I could mount up into the firmament.'

"She remained standing as I had often before seen her, perched on the riverbank, her face as red as her flaming shawl. I should have liked to have sketched her in my album. It would have been an ecstatic caricature. I turned my face away from her so as to be able to laugh.

"I then spoke to her of painting, as I would have done to a fellow artist, using the technical terms common among the devotees of the profession. She listened attentively to me, eagerly seeking to divine the sense of the obscure words, so as to penetrate my thoughts. From time to time she would exclaim: 'Oh! I understand; I understand. This is very interesting.' We returned home.

"The next day on seeing me she approached me eagerly, holding out her hand, and we became firm friends immediately.

"She was a brave creature with an elastic sort of a soul which became enthusiastic at a bound. She lacked equilibrium, like all women who are spinsters at the age of fifty. She seemed to be pickled in vinegary innocence, though her heart still retained something of youth and of girlish effervescence. She loved both nature and animals with a fervent ardor, a love like old wine, mellow through age, with a sensual love that she had never bestowed on men.

"One thing is certain: a mare roaming in a meadow with a foal at its side, a bird's nest full of young ones squeaking, with their open mouths and enormous heads, made her quiver with the most violent emotion.

"Poor solitary beings! Sad wanderers from table d'hôte to table d'hôte, poor beings, ridiculous and lamentable, I love you ever since I became acquainted with Miss Harriet!

"I soon discovered that she had something she would like to tell me but dared not, and I was amused at her timidity. When I started out in the morning with my box on my back she would accompany me as far as the end of the village, silent, but evidently struggling inwardly to find words with which to begin a conversation. Then she would leave me abruptly and, with jaunty step, walk away quickly.

"One day, however, she plucked up courage:

" 'I would like to see how you paint pictures. Will you show me? I have been very curious.'

"And she colored up as though she had given utterance to words extremely audacious.

"I conducted her to the bottom of the Petit-Val, where I had commenced a large picture.

"She remained standing near me, following all my gestures with concentrated attention. Then suddenly, fearing, perhaps, that she was disturbing me, she said to me: 'Thank you,' and walked away.

"But in a short time she became more familiar and accompanied me every day, her countenance exhibiting visible pleasure. She carried her folding stool under her arm, would not consent to my carrying it, and she sat always by my side. She would remain there for hours, immovable and mute, following with her eye the point of my brush in its every movement. When I would obtain by a large splotch of color spread on with a knife a striking and unexpected effect she would, in spite of herself, give vent to a half-suppressed 'Oh!' of astonishment, of joy, of admiration. She had the most tender respect for my canvases, an almost religious respect for that human reproduction of a part of nature's work divine. My studies appeared to her to be pictures of sanctity, and sometimes she spoke to me of God with the idea of converting me.

"Oh! He was a queer good-natured being, this God of hers. He was a sort of village philosopher without any great resources and without great power, for she always figured him to herself as a being quivering over injustices committed under her eyes and helpless to prevent them.

"She was, however, on excellent terms with him, affecting even to be the confidante of his secrets and of his whims. She said:

" 'God wills,' or, 'God does not will,' just like a sergeant announcing to a recruit: 'The colonel has commanded.'

"At the bottom of her heart she deplored my ignorance of the intention of the Eternal, which she strove, nay, felt herself compelled, to impart to me.

"Almost every day I found in my pockets, in my hat when I lifted it from the ground, in my box of colors, in my polished shoes standing in the mornings in front of my door those little pious brochures which she, no doubt, received directly from Paradise.

"I treated her as one would an old friend, with unaffected cordiality. But I soon perceived that she had changed somewhat in her manner, but for a while I paid little attention to it.

"When I walked about, whether to the bottom of the valley or through some country lanes, I would see her suddenly appear, as though she were returning from a rapid walk. She would then sit down abruptly, out of breath, as though she had been running or overcome by some profound emotion. Her face would be red, that English red which is denied to the people of all other countries; then without any reason she would grow pale, become the color of the ground and seem ready to faint away. Gradually, however, I would see her regain her ordinary color, whereupon she would begin to speak.

"Then without warning she would break off in the middle of a sentence, spring up from her seat and march off so rapidly and so strongly that it would sometimes put me to my wit's end to try and discover whether I had done or said anything to displease or offend her.

"I finally came to the conclusion that this arose from her early habits and training, somewhat modified, no doubt, in honor of me, since the first days of our acquaintanceship.

"When she returned to the farm after walking for hours on the wind-beaten coast her long curled hair would be shaken out and hanging loose, as though it had broken away from its bearings. It was seldom that this gave her any concern, though sometimes she looked as though she had been dining *sans cérémonie*, her locks having become disheveled by the breezes.

"She would then go up to her room in order to adjust what I called her glass lamps. When I would say to her in familiar gallantry which, however, always offended her:

"'You are as beautiful as a planet today, Miss Harriet,' a little blood would immediately mount into her cheeks, the blood of a young maiden, the blood of sweet fifteen.

"Then she would become abruptly savage and cease coming to watch me paint. But I always thought:

"'This is only a fit of temper she is passing through.'

"But it did not always pass away. When I spoke to her sometimes she would answer me, either with an air of affected indifference or in sullen anger, and she became by turns rude, impatient and nervous. For a time I never saw her except at meals, and we spoke but little. I concluded at length that I must have offended her in something, and accordingly I said to her one evening:

"'Miss Harriet, why is it that you do not act toward me as formerly? What have I done to displease you? You are causing me much pain!'

"She responded in an angry tone, in a manner altogether *sui generis*:

"'I am always with you the same as formerly. It is not true, not true,' and she ran upstairs and shut herself up in her room.

"At times she would look upon me with strange eyes. Since that time I have often said to myself that those condemned to death must look thus when informed that their last day has come. In her eye there lurked a species of folly, a folly at once mysterious and violent—even more, a fever, an exasperated desire, impatient, at once incapable of being realized and unrealizable!

"Nay, it seemed to me that there was also going on within her a combat in which her heart struggled against an unknown force that she wished to overcome—perhaps, even something else. But what could I know? What could I know?

III

"This was indeed a singular revelation.

"For some time I had commenced to work as soon as daylight appeared on a picture, the subject of which was as follows:

"A deep ravine, steep banks dominated by two declivities, lined with brambles and long rows of trees, hidden, drowned in milky vapor, clad in that misty robe which sometimes floats over valleys at break of day. At the extreme end of that thick and transparent fog you see coming, or rather already come, a human couple, a stripling and a maiden embraced, interlaced, she with head leaning on him, he inclined toward her, and lip to lip.

"A ray of the sun glistening through the branches has traversed the fog of dawn and illuminated it with a rosy reflection just behind the rustic lovers, whose vague shadows are reflected on it in clear silver. It was well done; yes indeed, well done.

"I was working on the declivity which led to the Val d'Etretat. This particular morning I had, by chance, the sort of floating vapor which was necessary for my purpose. Suddenly an object appeared in front of me, a kind of phantom; it was Miss Harriet. On seeing me she took to flight. But I called after her, saying: 'Come here; come here, mademoiselle, I have a nice little picture for you.'

"She came forward, though with seeming reluctance. I handed her my sketch. She said nothing but stood for a long time motionless, looking at it. Suddenly she burst into tears. She wept spasmodically, like men who have been struggling hard against shedding tears but who can do so no longer and abandon themselves to grief, though unwillingly. I got up, trembling, moved myself by the sight of a sorrow I did not comprehend, and I took her by the hand with a gesture of brusque affection, a true French impulse which impels one quicker than one thinks.

"She let her hands rest in mine for a few seconds, and I felt them quiver, as if her whole nervous system was twisting and turning. Then she withdrew her hands abruptly or, rather, tore them out of mine.

"I recognized that shiver as soon as I had felt it; I was deceived in nothing. Ah! The love shudder of a woman, whether she is fifteen or fifty years of age, whether she is one of the people or one of the *monde*, goes so straight to my heart that I never had any difficulty in understanding it!

"Her whole frail being trembled, vibrated, yielded. I knew it. She walked away before I had time to say a word, leaving me as surprised as if I had witnessed a miracle and as troubled as if I had committed a crime.

"I did not go in to breakfast. I took a walk on the banks of the Falaise, feeling that I could just as soon weep as laugh, looking on the adventure as both comic and deplorable and my position as ridiculous, fain to believe that I had lost my head.

"I asked myself what I ought to do. I debated whether I ought not to take my leave of the place, and almost immediately my resolution was formed.

"Somewhat sad and perplexed, I wandered about until dinnertime and entered the farmhouse just when the soup had been served up.

"I sat down at the table, as usual. Miss Harriet was there, munching away solemnly without speaking to anyone, without even lifting her eyes. She wore, however, her usual expression, both of countenance and manner.

"I waited patiently till the meal had been finished. Then, turning toward the landlady, I said: 'Madame Lecacheur, it will not be long now before I shall have to take my leave of you.'

"The good woman, at once surprised and troubled, replied in a quivering voice: 'My dear sir, what is it I have just heard you say? Are you going to leave us after I have become so much accustomed to you?'

"I looked at Miss Harriet from the corner of my eye. Her countenance did not change in the least, but the underservant came toward me with eyes wide open. She was a fat girl of about eighteen years of age, rosy, fresh, strong as a horse, yet possessing a rare attribute in one in her position—she was very neat and clean. I had kissed her at odd times in out-of-the-way corners in the manner of a mountain guide, nothing more.

"The dinner being over, I went to smoke my pipe under the apple trees, walking up and down at my ease from one end of the court to the other. All the reflections which I had made during the day, the strange discovery of the morning, that grotesque and passionate attachment for me, the recollections which that revelation had suddenly called up, recollections at once charming and perplexing, perhaps, also, that look which the servant had cast on me at the announcement of my departure—all these things, mixed up and combined, put me now in an excited bodily state with the tickling sensation of kisses on my lips, and in my veins something which urged me on to commit some folly.

"Night having come on, casting its dark shadows under the trees, I descried Céleste, who had gone to shut the hen coops at the other end of the inclosure. I darted toward her, running so noiselessly that she heard nothing, and as she got up from closing the small traps by which the chickens went in and out, I clasped her in my arms and rained on her coarse, fat face a shower of kisses. She made a struggle, laughing all the same, as she was accustomed to do in such circumstances. What made me suddenly loose my grip of her? Why did I at once experience a shock? What was it that I heard behind me?

"It was Miss Harriet who had come upon us, who had seen us and who stood in front of us, as motionless as a specter. Then she disappeared in the darkness.

"I was ashamed, embarrassed, more annoyed at having been surprised by her than if she had caught me committing some criminal act.

"I slept badly that night; I was worried and haunted by sad thoughts. I seemed to hear loud weeping, but in this I was no doubt deceived. Moreover, I thought several times that I heard someone walking up and down in the house and that someone opened my door from the outside.

"Toward morning I was overcome by fatigue, and sleep seized on me. I got up late and did not go downstairs until breakfast time, being still in a bewildered state, not knowing what kind of face to put on.

"No one had seen Miss Harriet. We waited for her at table, but she did not appear. At length Mother Lecacheur went to her room. The Englishwoman had gone out. She must have set out at break of day, as she was wont to do, in order to see the sunrise.

"Nobody seemed astonished at this, and we began to eat in silence.

"The weather was hot, very hot, one of those still, sultry days when not a leaf stirs. The table had been placed out of doors under an apple tree, and from time to time Sapeur had gone to the cellar to draw a jug of cider, everybody was so thirsty. Céleste brought the dishes from the kitchen, a ragout of mutton with potatoes, a cold rabbit and a salad. Afterward she placed before us a dish of strawberries, the first of the season.

"As I wanted to wash and freshen these, I begged the servant to go and bring a pitcher of cold water.

"In about five minutes she returned, declaring that the well was dry. She had lowered the pitcher to the full extent of the cord and had touched the bottom, but on drawing the pitcher up again it was empty. Mother Lecacheur, anxious to examine the thing for herself, went and looked down the hole. She returned announcing that one could see clearly something in the well, something altogether unusual. But this, no doubt, was pottles of straw which, out of spite, had been cast down it by a neighbor.

"I wished also to look down the well, hoping to clear up the mystery, and perched myself close to its brink. I perceived indistinctly a white object. What could it be? I then conceived the idea of lowering a lantern at the end of a cord. When I did so the yellow flame danced on the layers of stone and gradually became clearer. All four of us were leaning over the opening, Sapeur and Céleste having now joined us. The lantern rested on a black-and-white, indistinct mass, singular, incomprehensible. Sapeur exclaimed:

" 'It is a horse. I see the hoofs. It must have escaped from the meadow during the night and fallen in headlong.'

"But suddenly a cold shiver attacked my spine; I first recognized a foot, then a clothed limb; the body was entire, but the other limb had disappeared under the water.

"I groaned and trembled so violently that the light of the lamp danced hither and thither over the object, discovering a slipper.

" 'It is a woman! Who—who—can it be? It is Miss Harriet.'

"Sapeur alone did not manifest horror. He had witnessed many such scenes in Africa.

"Mother Lecacheur and Céleste began to scream and to shriek and ran away.

"But it was necessary to recover the corpse of the dead. I attached the boy securely by the loins to the end of the pulley rope; then I lowered him slowly and watched him disappear in the darkness. In the one hand he had a lantern and held onto the rope with the other. Soon I recognized his voice, which seemed to come from the center of the earth, crying:

" 'Stop.'

"I then saw him fish something out of the water. It was the other limb. He bound the two feet together and shouted anew:

" 'Haul up.'

"I commenced to wind him up, but I felt my arms strain, my muscles twitch, and was in terror lest I should let the boy fall to the bottom. When his head appeared over the brink I asked:

"'What is it?' as though I only expected that he would tell me what he had discovered at the bottom.

"We both got onto the stone slab at the edge of the well and, face to face, hoisted the body.

"Mother Lecacheur and Céleste watched us from a distance, concealed behind the wall of the house. When they saw issuing from the well the black slippers and white stockings of the drowned person they disappeared.

"Sapeur seized the ankles of the poor, chaste woman, and we drew it up, inclined, as it was, in the most immodest posture. The head was in a shocking state, bruised and black, and the long gray hair, hanging down, was tangled and disordered.

"'In the name of all that is holy, how lean she is!' exclaimed Sapeur in a contemptuous tone.

"We carried her into the room, and as the women did not put in an appearance, I, with the assistance of the lad, dressed the corpse for burial.

"I washed her disfigured face. By the touch of my hand an eye was slightly opened; it seemed to scan me with that pale stare, with that cold, that terrible look which corpses have, a look which seems to come from the beyond. I plaited up, as well as I could, her dishevelled hair, and I adjusted on her forehead a novel and singularly formed lock. Then I took off her dripping wet garments, baring, not without a feeling of shame, as though I had been guilty of some profanation, her shoulders and her chest and her long arms, slim as the twigs of branches.

"I next went to fetch some flowers, corn poppies, blue beetles, marguerites and fresh and perfumed herbs, with which to strew her funeral couch.

"Being the only person near her, it was necessary for me to perform the usual ceremonies. In a letter found in her pocket, written at the last moment, she asked that her body be buried in the village in which she had passed the last days of her life. A frightful thought then oppressed my heart. Was it not on my account that she wished to be laid at rest in this place?

"Toward the evening all the female gossips of the locality came to view the remains of the defunct, but I would not allow a single person to enter; I wanted to be alone, and I watched by the corpse the whole night.

"By the flickering light of the candles I looked at the body of this miserable woman, wholly unknown, who had died so lamentably and so far away from home. Had she left no friends, no relatives behind her? What had her infancy been? What had been her life? When had she come thither all alone, a wanderer, like a dog driven from home? What secrets of suffering and of despair were sealed up in that disagreeable body, in that spent and withered body, that impenetrable hiding place of a mystery which had driven her far away from affection and from love?

"How many unhappy beings there are! I felt that upon that human creature weighed the eternal injustice of implacable nature! Life was over with her without her ever having experienced, perhaps, that which sustains the most miserable of us all—to wit, the hope of being once loved! Otherwise why should she thus have concealed herself, have fled from the face of others?

Why did she love everything so tenderly and so passionately, everything living that was not a man?

"I recognized also that she believed in a God and that she hoped for compensation from him for the miseries she had endured. She had now begun to decompose and to become, in turn, a plant. She who had blossomed in the sun was now to be eaten up by the cattle, carried away in herbs and in the flesh of beasts, again to become human flesh. But that which is called the soul had been extinguished at the bottom of the dark well. She suffered no longer. She had changed her life for that of others yet to be born.

"Hours passed away in this silent and sinister communion with the dead. A pale light at length announced the dawn of a new day, and a bright ray glistened on the bed, shedding a dash of fire on the bedclothes and on her hands. This was the hour she had so much loved, when the waking birds began to sing in the trees.

"I opened the window to its fullest extent; I drew back the curtains so that the whole heavens might look in upon us. Then, bending toward the glassy corpse, I took in my hands the mutilated head and slowly, without terror or disgust, imprinted a long, long kiss upon those lips which had never before received the salute of love."

. . . .

Léon Chenal remained silent. The women wept. We heard on the box seat Count d'Etraille blow his nose from time to time. The coachman alone had gone to sleep. The horses, which felt no longer the sting of the whip, had slackened their pace and dragged softly along. And the four-in-hand, hardly moving at all, became suddenly torpid, as if laden with sorrow.

THE HOLE

CUTS AND WOUNDS WHICH CAUSED DEATH

That was the heading of the charge which brought Leopold Renard, upholsterer, before the Assize Court.

Round him were the principal witnesses, Mme Flamèche, widow of the victim, Louis Ladureau, cabinetmaker, and Jean Durdent, plumber.

Near the criminal was his wife, dressed in black, a little ugly woman who looked like a monkey dressed as a lady.

This is how Renard described the drama:

"Good heavens, it is a misfortune of which I am the first and last victim and with which my will has nothing to do. The facts are their own commentary, Monsieur le Président. I am an honest man, a hard-working man, an upholsterer in the same street for the last sixteen years, known, liked, respected and esteemed by all, as my neighbors have testified, even the porter, who is not *folâtre* every day. I am fond of work, I am fond of saving, I like honest men and respectable pleasures. That is what has ruined me, so much the worse for me; but as my will had nothing to do with it, I continue to respect myself.

"Every Sunday for the last five years my wife and I have spent the day at Passy. We get fresh air, not to say that we are fond of fishing—as fond of it as we are of small onions. Mélie inspired me with that passion, the jade; she is more enthusiastic than I am, the scold, and all the mischief in this business is her fault, as you will see immediately.

"I am strong and mild-tempered, without a pennyworth of malice in me. But she, oh la la! She looks insignificant, she is short and thin, but she does more mischief than a weasel. I do not deny that she has some good qualities; she has some, and those very important to a man in business. But her character! Just ask about it in the neighborhood; even the porter's wife, who has just sent me about my business—she will tell you something about it.

"Every day she used to find fault with my mild temper: 'I would not put up with this! I would not put up with that.' If I had listened to her, Monsieur le Président, I should have had at least three bouts of fisticuffs a month."

Mme Renard interrupted him: "And for good reasons too; they laugh best who laugh last."

He turned toward her frankly. "Oh! very well, I can blame you, since you were the cause of it."

Then, facing the president again, he said:

"I will continue. We used to go to Passy every Saturday evening, so as to be able to begin fishing at daybreak the next morning. It is a habit which has become second nature with us, as the saying is. Three years ago this summer I discovered a place, oh! such a spot! There, in the shade, were eight feet of water at least and perhaps ten, a hole with a *retour* under the bank, a regular retreat for fish and a paradise for any fisherman. I might look upon that hole as my property, Monsieur le Président, as I was its Christopher Columbus. Everybody in the neighborhood knew it, without making any opposition. They used to say: 'That is Renard's place'; and nobody would have gone to it, not even Monsieur Plumsay, who is renowned, be it said without any offense, for appropriating other people's places.

"Well, I went as usual to that place, of which I felt as certain as if I had owned it. I had scarcely got there on Saturday when I got into Delila, with my wife. Delila is my Norwegian boat which I had built by Fourmaise and which is light and safe. Well, as I said, we got into the boat and we were going to bait, and for baiting there is nobody to be compared with me, and they all know it. You want to know with what I bait? I cannot answer that question; it has nothing to do with the accident; I cannot answer, that is my secret. There are more than three hundred people who have asked me; I have been offered glasses of brandy and liquors, fried fish, matelots,[1] to make me tell! But just go and try whether the chub will come. Ah! they have patted my

---

[1] A preparation of several kinds of fish with a sharp sauce.

stomach to get at my secret, my recipe. Only my wife knows, and she will not tell it any more than I shall! Is not that so, Mélie?"

The president of the court interrupted him:

"Just get to the facts as soon as you can."

The accused continued: "I am getting to them; I am getting to them. Well, on Saturday, July eighth, we left by the five-twenty-five train, and before dinner we went to ground bait as usual. The weather promised to keep fine, and I said to Mélie: 'All right for tomorrow!' And she replied: 'It looks like it.' We never talk more than that together.

"And then we returned to dinner. I was happy and thirsty, and that was the cause of everything. I said to Mélie: 'Look here, Mélie, it is fine weather, so suppose I drink a bottle of *Casque à mèche*. That is a little white wine which we have christened so because if you drink too much of it it prevents you from sleeping and is the opposite of a nightcap. Do you understand me?

"She replied: 'You can do as you please, but you will be ill again and will not be able to get up tomorrow.' That was true, sensible, prudent and clear-sighted, I must confess. Nevertheless, I could not withstand it, and I drank my bottle. It all comes from that.

"Well, I could not sleep. By Jove! It kept me awake till two o'clock in the morning, and then I went to sleep so soundly that I should not have heard the angel shouting at the Last Judgment.

"In short, my wife woke me at six o'clock and I jumped out of bed, hastily put on my trousers and jersey, washed my face and jumped on board Delila. But it was too late, for when I arrived at my hole it was already taken! Such a thing had never happened to me in three years, and it made me feel as if I were being robbed under my own eyes. I said to myself, 'Confound it all! Confound it!' And then my wife began to nag at me. 'Eh! What about your *Casque à mèche!* Get along, you drunkard! Are you satisfied, you great fool?' I could say nothing, because it was all quite true, and so I landed all the same near the spot and tried to profit by what was left. Perhaps, after all, the fellow might catch nothing and go away.

"He was a little thin man in white linen coat and waistcoat and with a large straw hat, and his wife, a fat woman who was doing embroidery, was behind him.

"When she saw us take up our position close to their place she murmured: 'I suppose there are no other places on the river!' And my wife, who was furious, replied: 'People who know how to behave make inquiries about the habits of the neighborhood before occupying reserved spots.'

"As I did not want a fuss I said to her: 'Hold your tongue, Mélie. Let them go on, let them go on; we shall see.'

"Well, we had fastened Delila under the willow trees and had landed and were fishing side by side, Mélie and I, close to the two others; but here, monsieur, I must enter into details.

"We had only been there about five minutes when our male neighbor's float began to go down two or three times, and then he pulled out a chub as thick as my thigh, rather less, perhaps, but nearly as big! My heart beat and the perspiration stood on my forehead, and Mélie said to me: 'Well, you sot, did you see that?'

"Just then Monsieur Bru, the grocer of Poissy, who was fond of gudgeon fishing, passed in a boat and called out to me: 'So somebody has taken your usual place, Monsieur Renard?' And I replied: 'Yes, Monsieur Bru, there are some people in this world who do not know the usages of common politeness.'

"The little man in linen pretended not to hear, nor his fat lump of a wife, either."

Here the president interrupted him a second time: "Take care, you are insulting the widow, Madame Flamèche, who is present."

Renard made his excuses: "I beg your pardon, I beg your pardon; my anger carried me away. . . . Well, not a quarter of an hour had passed when the little man caught another chub and another almost immediately and another five minutes later.

"The tears were in my eyes, and then I knew that Madame Renard was boiling with rage, for she kept on nagging at me: 'Oh, how horrid! Don't you see that he is robbing you of your fish? Do you think that you will catch anything? Not even a frog, nothing whatever. Why, my hands are burning just to think of it.'

"But I said to myself: 'Let us wait until twelve o'clock. Then this poaching fellow will go to lunch, and I shall get my place again.' As for me, Monsieur le Président, I lunch on the spot every Sunday; we bring our provisions in Delila. But there! At twelve o'clock the wretch produced a fowl out of a newspaper, and while he was eating, actually he caught another chub!

"Mélie and I had a morsel also, just a mouthful, a mere nothing, for our heart was not in it.

"Then I took up my newspaper, to aid my digestion. Every Sunday I read the *Gil Blas* in the shade like that, by the side of the water. It is Columbine's day, you know, Columbine who writes the articles in the *Gil Blas*. I generally put Madame Renard into a passion by pretending to know this Columbine. It is not true, for I do not know her and have never seen her, but that does not matter; she writes very well, and then she says things straight out for a woman. She suits me, and there are not many of her sort.

"Well, I began to tease my wife, but she got angry immediately and very angry, and so I held my tongue. At that moment our two witnesses, who are present here, Monsieur Ladureau and Monsieur Durdent, appeared on the other side of the river. We knew each other by sight. The little man began to fish again, and he caught so many that I trembled with vexation, and his wife said: 'It is an uncommonly good spot, and we will come here always, Desiré.' As for me, a cold shiver ran down my back, and Madame Renard kept repeating: 'You are not a man; you have the blood of a chicken in your veins'; and suddenly I said to her: 'Look here, I would rather go away, or I shall only be doing something foolish.'

"And she whispered to me as if she had put a red-hot iron under my nose: 'You are not a man. Now you are going to run away and surrender your place! Off you go, Bazaine!'

"Well, I felt that, but yet I did not move while the other fellow pulled out a bream. Oh! I never saw such a large one before, never! And then my wife began to talk aloud, as if she were thinking, and you can see her trickery. She said: 'That is what one might call stolen fish, seeing that we baited the place ourselves. At any rate they ought to give us back the money we have spent on bait.'

"Then the fat woman in the cotton dress said in turn: 'Do you mean to call us thieves, madame?' And they began to explain, and then they came to words. Oh Lord! those creatures know some good ones. They shouted so loud that our two witnesses, who were on the other bank, began to call out by way of a joke: 'Less noise over there; you will prevent your husbands from fishing.'

"The fact is that neither of us moved any more than if we had been two tree stumps. We remained there, with our noses over the water, as if we had heard nothing; but, by Jove, we heard all the same. 'You are a mere liar.'

" 'You are nothing better than a streetwalker.'

" 'You are only a trollop.'

" 'You are a regular strumpet.'

"And so on and so on; a sailor could not have said more.

"Suddenly I heard a noise behind me and turned round. It was the other one, the fat woman, who had fallen on to my wife with her parasol. *Whack! whack!* Mélie got two of them, but she was furious, and she hits hard when she is in a rage, so she caught the fat woman by the hair and then, *thump, thump*. Slaps in the face rained down like ripe plums. I should have let them go on—women among themselves, men among themselves—it does not do to mix the blows, but the little man in the linen jacket jumped up like a devil and was going to rush at my wife. Ah! no, no, not that, my friend! I caught the gentleman with the end of my fist, *crash, crash*, one on the nose, the other in the stomach. He threw up his arms and legs and fell on his back into the river, just into the hole.

"I should have fished him out most certainly, Monsieur le Président, if I had had the time. But unfortunately the fat woman got the better of it, and she was drubbing Mélie terribly. I know that I ought not to have assisted her while the man was drinking his fill, but I never thought that he would drown and said to myself: 'Bah, it will cool him.'

"I therefore ran up to the women to separate them, and all I received was scratches and bites. Good lord, what creatures! Well, it took me five minutes, and perhaps ten, to separate those two viragoes. When I turned around there was nothing to be seen, and the water was as smooth as a lake. The others yonder kept shouting: 'Fish him out!' It was all very well to say that, but I cannot swim and still less dive!

"At last the man from the dam came and two gentlemen with boat hooks, but it had taken over a quarter of an hour. He was found at the bottom of the hole in eight feet of water, as I have said, but he was dead, the poor little man in his linen suit! There are the facts, such as I have sworn to. I am innocent, on my honor."

The witnesses having deposed to the same effect, the accused was acquitted.

THE INN

LIKE ALL THE LITTLE WOODEN INNS in the higher Alps, tiny *auberges* situated in the bare and rocky gorges which intersect the white summits of the mountains, the inn of Schwarenbach is a refuge for travelers who are crossing the Gemmi.

It is open six months in the year and is inhabited by the family of Jean Hauser. As soon as the snow begins to fall and fills the valley so as to make the road down to Loëche impassable, the father, with mother, daughter and the three sons, depart, leaving the house in charge of the old guide, Gaspard Hari, with the young guide, Ulrich Kunsi, and Sam, the great mountain dog.

The two men and the dog remain till spring in their snowy prison, with nothing before their eyes except immense, white slopes of the Balmhorn, surrounded by light, glistening summits and shut up, blocked up and buried by the snow which rises around them, enveloping and almost burying the little house up to the eaves.

It was the day on which the Hauser family were going to return to Loëche, as winter was approaching and the descent was becoming dangerous. Three mules started first, laden with baggage and led by the three sons. Then the mother, Jeanne Hauser, and her daughter Louise mounted a fourth mule and set off in their turn. The father followed them, accompanied by the two men in charge, who were to escort the family as far as the brow of the descent. First of all they skirted the small lake, now frozen over, at the foot of the mass of rocks which stretched in front of the inn; then they followed the valley which was dominated on all sides by snow-covered peaks.

A ray of sunlight glinted into that little white, glistening, frozen desert, illuminating it with a cold and dazzling flame. No living thing appeared among this ocean of hills; there was no stir in that immeasurable solitude, no noise disturbed the profound silence.

By degrees the young guide, Ulrich Kunsi, a tall, long-legged Swiss, left Daddy Hauser and old Gaspard behind in order to catch up with the mule which carried the two women. The younger one looked at him as he approached, as if she would call him with her sad eyes. She was a young, light-haired peasant girl, whose milk-white cheeks and pale hair seemed to have lost their color by long dwelling amid the ice. When Ulrich had caught up with the animal which carried the women he put his hand on the crupper and relaxed his speed. Mother Hauser began to talk to him and enumerated with minutest detail all that he would have to attend to during the winter. It was the first winter he would spend up there, while old Hari had already spent fourteen winters amid the snow at the inn of Schwarenbach.

Ulrich Kunsi listened without appearing to understand and looked incessantly at the girl. From time to time he replied: "Yes, Madame Hauser," but his thoughts seemed far away, and his calm features remained unmoved.

They reached Lake Daube, whose broad, frozen surface reached to the bottom of the valley. On the right the Daubenhorn showed its black mass, rising up in a peak above the enormous moraines of the Lömmeon glacier which soared above the Wildstrubel. As they approached the neck of the Gemmi, where the descent to Loëche begins, the immense horizon of the Alps of the Valais, from which the broad, deep valley of the Rhône separated them, came in view.

In the distance there was a group of white, unequal, flat or pointed mountain summits which glistened in the sun: the Mischabel with its twin peaks, the huge group of the Weisshorn, the heavy Brunegghorn, the lofty and formidable pyramid of Mont Cervin, slayer of men, and the Dent Blanche, that terrible coquette.

Then beneath them, as at the bottom of a terrible abyss, they saw Loëche, its houses looking like grains of sand which had been thrown into that enormous crevice which finishes and closes the Gemmi and which opens down below on to the Rhône.

The mule stopped at the edge of the path which turns and twists continually, zigzagging fantastically and strangely along the steep side of the mountain as far as the almost invisible little village at its feet. The women jumped into the snow, and the two old men joined them.

"Well," Father Hauser said, "good-by and keep up your spirits till next year, my friends," and old Hari replied: "Till next year."

They embraced each other, and then Mme Hauser in her turn offered her cheek, and the girl did the same. When Ulrich Kunsi's turn came he whispered in Louise's ear:

"Do not forget those up yonder," and she replied: "No," in such a low voice that he guessed what she had said without hearing it.

"Well, adieu," Jean Hauser repeated, "and don't fall in." Then, going before the two women, he commenced the descent, and soon all three disappeared at the first turn in the road, while the two men returned to the inn at Schwarenbach.

They walked slowly side by side without speaking. The parting was over, and they would be alone together for four or five months. Then Gaspard Hari began to relate his life last winter. He had remained with Michael Canol, who was too old now to stand it, for an accident might happen during that long solitude. They had not been dull, however; the only thing was to be resigned to it from the first, and in the end one would find plenty of distraction, games and other means of whiling away the time.

Ulrich Kunsi listened to him with his eyes on the ground, for in thought he was with those who were descending to the village. They soon came in sight of the inn which was scarcely visible, so small did it look, a mere black speck at the foot of that enormous billow of snow. When they opened the door Sam, the great curly dog, began to romp round them.

"Come, my boy," old Gaspard said, "we have no women now, so we must get our own dinner ready. Go and peel the potatoes." And they both sat down on wooden stools and began to put the bread into the soup.

The next morning seemed very long to Kunsi. Old Hari smoked and smoked beside the hearth, while the young man looked out of the window at the snow-covered mountain opposite the house. In the afternoon he went out and, going over the previous day's ground again, he looked for the traces of the mule that had carried the two women; then when he had reached the neck of the Gemmi he laid himself down on his stomach and looked at Loëche.

The village, in its rocky pit, was not yet buried under the snow, although the white masses came quite close to it, balked, however, of their prey by the pine woods which protected the hamlet. From his vantage point the low houses looked like paving stones in a large meadow. Hauser's little daughter was there now in one of those gray-colored houses. In which? Ulrich Kunsi was too far away to be able to make them out separately. How he would have liked to go down while he was yet able!

But the sun had disappeared behind the lofty crest of the Wildstrubel, and the young man returned to the chalet. Daddy Hari was smoking and, when he saw his mate come in, proposed a game of cards to him. They sat down opposite each other for a long time and played the simple game called brisque; then they had supper and went to bed.

The following days were like the first, bright and cold, without any more snow. Old Gaspard spent his afternoons in watching the eagles and other rare birds which ventured on to those frozen heights, while Ulrich journeyed regulargly to the neck of the Gemmi to look at the village. In the evening they played at cards, dice or dominoes and lost and won trifling sums, just to create an interest in the game.

One morning Hari, who was up first, called his companion. A moving cloud of white spray, deep and light, was falling on them noiselessly and burying them by degrees under a dark, thick coverlet of foam. This lasted four days and four nights. It was necessary to free the door and the windows, to dig out a passage and to cut steps to get over this frozen powder which a twelve-hour frost had made as hard as the granite of the moraines.

They lived like prisoners, not venturing outside their abode. They had divided their duties and performed them regularly. Ulrich Kunsi undertook the scouring, washing and everything that belonged to cleanliness. He also chopped up the wood, while Gaspard Hari did the cooking and attended to the fire. Their regular and monotonous work was relieved by long games at cards or dice, but they never quarreled and were always calm and placid. They were never even impatient or ill humored, nor did they ever use hard words, for they had laid in a stock of patience for this wintering on the top of the mountain.

Sometimes old Gaspard took his rifle and went after chamois and occasionally killed one. Then there was a feast in the inn at Schwarenbach, and they reveled in fresh meat. One morning he went out as usual. The thermometer outside marked eighteen degrees of frost, and as the sun had not yet risen, the hunter hoped to surprise the animals at the approaches to the Wildstrubel. Ulrich, being alone, remained in bed until ten o'clock. He was of a sleepy nature but would not have dared to give way like that to his inclination in the presence of the old guide, who was ever an early riser. He breakfasted leisurely with Sam, who also spent his days and nights in sleeping in front of the fire; then he felt low-spirited and even frightened at the solitude and was seized by a longing for his daily game of cards, as one is by the domination of an invincible habit. So he went out to meet his companion who was to return at four o'clock.

The snow had leveled the whole deep valley, filled up the crevasses, obliterated all signs of the two lakes and covered the rocks, so that between the high summits there was nothing but an immense white, regular, dazzling and frozen surface. For three weeks Ulrich had not been to the edge of the precipice from which he had looked down onto the village, and he wanted to go there before climbing the slopes which led to the Wildstrubel. Loëche was now covered by the snow, and the houses could scarcely be distinguished, hidden as they were by that white cloak.

Turning to the right, Ulrich reached the Lömmeon glacier. He strode along with a mountaineer's long swinging pace, striking the snow, which was as hard as a rock, with his iron-shod stick and with piercing eyes looking for the little black, moving speck in the distance on that enormous white expanse.

When he reached the end of the glacier he stopped, and asked himself whether the old man had taken that road, and then he began to walk along the moraines with rapid and uneasy steps. The day was declining; the snow was assuming a rosy tint, and a dry, frozen wind blew in rough gusts over its crystal surface. Ulrich uttered a long, shrill, vibrating call. His voice sped through the deathlike silence in which the mountains were sleeping; it reached into the distance over the profound and motionless waves of glacial foam, like the cry of a bird over the waves of the sea; then it died away, and nothing answered him.

He started off again. The sun had sunk behind the mountaintops which still were purpled with the reflection from the heavens, but the depths of the valley were becoming gray, and suddenly the young man felt frightened. It seemed to him as if the silence, the cold, the solitude, the wintry death of these mountains, were taking possession of him, were stopping and freezing his blood, making his limbs grow stiff and turning him into a motionless and frozen object, and he began to run rapidly toward the dwelling. The old man, he thought, would have returned during his absence. He had probably taken another road and would, no doubt, be sitting before the fire with a dead chamois at his feet.

He soon came in sight of the inn, but no smoke rose from it. Ulrich ran faster. Opening the door, he met Sam who ran up to him to greet him, but Gaspard Hari had not returned. Kunsi, in his alarm, turned round suddenly, as if he had expected to find his comrade hidden in a corner. Then he relighted the fire and made the soup, hoping every moment to see the old man come in. From time to time he went out to see if Gaspard were not in sight. It was night now, that wan night of the mountain, a livid night, with the crescent moon, yellow and dim, just disappearing behind the mountaintops and shining faintly on the edge of the horizon.

Then the young man went in and sat down to warm his hands and feet, while he pictured to himself every possible sort of accident. Gaspard might have broken a leg, have fallen into a crevasse, have taken a false step and dislocated his ankle. Perhaps he was lying on the snow, overcome and stiff with the cold, in agony of mind, lost and perhaps shouting for help, calling with all his might in the silence of the night.

But where? The mountain was so vast, so rugged, so dangerous in places, especially at that time of the year, that it would have required ten or twenty guides walking for a week in all directions to find a man in that immense space. Ulrich Kunsi, however, made up his mind to set out with Sam if Gaspard did not return by one in the morning, and he made his preparations.

He put provisions for two days into a bag, took his steel climbing irons, tied a long, thin, strong rope round his waist and looked to see that his iron-shod stick and his ax, which served to cut steps in the ice, were in order. Then he waited. The fire was burning on the hearth; the great dog was snoring in front of it, and the clock was ticking in its case of resounding wood, as regularly as a heart beating.

He waited, his ears on the alert for distant sounds, and shivered when the wind blew against the roof and the walls. It struck twelve, and he trembled. Then as he felt frightened and shivery, he put some water on the fire so that he might have hot coffee before starting. When the clock struck one he got up, woke Sam, opened the door and went off in the direction of the Wildstrubel. For five hours he ascended, scaling the rocks by means of his climbing irons, cutting into the ice, advancing continually and occasionally hauling up the dog, who remained below at the foot of some slope that was too steep for him, by means of the rope. About six o'clock he reached one of the summits to which old Gaspard often came after chamois, and he waited till it should be daylight.

The sky was growing pale overhead, and suddenly a strange light, springing, nobody could tell whence, suddenly illuminated the immense ocean of pale mountain peaks which stretched for many leagues around him. It seemed as if this vague brightness arose from the snow itself in order to spread itself into space. By degrees the highest and most distant summits assumed a delicate, fleshlike rose color, and the red sun appeared behind the ponderous giants of the Bernese Alps.

Ulrich Kunsi set off again, walking like a hunter, stooping and looking for any traces and saying to his dog: "Seek old fellow, seek!"

He was descending the mountain now, scanning the depths closely and from time to time shouting, uttering a loud, prolonged, familiar cry which soon died away in that silent vastness. Then he put his ear to the ground to listen.

He thought he could distinguish a voice, and so he began to run and shout again. But he heard nothing more and sat down, worn out and in despair. Toward midday he breakfasted and gave Sam, who was as tired as himself, something to eat also; then he recommenced his search.

When evening came he was still walking, having traveled more than thirty miles over the mountains. As he was too far away to return home and too tired to drag himself along any farther, he dug a hole in the snow and crouched in it with his dog under a blanket which he had brought with him. The man and the dog lay side by side, warming themselves one against the other, but frozen to the marrow nevertheless. Ulrich scarcely slept, his mind haunted by visions and his limbs shaking with cold.

Day was breaking when he got up. His legs were as stiff as iron bars, and his spirits so low that he was ready to weep, while his heart was beating so that he almost fell with excitement whenever he thought he heard a noise.

Suddenly he imagined that he also was going to die of cold in the midst of this vast solitude. The terror of such a death roused his energies and gave him renewed vigor. He was descending toward the inn, falling down and getting up again, and followed at a distance by Sam, who was limping on three legs. They did not reach Schwarenbach until four o'clock in the afternoon. The house was empty, and the young man made a fire, had something to eat and went to sleep, so worn out that he did not think of anything more.

He slept for a long time, for a very long time, the unconquerable sleep of exhaustion. But suddenly a voice, a cry, a name: "Ulrich," aroused him from his profound slumber and made him sit up in bed. Had he been dreaming? Was it one of those strange appeals which cross the dreams of disquieted minds? No, he heard it still, that reverberating cry which had entered at his ears and remained in his brain, thrilling him to the tips of his sinewy fingers. Certainly somebody had cried out and called: "Ulrich!" There was somebody there near the house, there could be no doubt of that, and he opened the door and shouted: "Is it you, Gaspard?" with all the strength of his lungs. But there was no reply, no murmur, no groan, nothing. It was quite dark, and the snow looked wan.

The wind had risen, that icy wind which cracks the rocks and leaves nothing alive on those deserted heights. It came in sudden gusts, more parching and more deadly than the burning wind of the desert, and again Ulrich shouted: "Gaspard! Gaspard! Gaspard!" Then he waited again. Everything was silent on the mountain! Then he shook with terror, and with a bound he was inside the inn. He shut and bolted the door and then fell into a chair, trembling all over, for he felt certain that his comrade had called him at the moment of dissolution.

He was certain of that, as certain as one is of conscious life or of taste when eating. Old Gaspard Hari had been dying for two days and three nights somewhere, in some hole in one of those deep, untrodden ravines whose whiteness is more sinister than subterranean darkness. He had been dying for two days and three nights and he had just then died, thinking of his comrade. His soul, almost before it was released, had taken its flight to the inn where Ulrich was sleeping, and it had called him by that terrible and mysterious power which the spirits of the dead possess. That voiceless soul had cried to the worn-out soul of the sleeper; it had uttered its last farewell, or its reproach, or its curse on the man who had not searched carefully enough.

And Ulrich felt that it was there, quite close to him, behind the wall, behind the door which he had just fastened. It was wandering about like a night bird which skims a lighted window with his wings, and the terrified young man was ready to scream with horror. He wanted to run away but did not dare go out; he did not dare and would never dare in the future, for that phantom would remain there day and night round the inn, as long as the old man's body was not recovered and deposited in the consecrated earth of a churchyard.

Daylight came, and Kunsi recovered some of his courage with the return of the bright sun. He prepared his meal, gave his dog some food and then remained motionless on a chair, tortured at heart as he thought of the old man lying on the snow. Then as soon as night once more covered the mountains, new terrors assailed him. He now walked up and down the dark kitchen which was scarcely lighted by the flame of one candle. He walked from one end of it to the other with great strides, listening, listening to hear the terrible cry of the preceding night again break the dreary silence outside. He felt himself a lone, unhappy man, as no man had ever been alone before! Alone in this immense desert of snow, alone five thousand feet above the inhabited earth, above human habitations, above that stirring, noisy, palpitating life, alone under an icy sky! A mad longing impelled him to run away, no matter where, to get down to Loëche by flinging himself over the precipice, but he did not even dare to open the door, as he felt sure that the other, the *dead*, man would bar his road, so that he might not be obliged to remain up there alone.

Toward midnight, tired with walking, worn out by grief and fear, he fell into a doze in his chair, for he was afraid of his bed, as one is of a haunted spot. But suddenly the strident cry of the preceding evening pierced his ears, so shrill that Ulrich stretched out his arms to repulse the ghost, and he fell onto his back with his chair.

Sam, who was awakened by the noise, began to howl as frightened dogs do and trotted all about the house, trying to find out where the danger came from. When he got to the door he sniffed beneath it, smelling vigorously, with his coat bristling and his tail stiff while he growled angrily. Kunsi, who was terrified, jumped up and, holding his chair by one leg, cried: "Don't come in; don't come in, or I shall kill you." And the dog, excited by this threat, barked angrily at that invisible enemy who defied his master's voice. By degrees, however, he quieted down, came back and stretched himself in front of the fire. But he was uneasy and kept his head up and growled between his teeth.

Ulrich, in turn, recovered his senses, but as he felt faint with terror, he went and got a bottle of brandy out of the sideboard and drank off several glasses, one after another, at a gulp. His ideas became vague, his courage revived, and a feverish glow ran through his veins.

He ate scarcely anything the next day and limited himself to alcohol; so he lived for several days, like a drunken brute. As soon as he thought of Gaspard Hari he began to drink again and went on drinking until he fell onto the floor, overcome by intoxication. And there he remained on his face, dead drunk, his limbs benumbed, and snoring with his face to the ground. But scarcely had he digested the maddening and burning liquor than the same cry, "Ulrich," woke him like a bullet piercing his brain, and he got up, still staggering, stretching out his hands to save himself from falling and calling to Sam to help him. And the dog, who appeared to be going mad like his master, rushed to the door, scratched it with his claws and gnawed it with his long white teeth, while the young man, his neck thrown back and his head in the air, drank the brandy in gulps, as if it were cold water, so that it might by and by send his thoughts, his frantic terror and his memory to sleep again.

In three weeks he had consumed all his stock of ardent spirits. But his continual drunkenness only lulled his terror, which awoke more furiously than ever as soon as it was impossible for him to calm it by drinking. His fixed idea which had been intensified by a month of drunkenness and which was continually increasing in his absolute solitude penetrated him like a gimlet. He now walked about his house like a wild beast in its cage, putting his ear to the door to listen if the other were there and defying him through the wall. Then as soon as he dozed, overcome by fatigue, he heard the voice which made him leap to his feet.

At last one night, as cowards do when driven to extremity, he sprang to the door and opened it to see who was calling him and to force him to keep quiet. But such a gust of cold wind blew into his face that it chilled him to the bone. He closed and bolted the door again immediately without noticing that Sam had rushed out. Then as he was shivering with cold, he threw some wood on the fire and sat down in front of it to warm himself. But suddenly he started, for somebody was scratching at the wall and crying. In desperation he called out: "Go away!" but was answered by another long, sorrowful wail.

Then all his remaining senses forsook him from sheer fright. He repeated: "Go away!" and turned round to find some corner in which to hide, while the other person went round the house still crying and rubbing against the wall. Ulrich went to the oak sideboard which was full of plates and dishes and of provisions and, lifting it up with superhuman strength, he dragged it to the door so as to form a barricade. Then piling up all the rest of the furniture, the mattresses, paillasses and chairs, he stopped up the windows as men do when assailed by an enemy.

But the person outside now uttered long, plaintive, mournful groans, to which the young man replied by similar groans, and thus days and nights passed without their ceasing to howl at each other. The one was continually walking round the house and scraped the walls with his nails so vigorously that it seemed as if he wished to destroy them, while the other, inside, followed all his movements, stooping down and holding his ear to the walls and replying to all his appeals with terrible cries. One evening, however, Ulrich heard nothing more, and he sat down, so overcome by fatigue that he went to sleep immediately and awoke in the morning without a thought, without any recollection of what had happened, just as if his head had been emptied during his heavy sleep. But he felt hungry, and he ate.

The winter was over, and the Gemmi pass was practicable again, so the Hauser family started off to return to their inn. As soon as they had reached the top of the ascent the women mounted their mule and spoke about the two men whom they would meet again shortly. They were, indeed, rather surprised that neither of them had come down a few days before, as soon as the road became passable, in order to tell them all about their long winter sojourn. At last, however, they saw the inn, still covered with snow, like a quilt. The door and the windows were closed, but a little smoke was coming out of the chimney, which reassured old Hauser; on going up to the door, however, he saw the skeleton of an animal which had been torn to pieces by the eagles, a large skeleton lying on its side.

They all looked closely at it, and the mother said: "That must be Sam." Then she shouted: "Hi! Gaspard!" A cry from the interior of the house answered her, so sharp a cry that one might have thought some animal uttered it. Old Hauser repeated: "Hi! Gaspard!" and they heard another cry, similar to the first.

Then the three men, the father and the two sons, tried to open the door, but it resisted their efforts. From the empty cow stall they took a beam to serve as a battering-ram and hurled it against the door with all their might. The wood gave way, and the boards flew into splinters; then the house was shaken by a loud voice, and inside, behind the sideboard which was overturned, they saw a man standing upright, his hair falling onto his shoulders and a beard descending to his breast, with shining eyes and nothing but rags to cover him. They did not recognize him, but Louise Hauser exclaimed: "It is Ulrich, Mother." And her mother declared that it was Ulrich, although his hair was white.

He allowed them to go up to him and to touch him, but he did not reply to any of their questions, and they were obliged to take him to Loëche, where the doctors found that he was mad. Nobody ever knew what had become of his companion.

Little Louise Hauser nearly died that summer of decline, which the medical men attributed to the cold air of the mountains.

A FAMILY

I WAS GOING to see my friend Simon Radevin once more, for I had not seen him for fifteen years. Formerly he was my most intimate friend, and I used to spend long, quiet and happy evenings with him. He was one of those men to whom one tells the most intimate affairs of the heart and in whom one finds, when quietly talking, rare, clever, ingenious and refined thoughts—thoughts which stimulate and capture the mind.

For years we had scarcely been separated: we had lived, traveled, thought and dreamed together, had liked the same things with the same liking, admired the same books, comprehended the same works, shivered with the same sensations and very often laughed at the same individuals, whom we understood completely by merely exchanging a glance.

Then he married—quite unexpectedly married a little girl from the provinces, who had come to Paris in search of a husband. How ever could that little, thin, insipidly fair girl, with her weak hands, her light, vacant eyes and her clear, silly voice, who was exactly like a hundred thousand marriageable dolls, have picked up that intelligent, clever young fellow? Can anyone understand these things? No doubt he had hoped for happiness, simple, quiet and long-enduring happiness, in the arms of a good, tender and faithful woman; he had seen all that in the transparent looks of that schoolgirl with light hair.

He had not dreamed of the fact that an active, living and vibrating man grows tired as soon as he has comprehended the stupid reality of a commonplace life, unless, indeed, he becomes so brutalized as to be callous to externals.

What would he be like when I met him again? Still lively, witty, lighthearted and enthusiastic, or in a state of mental torpor through provincial life? A man can change a great deal in the course of fifteen years!

The train stopped at a small station, and as I got out of the carriage a stout, a very stout man with red cheeks and a big stomach rushed up to me with open arms, exclaiming: "George!"

I embraced him, but I had not recognized him, and then I said in astonishment: "By Jove! You have not grown thin!"

And he replied with a laugh: "What did you expect? Good living, a good table and good nights! Eating and sleeping, that is my existence!"

I looked at him closely, trying to find the features I held so dear in that broad face. His eyes alone had not altered, but I no longer saw the same look in them, and I said to myself: "If looks be the reflection of the mind, the thoughts in that head are not what they used to be—those thoughts which I knew so well."

Yet his eyes were bright, full of pleasure and friendship, but they had not that clear, intelligent expression which tells better than do words the value of the mind. Suddenly he said to me:

"Here are my two eldest children." A girl of fourteen, who was almost a woman, and a boy of thirteen, in the dress of a pupil from a lycée, came forward in a hesitating and awkward manner, and I said in a low voice: "Are they yours?"

"Of course they are," he replied, laughing.

"How many have you?"

"Five! There are three more indoors."

He said that in a proud, self-satisfied, almost triumphant manner, and I felt profound pity, mingled with a feeling of vague contempt, for this vainglorious and simple reproducer of his species who spent his nights in his country house in uxorious pleasures.

I got into a carriage, which he drove himself, and we set off through the town, a dull, sleepy, gloomy town where nothing was moving in the streets save a few dogs and two or three maidservants. Here and there a shopkeeper standing at his door took off his hat, and Simon returned the salute and told me the man's name—no doubt to show me that he knew all the inhabitants personally. The thought struck me that he was thinking of becoming a candidate for the Chamber of Deputies, that dream of all who have buried themselves in the provinces.

We were soon out of the town; the carriage turned into a garden which had some pretensions to a park and stopped in front of a turreted house which tried to pass for a château.

"That is my den," Simon said, so that he might be complimented on it, and I replied that it was delightful.

A lady appeared on the steps, dressed up for a visitor, her hair done for a visitor and with phrases ready prepared for a visitor. She was no longer the light-haired insipid girl I had seen in church fifteen years previously, but a stout lady in curls and flounces, one of those ladies of uncertain age, without intellect, without any of those things which constitute a woman. In short she was a mother, a stout, commonplace mother, a human layer and brood mare, a machine of flesh which procreates, without mental care save for her children and her housekeeping book.

She welcomed me, and I went into the hall where three children, ranged according to their height, were ranked for review like firemen before a mayor. "Ah! ah! so there are the others?" said I. And Simon, who was radiant with pleasure, named them: "Jean, Sophie and Gontran."

The door of the drawing room was open. I went in, and in the depths of an easy chair I saw something trembling, a man, an old, paralyzed man. Mme Radevin came forward and said: "This is my grandfather, monsieur; he is eighty-seven." And then she shouted into the shaking old man's ears: "This is a friend of Simon's, grandpapa."

The old gentleman tried to say "Good day" to me, and he muttered: "Oua, oua, oua," and waved his hand.

I took a seat, saying: "You are very kind, monsieur."

Simon had just come in, and he said with a laugh: "So! You have made Grandpapa's acquaintance. He is priceless, is that old man. He is the delight of the children, and he is so greedy that he almost kills himself at every meal. You have no idea what he would eat if he were allowed to do as he pleased. But you will see, you will see. He looks all the sweets over as if they were so many girls. You have never seen anything funnier; you will see it presently."

I was then shown to my room to change my dress for dinner, and hearing a great clatter behind me on the stairs, I turned round and saw that all the children were following me behind their father—to do me honor, no doubt.

My windows looked out onto a plain, a bare, interminable plain, an ocean of grass, of wheat and of oats without a clump of trees or any rising ground, a striking and melancholy picture of the life which they must be leading in that house.

A bell rang; it was for dinner, and so I went downstairs. Mme Radevin took my arm in a ceremonious manner, and we went into the dining room. A footman wheeled in the old man's armchair, who gave a greedy and curious look at the dessert as with difficulty he turned his shaking head from one dish to the other.

Simon rubbed his hands, saying: "You will be amused." All the children understood that I was going to be indulged with the sight of their greedy grandfather and they began to laugh accordingly, while their mother merely smiled and shrugged her shoulders. Simon, making a speaking trumpet of his hands, shouted at the old man: "This evening there is sweet rice cream," and the wrinkled face of the grandfather brightened; he trembled violently all over, showing that he had understood and was very pleased. The dinner began.

"Just look!" Simon whispered. The grandfather did not like the soup and refused to eat it, but he was made to, on account of his health. The footman forced the spoon into his mouth, while the old man blew energetically, so as not to swallow the soup, which was thus scattered like a stream of water onto the table and over his neighbors. The children shook with delight at the spectacle, while their father, who was also amused, said: "Isn't the old man funny?"

During the whole meal they were all taken up solely with him. With his eyes he devoured the dishes which were put on the table and with trembling hands tried to seize them and pull them to him. They put them almost within his reach to see his useless efforts, his trembling clutches at them, the piteous appeal of his whole nature, of his eyes, of his mouth and of his nose as he smelled them. He slobbered onto his table napkin with eagerness while uttering inarticulate grunts, and the whole family was highly amused at this horrible and grotesque scene.

Then they put a tiny morsel onto his plate, which he ate with feverish gluttony in order to get something more as soon as possible. When the rice cream was brought in he nearly had a fit and groaned with greediness. Gontran called out to him: "You have eaten too much already; you will have no more." And they pretended not to give him any. Then he began to cry—cry and tremble more violently than ever, while all the children laughed. At last, however, they gave him his helping, a very small piece. As he ate the first mouthful of the pudding he made a comical and greedy noise in his throat and a movement with his neck like ducks do when they swallow too large a morsel, and then, when he had done, he began to stamp his feet so as to get more.

I was seized with pity for this pitiable and ridiculous Tantalus and interposed on his behalf. "Please, will you not give him a little more rice?"

But Simon replied: "Oh no, my dear fellow; if he were to eat too much, it might harm him at his age."

I held my tongue and thought over these words. Oh, ethics! Oh, logic!

Oh, wisdom! At his age! So they deprived him of his only remaining pleasure out of regard for his health! His health! What would he do with it, inert and trembling wreck that he was? They were taking care of his life, so they said. His life? How many days? Ten, twenty, fifty or a hundred? Why? For his own sake? Or to preserve, for some time longer, the spectacle of his impotent greediness in the family?

There was nothing left for him to do in this life, nothing whatever. He had one single wish left, one sole pleasure; why not grant him that last solace constantly, until he died?

After playing cards for a long time I went up to my room and to bed; I was low-spirited and sad, sad, sad! I sat at my window, but I heard nothing but the beautiful warbling of a bird in a tree, somewhere in the distance. No doubt the bird was singing thus in a low voice during the night to lull his mate, who was sleeping on her eggs.

And I thought of my poor friend's five children and to myself pictured him snoring by the side of his ugly wife.

BELLFLOWER[1]

How STRANGE are those old recollections which haunt us without our being able to get rid of them!

This one is so very old that I cannot understand how it has clung so vividly and tenaciously to my memory. Since then I have seen so many sinister things, either affecting or terrible, that I am astonished at not being able to pass a single day without the face of Mother Bellflower recurring to my mind's eye, just as I knew her formerly long, long ago, when I was ten or twelve years old.

She was an old seamstress who came to my parents' house once a week, every Thursday, to mend the linen. My parents lived in one of those country houses called châteaux, which are merely old houses with pointed roofs, to which are attached three or four adjacent farms.

The village, a large village, almost a small market town, was a few hundred yards off and nestled round the church, a red brick church, which had become black with age.

Well, every Thursday Mother Bellflower came between half-past six and seven in the morning and went immediately into the linen room and began to work. She was a tall, thin, bearded or rather hairy woman, for she had a beard all over her face, a surprising, an unexpected beard, growing in improbable tufts, in curly bunches which looked as if they had been sown by a madman over that great face, the face of a gendarme in petticoats. She had them on her nose, under her nose, round her nose, on her chin, on her cheeks, and her eyebrows, which were extraordinarily thick and long and

---
[1] Clochette.

quite gray, bushy and bristling, looked exactly like a pair of mustaches stuck on there by mistake.

She limped, not like lame people generally do, but like a ship pitching. When she planted her great bony, vibrant body on her sound leg, she seemed to be preparing to mount some enormous wave, and then suddenly she dipped as if to disappear in an abyss and buried herself in the ground. Her walk reminded one of a ship in a storm, and her head, which was always covered with an enormous white cap, whose ribbons fluttered down her back, seemed to traverse the horizon from north to south and from south to north at each limp.

I adored Mother Bellflower. As soon as I was up I used to go into the linen room, where I found her installed at work with a foot warmer under her feet. As soon as I arrived she made me take the foot warmer and sit upon it, so that I might not catch cold in that large chilly room under the roof.

"That draws the blood from your head," she would say to me.

She told me stories while mending the linen with her long, crooked, nimble fingers; behind her magnifying spectacles, for age had impaired her sight, her eyes appeared enormous to me, strangely profound, double.

As far as I can remember from the things which she told me and by which my childish heart was moved, she had the large heart of a poor woman. She told me what had happened in the village, how a cow had escaped from the cow house and had been found the next morning in front of Prosper Malet's mill looking at the sails turning, or about a hen's egg which had been found in the church belfry without anyone being able to understand what creature had been there to lay it, or the queer story of Jean Pila's dog who had gone ten leagues to bring back his master's breeches which a tramp had stolen while they were hanging up to dry out of doors after he had been caught in the rain. She told me these simple adventures in such a manner that in my mind they assumed the proportions of never-to-be-forgotten dramas, of grand and mysterious poems; and the ingenious stories invented by the poets, which my mother told me in the evening, had none of the flavor, none of the fullness or of the vigor of the peasant woman's narratives.

Well, one Thursday when I had spent all the morning in listening to Mother Clochette, I wanted to go upstairs to her again during the day after picking hazelnuts with the manservant in the wood behind the farm. I remember it all as clearly as what happened only yesterday.

On opening the door of the linen room I saw the old seamstress lying on the floor by the side of her chair, her face turned down and her arms stretched out, but still holding her needle in one hand and one of my shirts in the other. One of her legs in a blue stocking, the longer one no doubt, was extended under her chair, and her spectacles glistened by the wall, where they had rolled away from her.

I ran away uttering shrill cries. They all came running, and in a few minutes I was told that Mother Clochette was dead.

I cannot describe the profound, poignant, terrible emotion which stirred my childish heart. I went slowly down into the drawing room and hid myself in a dark corner in the depths of a great old armchair, where I knelt and wept. I remained there for a long time, no doubt, for night came on. Suddenly someone came in with a lamp—without seeing me, however—and I heard my father and mother talking with the medical man, whose voice I recognized.

He had been sent for immediately, and he was explaining the cause of the accident, of which I understood nothing, however. Then he sat down and had a glass of liqueur and a biscuit.

He went on talking, and what he then said will remain engraved on my mind until I die! I think that I can give the exact words which he used.

"Ah!" he said. "The poor woman! she broke her leg the day of my arrival here. I had not even had time to wash my hands after getting off the diligence before I was sent for in all haste, for it was a bad case, very bad.

"She was seventeen and a pretty girl, very pretty! Would anyone believe it? I have never told her story before; in fact, no one but myself and one other person, who is no longer living in this part of the country, ever knew it. Now that she is dead I may be less discreet.

"A young assistant teacher had just come to live in the village; he was good looking and had the bearing of a soldier. All the girls ran after him, but he was disdainful. Besides that, he was very much afraid of his superior, the schoolmaster, old Grabu, who occasionally got out of bed the wrong foot first.

"Old Grabu already employed pretty Hortense, who has just died here and who was afterward nicknamed Clochette. The assistant master singled out the pretty young girl who was no doubt flattered at being chosen by this disdainful conqueror; at any rate, she fell in love with him, and he succeeded in persuading her to give him a first meeting in the hayloft behind the school at night after she had done her day's sewing.

"She pretended to go home, but instead of going downstairs when she left the Grabus', she went upstairs and hid among the hay to wait for her lover. He soon joined her, and he was beginning to say pretty things to her, when the door of the hayloft opened and the schoolmaster appeared and asked: 'What are you doing up there, Sigisbert?' Feeling sure that he would be caught, the young schoolmaster lost his presence of mind and replied stupidly: 'I came up here to rest a little among the bundles of hay, Monsieur Grabu.'

"The loft was very large and absolutely dark. Sigisbert pushed the frightened girl to the farther end and said: 'Go there and hide yourself. I shall lose my situation, so get away and hide yourself.'

"When the schoolmaster heard the whispering he continued: 'Why, you are not by yourself.'

"'Yes, I am, Monsieur Grabu!'

"'But you are not, for you are talking.'

"'I swear I am, Monsieur Grabu.'

"'I will soon find out,' the old man replied and, double-locking the door, he went down to get a light.

"Then the young man, who was a coward such as one sometimes meets, lost his head, and he repeated, having grown furious all of a sudden: 'Hide yourself, so that he may not find you. You will deprive me of my bread for my whole life; you will ruin my whole career! Do hide yourself!'

"They could hear the key turning in the lock again, and Hortense ran to the window which looked out onto the street, opened it quickly and then in a low and determined voice said: 'You will come and pick me up when he is gone,' and she jumped out.

"Old Grabu found nobody and went down again in great surprise! A quarter of an hour later Monsieur Sigisbert came to me and related his adventure. The girl had remained at the foot of the wall, unable to get up, as she had fallen from the second story, and I went with him to fetch her. It was raining in torrents, and I brought the unfortunate girl home with me, for the right leg was broken in three places, and the bones had come out through the flesh. She did not complain and merely said with admirable resignation: 'I am punished, well punished!'

"I sent for assistance and for the workgirl's friends and told them a made-up story of a runaway carriage which had knocked her down and lamed her outside my door. They believed me, and the gendarmes for a whole month tried in vain to find the author of this accident.

"That is all! Now I say that this woman was a heroine and had the fiber of those who accomplish the grandest deeds in history.

"That was her only love affair, and she died a virgin. She was a martyr, a noble soul, a sublimely devoted woman! And if I did not absolutely admire her I should not have told you this story, which I would never tell anyone during her life; you understand why."

The doctor ceased; Mamma cried, and Papa said some words which I did not catch; then they left the room, and I remained on my knees in the armchair and sobbed, while I heard a strange noise of heavy footsteps and something knocking against the side of the staircase.

They were carrying away Clochette's body.

IN THE WOOD

THE MAYOR was just going to sit down to breakfast, when he was told that the rural policeman was waiting for him at the *mairie* with two prisoners. He went there immediately and found old Hochedur standing up and watching a middle-class couple of mature years with stern looks.

The man, a fat old fellow with a red nose and white hair, seemed utterly dejected, while the woman, a little roundabout, stout creature with shining cheeks, looked at the agent who had arrested them with defiant eyes.

"What is it? What is it, Hochedur?"

The rural policeman made his deposition. He had gone out that morning at his usual time in order to patrol his beat from the forest of Champioux as far as the boundaries of Argenteuil. He had not noticed anything unusual in the country except that it was a fine day and that the wheat was doing well, when the son of old Bredel, who was going over his vines a second time, called out to him: "Here, Daddy Hochedur, go and have a look into the skirts of the wood, in the first thicket, and you will catch a pair of pigeons there who must be a hundred and thirty years old between them!"

He went in the direction that had been indicated to him and had gone into the thicket. There he heard words and gasps which made him suspect a flagrant breach of morality. Advancing, therefore, on his hands and knees as if to surprise a poacher, he had arrested this couple at the very moment when they were going to abandon themselves to their natural instincts.

The mayor looked at the culprits in astonishment, for the man was certainly sixty and the woman fifty-five at least. So he began to question them, beginning with the man, who replied in such a weak voice that he could scarcely be heard.

"What is your name?"

"Nicolas Beaurain."

"Your occupation?"

"Haberdasher in the Rue des Martyrs, in Paris."

"What were you doing in the wood?"

The haberdasher remained silent, with his eyes on his fat stomach and his hands resting on his thighs, and the mayor continued:

"Do you deny what the officer of the municipal authorities states?"

"No, monsieur."

"So you confess it?"

"Yes, monsieur."

"What have you to say in your defense?"

"Nothing, monsieur."

"Where did you meet the partner in your misdemeanor?"

"She is my wife, monsieur."

"Your wife?"

"Yes, monsieur."

"Then—then—you do not live together in Paris?"

"I beg your pardon, monsieur, but we are living together!"

"But in that case you must be mad, altogether mad, my dear sir, to get caught like that in the country at ten o'clock in the morning."

The haberdasher seemed ready to cry with shame, and he murmured: "It was she who enticed me! I told her it was stupid, but when a woman has got a thing into her head, you know, you cannot get it out."

The mayor, who liked open speaking, smiled and replied:

"In your case the contrary ought to have happened. You would not be here if she had had the idea only in her head."

Then M. Beaurain was seized with rage and, turning to his wife, he said: "Do you see to what you have brought us with your poetry? And now we shall have to go before the courts at our age for a breach of morals! And we shall have to shut up the shop, sell our good will and go to some other neighborhood! That's what it has come to!"

Mme Beaurain got up and, without looking at her husband, explained herself without any embarrassment, without useless modesty and almost without hesitation.

"Of course, monsieur, I know that we have made ourselves ridiculous. Will you allow me to plead my case like an advocate, or rather like a poor woman? And I hope that you will be kind enough to send us home and to spare us the disgrace of a prosecution.

"Years ago, when I was young, I made Monsieur Beaurain's acquaintance on Sunday in this neighborhood. He was employed in a draper's shop, and I was a saleswoman in a ready-made clothing establishment. I remember it as if it were yesterday. I used to come and spend Sundays here occasionally with a friend of mine, Rose Levèque, with whom I lived in the Rue Pigalle, and Rose had a sweetheart, while I had not. He used to bring us here, and one Saturday he told me, laughing, that he should bring a friend with him the next day. I quite understood what he meant, but I replied that it would be no good, for I was virtuous, monsieur.

"The next day we met Monsieur Beaurain at the railway station. In those days he was good looking, but I had made up my mind not to yield to him, and I did not yield. Well, we arrived at Bezons. It was a lovely day, the sort of day that tickles your heart. When it is fine even now, just as it used to be formerly, I grow quite foolish, and when I am in the country I utterly lose my head. The verdure, the swallows flying so swiftly, the smell of the grass, the scarlet poppies, the daisies, all that makes me quite excited! It is like champagne when one is not used to it!

"Well, it was lovely weather, warm and bright, and it seemed to penetrate into your body by your eyes when you looked and by your mouth when you breathed. Rose and Simon hugged and kissed each other every minute, and that gave me something to look at! Monsieur Beaurain and I walked behind them without speaking much, for when people do not know each other well they cannot find much to talk about. He looked timid, and I liked to see his embarrassment. At last we got to the little wood; it was as cool as in a bath there, and we all four sat down. Rose and her lover joked me because I looked rather stern, but you will understand that I could not be otherwise. And then they began to kiss and hug again without putting any more restraint upon themselves than if we had not been there. Then they whispered together and got up and went off among the trees without saying a word. You may fancy how I felt, alone with this young fellow whom I saw for the first time. I felt so confused at seeing them go that it gave me courage and I began to talk. I asked him what his business was, and he said he was a linen draper's assistant, as I told you just now. We talked for a few minutes, and that made him bold, and he wanted to take liberties with me, but I told him sharply to keep his own place. Is not that true, Monsieur Beaurain?"

M. Beaurain, who was looking at his feet in confusion, did not reply, and she continued: "Then he saw that I was virtuous and he began to make love to me nicely, like an honorable man, and from that time he came every Sunday, for he was very much in love with me. I was very fond of him also, very fond of him! He was a good-looking fellow formerly, and in short he married me the next September, and we started business in the Rue des Martyrs.

"It was a hard struggle for some years, monsieur. Business did not prosper, and we could not afford many country excursions, and then we became unaccustomed to them. One has other things in one's head and thinks more of the cashbox than of pretty speeches when one is in business. We were growing old by degrees without perceiving it, like quiet people who do not think much about love. But one does not regret anything as long as one does not notice what one has lost.

"And after that, monsieur, business went better, and we became tranquil as to the future! Then, you see, I do not exactly know what passed within me —no, I really do not know—but I began to dream like a little boarding-school girl. The sight of the little carts full of flowers which are peddled about the streets made me cry; the smell of violets sought me out in my easy chair, behind my cashbox, and made my heart beat! Then I used to get up and go onto the doorstep to look at the blue sky between the roofs. When one looks at the sky from a street it seems like a river flowing over Paris, winding as it goes, and the swallows pass to and fro in it like fish. These sort of things are very stupid at my age! But what can one do, monsieur, when one has worked all one's life? A moment comes in which one perceives that one could have done something else, and then one regrets. Oh yes! One feels great regret! Just think that for twenty years I might have gone and had kisses in the wood, like other women. I used to think how delightful it would be to lie under the trees loving someone! And I thought of it every day and every night! I dreamed of the moonlight on the water, until I felt inclined to drown myself.

"I did not venture to speak to Monsieur Beaurain about this at first. I knew that he would make fun of me and send me back to sell my needles and cotton! And then, to speak the truth, Monsieur Beaurain never said much to me, but when I looked in the glass I also understood quite well that I also no longer appealed to anyone!

"Well, I made up my mind, and I proposed an excursion into the country to him to the place where we had first become acquainted. He agreed without any distrust, and we arrived here this morning about nine o'clock.

"I felt quite young again when I got among the corn, for a woman's heart never grows old! And really I no longer saw my husband as he is at present, but just like he was formerly! That I will swear to you, monsieur. As true as I am standing here, I was intoxicated. I began to kiss him, and he was more surprised than if I had tried to murder him. He kept saying to me: 'Why, you must be mad this morning! What is the matter with you?' I did not listen to him; I only listened to my own heart, and I made him come into the wood with me. There is the story. I have spoken the truth, Monsieur le Maire, the whole truth."

The mayor was a sensible man. He rose from his chair, smiled and said: "Go in peace, madame, and sin no more—under the trees."

THE MARQUIS DE FUMEROL

Roger de Toumeville was sitting astride a chair in the midst of his friends and talking; he held a cigar in his hand and from time to time took a whiff and blew out a small cloud of smoke.

"We were at dinner when a letter was brought in, and my father opened it. You know my father who thinks that he is king of France *ad interim*. I call him Don Quixote, because for twelve years he has been running a tilt against the windmill of the Republic without quite knowing whether it was in the name of Bourbon or of Orléans. At present he is holding the lance in the name of Orléans alone, because there is nobody else left. In any case, he thinks himself the first gentleman in France, the best known, the most influential, the head of the party, and as he is an irremovable senator, he thinks that the neighboring kings' thrones are very insecure.

"As for my mother, she is my father's inspiration, the soul of the kingdom and of religion, the right arm of God on earth and the scourge of evil thinkers.

"Well, this letter was brought in while we were at dinner. My father opened and read it, and then he said to my mother: 'Your brother is dying.' She grew very pale. My uncle was scarcely ever mentioned in the house, and I did not know him at all; all I knew from public talk was that he had led and was still leading the life of a buffoon. After having spent his fortune with an incalculable number of women, he had only retained two mistresses, with whom he was living in small apartments in the Rue des Martyrs.

"An ex-peer of France and ex-colonel of cavalry, it was said that he believed in neither God nor devil. Having no faith, therefore, in a future life, he had abused this present life in every way and had become a living wound to my mother's heart.

"'Give me that letter, Paul,' she said, and when she had read it I asked for it in my turn. Here it is:

"Monsieur le Comte: *I think I ought to let you know that your brother-in-law, Count Fumerol, is going to die. Perhaps you would make preparations and not forget that I told you.*

"*Your servant,* Mélani."

"'We must think,' my father murmured. 'In my position I ought to watch over your brother's last moments.'

"My mother continued: 'I will send for Abbé Poivron and ask his advice, and then I will go to my brother's with him and Roger. Stop here, Paul, for you must not compromise yourself, but a woman can and ought to do these things. For a politician in your position, it is another matter. It would be a fine thing for one of your opponents to be able to bring one of your most laudable actions up against you.'

"'You are right!' my father said. 'Do as you think best, my dear wife.'

"A quarter of an hour later the Abbé Poivron came into the drawing room, and the situation was explained to him, analyzed and discussed in all its bearings. If the Marquis de Fumerol, one of the greatest names in France, were to die without the succor of religion it would assuredly be a terrible blow to the nobility in general, to the Count de Tourneville in particular, and the freethinkers would be triumphant. The evilly disposed newspapers would sing songs of victory for six months; my mother's name would be dragged through the mire and brought into the slander of socialistic journals and my father's would be bespattered. It was impossible that such a thing should occur.

"A crusade was therefore immediately decided upon, which was to be led by the Abbé Poivron, a little fat, clean, slightly scented priest, the faithful vicar of a large church in a rich and noble quarter.

"The landau was ordered, and we three started, my mother, the curé and I, to administer the last sacraments to my uncle.

"It had been decided that first of all we should see Madame Mélani who had written the letter and who was most likely the porter's wife or my uncle's servant, and I got down as a scout in front of a seven-storied house and went into a dark passage, where I had great difficulty in finding the porter's den. He looked at me distrustfully, and I said:

"'Madame Mélani, if you please.'

"'Don't know her!'

"'But I have received a letter from her.'

"'That may be, but I don't know her. Are you asking for some kept woman?'

"'No, a servant probably. She wrote me about a place.'

"'A servant—a servant? Perhaps it is the marquis's. Go and see, the fifth story on the left.'

"As soon as he found I was not asking for a kept woman he became more friendly and came as far as the passage with me. He was a tall thin man with white whiskers, the manners of a beadle, and majestic in movement.

"I climbed up a long spiral staircase whose balusters I did not venture to touch, and I gave three discreet knocks at the left-hand door on the fifth story. It opened immediately, and an enormous dirty woman appeared before me, who barred the entrance with her open arms which she placed upon the two doorposts and grumbled out:

"'What do you want?'

"'Are you Madame Mélani?'

"'Yes.'

"'I am the Viscount de Tourneville.'

"'Ah! All right! Come in.'

"'Well, the fact is, my mother is downstairs with a priest.'

"'Oh! All right; go and bring them up, but take care of the porter.'

"I went downstairs and came up again with my mother who was followed by the abbé, and I fancied that I heard other footsteps behind us. As soon as we were in the kitchen, Mélani offered us chairs, and we all four sat down to deliberate.

"'Is he very ill?' my mother asked.

"'Oh yes, madame; he will not be here long.'

"'Does he seem disposed to receive a visit from a priest?'

"'Oh! I do not think so.'

"'Can I see him?'

"'Well—yes—madame—only—only—those young ladies are with him.'

"'What young ladies?'

"'Why—why—his lady friends, of course.'

"'Oh!' Mamma had grown scarlet, and the Abbé Poivron had lowered his eyes.

"The affair began to amuse me, and I said: 'Suppose I go in first? I shall see how he receives me, and perhaps I shall be able to prepare his heart for you.'

"My mother, who did not suspect any trick, replied: 'Yes, go, my dear.'

"But a woman's voice cried out: 'Mélani!'

"The fat servant ran out and said: 'What do you want, Mademoiselle Claire?'

"'The omelet, quickly.'

"'In a minute, mademoiselle.' And coming back to us, she explained this summons.

"'They ordered a cheese omelet at two o'clock as a slight collation.' And immediately she began to break eggs into a salad bowl and began to whip them vigorously, while I went out onto the landing and pulled the bell so as to announce my official arrival. Mélani opened the door to me and made me sit down in an anteroom while she went to tell my uncle that I had come. Then she came back and asked me to go in, while the abbé hid behind the door so that he might appear at the first sign.

"I was certainly very much surprised at seeing my uncle, for he was very handsome, very solemn and very elegant—the old rake.

"Sitting, almost lying, in a large armchair, his legs wrapped in blankets, with his hands, his long white hands, over the arms of the chair, he was waiting for death with biblical dignity. His white beard fell on his chest, and his hair which was also white mingled with it on his cheeks.

"Standing behind his armchair as if to defend him against me were two young women, two stout young women, who looked at me with the bold eyes of prostitutes. In their petticoats and morning wrappers, with bare arms, with coal-black hair twisted up onto the napes of their necks, with embroidered oriental slippers which showed their ankles and silk stockings, they looked like the immoral figures of some symbolical painting by the side of the dying man. Between the easy chair and the bed there was a table covered with a white cloth on which two plates, two glasses, two forks and two knives were waiting for the cheese omelet which had been ordered some time before of Mélani.

"My uncle said in a weak, almost breathless, but clear voice: 'Good morning, my child; it is rather late in the day to come to see me; our acquaintanceship will not last long.'

"I stammered out: 'It was not my fault, Uncle,' and he replied: 'No; I know that. It is your father's and mother's fault more than yours. How are they?'

"'Pretty well, thank you. When they heard that you were ill they sent me to ask after you.'

"'Ah! Why did they not come themselves?'

"I looked up at the two girls and said gently: 'It is not their fault if they could not come, Uncle. But it would be difficult for my father and impossible for my mother to come in here.' The old man did not reply but raised his hand toward mine, and I took the pale, cold hand and kept it in my own.

"The door opened; Mélani came in with the omelet and put it on the table, and the two girls immediately sat down in front of their plates and began to eat without taking their eyes off me.

"Then I said: 'Uncle, it would be a great pleasure for my mother to embrace you.'

"'I also,' he murmured, 'should like——' He said no more, and I could think of nothing to propose to him, and nothing more was heard except the noise of the plates and the slight sound of eating mouths.

"Now the abbé, who was listening behind the door, seeing our embarrassment and thinking we had won the game, thought the time had come to interpose and showed himself. My uncle was so stupefied at that apparition that at first he remained motionless; then he opened his mouth as if he meant to swallow up the priest and cried out in a strong, deep, furious voice: 'What are you doing here?'

"The abbé, who was used to difficult situations, came forward, murmuring: 'I have come in your sister's name, Monsieur le Marquis; she has sent me—she would be so happy, monsieur——'

"But the marquis was not listening. Raising one hand, he pointed to the door with a proud and tragic gesture and said angrily and gasping for breath: 'Leave this room—go out—robber of souls. Go out from here, you violator of consciences! Go out from here, you picklock of dying men's doors!'

"The abbé went backward, and I, too, went to the door, beating a retreat with him, and the two little women who were avenged got up, leaving their omelet half eaten, and stood on either side of my uncle's armchair, putting their hands on his arms to calm him and to protect him against the criminal enterprises of the family and of religion.

"The abbé and I rejoined my mother in the kitchen, and Mélani again offered us chairs. 'I knew quite well that you would fail that way; we must try some other means, otherwise he will escape us.' And we began deliberating afresh, my mother being of one opinion and the abbé of another, while I held a third.

"We had been discussing the matter in a low voice for half an hour, perhaps, when a great noise of furniture being moved and of cries uttered by my uncle, more vehement and terrible even than the former had been, made us all jump up.

"Through the doors and walls we could hear him shouting: 'Go out—out—rascals—humbugs; get out, scoundrels—get out—get out!'

"Mélani rushed in but came back immediately to call me to help her, and I hastened in. Opposite to my uncle who was terribly excited by anger, almost standing up and vociferating, two men, one behind the other, seemed to be waiting till he should be dead with rage.

"By his long, ridiculous coat, his pointed English shoes, by his manners—like those of a tutor out of a situation—by his high collar, white necktie and straight hair, by his humble face, I immediately recognized the first as a Protestant minister.

"The second was the porter of the house who belonged to the Reformed religion and had followed us. Having known of our defeat, he had gone to fetch his own pastor in hope of a better fate. My uncle seemed mad with rage! If the sight of the Catholic priest, of the priest of his ancestors, had irritated the Marquis de Fumerol, who had become a freethinker, the sight of his porter's minister made him altogether beside himself. I therefore took the two men by the arm and threw them out of the room so violently that they fell up against each other twice between the two doors which led to the staircase; then I disappeared in my turn and returned to the kitchen, which was our headquarters, in order to take counsel with my mother and the abbé.

"But Mélani came back in terror, sobbing out: 'He is dying—he is dying. Come immediately—he is dying.'

"My mother rushed out. My uncle had fallen onto the carpet, full length along the floor, and did not move. I fancy he was already dead. My mother was superb at that moment! She went straight up to the two girls who were kneeling by the body and trying to raise it up and, pointing to the door with irresistible authority, dignity and majesty, she said: 'Now it is for you to go out.'

"And they went out without a protest and without saying a word. I must add that I was getting ready to turn them out as unceremoniously as I had done the parson and the porter.

"Then the Abbé Poivron administered extreme unction to my uncle with all the customary prayers and remitted all his sins, while my mother sobbed, kneeling near her brother. Suddenly, however, she exclaimed: 'He recognized me; he pressed my hand; I am sure he recognized me and thanked me! O God, what happiness!'

"Poor Mamma! If she had known or guessed to whom those thanks ought to have been addressed!

"They laid my uncle on his bed; he was certainly dead that time.

"'Madame,' Mélani said, 'we have no sheets to bury him in; all the linen belongs to those two young ladies,' and when I looked at the omelet which they had not finished, I felt inclined to laugh and to cry at the same time. There are some strange moments and some strange sensations in life occasionally!

"We gave my uncle a magnificent funeral with five speeches at the grave. Baron de Croiselles, the senator, showed in admirable terms that God always returns victorious into well-born souls which have gone astray for a moment. All the members of the Royalist and Catholic party followed the funeral procession with triumphant enthusiasm, speaking of that beautiful death after a somewhat restless life."

Viscount Roger ceased speaking, and those around him laughed. Then somebody said: "Bah! That is the story of all conversions *in extremis*."

SAVED

THE LITTLE MARQUISE DE RENNEDON came rushing in like a ball through the window. She began to laugh before she spoke, to laugh till she cried, like she had done a month previously, when she had told her friend that she had betrayed the marquis in order to have her revenge, but only once, just because he was really too stupid and too jealous.

The little Baroness de Grangerie had thrown the book which she was reading onto the sofa and looked at Annette curiously. She was already laughing herself, and at last she asked:

"What have you been doing now?"

"Oh, my dear!—my dear! It is too funny—too funny. Just fancy—I am saved!—saved!—saved!"

"How do you mean, saved?"

"Yes, saved!"

"From what?"

"From my husband, my dear, saved! Delivered! free! free! free!"

"How free? In what?"

"In what? Divorce! yes, a divorce! I have my divorce!"

"You are divorced?"

"No, not yet; how stupid you are! One does not get divorced in three hours! But I have my proofs that he has deceived me—caught in the very act —just think!—in the very act. I have got him tight."

"Oh, do tell me all about it! So he deceived you?"

"Yes, that is to say no—yes and no—I do not know. At any rate I have proofs, and that is the chief thing."

"How did you manage it?"

"How did I manage it? This is how! I have been energetic, very energetic. For the last three months he has been odious, altogether odious, brutal, coarse, a despot—in one word, vile. So I said to myself: This cannot last, I must have a divorce! But how?—for it is not very easy. I tried to make him beat me, but he would not. He vexed me from morning till night, made me go out when I did not wish to and to remain at home when I wanted to dine out; he made my life unbearable for me from one week's end to the other, but he never struck me.

"Then I tried to find out whether he had a mistress. Yes, he had one, but he took a thousand precautions in going to see her, and they could never be caught together. Guess what I did then?"

"I cannot guess."

"Oh! you could never guess. I asked my brother to procure me a photograph of the creature."

"Of your husband's mistress?"

"Yes. It cost Jacques fifteen louis,[1] the price of an evening, from seven o'clock till midnight, including a dinner, at three louis an hour, and he obtained the photograph into the bargain."

"It appears to me that he might have obtained it anyhow by means of some artifice and without—without—without being obliged to take the original at the same time."

"Oh! she is pretty, and Jacques did not mind the least. And then I wanted some details about her, physical details about her figure, her breast, her complexion, a thousand things, in fact."

"I do not understand you."

"You shall see. When I had learned all that I wanted to know I went to a —how shall I put it?—to a man of business—you know—one of those men who transact business of all sorts—agents of—of—of publicity and complicity—one of those men—well, you understand what I mean."

"Pretty nearly, I think. And what did you say to him?"

"I said to him, showing the photograph of Clarisse (her name is Clarisse): 'Monsieur, I want a lady's maid who resembles this photograph. I require one who is pretty, elegant, neat and sharp. I will pay her whatever is necessary, and if it costs me ten thousand francs,[2] so much the worse. I shall not require her for more than three months.'

"The man looked extremely astonished and said: 'Do you require a maid of an irreproachable character, madame?' I blushed and stammered: 'Yes, of course, for honesty.' He continued: 'And—then—as regards morals?' I did not venture to reply, so I only made a sign with my head which signified *No*. Then suddenly I comprehended that he had a horrible suspicion and, losing my presence of mind, I exclaimed: 'Oh! monsieur—it is for my husband, in order that I may surprise him.'

"Then the man began to laugh, and from his looks I gathered that I had regained his esteem. He even thought I was brave, and I would willingly have made a bet that at that moment he was longing to shake hands with me. However, he said to me. 'In a week, madame, I shall have what you require, I will answer for my success, and you shall not pay me until I have succeeded. So this is a photograph of your husband's mistress?'

" 'Yes, monsieur.'

" 'A handsome woman, and not too stout. And what scent?'

"I did not understand and repeated: 'What scent?'

"He smiled: 'Yes, madame, perfume is essential in tempting a man, for

---

[1] $60.

[2] $2000.

it unconsciously brings to his mind certain reminiscences which dispose him to action; the perfume creates an obscure confusion in his mind and disturbs and energizes him by recalling his pleasures to him. You must also try to find out what your husband is in the habit of eating when he dines with his lady, and you might give him the same dishes the day you catch him. Oh! we have got him, madame, we have got him.'

"I went away delighted, for here I had lighted on a very intelligent man.

"Three days later I saw a tall dark girl arrive at my house; she was very handsome, and her looks were modest and bold at the same time, the peculiar look of a female rake. She behaved very properly toward me, and as I did not exactly know what she was I called her mademoiselle, but she said immediately: 'Oh! pray, madame, only call me Rose.' And she began to talk.

"'Well, Rose, you know why you have come here?'

"'I can guess it, madame.'

"'Very good, my girl—and that will not be too much bother for you?'

"'Oh! madame, this will be the eighth divorce that I shall have caused; I am used to it.'

"'Why, that is capital. Will it take you long to succeed?'

"'Oh! madame, that depends entirely on Monsieur's temperament. When I have seen Monsieur for five minutes alone I shall be able to tell you exactly.'

"'You will see him soon, my child, but I must tell you that he is not handsome.'

"'That does not matter to me, madame. I have already separated some very ugly ones. But I must ask you, madame, whether you have discovered his favorite perfume?'

"'Yes, Rose—verbena.'

"'So much the better, madame, for I am also very fond of that scent! Can you also tell me, madame, whether Monsieur's mistress wears silk underclothing and nightdresses?'

"'No, my child, cambric and lace.'

"'Oh! then she is altogether of superior station, for silk underclothing is getting quite common.'

"'What you say is quite true!'

"'Well, madame, I will enter your service.' And so as a matter of fact she did immediately, and as if she had done nothing else all her life.

"An hour later my husband came home. Rose did not even raise her eyes to him, but he raised his eyes to her. She already smelled strongly of verbena. In five minutes she left the room, and he immediately asked me: 'Who is that girl?'

"'Why—my new lady's maid.'

"'Where did you pick her up?'

"'Baroness de Grangerie got her for me with the best references.'

"'Ah! she is rather pretty!'

"'Do you think so?'

"'Why, yes—for a lady's maid.'

"I was delighted, for I felt that he was already biting, and that same evening Rose said to me: 'I can now promise you that it will not take more than a fortnight. Monsieur is very easily caught!'

"'Ah! you have tried already?'

"'No, madame, he only asked what my name was, so that he might hear what my voice was like.'

"'Very well, my dear Rose. Get on as quick as you can.'

"'Do not be alarmed, madame; I shall only resist long enough not to make myself depreciated.'

"At the end of a week my husband scarcely ever went out; I saw him roaming about the house the whole afternoon, and what was most significant in the matter was that he no longer prevented me from going out. And I, I was out of doors nearly the whole day long—in order—in order to leave him at liberty.

"On the ninth day, while Rose was undressing me, she said to me with a timid air: 'It happened this morning, madame.'

"I was rather surprised, or rather overcome even, not at the part itself but at the way in which she told me, and I stammered out: 'And—and—it went off well?'

"'Oh yes, very well, madame. For the last three days he has been pressing me, but I did not wish matters to proceed too quickly. You will tell me when you want us to be caught, madame.'

"'Yes, certainly. Here! Let us say Thursday.'

"'Very well, madame, I shall grant nothing more till then, so as to keep Monsieur on the alert.'

"'You are sure not to fail?'

"'Oh, quite sure, madame. I will excite him, so as to make him be there at the very moment which you may appoint.'

"'Let us say five o'clock then.'

"'Very well, madame, and where?'

"'Well—in my bedroom.'

"'Very good, madame, in your bedroom.'

"You will understand what I did then, my dear. I went and fetched Mamma and Papa first of all and then my uncle d'Orvelin, the president, and Monsieur Raplet, the judge, my husband's friend. I had not told them what I was going to show them, but I made them all go on tiptoe as far as the door of my room. I waited till five o'clock exactly, and oh, how my heart beat! I had made the porter come upstairs as well, so as to have an additional witness! And then—and then at the moment when the clock began to strike I opened the door wide. Ah! ah! ah! Here he was, evidently—it was quite evident, my dear. Oh, what a head! If you had only seen his head! And he turned round, the idiot! Oh! how funny he looked—I laughed, I laughed. And papa was angry and wanted to give my husband a beating. And the porter, a good servant, helped him to dress himself before us—before us.

He buttoned his braces for him—what a joke it was! As for Rose, she was perfect, absolutely perfect. She cried—oh! she cried very well. She is an invaluable girl. If you ever want her, don't forget!

"And here I am. I came immediately to tell you of the affair directly. I am free. Long live divorce!"

And she began to dance in the middle of the drawing room, while the little baroness, who was thoughtful and put out, said:

"Why did you not invite me to see it?"

THE SIGNAL

The little Marchioness de Rennedon was still asleep in her dark and perfumed bedroom.

In her soft, low bed, between sheets of delicate cambric, fine as lace and caressing as a kiss, she was sleeping alone and tranquil, the happy and profound sleep of divorced women.

She was awakened by loud voices in the little blue drawing room, and she recognized her dear friend, the little Baroness de Grangerie, who was disputing with the lady's maid because the latter would not allow her to go into the marchioness's room. So the little marchioness got up, opened the door, drew back the door hangings and showed her head, nothing but her fair head, hidden under a cloud of hair.

"What is the matter with you that you have come so early?" she asked. "It is not nine o'clock yet."

The little baroness, who was very pale, nervous and feverish, replied: "I must speak to you. Something horrible has happened to me."

"Come in, my dear."

She went in; they kissed each other, and the little marchioness got back into her bed, while the lady's maid opened the windows to let in light and air. Then when she had left the room Madame de Rennedon went on: "Well, tell me what it is."

Baroness de Grangerie began to cry, shedding those pretty bright tears which make women more charming. She sobbed out without wiping her eyes, so as not to make them red: "Oh, my dear, what has happened to me is abominable, abominable. I have not slept all night, not a minute; do you hear? Not a minute. Here, just feel my heart how it is beating."

And, taking her friend's hand, she put it on her breast, on that firm, round covering of women's hearts which often suffices men and prevents them from seeking beneath. But her heart was really beating violently.

She continued: "It happened to me yesterday during the day at about four o'clock—or half-past four; I cannot say exactly. You know my apartments, and you know that my little drawing room, where I always sit, looks on to the Rue Saint-Lazare and that I have a mania for sitting at the window to look at the people passing. The neighborhood of the railway station is very gay, so full of motion and lively—just what I like! So yesterday I was sitting in the low chair which I have placed in my window recess; the window was open, and I was not thinking of anything, simply breathing the fresh air. You remember how fine it was yesterday!

"Suddenly I remarked a woman sitting at the window opposite—a woman in red. I was in mauve, you know, my pretty mauve costume. I did not know the woman, a new lodger, who had been there a month, and as it has been raining for a month, I had not yet seen her, but I saw immediately that she was a bad girl. At first I was very much shocked and disgusted that she should be at the window just as I was, and then by degrees it amused me to watch her. She was resting her elbows on the window ledge and looking at the men, and the men looked at her also, all or nearly all. One might have said that they knew of her presence by some means as they got near the house, that they scented her, as dogs scent game, for they suddenly raised their heads and exchanged a swift look with her, a sort of freemason's look. Hers said: 'Will you?' Theirs replied: 'I have no time,' or else: 'Another day,' or else: 'I have not got a sou,' or else: 'Hide yourself, you wretch!'

"You cannot imagine how funny it was to see her carrying on such a piece of work, though after all it is her regular business.

"Occasionally she shut the window suddenly, and I saw a gentleman go in. She had caught him like a fisherman hooks a gudgeon. Then I looked at my watch and I found that they never stopped longer than from twelve to twenty minutes. In the end she really infatuated me, the spider! And then the creature is so ugly.

"I asked myself: 'How does she manage to make herself understood so quickly, so well and so completely? Does she add a sign of the head or a motion of the hands to her looks?' And I took my opera glasses to watch her proceedings. Oh! They were very simple: first of all a glance, then a smile, then a slight sign with the head which meant: 'Are you coming up?' But it was so slight, so vague, so discreet, that it required a great deal of knack to succeed as she did. And I asked myself: 'I wonder if I could do that little movement from below upward, which was at the same time bold and pretty, as well as she does,' for her gesture was very pretty.

"I went and tried it before the looking glass and, my dear, I did it better than she, a great deal better! I was enchanted and resumed my place at the window.

"She caught nobody more then, poor girl, nobody. She certainly had no luck. It must really be very terrible to earn one's bread in that way, terrible and amusing occasionally, for really some of these men one meets in the street are rather nice.

"After that they all came on my side of the road and none on hers; the sun had turned. They came one after the other, young, old, dark, fair, gray, white. I saw some who looked very nice, really very nice, my dear, far better than my husband or than yours—I mean than your late husband, as you have got a divorce. Now you can choose.

"I said to myself: 'If I give them the sign will they understand me, who am a respectable woman?' And I was seized with a mad longing to make that sign to them. I had a longing, a terrible longing; you know, one of those longings which one cannot resist! I have some like that occasionally. How silly such things are, don't you think so? I believe that we women have the souls of monkeys. I have been told (and it was a physician who told me) that the brain of a monkey is very like ours. Of course we must imitate someone or other. We imitate our husbands when we love them during the first months after our marriage, and then our lovers, our female friends, our confessors when they are nice. We assume their ways of thought, their manners of speech, their words, their gestures, everything. It is very foolish.

"However, as for me, when I am much tempted to do a thing I always do it and so I said to myself: 'I will try it once, on one man only, just to see. What can happen to me? Nothing whatever! We shall exchange a smile and that will be all, and I shall deny it most certainly.'

"So I began to make my choice. I wanted someone nice, very nice, and suddenly I saw a tall, fair, very good-looking fellow coming alone. I like fair men, as you know. I looked at him; he looked at me. I smiled; he smiled. I made the movement, oh, so faintly; he replied yes with his head, and there he was, my dear! He came in at the large door of the house.

"You cannot imagine what passed through my mind then! I thought I should go mad. Oh, how frightened I was! Just think, he will speak to the servants! To Joseph, who is devoted to my husband! Joseph would certainly think that I had known that gentleman for a long time.

"What could I do, just tell me? And he would ring in a moment. What could I do, tell me? I thought I would go and meet him and tell him he had made a mistake and beg him to go away. He would have pity on a woman, on a poor woman. So I rushed to the door and opened it just at the moment when he was going to ring the bell, and I stammered out quite stupidly: 'Go away, monsieur, go away; you have made a mistake, a terrible mistake. I took you for one of my friends whom you are very like. Have pity on me, monsieur.'

"But he only began to laugh, my dear, and replied: 'Good morning, my dear, I know all about your little story; you may be sure. You are married and so you want forty francs instead of twenty, and you shall have them, so just show the way.'

"And he pushed me in, closed the door, and as I remained standing before him, horror-struck, he kissed me, put his arm round my waist and made me go back into the drawing room, the door of which had remained open. Then he began to look at everything, like an auctioneer, and continued: 'By Jove, it is very nice in your rooms, very nice. You must be very down on your luck just now to do the window business!'

"Then I began to beg him again. 'Oh, monsieur, go away, please go away! My husband will be coming in soon; it is just his time. I swear that you have made a mistake!' But he answered quite coolly: 'Come, my beauty, I have had enough of this nonsense, and if your husband comes in I will give him five francs to go and have a drink at the café opposite.' And then, seeing

Raoul's photograph on the chimney piece, he asked me: 'Is that your—your husband?'

" 'Yes, that is he.'

" 'He looks like a nice, disagreeable sort of fellow. And who is this? One of your friends?'

"It was your photograph, my dear, you know, the one in ball dress. I did not know any longer what I was saying and I stammered: 'Yes, it is one of my friends.'

" 'She is very nice; you shall introduce me to her.'

"Just then the clock struck five, and Raoul comes home every day at half-past! Suppose he were to come home before the other had gone; just fancy what would have happened! Then—then I completely lost my head—altogether. I thought—I thought—that—that—the best thing would be—to get rid of—of this man—as quickly as possible. The sooner it was over—you understand."

. . . .

The little Marchioness de Rennedon had begun to laugh, to laugh madly, with her head buried in her pillow, so that the whole bed shook, and when she was a little calmer she asked:

"And—and—was he good looking?"

"Yes."

"And yet you complain?"

"But—but—don't you see, my dear, he said—he said—he should come again tomorrow—at the same time—and I—I am terribly frightened. You have no idea how tenacious he is and obstinate. What can I do—tell me—what can I do?"

The little marchioness sat up in bed to reflect, and then she suddenly said: "Have him arrested!"

The little baroness looked stupefied and stammered out: "What do you say? What are you thinking of? Have him arrested? Under what pretext?"

"That is very simple. Go to the commissary of police and say that a gentleman has been following you about for three months, that he had the insolence to go up to your apartments yesterday, that he has threatened you with another visit tomorrow and that you demand the protection of the law, and they will give you two police officers who will arrest him."

"But, my dear, suppose he tells——"

"They will not believe him, you silly thing, if you have told your tale cleverly to the commissary, but they will believe you, who are an irreproachable woman, and in society."

"Oh! I shall never dare to do it."

"You must dare, my dear, or you are lost."

"But think that he will—he will insult me if he is arrested."

"Very well, you will have witnesses, and he will be sentenced."

"Sentenced to what?"

"To pay damages. In such cases one must be pitiless!"

"Ah! Speaking of damages—there is one thing that worries me very much—very much indeed. He left me two twenty-franc pieces on the mantelpiece."
"Two twenty-franc pieces?"
"Yes."
"No more?"
"No."
"That is very little. It would have humiliated me. Well?"
"Well? What am I to do with that money?"

The little marchioness hesitated for a few seconds, and then she replied in a serious voice:

"My dear—you must make—you must make your husband a little present with it. That will be only fair!"

THE DEVIL

THE PEASANT WAS STANDING OPPOSITE the doctor, by the bedside of the dying old woman, and she, calmly resigned and quite lucid, looked at them and listened to their talking. She was going to die and she did not rebel at it, for her life was over—she was ninety-two.

The July sun streamed in at the window and through the open door and cast its hot flames onto the uneven brown clay floor which had been stamped down by four generations of clodhoppers. The smell of the fields came in also, driven by the brisk wind and parched by the noontide heat. The grasshoppers chirped themselves hoarse, filling the air with their shrill noise, like that of the wooden crickets which are sold to children at fair time.

The doctor raised his voice and said: "Honoré, you cannot leave your mother in this state; she may die at any moment." And the peasant, in great distress, replied: "But I must get in my wheat, for it has been lying on the ground a long time, and the weather is just right for it; what do you say about it, Mother?" And the dying woman, still possessed by her Norman avariciousness, replied yes with her eyes and her forehead and so urged her son to get in his wheat and to leave her to die alone. But the doctor got angry and, stamping his foot, he said: "You are no better than a brute; do you hear? And I will not allow you to do it. Do you understand? And if you must get in your wheat today, go and fetch Rapet's wife and make her look after your mother. I *will* have it. And if you do not obey me I will let you die like a dog when you are ill in your turn; do you hear me?"

The peasant, a tall thin fellow with slow movements who was tormented by indecision, by his fear of the doctor and his keen love for saving, hesitated, calculated and stammered out: "How much does La Rapet charge for attending sick people?"

"How should I know?" the doctor cried. "That depends upon how long she is wanted for. Settle it with her, by Jove! But I want her to be here within an hour; do you hear?"

THE DEVIL

So the man made up his mind. "I will go for her," he replied; "don't get angry, Doctor." And the latter left, calling out as he went: "Take care, you know, for I do not joke when I am angry!" And as soon as they were alone the peasant turned to his mother and said in a resigned voice: "I will go and fetch La Rapet, as the man will have it. Don't go off while I am away."

And he went out in his turn.

La Rapet, who was an old washerwoman, watched the dead and the dying of the neighborhood, and then as soon as she had sewn her customers into that linen cloth from which they would emerge no more, she went and took up her irons to smooth the linen of the living. Wrinkled like a last year's apple, spiteful, envious, avaricious with a phenomenal avarice, bent double, as if she had been broken in half across the loins by the constant movement of the iron over the linen, one might have said that she had a kind of monstrous and cynical affection for a death struggle. She never spoke of anything but of the people she had seen die, of the various kinds of deaths at which she had been present, and she related, with the greatest minuteness, details which were always the same, just like a sportsman talks of his shots.

When Honoré Bontemps entered her cottage he found her preparing the starch for the collars of the village women, and he said: "Good evening; I hope you are pretty well, Mother Rapet."

She turned her head round to look at him and said: "Fairly well, fairly well, and you?"

"Oh, as for me, I am as well as I could wish, but my mother is very sick."

"Your mother?"

"Yes, my mother!"

"What's the matter with her?"

"She is going to turn up her toes; that's what's the matter with her!"

The old woman took her hands out of the water and asked with sudden sympathy: "Is she as bad as all that?"

"The doctor says she will not last till morning."

"Then she certainly is very bad!" Honoré hesitated, for he wanted to make a few preliminary remarks before coming to his proposal, but as he could hit upon nothing, he made up his mind suddenly.

"How much are you going to ask to stop with her till the end? You know that I am not rich, and I cannot even afford to keep a servant girl. It is just that which has brought my poor mother to this state, too much work and fatigue! She used to work for ten, in spite of her ninety-two years. You don't find any made of that stuff nowadays!"

La Rapet answered gravely: "There are two prices: forty sous by day and three francs by night for the rich, and twenty sous by day and forty by night for the others. You shall pay me the twenty and forty." But the peasant reflected, for he knew his mother well. He knew how tenacious of life, how vigorous and unyielding she was. He knew, too, that she might last another week, in spite of the doctor's opinion, and so he said resolutely: "No, I would rather you would fix a price until the end. I will take my chance one way or the other. The doctor says she will die very soon. If that happens, so much the better for you and so much the worse for me, but if she holds out till tomorrow or longer, so much the better for me and so much the worse for you!"

The nurse looked at the man in astonishment, for she had never treated a death as a speculative job, and she hesitated, tempted by the idea of the possible gain. But almost immediately she suspected that he wanted to juggle her. "I can say nothing until I have seen your mother," she replied.

"Then come with me and see her."

She washed her hands and went with him immediately. They did not speak on the road; she walked with short, hasty steps, while he strode on with his long legs, as if he were crossing a brook at every step. The cows lying down in the fields, overcome by the heat, raised their heads heavily and lowed feebly at the two passers-by, as if to ask them for some green grass.

When they got near the house Honoré Bontemps murmured: "Suppose it is all over?" And the unconscious wish that it might be so showed itself in the sound of his voice.

But the old woman was not dead. She was lying on her back on her wretched bed, her hands covered with a pink cotton counterpane, horribly thin, knotty paws, like some strange animal's or like crabs' claws, hands closed by rheumatism, fatigue and the work of nearly a century which she had accomplished.

La Rapet went up to the bed and looked at the dying woman, felt her pulse, tapped her on the chest, listened to her breathing and asked her questions so as to hear her speak; then, having looked at her for some time longer, she went out of the room, followed by Honoré. His decided opinion was that the old woman would not last out the night, and he asked: "Well?" And the sick nurse replied: "Well, she may last two days, perhaps three. You will have to give me six francs, everything included."

"Six francs! Six francs!" he shouted. "Are you out of your mind? I tell you that she cannot last more than five or six hours!" And they disputed angrily for some time, but as the nurse said she would go home as the time was slipping away, and as his wheat would not come to the farmyard of its own accord, he agreed to her terms at last.

"Very well then, that is settled; six francs, including everything, until the corpse is taken out."

"That is settled, six francs."

And he went away with long strides to the wheat which was lying on the ground under the hot sun which ripens the grain, while the sick nurse returned to the house.

She had brought some work with her, for she worked without stopping by the side of the dead and dying, sometimes for herself, sometimes for the family who employed her as seamstress also, paying her rather more in that capacity. Suddenly she asked:

"Have you received the last sacrament, Mother Bontemps?"

The old peasant woman said no with her head, and La Rapet, who was very devout, got up quickly. "Good heavens, is it possible? I will go and fetch the curé," and she rushed off to the parsonage so quickly that the urchins in the street thought some accident had happened when they saw her trotting off like that.

The priest came immediately in his surplice, preceded by a choirboy, who rang a bell to announce the passage of the Host through the parched and quiet country. Some men, working at a distance, took off their large hats and remained motionless until the white vestment had disappeared behind some farm buildings; the women who were making up the sheaves stood up to make the sign of the cross; the frightened black hens ran away along the ditch until they reached a well-known hole through which they suddenly disappeared, while a foal, which was tied up in a meadow, took fright at the sight of the surplice and began to gallop round at the length of its rope, kicking violently. The choirboy, in his red cassock, walked quickly, and the priest, the square biretta on his bowed head, followed him, muttering some prayers. Last of all came La Rapet, bent almost double, as if she wished to prostrate herself; she walked with folded hands, as if she were in church.

Honoré saw them pass in the distance, and he asked: "Where is our priest going to?" And his man, who was more acute, replied: "He is taking the sacrament to your mother, of course!"

The peasant was not surprised and said: "That is quite possible," and went on with his work.

Mother Bontemps confessed, received absolution and extreme unction, and the priest took his departure, leaving the two women alone in the suffocating cottage. La Rapet began to look at the dying woman and to ask herself whether it could last much longer.

The day was on the wane, and a cooler air came in stronger puffs, making a view of Epinal, which was fastened to the wall by two pins, flap up and down. The scanty window curtains, which had formerly been white but were now yellow and covered with flyspecks, looked as if they were going to fly off and seemed to struggle to get away, like the old woman's soul.

Lying motionless, with her eyes open, the old mother seemed to await the death which was so near and which yet delayed its coming, with perfect indifference. Her short breath whistled in her throat. It would stop altogether soon, and there would be one woman less in the world, one whom nobody would regret.

At nightfall Honoré returned, and when he went up to the bed and saw that his mother was still alive he asked: "How is she?" just as he had done formerly when she had been sick. Then he sent La Rapet away, saying to her: "Tomorrow morning at five o'clock without fail." And she replied: "Tomorrow at five o'clock."

She came at daybreak and found Honoré eating his soup, which he had made himself, before going to work.

"Well, is your mother dead?" asked the nurse.

"She is rather better, on the contrary," he replied with a malignant look out of the corners of his eyes. Then he went out.

La Rapet was seized with anxiety and went up to the dying woman, who was in the same state, lethargic and impassive, her eyes open and her hands clutching the counterpane. The nurse perceived that this might go on thus for two days, four days, eight days, even, and her avaricious mind was seized with fear. She was excited to fury against the cunning fellow who had tricked her and against the woman who would not die.

Nevertheless, she began to sew and waited with her eyes fixed on the wrinkled face of Mother Bontemps. When Honoré returned to breakfast he seemed quite satisfied and even in a bantering humor, for he was carrying in his wheat under very favorable circumstances.

La Rapet was getting exasperated; every passing minute now seemed to her so much time and money stolen from her. She felt a mad inclination to choke this old ass, this headstrong old fool, this obstinate old wretch—to stop that short, rapid breath, which was robbing her of her time and money, by squeezing her throat a little. But then she reflected on the danger of doing so, and other thoughts came into her head, so she went up to the bed and said to her: "Have you ever seen the devil?"

Mother Bontemps whispered: "No."

Then the sick nurse began to talk and to tell her tales likely to terrify her weak and dying mind. "Some minutes before one dies the devil appears," she said, "to all. He has a broom in his hand, a saucepan on his head, and he utters loud cries. When anybody has seen him all is over, and that person has only a few moments longer to live"; and she enumerated all those to whom the devil had appeared that year: Josephine Loisel, Eulalie Ratier, Sophie Padagnau, Séraphine Grospied.

Mother Bontemps, who was at last most disturbed in mind, moved about, wrung her hands and tried to turn her head to look at the other end of the room. Suddenly La Rapet disappeared at the foot of the bed. She took a sheet out of the cupboard and wrapped herself up in it; then she put the iron pot onto her head so that its three short, bent feet rose up like horns, took a broom in her right hand and a tin pail in her left, which she threw up suddenly so that it might fall to the ground noisily.

Certainly when it came down it made a terrible noise. Then, climbing onto a chair, the nurse showed herself, gesticulating and uttering shrill cries into the pot which covered her face, while she menaced the old peasant woman, who was nearly dead, with her broom.

Terrified, with a mad look on her face, the dying woman made a superhuman effort to get up and escape; she even got her shoulders and chest out of bed; then she fell back with a deep sigh. All was over, and La Rapet calmly put everything back into its place; the broom into the corner by the cupboard, the sheet inside it, the pot onto the hearth, the pail onto the floor and the chair against the wall. Then with a professional air she closed the dead woman's enormous eyes, put a plate on the bed and poured some holy water into it, dipped the twig of boxwood into it and, kneeling down, she fervently repeated the prayers for the dead, which she knew by heart, as a matter of business.

When Honoré returned in the evening, he found her praying. He calculated immediately that she had made twenty sous out of him, for she had only spent three days and one night there, which made five francs altogether, instead of the six which he owed her.

THE VENUS OF BRANIZA

SOME YEARS AGO there lived in Braniza a celebrated Talmudist, renowned no less on account of his beautiful wife than for his wisdom, his learning and his fear of God. The Venus of Braniza deserved that name thoroughly; she deserved it for herself on account of her singular beauty, and even more as the wife of a man deeply versed in the Talmud, for the wives of the Jewish philosophers are, as a rule, ugly or possess some bodily defect.

The Talmud explains this in the following manner: It is well known that marriages are made in heaven, and at the birth of a boy a divine voice calls out the name of his future wife and vice versa. But just as a good father tries to get rid of his good wares out of doors and only uses the damaged stuff at home for his children, so God bestows on the Talmudists those women whom other men would not care to have.

Well, God made an exception in the case of our Talmudist and had bestowed a Venus on him, perhaps only in order to confirm the rule by means of this exception and to make it appear less hard. This philosopher's wife was a woman who would have done honor to any king's throne or to a pedestal in any sculpture gallery. Tall, and with a wonderfully voluptuous figure, she carried a strikingly beautiful head, surrounded by thick black plaits, on her proud shoulders. Two large dark eyes languished and glowed beneath long lashes, and her beautiful hands looked as if they were carved out of ivory.

This glorious woman, who seemed to have been designed by nature to rule, to see slaves at her feet, to provide occupation for the painter's brush, the sculptor's chisel and the poet's pen, lived the life of a rare and beautiful flower shut up in a hothouse. She would sit the whole day long wrapped up in her costly furs, looking down dreamily into the street.

She had no children; her husband, the philosopher, studied and prayed and studied again from early morning until late at night; his mistress was the "Veiled Beauty," as the Talmudists call the Kabbalah. She paid no attention to her house for she was rich, and everything went of its own accord, like a clock which has only to be wound up once a week; nobody came to see her, and she never went out of the house; she sat and dreamed and brooded and—yawned.

.   .   .   .

One day when a terrible storm of thunder and lightning had spent its fury over the town and all windows had been opened in order to let the Messias in, the Jewish Venus was sitting as usual in her comfortable easy chair, shivering in spite of her furs and thinking. Suddenly she fixed her glowing eyes on her husband who was sitting before the Talmud, swaying his body backward and forward, and said suddenly:

"Just tell me, when will Messias, the son of David, come?"

"He will come," the philosopher replied, "when all the Jews have become either altogether virtuous or altogether vicious, says the Talmud."

"Do you believe that all the Jews will ever become virtuous?" the Venus continued.

"How am I to believe that?"

"So Messias will come when all the Jews have become vicious?"

The philosopher shrugged his shoulders and lost himself again in the labyrinth of the Talmud out of which, so it is said, only one man returned in perfect sanity. The beautiful woman at the window again looked dreamily out into the heavy rain, while her white fingers played unconsciously with the dark furs of her splendid robe.

.   .   .   .

One day the Jewish philosopher had gone to a neighboring town, where an important question of ritual was to be decided. Thanks to his learning, the question was settled sooner than he had expected, and instead of returning the next morning, as he had intended, he came back the same evening with a friend who was no less learned than himself. He got out of the carriage at his friend's house and went home on foot. He was not a little surprised when he saw his windows brilliantly illuminated and found an officer's servant comfortably smoking his pipe in front of his house.

"What are you doing here?" he asked in a friendly manner but with some curiosity, nevertheless.

"I am on guard lest the husband of the beautiful Jewess should come home unexpectedly."

"Indeed? Well, mind and keep a good lookout."

Saying this, the philosopher pretended to go away but went into the house through the garden entrance at the back. When he got into the first room he found a table laid for two, which had evidently only been left a short time previously. His wife was sitting as usual at her bedroom window, wrapped in her furs, but her cheeks were suspiciously red, and her dark eyes had not their usual languishing look but now rested on her husband with a gaze which expressed at the same time satisfaction and mockery. At that moment his foot stuck against an object on the floor which gave out a strange sound. He picked it up and examined it in the light. It was a pair of spurs.

"Who has been here with you?" asked the Talmudist.

The Jewish Venus shrugged her shoulders contemptuously but did not reply.

"Shall I tell you? The captain of hussars has been with you."

"And why should he not have been here with me?" she said, smoothing the fur on her jacket with her white hand.

"Woman! are you out of your mind?"

"I am in full possession of my senses," she replied, and a knowing smile hovered round her red voluptuous lips. "But must I not also do my part in order that Messias may come and redeem us poor Jews?"

THE RABBIT

OLD LECACHEUR appeared at the door of his house at his usual hour, between five and a quarter past five in the morning, to look after his men who were going to work.

With a red face, only half awake, his right eye open and the left nearly closed, he was buttoning his braces over his fat stomach with some difficulty, all the time looking into every corner of the farmyard with a searching glance. The sun was darting his oblique rays through the beech trees by the side of the ditch and the apple trees outside, making the cocks crow on the dunghill and the pigeons coo on the roof. The smell of the cow stalls came through the open door, mingling in the fresh morning air with the pungent odor of the stable where the horses were neighing, with their heads turned toward the light.

As soon as his trousers were properly fastened Lecacheur came out and went first of all toward the hen house to count the morning's eggs, for he had been suspecting thefts for some time. But the servant girl ran up to him with lifted arms and cried:

"Master! Master! They have stolen a rabbit during the night."

"A rabbit?"

"Yes, master, the big gray rabbit, from the hutch on the left." Whereupon the farmer quite opened his left eye and said simply:

"I must see that."

And off he went to inspect it. The hutch had been broken open and the rabbit was gone. Then he became thoughtful, closed his left eye again, scratched his nose and after a little consideration said to the frightened girl who was standing stupidly before him:

"Go and fetch the gendarmes; say I expect them as soon as possible."

Lecacheur was mayor of the village, Pairgry-le Gras, and ruled it like a tyrant on account of his money and position. As soon as the servant had disappeared in the direction of the village, which was only about five hundred yards off, he went into the house to have his morning coffee and to discuss the matter with his wife. He found her on her knees in front of the fire, trying to get it to burn up quickly. As soon as he got to the door he said:

"Somebody has stolen the gray rabbit."

She turned round so quickly that she found herself sitting on the floor and, looking at her husband with distressed eyes, she said:

"What is it, Cacheux! Somebody has stolen a rabbit?"

"The big gray one."

She sighed. "How sad! Who can have done it?"

She was a little, thin, active, neat woman, who knew all about farming. But Lecacheur had his own ideas about the matter.

"It must be that fellow Polyte."

His wife got up suddenly and said in a furious voice:

"He did it! He did it! You need not look for anyone else. He did it! You have said it, Cacheux!"

All her peasant's fury, all her avarice, all the rage of a saving woman against the man of whom she had always been suspicious and against the girl whom she had always suspected, could be seen in the contraction of her mouth, in the wrinkles in her cheeks and in the forehead of her thin, exasperated face.

"And what have you done?" she asked.

"I have sent for the gendarmes."

This Polyte was a laborer who had been employed on the farm for a few days and had been dismissed by Lecacheur for an insolent answer. He was an old soldier and was supposed to have retained his habits of marauding and debauchery from his campaigns in Africa. He did anything for a livelihood, but whether working as a mason, a navvy, a reaper, whether he broke stones or lopped trees, he was always lazy. So he remained in no position long and had, at times, to change his neighborhood to obtain work.

From the first day that he came to the farm Lecacheur's wife had detested him, and now she was sure that he had committed the robbery.

In about half an hour the two gendarmes arrived. Brigadier Sénateur was very tall and thin, and Gendarme Lenient, short and fat. Lecacheur made them sit down and told them the affair, and then they went and saw the scene of the theft, in order to verify the fact that the hutch had been broken open and to collect all the proofs they could. When they got back to the kitchen the mistress brought in some wine, filled their glasses and asked with a distrustful look:

"Shall you catch him?"

The brigadier, who had his sword between his legs, appeared thoughtful. Certainly he was sure of taking him if he was pointed out to him, but if not, he could not himself answer for being able to discover him. After reflecting for a long time he put this simple question:

"Do you know the thief?"

And Lecacheur replied with a look of Normandy slyness in his eyes:

"As for knowing him, I do not, as I did not see him commit the robbery. If I had seen him I should have made him eat it raw, skin and flesh, without a drop of cider to wash it down. As for saying who it is, I cannot, although I believe it is that good-for-nothing Polyte."

Then he related at length his troubles with Polyte, his leaving his service, his bad reputation, things which had been told him, accumulating insignificant and minute proofs. Then the brigadier, who had been listening very attentively while he emptied his glass and filled it again, turned to his gendarme with an indifferent air and said:

"We must go and look in the cottage of Severin's wife." At which the gendarme smiled and nodded three times.

Then Mme Lecacheur came to them and very quietly, with all a peasant's cunning, questioned the brigadier in her turn. The shepherd Severin, a simpleton, a sort of brute who had been brought up from youth among his bleating flocks and who knew of scarcely anything besides them in the world, had nevertheless preserved the peasant's instinct for saving at the bottom of his heart. For years and years he had hidden in hollow trees and crevices in the rocks all that he earned, either as shepherd or by curing the fractures of animals (for the bonesetter's secret had been handed down to him by the old shepherd whose place he took) by touch or advice, for one day he bought a small property consisting of a cottage and a field for three thousand francs.

A few months later it became known that he was going to marry a servant notorious for her bad morals, the innkeeper's servant. The young fellows said that the girl, knowing that he was pretty well off, had been to his cottage every night and had taken him, bewitched him, led him on to matrimony little by little, night by night.

And then, having been to the mayor's office and to church, she lived in the house which her man had bought, while he continued to tend his flocks day and night on the plains.

And the brigadier added:

"Polyte has been sleeping with her for three weeks, for the thief has no place of his own to go to!"

The gendarme made a little joke:

"He takes the shepherd's blankets."

Mme Lecacheur, seized by a fresh access of rage, of rage increased by a married woman's anger against debauchery, exclaimed:

"It is she, I am sure. Go there. Ah! The blackguard thieves!"

But the brigadier was quite unmoved.

"A minute," he said. "Let us wait until twelve o'clock; as Polyte goes and dines there every day, I shall catch them with it under their noses."

The gendarme smiled, pleased at his chief's idea, and Lecacheur also smiled now, for the affair of the shepherd struck him as very funny: deceived husbands are always amusing.

.   .   .   .

Twelve o'clock had just struck when the brigadier, followed by his man, knocked gently three times at the door of a small, lonely house situated at the corner of a wood, some five hundred yards from the village.

They stood close against the wall so as not to be seen from within and waited. As nobody answered, the brigadier knocked again in a minute or two. It was so quiet that the house seemed uninhabited, but Lenient, the gendarme, who had very quick ears, said that he heard somebody moving about inside. Sénateur got angry. He would not allow anyone to resist the authority of the law for a moment and, knocking at the door with the hilt of his sword, he cried out:

"Open the door in the name of the law."

As this order had no effect, he roared out:

"If you do not obey I shall smash the lock. I am the brigadier of the gendarmery, by God! Here, Lenient."

He had not finished speaking when the door opened and Sénateur saw before him a fat girl with a very red color, blowzy, with pendent breasts, big stomach and broad hips, a sort of sanguine and sensual female, the wife of the shepherd Severin. He entered the cottage.

"I have come to pay you a visit, as I want to make a little search," he said, and he looked about him. On the table there was a plate, a jug of cider and a glass half full, which proved that a meal had been going on. Two knives were lying side by side, and the shrewd gendarme winked at his superior officer.

"It smells good," the latter said.

"One might swear that it was stewed rabbit," Lenient added, much amused.

"Will you have a glass of brandy?" the peasant woman asked.

"No, thank you; I only want the skin of the rabbit that you are eating."

She pretended not to understand, but she was trembling.

"What rabbit?"

The brigadier had taken a seat and was calmly wiping his forehead.

"Come, come, you are not going to try and make us believe that you live on couch grass. What were you eating there all by yourself for your dinner?"

"I? Nothing whatever, I swear to you. A mite of butter on my bread."

"You are a novice, my good woman—*a mite of butter on your bread*. You are mistaken; you ought to have said: a mite of butter on the rabbit. By God, your butter smells good! It is special butter, extra-good butter, butter fit for a wedding, certainly not household butter!"

The gendarme was shaking with laughter and repeated:

"Not household butter, certainly."

As Brigadier Sénateur was a joker, all the gendarmes had grown facetious, and the officer continued:

"Where is your butter?"

"My butter?"

"Yes, your butter."

"In the jar."

"Then where is the butter jar?"

"Here it is."

She brought out an old cup, at the bottom of which there was a layer of rancid salt butter. The brigadier smelled it and said with a shake of his head:

"It is not the same. I want the butter that smells of the rabbit. Come, Lenient, open your eyes; look under the sideboard, my good fellow, and I will look under the bed."

Having shut the door, he went up to the bed and tried to move it, but it was fixed to the wall and had not been moved for more than half a century, apparently. Then the brigadier stooped and made his uniform crack. A button had flown off.

"Lenient," he said.

"Yes, Brigadier?"

"Come here, my lad, and look under the bed; I am too tall. I will look after the sideboard."

He got up and waited while his man executed his orders.

Lenient, who was short and stout, took off his kepi, laid himself on his stomach and, putting his face on the floor, looked at the black cavity under the bed. Then suddenly he exclaimed:

"All right, here we are!"

"What have you got? The rabbit?"

"No, the thief."

"The thief! Pull him out, pull him out!"

The gendarme had put his arms under the bed and laid hold of something. He pulled with all his might, and at last a foot shod in a thick boot appeared, which he was holding in his right hand. The brigadier grabbed it, crying:

"Pull, pull!"

And Lenient, who was on his knees by that time, was pulling at the other leg. But it was a hard job, for the prisoner kicked out hard and arched up his back across the bed.

"Courage! Courage! Pull! Pull!" Sénateur cried, and they pulled with all their strength—so hard that the wooden bar gave way and the victim came out as far as his head. At last they got that out also and saw the terrified and furious face of Polyte, whose arms remained stretched out under the bed.

"Pull away!" the brigadier kept on exclaiming. Then they heard a strange noise as the arms followed the shoulders and the hands the arms. In the hands was the handle of a saucepan and at the end of the handle the pan itself, which contained stewed rabbit.

"Good lord! Good lord!" the brigadier shouted in his delight, while Lenient took charge of the man. The rabbit's skin, an overwhelming proof, was discovered under the mattress, and the gendarmes returned in triumph to the village with their prisoner and their booty.

.   .   .   .

A week later, as the affair had made much stir, Lecacheur, on going into the *mairie* to consult the schoolmaster, was told that the shepherd Severin had been waiting for him for more than an hour. He found him sitting on a chair in a corner with his stick between his legs. When he saw the mayor he got up, took off his cap and said:

"Good morning, Maître Cacheux," and then he remained standing, timid and embarrassed.

"What do you want?" the former said.

"This is it, monsieur. Is it true that somebody stole one of your rabbits last week?"

"Yes, it is quite true, Severin."

"Who stole the rabbit?"

"Polyte Ancas, the laborer."

"Right! Right! And is it also true that it was found under my bed?"

"What do you mean, the rabbit?"

"The rabbit and then Polyte."

"Yes, my poor Severin, quite true, but who told you?"

"Pretty well everybody. I understand! And I suppose you know all about marriages, as you marry[1] people?"

"What about marriage?"

"With regard to one's rights."

"What rights?"

"The husband's rights and then the wife's rights."

"Of course I do."

"Oh! Then just tell me, M'sieu Cacheux, has my wife the right to go to bed with Polyte?"

"What do you mean by going to bed with Polyte?"

"Yes, has she any right before the law, and seeing that she is my wife, to go to bed with Polyte?"

"Why, of course not, of course not."

"If I catch him there again shall I have the right to thrash him and her also?"

"Why—why—why, yes."

"Very well, then; I will tell you why I want to know. One night last week, as I had my suspicions, I came in suddenly, and they were not behaving properly. I chucked Polyte out to go and sleep somewhere else, but that was all, as I did not know what my rights were. This time I did not see them; I only heard of it from others. That is over, and we will not say any more about it; but if I catch them again—by God! if I catch them again—I will make them lose all taste for such nonsense, Maître Cacheux, as sure as my name is Severin."

LA MORILLONNE

They called her "La Morillonne,"[1] not only on account of her black hair and of a complexion which resembled autumnal leaves, but because of her thick purple lips which were like blackberries when she curled them.

That she should be as dark as this in a district where everybody was fair and born of parents who had tow-colored hair and butterlike complexions was one of the mysteries of atavism. A female ancestor must have had intimacy with one of those traveling tinkers who have gone about the country from time immemorial with faces the color of bister and indigo, crowned by a wisp of light hair.

From that ancestor she derived not only her dark complexion, but also her dark soul and her deceitful eyes, whose depths were at times illuminated by flashes of every vice, the eyes of an obstinate and malicious animal.

[1] In France the civil marriage is compulsory.
[1] A sort of black grape.—Editor.

Handsome? Certainly not, or even pretty. Ugly, with an absolute ugliness! Such a false look! Her nose was flat, having been smashed by a blow, while her unwholesome-looking mouth was always slobbering with greediness or uttering something vile. Her hair was thick and untidy, a regular nest for vermin, and she had a thin, feverish body, with a limping walk. In short, she was a perfect monster, and yet all the young men of the neighborhood had made love to her, and whoever had been so honored longed for her society again.

From the time that she was twelve she had been the mistress of every fellow in the village. She had corrupted boys of her own age in every conceivable manner and place.

Young men at the risk of imprisonment and even steady, old, notable and venerable men, such as the farmer at Eclausiaux, M. Martin, the ex-mayor, and other highly respectable citizens, had been taken by the manners of that slut. The reason why the rural policeman was not severe upon them, in spite of his love for summoning people before the magistrates, was, so people said, that he would have been obliged to take out a summons against himself.

The consequence was that she had grown up without being interfered with and was the mistress of every fellow in the village, as said the schoolmaster, who had himself been one of *the fellows*. But the most curious part of the business was that no one was jealous. They handed her on from one to the other, and when someone expressed his astonishment at this to her one day she said to this unintelligent stranger:

"Is everybody not satisfied?"

And then how could any of them, even if he had been jealous, have monopolized her? They had no hold on her. She was not selfish, and though she accepted all gifts, whether in kind or in money, she never asked for anything and she even appeared to prefer paying herself after her own fashion, by stealing. All she seemed to care about as her reward was pilfering, and a crown put into her hand gave her less pleasure than a halfpenny which she had stolen. Neither was it any use to dream of ruling her, of being the sole male or proud master of the hen roost, for none of them, no matter how broad shouldered he was, would have been capable of it. Some had tried to vanquish her but in vain.

How then could any of them claim to be her master? It would have been the same as wishing to have the sole right of baking bread in the common oven in which the whole village baked.

But there was one exception, and that was Bru, the shepherd.

He lived in the fields in a movable hut, feeding on cakes made of unleavened dough which he kneaded on a stone and baked in the hot ashes, now here, now there, in a hole dug out in the ground and heated with dead wood. Potatoes, milk, hard cheese, blackberries and a small cask of old gin distilled by himself were his daily food. He knew nothing about love, although he was accused of all sorts of horrible things. But nobody dared abuse him to his face; in the first place, because Bru was a spare and sinewy man, who handled his shepherd's crook like a drum major does his staff; secondly, because of his three sheep dogs who had teeth like wolves and obeyed nobody but their master, and lastly, for fear of the evil eye. For Bru, it appeared, knew spells which would blight the corn, give the sheep foot rot, cattle the rinderpest, make cows die in calving and set fire to the ricks and stacks.

But as Bru was the only one who did not thirst after La Morillonne, naturally one day she began to think of him and declared that she, at any rate, was not afraid of his evil eye. So she went after him.

"What do you want?" he said, and she replied boldly:

"What do I want? I want you."

"Very well," he said, "but then you must belong to me alone."

"All right," was her answer, "if you think you can please me."

He smiled and took her into his arms, and she was away from the village for a whole week. She had, in fact, become Bru's exclusive property.

The village grew excited. They were not jealous of one another but they were of him. What! Could she not resist him? Of course he had charms and spells against every imaginable thing. Then they grew furious; next they grew bold and watched from behind a tree. She was still as lively as ever, but he, poor fellow, seemed to have suddenly fallen ill and required nursing at her hands. The villagers, however, felt no compassion for the poor shepherd, and one of them, more courageous than the rest, advanced toward the hut with his gun in his hand.

"Tie up your dogs," he cried out from a distance; "fasten them up, Bru, or I shall shoot them."

"You need not be frightened of the dogs," La Morillonne replied; "I will be answerable for it that they will not hurt you," and she smiled as the young man with the gun went toward her.

"What do you want?" the shepherd said.

"I can tell you," she replied. "He wants me and I am very willing. There!"

Bru began to cry, and she continued:

"You are a good-for-nothing."

And she went off with the lad. Bru seized his crook, seeing which the young fellow raised his gun.

"Seize him! Seize him!" the shepherd shouted, urging on his dogs, while the other had already got his finger on the trigger to fire at them. But La Morillonne pushed down the muzzle and called out:

"Here, dogs! Here! Prr, prr, my beauties!"

And the three dogs rushed up to her, licked her hands and frisked about as they followed her, while she called to the shepherd from the distance:

"You see, Bru, they are not at all jealous!"

And then with a short and evil laugh she added:

"They are my property now."

EPIPHANY

"Ah!" said Captain the Count de Garens, "I should rather think that I do remember that Epiphany supper during the war!

"At the time I was quartermaster of cavalry, and for a fortnight I had been lurking about as a scout in front of the German advance guard. The evening before we had cut down a few Uhlans and had lost three men, one of whom was that poor little Raudeville. You remember Joseph de Raudeville well, of course.

"Well, on that day my captain ordered me to take six troopers and occupy the village of Porterin, where there had been five fights in three weeks, and to hold it all night. There were not twenty houses left standing, nay, not a dozen, in that wasps' nest. So I took ten troopers and set out at about four o'clock; at five o'clock, while it was still pitch dark, we reached the first houses of Porterin. I halted and ordered Marchas—you know Pierre de Marchas who afterward married little Martel-Auvelin, the daughter of the Marquis de Martel-Auvelin—to go alone into the village and to report to me what he saw.

"I had chosen nothing but volunteers and all of good family. When on service it is pleasant not to be forced into intimacy with unpleasant fellows. This Marchas was as sharp as possible, as cunning as a fox and as supple as a serpent. He could scent the Prussians as well as a dog can scent a hare, could find victuals where we should have died of hunger without him and could obtain information from everybody—information which was always reliable—with incredible cleverness.

"In ten minutes he returned. 'All right,' he said; 'there have been no Prussians here for three days. It is a sinister place, is this village. I have been talking to a Sister of Mercy, who is attending to four or five wounded men in an abandoned convent.'

"I ordered them to ride on, and we penetrated into the principal street. On the right and left we could vaguely see roofless walls, hardly visible in the profound darkness. Here and there a light was burning in a room; some family had remained to keep its house standing as long as they were able, a family of brave, or of poor, people. The rain began to fall, a fine, icy-cold rain, which froze us before it wetted us through by merely touching our cloaks. The horses stumbled against stones, against beams, against furniture. Marchas guided us, going before us on foot and leading his horse by the bridle.

"'Where are you taking us to?' I asked him. And he replied: 'I have a place for us to lodge in, and a rare good one.' And soon we stopped before a small house, evidently belonging to some person of the middle class, completely shut up, built onto the street with a garden in the rear.

"Marchas broke open the lock by means of a big stone which he picked up near the garden gate; then he mounted the steps, smashed in the front door with his feet and shoulders, lighted a bit of wax candle, which he was never without, and preceded us into the comfortable apartments of some rich, private individual, guiding us with admirable assurance, just as if he had lived in this house which he now saw for the first time.

"Two troopers remained outside to take care of our horses; then Marchas said to stout Ponderel, who followed him: 'The stables must be on the left; I saw that as we came in; go and put the animals up there, for we do not want them,' and then, turning to me, he said: 'Give your orders, confound it all!'

"Marchas always astonished me, and I replied with a laugh: 'I shall post my sentinels at the country approaches and I will return to you here.'

"'How many men are you going to take?'

"'Five. The others will relieve them at five o'clock in the evening.'

"'Very well. Leave me four to look after provisions, to do the cooking and to set the table. I will go and find out where the wine is hidden away.'

"I went off to reconnoiter the deserted streets, until they ended in the open country, so as to post my sentries there.

"Half an hour later I was back and found Marchas lounging in a great armchair, the covering of which he had taken off, from love of luxury, as he said. He was warming his feet at the fire and smoking an excellent cigar, whose perfume filled the room. He was alone, his elbows resting on the arms of the chair, his cheeks flushed, his eyes bright, and looking delighted.

"I heard the noise of plates and dishes in the next room, and Marchas said to me, smiling in a beatific manner: 'This is famous; I found the champagne under the flight of steps outside, the brandy—fifty bottles of the very finest—in the kitchen garden under a pear tree which did not look to me to be quite straight when I looked at it by the light of my lantern. As for solids, we have two fowls, a goose, a duck and three pigeons. They are being cooked at this moment. It is a delightful part of the country.'

"I had sat down opposite to him, and the fire in the grate was burning my nose and cheeks.

"'Where did you find this wood?' I asked.

"'Splendid wood,' he replied. 'The owner's carriage. It is the paint which is causing all this flame, an essence of alcohol and varnish. A capital house!'

"I laughed for I found the creature was funny, and he went on: 'Fancy this being the Epiphany! I have had a bean put into the goose, but there is no queen; it is really very annoying!' And I repeated like an echo: 'It is annoying, but what do you want me to do in the matter?'

"'To find some, of course.'

"'Some women. Women? You must be mad!'

"'I managed to find the brandy under the pear tree and the champagne under the steps, and yet there was nothing to guide me, while as for you, a petticoat is a sure sign. Go and look, old fellow.'

"He looked so grave, so convinced, that I could not tell whether he was joking or not. So I replied: 'Look here, Marchas, are you having a joke with me?'

"'I never joke on duty.'

"'But where the devil do you expect me to find any women?'

" 'Where you like; there must be two or three remaining in the neighborhood, so ferret them out and bring them here.'

"I got up, for it was too hot in front of the fire, and Marchas went on: 'Do you want an idea?'

" 'Yes.'

" 'Go and see the priest.'

" 'The priest? What for?'

" 'Ask him to supper and beg him to bring a woman with him.'

" 'The priest! A woman! Ha! ha! ha!'

"But Marchas continued with extraordinary gravity: 'I am not laughing; go and find the priest and tell him how we are situated, and, as he must be horribly dull, he will come. But tell him that we want one woman at least, a lady, of course, since we are all men of the world. He is sure to have the names of his female parishioners on the tips of his fingers, and if there is one to suit us and you manage it well he will indicate her to you.'

" 'Come, come, Marchas, what are you thinking of?'

" 'My dear Garens, you can do this quite well. It will be very funny. We are well bred, by Jove, and we will put on our most distinguished manners and our grandest style. Tell the abbé who we are, make him laugh, soften him, seduce him and persuade him!'

" 'No, it is impossible.'

"He drew his chair close to mine, and as he knew my weak side, the scamp continued: 'Just think what a swagger thing it will be to do and how amusing to tell about; the whole army will talk about it, and it will give you a famous reputation.'

"I hesitated, for the adventure rather tempted me. He persisted: 'Come, my little Garens. You are in command of this detachment and you alone can go and call on the head of the church in this neighborhood. I beg of you to go, and I promise you that after the war I will relate the whole affair in verse in the *Revue des Deux Mondes*. You owe this much to your men, for you have made them march enough during the last month.'

"I got up at last and asked: 'Where is the parsonage?'

" 'Take the second turning at the end of the street; you will then see an avenue, and at the end of the avenue you will find the church. The parsonage is beside it.' As I departed he called out: 'Tell him the bill of fare to make him hungry!'

"I discovered the ecclesiastic's little house without any difficulty; it was by the side of a large, ugly brick church. As there was neither bell nor knocker, I knocked at the door with my fist, and a loud voice from inside asked: 'Who is there?' to which I replied: 'A quartermaster of hussars.'

"I heard the noise of bolts and a key being turned. Then I found myself face to face with a tall priest with a large stomach, the chest of a prize fighter, formidable hands projecting from turned-up sleeves, a red face and the looks of a kind man. I gave him a military salute and said: 'Good day, Monsieur l'Abbé.'

"He had feared a surprise, some marauders' ambush, and he smiled as he replied: 'Good day, my friend; come in.' I followed him into a small room, with a red tiled floor, in which a small fire was burning, very different to Marchas' furnace. He gave me a chair and said: 'What can I do for you?'

"'Monsieur, allow me first of all to introduce myself,' and I gave him my card, which he took and read half aloud: 'The Comte de Garens.'

"I continued: 'There are eleven of us here, Monsieur l'Abbé, five on grand guard and six installed at the house of an unknown inhabitant. The names of the six are Garens (that is I), Pierre de Marchas, Ludovic de Ponderel, Baron d'Etreillis, Karl Massouligny, the painter's son, and Joseph Herbon, a young musician. I have come to ask you, in their name and my own, to do us the honor of supping with us. It is an Epiphany supper, Monsieur l'Abbé, and we should like to make it a little cheerful.'

"The priest smiled and murmured: 'It seems to me to be hardly a suitable occasion for amusing oneself.'

"I replied: 'We are fighting every day, monsieur. Fourteen of our comrades have been killed in a month, and three fell as late as yesterday. That is war. We stake our life every moment; have we not, therefore, the right to amuse ourselves freely? We are Frenchmen; we like to laugh, and we can laugh everywhere. Our fathers laughed on the scaffold! This evening we should like to brighten ourselves up a little, like gentlemen, and not like soldiers; you understand me, I hope. Are we wrong?'

"He replied quickly: 'You are quite right, my friend, and I accept your invitation with great pleasure.' Then he called out: 'Hermance!'

"An old, bent, wrinkled, horrible peasant woman appeared and said: 'What do you want?'

"'I shall not dine at home, my daughter.'

"'Where are you going to dine then?'

"'With some gentlemen, hussars.'

"I felt inclined to say: 'Bring your servant with you,' just to see Marchas' face, but I did not venture to and continued: 'Do you know anyone among your parishioners, male or female, whom I could invite as well?' He hesitated, reflected and then said: 'No, I do not know anybody!'

"I persisted: 'Nobody? Come, monsieur, think; it would be very nice to have some ladies, I mean to say, some married couples! I know nothing about your parishioners. The baker and his wife, the grocer, the—the—the—watchmaker—the—shoemaker—the—the chemist with his wife. We have a good spread and plenty of wine, and we should be enchanted to leave pleasant recollections of ourselves behind us with the people here.'

"The priest thought again for a long time and then said resolutely: 'No, there is nobody.'

"I began to laugh. 'By Jove, Monsieur l'Abbé, it is very vexing not to have an Epiphany queen, for we have the bean. Come, think. Is there not a married mayor, or a married deputy mayor, or a married municipal councilor or schoolmaster?'

"'No, all the ladies have gone away.'

"'What? Is there not in the whole place some good tradesman's wife, with her good tradesman, to whom we might give this pleasure, for it would be a pleasure to them, a great pleasure under present circumstances?'

"But suddenly the abbé began to laugh, and he laughed so violently that he fairly shook and exclaimed: 'Ha! ha! ha! I have got what you want, yes. I have got what you want! Ha! ha! ha! We will laugh and enjoy ourselves, my children; we will have some fun. How pleased the ladies will be, I say, how delighted they will be. Ha! ha! Where are you staying?'

"I described the house, and he understood where it was. 'Very good,' he said. 'It belongs to Monsieur Bertin-Lavaille. I will be there in half an hour with four ladies. Ha! ha! ha! Four ladies!'

"He went out with me, still laughing, and left me, repeating: 'That is capital; in half an hour at Bertin-Lavaille's house.'

"I returned quickly, very much astonished and very much puzzled. 'Covers for how many?' Marchas asked as soon as he saw me.

"'Eleven. There are six of us hussars besides the priest and four ladies.'

"He was thunderstruck, and I triumphant, and he repeated: 'Four ladies! Did you say four ladies?'

"'I said four women.'

"'Real women?'

"'Real women.'

"'Well, accept my compliments!'

"'I will, for I deserve them.'

"He got out of his armchair, opened the door, and I saw a beautiful white tablecloth on a long table, round which three hussars in blue aprons were setting out the plates and glasses. 'There are some women coming!' Marchas cried. And the three men began to dance and to cheer with all their might.

"Everything was ready, and we were waiting. We waited for nearly an hour, while a delicious smell of roast poultry pervaded the whole house. At last, however, a knock against the shutters made us all jump up at the same moment. Stout Ponderel ran to open the door, and in less than a minute a little Sister of Mercy appeared in the doorway. She was thin, wrinkled and timid and successively saluted the four bewildered hussars who saw her enter. Behind her the noise of sticks sounded on the tiled floor in the vestibule. As soon as she had come into the drawing room I saw three old heads in white caps following each other one by one, balancing themselves with different movements, one canting to the right, while the other canted to the left. Then three worthy women showed themselves, limping, dragging their legs behind them, crippled by illness and deformed through old age, three infirm old women, past service, the only three pensioners who were able to walk in the establishment which Sister Saint-Benedict managed.

"She had turned round to her invalids, full of anxiety for them, and then, seeing my quartermaster's stripes, she said to me: 'I am much obliged to you for thinking of these poor women. They have very little pleasure in life, and you are at the same time giving them a great treat and doing them a great honor.'

"I saw the priest, who had remained in the obscurity of the passage and who was laughing heartily, and I began to laugh in my turn, especially when I saw Marchas' face. Then, motioning the nun to the seats, I said: 'Sit down, Sister; we are very proud and very happy that you have accepted our unpretentious invitation.'

"She took three chairs which stood against the wall, set them before the fire, led her three old women to them, settled them on them, took their sticks and shawls which she put into a corner and then, pointing to the first, a thin woman with an enormous stomach who was evidently suffering from the dropsy, she said: 'This is Mother Paumelle, whose husband was killed by falling from a roof and whose son died in Africa; she is sixty years old.' Then she pointed to another, a tall woman, whose head shook unceasingly: 'This is Mother Jean-Jean, who is sixty-seven. She is nearly blind, for her face was terribly singed in a fire, and her right leg was half burned off.'

"Then she pointed to the third, a sort of dwarf, with protruding round, stupid eyes, which she rolled incessantly in all directions. 'This is La Putois, an idiot. She is only forty-four.'

"I bowed to the three women as if I were being presented to some Royal Highness and, turning to the priest, I said: 'You are an excellent man, Monsieur l'Abbé, and we all owe you a debt of gratitude.'

"Everybody was laughing, in fact, except Marchas, who seemed furious, and just then Karl Massouligny cried: 'Sister Saint-Benedict, supper is on the table!'

"I made her go first with the priest, then I helped up Mother Paumelle, whose arm I took, and dragged her into the next room, which was no easy task, for her swollen stomach seemed heavier than a lump of iron.

"Stout Ponderel gave his arm to Mother Jean-Jean, who bemoaned her crutch, and little Joseph Herbon took the idiot, La Putois, to the dining room, which was filled with the odor of the viands.

"As soon as we were opposite our plates the sister clapped her hands three times, and, with the precision of soldiers presenting arms, the women made a rapid sign of the cross, and then the priest slowly repeated the Benedictus in Latin. Then we sat down and the two fowls appeared, brought in by Marchas, who chose to wait rather than to sit down as a guest at this ridiculous repast.

"But I cried: 'Bring the champagne at once!' And a cork flew out with the noise of a pistol, and in spite of the resistance of the priest and the kind sister, the three hussars sitting by the side of the three invalids emptied their three full glasses down their throats by force.

"Massouligny, who possessed the faculty of making himself at home and of being on good terms with everyone wherever he was, made love to Mother Paumelle in the drollest manner. The dropsical woman who had retained her cheerfulness in spite of her misfortunes answered him banteringly in a high falsetto voice which seemed to be assumed, and she laughed so heartily at her neighbor's jokes that her large stomach looked as if it were going to rise up and get onto the table. Little Herbon had seriously undertaken the task of making the idiot drunk, and Baron d'Etreillis, whose wits were not always particularly sharp, was questioning old Jean-Jean about the life, the habits and the rules in the hospital.

"The nun said to Massouligny in consternation: 'Oh! oh! You will make her ill; pray do not make her laugh like that, monsieur. Oh, monsieur.' Then she got up and rushed at Herbon to take a full glass out of his hands which he was hastily emptying down La Putois's throat, while the priest shook with laughter, and said to the sister: 'Never mind, just this once it will not hurt her. Do leave them alone.'

"After the two fowls they ate the duck, which was flanked by the three pigeons and a blackbird, and then the goose appeared, smoking, golden-colored and diffusing a warm odor of hot, browned fat meat. La Paumelle, who was getting lively, clapped her hands; La Jean-Jean left off answering the baron's numerous questions, and La Putois uttered grunts of pleasure, half cries and half sighs, like little children do when one shows them sweets. 'Allow me to carve this bird,' the abbé said. 'I understand these sort of operations better than most people.'

" 'Certainly, Monsieur l'Abbé, and the sister said: 'How would it be to open the window a little; they are too warm, and I am afraid they will be ill.'

"I turned to Marchas. 'Open the window for a minute.' He did so; the cold outer air as it came in made the candles flare and the smoke from the goose, which the abbé was scientifically carving, with a table napkin round his neck, whirl about. We watched him doing it without speaking now, for we were interested in his attractive handiwork and also seized with renewed appetite at the sight of that enormous golden-colored bird, whose limbs fell one after another into the brown gravy at the bottom of the dish. At that moment, in the midst of greedy silence which kept us all attentive, the distant report of a shot came in at the open window.

"I started to my feet so quickly that my chair fell down behind me, and I shouted: 'Mount, all of you! You, Marchas, will take two men and go and see what it is. I shall expect you back here in five minutes.' And while the three riders went off at full gallop through the night I got into the saddle with my three remaining hussars in front of the steps of the villa, while the abbé, the sister and the three old women showed their frightened faces at the window.

"We heard nothing more, except the barking of a dog in the distance. The rain had ceased, and it was cold, very cold. Soon I heard the gallop of a horse, of a single horse, coming back. It was Marchas, and I called out to him: 'Well?'

" 'It is nothing; François has wounded an old peasant who refused to answer his challenge and who continued to advance in spite of the order to keep off. They are bringing him here, and we shall see what is the matter.'

"I gave orders for the horses to be put back into the stable, and I sent my two soldiers to meet the others and returned to the house. Then the abbé, Marchas and I took a mattress into the room to put the wounded man on;

the sister tore up a table napkin in order to make lint, while the three frightened women remained huddled up in a corner.

"Soon I heard the rattle of sabers on the road and I took a candle to show a light to the men who were returning. They soon appeared, carrying that inert, soft, long and sinister object which a human body becomes when life no longer sustains it.

"They put the wounded man on the mattress that had been prepared for him, and I saw at the first glance that he was dying. He had the death rattle and was spitting up blood which ran out of the corners of his mouth, forced out of his lungs by his gasps. The man was covered with it! His cheeks, his beard, his hair, his neck and his clothes seemed to have been rubbed, to have been dipped in a red tub; the blood had congealed on him and had become a dull color which was horrible to look at.

"The old man, wrapped up in a large shepherd's cloak, occasionally opened his dull, vacant eyes. They seemed stupid with astonishment, like the eyes of hunted animals which fall at the sportsman's feet, half dead before the shot, stupefied with fear and surprise.

"The abbé exclaimed: 'Ah! There is old Placide, the shepherd from Les Marlins. He is deaf, poor man, and heard nothing. Ah! O God! They have killed the unhappy man!' The sister had opened his blouse and shirt and was looking at a little blue hole in the middle of his chest which was not bleeding any more. 'There is nothing to be done,' she said.

"The shepherd was gasping terribly and bringing up blood with every breath. In his throat to the very depth of his lungs, they could hear an ominous and continued gurgling. The abbé, standing in front of him, raised his right hand, made the sign of the cross and in a slow and solemn voice pronounced the Latin words which purify men's souls. But before they were finished the old man was shaken by a rapid shudder, as if something had broken inside him; he no longer breathed. He was dead.

"When I turned round I saw a sight which was even more horrible than the death struggle of this unfortunate man. The three old women were standing up huddled close together, hideous and grimacing with fear and horror. I went up to them, and they began to utter shrill screams, while La Jean-Jean, whose leg had been burned and could no longer support her, fell to the ground at full length.

"Sister Saint-Benedict left the dead man, ran up to her infirm old women and without a word or a look for me wrapped their shawls round them, gave them their crutches, pushed them to the door, made them go out and disappeared with them into the dark night.

"I saw that I could not even let a hussar accompany them, for the mere rattle of a sword would have sent them mad with fear.

"The abbé was still looking at the dead man, but at last he turned to me and said:

"'Oh! What a horrible thing.'"

SIMON'S PAPA

Noon had just struck. The school door opened and the youngsters streamed out, tumbling over one another in their haste to get out quickly. But instead of promptly dispersing and going home to dinner as was their daily wont, they stopped a few paces off, broke up into knots and set to whispering.

The fact was that that morning Simon, the son of La Blanchotte, had, for the first time, attended school.

They had all of them in their families heard of La Blanchotte, and although in public she was welcome enough, the mothers among themselves treated her with compassion of a somewhat disdainful kind, which the children had caught without in the least knowing why.

As for Simon himself, they did not know him, for he never went abroad and did not play around with them through the streets of the village or along the banks of the river. So they loved him but little, and it was with a certain delight, mingled with astonishment, that they gathered in groups this morning, repeating to each other this sentence, concocted by a lad of fourteen or fifteen who appeared to know all about it, so sagaciously did he wink: "You know Simon—well, he has no papa."

La Blanchotte's son appeared in his turn upon the threshold of the school.

He was seven or eight years old, rather pale, very neat, with a timid and almost awkward manner.

He was making his way back to his mother's house when the various groups of his schoolfellows, perpetually whispering and watching him with the mischievous and heartless eyes of children bent upon playing a nasty trick, gradually surrounded him and ended by inclosing him altogether. There he stood amid them, surprised and embarrassed, not understanding what they were going to do with him. But the lad who had brought the news, puffed up with the success he had met with, demanded:

"What do you call yourself?"

He answered: "Simon."

"Simon what?" retorted the other.

The child, altogether bewildered, repeated: "Simon."

The lad shouted at him: "You must be named Simon something! That is not a name—Simon indeed."

And he, on the brink of tears, replied for the third time:

"I am named Simon."

The urchins began laughing. The lad triumphantly lifted up his voice: "You can see plainly that he has no papa."

A deep silence ensued. The children were dumfounded by this extraordinary, impossibly monstrous thing—a boy who had not a papa; they looked upon him as a phenomenon, an unnatural being, and they felt rising in them the hitherto inexplicable pity of their mothers for La Blanchotte. As for

Simon, he had propped himself against a tree to avoid falling, and he stood there as if paralyzed by an irreparable disaster. He sought to explain, but he could think of no answer for them, no way to deny this horrible charge that he had no papa. At last he shouted at them quite recklessly: "Yes, I have one."

"Where is he?" demanded the boy.

Simon was silent; he did not know. The children shrieked, tremendously excited. These sons of toil, nearly related to animals, experienced the cruel craving which makes the fowls of a farmyard destroy one of their own kind as soon as it is wounded. Simon suddenly spied a little neighbor, the son of a widow, whom he had always seen, as he himself was to be seen, quite alone with his mother.

"And no more have you," he said, "no more have you a papa."

"Yes," replied the other, "I have one."

"Where is he?" rejoined Simon.

"He is dead," declared the brat with superb dignity; "he is in the cemetery, is my papa."

A murmur of approval rose amid the scapegraces, as if the fact of possessing a papa dead in a cemetery made their comrade big enough to crush the other one who had no papa at all. And these rogues, whose fathers were for the most part evildoers, drunkards, thieves and ill treaters of their wives, hustled each other as they pressed closer and closer to Simon as though they, the legitimate ones, would stifle in their pressure one who was beyond the law.

The lad next Simon suddenly put his tongue out at him with a waggish air and shouted at him:

"No papa! No papa!"

Simon seized him by the hair with both hands and set to work to demolish his legs with kicks, while he bit his cheek ferociously. A tremendous struggle ensued between the two boys, and Simon found himself beaten, torn, bruised, rolled on the ground in the middle of the ring of applauding little vagabonds. As he arose, mechanically brushing his little blouse all covered with dust with his hand, someone shouted at him:

"Go and tell your papa."

He then felt a great sinking in his heart. They were stronger than he; they had beaten him, and he had no answer to give them for he knew it was true that he had no papa. Full of pride, he tried for some moments to struggle against the tears which were suffocating him. He had a choking fit, and then without cries he began to weep with great sobs which shook him incessantly. Then a ferocious joy broke out among his enemies, and, just like savages in fearful festivals, they took one another by the hand and danced in a circle about him as they repeated in refrain:

"No papa! No papa!"

But suddenly Simon ceased sobbing. Frenzy overtook him. There were stones under his feet; he picked them up and with all his strength hurled them at his tormentors. Two or three were struck and ran away yelling, and so formidable did he appear that the rest became panic-stricken. Cowards, like a jeering crowd in the presence of an exasperated man, they broke up and fled. Left alone, the little thing without a father set off running toward the fields, for a recollection had been awakened which nerved his soul to a great determination. He made up his mind to drown himself in the river.

He remembered, in fact, that eight days ago a poor devil who begged for his livelihood had thrown himself into the water because he had no more money. Simon had been there when they fished him out again, and the sight of the fellow who had seemed to him so miserable and ugly had then impressed him—his pale cheeks, his long drenched beard and his open eyes being full of calm. The bystanders had said:

"He is dead."

And someone had added:

"He is quite happy now."

So Simon wished to drown himself also because he had no father, just as the wretched being did who had no money.

He reached the water and watched it flowing. Some fishes were rising briskly in the clear stream and occasionally made little leaps and caught the flies on the surface. He stopped crying in order to watch them, for their feeding interested him vastly. But at intervals, as in the lulls of a tempest, when tremendous gusts of wind snap off trees and then die away, this thought would return to him with intense pain:

"I am about to drown myself because I have no papa."

It was very warm and fine weather. The pleasant sunshine warmed the grass; the water shone like a mirror, and Simon enjoyed for some minutes the happiness of that languor which follows weeping, desirous even of falling asleep there upon the grass in the warmth of noon.

A little green frog leaped from under his feet. He endeavored to catch it. It escaped him. He pursued it and lost it three times following. At last he caught it by one of its hind legs and began to laugh as he saw the efforts the creature made to escape. It gathered itself up on its large legs and then with a violent spring suddenly stretched them out as stiff as two bars.

Its eyes stared wide open in their round, golden circle, and it beat the air with its front limbs, using them as though they were hands. It reminded him of a toy made with straight slips of wood nailed zigzag, one on the other, which by a similar movement regulated the exercise of the little soldiers fastened thereon. Then he thought of his home and of his mother and, overcome by great sorrow, he again began to weep. His lips trembled, and he placed himself on his knees and said his prayers as before going to bed. But he was unable to finish them, for such hurried and violent sobs overtook him that he was completely overwhelmed. He thought no more; he no longer heeded anything around him but was wholly given up to tears.

Suddenly a heavy hand was placed upon his shoulder, and a rough voice asked him:

"What is it that causes you so much grief, my fine fellow?"

Simon turned round. A tall workman with a black beard and hair all curled was staring at him good-naturedly. He answered with his eyes and throat full of tears:

"They have beaten me because—I—I have no papa—no papa."

"What?" said the man, smiling. "Why, everybody has one."

The child answered painfully amid his spasms of grief:

"But I—I—I have none."

Then the workman became serious. He had recognized La Blanchotte's son, and although a recent arrival to the neighborhood, he had a vague idea of her history.

"Well," he said, "console yourself, my boy, and come with me home to your mother. She will give you a papa."

And so they started on the way, the big one holding the little one by the hand. The man smiled afresh, for he was not sorry to see this Blanchotte, who by popular report was one of the prettiest girls in the countryside, and, perhaps, he said to himself at the bottom of his heart, that a lass who had erred once might very well err again.

They arrived in front of a very neat little white house.

"There it is," exclaimed the child, and he cried: "Mamma."

A woman appeared, and the workman instantly left off smiling, for he at once perceived that there was no more fooling to be done with the tall pale girl who stood austerely at her door as though to defend from one man the threshold of that house where she had already been betrayed by another. Intimidated, his cap in his hand, he stammered out:

"See, madame, I have brought you back your little boy who had lost himself near the river."

But Simon flung his arms about his mother's neck and told her, as he again began to cry:

"No, Mamma, I wished to drown myself because the others had beaten me—had beaten me—because I have no papa."

A burning redness covered the young woman's cheeks, and, hurt to the quick, she embraced her child passionately, while the tears coursed down her face. The man, much moved, stood there, not knowing how to get away. But Simon suddenly ran to him and said:

"Will you be my papa?"

A deep silence ensued. La Blanchotte, dumb and tortured with shame, leaned against the wall, her hands upon her heart. The child, seeing that no answer was made him, replied:

"If you do not wish it I shall return to drown myself."

The workman took the matter as a jest and answered, laughing:

"Why, yes, I wish it certainly."

"What is your name then," went on the child, "so that I may tell the others when they wish to know your name?"

"Philip," answered the man.

Simon was silent a moment so that he might get the name well into his memory; then he stretched out his arms, quite consoled, and said:

"Well then, Philip, you are my papa."

The workman, lifting him from the ground, kissed him hastily on both cheeks and then strode away quickly.

When the child returned to school next day he was received with a spiteful laugh, and at the end of school, when the lads were on the point of recommencing, Simon threw these words at their heads as he would have done a stone: "He is named Philip, my papa."

Yells of delight burst out from all sides. "Philip who? Philip what? What on earth is Philip? Where did you pick up your Philip?"

Simon answered nothing and, immovable in faith, he defied them with his eye, ready to be martyred rather than fly before them. The schoolmaster came to his rescue, and he returned home to his mother.

For a space of three months the tall workman, Philip, frequently passed by La Blanchotte's house and sometimes made bold to speak to her when he saw her sewing near the window. She answered him civilly, always sedately, never joking with him or permitting him to enter her house. Notwithstanding this, being, like all men, a bit of a coxcomb, he imagined that she was often rosier than usual when she chatted with him.

But a fallen reputation is so difficult to recover and always remains so fragile that, in spite of the shy reserve La Blanchotte maintained, they already gossiped in the neighborhood.

As for Simon, he loved his new papa much and walked with him nearly every evening when the day's work was done. He went regularly to school and mixed in a dignified way with his schoolfellows without ever answering them back.

One day, however, the lad who had first attacked him said to him:

"You have lied. You have not a papa named Philip."

"Why do you say that?" demanded Simon, much disturbed.

The youth rubbed his hands. He replied:

"Because if you had one he would be your mamma's husband."

Simon was confused by the truth of this reasoning; nevertheless, he retorted:

"He is my papa all the same."

"That can very well be," exclaimed the urchin with a sneer, "but that is not being your papa altogether."

La Blanchotte's little one bowed his head and went off dreaming in the direction of the forge belonging to old Loizon, where Philip worked.

This forge was entombed in trees. It was very dark there; the red glare of a formidable furnace alone lit up with great flashes five blacksmiths who hammered upon their anvils with a terrible din. Standing enveloped in flame, they worked like demons, their eyes fixed on the red-hot iron they were pounding and their dull ideas rising and falling with their hammers.

Simon entered without being noticed and quietly plucked his friend by the sleeve. Philip turned round. All at once the work came to a standstill, and the men looked on very attentively. Then in the midst of this unaccustomed silence rose the little slender pipe of Simon:

"Philip, explain to me what the lad at La Michande has just told me, that you are not altogether my papa."

"And why that?" asked the smith.

The child replied in all innocence:

"Because you are not my mamma's husband."

No one laughed. Philip remained standing, leaning his forehead upon the back of his great hands which held the handle of his hammer upright upon the anvil. He mused. His four companions watched him, and, like a tiny mite among these giants, Simon anxiously waited. Suddenly one of the smiths, voicing the sentiment of all, said to Philip:

"All the same La Blanchotte is a good and honest girl, stalwart and steady in spite of her misfortune, and one who would make a worthy wife for an honest man."

"That is true," remarked the three others.

The smith continued:

"Is it the girl's fault if she has fallen? She had been promised marriage, and I know more than one who is much respected today and has sinned every bit as much."

"That is true," responded the three men in chorus.

He resumed:

"How hard she has toiled, poor thing, to educate her lad all alone, and how much she has wept since she no longer goes out, save to church, God only knows."

"That also is true," said the others.

Then no more was heard save the roar of the bellows which fanned the fire of the furnace. Philip hastily bent himself down to Simon.

"Go and tell your mamma that I shall come to speak to her."

Then he pushed the child out by the shoulders. He returned to his work, and in unison the five hammers again fell upon their anvils. Thus they wrought the iron until nightfall, strong, powerful, happy, like Vulcans, satisfied. But as the great bell of a cathedral resounds upon feast days above the jingling of the other bells, so Philip's hammer, dominating the noise of the others, clanged second after second with a deafening uproar. His eye on the fire, he plied his trade vigorously, erect amid the sparks.

The sky was full of stars as he knocked at La Blanchotte's door. He had his Sunday blouse on, a fresh shirt, and his beard was trimmed. The young woman showed herself upon the threshold and said in a grieved tone:

"It is ill to come thus when night has fallen, Mr Philip."

He wished to answer but stammered and stood confused before her.

She resumed:

"And you understand quite well that it will not do that I should be talked about any more."

Then he said all at once:

"What does that matter to me, if you will be my wife!"

No voice replied to him, but he believed that he heard in the shadow of the room the sound of a body falling. He entered very quickly, and Simon, who had gone to his bed, distinguished the sound of a kiss and some words that his mother said very softly. Then he suddenly found himself lifted up by the hands of his friend who, holding him at the length of his herculean arms, exclaimed to him:

"You will tell your schoolfellows that your papa is Philip Remy, the blacksmith, and that he will pull the ears of all who do you any harm."

On the morrow, when the school was full and lessons about to begin, little Simon stood up quite pale, with trembling lips.

"My papa," he said in a clear voice, "is Philip Remy, the blacksmith, and he has promised to box the ears of all who do me any harm."

This time no one laughed any longer, for he was very well known, was Philip Remy, the blacksmith, and he was a papa of whom anyone in the world would be proud.

WAITER, A BOCK![1]

WHY, ON THIS PARTICULAR EVENING, did I enter a certain beer shop? I cannot explain it. It was bitterly cold. A fine rain, a watery mist, floated about, veiling the gas jets in a transparent fog, making the pavements under the shadow of the shop fronts glitter, which revealed the soft slush and the soiled feet of the passers-by.

I was going nowhere in particular; was simply having a short walk after dinner. I had passed the Credit Lyonnais, the Rue Vivienne and several other streets. Suddenly I descried a large café, which was more than half full. I walked inside with no object in mind. I was not the least thirsty.

By a searching glance I detected a place where I would not be too much crowded. So I went and sat down by the side of a man who seemed to me to be old and who smoked a halfpenny clay pipe, which had become as black as coal. From six to eight beer saucers were piled up on the table in front of him, indicating the number of bocks he had already absorbed. With that same glance I had recognized in him a "regular toper," one of those frequenters of beerhouses who come in the morning as soon as the place is open and only go away in the evening when it is about to close. He was dirty, bald to about the middle of the cranium, while his long gray hair fell over the neck of his frock coat. His clothes, much too large for him, appeared to have been made for him at a time when he was very stout. One could guess that his pantaloons were not held up by braces and that this man could not take ten paces without having to pull them up and readjust them. Did he wear a vest? The mere thought of his boots and the feet they enveloped filled me with horror. The frayed cuffs were as black at the edges as were his nails.

As soon as I had sat down near him this queer creature said to me in a tranquil tone of voice:

"How goes it with you?"

I turned sharply round to him and closely scanned his features, whereupon he continued:

[1] Bavarian beer.

"I see you do not recognize me."

"No, I do not."

"Des Barrets."

I was stupefied. It was Count Jean des Barrets, my old college chum.

I seized him by the hand, so dumfounded that I could find nothing to say. I at length managed to stammer out:

"And you, how goes it with you?"

He responded placidly:

"With me? Just as I like."

He became silent. I wanted to be friendly and I selected this phrase:

"What are you doing now?"

"You see what I am doing," he answered, quite resignedly.

I felt my face getting red. I insisted:

"But every day?"

"Every day is alike to me," was his response, accompanied with a thick puff of tobacco smoke.

He then tapped on the top of the marble table with a sou to attract the attention of the waiter and called out:

"Waiter, two bocks."

A voice in the distance repeated:

"Two bocks instead of four."

Another voice, more distant still, shouted out:

"Here they are, sir, here they are."

Immediately there appeared a man with a white apron carrying two bocks, which he set down foaming on the table, the foam running over the edge onto the sandy floor.

Des Barrets emptied his glass at a single draught and replaced it on the table, sucking in the drops of beer that had been left on his mustache. He next asked:

"What is there new?"

"I know of nothing new, worth mentioning, really," I stammered. "But nothing has grown old for me; I am a commercial man."

In an equable tone of voice he said:

"Indeed—does that amuse you?"

"No, but what do you mean by that? Surely you must do something!"

"What do you mean by that?"

"I only mean, how do you pass your time?"

"What's the use of occupying myself with anything? For my part, I do nothing at all, as you see, never anything. When one has not got a sou one can understand why one has to go to work. What is the good of working? Do you work for yourself or for others? If you work for yourself you do it for your own amusement, which is all right; if you work for others you reap nothing but ingratitude."

Then, sticking his pipe into his mouth, he called out anew:

"Waiter, a bock! It makes me thirsty to keep calling so. I am not accustomed to that sort of thing. Yes, I do nothing; I let things slide and I am growing old. In dying I shall have nothing to regret. If so, I should remember nothing outside this public house. I have no wife, no children, no cares, no sorrows, nothing. That is the very best thing that could happen to one."

He then emptied the glass which had been brought him, passed his tongue over his lips and resumed his pipe.

I looked at him, stupefied, and asked him:

"But you have not always been like that?"

"Pardon me, sir; ever since I left college."

"It is not a proper life to lead, my dear sir; it is simply horrible. Come, you must indeed have done something; you must have loved something; you must have friends."

"No, I get up at noon; I come here; I have my breakfast; I drink my bock; I remain until evening; I have my dinner; I drink bock. Then about one in the morning I return to my couch, because the place closes up. And it is this latter that embitters me more than anything. For the last ten years I have passed six tenths of my time on this bench in my corner and the other four tenths in my bed, never changing. I talk sometimes with the habitués."

"But on arriving in Paris what did you do at first?"

"I paid my devoirs to the Café de Medicis."

"What next?"

"Next? I crossed the water and came here."

"Why did you take even that trouble?"

"What do you mean? One cannot remain all one's life in the Latin Quarter. The students make too much noise. But I do not move about any longer. Waiter, a bock."

I now began to think that he was making fun of me, and I continued:

"Come now, be frank. You have been the victim of some great sorrow; despair in love, no doubt! It is easy to see that you are a man whom misfortune has hit hard. What age are you?"

"I am thirty years of age, but I look to be forty-five at least."

I looked him straight in the face. His shrunken figure, badly cared for, gave one the impression that he was an old man. On the summit of his cranium a few long hairs shot straight up from a skin of doubtful cleanness. He had enormous eyelashes, a large mustache and a thick beard. Suddenly I had a kind of vision—I know not why—the vision of a basin filled with noisome water, the water which should have been applied to that poll. I said to him:

"Verily, you look to be more than that age. Of a certainty you must have experienced some great disappointment."

He replied:

"I tell you that I have not. I am old because I never take air. There is nothing that vitiates the life of a man more than the atmosphere of a café."

I could not believe him.

"You must surely have been married as well? One could not get baldheaded as you are without having been much in love."

He shook his head, sending down his back little hairs from the scalp.

"No, I have always been virtuous."

And, raising his eyes toward the luster which beat down on our heads, he said:

"If I am bald-headed it is the fault of the gas. It is the enemy of hair. Waiter, a bock. You must be thirsty also?"

"No, thank you. But you certainly interest me. When did you have your first discouragement? Your life is not normal; is not natural. There is something under it all."

"Yes, and it dates from my infancy. I received a heavy blow when I was very young. It turned my life into darkness, which will last to the end."

"How did it come about?"

"You wish to know about it? Well then, listen. You recall, of course, the castle in which I was brought up, seeing that you used to visit it for five or six months during the vacations. You remember that large gray building in the middle of a great park and the long avenues of oaks, which opened toward the four cardinal points? You remember my father and my mother, both of whom were ceremonious, solemn and severe?

"I worshiped my mother; I was suspicious of my father, but I respected both, accustomed always as I was to see everyone bow before them. In the country they were Monsieur le Comte and Madame la Comtesse, and our neighbors, the Tannemares, the Ravelets, the Brennevilles, showed the utmost consideration for them.

"I was then thirteen years old, happy, satisfied with everything, as one is at that age, and full of joy and vivacity.

"Now toward the end of September, a few days before entering the lycée, while I was enjoying myself in the mazes of the park, climbing the trees and swinging on the branches, I saw crossing an avenue my father and mother, who were walking together.

"I recall the thing as though it were yesterday. It was a very windy day. The whole line of trees bent under the pressure of the wind, moaned and seemed to utter cries—cries dull, yet deep—so that the whole forest groaned under the gale.

"Evening had come on, and it was dark in the thickets. The agitation of the wind and the branches excited me, made me skip about like an idiot and howl in imitation of the wolves.

"As soon as I perceived my parents I crept furtively toward them under the branches, in order to surprise them, as though I had been a veritable wolf. But suddenly seized with fear, I stopped a few paces from them. My father, a prey to the most violent passion, cried:

"'Your mother is a fool; moreover, it is not your mother that is the question; it is you. I tell you that I want money, and I will make you sign this.'

"My mother responded in a firm voice:

"'I will not sign it. It is Jean's fortune; I shall guard it for him and I will not allow you to devour it with strange women, as you have your own heritage.'

"Then my father, full of rage, wheeled round and seized his wife by the throat and began to slap her full in the face with the disengaged hand.

"My mother's hat fell off; her hair became disheveled and fell down her back; she essayed to parry the blows but could not escape from them. And my father, like a madman, banged and banged at her. My mother rolled over on the ground, covering her face in both her hands. Then he turned her over on her back in order to batter her still more, pulling away the hands which were covering her face.

"As for me, my friend, it seemed as though the world had come to an end, that the eternal laws had changed. I experienced the overwhelming dread that one has in presence of things supernatural, in presence of irreparable disaster. My boyish head whirled round and soared. I began to cry with all my might without knowing why, a prey to terror, to grief, to a dreadful bewilderment. My father heard me. I believed that he wanted to kill me, and I fled like a hunted animal, running straight in front of me through the woods.

"I ran perhaps for an hour, perhaps for two; I know not. Darkness had set in; I tumbled over some thick herbs, exhausted, and I lay there lost, devoured by terror, eaten up by a sorrow capable of breaking forever the heart of a child. I became cold; I became hungry. At length day broke. I dared neither get up, walk, return home or save myself, fearing to encounter my father whom I did not wish to see again.

"I should probably have died of misery and of hunger at the foot of a tree if the guard had not discovered me and led me by force.

"I found my parents wearing their ordinary aspect. My mother alone spoke to me:

"'How you have frightened me, you naughty boy; I have been the whole night sleepless.'

"I did not answer but began to weep. My father did not utter a single word.

"Eight days later I entered the lycée.

"Well, my friend, it was all over with me. I had witnessed the other side of things, the bad side; I have not been able to perceive the good side since that day. What things have passed in my mind, what strange phenomena have warped my ideas, I do not know. But I no longer have a taste for anything, a wish for anything, a love for anybody, a desire for anything whatever, no ambition, no hope. And I always see my poor mother lying on the ground in the avenue while my father was maltreating her. My mother died a few years after; my father lives still. I have not seen him since. Waiter, a bock."

A waiter brought him his bock, which he swallowed at a gulp. But in taking up his pipe again, trembling as he was, he broke it. Then he made a violent gesture:

"Zounds! This is indeed a grief, a real grief. I have had it for a month, and it was coloring so beautifully!"

Then he went off through the vast saloon which was now full of smoke and of people drinking, calling out:

"Waiter, a bock—and a new pipe."

THE SEQUEL TO A DIVORCE

CERTAINLY, although he had been engaged in the most extraordinary, most unlikely, most extravagant and funniest cases and had won legal games without a trump in his hand, although he had worked out the obscure law of divorce as if it had been a California gold mine, Maître[1] Garrulier, the celebrated, the only Garrulier, could not check a movement of surprise, or a disheartening shake of the head or a smile when the Countess de Baudémont explained her affairs to him for the first time.

He had just opened his correspondence, and his slender hands on which he bestowed the greatest attention buried themselves in a heap of female letters, and one might have thought oneself in the confessional of a fashionable preacher, so impregnated was the atmosphere with delicate perfumes.

Immediately, even before she had said a word, with the sharp glance of a practiced man of the world, that look which made beautiful Mme de Serpenoise say: "He strips your heart bare!" the lawyer had classed her in the third category. Those who suffer came into his first category; those who love, into the second, and those who are bored, into the third—and she belonged to the latter.

She was a pretty windmill, whose sails turned and flew round and fretted the blue sky with a delicious shiver of joy, as it were, and had the brain of a bird, in which four correct and healthy ideas cannot exist side by side and in which all dreams and every kind of folly are engulfed, like a great kaleidoscope.

Incapable of hurting a fly, emotional, charitable, with a feeling of tenderness for the street girl who sells bunches of violets for a penny, for a cab horse which a driver is ill using, for a melancholy pauper's funeral, when the body, without friends or relations to follow it, is being conveyed to the common grave, doing anything that might afford five minutes' amusement, not caring if she made men miserable for the rest of their days and taking pleasure in kindling passions which consumed men's whole being, looking upon life as too short to be anything else than one uninterrupted round of gaiety and enjoyment, she thought that people might find plenty of time for being serious and reasonable in the evening of life, when they are at the bottom of the hill and their looking glasses reveal a wrinkled face surrounded with white hair.

A thoroughbred Parisian whom one would follow to the end of the world like a poodle, a woman whom one adores with the head, the heart and the senses until one is nearly driven mad as soon as one has inhaled the delicate perfume that emanates from her dress and hair or touched her skin and heard her laugh, a woman for whom one would fight a duel and risk one's life with-

---

[1] Title given to advocates in France.

out a thought, for whom a man would remove mountains and sell his soul to the devil several times over, if the devil were still in the habit of frequenting the places of bad repute on this earth.

She had perhaps came to see this Garrulier, whom she had so often heard mentioned at five o'clock teas, so as to be able to describe him to her female friends subsequently in droll phrases, imitating his gestures and the unctuous inflections of his voice in order, perhaps, to experience some new sensation or, perhaps, for the sake of dressing like a woman who was going to try for a divorce, and certainly the whole effect was perfect. She wore a splendid cloak embroidered with jet—which gave an almost serious effect to her golden hair, to her small, slightly turned-up nose with its quivering nostrils and to her large eyes, full of enigma and fun—over a dark dress which was fastened at the neck by a sapphire and a diamond pin.

The barrister did not interrupt her but allowed her to get excited and to chatter, to enumerate her causes for complaint against poor Count de Baudémont, who certainly had no suspicion of his wife's escapade and who would have been very much surprised if anyone told him of it at that moment, when he was taking his fencing lesson at the club.

When she had quite finished he said coolly, as if he were throwing a pail of water on some burning straw:

"But, madame, there is not the slightest pretext for a divorce in anything that you have told me here. The judges would ask me whether I took the law courts for a theater and intended to make fun of them."

And seeing how disheartened she was, that she looked like a child whose favorite toy had been broken, that she was so pretty that he would have liked to kiss her hands in his devotion, and as she seemed to be witty and very amusing, and as, moreover, he had no objection to such visits being prolonged, when papers had to be looked over, while sitting close together, Maître Garrulier appeared to be considering. Taking his chin in his hand, he said:

"However, I will think it over; there is sure to be some dark spot that can be made out worse. Write to me and come and see me again."

In the course of her visits that black spot had increased so much, and Countess de Baudémont had followed her lawyer's advice so punctually and had played on the various strings so skillfully that a few months later, after a lawsuit which is still spoken of, in the course of which the president had to take off his spectacles and to use his pocket handkerchief noisily, the divorce was pronounced in favor of the Countess Marie Anne Nicole Bournet de Baudémont, née de Tanchart de Peothus.

The count, who was nonplused at such an adventure turning out so seriously, first of all flew into a terrible rage, rushed off to the lawyer's office and threatened to cut off his knavish ears for him. But when his access of fury was over and he thought of it, he shrugged his shoulders and said:

"All the better for her if it amuses her!"

Then he bought Baron Silberstein's yacht and with some friends got up a cruise to Ceylon and India.

Marie Anne began by triumphing and felt as happy as a schoolgirl going home for the holidays; she committed every possible folly and soon, tired, satiated and disgusted, began to yawn, cried and found out that she had sacrificed her happiness, like a millionaire who has gone mad and has cast his bank notes and shares into the river, and that she was nothing more than a disabled waif and stray. Consequently, she now married again, as the solitude of her home made her morose from morning till night; and then, besides, she found a woman requires a mansion when she goes into society, to race meetings or to the theater.

And so while she became a marchioness and pronounced her second "Yes" before a very few friends at the office of the mayor of the English urban district, malicious people in the Faubourg were making fun of the whole affair and affirming this and that, whether rightly or wrongly, and comparing the present husband with the former one, even declaring that he had partially been the cause of the former divorce. Meanwhile M. de Baudémont was wandering over the four quarters of the globe, trying to overcome his homesickness and to deaden his longing for love, which had taken possession of his heart and of his body, like a slow poison.

He traveled through the most out-of-the-way places and the most lovely countries and spent months and months at sea and plunged into every kind of dissipation and debauchery. But neither the supple forms nor the luxurious gestures of the bayaderes, nor the large passive eyes of the Creoles, nor flirtations with English girls with hair the color of new cider, nor nights of waking dreams, when he saw new constellations in the sky, nor dangers during which a man thinks it is all over with him and mutters a few words of prayer in spite of himself, when the waves are high and the sky black, nothing was able to make him forget that little Parisian woman who smelled so sweet that she might have been taken for a bouquet of rare flowers; who was so coaxing, so curious, so funny; who never had the same caprice, the same smile or the same look twice and who, at bottom, was worth more than many others, either saints or sinners.

He thought of her constantly during long hours of sleeplessness. He carried her portrait about with him in the breast pocket of his pea jacket—a charming portrait in which she was smiling and showing her white teeth between her half-open lips. Her gentle eyes with their magnetic look had a happy, frank expression, and from the mere arrangement of her hair one could see that she was fair among the fair.

He used to kiss that portrait of the woman who had been his wife, as if he wished to efface it, would look at it for hours and then throw himself down on the netting and sob like a child as he looked at the infinite expanse before him, seeming to see their lost happiness, the joys of their perished affections and the divine remembrance of their love in the monotonous waste of green waters. And he tried to accuse himself for all that had occurred and not to be angry with her, to think that his grievances were imaginary and to adore her in spite of everything and always.

And so he roamed about the world, tossed to and fro, suffering and hoping he knew not what. He ventured into the greatest dangers and sought for death just as a man seeks for his mistress, and death passed close to him without touching him, perhaps amused at his grief and misery.

For he was as wretched as a stonebreaker, as one of those poor devils who work and nearly break their backs over the hard flints the whole day long under the scorching sun or the cold rain, and Marie Anne herself was not happy, for she was pining for the past and remembered their former love.

At last, however, he returned to France, changed, tanned by exposure, sun and rain and transformed as if by some witch's philter.

Nobody would have recognized the elegant and effeminate clubman in this corsair with broad shoulders, a skin the color of tan, with very red lips, who rolled a little in his walk, who seemed to be stifled in his black dress coat but who still retained the distinguished manners and bearing of a nobleman of the last century, one of those who, when he was ruined, fitted out a privateer and fell upon the English wherever he met them, from St Milo to Calcutta. And wherever he showed himself his friends exclaimed:

"Why! Is that you? I should never have known you again!"

He was very nearly starting off again immediately; he even telegraphed orders to Havre to get the steam yacht ready for sea directly, when he heard that Marie Anne had married again.

He saw her in the distance at the Théâtre Français one Tuesday, and when he noticed how pretty, how fair, how desirable she was—looking so melancholy, with all the appearance of an unhappy soul that regrets something—his determination grew weaker, and he delayed his departure from week to week and waited, without knowing why, until at last, worn out with the struggle, watching her wherever she went, more in love with her than he had ever been before, he wrote her long, mad, ardent letters in which his passion overflowed like a stream of lava.

He altered his handwriting, as he remembered her restless brain and her many whims. He sent her the flowers which he knew she liked best and told her that she was his life, that he was dying of waiting for her, of longing for her, for her, his idol.

At last, very much puzzled and surprised, guessing—who knows?—from the instinctive beating of her heart and her general emotion that it must be he this time, he whose soul she had tortured with such cold cruelty, and knowing that she could make amends for the past and bring back their former love, she replied to him and granted him the meeting that he asked for. She fell into his arms, and they both sobbed with joy and ecstasy. Their kisses were those which lips give only when they have lost each other and found each other again at last, when they meet and exhaust themselves in each other's looks, thirsting for tenderness, love and enjoyment.

. . . .

Last week Count de Baudémont carried off Marie Anne quietly and coolly, just like one resumes possession of one's house on returning from a journey and drives out the intruders. And when Maître Garrulier was told of this unheard-of scandal he rubbed his hands—the long, delicate hands of a sensual prelate—and exclaimed:

"That is absolutely logical, and I should like to be in their place."

THE CLOWN

THE HAWKERS' COTTAGE stood at the end of the Esplanade, on the little promontory where the jetty is and where all the winds, all the rain and all the spray met. The hut, both walls and roof, was built of old planks, more or less covered with tar; its chinks were stopped with oakum, and dry wreckage was heaped up against it. In the middle of the room an iron pot stood on two bricks and served as a stove when they had any coal, but as there was no chimney, it filled the room, which was ventilated only by a low door, with acrid smoke, and there the whole crew lived, eighteen men and one woman. Some had undergone various terms of imprisonment, and nobody knew what the others had done, but though they were all more or less suffering from some physical defect and were virtually old men, they were still all strong enough for hauling. For Chamber of Commerce tolerated them there and allowed them that hovel to live in, on condition that they should be ready to haul by day and by night.

For every vessel they hauled each got a penny by day and twopence by night. It was not certain, however, on account of the competition of retired sailors, fishermen's wives, laborers who had nothing to do, people who were all stronger than those half-starved wretches in the hut.

And yet they lived there, those eighteen men and one woman. Were they happy? Certainly not. Hopeless? Not that, either, for they occasionally got a little beside their scanty pay, and then they stole occasionally, fish, lumps of coal, things without any value to those who lost them, but of great value to the poor, beggarly thieves.

The eighteen supported the woman, and there was no jealousy on her account! She had no special favorite among them.

She was a fat woman of about forty, chubby faced and puffy, of whom Daddy la Bretagne, who was one of the eighteen, used to say: "She does us honor."

If she had had a favorite among them Daddy la Bretagne would certainly have had the greatest right to that privilege, for although he was one of the most crippled among them, being partially paralyzed in his legs, he showed himself as skillful and strong-armed as any of them, and in spite of his infirmities, he always managed to secure a good place in the row of haulers. None of them knew as well as he how to inspire visitors with pity during the season and to make them put their hands into their pockets. He was a past master at cadging, so that among those empty stomachs and penniless rascals he had windfalls of victuals and coppers more frequently than fell rightly to his share. But he did not make use of them in order to monopolize their common mistress.

"I am just," he used to say. "Let each of us have his spoonful in turn and no more, when we are all eating out of the same dish."

With the coal he picked up he used to make a good fire for the whole band in the iron pot, over which he cooked whatever he brought home with him, without anyone complaining about it, for he used to say:

"It gives you a good fire at which to warm yourselves for nothing, and the smell of my stew into the bargain."

As for his money, he spent it in drink with the trollop, and afterward, what was left of it, with the others.

"You see," he used to say, "I am just, and more than just. I give her up to you because it is your right."

The consequence was that they all liked Daddy la Bretagne, so that he gloried in it and said proudly:

"What a pity that we are living under the Republic! These fellows would think nothing of making me king."

And one day when he said this his trollop replied: "The king is here, old fellow!" And at the same time she presented a new comrade to them who was no less ragged or wretched looking than the eighteen, but quite young by the side of him. He was a tall thin fellow of about forty and without a gray streak in his long hair. He was dressed only in a pair of trousers and a shirt, which he wore outside them, like a blouse, and the trollop said:

"Here, Daddy la Bretagne, you have two knitted vests on, so just give him one."

"Why should I?" the hauler asked.

"Because I choose you to," the woman replied. "I have been living with you set of old men for a long time, so now I want to have a young one; there he is, so you must give him a vest and keep him here, or I shall throw you up. You may take it or leave it, as you like; do you understand me?"

The eighteen looked at each other, openmouthed, and good Daddy la Bretagne scratched his head and then said:

"What she asks is quite right, and we must give way," he replied.

Then they explained themselves and came to an understanding. The poor devil did not come like a conqueror, for he was a wretched clown who had just been released from prison, where he had undergone three years' hard labor for an attempted outrage on a girl, but with one exception, the best fellow in the world, so people declared.

"And something nice for me," the trollop said, "for I can assure you that I mean him to reward me for anything I may do for him."

From that time the household of eighteen persons was increased to nineteen, and at first all went well. The clown was very humble and tried not to be burdensome to them. Fed, clothed and supplied with tobacco, he tried not to be too exacting in the other matter, and if needful, he would have hauled like the others, but the woman would not allow it.

"You shall not fatigue yourself, my little man," she said. "You must reserve yourself entirely for home."

And he did as she wished.

And soon the eighteen, who had never been jealous of each other, grew jealous of the favored lover. Some tried to pick a quarrel with him. He resisted. The best fellow in the world, no doubt, but he was not going to be taken for a mussel shut up in its shell, for all that. Let them call him as lazy as a priest if they liked; he did not mind that, but when they put hairs into his coffee, armfuls of rushes among his wreckage and filth into his soup, they had better look out!

"None of that, all the lot of you, or you will see what I can do," he used to say.

They repeated their practical jokes, however, and he thrashed them. He did not try to find out who the culprits were but attacked the first one he met, so much the worse for him. With a kick from his wooden clog (it was his specialty) he smashed their noses into a pulp, and having thus acquired the knowledge of his strength and urged on by his trollop, he soon became a tyrant. The eighteen felt that they were slaves, and their former paradise, where concord and perfect equality had reigned, became a hell, and that state of things could not last.

"Ah!" Daddy la Bretagne growled, "if only I were twenty years younger, I would nearly kill him! I have my Breton's hot head still, but my confounded legs are no good any longer."

And he boldly challenged the clown to a duel in which the latter was to have his legs tied, and then both of them were to sit on the ground and hack at each other with knives.

"Such a duel," he said, "would be perfectly fair!" he replied, kicking him in the side with one of his clogs, and the woman burst out laughing and said:

"At any rate you cannot compete with him on equal terms as regards myself, so do not worry yourself about it."

Daddy la Bretagne was lying in his corner and spitting blood, and none of the rest spoke. What could the others do when he, the blusterer of them all, had been served so? The jade had been right when she had brought in the intruder and said:

"The king is here, old fellow."

Only she ought to have remembered that, after all, she alone kept his subjects in check, and as Daddy la Bretagne said, by a right object. With her to console them they would no doubt have borne anything, but she was foolish enough to cut down their food and not to fill their common dish as full as it used to be. She wanted to keep everything for her lover, and that raised the exasperation of the eighteen to its height. So one night when she and the clown were asleep among all these fasting men, the eighteen threw themselves on them. They wrapped the despot's arms and legs up in tarpaulin, and in the presence of the woman who was firmly bound they flogged him till he was black and blue.

"Yes," old Bretagne said to me himself. "Yes, monsieur, that was our revenge. The king was guillotined in 1793, and so we guillotined our king also."

And he concluded with a sneer, saying: "But we wished to be just, and as it was not his head that had made him our king, by Jove, we settled him."

THE MAD WOMAN

"I CAN TELL YOU a terrible story about the Franco-Prussian War," M. d'Endolin said to some friends assembled in the smoking room of Baron de Ravot's château. "You know my house in the Faubourg de Cormeil. I was living there when the Prussians came, and I had for a neighbor a kind of mad woman who had lost her senses in consequence of a series of misfortunes. At the age of seven and twenty she had lost her father, her husband and her newly born child, all in the space of a month.

"When death has once entered into a house it almost invariably returns immediately, as if it knew the way, and the young woman, overwhelmed with grief, took to her bed and was delirious for six weeks. Then a species of calm lassitude succeeded that violent crisis, and she remained motionless, eating next to nothing and only moving her eyes. Every time they tried to make her get up she screamed as if they were about to kill her, and so they ended by leaving her continually in bed and only taking her out to wash her, to change her linen and to turn her mattress.

"An old servant remained with her to give her something to drink or a little cold meat from time to time. What passed in that despairing mind? No one ever knew, for she did not speak at all now. Was she thinking of the dead? Was she dreaming sadly, without any precise recollection of anything that had happened? Or was her memory as stagnant as water without any current? But however this may have been, for fifteen years she remained thus inert and secluded.

"The war broke out, and in the beginning of December the Germans came to Cormeil. I can remember it as if it were but yesterday. It was freezing hard enough to split the stones, and I myself was lying back in an armchair, being unable to move on account of the gout, when I heard their heavy and regular tread and could see them pass from my window .

"They defiled past interminably, with that peculiar motion of a puppet on wires, which belongs to them. Then the officers billeted their men on the inhabitants, and I had seventeen of them. My neighbor, the crazy woman, had a dozen, one of whom was the commandant, a regular violent, surly swashbuckler.

"During the first few days everything went on as usual. The officers next door had been told that the lady was ill, and they did not trouble themselves about that in the least, but soon that woman whom they never saw irritated them. They asked what her illness was and were told that she had been in bed for fifteen years in consequence of terrible grief. No doubt they did not believe it and thought that the poor mad creature would not leave her bed out of pride, so that she might not come near the Prussians or speak to them or even see them.

"The commandant insisted upon her receiving him. He was shown into the room and said to her roughly: 'I must beg you to get up, madame, and come downstairs so that we may all see you.' But she merely turned her vague eyes on him without replying, and so he continued: 'I do not intend to tolerate any insolence, and if you do not get up of your own accord I can easily find means to make you walk without any assistance.'

"But she did not give any signs of having heard him and remained quite motionless. Then he got furious, taking that calm silence for a mark of supreme contempt, so he added: 'If you do not come downstairs tomorrow——' And then he left the room.

"The next day the terrified old servant wished to dress her, but the mad woman began to scream violently and resisted with all her might. The officer ran upstairs quickly, and the servant threw herself at his feet and cried: 'She will not come down, monsieur; she will not. Forgive her, for she is so unhappy.'

"The soldier was embarrassed, as in spite of his anger he did not venture to order his soldiers to drag her out. But suddenly he began to laugh and gave some orders in German, and soon a party of soldiers was seen coming out, supporting a mattress as if they were carrying a wounded man. On that bed, which had been unmade, the mad woman, who was still silent, was lying quite quietly, for she was quite indifferent to anything that went on, as long as they let her lie. Behind her a soldier was carrying a parcel of feminine attire, and the officer said, rubbing his hands: 'We will just see whether you cannot dress yourself alone and take a little walk.'

"And then the procession went off in the direction of the forest of Imauville; in two hours the soldiers came back alone, and nothing more was seen of the mad woman. What had they done with her? Where had they taken her to? No one knew.

"The snow was falling day and night and enveloped the plain and the woods in a shroud of frozen foam, and the wolves came and howled at our very doors.

"The thought of that poor lost woman haunted me, and I made several applications to the Prussian authorities in order to obtain some information and was nearly shot for doing so. When spring returned the army of occupation withdrew, but my neighbor's house remained closed, and the grass grew thick in the garden walks. The old servant had died during the winter, and nobody troubled any longer about the occurrence; I alone thought about it constantly. What had they done with the woman? Had she escaped through the forest? Had somebody found her and taken her to a hospital without being able to obtain any information from her? Nothing happened to relieve my doubts, but by degrees time assuaged my fears.

"Well, in the following autumn the woodcock were very plentiful, and as my gout had left me for a time, I dragged myself as far as the forest. I had already killed four or five of the long-billed birds, when I knocked over one which fell into a ditch full of branches, and I was obliged to get into it in order to pick it up, and I found that it had fallen close to a dead, human body. Immediately the recollection of the mad woman struck me like a blow in the chest. Many other people had perhaps died in the wood during that disastrous year, but though I do not know why, I was sure, sure, I tell you, that I should see the head of that wretched maniac.

"And suddenly I understood; I guessed everything. They had abandoned her on that mattress in the cold, deserted wood, and, faithful to her fixed idea, she had allowed herself to perish under that thick and light counterpane of snow without moving either arms or legs.

"Then the wolves had devoured her, and the birds had built their nests with the wool from her torn bed, and I took charge of her bones. I only pray that our sons may never see any wars again."

MADEMOISELLE

HE HAD BEEN REGISTERED under the names of Jean Marie Mathieu Valot, but he was never called anything but Mademoiselle. He was the idiot of the district, but not one of those wretched, ragged idiots who live on public charity. He lived comfortably on a small income which his mother had left him and which his guardian paid him regularly, so he was rather envied than pitied. And then he was not one of those idiots with wild looks and the manners of an animal, for he was by no means an unpleasing object, with his half-open lips and smiling eyes, and especially in his constant make-up in female dress. For he dressed like a girl and showed by that how little he objected to being called Mademoiselle.

And why should he not like the nickname which his mother had given him affectionately when he was a mere child, so delicate and weak and with a fair complexion—a poor little diminutive lad, not as tall as many girls of the same age? It was in pure love that in his earlier years his mother whispered that tender Mademoiselle to him, while his old grandmother used to say jokingly:

"The fact is, that as for the male element in him, it is really not worth mentioning in a Christian—no offense to God in saying so." And his grandfather, who was equally fond of a joke, used to add: "I only hope it will not disappear as he grows up."

And they treated him as if he had really been a girl and coddled him, the more so as they were very prosperous and did not require to toil to keep things together.

When his mother and grandparents were dead Mademoiselle was almost as happy with his paternal uncle, an unmarried man who had carefully attended the idiot and who had grown more and more attached to him by dint of looking after him, and the worthy man continued to call Jean Marie Mathieu Valot Mademoiselle.

He was called so in all the country round as well, not with the slightest intention of hurting his feelings, but, on the contrary, because all thought they would please the poor gentle creature who harmed nobody in doing so.

The very street boys meant no harm by it, accustomed as they were to call the tall idiot in a frock and cap by the nickname, but it would have struck them as very extraordinary and would have led them to rude fun if they had seen him dressed like a boy.

Mademoiselle, however, took care of that, for his dress was as dear to him as his nickname. He delighted in wearing it and, in fact, cared for nothing else, and what gave it a particular zest was that he knew that he was not a girl and that he was living in disguise. And this was evident by the exaggerated feminine bearing and walk he put on, as if to show that it was not natural to him. His enormous, carefully filled cap was adorned with large variegated ribbons. His petticoat, with numerous flounces, was distended behind by many hoops. He walked with short steps and with exaggerated swaying of the hips, while his folded arms and crossed hands were distorted into pretensions of comical coquetry.

On such occasions if anybody wished to make friends with him it was necessary to say:

"Ah, Mademoiselle, what a nice girl you make."

That put him into a good humor, and he used to reply, much pleased:

"Don't I? But people can see I only do it for a joke."

But, nevertheless, when they were dancing at village festivals in the neighborhood he would always be invited to dance as Mademoiselle and would never ask any of the girls to dance with him, and one evening when somebody asked him the reason for this he opened his eyes wide, laughed as if the man had said something very stupid and replied:

"I cannot ask the girls because I am not dressed like a lad. Just look at my dress, you fool!"

As his interrogator was a judicious man, he said to him:

"Then dress like one, Mademoiselle."

He thought for a moment and then said with a cunning look:

"But if I dress like a lad I shall no longer be a girl, and then, I am a girl," and he shrugged his shoulders as he said it.

But the remark seemed to make him think.

For some time afterward when he met the same person he would ask him abruptly:

"If I dress like a lad will you still call me Mademoiselle?"

"Of course I shall," the other replied. "You will always be called so."

The idiot appeared delighted, for there was no doubt that he thought more of his nickname than he did of his dress, and the next day he made his appearance in the village square without his petticoats and dressed as a man. He had taken a pair of trousers, a coat and a hat from his guardian's clothes press. This created quite a revolution in the neighborhood, for the people who had been in the habit of smiling at him kindly when he was dressed as a woman looked at him in astonishment and almost in fear, while the indulgent could not help laughing and visibly making fun of him.

The involuntary hostility of some and the too-evident ridicule of others, the disagreeable surprise of all, were too palpable for him not to see it and to be hurt by it, and it was still worse when a street urchin said to him in a jeering voice as he danced round him:

"Oh! Oh! Mademoiselle, you wear trousers! Oh! Oh! Mademoiselle!"

And it grew worse and worse, when a whole band of these vagabonds were on his heels, hooting and yelling after him, as if he had been somebody in a masquerading dress during the carnival.

It was quite certain that the unfortunate creature looked more in disguise now than he had formerly. By dint of living like a girl and by even exaggerating the feminine walk and manners, he had totally lost all masculine looks and ways. His smooth face, his long flax-like hair, required a cap with ribbons and became a caricature under the high chimney-pot hat of the old doctor, his grandfather.

Mademoiselle's shoulders, and especially his swelling stern, danced about wildly in this old-fashioned coat and wide trousers. And nothing was as funny as the contrast between his quiet dress and slow trotting pace, the winning way he used his head and the conceited movements of his hands, with which he fanned himself like a girl.

Soon the older lads and the girls, the old women, men of ripe age and even the judicial councilor joined the little brats and hooted Mademoiselle, while the astonished idiot ran away and rushed into the house with terror. There he took his poor head between both hands and tried to comprehend the matter. Why were they angry with him? For it was quite evident that they were angry with him. What wrong had he done and whom had he injured by dressing as a boy? Was he not a boy, after all? For the first time in his life he felt a horror for his nickname, for had he not been insulted through it? But immediately he was seized with a horrible doubt.

"Suppose that, after all, I am a girl?"

He would have liked to ask his guardian about it but he did not like to, for he somehow felt, although only obscurely, that he, worthy man, might not tell him the truth out of kindness. And, besides, he preferred to find out for himself without asking anyone.

All his idiot's cunning, which had been lying latent up till then because he never had any occasion to make use of it, now came out and urged him to a solitary and dark action.

The next day he dressed himself as a girl again and made his appearance as if he had perfectly forgotten his escapade of the day before, but the people, especially the street boys, had not forgotten it. They looked at him sideways, and even the best of them could not help smiling, while the little blackguards ran after him and said:

"Oh! Oh! Mademoiselle, you had on a pair of breeches!"

But he pretended not to hear or even to guess to what they were alluding. He seemed as happy and glad to look about him as he usually did, with half-open lips and smiling eyes. As usual, he wore an enormous cap with variegated ribbons and the same large petticoats; he walked with short, mincing steps, swaying and wriggling his hips and gesticulating like a coquette and licked his lips when they called him Mademoiselle, while really he would have liked to have jumped at the throats of those who called him so.

Days and months passed, and by degrees those about him forgot all about his strange escapade. But he had never left off thinking about it or trying to find out—for which he was ever on the alert—how he could ascertain his qualities as a boy and how to assert them victoriously. Really innocent, he had reached the age of twenty without knowing anything or without ever having any natural impulse, but being tenacious of purpose, curious and dissembling, he asked no questions but observed all that was said and done.

Often at their village dances he had heard young fellows boasting about girls whom they had seduced and girls praising such and such a young fellow, and often, also, after a dance he saw the couples go away together, with their arms round each other's waists. They had no suspicions of him, and he listened and watched, until at last he discovered what was going on.

And then one night when dancing was over and the couples were going away with their arms round each other's waists, a terrible screaming was heard at the corner of the wood through which those going to the next village had to pass. It was Josephine, pretty Josephine, and when her screams were heard they ran to her assistance and arrived only just in time to rescue her, half strangled, from Mademoiselle's clutches.

The idiot had watched her and had thrown himself upon her in order to treat her as the other young fellows did the girls, but she resisted him so stoutly that he took her by the throat and squeezed it with all his might until she could not breathe and was nearly dead.

In rescuing Josephine from him they had thrown him on the ground, but he jumped up again immediately, foaming at the mouth and slobbering and exclaimed:

"I am not a girl any longer; I am a young man. I am a young man, I tell you."

A BAD ERROR

I MADE Mme Jadelle's acquaintance in Paris this winter. She pleased me infinitely at once. You know her as well as I—no—pardon me—nearly as well as I. You know that she is poetic and fantastic at one and the same time. You know she is free in her manner and of impressionable heart, impulsive, courageous, venturesome, audacious—above all, prejudiced and yet, in spite of that, sentimental, delicate, easily hurt, tender and modest.

She was a widow, and I adore widows, from sheer laziness. I was on the lookout for a wife, and I paid her my court. I knew her, and more than that, she pleased me. The moment came when I believed it would do to risk my proposal. I was in love with her and in danger of becoming too much so. When one marries he should not love his wife too much, or he is likely to make himself foolish; his vision is distorted, and he becomes silly and brutal at the same time. A man must assert himself. If he loses his head at first he risks being a nobody a year later.

So one day I presented myself at her house with light gloves on and I said to her: "Madame, I have the honor of loving you, and I have come to ask you if there is any hope of my pleasing you enough to warrant your placing your happiness in my care and taking my name."

She answered quietly: "What a question, sir! I am absolutely ignorant of whether you will please me sooner or later or whether you will not, but I ask nothing better than to make a trial of it. As a man, I do not find you bad. It remains to be seen how you are at heart and in character and habits. For the most part marriages are tempestuous or criminal because people are not careful enough in yoking themselves together. Sometimes a mere nothing is sufficient, a mania or tenacious opinion upon some moral or religious point, no matter what, a gesture which displeases or some little fault or disagreeable quality, to turn an affianced couple, however tender and affectionate, into a pair of irreconcilable enemies, incensed with, but chained to, each other until death. I will not marry, sir, without knowing the depths and corners and recesses of the soul of the man with whom I am to share my existence. I wish to study him at leisure, at least for some months.

"Here is what I propose. You will come and pass the summer in my house at De Lauville, my country place, and we shall see then if we are fitted to live side by side—I see you laugh! You have a bad thought. Oh, sir, if I were not sure of myself I would never make this proposition. I have for love, what you call love, you men, such a scorn, such a disgust, that a fall is impossible for me. Well, do you accept?"

I kissed her hand.

"When shall we start, madame?"

"The tenth of May."

"It is agreed."

A month later I was installed at her house. She was truly a singular woman. From morning until evening she was studying me. As she was fond of horses, we passed each day in riding through the wood, talking about everything, but she was always trying to probe my innermost thoughts, to which end she observed my slightest movement.

As for me, I became foolishly in love and did not trouble myself about the fitness of our characters. But I soon perceived that even my sleep was put under inspection. Someone slept in a little room adjoining mine, entering very late and with infinite precaution. This espionage for every instant finally made me impatient. I wished to hasten the conclusion and one evening thought of a way of bringing it about. She had received me in such a way that I had abstained from any new essay, but a violent desire invaded me to make her pay in some fashion for this restricted regime to which I had submitted, and I thought I knew a way.

You know Cesarine, her chambermaid, a pretty girl from Granville, where all the women are pretty, and as blond as her mistress was brunette? Well, one afternoon I drew the little soubrette into my room and, putting a hundred francs in her hand, I said to her:

"My dear child, I do not wish you to do anything villainous, but I desire the same privilege toward your mistress that she takes toward me."

The little maid laughed with a sly look as I continued:

"I am watched day and night, I know. I am watched as I eat, drink, dress myself, shave and put on my socks, and I know it."

The little girl stammered: "Yes sir." Then she was silent. I continued:

"You sleep in the room next to mine to see if I snore or if I dream aloud; you cannot deny it!"

"Yes sir." Then she was silent again.

I became excited. "Oh well, my girl," I said, "you understand that it is not fair for everything to be known about me, while I know nothing of the person who is to be my wife. I love her with all my soul. She has the face, the heart and mind that I have dreamed of, and I am the happiest of men on this account; nevertheless, there are some things I would like to know better."

Cesarine decided to put my bank note in her pocket. I understood that the bargain was concluded.

"Listen, my girl," I said. "We men—we care much for certain—certain details—physical details, which do not hinder a woman from being charming but which can change her price in our eyes. I do not ask you to say anything bad of your mistress or even to disclose to me her defects, if she has any. Only answer me frankly four or five questions, which I am going to put to you. You know Madame Jadelle as well as you do yourself, since you dress and undress her every day. Now then, tell me this: Is she as plump as she has the appearance of being?"

The little maid did not answer.

I continued: "You cannot, my child, be ignorant of the fact that women put cotton padding, you know, where—where—where they nourish their infants and also where they sit. Tell me, does she use padding?"

Cesarine lowered her eyes. Finally she said timidly: "Ask whatever you want to, sir, I will answer all at one time."

"Well, my girl, there are some women whose knees meet, so much so that they touch with each step that they take, and there are others who have them far apart, which makes their limbs like the arches of a bridge, so that one might view the landscape between them. This is the prettier of the two fashions. Tell me, how are your mistress's limbs?"

Still the maid said nothing.

I continued: "There are some who have necks so beautiful that they form a great fold underneath. And there are some that have large arms with a thin figure. There are some that are very large before and nothing at all behind, and there are some large behind and nothing at all in front. All this is very pretty, very pretty, but I wish to know just how your mistress is made. Tell me frankly, and I will give you much more money."

Cesarine looked at me out of the corner of her eye and, laughing with all her heart, answered: "Sir, aside from being dark, Mistress is made exactly like me."

Then she fled.

I had been made sport of. This was the time I found myself ridiculous, and I resolved to avenge myself at least upon this impertinent maid.

An hour later I entered the little room with precaution, where she listened to my sleeping, and unscrewed the bolts.

Toward midnight she arrived at her post of observation. I followed her immediately. On perceiving me she was going to cry out, but I put my hand over her mouth and, without too great effort, I convinced myself that if she had not lied Mme Jadelle was very well made.

I even put much zest into this authentication which, though pushed a little far, did not seem to displease Cesarine. She was, in very fact, a ravishing specimen of the Norman peasant race, strong and fine at the same time. She was wanting perhaps in certain delicate attentions that Henry VI would have scorned, but I revealed them to her quickly, and as I adore perfumes, I gave her a box the next evening with a flask of lavender water.

We were soon more closely bound to each other than I could have believed, almost friends. She became an exquisite mistress, naturally *spirituelle* and broken to pleasure. She had been a courtesan of great merit in Paris.

The delights which she brought me enabled me to await Mme Jadelle's conclusion of proof without impatience. I became an incomparable character, supple, docile and complacent. My fiancée found me delightful beyond a doubt, and I judged from certain signs that I was soon to be accepted. I was certainly the happiest man in the world, awaiting tranquilly the legal kiss of the woman I loved, in the arms of a young and beautiful girl for whom I had much fondness.

It is here, madame, that I must ask your forbearance a little; I have arrived at a delicate point.

One evening as we were returning from a horseback ride, Mme Jadelle complained sharply that her grooms had not taken certain measures prescribed by her for the horse she rode. She repeated many times: "Let them take care, I have a way of surprising them."

I passed a calm night in my bed. I awoke early, full of ardor and energy. Then I dressed myself.

I was in the habit of going up on the tower of the house each morning to smoke a cigarette. This was reached by a limestone staircase lighted by a large window at the top of the first story.

I advanced without noise, my feet encased in morocco slippers with wadded soles, and was climbing the first steps when I perceived Cesarine bending out the window, looking down below.

Not that I saw Cesarine entirely, but only a part of Cesarine, and that the lower part. I loved this part just as much; of Mme Jadelle I would have preferred, perhaps, the upper. She was thus so charming, so round, this part which offered itself to me, and only slightly clothed in a white skirt.

I approached so softly that the girl heard nothing. I put myself on my knees; with infinite precaution I took hold of the two sides of the skirt and, quickly, I raised it. I recognized there the full, fresh, plump, sweet ischial tuberosities of my mistress and threw there—your pardon, madame—I threw there a tender kiss, a kiss of a lover who dares anything.

I was surprised. It was verbena! But I had no time for reflection. I received a sudden blow, or rather a push in the face which seemed to break my nose. I uttered a cry that made my hair rise. The person had turned around—it was Mme Jadelle!

She was fighting the air with her hands, like a woman who had lost consciousness. She gasped for some seconds, made a gesture of using a horsewhip and then fled.

Ten minutes later Cesarine, stupefied, brought me in a letter. I read:

Mme Jadelle hopes that M. de Brives will immediately rid her of his presence.

I departed. Well, I am not yet consoled. I have attempted every means and all explanations to obtain a pardon for my misunderstanding, but all proceedings have been nipped in the bud.

Since that moment, you see, I have in my—in my heart a scent of verbena which gives me an immoderate desire to smell the perfume again.

THE PORT

HAVING SAILED from Havre on the third of May, 1882, for a voyage in the China seas, the square-rigged three-master, Notre Dame des Vents, made her way back into the port of Marseilles on the eighth of August, 1886, after an absence of four years. When she had discharged her first cargo in the Chinese port for which she was bound she had immediately found a new freight for Buenos Aires, and from that place had conveyed goods to Brazil.

Other passages, then damage repairs, calms ranging over several months, gales which knocked her out of her course—all the accidents, adventures and misadventures of the sea, in short—had kept far from her country this Norman three-master which had come back to Marseilles with her hold full of tin boxes containing American preserves.

At her departure she had on board, besides the captain and the mate, fourteen sailors, eight Normans and six Britons. On her return there were left only five Britons and four Normans; the other Briton had died while on the way; the four Normans, having disappeared under various circumstances, had been replaced by two Americans, a Negro and a Norwegian carried off one evening from a tavern in Singapore.

The big vessel, with reefed sails and yards crossed over her masts, drawn by a tug from Marseilles, rocking over a sweep of rolling waves which subsided gently into calm water, passed in front of the Château d'If and then under all the gray rocks of the roadstead, which the setting sun covered with a golden vapor. She entered the ancient port in which are packed together, side by side, ships from every port of the world, pell-mell, large and small, of every shape and every variety of rigging, soaking like a bouillabaisse of boats in this basin too limited in extent, full of putrid water where shells touch each other, rub against each other and seem to be pickled in the juice of the vessels.

Notre Dame des Vents took up her station between an Italian brig and an English schooner which made way to let this comrade slip in between them; then, when all the formalities of the customhouse and of the port had been complied with, the captain authorized two thirds of his crew to spend the night on shore.

It was already dark. Marseilles was lighted up. In the heat of this summer's evening a flavor of cooking with garlic floated over the noisy city, filled with the clamor of voices, of rolling vehicles, of the crackling of whips and of southern mirth.

As soon as they felt themselves on shore the ten men whom the sea had been tossing about for some months past proceeded along quite slowly with the hesitating steps of persons who are out of their element, unaccustomed to cities, two by two, in procession.

They swayed from one side to another as they walked, looked about them, smelling out the lanes opening out on the harbor, rendered feverish by the amorous appetite which had been growing to maturity in their bodies during the last sixty-six days at sea. The Normans strode on in front, led by Célestin Duclos, a tall young fellow, sturdy and waggish, who served as a captain for the others every time they set forth on land. He divined the places worth visiting, found out byways after a fashion of his own and did not take much part in the squabbles so frequent among sailors in seaport towns. But once he was caught in one, he was afraid of nobody.

After some hesitation as to which of the obscure streets that led down to the waterside and from which arose heavy smells, a sort of exhalation from closets, they ought to enter, Célestin gave the preference to a kind of winding passage, where gleamed over the doors projecting lanterns bearing enormous numbers on their rough, colored glass. Under the narrow arches at the entrance to the houses women wearing aprons, like servants, seated on straw chairs, rose up on seeing them coming near, taking three steps toward the gutter which separated the street in halves and so cutting off the path from this file of men who sauntered along at their leisure, humming and sneering, already getting excited by the vicinity of those dens of prostitutes.

Sometimes at the end of a hall, behind a second open door which presented itself unexpectedly, covered over with dark leather, would appear a big wench, undressed, whose heavy thighs and fat calves abruptly outlined themselves under her coarse white cotton wrapper. Her short petticoat had the appearance of a puffed-out girdle, and the soft flesh of her breast, her shoulders and her arms made a rosy stain on a black velvet corsage with edgings of gold lace. She kept calling out from her distant corner, "Will you come here, my pretty boys?" And sometimes she would go out herself to catch hold of one of them and to drag him toward her door with all her strength, fastening on him like a spider drawing forward an insect bigger than itself. The man, excited by the struggle, would offer a mild resistance, and the rest would stop to look on, undecided between the longing to go in at once and that of lengthening this appetizing promenade. Then when the woman, after desperate efforts, had brought the sailor to the threshold of her abode in which the entire band would be swallowed up after him, Célestin Duclos, who was a judge of houses of this sort, suddenly exclaimed: "Don't go in there, Marchand! That's not the place."

The man thereupon, obeying this direction, freed himself with a brutal shake, and the comrades formed themselves into a band once more, pursued by the filthy insults of the exasperated wench, while other women all along the alley in front of them came out past their doors, attracted by the noise, and in hoarse voices threw out to them invitations coupled with promises. They went on then, more and more stimulated by the combined effects of the coaxings and the seductions held out as baits to them by the choir of portresses of love all over the upper part of the street and the ignoble maledictions hurled at them by the choir at the lower end—the despised choir of disappointed wenches. From time to time they met another band—soldiers marching along with spurs jingling at their heels, sailors marching again, isolated citizens, clerks in business houses. On all sides might be some fresh streets, narrow and studded all over with those equivocal lanterns. They pursued their way still through this labyrinth of squalid habitation, over those greasy pavements through which putrid water was oozing, between those walls filled with women's flesh.

At last Duclos made up his mind and, drawing up before a house of rather attractive exterior, made all his companions follow him in there.

II

Then followed a scene of thoroughgoing revelry. For four hours the six sailors gorged themselves with love and wine. Six months' pay was thus wasted.

In the principal room in the tavern they were installed as masters, gazing with malignant glances at the ordinary customers who were seated at the little tables in the corners, where one of the girls, who was left free to come and go, dressed like a big baby or a singer at a café concert, went about serving them and then seated herself near them. Each man, on coming in, had selected his partner, whom he kept all the evening, for the vulgar taste is not changeable. They had drawn three tables close up to them, and after the first bumper the procession, divided into two parts, increased by as many women as there were seamen, had formed itself anew on the staircase. On the wooden steps the four feet of each couple kept tramping from time to time, while the several files of lovers were swallowed up behind the narrow doors leading into the different rooms.

Then they came down again to have a drink and, after they had returned to the rooms, descended the stairs once more.

Now almost intoxicated, they began to howl. Each of them, with bloodshot eyes and his chosen female companion on his knee, sang or bawled, struck the table with his fist, shouted while swilling wine down his throat, setting free the brute within. In the midst of them Célestin Duclos, pressing close to him a big damsel with red cheeks who sat astride over his legs, gazed at her ardently. Less tipsy than the others, not that he had taken less drink, he was as yet occupied with other thoughts and, more tender than his comrades, he tried to get up a chat. His thoughts wandered a little, escaped him and then came back and disappeared again without allowing him to recollect exactly what he meant to say.

"What time—what time—how long are you here?"

"Six months," the girl answered.

He seemed to be satisfied with her, as if this were a proof of good conduct, and he went on questioning her:

"Do you like this life?"

She hesitated, then in a tone of resignation:

"One gets used to it. It is not more worrying than any other kind of life. To be a servant girl or else a scrub is always a nasty occupation."

He looked as if he also approved of this truthful remark.

"You are not from this place?" he said.

She answered merely by shaking her head.

"Do you come from a distance?"

She nodded, still without opening her lips.

"Where is it you come from?"

She appeared to be thinking, to be searching her memory, then said falteringly:

"From Perpignan."

He was once more perfectly satisfied and said:

"Ah yes!"

In her turn she asked:

"And you, are you a sailor?"

"Yes, my beauty."

"Do you come from a distance?"

"Ah yes! I have seen countries, ports and everything."

"You have been round the world, perhaps?"

"I believe you, twice rather than once."

Again she seemed to hesitate, to search in her brain for something that she had forgotten, then in a tone somewhat different, more serious:

"Have you met many ships in your voyages?"

"I believe you, my beauty."

"You did not happen to see the Notre Dame des Vents?"

He chuckled.

"No later than last week."

She turned pale, all the blood leaving her cheeks, and asked:

"Is that true, perfectly true?"

" 'Tis true as I tell you."

"Honor bright! You are not telling me a lie?"
He raised his hand.
"Before God, I'm not!" he said.
"Then do you know whether Célestin Duclos is still on her?"
He was astonished, uneasy, and wished, before answering, to learn something further.
"Do you know him?"
She became distrustful in turn.
"Oh! 'Tis not myself—'tis a woman who is acquainted with him."
"A woman from this place?"
"No, from a place not far off."
"In the street? What sort of a woman?"
"Why then, a woman—a woman like myself."
"What has she to say to him, this woman?"
"I believe she is a countrywoman of his."
They stared into one another's eyes, watching one another, feeling, divining that something of a grave nature was going to arise between them.
He resumed:
"I could see her there, this woman."
"What would you say to her?"
"I would say to her—I would say to her—that I had seen Célestin Duclos."
"He is quite well—isn't he?"
"As well as you or me. He is a strapping young fellow."
She became silent again, trying to collect her ideas; then slowly:
"Where has the Notre Dame des Vents gone to?"
"Why, just to Marseilles."
She could not repress a start.
"Is that really true?"
"'Tis really true."
"Do you know Duclos?"
"Yes, I do know him."
She still hesitated; then in a very gentle tone:
"Good! That's good!"
"What do you want with him?"
"Listen—you will tell him—nothing!"
He stared at her, more and more perplexed. At last he put this question to her:
"Do you know him, too, yourself?"
"No," she said.
"Then what do you want with him?"
Suddenly she made up her mind what to do, left her seat, rushed over to the bar where the landlady of the tavern presided, seized a lemon which she tore open and shed its juice into a glass, then she filled this glass with pure water and, carrying it across to him:
"Drink this!"
"Why?"

"To make it pass for wine. I will talk to you afterward."
He drank it without further protest, wiped his lips with the back of his hand, then observed:
"That's all right. I am listening to you."
"You will promise not to tell him you have seen me or from whom you learned what I am going to tell you. You must swear not to do so."
He raised his hand.
"All right. I swear I will not."
"Before God?"
"Before God."
"Well, you will tell him that his father died, that his mother died, that his brother died, the whole three in one month, of typhoid fever, in January 1883—three years and a half ago."
In his turn he felt all his blood set in motion through his entire body, and for a few seconds he was so much overpowered that he could make no reply; then he began to doubt what she had told him and asked:
"Are you sure?"
"I am sure."
"Who told it to you?"
She laid her hands on his shoulders and, looking at him out of the depths of her eyes:
"You swear not to blab?"
"I swear that I will not."
"I am his sister!"
He uttered that name in spite of himself:
"Françoise?"
She contemplated him once more with a fixed stare, then, excited by a wild feeling of terror, a sense of profound horror, she faltered in a very low tone, almost speaking into his mouth:
"Oh! Oh! It is you, Célestin."
They no longer stirred; their eyes riveted in one another.
Around them his comrades were still yelling. The sounds made by glasses, by fists, by heels keeping time to the choruses and the shrill cries of the women, mingled with the roar of their songs.
He felt her leaning on him, clasping him, ashamed and frightened, his sister. Then in a whisper, lest anyone might hear him, so hushed that she could scarcely catch his words:
"What a misfortune! I have made a nice piece of work of it!"
The next moment her eyes were filled with tears, and she faltered:
"Is that my fault?"
But all of a sudden he said:
"So then they are dead?"
"They are dead."
"The father, the mother and the brother?"
"The three in one month, as I told you. I was left by myself with nothing but my clothes, for I was in debt to the apothecary and the doctor and for

the funeral of the three and had to pay what I owed with the furniture.

"After that I went as a servant to the house of Maître Cacheux—you know him well—the cripple. I was just fifteen at the time, for you went away when I was not quite fourteen. I tripped with him. One is so senseless when one is young. Then I went as a nursery maid to the notary who debauched me, also, and brought me to Havre, where he took a room for me. After a little while he gave up coming to see me. For three days I lived without eating a morsel of food, and then, not being able to get employment, I went to a house, like many others. I, too, have seen different places—ah, and dirty places! Rouen, Evreux, Lille, Bordeaux, Perpignan, Nice and then Marseilles, where I am now!"

The tears started from her eyes, flowed over her nose, wet her cheeks and trickled into her mouth.

She went on:

"I thought you were dead, too, my poor Célestin."

He said:

"I would not have recognized you myself—you were such a little thing then, and here you are so big! But how is it that you did not recognize me?"

She answered with a despairing movement of her hands:

"I see so many men that they all seem to me alike."

He kept his eyes still fixed on her intently, oppressed by an emotion that dazed him and filled him with such pain as to make him long to cry like a little child that has been whipped. He still held her in his arms, while she sat astride on his knees, with his open hands against the girl's back; and now by sheer dint of looking continually at her he at length recognized her, the little sister left behind in the country with all those whom she had seen die, while he had been tossing on the seas. Then suddenly taking between his big seaman's paws this head found once more, he began to kiss her, as one kisses kindred flesh. And after that, sobs, a man's deep sobs, heaving like great billows, rose up in his throat, resembling the hiccups of drunkenness.

He stammered:

"And this is you—this is you, Françoise—my little Françoise!"

Then all at once he sprang up, began swearing in an awful voice and struck the table such a blow with his fist that the glasses were knocked down and smashed. After that he advanced three steps, staggered, stretched out his arms and fell on his face. And he rolled on the floor, crying out, beating the boards with his hands and feet and uttering such groans that they seemed like a death rattle.

All those comrades of his stared at him and laughed.

"He's not a bit drunk," said one.

"He ought to be put to bed," said another.

"If he goes out we'll all be run in together."

Then as he had money in his pockets, the landlady offered to let him have a bed, and his comrades, themselves so much intoxicated that they could not stand upright, hoisted him up the narrow stairs to the apartment of the woman who had just been in his company and who remained sitting on a chair at the foot of that bed of crime, weeping quite as freely as he had wept, until the morning dawned.

CHÂLI

ADMIRAL DE LA VALLÉE, who seemed to be half asleep in his armchair, said in a voice which sounded like an old woman's:
"I had a very singular little love adventure once; would you like to hear it?"
He spoke from the depths of his great armchair with that everlasting dry, wrinkled smile on his lips, that smile à la Voltaire, which made people take him for a terrible skeptic.

I

"I was thirty years of age and a first lieutenant in the navy, when I was intrusted with an astronomical expedition to Central India. The English government provided me with all the necessary means for carrying out my enterprise, and I was soon busied with a few followers in that vast, strange, surprising country.

"It would take me ten volumes to relate that journey. I went through wonderfully magnificent regions, was received by strangely handsome princes and was entertained with incredible magnificence. For two months it seemed to me as if I were walking in a fairy kingdom on the back of imaginary elephants. In the midst of wild forests I discovered extraordinary ruins, delicate and chiseled like jewels, fine as lace and enormous as mountains, those fabulous, divine monuments which are so graceful that one falls in love with their form as with a woman, feeling a physical and sensual pleasure in looking at them. As Victor Hugo says, 'Whilst wide awake I was walking in a dream.'

"Toward the end of my journey I reached Ganhard, which was formerly one of the most prosperous towns in Central India but is now much decayed. It is governed by a wealthy, arbitrary, violent, generous and cruel prince. His name is Rajah Maddan, a true oriental potentate, delicate and barbarous, affable and sanguinary, combining feminine grace with pitiless ferocity.

"The city lies at the bottom of a valley, on the banks of a little lake surrounded by pagodas which bathe their walls in the water. At a distance the city looks like a white spot which grows larger as one approaches it, and by degrees you discover the domes and spires, the slender and graceful summits of Indian monuments.

"At about an hour's distance from the gates I met a superbly caparisoned elephant surrounded by a guard of honor which the sovereign had sent me, and I was conducted to the palace with great ceremony.

"I should have liked to have taken the time to put on my gala uniform, but royal impatience would not admit of it. He was anxious to make my acquaintance, to know what he might expect from me.

"I was ushered into a great hall surrounded by galleries, in the midst of bronze-colored soldiers in splendid uniforms, while all about were standing men dressed in striking robes, studded with precious stones.

"I saw a shining mass, a kind of setting sun reposing on a bench like our garden benches without a back; it was the rajah who was waiting for me, motionless, in a robe of the purest canary color. He had some ten or fifteen million francs' worth of diamonds on him, and by itself, on his forehead, glistened the famous star of Delhi, which has always belonged to the illustrious dynasty of the Pariharas of Mundore, from whom my host was descended.

"He was a man of about five and twenty, who seemed to have some Negro blood in his veins, although he belonged to the purest Hindu race. He had large, almost motionless, rather vague eyes, fat lips, a curly beard, low forehead and dazzling sharp white teeth, which he frequently showed with a mechanical smile. He got up and gave me his hand in the English fashion and then made me sit down beside him on a bench which was so high that my feet hardly touched the ground and on which I was very uncomfortable.

"He immediately proposed a tiger hunt for the next day; war and hunting were his chief occupations, and he could hardly understand how one could care for anything else. He was evidently fully persuaded that I had only come all that distance to amuse him a little and to be the companion of his pleasures.

"As I stood greatly in need of his assistance, I tried to flatter his tastes, and he was so pleased with me that he immediately wished to show me how his trained boxers fought and led the way into a kind of arena situated within the palace.

"At his command two naked men appeared, their hands covered with steel claws. They immediately began to attack each other, trying to strike one another with these sharp weapons which left long cuts from which the blood flowed freely down their dark skins.

"It lasted for a long time, till their bodies were a mass of wounds, and the combatants were tearing each other's flesh with these pointed blades. One of them had his jaw smashed, while the ear of the other was split into three pieces.

"The prince looked on with ferocious pleasure, uttered grunts of delight and imitated all their movements with careless gestures, crying out constantly:

"'Strike, strike hard!'

"One fell down unconscious and had to be carried out of the arena, covered with blood, while the rajah uttered a sigh of regret because it was over so soon.

"He turned to me to know my opinion; I was disgusted, but I congratulated him loudly. He then gave orders that I was to be conducted to Kuch-Mahal (the palace of pleasure), where I was to be lodged.

"This bijou palace was situated at the extremity of the royal park, and one of its walls was built into the sacred lake of Vihara. It was square, with three rows of galleries with colonnades of most beautiful workmanship. At each angle there were light, lofty or low towers, standing either singly or in pairs;

no two were alike, and they looked like flowers growing out of that graceful plant of oriental architecture. All were surmounted by fantastic roofs, like coquettish ladies' caps.

"In the middle of the edifice a large dome raised its round cupola, like a woman's bosom, beside a beautiful clock tower.

"The whole building was covered with sculpture from top to bottom, with exquisite arabesques which delighted the eye, motionless processions of delicate figures whose attitudes and gestures in stone told the story of Indian manners and customs.

"The rooms were lighted by windows with dentelated arches, looking on to the gardens. On the marble floor were designs of graceful bouquets in onyx, lapis lazuli and agate.

"I had scarcely had time to finish my toilet when Haribada, a court dignitary who was specially charged to communicate between the prince and me, announced his sovereign's visit.

"The saffron-colored rajah appeared, again shook hands with me and began to tell me a thousand different things, constantly asking me for my opinion, which I had great difficulty in giving him. Then he wished to show me the ruins of the former palace at the other extremity of the gardens.

"It was a real forest of stones inhabited by a large tribe of apes. On our approach the males began to run along the walls, making the most hideous faces at us, while the females ran away, carrying off their young in their arms. The rajah shouted with laughter and pinched my arm to draw my attention and to testify his own delight and sat down in the midst of the ruins, while around us, squatting on the top of the walls, perching on every eminence, a number of animals with white whiskers put out their tongues and shook their fists at us.

"When he had seen enough of this the yellow rajah rose and began to walk sedately on, keeping me always at his side, happy at having shown me such things on the very day of my arrival and reminding me that a grand tiger hunt was to take place the next day in my honor.

"I was present at it, at a second, a third, at ten, twenty in succession. We hunted all the animals which the country produces in turn: the panther, the bear, elephant, antelope and the crocodile—half the beasts in creation, I should say. I was disgusted at seeing so much blood flow and tired of this monotonous pleasure.

"At length the prince's ardor abated and, at my urgent request, he left me a little leisure for work, contenting himself by loading me with costly presents. He sent me jewels, magnificent stuffs, and well-broken animals of all sorts, which Haribada presented to me with apparently as grave respect as if I had been the sun himself, although he heartily despised me at the bottom of his heart.

"Every day a procession of servants brought me, in covered dishes, a portion of each course that was served at the royal table. Every day he seemed to take an extreme pleasure in getting up some new entertainment for me— dances by the bayaderes, jugglers, reviews of the troops—and I was obliged to pretend to be most delighted with it so as not to hurt his feelings when he wished to show me his wonderful country in all its charm and all its splendor.

"As soon as I was left alone for a few moments I either worked or went to see the monkeys, whose company pleased me a great deal better than that of their royal master.

"One evening, however, on coming back from a walk, I found Haribada outside the gate of my palace. He told me in mysterious tones that a gift from the king was waiting for me in my abode, and he said that his master begged me to excuse him for not having sooner thought of offering me that of which I had been deprived for such a long time.

"After these obscure remarks the ambassador bowed and withdrew.

"When I went in I saw six little girls standing against the wall, motionless, side by side, like smelts on a skewer. The eldest was perhaps ten and the youngest eight years old. For the first moment I could not understand why this girls' school had taken up its abode in my rooms; then, however, I divined the prince's delicate attention: he had made me a present of a harem and had chosen it very young from an excess of generosity. There the more unripe the fruit is, in the higher estimation it is held.

"For some time I remained confused, embarrassed and ashamed in the presence of these children who looked at me with great grave eyes which seemed already to divine what I might want of them.

"I did not know what to say to them; I felt inclined to send them back, but I could not return the presents of a prince; it would have been a mortal insult. I was obliged, therefore, to install this troop of children in my palace.

"They stood motionless, looking at me, waiting for my orders, trying to read my thoughts in my eyes. Confound such a present! How absurdly it was in my way. At last, thinking that I must be looking rather ridiculous, I asked the eldest her name.

"'Châli,' she replied.

"This little creature, with her beautiful skin which was slightly yellow, like old ivory, was a marvel, a perfect statue, with her face and its long and severe lines.

"I then asked, in order to see what she would reply and also, perhaps, to embarrass her:

"'What have you come here for?'

"She replied in her soft, harmonious voice: 'I have come to be altogether at my lord's disposal and to do whatever he wishes.' She was evidently quite resigned.

"I put the same question to the youngest, who answered immediately in her shrill voice:

"'I am here to do whatever you ask me, my master.'

"This one was like a little mouse and was very taking, just as they all were, so I took her in my arms and kissed her. The others made a movement to go away, thinking, no doubt, that I had made my choice, but I ordered them to stay and, sitting down in the Indian fashion, I made them all sit round me and began to tell them fairy tales, for I spoke their language tolerably well.

"They listened very attentively and trembled, wringing their hands in agony. Poor little things, they were not thinking any longer of the reason why they were sent to me.

"When I had finished my story I called Latchmân, my confidential servant, and made him bring sweetmeats and cakes, of which they ate enough to make themselves ill. Then, as I began to find the adventure rather funny, I organized games to amuse my wives.

"One of these diversions had an enormous success. I made a bridge of my legs, and the six children ran underneath, the smallest beginning and the tallest always knocking against them a little, because she did not stoop enough. It made them shout with laughter, and these young voices sounding through the low vaults of my sumptuous palace seemed to wake it up and to people it with childlike gaiety and life.

"Next I took great interest in seeing to the sleeping apartments of my innocent concubines, and in the end I saw them safely locked up under the surveillance of four female servants whom the prince had sent me at the same time, in order to take care of my sultanas.

"For a week I took the greatest pleasure in acting the part of a father toward these living dolls. We had capital games of hide-and-seek and puss in the corner, which gave them the greatest pleasure. Every day I taught them a new game to their intense delight.

"My house now seemed to be one large nursery, and my little friends, dressed in beautiful silk stuffs and in materials embroidered with gold and silver, ran up and down the long galleries and the quiet rooms like little human animals.

"Châli was an adorable little creature, timid and gentle, who soon got to love me ardently, with some degree of shame, with hesitation, as if afraid of European morality, with reserve and scruples and yet with passionate tenderness. I cherished her as if I had been her father.

"The others continued to play in the palace like a lot of happy kittens, but Châli never left me except when I went to the prince.

"We passed delicious hours together in the ruins of the old castle, among the monkeys, who had become our friends.

"She used to lie on my knees and remain there, turning all sorts of things over in her little sphinx's head, or perhaps not thinking of anything, retaining that beautiful, charming, hereditary pose of that noble and dreamy people, the hieratic pose of the sacred statues.

"In a large brass dish I had one day brought provisions, cakes, fruits. The apes came nearer and nearer, followed by their young ones, who were more timid; at last they sat down round us in a circle without daring to come any nearer, waiting for me to distribute my delicacies Then almost invariably a male more daring than the rest would come to me with outstretched hand, like a beggar, and I would give him something which he would take to his wife. All the others immediately began to utter furious cries, cries of rage and jealousy, and I could not make the terrible racket cease except by throwing each one his share.

"As I was very comfortable in the ruins, I had my instruments brought there so that I might be able to work. As soon, however, as they saw the copper fittings on my scientific instruments, the monkeys, no doubt taking them for some deadly engines, fled on all sides, uttering the most piercing cries.

"I often spent my evenings with Châli on one of the external galleries that looked on to the lake of Vihara. One night in silence we looked at the bright moon gliding over the sky, throwing a mantle of trembling silver over the water and, on the further shore, upon the row of small pagodas like carved mushrooms with their stalks in the water. Taking the thoughtful head of my little mistress between my hands, I printed a long, soft kiss on her polished brow, on her great eyes which were full of the secret of that ancient and fabulous land and on her calm lips which opened to my caress. I felt a confused, powerful, above all a poetical, sensation, the sensation that I possessed a whole race in this little girl, that mysterious race from which all the others seem to have taken their origin.

"The prince, however, continued to load me with presents. One day he sent me a very unexpected object which excited a passionate admiration in Châli. It was merely one of those cardboard boxes, covered with shells stuck on outside, which can be bought at any European seaside resort for a penny or two. But there it was a jewel beyond price, and, no doubt, was the first that had found its way into the kingdom. I put it on a table and left it there, wondering at the value which was set upon this trumpery article out of a bazaar.

"But Châli never got tired of looking at it, of admiring it ecstatically. From time to time she would say to me, 'May I touch it?' And when I had given her permission she raised the lid, closed it again with the greatest precaution, touched the shells very gently, and the contact seemed to give her real physical pleasure.

"However, I had finished my scientific work, and it was time for me to return. I was a long time in making up my mind, kept back by my tenderness for my little friend, but at last I was obliged to fix the day of my departure.

"The prince got up fresh hunting excursions and fresh wrestling matches, and after a fortnight of these pleasures I declared that I could stay no longer, and he gave me my liberty.

"My farewell from Châli was heart-rending. She wept, lying beside me with her head on my breast, shaken with sobs. I did not know how to console her; my kisses were no good.

"All at once an idea struck me and, getting up, I went and got the shell box and, putting it into her hands, I said, 'That is for you; it is yours.'

"Then I saw her smile at first. Her whole face was lighted up with internal joy, with that profound joy which comes when impossible dreams are suddenly realized, and she embraced me ardently.

"All the same she wept bitterly when I bade her a last farewell.

"I gave paternal kisses and cakes to all the rest of my wives, and then I left for home.

II

"Two years had passed when my duties again called me to Bombay, and because I knew the country and the language well, I was left there to undertake another mission.

"I finished what I had to do as quickly as possible, and as I had a considerable amount of spare time on my hands, I determined to go and see my friend Rajah Maddan and my dear little Châli once more, though I expected to find her much changed.

"The rajah received me with every demonstration of pleasure and hardly left me for a moment during the first day of my visit. At night, however, when I was alone I sent for Haribada, and after several misleading questions I said to him:

" 'Do you know what has become of little Châli whom the rajah gave me?'

"He immediately assumed a sad and troubled look and said, in evident embarrassment:

" 'We had better not speak of her.'

" 'Why? She was a dear little woman.'

" 'She turned out badly, sir.'

" 'What—Châli? What has become of her? Where is she?'

" 'I mean to say that she came to a bad end.'

" 'A bad end! Is she dead?'

" 'Yes. She committed a very dreadful action.'

"I was very much distressed. I felt my heart beat; my breast was oppressed with grief, and I insisted on knowing what she had done and what had happened to her.

"The man became more and more embarrassed and murmured: 'You had better not ask about it.'

" 'But I want to know.'

" 'She stole——'

" 'Who—Châli? What did she steal?'

" 'Something that belonged to you.'

" 'To me? What do you mean?'

" 'The day you left she stole that little box which the prince had given you; it was found in her hands.'

" 'What box are you talking about?'

" 'The box covered with shells.'

" 'But I gave it to her.'

"The Hindu looked at me with stupefaction and then replied: 'Well, she declared with the most sacred oaths that you had given it to her, but nobody could believe that you could have given a king's present to a slave, and so the rajah had her punished.'

" 'How was she punished? What was done to her?'

" 'She was tied up in a sack and thrown into the lake from this window, from the window of the room in which we are, where she had committed the theft.'

"I felt the most terrible grief that I ever experienced and made a sign to Haribada to go away so that he might not see my tears. I spent the night on the gallery which looked on to the lake, on the gallery where I had so often held the poor child on my knees, and pictured to myself her pretty little body lying decomposed in a sack in the dark waters beneath me.

"The next day I left again, in spite of the rajah's entreaties and evident vexation, and I now still feel as if I had never loved any woman but Châli."

JEROBOAM

ANYONE WHO SAID, or even insinuated, that the Reverend William Greenfield, vicar of St Sampson's, Tottenham, did not make his wife Anna perfectly happy, would certainly have been very malicious. In their twelve years of married life he had honored her with twelve children, and could anybody ask more of a saintly man?

Saintly even to heroism, in truth! For his wife Anna, who was endowed with invaluable virtues, which made her a model among wives and a paragon among mothers, had not been equally endowed physically. In one word, she was hideous. Her hair, which though thin was coarse, was the color of the national half-and-half, but of thick half-and-half which looked as if it had been already swallowed several times. Her complexion, which was muddy and pimply, looked as if it were covered with sand mixed with brick dust. Her teeth, which were long and protruding, seemed to start out of their sockets in order to escape from that almost lipless mouth whose sulphurous breath had turned them yellow. Evidently Anna suffered from bile.

Her china-blue eyes looked different ways, one very much to the right and the other very much to the left, with a frightened squint, no doubt in order that they might not see her nose, of which they felt ashamed. They were quite right! Thin, soft, long, pendent, sallow and ending in a violent knob, it irresistibly reminded those who saw it of something both ludicrous and indescribable. Her body, through the inconceivable irony of nature, was at the same time thin and flabby, wooden and chubby, without either the elegance of slimness or the rounded curves of stoutness. It might have been taken for a body which had formerly been fat but which had now grown thin, while the covering had remained stretched on the framework.

She was evidently nothing but skin and bone, but had too much bone and too little skin.

It will be seen that the reverend gentleman had done his duty, his whole duty, in fact, more than his duty, in sacrificing a dozen times on this altar. Yes, a dozen times bravely and loyally! His wife could not deny it or dispute the number, because the children were there to prove it. A dozen times, and not one less!

And, alas! Not once more. This was the reason why, in spite of appearances, Mrs Anna Greenfield ventured to think, in the depths of her heart, that the Reverend William Greenfield, vicar of St Sampson's, Tottenham, had not made her perfectly happy. She thought so all the more as, for four years now, she had been obliged to renounce all hope of that annual sacrifice which had been so easy and so regular formerly, but which had now fallen into disuse. In fact, at the birth of her twelfth child the reverend gentleman had expressly said to her:

"God has greatly blessed our union, my dear Anna. We have reached the sacred number of the Twelve Tribes of Israel. Were we now to persevere in the works of the flesh, it would be mere debauchery, and I cannot suppose that you would wish me to end my exemplary life in lustful practices."

His wife blushed and looked down, and the holy man, with that legitimate pride of virtue which is its own reward, audibly thanked heaven that he was "not as other men are."

A model among wives and a paragon of mothers, Anna lived with him for four years on those terms without complaining to anyone. She contented herself by praying fervently to God that He would inspire her husband with the desire to begin a second series of the Twelve Tribes. At times even, in order to make her prayers more efficacious, she tried to compass that end by culinary means. She spared no pains and gorged the reverend gentleman with highly seasoned dishes—hare soup, oxtails stewed in sherry, the green fat in turtle soup, stewed mushrooms, Jerusalem artichokes, celery and horse-radish, hot sauces, truffles, hashes with wine and cayenne pepper in them, curried lobsters, pies made of cocks' combs, oysters and the soft roe of fish. These dishes were washed down by strong beer and generous wines, Scotch ale, burgundy, dry champagne, brandy, whisky and gin—in a word, by that numberless array of alcoholic drinks with which the English people love to heat their blood.

As a matter of fact, the reverend gentleman's blood became very heated, as was shown by his nose and cheeks. But in spite of this the powers above were inexorable, and he remained quite indifferent as regards his wife, who was unhappy and thoughtful at the sight of that protruding nasal appendage which, alas, was alone in its glory.

She became thinner and, at the same time, flabbier than ever. She almost began to lose her trust in God, when suddenly she had an inspiration: Was it not, perhaps, the work of the devil?

She did not care to inquire too closely into the matter, as she thought it a very good idea. It was this.

Go to the Universal Exhibition in Paris, and there, perhaps, you will discover how to make yourself loved.

Decidedly luck favored her, for her husband immediately gave her permission to go. As soon as she got into the Esplanade des Invalides she saw the Algerian dancers and said to herself:

"Surely this would inspire William with the desire to be the father of the thirteenth tribe!"

But how could she manage to get him to be present at such abominable orgies? For she could not hide from herself that it was an abominable exhibition, and she knew how scandalized he would be at their voluptuous movements. She had no doubt that the devil had led her there, but she could not take her eyes off the scene, and it gave her an idea. So for nearly a fortnight you might have seen the poor, unattractive woman sitting and attentively and curiously watching the swaying hips of the Algerian women. She was learning.

The evening of her return to London she rushed into her husband's bedroom, disrobed herself in an instant, retaining only a thin gauze covering, and for the first time in her life appeared before him in all the ugliness of seminudity.

"Come, come," the saintly man stammered out, "are you—are you mad, Anna? What demon possesses you? Why inflict the disgrace of such a spectacle on me?"

But she did not listen to him, did not reply, and suddenly began to sway her hips about like an *almah*.[1] The reverend gentleman could not believe his eyes; in his stupefaction he did not think of covering them with his hands or even of shutting them. He looked at her, stupefied and dumfounded, a prey to the hypnotism of ugliness. He watched her as she advanced and retired, as she swayed and skipped and wriggled and postured in extraordinary attitudes. For a long time he sat motionless and almost unable to speak. He only said in a low voice:

"Oh lord! To think that twelve times—twelve times—a whole dozen!"

Then she fell into a chair, panting and worn out and saying to herself:

"Thank heaven! William looks as he used to do formerly on the days that he honored me. Thank heaven! There will be a thirteenth tribe, and then a fresh series of tribes, for William is very methodical in all that he does!"

But William merely took a blanket off the bed and threw it over her, saying in a voice of thunder:

"Your name is no longer Anna, Mrs Greenfield; for the future you shall be called Jezebel. I only regret that I have twelve times mingled my blood with your impure blood." And then, seized by pity, he added: "If you were only in a state of inebriety, of intoxication, I could excuse you."

"Oh, William!" she exclaimed repentantly, "I am in that state. Forgive me, William—forgive a poor drunken woman!"

"I will forgive you, Anna," he replied, and he pointed to a washbasin, saying: "Cold water will do you good, and when your head is clear remember the lesson which you must learn from this occurrence."

"What lesson?" she asked humbly.

"That people ought never to depart from their usual habits."

"But why then, William," she asked timidly, "have you changed your habits?"

"Hold your tongue!" he cried. "Hold your tongue, Jezebel! Have you not got over your intoxication yet? For twelve years I certainly followed the

---

[1] Egyptian dancing girl.—(Translator.)

divine precept: 'increase and multiply,' once a year. But since then I have grown accustomed to something else, and I do not wish to alter my habits."

And the Reverend William Greenfield, vicar of St Sampson's, Tottenham, the saintly man whose blood was inflamed by heating food and liquor, whose ears were like full-blown poppies and who had a nose like a tomato, left his wife and, as had been his habit for four years, went to make love to Polly, the servant.

"Now, Polly," he said, "you are a clever girl, and I mean through you to teach Mrs Greenfield a lesson she will never forget. I will try and see what I can do for you."

And to accomplish this he took her to Mrs Greenfield, called the latter his little Jezebel and said to her with an unctuous smile:

"Call me Jeroboam! You don't understand why? Neither do I, but that does not matter. Take off all your things, Polly, and show yourself to Mrs Greenfield."

The servant did as she was bidden, and the result was that Mrs Greenfield never again hinted to her husband the desirability of laying the foundations of a thirteenth tribe.

VIRTUE IN THE BALLET

IT IS A STRANGE FEELING of pleasure that the writer about the stage and about theatrical characters in general feels when he occasionally discovers a good, honest human heart in the twilight behind the scenes. Of all the witches and semi-witches of that eternal Walpurgis Night, whose boards represent the world, the ladies of the ballet have at all times and in all places been regarded at least like saints, although Hackländer repeatedly tried in vain in his earlier novels to convince us that true virtue appears in tights and short petticoats and is only to be found in ballet girls. I fear that the popular voice is right as a general rule, but it is equally true that here and there one finds a pearl in the dust and even in the dirt. The short story that I am about to tell will best justify my assertion.

Whenever a new, youthful dancer appeared at the Vienna Opera House the habitués began to go after her and did not rest until the fresh young rose had been plucked by some hand or other, though often it was old and trembling. For how could those young and pretty, sometimes even beautiful, girls —with every right to life, love and pleasure, but poor and on a very small salary—resist the seduction of the smell of flowers and of the flash of diamonds? And if one resisted it, it was love, some real, strong passion that gave her the strength, generally, however, only to go after luxury all the more shamelessly and selfishly when her lover forsook her.

At the beginning of the winter season of 185— the pleasing news was spread among the habitués that a girl of dazzling beauty was going to appear very shortly in the ballet at the Court Theater. When the evening came nobody had yet seen the much-discussed phenomenon, but report spread her name from mouth to mouth. It was Satanella. The moment the troupe of elastic figures in fluttering petticoats jumped onto the stage every opera glass in the boxes and stalls was directed on the stage, and at the same instant the new dancer was discovered, although she timidly kept in the background.

She was one of those girls who seem crowned with the bright halo of virginity but at the same time present a splendid type of womanhood. She had the voluptuous form of Ruben's second wife, whom they called, not untruly, a reincarnated Helen, and her head with its delicate nose, its small, full mouth and its dark, inquiring eyes reminded people of the celebrated picture of the Flemish Venus in the Belvedere in Vienna.

She took the old guard of the Vienna Court Theater by storm, and the very next morning a perfect shower of billets-doux, jewels and bouquets fell into the poor ballet girl's attic. For a moment she was dazzled by all this splendor and looked at the gold bracelets, the brooches set with rubies and emeralds, and at the sparkling earrings, with flushed cheeks. Then an unspeakable terror of being lost and of sinking into degradation seized her, and she pushed the jewels away and was about to send them back. But as is usual in such cases, her mother intervened in favor of the generous gentlemen, and so the jewels were accepted, but the notes which accompanied them were not answered. A second and a third discharge of Cupid's artillery followed without making any impression on that virtuous girl; in consequence a great number of her admirers grew quiet, though some continued to send her presents and to assail her with love letters. One had the courage to go still farther.

He was a wealthy banker who had called on the mother of Henrietta, as we shall call the fair-haired ballet girl, and then one evening, quite unexpectedly, on the girl herself. He by no means met with the reception which he had expected from the pretty girl in the faded cotton gown. Henrietta treated him with a certain amount of good-humored respect, which had a much more unpleasant effect on him than that coldness and prudery which is often coexistent with coquetry and selfish speculation among a certain class of women. In spite of everything, however, he soon went to see her daily and lavished his wealth on the beautiful dancer without request on her part and gave her no chance of refusing, for he relied on the mother for everything. The mother took pretty, small apartments for her daughter and herself in the Kärntnerstrasse and furnished them elegantly, hired a cook and housemaid, made an arrangement with a fly driver, and lastly, clothed her daughter's lovely lines in silk, velvet and valuable lace.

Henrietta persistently held her tongue at all this; only once she said to her mother in the presence of the Stock Exchange Jupiter:

"Have you won a prize in the lottery?"

"Of course I have," her mother replied with a laugh.

The girl, however, had given away her heart long before, and, contrary to all precedent, to a man of whose very name she was ignorant, who sent her no diamonds and not even flowers. But he was young and good looking and stood, so retiringly and so evidently in love, at the small side door of the opera house every night when she got out of her antediluvian and rickety fly and also when she got into it again after the performance that she could not help noticing him. Soon he began to follow her wherever she went, and once he summoned up courage to speak to her, when she had been to see a friend in a remote suburb. He was very nervous, but she thought all that he said very clear and logical, and she did not hesitate for a moment to confess that she returned his love.

"You have made me the happiest and at the same time the most wretched of men," he said after a pause.

"What do you mean?" she said innocently.

"Do you not belong to another man?" he asked her in a sad voice.

She shook her abundant light curls.

"Up till now I have belonged to myself alone, and I will prove it to you by requesting you to call upon me frequently and without restraint. Everyone shall know that we are lovers. I am not ashamed of belonging to an honorable man, but I will not sell myself."

"But your splendid apartments and your dresses," her lover interposed shyly; "you cannot pay for them out of your salary."

"My mother has won a large prize in the lottery or made a hit on the Stock Exchange." And with these words the determined girl cut short all further explanations.

That same evening the young man paid his first visit, to the horror of the girl's mother who was so devoted to the Stock Exchange, and he came again the next day and nearly every day. Her mother's reproaches were of no more avail than Jupiter's furious looks, and when the latter one day asked for an explanation as to certain visits, the girl said proudly:

"That is very soon explained. He loves me as I love him, and I presume you can guess the rest."

And he certainly did guess the rest and disappeared, and with him the shower of gold ceased.

The mother cried and the daughter laughed. "I never gave the worn-out old rake any hopes, and what does it matter to me what bargain you made with him? I always thought that you had been lucky on the Stock Exchange. Now, however, we must seriously consider about giving up our apartments and make up our minds to live as we did before."

"Are you really capable of making such a sacrifice for me, to renounce luxury and to have my poverty?" her lover said.

"Certainly I am! Is not that a matter of course when one loves?" the ballet girl replied in surprise.

"Then let me inform you, my dear Henrietta," he said, "that I am not so poor as you think; I only wished to find out whether I could make myself loved for my own sake, and I have done so. I am Count L——, and though I am a minor and dependent on my parents, yet I have enough to be able to retain your pretty rooms for you and to offer you, if not a luxurious, at any rate a comfortable existence."

On hearing this the mother dried her tears immediately. Count L—— became the girl's acknowledged lover, and they passed the happiest hours together. Unselfish as the girl was, she was yet such a thoroughly ingenuous Viennese that whenever she saw anything that took her fancy, whether it was a dress, a cloak or one of those pretty little ornaments for a side table, she used to express her admiration in such terms as forced her lover to make her a present of the object in question. In this way Count L—— incurred enormous debts, which his father paid repeatedly; at last, however, he inquired into the cause of all this extravagance, and when he discovered it he gave his son the choice of giving up his connection with the dancer or of relinquishing all claims on the paternal money box.

It was a sorrowful evening when Count L—— told his mistress of his father's determination.

"If I do not give you up I shall be able to do nothing for you," he said at last, "and I shall not even known how I should manage to live myself, for my father is just the man to allow me to want if I defy him. That, however, is a very secondary consideration, but as a man of honor, I cannot bind you, who have every right to luxury and enjoyment, to myself from the moment when I cannot even keep you from want, and so I must set you at liberty."

"But I will not give you up," Henrietta said proudly.

The young count shook his head sadly.

"Do you love me?" the ballet girl said quickly.

"More than my life."

"Then we will not separate, as long as I have anything," she continued.

And she would not give up her connection with him, and when his father actually turned Count L—— into the street she took her lover into her own lodgings. He obtained a situation as a copying clerk in a lawyer's office, and she sold her valuable dresses and jewels. Thus they lived for more than a year.

The young man's father did not appear to trouble his head about them but, nevertheless, he knew everything that went on in their small home and knew every article that the ballet girl sold. At last, softened by such love and strength of character, he himself made the first advances to a reconciliation with his son.

At the present time Henrietta wears the diamonds which formerly belonged to the old countess, and it is long since she was a ballet girl. Now she sits by the side of her husband in a carriage on whose panels their armorial bearings are painted.

THE DOUBLE PINS

Ah, my dear fellow, what jades women are!"

"What makes you say that?"

"Because they have played me an abominable trick."

"You?"

"Yes, me."

THE DOUBLE PINS

"Women or a woman?"

"Two women."

"Two women at once?"

"Yes."

"What was the trick?"

The two young men were sitting outside a café on the boulevard and drinking liqueurs mixed with water, those aperients which look like infusions of all the tints in a box of water colors. They were nearly the same age: twenty-five to thirty. One was dark and the other fair, and they had the same semi-elegant look of stockjobbers, of men who go to the Stock Exchange and into drawing rooms, who are to be seen everywhere, who live everywhere and love everywhere. The dark one continued:

"I have told you of my connection with that little woman, a tradesman's wife, whom I met on the beach at Dieppe?"

"Yes."

"My dear fellow, you know how it is. I had a mistress in Paris whom I love dearly, an old friend, a good friend, who is virtually a habit, in fact, one I value very much."

"Your habit?"

"Yes, my habit and hers also. She is married to an excellent man, whom I also value very much, a very cordial fellow and a capital companion! I may say that my life is bound up with that house."

"Well?"

"Well! They could not manage to leave Paris, and I found myself a widower at Dieppe."

"Why did you go to Dieppe?"

"For a change of air. One cannot remain on the boulevards the whole time."

"And then?"

"Then I met the little woman I mentioned to you on the beach there."

"The wife of that head of a public office?"

"Yes, she was dreadfully dull; her husband only came every Sunday, and he is horrible! I understood her perfectly, and we laughed and danced together."

"And the rest?"

"Yes, but that came later. However, we met and we liked each other. I told her I liked her, and she made me repeat it so that she might understand it better, and she put no obstacles in my way."

"Did you love her?"

"Yes, a little! She is very nice."

"And what about the other?"

"The other was in Paris! Well, for six weeks it was very pleasant, and we returned here on the best of terms. Do you know how to break with a woman when that woman has not wronged you in any way?"

"Yes, perfectly well."

"How do you manage it?"

"I give her up."

"How do you do it?"

"I do not see her any longer."

"But supposing she comes to you?"

"I am not at home."

"And if she comes again?"

"I say I am not well."

"If she looks after you?"

"I play her some dirty trick."

"And if she puts up with it?"

"I write her husband anonymous letters so that he may look after her on the days that I expect her."

"That is serious! I cannot resist and do not know how to bring about a rupture, and so I have a collection of mistresses. There are some whom I do not see more than once a year, others every ten months, others on those days when they want to dine at a restaurant; those whom I have put at regular intervals do not worry me, but I often have great difficulty with the fresh ones so as to keep them at proper intervals."

"And then?"

"And then—then this little woman was all fire and flame, without any fault of mine, as I told you! As her husband spends all the whole day at the office, she began to come to me unexpectedly, and twice she nearly met my regular one on the stairs."

"The devil!"

"Yes; so I gave each of them her days, regular days, to avoid confusion. Saturday and Monday for the old one, Tuesday, Friday and Sunday for the new one."

"Why did you show her the preference?"

"Ah! My dear friend, she is younger."

"So that only gave you two days to yourself in a week."

"That is enough for one."

"Allow me to compliment you on that."

"Well, just fancy that the most ridiculous and most annoying thing in the world happened to me. For four months everything had been going on perfectly; I felt quite safe and I was really very happy, when suddenly, last Monday, the crash came.

"I was expecting my regular one at the usual time, a quarter past one, and was smoking a good cigar, dreaming, very well satisfied with myself, when I suddenly saw that it was past the time. I was much surprised, for she is very punctual, but I thought that something might have accidentally delayed her. However, half an hour passed, then an hour, an hour and a half, and then I knew that something must have detained her—a sick headache, perhaps, or some annoying visitor. That sort of waiting is very vexatious, very annoying and enervating. At last I made up my mind to go out and, not knowing what to do, I went to her and found her reading a novel.

" 'Well,' I said to her. And she replied quite calmly:

" 'My dear, I could not come; I was hindered.'

" 'How?'

" 'By something else.'

" 'What was it?'

" 'A very annoying visit.'

"I saw she would not tell me the true reason, and as she was very calm, I did not trouble myself any more about it, hoping to make up for lost time with the other next day. On the Tuesday I was very excited and amorous in expectation of the public official's little wife, and I was surprised that she did not come before the appointed time. I looked at the clock every moment and watched the hands impatiently, but the quarter passed, then the half-hour, then two o'clock. I could not sit still any longer and walked up and down very soon in great strides, putting my face against the window and my ears to the door, to listen whether she was not coming upstairs.

"Half-past two, three o'clock! I seized my hat, rushed to her house. She was reading a novel, my dear fellow! 'Well!' I said anxiously, and she replied as calmly as usual:

" 'I was hindered and could not come.'

" 'By what?'

" 'An annoying visit.'

"Of course I immediately thought that they both knew everything, but she seemed so calm and quiet that I set aside my suspicions and thought it was only some strange coincidence, as I could not believe in such dissimulation on her part. And so after half an hour's friendly talk, which was, however, interrupted a dozen times by her little girl coming in and out of the room, I went away very much annoyed. Just imagine the next day."

"The same thing happened?"

"Yes, and the next also. And that went on for three weeks without any explanation, without anything explaining such strange conduct to me, the secret of which I suspected, however."

"They knew everything?"

"I should think so, by George. But how? Ah! I had a great deal of anxiety before I found it out."

"How did you manage it at last?"

"From their letters, for on the same day they both gave me their dismissal in identical terms."

"Well?"

"This is how it was: You know that women always have an array of pins about them. I know hairpins; I doubt them and look after them, but the others are much more treacherous, those confounded little black-headed pins which look all alike to us, great fools that we are, but which they can distinguish, just as we can distinguish a horse from a dog.

"Well, it appears that one day my official's little wife left one of those telltale instruments pinned to the paper close to my looking glass. My usual one had immediately seen this little black speck, no bigger than a flea, had taken it out without saying a word and had left one of her pins, which was also black but of a different pattern, in the same place.

"The next day the official's wife wished to recover her property and immediately recognized the substitution. Then her suspicions were aroused, and she put in two and crossed them. My original one replied to this telegraphic signal by three black pellets, one on the top of the other, and as soon as this method had begun they continued to communicate with one another without saying a word, just to spy on each other. Then it appears that the regular one, being bolder, wrapped a tiny piece of paper round the little wire point and wrote upon it:

"C. D., Poste Restante, Boulevard Malherbes.

"Then they wrote to each other. You understand that was not everything that passed between them. They set to work with precaution, with a thousand stratagems, with all the prudence that is necessary in such cases, but the regular one made a bold stroke and made an appointment with the other. I do not know what they said to each other; all that I know is that I had to pay the costs of their interview. There you have it all!"

"Is that all?"
"Yes."
"And you do not see them any more?"
"I beg your pardon, I see them as friends, for we have not quarreled altogether."
"And have they met again?"
"Yes, my dear fellow, they have become intimate friends."
"And has not that given you an idea?"
"No, what idea?"
"You great booby! The idea of making them put back the pins where they found them."

HOW HE GOT THE LEGION OF HONOR

SOME PEOPLE are born with a predominant instinct, with some vocation or some desire which demands recognition as soon as they begin to speak or to think.

Ever since he was a child M. Caillard had only had one idea in his head—to be decorated. When he was still quite a small boy he used to wear a zinc Cross of the Legion of Honor in his tunic, just like other children wear a soldier's cap, and he took his mother's hand in the street with a proud look, sticking out his little chest with its red ribbon and metal star so that it might show to advantage.

His studies were not a success, and he failed in his examination for bachelor of arts; so not knowing what to do, he married a pretty girl, for he had plenty of money of his own.

They lived in Paris, like many rich middle-class people do, mixing with their own particular set without going among other people, proud of knowing a deputy, who might perhaps be a minister someday, while two chiefs of division were among their friends.

But M. Caillard could not get rid of his one absorbing idea, and he felt constantly unhappy because he had not the right to wear a little bit of colored ribbon in his buttonhole.

When he met any men who were decorated on the boulevards, he looked at them askance, with intense jealousy. Sometimes, when he had nothing to do in the afternoon, he would count them and say to himself: "Just let me see how many I shall meet between the Madeleine and the Rue Drouot."

Then he would walk slowly, looking at every coat with a practiced eye for the little bit of red ribbon, and when he had got to the end of his walk he always said the numbers out loud. "Eight officers and seventeen knights. As many as that! It is stupid to sow the cross broadcast in that fashion. I wonder how many I shall meet going back?"

And he returned slowly, unhappy when the crowd of passers-by interfered with his seeing them.

He knew the places where most of them were to be found. They swarmed in the Palais Royal. Fewer were seen in the Avenue de l'Opera than in the Rue de la Paix, while the right side of the boulevard was more frequented by them than the left.

They also seemed to prefer certain cafés and theaters. Whenever he saw a group of white-haired old gentlemen standing together in the middle of the pavement, interfering with the traffic, he used to say to himself: "They are officers of the Legion of Honor," and he felt inclined to take off his hat to them.

He had often remarked that the officers had a different bearing from mere knights. They carried their heads higher, and you felt that they enjoyed greater official consideration and a more widely extended importance.

Sometimes again the worthy man would be seized with a furious hatred for everyone who was decorated; he felt like a Socialist toward them. Then, when he got home, excited at meeting so many crosses—just like a poor, hungry wretch is on passing some dainty provision shop—he used to ask in a loud voice:

"When shall we get rid of this wretched government?" And his wife would be surprised and ask:

"What is the matter with you today?"

"I am indignant," he would reply, "at the injustice I see going on around us. Oh! The Communards were certainly right!"

After dinner he would go out again and look at the shops where all the decorations were sold and examine all the emblems of various shapes and colors. He would have liked to possess them all and to have walked gravely at the head of a procession with his crush hat under his arm and his breast covered with decorations, radiant as a star, amid a buzz of admiring whispers and a hum of respect. But alas! He had no right to wear any decoration whatever.

He used to say to himself: "It is really too difficult for any man to obtain the

Legion of Honor unless he is some public functionary. Suppose I try to get appointed an officer of the Academy!"

But he did not know how to set about it and spoke to his wife on the subject, who was stupefied.

"Officer of the Academy! What have you done to deserve it?"

He got angry. "I know what I am talking about; I only want to know how to set about it. You are quite stupid at times."

She smiled. "You are quite right; I don't understand anything about it."

An idea struck him: "Suppose you were to speak to Monsieur Rosselin, the deputy, he might be able to advise me. You understand I cannot broach the subject to him directly. It is rather difficult and delicate but, coming from you, it might seem quite natural."

Mme Caillard did what he asked her, and M. Rosselin promised to speak to the minister about it. Then Caillard began to worry him till the deputy told him he must make a formal application and put forward his claims.

"What were his claims?" he said. "He was not even a bachelor of arts."

However, he set to work and produced a pamphlet with the title, *The People's Right to Instruction*, but he could not finish it for want of ideas.

He sought for easier subjects and began several in succession. The first was, *The Instruction of Children by Means of the Eye*. He wanted gratuitous theaters to be established in every poor quarter of Paris for little children. Their parents were to take them there when they were quite young, and by means of a magic lantern all the notions of human knowledge were to be imparted to them. There were to be regular courses. The sight would educate the mind, while the pictures would remain impressed on the brain, and thus science would, so to say, be made visible. What could be more simple than to teach universal history, natural history, geography, botany, zoology, anatomy, etc., etc., thus?

He had his ideas printed in tract form and sent a copy to each deputy, ten to each minister, fifty to the president of the Republic, ten to each Parisian and five to each provincial newspaper.

Then he wrote on *Street Lending Libraries*. His idea was to have little carts full of books drawn about the streets, like orange carts are. Every householder or lodger would have a right to ten volumes a month by means of a halfpenny subscription.

"The people," M. Caillard said, "will only disturb itself for the sake of its pleasures, and since it will not go to instruction, instruction must come to it," etc., etc.

His essays attracted no attention, but he sent in his application and he got the usual formal official reply. He thought himself sure of success, but nothing came of it.

Then he made up his mind to apply personally. He begged for an interview with the minister of public instruction, and he was received by a young subordinate, already very grave and important, who kept touching the buttons of electric bells to summon ushers and footmen and officials inferior to himself. He declared to M. Caillard that his matter was going on quite favorably and advised him to continue his remarkable labors. So M. Caillard set at it again.

M. Rosselin, the deputy, seemed now to take a great interest in his success and gave him a lot of excellent, practical advice. Rosselin was decorated, although nobody knew exactly what he had done to deserve such a distinction.

He told Caillard what new studies he ought to undertake; he introduced him to learned societies which took up particularly obscure points of science, in the hope of gaining credit and honors thereby, and he even took him under his wing at the Ministry.

One day when he came to lunch with his friend (for several months past he had constantly taken his meals there), he said to him in a whisper as he shook hands: "I have just obtained a great favor for you. The Committee on Historical Works is going to intrust you with a commission. There are some researches to be made in various libraries in France."

Caillard was so delighted that he could scarcely eat or drink, and a week later he set out. He went from town to town, studying catalogues, rummaging in lofts full of dusty volumes, and was a bore to all the librarians.

One day, happening to be at Rouen, he thought he should like to embrace his wife, whom he had not seen for more than a week, so he took the nine o'clock train, which would land him at home by twelve at night.

He had his latchkey, so he went in without making any noise, delighted at the idea of the surprise he was going to give her. She had locked herself in. How tiresome! However, he cried out through the door:

"Jeanne, it is I."

She must have been very frightened, for he heard her jump out of bed and speak to herself, as if she were in a dream. Then she went to her dressing room, opened and closed the door and went quickly up and down her room, barefoot, two or three times, shaking the furniture till the vases and glasses sounded. Then at last she asked:

"Is it you, Alexander?"

"Yes, yes," he replied; "make haste and open the door."

As soon as she had done so she threw herself into his arms, exclaiming:

"Oh! What a fright! What a surprise! What a pleasure!"

He began to undress himself methodically, like he did everything, and from a chair he took his overcoat, which he was in the habit of hanging up in the hall. But suddenly he remained motionless, struck dumb with astonishment—there was a red ribbon in the buttonhole!

"Why," he stammered, "this—this—this overcoat has got the rosette in it!"

In a second his wife threw herself on him and, taking it from his hands, she said:

"No! You have made a mistake—give it to me."

But he still held it by one of the sleeves without letting it go, repeating in a half-dazed manner:

"Oh! Why? Just explain. Whose overcoat is it? It is not mine, as it has the Legion of Honor on it."

She tried to take it from him, terrified, and hardly able to say:

"Listen—listen—give it me. I must not tell you—it is a secret—listen to me."

But he grew angry and turned pale:

"I want to know how this overcoat comes to be here. It does not belong to me."

Then she almost screamed at him:

"Yes, it does; listen—swear to me—well—you are decorated."

She did not intend to joke at his expense.

He was so overcome that he let the overcoat fall and dropped into an armchair.

"I am—you say I am—decorated?"

"Yes, but it is a secret, a great secret."

She had put the glorious garment into a cupboard and came to her husband, pale and trembling.

"Yes," she continued, "it is a new overcoat that I have had made for you. But I swore that I would not tell you anything about it, as it will not be officially announced for a month or six weeks, and you were not to have known till your return from your business journey. Monsieur Rosselin managed it for you."

"Rosselin!" he contrived to utter in his joy. "He has obtained the decoration for me? He—— Oh!"

And he was obliged to drink a glass of water.

A little piece of white paper had fallen to the floor out of the pocket of the overcoat. Caillard picked it up; it was a visiting card, and he read out:

"Rosselin—deputy."

"You see how it is?" said his wife.

He almost cried with joy, and a week later it was announced in the *Journal Officiel* that M. Caillard had been awarded the Legion of Honor on account of his exceptional services.

A CRISIS

A BIG FIRE WAS BURNING, and the tea table was set for two. The Count de Sallure threw his hat, gloves and fur coat on a chair, while the countess, who had removed her opera cloak, was smiling amiably at herself in the glass and arranging a few stray curls with her jeweled fingers. Her husband had been looking at her for the past few minutes, as if on the point of saying something, but hesitating; finally he said:

"You have flirted outrageously tonight!" She looked him straight in the eyes with an expression of triumph and defiance on her face.

"Why, certainly," she answered. She sat down, poured out the tea, and her husband took his seat opposite her.

"It made me look quite—ridiculous!"

"Is this a scene?" she asked, arching her brows. "Do you mean to criticize my conduct?"

"Oh no, I only meant to say that Monsieur Burel's attentions to you were positively improper, and if I had the right—I—would not tolerate it."

"Why, my dear boy, what has come over you? You must have changed your views since last year. You did not seem to mind who courted me and who did not a year ago. When I found out that you had a mistress, a mistress whom you loved passionately, I pointed out to you then, as you did me to-night (but I had good reasons), that you were compromising yourself and Madame de Servy, that your conduct grieved me and made me look ridiculous; what did you answer me? That I was perfectly free, that marriage between two intelligent people was simply a partnership, a sort of social bond, but not a moral bond. Is it not true? You gave me to understand that your mistress was far more captivating than I, that she was more womanly; that is what you said: 'more womanly.' Of course you said all this in a very nice way, and I acknowledge that you did your very best to spare my feelings, for which I am very grateful to you, I assure you, but I understand perfectly what you meant.

"We then decided to live practically separated; that is, under the same roof but apart from each other. We had a child, and it was necessary to keep up appearances before the world, but you intimated that if I chose to take a lover you would not object in the least, providing it was kept secret. You even made a long and very interesting discourse on the cleverness of women in such cases; how well they could manage such things, etc., etc. I understood perfectly, my dear boy. You loved Madame de Servy very much at that time, and my conjugal—legal—affection was an impediment to your happiness, but since then we have lived on the very best of terms. We go out in society together, it is true, but here in our own house we are complete strangers. Now for the past month or two you act as if you were jealous, and I do not understand it."

"I am not jealous, my dear, but you are so young, so impulsive, that I am afraid you will expose yourself to the world's criticisms."

"You make me laugh! Your conduct would not bear a very close scrutiny. You had better not preach what you do not practice."

"Do not laugh, I pray. This is no laughing matter. I am speaking as a friend, a true friend. As to your remarks, they are very much exaggerated."

"Not at all. When you confessed to me your infatuation for Madame de Servy, I took it for granted that you authorized me to imitate you. I have not done so."

"Allow me to——"

"Do not interrupt me. I have not done so. I have no lover—as yet. I am looking for one, but I have not found one to suit me. He must be very nice —nicer than you are—that is a compliment, but you do not seem to appreciate it."

"This joking is entirely uncalled for."

"I am not joking at all; I am in dead earnest. I have not forgotten a single word of what you said to me a year ago, and when it pleases me to do so, no matter what you may say or do, I shall take a lover. I shall do it without your even suspecting it—you will be none the wiser—like a great many others."

"How can you say such things?"

"How can I say such things? But, my dear boy, you were the first one to laugh when Madame de Gers joked about poor, unsuspecting Monsieur de Servy."

"That might be, but it is not becoming language for you."

"Indeed! You thought it a good joke when it concerned Monsieur de Servy, but you do not find it so appropriate when it concerns you. What a queer lot men are! However, I am not fond of talking about such things; I simply mentioned it to see if you were ready."

"Ready—for what?"

"Ready to be deceived. When a man gets angry on hearing such things he is not quite ready. I wager that in two months you will be the first one to laugh if I mention a deceived husband to you. It is generally the case when you are the deceived one."

"Upon my word, you are positively rude tonight; I have never seen you that way."

"Yes—I have changed—for the worse, but it is your fault."

"Come, my dear, let us talk seriously. I beg of you, I implore you not to let Monsieur Burel court you as he did tonight."

"You are jealous; I knew it."

"No, no, but I do not wish to be looked upon with ridicule, and if I catch that man devouring you with his eyes like he did tonight—I—I will thrash him!"

"Could it be possible that you are in love with me?"

"Why not? I am sure I could do much worse."

"Thanks. I am sorry for you—because I do not love you any more."

The count got up, walked around the tea table and, going behind his wife, he kissed her quickly on the neck. She sprang up and with flashing eyes said: "How dare you do that? Remember, we are absolutely nothing to each other; we are complete strangers."

"Please do not get angry; I could not help it; you look so lovely tonight."

"Then I must have improved wonderfully."

"You look positively charming; your arms and shoulders are beautiful, and your skin——"

"Would captivate Monsieur Burel."

"How mean you are! But really, I do not recall ever having seen a woman as captivating as you are."

"You must have been fasting lately."

"What's that?"

"I say, you must have been fasting lately."

"Why—what do you mean?"

"I mean just what I say. You must have fasted for some time, and now you are famished. A hungry man will eat things which he will not eat at any other time. I am the neglected—dish, which you would not mind eating tonight."

"Marguerite! Whoever taught you to say those things?"

"You did. To my knowledge you have had four mistresses. Actresses, society women, gay women, etc., so how can I explain your sudden fancy for me, except by your long fast?"

"You will think me rude, brutal, but I have fallen in love with you for the second time. I love you madly!"

"Well, well! Then you—wish to——"

"Exactly."

"Tonight?"

"Oh, Marguerite!"

"There, you are scandalized again. My dear boy, let us talk quietly. We are strangers, are we not? I am your wife, it is true, but I am—free. I intended to engage my affection elsewhere, but I will give you the preference, providing—I receive the same compensation."

"I do not understand you; what do you mean?"

"I will speak more clearly. Am I as good looking as your mistresses?"

"A thousand times better."

"Better than the nicest one?"

"Yes, a thousand times."

"How much did she cost you in three months?"

"Really—what on earth do you mean?"

"I mean, how much did you spend on the costliest of your mistresses, in jewelry, carriages, suppers, etc., in three months?"

"How do I know?"

"You ought to know. Let us say, for instance, five thousand francs a month —is that about right?"

"Yes—about that."

"Well, my dear boy, give me five thousand francs and I will be yours for a month, beginning from tonight."

"Marguerite! Are you crazy?"

"No, I am not, but just as you say. Good night!"

The countess entered her boudoir. A vague perfume permeated the whole room. The count appeared in the doorway.

"How lovely it smells in here!"

"Do you think so? I always use Peau d'Espagne; I never use any other perfume."

"Really? I did not notice—it is lovely."

"Possibly, but be kind enough to go; I want to go to bed."

"Marguerite!"

"Will you please go?"

The count came in and sat on a chair.

Said the countess: "You will not go? Very well."

She slowly took off her waist, revealing her white arms and neck, then she lifted her arms above her head to loosen her hair.

The count took a step toward her.

The countess: "Do not come near me or I shall get real angry, do you hear?"

He caught her in his arms and tried to kiss her. She quickly took a tumbler of perfumed water standing on the toilet table and dashed it into his face.

He was terribly angry. He stepped back a few paces and murmured: "How stupid of you!"

"Perhaps—but you know my conditions—five thousand francs!"

"Preposterous!"

"Why, pray?"

"Why? Because—whoever heard of a man paying his wife?"

"Oh! How horribly rude you are!"

"I suppose I am rude, but I repeat, the idea of paying one's wife is preposterous! Positively stupid!"

"Is it not much worse to pay a gay woman? It certainly would be stupid when you have a wife at home."

"That may be, but I do not wish to be ridiculous."

The countess sat down on the bed and took off her stockings, revealing her bare, pink feet.

The count approached a little nearer and said tenderly:

"What an odd idea of yours, Marguerite!"

"What idea?"

"To ask me for five thousand francs!"

"Odd? Why should it be odd? Are we not strangers? You say you are in love with me; all well and good. You cannot marry me, as I am already your wife, so you buy me. *Mon Dieu!* Have you not bought other women? Is it not much better to give me that money than to a strange woman who would squander it? Come, you will acknowledge that it is a novel idea to actually pay your own wife! An intelligent man like you ought to see how amusing it is; besides, a man never really loves anything unless it costs him a lot of money. It would add new zest to our—conjugal love, by comparing it with your—illegitimate love. Am I not right?"

She went toward the bell.

"Now then, sir, if you do not go I will ring for my maid!"

The count stood perplexed, displeased, and suddenly taking a handful of bank notes out of his pocket, he threw them at his wife, saying:

"Here are six thousand, you witch, but remember——"

The countess picked up the money, counted it and said:

"What?"

"You must not get used to it."

She burst out laughing and said to him:

"Five thousand francs each month, or else I shall send you back to your actresses, and if you are pleased with me—I shall ask for more."

GRAVEYARD SIRENS

THE FIVE FRIENDS had finished their dinner; there were two bachelors and three married men, all middle-aged and wealthy. They assembled thus once a month in memory of old times and lingered to gossip over their coffee till late at night. Many a happy evening was spent in this way, for they were fond of one another's society and had remained closely united. Conversation among them was a sort of review of the daily papers, commenting on everything that interests and amuses Parisians. One of the cleverest, Joseph de Bardon, was a bachelor. He lived the life of a *boulevardier* most thoroughly and fantastically, without being debauched or depraved. It interested him, and as he was still young, being barely forty, he enjoyed it keenly. A man of the world in the broadest and best sense of the word, he possessed a great deal of wit without much depth, a general knowledge without real learning, quick perception without serious penetration; but his adventures and observations furnished him many amusing stories, which he told with so much philosophy and humor that society voted him very intellectual.

He was a favorite after-dinner speaker, always having some story to relate to which his friends looked forward. Presently he began to tell a story without being asked. Leaning on the table with a half-filled glass of brandy in front of his plate, in the smoky atmosphere filled with the fragrance of coffee, he seemed perfectly at ease, just as some beings are entirely at home in certain places and under certain conditions—as a goldfish in its aquarium, for instance, or a nun in her cloister.

Puffing at his cigar, he said:

"A rather curious thing happened to me a little while ago."

All exclaimed at once: "Tell us about it!"

Presently he continued:

"You all know how I love to roam around the city like a collector in search of antiquities. I enjoy watching people and things. About the middle of September, the weather being very fine, I went for a walk one afternoon without a definite purpose. Why do we men always have the vague impulse to call on some pretty woman? We review them in our mind, compare their respective charms, the interest they arouse in us, and finally decide in favor of the one that attracts us most.

"But when the sun shines brightly and the air is balmy sometimes we altogether lose the desire for calling.

"That day the sun was bright and the air balmy, so I simply lighted a cigar and started for the Boulevard Extérieur. As I was sauntering along I thought I would take a look around the cemetery at Montmartre. Now I have always liked cemeteries because they sadden and rest me, and I need that influence at times. Besides, many of my friends are laid to rest there, and I go to see them once in a while.

"As it happens, I once buried a romance in this particular cemetery—an old love of mine, a charming little woman whose memory awakens all kinds of regrets in me. I often dream beside her grave. All is over for her now!

"I like graveyards because they are such immense, densely populated cities. Just think of all the bodies buried in that small space, of the countless generations of Parisians laid there forever, eternally entombed in the little vaults of their little graves marked by a cross or a stone, while the living—fools that they are!—take up so much room and make such a fuss.

"Cemeteries have some monuments quite as interesting as those to be seen in the museums. Cavaignac's tomb I liken, without comparing it, to that masterpiece of Jean Gonjon, the tombstone of Louis de Brézé in the subterranean chapel in the cathedral of Rouen. My friends, all so-called modern and realistic art originated there. That reproduction of Louis de Brézé is more lifelike and terrible, more convulsed with agony, than any one of the statues that decorate modern tombs.

"In Montmartre is Baudin's monument, and it is quite imposing; also the tombs of Gautier and Murger, where the other day I found a solitary wreath of yellow immortelles laid there—by whom do you suppose? Perhaps by the last *grisette*, grown old and possibly become a janitress in the neighborhood! It's a pretty little statue by Millet, but it is ruined by neglect and accumulated filth. Sing of youth, O Murger!

"Well, I entered the cemetery filled with a certain sadness, not too poignant, a feeling suggesting such thoughts as this: The place is not very cheerful, but I'm not to be put here yet.

"The impression of autumn, a warm dampness smelling of dead leaves, the pale, anemic rays of the sun, intensified and poetized the solitude of this place, which reminds one of death and of the end of all things.

"I walked slowly along the alleys of graves where neighbors no longer visit, no longer sleep together or read the papers. I began reading the epitaphs. There is nothing more amusing in the world. Labiche and Meilhac have never made me laugh as much as some of these tombstone inscriptions. I tell you these crosses and marble slabs on which the relatives of the dead have poured out their regrets and their wishes for the happiness of the departed, their hopes of reunion—the hypocrites!—make better reading than Balzac's funniest tales! But what I love in Montmartre are the abandoned plots filled with yew trees and cypress, the resting place of those departed long ago. However, the green trees nourished by the bodies will soon be felled to make room for those that have recently passed away, whose graves will be there under little marble slabs.

"After loitering awhile I felt tired and decided to pay my faithful tribute to my little friend's memory. When I reached the grave my heart was very sad. Poor child! She was so sweet and loving, so fair and white—and now—should her grave be reopened . . .

"Bending over the iron railing, I murmured a prayer which she probably never heard, and I turned to leave, when I caught sight of a woman in deep mourning kneeling beside a neighboring grave. Her crape veil was thrown back, disclosing her blonde hair which seemed illumined under the darkness of her hat. I forgot to leave.

"She seemed bowed with sorrow. She had buried her face in her hands, apparently lost in deep thought. With closed lids, as rigid as a statue, she was living over torturing memories and seemed herself a corpse mourning a corpse. Presently I saw that she was weeping, as there was a convulsive movement of her back and shoulders. Suddenly she uncovered her face. Her eyes, brimming with tears, were charming. For a moment she gazed around, as if awakening from a nightmare. She saw me looking at her and quickly hid her face again, greatly abashed. Now with convulsive sobs she bent her head slowly over the tombstone. She rested her forehead against it, and her veil, falling around her, covered the whiteness of the beloved sepulcher with a dark shroud. I heard her moan and then saw her fall to the ground in a faint.

"I rushed to her side and began slapping her hands and breathing on her temples, while reading this simple inscription on the tombstone:

"*Here lies Louis-Théodore Carrel, captain in the Marine Infantry, killed by the enemy in Tonkin. Pray for his soul.*

"This death was quite recent. I was moved almost to tears and renewed my efforts to revive the poor girl. At last she came to. I am not so very bad looking, and my face must have shown how upset I was, for her very first glance showed me that she was likely to be grateful for my care. Between sobs she told me of her marriage to the officer who had been killed in Tonkin within a year after their wedding. He had married her for love, she being an orphan and possessing nothing above the required dowry.

"I consoled her, comforted her and assisted her to her feet, saying:

"'You must not stay here. Come away.'

"'I am unable to walk,' she whispered.

"'Let me help you,' I said.

"'Thank you, you are very kind,' she murmured. 'Did you also come to mourn someone?'

"'Yes, madame.'

"'A woman?'

"'Yes, madame.'

"'Your wife?'

"'A friend.'

"'One may love a friend just as much as a wife, for passion knows no law,' said the lady.

"'Yes, madame,' I replied.

"And so we left the spot together, she leaning on me and I almost carrying her through the alleys. As we came out she murmured:

"'I'm afraid that I'm going to faint.'

"'Wouldn't you like to take something, madame?' I inquired.

"'Yes,' she said, 'I would.'

"I discovered a restaurant near at hand, where the friends of the dead gather to celebrate the end of their painful duty. We went in, and I made her drink a cup of hot tea, which appeared to give her renewed strength.

"A faint smile dawned on her lips, and she began telling me about herself: how terrible it was to go through life all alone, to be alone at home day and night, to have no one on whom to lavish love, confidence and intimacy.

"It all seemed sincere and sounded well coming from her. I was softened. She was very young, perhaps twenty. I paid her several compliments that appeared to please her, and as it was growing dark, I offered to take her home in a cab. She accepted. In the carriage we were so close to each other that we could feel the warmth of our bodies through our clothing, which really is the most intoxicating thing in the world.

"When the cab stopped in front of her home she said:

"'I hardly feel able to walk upstairs, for I live on the fourth floor. You have already been so kind that I am going to ask you to assist me to my rooms.'

"I consented gladly. She walked up slowly, breathing heavily at each step. In front of her door she added:

"'Do come in for a few minutes so that I can thank you again for your kindness.'

"And I, of course, followed her.

"Her apartment was modest, even a trifle poor, but well kept and in good taste.

"We sat down side by side on a small divan, and she again began to speak of her loneliness.

"Then she rang for the maid, so as to offer me some refreshments. But the girl failed to appear, and I joyfully concluded that this maid probably came only in the morning and was a sort of scrubwoman.

"She had taken off her hat. How pretty she was! Her clear eyes looked steadily at me, so clear and so steady that a great temptation came to me to which I promptly yielded. Clasping her in my arms, I kissed her again and again on her half-closed lids.

"She repelled me, struggling to free herself and repeating:

"'Do stop—do end it.'

"What did she mean to imply by this word? Under such conditions, to 'end' could have at least two meanings. In order to silence her I passed from her eyes to her lips and gave to the word 'end' the conclusion I preferred. She did not resist very much, and as our eyes met after this insult to the memory of the departed captain, I saw that her expression was one of tender resignation, which quickly dispelled my misgivings.

"Then I grew attentive and gallant. After an hour's chat I asked her:

"'Where do you dine?'

"'In a small restaurant near by.'

"'All alone?'

"'Why, yes.'

"'Will you take dinner with me?'

"'Where?'"

" 'In a good restaurant on the boulevard.'

"She hesitated a little but at last consented, consoling herself with the argument that she was so desperately lonely and adding, 'I must put on a lighter gown.'

"She retired to her room, and when she emerged she was dressed in a simple gray frock that made her look exquisitely slender. She apparently had different costumes for street and for cemetery wear!

"Our dinner was most pleasant and cordial. She drank some champagne, thereby becoming very animated and lively, and we returned to her apartment together.

"This liaison, begun among tombstones, lasted about three weeks. But man tires of everything and especially of women. So I pleaded an urgent trip and left her. Of course I managed to be generous, for which she was duly thankful, making me promise and even swear that I would come back, for she really seemed to care a little for me.

"In the meantime I found other attachments, and a month or so went by without the memory of this love being vivid enough to bring me back to her. Still, I had not forgotten her. She haunted me like a mystery, a psychological problem, an unsolved question.

"I can't tell why, but one day I imagined that I should find her in the cemetery. So I went back. I walked around a long time without meeting anyone but the usual visitors of the place, mourners who had not broken off all relations with their dead. The grave of the captain killed in Tonkin was deserted, without flowers or wreaths.

"As I was passing through another part of this great city of death I suddenly saw a couple in deep mourning coming toward me through one of the narrow paths hedged with crosses. When they drew near, oh, surprise! I recognized—her! She saw me and blushed. As I brushed past her she gave me a little wink that meant clearly: Don't recognize me, and also seemed to say: Do come back.

"The man who accompanied her was about fifty years old, fine looking and distinguished, an officer of the Legion of Honor. He was leading her just as I had, when we left the cemetery together.

"I was utterly nonplused, reluctant to believe what my eyes had just seen, and I wondered to what strange tribe of creatures this graveyard huntress belonged. Was she merely a clever courtesan, an inspired prostitute, who haunted cemeteries for men disconsolate at the loss of some woman, a mistress or a wife, and hungering for past caresses? Is it a profession? Are the cemeteries worked like the streets? Are there graveyard sirens? Or had she alone the idea—wonderful for its deep philosophy—to profit by the amorous regrets awakened in these awful places? I would have given a great deal to know whose widow she was that day!"

GROWING OLD

The two friends had finished dinner. From the window of the café they saw the boulevard full of people. They felt the warm zephyrs which prevail in Paris on sweet summer nights and make travelers raise their heads and desire to go out, to go down, one knows not where, under the leaves and dream of rivers lighted by the moon, of glowworms and of nightingales.

One of them, Henry Simon, sighed profoundly and said:

"Ah! I am getting old. It is sad. Formerly on evenings like this I felt the devil in my body. Now I feel only regrets. How quickly life goes!"

He was already a little stout and very bald; he was perhaps forty-five years old.

The other, Peter Carnier, was older but thinner and more lively; he replied:

"As for me, my friend, I have grown old without perceiving it the least in the world. I was always gay, a jolly fellow, vigorous and all the rest. Now as one looks at himself each day in the mirror he does not perceive the work that age is accomplishing, because it is slow and regular and modifies his visage so gradually that the transition is unseen. Only for this we should die of chagrin after but two or three years' ravages. But we are not able to appreciate them. In order to take a reckoning it would be necessary to go six months without looking at ourselves; and then what a blow!

"And the women, my dear, how I pity them, the poor beings. All their happiness, all their power, all their life, is in their beauty, which lasts but ten years.

"I then grew old without suspecting it; I believed myself a young man, although I was nearly fifty years old. Never having felt an infirmity of any sort, I went along, happy and tranquil.

"The revelation of my decadence came to me in a simple but terrible fashion, which made me downcast for nearly six months. Since then I have accepted the part.

"I have often been in love, like all men, but once in particular. I met her at the seashore at Etretat about twelve years ago, a little after the war. There is nothing so pretty as this shore in the morning at the bathing hour. It is small, rounded like a horseshoe, incased in those high, white cliffs, pierced with those singular holes they call ports, one enormous one extending into the sea like a giant's leg, the other opposite, squat and round. A crowd of women assembles here on the right side of the shuffleboard, which they cover like a bright garden with their brilliant costumes—this box between the high rocks. The sun falls full upon the coast, upon umbrellas of all shades, upon the sea of a greenish blue. And all is gay, charming, smiling, to the eyes. You seat yourself near the water to watch the bathers. They descend in a bathrobe of flannel which they throw off with a pretty motion upon reaching the fringe of the foam from the short waves; they go into the sea with a little rapid step which is arrested sometimes by a delicious cold shiver or a slight suffocation.

"Few can stand this trial of the bath. It is there that one can judge them from the calf to the throat. The going out especially reveals the weak, although salt water may be a powerful help to flabby flesh.

"The first time that I saw this young woman thus I was delighted, ravished. She held good; she held firm. Then there are some faces whose charm enters into us suddenly, invades us at a single blow. It seemed to me that I had found the woman that I was born to love. I had that sensation, and it was like a shock.

"I had myself presented and was immediately captured as I never was before. She ravaged my heart. It is a frightful and delicious thing, the undergoing thus the domination of a woman. It is almost a punishment and, at the same time, an unbelievable happiness. Her look, her smile, her hair at the nape of the neck when the breeze moved it, all the little lines of her face, the least movement of her features delighted me and made me extremely fond of her. She took possession of me through all my being, by her gestures, her attitudes, even by the things she carried, which became bewitching to me. I would wait to see her veil thrown upon some piece of furniture, her gloves upon an armchair. Her costumes seemed to me inimitable. No one had hats like hers.

"She was married, and the husband came every Saturday to remain until Monday. He seemed to me very indifferent. I was not at all jealous of him; I know not why, but never a being seemed to have less importance in life or attract less of my attention than this man.

"How I loved her! And how beautiful she was, and gracious and young! She was youth, elegance and freshness even. Never before had I felt what a pretty being a woman is, so distinguished and delicate, so full of charm and grace! Never had I understood what a seducing beauty there is in the curve of her cheek, in the movement of her lips, in the round folds of her little ear, in the form of that simple organ which we call the nose.

"This lasted three months, and then I departed for America, my heart bruised and full of despair. But the thought of her remained in me persistent, triumphant. She possessed me at a distance as she had when I was near her.

"Some years passed. I had not forgotten her. Her charming image remained before my eyes and in my heart. My tenderness remained faithful to her, a tranquil tenderness now, something like a much loved memory of the most beautiful, most attractive thing I had met in life.

"Twelve years are such a little thing in a man's existence! One scarcely feels them pass! They go one after another, these years, gently and quickly, slowly or hurriedly, each long but so soon finished! And they add so rapidly and leave so little trace behind them; they vanish so completely that in looking back over the time passed one cannot perceive anything and cannot comprehend how it is that they have made him old. It seemed to me truly that only a few months separated me from that charming season on the beach at Etretat.

"Last spring I went to dine at Maisons-Lafitte at the house of some friends. Just as the train was starting a large woman got into my car, followed by four little girls. I scarcely glanced at this large, round mother, with a face like a full moon incased in a beribboned hat.

"She breathed heavily, being out of breath from a quick walk. The children began to babble. I opened my newspaper and began to read.

"We were just passing Asnières when my neighbor said to me suddenly:

" 'Pardon me, sir, but are you not Monsieur Carnier?'

" 'Yes, madame.'

"Then she began to laugh, the laugh of a contented, brave woman, but a little sad, nevertheless.

" 'You do not recognize me?' she said.

"I hesitated. I fully believed that I had somewhere seen that face, but where? And when? I answered:

" 'Yes—and no—I certainly do recognize you but cannot recall your name.'

"She blushed a little as she said: 'Madame Julie Lefevre.'

"Never have I received such a blow. For a second it seemed to me that all was finished for me. I felt that a veil had been torn away from before my eyes and that I was about to discover something frightful and wounding.

"It was she! That great, gross, common woman, she? And she had borne these four girls since I had seen her. And these four beings astonished me as much as the mother herself. They had come from her; they were tall already, had taken her place in life. She no longer counted, she, that marvel of coquettish, refined grace. I had seen her yesterday, it seemed to me, and I found her again like this! Was it possible? A violent grief attacked my heart, and also a revolt against Nature even, an unreasonable indignation against her brutal work, so infamous and destructive.

"I looked at her, aghast. Then I took her by the hand, and the tears mounted to my eyes. I wept for her young; I wept for her dead. For I was not acquainted with this large lady.

"She, also affected, stammered:

" 'I am much changed, am I not? What can we expect after so long? You see, I have become a mother, nothing but a mother, a good mother. Adieu to all else; it is finished. Oh! I never thought that you would not recognize me if we met! And you, too, are changed; it took me some time to be sure that I was not deceived. You are quite gray. Think of it. Twelve years! Twelve years! My eldest daughter is already ten years old.'

"I looked at the child. I found in her something of the former charm of her mother, but something still undecisive, not yet formed, but near at hand. And life appeared as rapid to me as a train which passes.

"We arrived at Maisons-Lafitte. I kissed the hand of my old friend. I had found nothing to say to her but the most frightful commonplaces. I was too upset to talk.

"That evening, all alone in my room, I looked at myself for a long time in my glass. And I ended by recalling myself as I was, of looking back in thought to my brown mustache and my black hair and the physiognomy of my young face. Now I was old. Adieu!"

A FRENCH ENOCH ARDEN

The sea lashes the shore with its short and monstrous waves. Little white clouds are scudding quickly across the great blue sky, swept by a rapid wind, like birds, and the village, in the fold of the valley which runs down to the ocean, lies broiling in the sun.

Quite at the entrance is the house of the Martin-Levesques, alone, at the side of the road. It is a little fisherman's cottage with clay walls and a thatched roof adorned with blue iris flowers. A garden as big as a handkerchief, where sprout some onions, a few cabbages, some parsley, some chervil, squares itself before the door. A hedge hems it in along the roadside.

The man has gone fishing, and the woman before the lodge is repairing the meshes of a big brown net hung on the wall like a great spider's web. A little girl of fourteen at the garden entrance, seated in a cane chair, leaning backward and resting her arm on the fence, is mending linen, the linen of the poor, already pieced and patched.

Another small girl, a year younger, is rocking in her arms a very little baby, yet without gestures or words, and the two youngsters of two or three years sitting on the ground are playing garden with their clumsy hands and throwing fistfuls of dust in each other's face.

"No one speaks. Only the little rascal whom the girl is trying to put to sleep cries steadily with a sharp, weak little voice. A cat is sleeping at the window, and some blooming gillyflowers make, at the foot of the wall, a fine cushion of white blossoms, over which flies are buzzing.

The little girl who is sewing near the entrance calls suddenly:
"Mamma."
"What is the matter with you?" replied the mother.
"There he is again."

She had been uneasy since morning because there was a man prowling about the house, an old man who seemed to be poor. They had observed him as they were going with their father to the boat to see him embark. He was seated on the edge of the ditch opposite their gate, and when they came back they found him still there, looking at the house.

He seemed ill and very wretched. He had not stirred for more than an hour; then, seeing he would be considered a malefactor, he had risen and departed, dragging one leg.

But soon they had seen him return with his slow and weary step, and again he had sat down, a little farther away this time, as if to watch them.

The mother and daughters were afraid. The mother especially, because she was of a timorous nature and because her husband Levesque was not expected to come from the sea until nightfall.

Her husband's name was Levesque; hers was Martin, and they were called the Martin-Levesques. This is why: She had married for her first husband a man named Martin, who went to Newfoundland every summer fishing for cod.

After two years of married life she had a little girl by him, and another, three months after the craft which carried her husband, the Two Sisters, a three-masted bark from Dieppe, disappeared.

No news was ever received from it; none of its crew ever came back; it was considered to be a total wreck.

The Martin woman waited for her second husband ten years, bringing up her children with great difficulty; then as she was a good, strong woman, a fisherman of the neighborhood, Levesque, a widower with a boy, asked her in marriage. She married him and had two children by him in three years.

They lived painfully, laboriously. Bread was dear and meat almost unknown in the household. They ran in debt at times with the baker, in winter, during the stormy months. The little ones were well, nevertheless. People said:

"They are brave folk, the Martin-Levesques. The wife is a hard worker, and Levesque has not his equal for fishing."

The little girl seated at the gate repeated: "You would think that he knew us. Perhaps it is some poor man from Epreville or from Auzebogo."

But the mother was not deceived. No, no, it wasn't anyone of the country, surely!

As he moved no more than a stake, and as he kept his eyes glued to the Martin-Levesques' cottage, the woman became furious and, fear making her brave, she seized a shovel and went out of the door.

"What are you doing there?" she called to the vagabond.

He answered in a gruff voice:

"I am taking the fresh air! Does that do you any harm?"

She replied:

"Why are you spying like this on my house?"

The man replied:

"I am not injuring anybody. Isn't it permitted to sit down by the roadside?"

Not finding an answer ready, she went back into the house.

The day passed slowly. Toward noon the man disappeared, but he came by again toward five o'clock. They did not see any more of him during the evening.

Levesque returned at dusk. They told him about it. He remarked:

"It is some skulker or good-for-nothing."

He went to bed, undisturbed, while his wife dreamed of this prowler who had looked at her so strangely.

When day came there was a great wind, and the sailor, seeing that he could not start out to sea, helped his wife at mending nets.

About nine o'clock the eldest daughter, a Martin, who had gone out to get some bread, came back running with a frightened air and cried:

"Ma, there he is again!"

The mother was startled and, very pale, said to her husband:

"Go and speak to him, Levesque, so that he won't watch us like this, because it worries me to death."

And Levesque, a big sailor with a complexion like a brick, a thickened beard, blue eyes, strong neck, always wearing woolen garments on account of the wind and rain at sea, walked out quietly and approached the straggler.

And they began to talk.

The mother and the children looked on from the distance, anxious and trembling.

Suddenly the unknown rose and came toward the house with Levesque. The wife, terrified, drew back.

Her husband said to her:

"Give him a piece of bread and a glass of cider. He hasn't eaten anything since the day before yesterday."

They both entered the house, followed by the woman and the children. The vagabond sat down and began to eat, with his head lowered beneath the glances.

The mother, standing up, scrutinized him. The two big girls, the Martins, leaning against the door, one of them holding the latest baby, fixed their eager eyes upon him, and the two boys, seated in the ashes of the fireplace, had stopped playing with the black kettle to look at this stranger too.

Levesque, having taken a chair, asked him:

"Do you come from a distance?"

"I have come from Cette."

"On foot as far as that?"

"Yes, on foot. A man has to walk when he cannot afford to ride."

"And where are you going?"

"I was coming here."

"You know someone here?"

"That might be."

They were silent. He ate slowly, although he was famished, and he took a sip of cider after each mouthful of bread. He had a worn, wrinkled face and seemed to have suffered much.

Levesque brusquely asked him:

"What is your name?"

"My name is Martin."

A strange shudder shook the mother. She took a step forward, as if to scan the vagabond more closely, and stood opposite him with her arms hanging down and her mouth open. Nobody said anything further. Levesque finally resumed:

"Are you from here?"

He answered: "I am from here." And as he raised his head the woman's eyes and his met and remained fixed upon each other, as if their glances were fastened.

She suddenly said in a changed voice, low and trembling:

"It is you, my husband?"

He slowly replied:

"Yes, it is I."

He did not move, continuing to masticate the bread.
Levesque, more surprised than moved, stammered:
"It is you, Martin?"
The other man said simply:
"Yes, it is I."
And the second husband asked:
"Where have you come from?"
He first told his story.
"From the coast to Africa; I was wrecked on a reef. Three of us were saved, Picard, Vatinel and me. And then we were captured by savages who held us twelve years. Picard and Vatinel are dead. An English traveler passing that way took me and brought me to Cette, and here I am."
The woman began to weep, her face in her apron.
Levesque said:
"What shall we do now?"
Martin asked:
"You are her husband?"
Levesque replied:
"Yes, I am."
They looked at each other and were silent.
Then Martin, gazing at the children in a circle around him, nodded toward two little girls.
"Those are mine."
Levesque said:
"They are yours."
He did not rise; he did not kiss them; he merely remarked:
"Good God! How tall they are."
Levesque repeated:
"What shall we do?"
Martin, perplexed, could not tell. Finally he decided:
"I will do as you wish. I don't want to injure you. It is vexing all the same, considering the house. I have two children; you have three, each his own. But the mother, is she yours or mine? I will consent to whatever you wish, but the house is mine, since my father left it to me, since I was born here and since there are papers for it at the notary's."
The woman still wept with little sobs stifled in the blue cloth of her apron. The two tall girls drew near and looked at their father with uneasiness.
He had finished eating. But Levesque had an idea:
"We must go to the priest; he will decide."
Martin rose, and as he approached his wife she threw herself sobbing upon his breast.
"My husband! You are here! Martin, my poor Martin, you are here!"
And she held him in her arms, suddenly pierced by a breath of olden times, by a great shock of memories which recalled to her the days when she was twenty and their first embraces.
Martin, himself moved, kissed her on the cap. The two children in the

corner began to howl together, seeing their mother weep, and the last born, in the arms of the second Martin girl, shrieked with the sharp sound of a cracked fife.

Levesque, standing up, waited.

"Come," he said, "we must get this straightened out."

Martin released his wife, and as he looked at his two daughters their mother said to them:

"Kiss your father, at least."

They approached him together, astonished and a little afraid. And he kissed them one after the other on both cheeks with a big peasant's smack. And seeing this unknown approach, the little child uttered such piercing cries that it almost went into convulsions.

Then the two men went out together.

As they passed the Café du Commerce Levesque asked:

"Shall we have a little drop?"

"I would like it very much," said Martin.

They entered and sat down in a room which was vacant.

"Ho! Chicot, two bottles of wine, good wine. This is Martin who has come back, Martin of the Two Sisters, which was lost."

And the tavern keeper, three glasses in one hand and a carafe in the other, approached, large of paunch, ruddy, fat, and asked with a quiet air:

"What? You here, Martin?"

Martin replied: "I am here."

JULIE ROMAIN

IN THE SPRINGTIME two years ago I was walking along the shores of the Mediterranean. What is more charming than to dream while walking over a lonely road? One enjoys the sunlight and the caressing wind when climbing the mountains or strolling by the seashore. And in his daydreams what illusions, what love poems, what adventures pass in two hours through the mind of one who idles along a road. Every possible hope, confused and joyous, penetrates him with the warm, light air; he inhales them with the breeze, and they give birth in his being to an appetite for happiness that increases like the hunger he acquires in walking. Sweet and fleeting thoughts sing in his soul as he comes closer to nature.

I followed the road that leads from Saint-Raphaël to Italy, or rather, I made my way through that superb and changing scenery which seems made to be celebrated in all the love poems of the earth. It seemed to me a pity to think that from Cannes to Monaco scarcely anyone comes into this part of country save to make trouble, to juggle with money or to display under this delicious sky and in this garden of roses and oranges base vanities, stupid pretensions and vile covetousness and to show the human mind as it is—servile, ignorant, arrogant and grasping.

Suddenly in one of the curves of the ravishing bays I saw a group of villas, four or five only, fronting on the sea at the foot of the mountain. Behind them was a wild forest of pines which covered two great valleys apparently without roads or outlet. Involuntarily I stopped in front of the gate of one of these chalets, so pretty was it, a little white cottage with brown decorations, covered with roses that climbed to the roof. The garden was filled with flowers of all colors and every size, coquettishly arranged in studied disorder. The lawn was dotted with flower beds; a vase with trailing vines stood on the step of the veranda, and over the windows hung clusters of purple grapes, while the stone balustrade that surrounded this charming dwelling was covered with enormous red morning-glories that looked like spots of blood. Behind the house stretched a long alley of orange trees in flower, which reached as far as the foot of the mountain.

On the door of the villa in small, gilt letters I read this name: "Villa d'Antan." I asked myself what poet or fairy inhabited the place, what inspired recluse had discovered it and created this dream of a dwelling that appeared to spring from masses of flowers.

A workman was breaking stones on the road at a short distance. I asked him the name of the proprietor of the chalet. He replied that it belonged to the famous Mme Julie Romain.

Julie Romain! In my childhood I had often heard her spoken of, the great actress, the rival of Rachel! No woman had been more applauded or more loved—more loved, above all! How many duels had been fought and how many suicides had been committed because of her, and how many wild adventures had been undertaken for her sake! What was her age now, that seductress? Sixty—no, seventy—seventy-five years. Julie Romain! Here, in this house! I recalled again the emotion created throughout France (I was twelve years old then) by her flight to Sicily with one lover, a poet, after her notorious quarrel with another adorer.

She fled with her new love one evening after a first-night representation during which the audience had applauded her for half an hour and called her out eleven times in succession. She went away with the poet in a post chaise, as was the custom then; they had crossed the sea in order to love in that antique island, daughter of Greece, under the immense grove of orange trees that surrounds Palermo, which is called the "Conque d'Ov."

Their ascent of Etna was gossiped about, and also how they hung over the immense crater, arm in arm, cheek against cheek, as if they desired to throw themselves into the gulf of fire.

He was dead now, the writer of affecting verses, of poems so brilliant that they dazzled a whole generation, and so subtle and mysterious that they opened a new world to other poets.

The other lover was dead also, the abandoned one, who created for her those musical expressions that remain in all hearts, expressions of triumph and despair that are at once intoxicating and heart-rending.

She lived here, in this house veiled with flowers!

I hesitated no longer. I rang the bell. A domestic came to open the door, a boy of eighteen years, awkward and shy, with hands that appeared to be in his way. I wrote on my card a gallant compliment to the old actress and an ardent prayer that she would receive me. Perhaps she might know my name and allow me to see her.

The young valet disappeared but soon returned and asked me to follow him. He showed me into a neat drawing room, correct in every detail in the style of Louis Philippe, with furniture of a cold and cumbersome fashion, the coverings of which were being removed in my honor by a little maid of about sixteen years, with a slender figure but not much beauty.

Then the servants left me alone. I looked around the room with interest. On the walls hung three portraits, one was of the actress in a celebrated role, another was of the poet-lover wearing a long frock coat, tight at the waist, and the ruffled shirt of those days, and the third was of the musician, seated before a clavichord. The lady was blonde and charming in her portrait, but her pose was a little affected, as was the fashion of that day. Her charming mouth and blue eyes smiled graciously, and the technique of the painting was of a high degree of excellence. Those three remarkable faces seemed to be looking already at the next generation, and their surroundings had an air of a day that was past and of individualities that were no more.

A door opened, and a little woman entered. She was very old, very small, with eyebrows and bands of white hair. Somehow she reminded me of a white mouse, quick and furtive in her movements. She gave me her hand and, with a voice that was still fresh, vibrating and sonorous, she said graciously: "Thank you, monsieur. It is very kind of the men of today to remember the women of yesterday! Be seated!"

I told her that her house had attracted me, that I had tried to learn the name of the proprietor and, having learned it, I could not resist the desire to ring her bell.

"Your visit gives me the greater pleasure, monsieur," she said, "as it is the first time such an event has happened. When your card was handed to me with the gracious compliment it carried, I was as startled as if someone had announced an old friend who had been gone these twenty years. I am forgotten, truly forgotten; no one remembers me; no one will think of me until the day of my death; then all the papers will talk for three days of Julie Romain, telling anecdotes, giving details and souvenirs and scandals and, perhaps, pompous eulogies. Then that will be the end of me!"

She was silent a moment and then resumed: "And that will not be long now. In a few months, in a few days, perhaps, the little woman who is now alive will be nothing but a corpse!"

She raised her eyes to her portrait, which met her gaze as if smiling at that withered caricature of itself; then she looked at the two men, the scornful poet and the inspired musician, both of whom seemed to say: "What does that ruin ask of us?"

An indescribable, keen, irresistible sadness seized my heart, the sadness that overwhelms those whose lives are finished and who struggle still with memories, as a drowning man struggles in deep water.

From the place where I sat I could see brilliant and swiftly moving carriages passing along the road, going from Nice to Monte Carlo. And seated inside were beautiful young women, rich and happy, and men, smiling and satisfied. She followed my glance and, comprehending my thought, murmured with a resigned smile: "It is not possible to be and to have been at the same time."

"How beautiful life must have been for you!" I said.

She sighed deeply. "Yes, beautiful and sweet! It is for that reason that I regret it so much."

I saw that she was disposed to talk of herself, so softly and with delicate precautions, as one would touch a painful wound, I began to question her. She spoke of her success, of her intoxicating joys, of her friends, of her whole triumphant existence.

"Your greatest joy and your deepest happiness—did you owe them to the theater, madame?" I asked.

"Oh no!" she replied quickly.

I smiled and she added, raising her eyes with a sad look to the portraits of the two men:

"I owed my greatest happiness to them."

I could not refrain from asking her to which one she owed it.

"To both, monsieur! I even confuse them in my mind sometimes, and besides, I feel remorse toward one of them to this day."

"Then, madame, it is not to them but to the act of love itself that you owe your gratitude. They have merely been love's instruments."

"That is possible. But, ah, what wonderful instruments!"

"Are you certain that you have not been loved—that you would not have been loved as well, and perhaps better, by a simple man, one who was not great but who would have offered you his whole life, his whole heart, his his whole being, every thought and every hour? With those two you had two formidable rivals—music and poetry."

She cried out with force, with that youthful voice which could still thrill the soul: "No, monsieur, no! A simpler man might have loved me better, perhaps, but he would not have loved me as those two did. Ah! But they knew how to sing the music of love as no other man in the world could have sung it.

"How they intoxicated me! Is it possible that any other man could have found that which they found in words and in sounds? Is it enough to love if one does not know how to put into love all the poetry and all the music of the sky and the earth? They knew, those two, how to make a woman ecstatic with joy, and with their songs and their words as well as with their deeds. Yes, there was perhaps more of illusion than reality in our passion, but those illusions lift you to the clouds, whereas realities alone always leave you on the earth. If others loved me more it was through them alone that I learned, felt and adored love!"

Suddenly she began to weep noiselessly tears of bitter sorrow. I appeared not to notice it and looked far away out of the window. After a few moments she went on:

"You see, monsieur, with most people the heart grows old with the body. With me that has not happened. My poor body is seventy-five years old, but my heart is only twenty. And that is the reason why I live all alone, with my flowers and my dreams."

Again a long silence fell between us. After a time she calmed herself and again spoke smilingly:

"How you would laugh at me, monsieur, if you knew how I pass my evenings when the weather is fine! I am ashamed of my folly and pity myself at the same time."

It was useless for me to beg her to tell me; she would not do so; then I rose to go, at which she cried, "What! so soon?"

I told her that I had intended to dine at Monte Carlo, and at once she asked a little timidly: "Would you not like to dine with me? It would give me very much pleasure."

I accepted her invitation immediately. She appeared delighted and rang the bell; then when she had given a few orders to the little maid, she said she would like to show me her house.

A kind of glass-covered veranda, full of plants, opened from the dining room and permitted one to see, from one end to the other, the long alley of orange trees, extending to the foot of the mountains. A low seat, hidden under the shrubbery, indicated that the aged actress often came to sit there.

Then we went into the garden to look at the flowers. Evening came on softly, one of those calm, warm evenings that brings forth all the perfumes of the earth. It was almost dark when we placed ourselves at the table. The dinner was excellent, and we sat long over it. We became quite intimate friends. A profound sympathy for her had sprung up in my heart. She drank a glass of wine and became more friendly and confidential.

"Let us go out and look at the moon," she said at last. "I adore the moon, the lovely moon! It has been the witness of my greatest joys. It seems to me that all my sweetest memories are treasured there and that I have only to look at it in order to have them come back to me. And sometimes, in the evening, I arrange for myself a pretty scene, so pretty—if you only knew! But no, you would laugh at me too much. I cannot tell you—I don't dare—no—no, I cannot tell you."

"Ah, madame, continue, I pray!" I begged of her. "What is your little secret? Tell me! I promise you not to laugh—I swear it!"

She hesitated; I took her hands, her poor little hands, so thin and cold, and kissed them one after the other many times, as her lovers were wont to do in former days. She was moved, though she still hesitated.

"You promise me not to laugh?" she said timidly.

"Yes, I swear it, madame!"

"Well then, come!" she said with a smile.

We rose from the table, and as the awkward youth in green livery drew back the chair behind her she spoke a few low, quick words in his ear.

He replied respectfully, "Yes, madame, immediately."

She took my arm and led me upon the veranda. The orange tree walk was a beautiful sight. The moon cast a slender line of silver among the trees, a long line of light that fell on the yellow sand between the dense and rounded branches. As the trees were in bloom, their delicious and penetrating perfume filled the air, and among the dark foliage were thousands of fireflies whose tiny flames looked like the seed of stars.

"Oh, what an ideal environment for a scene of love!" I cried.

She smiled. "Is it not? Is it not? You will see presently!"

She made me sit down beside her and murmured:

"The memory of such scenes is what makes me regret life. But you hardly dream of those things, you men of today. You are merely money-makers, businessmen. You don't know how to talk to us even. When I say 'us,' I mean women who are young. Love affairs have become merely liaisons, which originate often in an unacknowledged bill of the dressmaker. If you find the bill more important than the woman, you disappear, but if you esteem the woman of greater value than the bill, you pay! Nice manners, and charming affections!"

She took my hand. "Look!" she said.

I was astonished and transported with pleasure at the charming picture that appeared. Below us, at the end of the alley and in the full moonlight, a youth and a maiden were coming toward us, clasping each other around the waist. They advanced, their arms entwined, walking slowly in the moon's rays, the soft effulgence of which bathed them completely.

They disappeared in the darkness for a moment, then reappeared farther down the avenue.

The youth was dressed in a white satin costume of the last century, with a broad hat over which hung an ostrich feather. The maiden wore a skirt with wide hoops, and her head was dressed with the high, powdered coiffure affected by beautiful dames in the days of the Regency.

At last they came to a halt about a hundred steps away from us and, standing in the middle of the alley, they embraced after saluting each other gracefully.

Suddenly I recognized the two little servants! Then I was seized with one of those irresistible desires to laugh that shake one all over. I did not laugh, however. I resisted the impulse and waited to see the next scene in this extraordinary comedy.

The lovers now returned toward the end of the alley, and distance again made them appear charming. They withdrew farther and farther away and at last disappeared like figures in a dream. The alley seemed lonely without them.

I took my departure also. I left immediately so that I should not see them again, for I thought it probable that the spectacle was made to last a long time, in order to recall all the past—that past of love and scenic effect, that fictitious past, deceiving and seductive, falsely yet truly charming—to cause the tender heart to throb again in the romantic breast of the old actress and to use me as a final instrument.

AN UNREASONABLE WOMAN

A GREAT WIND was whistling outside, an autumn wind, groaning and galloping; one of those winds which kill the last leaves and carry them away to the clouds.

The hunters had finished their dinner and were still booted, red, animated and lighted up. They were those demi-Norman lords, half country squire, half peasant, rich and vigorous, shaped for cutting the horns of beeves when they stopped them in the market.

They had hunted all day on M. Blondel's estate, M. Blondel, the mayor of Eparville, and they were eating now around the great table in a kind of farm-villa of which their host was the proprietor.

They were talking like a whirlwind, laughing like a roar of wild animals and drinking like cisterns, their legs stretched out, their elbows on the cloth, their eyes shining under the flame of the lamps, heated by a hearth fire so formidable as to send to the ceiling its ruddy glow. They chatted of hunting and dogs. But they had come to the hour when other ideas come to men half tipsy, and all eyes followed the strong girl with plump cheeks who carried at the end of her red wrists great platters filled with food.

Suddenly a devil of a fellow, who had become a veterinary after having studied for a priest and who looked after all the animals of the district, by name Sejour, said:

"My eyes! Monsieur Blondel, you have a girl there who is not starved."

And a laugh made the echoes ring. Then an old nobleman, declassed, ruined by alcohol, M. de Varnetot, raised his voice.

"I once had a droll adventure with a girl like that. Wait, I must tell it to you. Every time I think of her it recalls Mirza, my dog which I sold to Count d'Haussonel and which returned every day when she was let out, because she was unable to leave me. Finally I got angry and begged the count to keep her chained. Do you know what the beast did? She died of grief.

"But to return to my maid; here is the story:

"I was then twenty-five years old and lived as a bachelor in my castle at Villebon. You know that when one is young and has an income and makes a beast of himself every evening he has his eye on all sides.

"I discovered a young girl who was in service at the house of Deboultot of Cauville. You know Deboultot well, you, Blondel. To be brief, she pleased me so much, the hussy, that I went one day to her master and made a business proposition to him. He gave me his servant, and I sold him my black mare Cocotte, which he had sought of me for two years. He extended his hand to me and said: 'It is agreed M. de Varnetot.' It was a bargain. The little one came to the castle, and I took my black mare to Cauville myself, and I let him have her for three hundred crowns.

"At first everything went as if on wheels. No one mistrusted anything.

Only Rose loved me a little too much for my taste. The child, you see, was not a nobody. She had something out of the common in her veins. She came from some girl who committed some error with her master.

"Briefly, she adored me. There were cajolings, endearments, little pet names and heaps of caresses—enough to make it a matter of reflection.

"I said to myself: 'This cannot last, or I would allow myself to be caught.' But they do not catch me easily. I am not one of those to be taken in with a couple of kisses. So I had my eyes opened when she announced to me that she was large.

"Pif! Pif! It was as if someone had put two shots from a gun into my breast. And she embraced me; she embraced me, I say, and laughed and danced as if she were mad. What? I said nothing the first day, but at night I reasoned with myself; I thought: 'It is just here; it is necessary to parry the blow and cut the thread; it is the only time.' You understand, I had my father and mother at Barneville, and my sister married to the Marquis d' Yspare, at Rollebec, two leagues from Villebon. There must not be any stories.

"But how was I to draw myself out of the affair? If she left the house something would be suspected, and people would talk. If I kept her there the condition would soon be recognized, and then I could not turn her away.

"I spoke to my uncle about it, the Baron de Creteuil, an old buck who has known more than one such case, and asked his advice. He responded tranquilly:

"'You must marry, my boy.'

"I made a leap. 'Marry, Uncle?' I said. 'Marry whom?'

"He shrugged his shoulders gently as he replied:

"'Whom you wish; that is your affair, not mine. If one is not stupid there is always somebody to be found.'

"I reflected for two weeks upon this idea and ended by saying to myself: 'My uncle is right.'

"Then I commenced to rack my brain to think of someone, when one evening the justice of the peace, with whom I was dining, said to me:

"'Mother Paumelle's son is into mischief again; it is true that a good dog shows his race.'

"This Mother Paumelle was a sly old gypsy of whom the youth could have all they desired. For six francs she would certainly have sold her soul, and her rake of a son followed in her footsteps.

"I went and found her and very gently made her understand the state of affairs. As I was somewhat embarrassed in my explanations, she demanded all at once:

"'Well, how much will you give to this little one?'

"She was malicious, this old woman, but as I was not stupid, I was prepared for business. I owned three pieces of wasteland beyond Sasseville which belong to my three farms in Villebon. The farmers were always complaining that it was too far away; in short, I took back the three fields, six acres in all, and as my farmers found fault, I returned to them, up to the end of each lease, all their rents in poultry. In this way the thing was settled. Then, having bought a piece on one side from my neighbor, Monsieur Aumonte, I had a little house constructed down there, the whole thing for about fifteen hundred francs in all. In this way I had got together a little farm, which had not cost me very much, that I could give to the little girl for a marriage portion.

"The old woman cried out: 'It is not enough, but I will wait; we will leave it without deciding anything.'

"The next day at daybreak the lad came to find me. I could scarcely recall his face, but when I saw him I was reassured; he was not bad for a peasant but had the air of a rude fellow.

"He looked at the affair from a distance, as if he were buying a cow. When we had agreed he wished to see the property, and we set out together over the fields. The scamp kept me going for three hours over the land; he surveyed it, measured it, took up the earth and crumbled it in his hands, as if he were afraid of being deceived in the merchandise. The house was not yet roofed; he exacted slate instead of thatch, because it needed less repairs! Then he said to me:

"'And the furniture; you must give that.'

"I protested: 'No. It is enough to give you a farm.'

"He sneered: 'Yes, a farm and a child.'

"I colored in spite of myself. He went on:

"'Come, now, you must give a bed, a table, the chest of drawers, three chairs and the kitchen dishes, or nothing can be done.'

"I consented to it.

"Then we started to return. He had not yet said a word about the girl. But suddenly, with a sly, constrained air, he asked:

"'But if she should die who would it go to, this farm?'

"I answered: 'To you, naturally.'

"That was what he had wanted to know since morning. Immediately he extended his hand to me with a satisfied appearance. We were of one accord.

"Oh! But I had difficulty in making Rose consent. She dragged herself at my feet, sobbed and kept repeating: 'It was you proposed it to me! It was you! It was you!' For more than a week she resisted in spite of my reasoning and my prayers. They are stupid, these women! As soon as they get love into their heads they understand nothing else. Wisdom is nothing; it is love above all and all for love!

"Finally I got angry and threatened to throw her out. Then she yielded, little by little, on the condition that I would allow her to come and see me from time to time.

"I myself conducted her to the altar, paid for the ceremony and gave the wedding dinner. I did the thing up grandly, in short. Then, 'Good-by, my children!' I went to pass six months with my brother in Touraine.

"When I returned I learned that she had been at the house every week asking for me. And I had scarcely been home an hour before I saw her coming with a baby in her arms. Believe me if you will, but it affected me in some way to see this little monkey. I believe I even embraced it.

"As for the mother, she was a wreck, a skeleton, a shadow. She looked thin and old. Ye gods! It was evident this marriage was not to her liking. I said to her mechanically:

"'Are you happy?'

"Then she began to weep like a fountain and with hiccups and sobs she cried:

"'I can never, never leave you now. I would rather die; I cannot.'

"She made a devil of a noise. I consoled her as well as I could and conducted her back to the gate.

"I learned that her husband beat her and that her mother-in-law made life hard for her, the old cabbagehead.

"Two days later she returned. She took me in her arms and dragged herself upon the earth. 'Kill me,' she said, 'but I will never go back down there.'

"This is exactly what Mirza would have said could she have spoken! These stories began to be very tiresome to me, and I went away again for another six months.

"When I returned—when I returned I learned that she had died three weeks before, having visited the castle every Sunday—just like Mirza. The child had also died eight days before.

"As for the husband, the cunning rascal, he inherited the property. He has turned out well since, it appears, and is now municipal counselor."

M. de Varnetot added, laughing:

"It is a fact that I made the fortune of that man!"

And M. Sejour, the veterinary, concluded gravely, carrying a glass of brandy to his lips:

"Say what you will, but with women like that, such things should not be."

ROSALIE PRUDENT

THERE WAS A MYSTERY in that affair about Rosalie Prudent, which neither the jury, nor the judge, nor the prosecuting attorney of the Republic himself could understand.

The girl Rosalie was a servant at the house of the Varambot family, of Mantes. She became *enceinte* and, unknown to her employers, had given birth to a child in the garret during the night and had then killed the child and buried it in the garden.

It was the ordinary story of most of the infanticides committed by servants. But one act remained inexplicable. The examination of the girl's room had resulted in the discovery of a complete layette for an infant, made by Rosalie herself, who had passed her nights during three months in cutting out the garments and sewing them. The grocer where she had bought her candles (paid for out of her wages), in order to perform this long task, came forward and testified to the fact of their purchase. In addition it was learned that the midwife of the town, informed by Rosalie of her condition, had given her all the advice and information necessary in case the child should be born at a time when aid was impossible to obtain. She had found a place, also, at Poissy for Rosalie Prudent, who foresaw her loss of situation, as the Varambots were severe on the subject of morality.

They appeared in court, the man and his wife, small provincials of moderate means, exasperated against the vulgar creature who had besmirched the immaculateness of their house. They would have liked to have seen her guillotined at once without trial, and they overwhelmed her with insults, which in their mouths became accusations.

The guilty one, a tall, handsome girl of lower Normandy, fairly well educated for her station, wept without ceasing and made no reply to them or to anyone. The court came to the conclusion that she had accomplished that act of barbarity in a moment of despair and insanity, since everything indicated that she had hoped to keep her infant and bring it up.

The judge tried once more to make her speak, to get her to acknowledge her crime and, having asked her with great kindness to do so, he made her understand at last that the jury sitting there to judge her did not wish her death but were ready to pity her.

The girl appeared to be making up her mind to speak at last.

"Tell us now at first who is the father of that child," said the judge.

Until that moment she had refused obstinately to divulge this fact. Now she replied suddenly, looking straight at her employers, who had come there in a rage to calumniate her.

"It is Monsieur Joseph, the nephew of Monsieur Varambot!"

Varambot and his wife started, and both cried at the same time:

"It is false! She lies! It is infamous!"

The judge bade them be silent and said:

"Continue, I beg of you, and tell us how it happened."

Then the girl began to speak hurriedly, seeming to find some comfort for her poor, solitary, bruised heart in giving vent to her sorrow before these severe-looking men, whom she had taken until then for enemies and inflexible judges.

"Yes, it was Monsieur Joseph Varambot—it happened when he came for his vacation last summer."

"What is the occupation of this Monsieur Joseph Varambot?"

"He is underofficer in the artillery, monsieur. He was two months at the house—two months of the summer. I wasn't thinking of anything when he began to look at me and then to say things to me and finally to make love to me the whole day long. I was easy, monsieur! He told me I was a handsome girl, that I pleased him, that I was to his taste. For myself, he pleased me, to be sure. What would you have done? Anyone listens to those things when one is alone—as I am. I am alone on the earth, monsieur. There is no one to whom I can talk—no one to whom I can tell my troubles. I have neither father, nor mother, nor brother nor sister—no one! He seemed like a brother who had come to me when he began to talk to me. And then he asked me to go down to the river one evening so that we might talk without making so much noise. And I went down there. Could I have known what would happen? He put his arms around my waist—of course I didn't want to—no, no! I couldn't help it. I wanted to cry; the air was so soft and warm—it was clear moonlight—I couldn't help it! No, I swear it to you, I couldn't help it—he did what he pleased. That lasted three weeks, as long as he remained. I would have followed him to the end of the world. But he went away, and I didn't know that I was *enceinte*—I didn't! I didn't know it until the month afterward."

She began to weep so violently that they were obliged to give her time to compose herself. Then the judge spoke in the tone of a father confessor: "Go on, my girl, go on."

She continued: "When I knew that I was *enceinte* I told Madame Boudin, the midwife, to whom one can tell these things, and I asked her what to do in case that happened without her. And then I made the clothes, night after night, until one o'clock in the morning; and then I looked for another place, for I knew very well I should be discharged, but I wished to remain in that house until the end, in order to economize the pennies, seeing that I had no money and that I would need it for the little one."

"Then you did not wish to kill him?"

"Oh! Surely not, monsieur."

"Why did you kill him then?"

"Here's how it happened. It came sooner than I thought it would. It took me in the kitchen as I was washing my dishes. Monsieur and Madame Varambot had retired already, so I went upstairs without trouble, holding to the banisters. I lay down on the floor in my room, so as not to soil the bed. That lasted perhaps one hour—but it may have been two or three—I can't tell, so much pain did I have—and then—and then it was over, and I took up my baby!

"Oh yes! I was happy, for sure! I did everything that Madame Boudin told me, everything! Then I laid him on the bed, and then another pain began, and it was a pain to kill anyone. If you knew what that was, you others, you wouldn't do as much I'm sure! I fell on my knees, and then on my back on the floor, and then it began all over again, and that, too, lasted one hour, or perhaps two, and there I was all alone. Finally there came another little one, yes, another, two of them, like that! I took it up as I took the first one, and I put it on the bed by the side of the other. One—two! Can it be possible, I said? Two babies! And I, who earn twenty francs a month! Say—was it possible for me to take care of them? To care for one—yes, I might do that by depriving myself, but not two!

"The thought of that turned my head. What do I know about it, I? Could I choose, say? Do I know? I saw myself come to my last day! I couldn't keep two, so I put the pillow on them without knowing what I was doing, and I threw myself on the bed and upon them too. And I stayed there, rolling and crying, until daylight, which I saw through the window. I looked at them—they were both dead under the pillow, quite dead. Then I took them under my arm. I went down the stairs and out in the garden; I took the gardener's spade and I buried them in the ground, as deep as I could, one here and the other there, not together, so that they could not talk of their mother, if they do talk, the little dead children. Do I know?

"And then I went back to my bed, and I was so sick that I could not get up. They made the doctor come, and he understood everything. That is the truth, Monsieur the Judge. Do what you want to me. I am ready."

During her speech half of the jurymen had been wiping their eyes over and over again, trying to hide their emotion. All the women in the courtroom were sobbing.

"At what spot in the garden did you bury the other infant?" asked the judge.

"Which one did you find?" Rosalie inquired.

"The one that was under the artichokes."

"Ah! The other is buried under the strawberries beside the well!" The poor girl began again to sob so loud that it was enough to break one's heart to hear her. The jury acquitted her.

HIPPOLYTE'S CLAIM

THE FAT JUSTICE OF THE PEACE, with one eye closed and the other half open, is listening with evident displeasure to the plaintiffs. Once in a while he gives a sort of grunt that foretells his opinion, and in a thin voice resembling that of a child, he interrupts them to ask questions. He has just rendered judgment in the case of M. Joly against M. Petitpas, the contestants having come to court on account of the boundary of a field which had been accidentally overstepped by M. Petitpas's farm hand, while the latter was plowing.

Now he calls the case of Hippolyte Lacour, vestryman and ironmonger, against Mme Céleste Césarine Luneau, widow of Anthime Isidore Luneau.

Hippolyte Lacour is forty-five years old; he is tall and gaunt, with a clean-shaven face and long hair, and he speaks in a slow, singsong voice.

Mme Luneau appears to be about forty years of age. She is built like a prize fighter, and her plain dress is stretched tightly over her portly form. Her enormous hips hold up her overflowing bosom in front, while in the back they support the great rolls of flesh that cover her shoulders. Her face, with strongly cut features, rests on a short, fat neck, and her strong voice is pitched at a key that makes the windows and the eardrums of her auditors vibrate. She is about to become a mother, and her huge form protrudes like a mountain.

The witnesses for the defense are waiting to be called.

His Honor begins: Hippolyte Lacour, state your complaint.

The plaintiff speaks: Your honor, it will be nine months on Saint Michael's Day that the defendant came to me one evening, after I had rung the Angelus, and began an explanation relating to her barrenness.

THE JUSTICE OF THE PEACE: Kindly be more explicit.

HIPPOLYTE: Very well, your honor. Well, she wanted to have a child and desired my participation. I didn't raise any objection, and she promised to give me one hundred francs. The thing was all cut and dried, and now she refuses to acknowledge my claim, which I renew before your honor.

The Justice: I don't understand in the least. You say that she wanted a child? What kind of child? Did she wish to adopt one?

Hippolyte: No, your honor, she wanted a new one.

The Justice: What do you mean by a new one?

Hippolyte: I mean a newborn child, one that we were to beget as if we were man and wife.

The Justice: You astonish me. To what end did she make this abnormal proposition?

Hippolyte: Your honor, at first I could not make out her reasons and was taken a little aback. But as I don't do anything without thoroughly investigating beforehand, I called on her to explain matters to me, which she did. You see, her husband, Anthime Isidore, whom you knew as well as you know me, had died the week before, and his money reverted to his family. This greatly displeased her on account of the loss it meant, so she went to a lawyer who told her all about what might happen if a child should be born to her after ten months. I mean by this that if she gave birth to a child inside of the ten months following the death of Anthime Isidore, her offspring would be considered legitimate and would entitle her to the inheritance. She made up her mind at once to run the risk and came to me after church, as I have already had the honor of telling you, seeing that I am the father of eight living children, the eldest of whom is a grocer in Caen, department of Calvados, and legitimately married to Victoire-Elisabeth Rabou——

The Justice: These details are superfluous. Go back to the subject.

Hippolyte: I am getting there, your honor. So she said to me: "If you succeed I'll give you one hundred francs as soon as I get the doctor's report." Well, your honor, I made ready to give entire satisfaction, and after eight weeks or so I learned with pleasure that I had succeeded. But when I asked her for the hundred francs she refused to pay me. I renewed my demands several times, never getting so much as a pin. She even called me a liar and a weakling, a libel which can be destroyed by glancing at her.

The Justice: Defendant, what have you to say?

Mme Luneau: Your honor, I say that this man is a liar.

The Justice: How can you prove this assertion?

Mme Luneau [*red in the face, choking and stammering*]: How can I prove it? What proofs have I? I haven't a single real proof that the child isn't his. But, your honor, it isn't his; I swear it on the head of my dead husband.

The Justice: Well, whose is it then?

Mme Luneau [*stammering with rage*]: How do I know? How do—do I know? Everybody's, I suppose. Here are my witnesses, your honor. They're all here, the six of them. Now make them testify, make them testify. They'll tell——

The Justice: Collect yourself, Madame Luneau, collect yourself and reply calmly to my questions. What reasons have you to doubt that this man is the father of the child you are carrying?

HIPPOLYTE'S CLAIM

Mme Luneau: What reasons? I have a hundred to one, a hundred? No, two hundred, five hundred, ten thousand, a million and more reasons to believe he isn't. After the proposal I made to him, with the promise of one hundred francs, didn't I learn that he wasn't the father of his own children, your honor, not the father of one of 'em?

Hippolyte [*calmly*]: That's a lie.

Mme Luneau [*exasperated*]: A lie! A lie, is it? I guess his wife has been seen by everybody around here. Call my witnesses, your honor, and make them testify.

Hippolyte [*calmly*]: It's a lie.

Mme Luneau: It's a lie, is it? How about the red-haired ones then? I suppose they're yours too?

The Justice: Kindly refrain from personal attacks, or I shall be obliged to call you to order.

Mme Luneau: Well, your honor, I had my doubts about him, and said I to myself, two precautions are better than one, so I explained my position to Césaire Lepic, the witness who is present. Says he to me, "At your disposal, Madame Luneau," and he lent me his assistance in case Hippolyte should turn out to be unreliable. But as soon as the other witnesses heard that I wanted to make sure against any disappointment, I could have had more than a hundred, your honor, if I had wanted them. That tall one over there, Lucas Chandelier, swore at the time that I oughtn't to give Hippolyte Lacour a cent, for he hadn't done more than the rest of them who had obliged me for nothing.

Hippolyte: What did you promise for? I expected the money, your honor. No mistake with me—a promise given, a promise kept.

Mme Luneau [*beside herself*]: One hundred francs! One hundred francs! One hundred francs for that, you liar! The others there didn't ask a red cent! Look at 'em, all six of 'em! Make them testify, your honor; they'll tell, sure. [*To Hippolyte.*] Look at 'em, you liar! they're as good as you. They're only six, but I could have had one, two, three, five hundred of 'em for nothing, too, you robber!

Hippolyte: Well, even if you'd had a hundred thousand——

Mme Luneau: I could, if I'd wanted 'em.

Hippolyte: I did my duty, so it doesn't change matters.

Mme Luneau [*slapping her protuberant form with both hands*]: Then prove that it's you that did it; prove it, you robber! I defy you to prove it!

Hippolyte [*calmly*]: Maybe I didn't do any more than anybody else. But you promised me a hundred francs for it. What did you ask the others for afterward? You had no right to. I guess I could have done it alone.

Mme Luneau: It is not true, robber! Call my witnesses, your honor; they'll answer, sure.

The justice calls the witnesses in behalf of the defense. Six red, awkward individuals appear.

The Justice: Lucas Chandelier, have you any reason to suppose that you are the father of the child Madame Luneau is carrying?

Lucas Chandelier: Yes sir.
The Justice: Célestin-Pierre Sidoine, have you any reason to suppose that you are the father of the child Madame Luneau is carrying?
Célestin-Pierre Sidoine: Yes sir.
The four other witnesses testify to the same effect.

The justice, after a pause, pronounces judgment: Whereas the plaintiff has reasons to believe himself the father of the child which Madame Luneau desired, Lucas Chandelier, Célestin-Pierre Sidoine and others have similar, if not conclusive, reasons to lay claim to the child.

But whereas Madame Luneau had previously asked the assistance of Hippolyte Lacour for a duly stated consideration:

And whereas one may not question the absolute good faith of Hippolyte Lacour, though it is questionable whether he had a perfect right to enter into such an agreement, seeing that the plaintiff is married and compelled by the law to remain faithful to his lawful spouse:

Therefore the court condemns Madame Luneau to pay an indemnity of twenty-five francs to Hippolyte Lacour for loss of time and unjustifiable abduction.

BENOIST

It all came over him one Sunday after Mass. He went out of church and followed the crossroad that led to his house, when he found himself behind the Martin girl who was also returning home.

The father walked beside his daughter with the important step of a rich farmer. Disdaining the blouse, he wore a kind of waistcoat of gray cloth and had on his head a melon-shaped hat with a wide brim. She, laced in a corset which she only wore once a week, walked very straight, her waist drawn in, her shoulders large, hips projecting, switching a little. Her hat was all flowers, the confection of an Yvetot milliner, and she showed her round, strong, supple neck, where little tendrils of hair were fluttering, moistened by the air and sun.

Benoist saw only her back, but he knew her face well, which was the reason he had noticed her still further. Suddenly he said to himself: "My, but she is pretty, just the same, that Martin girl!"

He looked at her as she walked along, admiring her crudely and feeling himself moved with desire. He had no need of seeing her face, none at all. He planted his eyes upon her figure, repeating to himself, as if he were speaking: "She is a pretty girl!"

The Martin girl turned to the right to enter Martinère, the farm of John Martin, her father. As she turned she looked back and saw Benoist, who looked queer to her. She cried out: "Good morning, Benoist." He answered: "Good morning, Mademoiselle Martin; good morning, Monsieur Martin," and passed on.

When he entered his house the soup was on the table. He seated himself opposite his mother, beside the hired man and boy, while the maidservant went to draw the cider. He ate a few spoonfuls then pushed his plate aside. His mother asked:

"What is the matter; don't you feel well?"

He answered: "No, I have something like a burning in my stomach and I have no appetite."

He watched the others eat, breaking off from time to time a mouthful of bread which he carried slowly to his lips and masticated a long time. He kept thinking of the Martin girl: "All the same, she is a pretty girl." And strange to say, he had never perceived it until this time, and now it had come to him so suddenly and so strongly that he was unable to eat any more. He scarcely touched the stew.

His mother said to him: "Come now, Benoist, do eat a little; it is a side of mutton and very good. When one has no appetite it is well to force oneself a little sometimes."

He swallowed a mouthful then pushed back his plate: "No, I cannot, decidedly."

Upon rising he made a tour of the farm and gave the boy a half holiday, promising to drive up the cattle in passing. The country was empty; it was a day of repose. From place to place in a field of clover the cows moved slowly, with bodies expanded, ruminating under the full sun. Some detached plows were standing in a corner of a plowed field, and the upturned earth, ready for the seed, displayed its large brown ridges in the midst of patches of yellow where bits of wheat and oat straw were left to decay after a late reaping.

An autumn wind, somewhat dry, was blowing over the plain, announcing a cool evening after sunset. Benoist sat down beside a ditch, put his hat on his knees as if he needed the air on his head and said aloud in the silence of the field: "When it comes to pretty girls, there is a pretty girl!"

He thought of her still in the evening in his bed and again on waking the next day. He was not sad; he was not discontented; he could not have told what was the trouble with him. But there was something which held him, something that fastened to his soul, an idea which would not leave him and which made a kind of tickling in his heart.

Sometimes we find a large fly shut up in a room. We hear it flying around and buzzing until the noise possesses us, irritates us. Suddenly it stops; we forget about it, but again it starts, forcing our attention. We can neither catch it nor kill it nor make it stay in place. Finally we resign ourselves to its humming. So the remembrance of the Martin girl agitated Benoist's mind; it was like an imprisoned fly.

Then a desire to see her again took possession of him, and he passed and repassed before the Martin farm. He saw her at last, hanging some linen upon a line between two apple trees.

It was warm, and she was protected only by a short skirt and a chemise, which showed to advantage the white arch made by her arms as she pinned up the napkins. He lay flat beside the ditch for more than an hour after she had gone. He returned to find himself more haunted than before.

For a month his mind was full of her, so that he trembled when her name was mentioned before him. He could not eat and had night sweats which hindered his sleeping. On Sunday at Mass he could not keep his eyes away from her. She perceived it and smiled at him, flattered at being appreciated.

Then one evening he suddenly met her in the road. She stopped on seeing him approach. He walked straight to her, suffocated by a fear that seized him, but resolved to speak to her. He commenced stammering:

"See here, Mademoiselle Martin, I can't endure this any longer."

And she answered him mockingly: "What is it that you cannot endure, Benoist?"

He replied: "That I think about you as long as there are hours in the day."

Placing her hands on her hips, she answered: "It is not I who force you to."

He murmured: "Yes, it is you, and I can neither sleep nor eat nor rest nor nothing."

Very low she said: "What do you think is necessary to cure you of it?"

He was struck dumb, his arms twitching, his eyes round, his mouth open. She struck him a sharp blow in the chest and ran away as fast as she could.

From this day they often met by the ditches or in the crossroad, generally at the close of day, when he was returning with his horses and she was driving the cows to the stable. He felt himself drawn, thrown toward her, by some great impulse of heart and body. He felt a desire to press her close, to strangle her, to eat her and make her a part of himself. And he had tremblings from powerlessness, from impatience and rage, from the fact that she was his complement, making together but one being.

There began to be gossip in the country. It was said they were promised to one another. Indeed, he had asked her if she would be his wife, and she had answered: "Yes." They were only waiting for an opportunity to speak of it to their parents.

Then suddenly she no longer came at certain hours to meet him. He could only get a glimpse of her at Mass on Sunday. And then one Sunday, after the sermon, the curate announced from the high pulpit that there was a promise of marriage between Victoire Adelaide Martin and Joseph Isidore Vallin.

Benoist felt as if he had raised blood. His ears buzzed; he could no longer hear anything, and he perceived after some time that he was weeping into his prayer book.

For a month he kept to his room. Then he began to work again. But he was not cured and still thought of her always. He shunned passing along the roads that surrounded her dwelling, not wishing to see even the trees of her yard, and this forced him to make a large circuit morning and evening.

She was now married to Vallin, the richest farmer in the district. Benoist no longer spoke to him, although they had been comrades since infancy.

Then one evening, as Benoist was passing across the common, he learned that she was *enceinte*. Instead of resenting this or its affecting him with a great grief, he found in it a kind of solace. It was finished now, well finished. They were more separated by this than by marriage. Truly, it was best so. Some months passed, and still some months. He saw her sometimes, walking to the village with slow step. She blushed on seeing him, lowered her head and hastened her steps. And he turned out of his way in order not to cross her and look into her eyes.

But he thought, with the same terror as on that first morning, of finding himself face to face with her and obliged to speak to her. What could he say after all he had said to her in former times, holding her hands and kissing the locks about her cheeks? He still often thought of their meeting place by the side of the ditch. It was villainous to do as she did after so many promises.

However, little by little, anger left his heart; there was no longer anything but sadness. And one day he took his old way by the farm where she lived. He saw the roof of the house from afar. She was in there! Living there with another! The apple trees were in blossom; the fowls were singing about the barnyard. The whole place seemed empty, the folk having gone to the fields for the spring work. He stopped near the fence and looked into the yard. The dog lay sleeping before his kennel. Three calves were walking slowly, one behind the other, toward the pool. A large turkey cock was wheeling about before the door, parading before the poultry after the manner of a stage singer.

Benoist leaned against a post and suddenly felt himself seized with a desire to weep. But just then he heard a cry, a great, appealing cry, coming from the house. He stood lost in amazement, his hands clinched upon the bars, ever listening. Another cry, prolonged, piercing, came to his ears and entered his soul and his flesh. It was she who was in trouble! She!

Finally he started hurriedly across the inclosure, pushed open the door and saw her stretched out upon the floor in agony, her face livid, her eyes haggard, seized with the pains of childbirth.

He stood there, paler and trembling more than she, murmuring: "I am here, my friend; here I am."

And she replied in gasps: "Oh, do not leave me, Benoist; do not leave me!"

He looked at her, not knowing what to say or what to do. She began to cry out again: "Oh! Oh! This tears me in two! Oh! Benoist!"

And she seemed frightfully tortured. Suddenly a furious desire to help her came over Benoist; he must appease her suffering, free her from this agony. He bent over and took her up and carried her to her bed. And although she groaned continually, he then undressed her, taking off her kerchief, her frock and her skirt. She began to bite her hands in order not to cry out. Then he did for her as he was accustomed to do for beasts, cows, sheep and mares: he aided her and received into his hands a large infant, which began to squall.

He wiped it and wrapped it in a cloth which was drying before the fire, then placed it on a pile of linen that lay on the table and returned to the mother. He put her on the floor again, changed the bed and put her in it. She whispered: "Thanks, Benoist, you have a brave heart." And she wept a little, as if some regret had seized her.

As for him, he loved her no longer, not at all. It was finished. Why? How?

He could not have told. What had come to pass had cured him better than ten years of absence.

She asked, weak and trembling: "What is it?"

He answered in a calm voice: "It is a girl, and a handsome one."

They were again silent. At the end of a few seconds the mother, in a feeble voice, said: "Show her to me, Benoist."

He went and got the little one and was presenting it to her, as if it were bread that had been blessed, when the door opened and Isidore Vallin appeared. He could not understand at first, then suddenly he guessed it all.

Benoist, somewhat disconcerted, murmured: "I was passing; I was just passing when I heard a cry—and I came. Here is your child, Vallin!"

Then the husband, with tears in his eyes, took the frail little monkey that was held out to him, embraced it and stood for some seconds overcome; then he placed the child on the bed and extended both hands to Benoist, saying: "Done now, Benoist; you see, between us all is said. If you wish we shall from this time be friends; just that, a pair of friends."

And Benoist replied: "I am willing; certainly—I am willing."

FECUNDITY

They were walking, these two old friends, in the garden all in blossom, where the gay springtime stirred with life.

One was a senator and the other a member of the French Academy, grave, both of them, full of reason and logic, but solemn—people of mark and reputation.

They were speaking at first of politics, exchanging thoughts, not upon ideas but men, personalities, which in these matters always precede reason. Then they rose to reminiscences; then they were silent, continuing to walk side by side, both softened by the sweetness of the air.

A great basket of radishes sent forth their odor, fresh and delicate. A heap of flowers of every kind and color threw their sweetness to the breeze, while a radiant ebony tree full of yellow berries scattered to the wind its fine powder, a golden smoke which reminded one of honey and which carried, like the caressing powder of the perfumer, its embalmed seed across space.

The senator stopped, breathed in the fertile sweetness that was floating by him, looked at the blossoming tree, resplendent as a sun, from which the pollen was now escaping. And he said:

"When one thinks that these imperceptible atoms, which smell good, can bring into existence in a hundred places, miles from here, plants of their own kind, can start the sap and fiber of the female trees, creating from a germ, as we mortals do, they seem mortal and they will be replaced by other beings of the same essence forever, like us!"

Then, planted before the radiant ebony tree whose vivifying perfume permeated every breath of air, the senator added, as if addressing it:

"Ah! My jolly fellow, if you were to count your children you would be woefully embarrassed. And behold! Here is one that accomplishes them easily, who lets himself go without remorse and disturbs himself little about it afterward."

The academician replied: "We do as much, my friend."

The senator answered: "Yes, I do not deny that; we do forget ourselves sometimes, but we know it, at least, and that constitutes our superiority."

The other man shook his head: "No, that is not what I mean; you see, my dear, there is scarcely a man who does not possess some unknown children, those children labeled *of unknown father*, whom he has created, as this tree reproduces itself, almost unconsciously.

"If it became necessary to establish the count of the women we have had, we should be, should we not? as embarrassed as this ebony tree, which you call upon to enumerate his descendants.

"From eighteen to forty, perhaps, bringing into line all our passing encounters and contacts of an hour, it can easily be admitted that we have had intimate relations with two or three hundred women. Ah well, my friend, among this number are you sure that you have not made fruitful at least one and that you have not, upon the streets or in prison, some blackguard son who robs and assassinates honest people, that is to say, people like us? Or perhaps a daughter in some bad place? Or perhaps, if she chanced to be abandoned by her mother, a cook in somebody's kitchen?

"Think further that nearly all women that we call 'public' possess one or two children whose father they do not know, children caught in the hazard of their embraces at ten or twenty francs. In every trade there is profit and loss. These castaways constitute the 'loss' of their profession. Who were their generators? You—I—all of us, the men who are 'all right!' These are the results of our joyous dinners to friends, of our evenings of gaiety, of the hours when our flesh contents us and pushes us on to the completion of adventure.

"Robbers, rovers, all these miserable creatures, in short, are our children. And how much better that is for us than if we were theirs, for they reproduce also, these beggars!

"For my part I have a villainous story upon my conscience which I would like to tell you. It brings me incessant remorse, and more than that, continual doubt and an unappeasable uncertainty which at times tortures me horribly.

"At the age of twenty-five I had undertaken, with one of my friends, now counselor of state, a journey through Brittany on foot.

"After fifteen or twenty days of forced march, after having visited the coasts of the north and a part of Finistère, we arrived at Douarnenez; from there, in a day's march, we reached the wildest point of the Raz by the bay of Trepasses, where we slept in some village whose name ends in *of*. When the morning came a strange fatigue held my comrade in bed. I say bed from habit, since our bed was composed simply of two boxes of straw.

"It was impossible to remain in such a place. I forced him to get up, and we came into Audierne toward four or five o'clock in the evening. The next day he was a little better. We set out again, but on the way he was taken with intolerable weariness, and it was with great difficulty that we were able to reach Pont l'Abbé.

"There at least there was an inn. My friend went to bed, and the doctor, whom we called from Quimper, found a high fever without quite determining the nature of it.

"Do you know Pont l'Abbé? No? Well, it is the most characteristic Breton town from Point Raz to Morbihan—a region which contains the essence of Breton morals and legends and customs. Today, even, this corner of the country has scarcely changed at all. I say 'today, even,' because I return there now every year, alas!

"An old castle bathes the foot of its towers in a dismal pond, sad with the call of wild birds. A river, deep enough for coasters, comes up to the town. In the streets, narrowed by the old houses, the men wear great hats and embroidered waistcoats and the four coats, one above the other; the first, about the size of the hand, covers at least the shoulder blades, while the last stops just below the breeches.

"The girls, who are large, pretty and fresh looking, wear a bodice of thick cloth which forms a breastplate and corset, constraining and leaving scarcely a suspicion of their swelling, martyrized busts. Their headdresses are also of strange fashion: over the temples two embroidered bands in color frame the face, binding the hair which falls in a sheet behind the head, and is mounted by a singular bonnet on the very summit, often of tissue of gold or silver.

"The servant at our inn was eighteen years old or more, with blue eyes, a pale blue, which were pierced with the two little black dots of the pupils, and with teeth short and white, which she showed always in laughing and which seemed made for biting granite.

"She did not know a word of French, speaking only the Breton patois, as do most of her compatriots.

"Well, my friend was no better, and although no malady declared itself, the doctor forbade his setting out, ordering complete rest. I spent the days near him, the little maid coming in frequently, bringing perhaps my dinner or some drink for him.

"I teased her a little, which seemed to amuse her, but we did not talk, naturally, since we could not understand each other.

"But one night, when I had remained near the sick man very late, I met, in going to my chamber, the girl entering hers. It was just opposite my open door. Then brusquely, without reflecting upon what I was doing and more in the way of a joke than anything, I seized her around the waist, and before she was over her astonishment I had taken her and shut her in my room. She looked at me, startled, excited, terrified, not daring to cry out for fear of scandal and of being driven out by her master at first and her father afterward.

"I had done this in laughter, but when I saw her there, the desire to possess her carried me away. There was a long and silent struggle, a struggle of body against body after the fashion of athletes, with arms drawn, contracted, twisted, respiration short, skin moist with perspiration. Oh! she fought valiantly, and sometimes we would hit a piece of furniture, a partition or a chair; then, always clutching each other, we would remain immovable for some seconds in the fear of some noise that would awaken someone; then we would commence again our exciting battle, I attacking, she resisting. Exhausted, finally, she fell, and I took her brutally upon the ground, upon the floor.

"As soon as she was released she ran to the door, drew the bolts and fled. I scarcely met her for some days following. She would not allow me to approach her. Then when my comrade was strong and we were to continue our journey, on the eve of our departure, she entered my apartment at midnight, barefooted, in her chemise, just as I was about to retire.

"She threw herself in my arms, drew me to her passionately and, until daylight, embraced me, caressed me, weeping and sobbing, giving me all the assurances of tenderness and despair that a woman can give when she does not know a word of our language.

"A week after this I had forgotten this adventure, so common and frequent when on a journey, the servants of the inns being generally destined to divert travelers thus.

"Thirty years passed without my thinking of, or returning to, Pont l'Abbé. Then in 1876, in the course of an excursion through Brittany, I happened to go there, as I was compiling a document which required statistics from the various parts of the country.

"Nothing seemed to have changed. The castle still soaked its gray walls in the pond at the entrance of the little town; the inn was there, too, although repaired, remodeled, with a modern air. On entering I was received by two young Bretons, of about eighteen, fresh and genteel, enlaced in their straight girdles of cloth and encapped with silver embroidery over their ears.

"It was about six o'clock in the evening. I had sat down to dine when the host, coming to serve me himself—fatality, without doubt—led me to ask him: 'Did you know the former master of this house? I passed a fortnight here once thirty years ago. I seem to be speaking to you from afar.'

"He answered: 'Those were my parents, sir.'

"Then I recounted the occasion of my stopping there, recalling my being detained by the illness of my comrade. He did not allow me to finish.

"'Oh! I remember that perfectly,' he said; 'I was fifteen or sixteen then. You slept in the room at the end of the hall and your friend in the one that is now mine, upon the street.'

"Then for the first time a lively remembrance of the pretty maid came back to me. I asked: 'You recall a genteel, pretty servant that your father had, who had, if I remember, sparkling eyes and fine teeth?'

"He replied: 'Yes sir; she died in childbed some time after.'

"And, pointing toward the courtyard where a thin, lame man was taking out some manure, he added: 'That is her son.'

"I began to laugh. 'He is not beautiful and does not resemble his mother at all. Takes after his father, no doubt.'

"The innkeeper replied: 'It may be, but they never knew who his father was. She died without telling, and no one here knew she had a lover. It was a famous surprise when we found it out. No one was willing to believe it.'

"A kind of disagreeable shiver went over me, one of those painful suggestions that touch the heart, like the approach of a heavy vexation. I looked at the man in the yard. He came now to draw some water for the horses and carried two pails, limping, making grievous effort with the limb that was shorter. He was ragged and hideously dirty, with long yellow hair, so matted that it hung in strings on his cheeks.

"The innkeeper added: 'He doesn't amount to anything but is taken care of by charity in the house. Perhaps he would have turned out better if he had been brought up like anybody. But you see how it is, sir? No father, no mother, no money! My parents took pity on him as a child, but after all—he was not theirs, you see.'

"I said nothing.

"I went to bed in my old room, and all night I could think of nothing but that frightful hostler, repeating to myself: 'What if that were my son? Could I have killed that girl and brought that creature into existence?'

"It was possible, surely. I resolved to speak to this man and to find out exactly the date of his birth. A difference of two months would arrest my doubts.

"I had him come to me the next day. But he could not speak French at all. He had the appearance of understanding nothing. Besides, he was absolutely ignorant of his age, which one of the maids asked him for me. And he held himself with the air of an idiot before me, rolling his cap in his knotty paws, laughing stupidly, with something of the old laugh of the mother in the corners of his mouth and eyes.

"But the host, becoming interested, went to look up his birth on the records. He entered into life eight months and twenty-six days after my departure from Pont l'Abbé, because I recalled perfectly arriving at Lorient on the fifteenth of August. The record said: 'Father unknown.' The mother was called Jeanne Karradec.

"Then my heart began to beat with pressing blows. I could not speak, so suffocated did I feel. And I looked at that brute, whose long yellow hair seemed dirty and more tangled than that of beasts. And the beggar, constrained by my look, ceased to laugh, turned his head and took himself off.

"Every day I would wander along the little river, sadly reflecting. But to what good? Nothing could help me. For hours and hours I would weigh all the reasons, good and bad, for and against the chances of my paternity, placing myself in inextricable positions, only to return again to the horrible suspicion, then to the conviction, more atrocious still, that this man was my son.

"I could not dine and I retired to my room. It was a long time before I could sleep. Then sleep came, a sleep haunted with insupportable visions. I could see this ninny laughing in my face and calling me 'Papa.' Then he would change into a dog and bite me in the calf of my leg; in vain I tried to free myself; he would follow me always and, in place of barking, he would speak, abusing me. Then he would go before my colleagues at the Academy called together for the purpose of deciding whether I was his father. And one of them cried: 'It is indubitable! See how he resembles him!'

"And in fact, I perceived that the monster did resemble me. And I awoke with this idea planted in my brain and with the foolish desire to see the man again and decide whether he did or did not have features in common with my own.

"I joined him as he was going to Mass (it was on Sunday) and gave him a hundred sous, scanning his face anxiously. He began to laugh in ignoble fashion, took the money; then, again constrained by my eye, he fled after having blurted out a word, almost inarticulate, which meant to say 'Thank you,' without doubt.

"That day passed for me in the same agony as the preceding. Toward evening I went to the proprietor and, with much caution, clothing of words, finesse and roundabout conversation, I told him that I had become interested in this poor being so abandoned by everybody and so deprived of everything and that I wished to do something for him.

"The man replied: 'Oh, don't worry about him, sir. He wants nothing; you will only make trouble for yourself. I employ him to clean the stable, and it is all that he can do. For that, I feed him, and he sleeps with the horses. He needs nothing more. If you have some old clothes give them to him, but they will be in pieces in a week.'

"I did not insist, reserving my opinion.

"The beggar returned that evening, horribly drunk, almost setting fire to the house, striking one of the horses a blow with a pickax and finally ended the score by going to sleep in the mud out in the rain, thanks to my generosity. They begged me the next day not to give him any more money. Liquor made him furious, and when he had two sous in his pocket he drank it. The innkeeper added: 'To give him money is the same as wishing to kill him.' This man had absolutely never had any money, save a few centimes thrown to him by travelers, and he knew no other destination for it but the alehouse.

"Then I passed some hours in my room with an open book which I made a semblance of reading, but without accomplishing anything except to look at this brute. My son! My son! I was trying to discover if he was anything like me. By force of searching I believed I recognized some similar lines in the brow and about the nose. And I was immediately convinced of a resemblance which only different clothing and the hideous mane of the man disguised.

"I could not stay there very long without becoming suspected, and I set out with breaking heart after having left with the innkeeper some money to sweeten the existence of his valet.

"For six years I lived with this thought, this horrible uncertainty, this abominable doubt. And each year I condemned myself to the punishment of seeing this brute wallow in his filth, imagining that he resembles me and of seeking, always in vain, to be helpful to him.

"And each year I come back more undecided, more tortured, more anxious. I have tried to have him instructed, but he is an idiot without resource. I have tried to render life less painful to him, but he is an irremediable drunkard and uses all the money that is given him for drink. And he knows very well how to sell his clothes and procure liquor.

"I have tried to arouse pity in his employer for him, that he might treat him more gently, offering him money always. The innkeeper, astonished, finally remarked very sagely: 'All this that you would like to do for him only ruins him. He must be kept like a prisoner. As soon as he has time given him or favors shown, he becomes unmanageable. If you wish to do good to abandoned children, choose one that will respond to your trouble.'

"What could I say to that?

"And if I should disclose a suspicion of the doubts which torture me, this creature would certainly turn rogue and exploit me, compromise me, ruin me. He would cry out to me, 'Papa,' as in my dream.

"And I tell myself that I have killed the mother and ruined this atrophied being, larva of the stable, hatched and bred of vileness, this man who, treated as others are, might have been like others.

"And you will not understand the sensation, strange, confused and intolerable, the fear I have in his presence, from thinking that this has come from me, that he belongs to me by that intimate bond which binds father to son, that, thanks to the terrible laws of heredity, he is a part of me in a thousand things, by his blood and his hair and his flesh, and that he has the same germs of sickness and the same ferments of passion.

"And I have ever an unappeasable need of seeing him, and the sight of him makes me suffer horribly, and from my window down there I look at him as he works in the dunghill of the beasts, repeating to myself: 'That is my son!'

"And I feel, sometimes, an intolerable desire to embrace him. But I have never even touched his sordid hand."

The academician was silent. And his companion, the political man, murmured: "Yes indeed; we ought to occupy ourselves a little more with the children who have no fathers."

Then a breath of wind traversing the great tree shook its berries and enveloped with a fine, odorous cloud the two old men, who took long draughts of the sweet perfume.

And the senator added: "It is good to be twenty-five years old, and it is even good to have children like that."

A WAY TO WEALTH

"Do you know what has become of Leremy?"
"He is captain of the Sixth Dragoons."
"And Pinson?"
"Subprefect."
"And Racollet?"

"Dead."

We hunted up other names which recalled to us young figures crowned with caps trimmed with gold braid. Later we found some of these comrades, bearded, bald, married, the fathers of many children; and these meetings, these changes, gave us some disagreeable shivers, as they showed us how short life is, how quickly everything changes and passes away.

My friend asked: "And Patience, the great Patience?"

I roared.

"Oh! If you want to hear about him, listen to me: Four or five weeks ago, as traveling inspector at Limoges, I was awaiting the dinner hour. Seated before the Grand Café in Theater Square, I closed my eyes wearily. The tradesmen were coming in in twos, or threes or fours, taking their absinthe or vermouth, talking in a loud voice of their business and that of others, laughing violently or lowering their voices when they communicated something important or delicate.

"I said to myself: 'What am I going to do after dinner?' And I thought of the long evening in this provincial town, of the slow, uninteresting walks through the unknown streets, of the overwhelming sadness which takes possession of the solitary traveler, of the people who pass, strangers in all things and through all things, the cut of their provincial coats, their hats, their trousers, their customs, local accent, their houses, shops and carriages of singular shape. And then the ordinary sounds to which one is not accustomed, the harassing sadness which presses itself upon you little by little until you feel as if you were lost in a dangerous country, which oppresses you and makes you wish yourself back at the hotel, the hideous hotel, where your room preserves a thousand suspicious odors, where the bed makes one hesitate and the basin has a hair glued in the dirt at the bottom.

"I thought about all this as I watched them light the gas, feeling my isolated distress increase by the falling of the shadows. What was I going to do after dinner? I was alone, entirely alone, and lamentably lonesome.

"A big man came in, seated himself at a neighboring table and commanded in a formidable voice:

"'Waiter, my bitters.'

"The 'my' in the phrase sounded like the report of a cannon. I understood immediately that everything in existence was his, belonged to him and not to any other, that he had his character and, by Jove! his appetite, his pantaloons, his no matter what, after his own fashion, absolute and more complete than important. He looked about him with a satisfied air. They brought him his bitters and he called:

"'My paper.'

"I asked myself: 'Which is his paper, I wonder?' The name of that would certainly reveal to me his opinions, his theories, his hobbies and his nature.

"The waiter brought the *Times*. I was surprised. Why the *Times*, a grave, somber, doctrinal, heavy journal? I thought:

"'He is then a wise man, of serious ways, regular habits, in short, a good commoner.'

"He placed on his nose some gold eyeglasses, turned around and, before commencing to read, cast another glance all around the room. He noticed me and immediately began to look at me in a persistent, uneasy fashion. I was on the point of asking him the reason for his attention, when he cried out from where he sat:

"'By my pipe, if it is not Gontran Lardois!'

"I answered: 'Yes sir, you have not deceived yourself.'

"Then he got up brusquely and came toward me with outstretched hands.

"'Ah, my old friend, how are you?' he asked.

"My greeting was constrained, not knowing him at all. Finally I stammered:

"'Why—very well—and you?'

"He began to laugh: 'It appears that you do not know me.'

"'No, not quite. It seems to me—however—'

"He tapped me on the shoulder.

"'There, there! Not to bother you any longer, I am Patience, Robert Patience, your chum, your comrade.'

"I recognized him. Yes, Robert Patience, my comrade at college. It was no other. I pressed the hand he extended to me and said:

"'Everything going well with you?'

"'With me? Like a charm.'

"His laugh rang with triumph. He inquired:

"'What has brought you here?'

"I explained to him that I was inspector of finances, making the rounds.

"He replied, observing my badge: 'Then you are successful?'

"I replied: 'Yes, rather; and you?'

"'Oh! I? Very, very!'

"'What are you doing now?'

"'I am in business.'

"'Then you are making money?'

"'Lots of it. I am rich. But come to lunch with me tomorrow at noon, number 17 Coq-qui-chante Street; then you will see my place.'

"He appeared to hesitate a second then continued:

"'You are still the good rounder of former times?'

"'Yes, I hope so.'

"'Not married?'

"'No.'

"'So much the better. And you are still as fond of fun and potatoes?'

"I commenced to find him deplorably commonplace. I answered, nevertheless: 'Yes.'

"'And pretty girls?'

"'As to that, yes.'

"He began to laugh with a good, hearty laugh.

"'So much the better; so much the better,' he said. 'You recall our first farce at Bordeaux, when we had supper at the Roupie coffeehouse? Ha! What a night!'

"I recalled that night, surely, and the memory of it amused me. Other facts were brought to mind and still others. One would say:

"'Do you remember the time we shut up the fawn in Father Latoque's cellar?'

"And he would laugh, striking his fist upon the table, repeating:

"'Yes—yes—yes—and you remember the mouth of the professor in geography, Monsieur Marin, when we sent off a cracker on the map of the world just as he was orating on the principal volcanoes of the earth?'

"Then brusquely I asked him:

"'And you, are you married?'

"He cried: 'For ten years, my dear fellow, and I have four children, most astonishing monkeys, but you will see them and their mother.'

"We were talking loud; the neighbors were looking around at us in astonishment. Suddenly my friend looked at his watch, a chronometer as large as a citron, and cried out:

"'Thunder! It is rude, but I shall have to leave you; I am not free this evening.'

"He rose, took both my hands and shook them, as if he wished to break off my arms, and said:

"'Tomorrow at noon, you remember?'

"'I remember.'

"I passed the morning at work at the house of the general treasurer. He wished to keep me for luncheon, but I told him that I had an appointment with a friend. He accompanied me out. I asked him:

"'Do you know where Coq-qui-chante Street is?'

"He answered: 'Yes, it is five minutes from here. As I have nothing to do, I will conduct you there.'

"And we set out on the way. Soon I noticed the street we sought. It was wide, pretty enough, at the border of the town and the country. I noticed the houses and perceived number 17. It was a kind of hotel with a garden at the back. The front, ornamented with frescoes in the Italian fashion, appeared to me in bad taste. There were goddesses hanging to urns and others whose secret beauties a cloud concealed. Two stone Cupids held up the number.

"I said to the treasurer: 'Here is where I am going.'

"And I extended my hand by way of leaving him. He made a brusque and singular gesture but said nothing, pressing the hand held out to him. I rang. A maid appeared. I said:

"'Monsieur Patience, if you please. Is he at home?'

"She replied: 'He is here, sir. Do you wish to speak with him?'

"'Yes.'

"The vestibule was ornamented with paintings from the brush of some local artist. Paul and Virginia were embracing under some palms drowned in a rosy light. A hideous oriental lantern hung from the ceiling. There were many doors, masked by showy hangings. But that which struck me particularly was the odor—a permeating, perfumed odor, recalling rice powder and the moldiness of cellars—an indefinable odor in a heavy atmosphere, as overwhelming as stifling, in which the human body becomes petrified. I ascended, behind the maid, a marble staircase which was covered by a carpet of some oriental kind and was led into a sumptuous drawing room.

"Left alone, I looked about me.

"The room was richly furnished, but with the pretension of an ill-bred parvenu. The engravings of the last century were pretty enough, representing women with high, powdered hair and very low-cut bodices surprised by gallant gentlemen in interesting postures. Another lady was lying on a great bed, toying with her foot with a little dog drowned in draperies. Another resisted her lover complacently, whose hand was in a suspicious place. One design showed four feet whose bodies could be divined, although concealed behind a curtain. The vast room, surrounded by soft divans, was entirely impregnated with this enervating odor which had already taken hold of me. There was something suspicious about these walls, these stuffs, this exaggerated luxury, in short, the whole place.

"I approached the window to look into the garden, of which I could see but the trees. It was large, shady, superb. A broad path was outlined on the turf, where a jet of water was playing in the air, brought in under some masonry some distance off. And suddenly three women appeared down there at the end of the garden, between two shapely shrubs. They were walking slowly, taking hold of each other's arms, clothed in long white dresses clouded with lace. Two of them were blonde and the other a brunette.

"They disappeared immediately among the trees. I remained transfixed, charmed, before this short but delightful apparition, which brought surging to my mind a whole poetic world. They were scarcely to be seen at all in that bower of leaves at the end of the park, so secluded and delicious. I must have dreamed, and these were the beautiful ladies of the last century wandering under the elm-tree hedge, the ladies whose light loves the clever gravures on the walls recalled. And I thought of those happy times, flowery, incorporeal, tender, when customs were so sweet and lips so easy.

"A great voice behind me made me leap back into the room. Patience had come in, radiant, extending both his hands.

"He looked at me out of the end of his eyes with the sly air of some amorous confidence and, with a large, comprehensive gesture, a Napoleonic gesture, pointed out his sumptuous drawing room, his park, with the three women passing again at the back, and in a triumphant voice that sang of pride said:

"'And when you think that I commenced with nothing—my wife and my sisters-in-law!'"

AM I INSANE?

AM I INSANE or jealous? I know not which, but I suffer horribly. I committed a crime, it is true, but is not insane jealousy, betrayed love and the terrible pain I endure enough to make anyone commit a crime without actually being a criminal?

AM I INSANE?

I have loved this woman to madness—and yet is it true? Did I love her? No, no! She owned me body and soul; I was her plaything; she ruled me by her smile, her look, the divine form of her body. It was all those things that I loved, but the woman contained in that body, I despise her, hate her. I always have hated her, for she is but an impure, perfidious creature in whom there was no soul; even less than that, she is but a mass of soft flesh in which dwells infamy!

The first few months of our union were deliciously strange. Her eyes were three different colors. No, I am not insane; I swear they were. They were gray at noon, shaded green at twilight and blue at sunrise. In moments of love they were blue, the pupils dilated and nervous. Her lips trembled, and often the tip of her pink tongue could be seen as that of a reptile ready to hiss. When she raised her heavy lids and I saw that ardent look, I shuddered, not only for the unceasing desire to possess her, but for the desire to kill this beast.

When she walked across the room each step resounded in my heart. When she disrobed and emerged infamous but radiant from the white mass of linen and lace, a sudden weakness seized me; my limbs gave way beneath me, and my chest heaved; I was faint, coward that I was!

Each morning when she awakened I waited for that first look; my heart filled with rage, hatred and disdain for this beast whose slave I was, but when she fixed those limpid blue eyes on me, that languishing look showing traces of lassitude, it was like a burning, unquenchable fire within me, inciting me to passion.

When she opened her eyes that day I saw a dull, indifferent look, a look devoid of desire, and I knew then she was tired of me. I saw it, knew it, felt right away that it was all over, and each hour and minute proved to me that I was right. When I beckoned her with my arms and lips she shrank from me.

"Leave me alone," she said. "You are horrid!"

Then I became suspicious, insanely jealous, but I am not insane, no indeed! I watched her slyly, not that she had betrayed me, but she was so cold that I knew another would soon take my place.

At times she would say:

"Men disgust me!" Alas! It was too true.

Then I became jealous of her indifference, of her thoughts, which I knew to be impure, and when she awakened sometimes with that same look of lassitude I suffocated with anger, and an irresistible desire to choke her and make her confess the shameful secrets of her heart took hold of me.

Am I insane? No.

One night I saw that she was happy. I felt, in fact I was convinced, that a new passion ruled her. As of old, her eyes shone; she was feverish, and her whole self fluttered with love.

I feigned ignorance, but I watched her closely. I discovered nothing, however. I waited a week, a month, almost a year. She was radiantly, ideally happy, as if soothed by some ephemeral caress.

At last I guessed. No, I am not insane; I swear I am not. How can I explain this inconceivable, horrible thing? How can I make myself understood? This is how I guessed.

She came in one night from a long ride on horseback and sank exhausted in a seat facing me. An unnatural flush tinted her cheeks, and her eyes—those eyes that I knew so well—had such a look in them. I was not mistaken; I had seen her look like that; she loved! But whom? What? I almost lost my head, and so as not to look at her I turned to the window. A valet was leading her horse to the stable, and she stood and watched him disappear; then she fell asleep almost immediately. I thought and thought all night. My mind wandered through mysteries too deep to conceive. Who can fathom the perversity and strange caprices of a sensual woman?

Every morning she rode madly through hills and dales and each time came back languid, exhausted. At last I understood. It was of the horse I was jealous—of the wind which caressed her face, of the drooping leaves and of the dewdrops, of the saddle which carried her! I resolved to be revenged. I became very attentive. Every time she came back from her ride I helped her down, and the horse made a vicious rush at me. She would pat him on the neck, kiss his quivering nostrils without even wiping her lips. I watched my chance.

One morning I got up before dawn and went to the path in the woods she loved so well. I carried a rope with me, and my pistols were hidden in my breast, as if I were going to fight a duel. I drew the rope across the path, tying it to a tree on each side, and hid myself in the grass. Presently I heard her horse's hoofs; then I saw her coming at a furious pace, her cheeks flushed, an insane look in her eyes. She seemed enraptured, transported into another sphere.

As the animal approached the rope he struck it with his fore feet and fell. Before she had struck the ground I caught her in my arms and helped her to her feet. I then approached the horse, put my pistol close to his ear and shot him—as I would a man.

She turned on me and dealt me two terrific blows across the face with her riding whip which felled me, and as she rushed at me again I shot her!

Tell me, am I insane?

FORBIDDEN FRUIT

BEFORE MARRIAGE they had loved each other chastely in the starlight. At first there was a charming meeting on the shore of the ocean. He found her delicious, the rosy young girl who passed him with her bright umbrellas and fresh costumes on the marine background. He loved this blonde, fragile creature in her setting of blue waves and immense skies. And he confounded the tenderness which this scarcely fledged woman caused to be born in him with the vague and powerful emotion awakened in his soul, in his heart and in his veins by the lovely salt air and the great seascape full of sun and waves.

She loved him because he paid her attention, because he was young and rich enough, genteel and delicate. She loved him because it is natural for young ladies to love young men who say tender words to them.

Then for three months they lived side by side, eye to eye and hand to hand. The greeting which they exchanged in the morning before the bath, in the freshness of the new day, and the adieu of the evening upon the sand under the stars, in the warmth of the calm night, murmured low and still lower, had already the taste of kisses, although their lips had never met.

They dreamed of each other as soon as they were asleep, thought of each other as soon as they awoke and, without yet saying so, called for and desired each other with their whole soul and body.

After marriage they adored each other above everything on earth. It was at first a kind of sensual, indefatigable rage, then an exalted tenderness made of palpable poesy, of caresses already refined and of inventions both genteel and ungenteel. All their looks signified something impure, and all their gestures recalled to them the ardent intimacy of the night.

Now, without confessing it, without realizing it, perhaps, they commenced to weary of one another. They loved each other, it is true, but there was nothing more to reveal, nothing more to do that had not often been done, nothing more to learn from each other, not even a new word of love, an unforeseen motion or an intonation, which sometimes is more expressive than a known word too often repeated.

They forced themselves, however, to relight the flame, enfeebled from the first embraces. They invented some new and tender artifice each day, some simple or complicated ruse, in the vain attempt to renew in their hearts the unappeasable ardor of the first days and in their veins the flame of the nuptial month.

From time to time, by dint of whipping their desire, they again found an hour of factitious excitement which was immediately followed by a disgusting lassitude.

They tried moonlight walks under the leaves in the sweetness of the night, the poesy of the cliffs bathed in mist, the excitement of public festivals.

Then one morning Henrietta said to Paul:

"Will you take me to dine at an inn?"

"Why, yes, my dearie."

"In a very well-known inn?"

"Yes."

He looked at her, questioning with his eye, understanding well that she had something in mind which she had not spoken.

She continued: "You know, an inn—how shall I explain it?—in a gallant inn, where people make appointments to meet each other?"

He smiled. "Yes. I understand, a private room in a large café?"

"That is it. But in a large café where you are known, where you have already taken supper—no, dinner—that is—I mean—I want—no, I do not dare say it!"

"Speak out, *chérie;* between us what can it matter? We are not like those who have little secrets from each other."

"No, I dare not."

"Oh! Come, now! Don't be so innocent. Say it."

"Well—oh! Well—I wish—I wish to be taken for your mistress—and that the waiters, who do not know that you are married, may look upon me as your mistress, and you, too—that for an hour you believe me your mistress in that very place where you have remembrances of—— That's all! And I myself will believe that I am your mistress. I want to commit a great sin—to deceive you—with yourself—there! It is very bad, but that is what I want to do. Do not make me blush—I feel that I am blushing—imagine—my wanting to take the trouble to dine with you in a place not quite the thing—in a private room where people devote themselves to love every evening—every evening. It is very bad. I am as red as a peony! Don't look at me!"

He laughed, very much amused, and responded:

"Yes, we will go this evening to a very chic place where I am known."

Toward seven o'clock they mounted the staircase of a large café on the boulevard, he smiling, with the air of a conqueror, she timid, veiled, but delighted. When they were in a little room furnished with four armchairs and a large sofa covered with red velvet, the steward, in black clothes, entered and presented the bill of fare. Paul passed it to his wife.

"What do you wish to eat?" he said.

"I don't know; what do they have that is good here?"

Then he read off the list of dishes while taking off his overcoat, which he handed to a waiter. Then he said:

"Serve this menu: Bisque soup, deviled chicken, sides of hare, duck, American style, vegetable salad and dessert. We will drink champagne."

The steward smiled and looked at the young lady. He took the card, murmuring: "Will Monsieur Paul have a cordial or some champagne?"

"Champagne, very dry."

Henrietta was happy to find that this man knew her husband's name. They sat down side by side upon the sofa and began to eat.

Ten candles lighted the room, reflected in a great mirror, mutilated by the thousands of names traced on it with a diamond, making on the clear crystal a kind of huge cobweb.

Henrietta drank glass after glass to animate her, although she felt giddy from the first one. Paul, excited by certain memories, kissed his wife's hand repeatedly. Her eyes were brilliant.

She felt strangely moved by this suspicious situation; she was excited and happy, although she felt a little defiled. Two grave waiters, mute, accustomed to seeing everything and forgetting all, entered only when it was necessary and went out in the moments of overflow, going and coming quickly and softly.

Toward the middle of the dinner Henrietta was tipsy, completely tipsy, and Paul, in his gaiety, pressed her knee with all his force. She prattled now, boldly, her cheeks red, her look lively and dizzy.

"Oh, come, Paul," she said, "confess now, won't you? I want to know all."
"What do you mean, *chérie?*"
"I dare not say it."
"But you must always——"
"Have you had mistresses—many of them—before me?"

He hesitated, a little perplexed, not knowing whether he ought to conceal his good fortunes or boast of them.

She continued: "Oh! I beg you to tell me; have you had many?"
"Why, some."
"How many?"
"I don't know. How can one know such things?"
"You cannot count them?"
"Why, no!"
"Oh! Then you have had very many?"
"Yes."
"How many, do you suppose?—somewhere near——"
"I don't know at all, my dear. Some years I had many and some only a few."
"How many a year, should you say?"
"Sometimes twenty or thirty, sometimes four or five only."
"Oh! That makes more than a hundred women in all."
"Yes, somewhere near."
"Oh! How disgusting!"
"Why disgusting?"
"Because it is disgusting—when one thinks of all those women—bare—and always—always the same thing. Oh! It is disgusting all the same—more than a hundred women."

He was shocked that she thought it disgusting and responded with that superior air which men assume to make women understand that they have said something foolish:

"Well, that is curious! If it is disgusting to have a hundred women, it is equally disgusting to have one."
"Oh no, not at all!"
"Why not?"
"Because with one woman there is intrigue, there is a love that attaches you to her, while with a hundred women there is filthiness, misconduct. I cannot understand how a man can meddle with all those girls who are so foul."
"No, they are very neat."
"One cannot be neat, carrying on a trade like that."
"On the contrary, it is because of their trade that they are neat."
"Oh, pshaw! When one thinks of the nights they pass with others! It is ignoble!"
"It is no more ignoble than drinking from a glass from which I know not who drank this morning, and that has been less thoroughly washed—you may be certain of it."
"Oh, be still; you are revolting."
"But why ask me then if I have had mistresses?"

"Then tell me, were your mistresses all girls, all of them—the whole hundred?"

"Why, no—no. Some were actresses—some little working girls—and some women of the world."

"How many of them were women of the world?"

"Six."

"Only six?"

"Yes."

"Were they pretty?"

"Yes, of course."

"Prettier than the girls?"

"No."

"Which did you prefer, girls or women of the world?"

"Women of the world."

"Oh! How filthy! Why?"

"Because I do not care much for amateur talent."

"Oh! Horror! You are abominable, do you know it? But tell me, is it very amusing to pass from one to another like that?"

"Yes, rather."

"Very?"

"Very."

"What is there amusing about it? Is it because they do not resemble each other?"

"They do not."

"Ah! The women do not resemble each other?"

"Not at all."

"In nothing?"

"In nothing."

"That is strange! In what respect do they differ?"

"In every respect."

"In body?"

"Yes, in body."

"In the whole body?"

"Yes, in the whole body."

"And in what else?"

"Why, in the manner of—of embracing, of speaking, of saying the least thing."

"Ah! And it is very amusing, this changing?"

"Yes."

"And are men different too?"

"That I do not know."

"You do not know?"

"No."

"They must be different."

"Yes, without doubt."

She remained pensive, her glass of champagne in her hand. It was full, and she drank it at a draught; then placing the glass upon the table, she threw both arms around her husband's neck and murmured in his mouth:

"Oh, my dear, how I love you!" He seized her in a passionate embrace.

A waiter, who was entering, drew back, closing the door, and the service was interrupted for about five minutes.

When the steward again appeared, with a grave, dignified air, bringing in the fruits for the dessert, she was holding another glassful between her fingers and, looking to the bottom of the yellow, transparent liquid, as if to see there things unknown and dreamed of, she murmured with a thoughtful voice:

"Oh yes! It must be very amusing, all the same!"

THE CHARM DISPELLED

THE BOAT WAS FILLED with people. As the passage promised to be good, many people of Havre were making a trip to Trouville.

They loosed the moorings; a last whistle announced the departure, and immediately the entire body of the vessel shook, while a sound of stirring water was heard all along the sides. The wheels turned for some seconds, stopped and then started gently. The captain upon his bridge having cried, "Go ahead!" through the tube which extends into the depths of the machinery, they now began to beat the waves with great rapidity.

We passed along the pier covered with people. Some that were on the boat waved their handkerchiefs, as if they were setting out for America, and the friends who remained behind responded in the same fashion.

The great July sun fell upon the red umbrellas, the bright costumes, the joyous faces and upon the ocean, scarcely moved by any undulations. As soon as they had left the port the little vessel made a sharp turn, pointing its nose directly for the far-off coast rising to meet the foam.

On our left was the mouth of the Seine, more than twelve miles wide. Here and there great buoys pointed out banks of sand, and one could see at a distance the fresh, muddy water of the river, which had not yet mingled with the salt brine, outlined in broad, yellow stripes upon the immense, pure green sheet of the open sea.

As soon as I boarded the boat I felt the need of walking up and down, like a sailor on his watch. Why? That I cannot say. But I began to circulate among the crowd of passengers on deck.

Suddenly someone called my name. I turned around. It was Henry Sidonie, whom I had not seen for ten years.

After we had shaken hands we resumed the walk of a bear in his cage, which I had been taking alone, while we talked of people and things. And we looked at the two lines of travelers seated on both sides of the boat, chatting all the while.

All at once Sidonie exclaimed with a veritable expression of rage: "It is crowded with English here! Nasty people!"

The boat was full of English, in fact. Men standing about scanned the horizon with an important air which seemed to say: "It is the English who are masters of the sea! Boom! Boom! Here we are!"

And the white veils upon their white hats had the air of flags in their self-sufficiency.

The thin young girls, whose boots recalled the naval construction of their country, wrapping their straight figures and thin arms in multicolored shawls, smiled vaguely at the radiant landscape. Their little heads, perched on the top of their long bodies, wearing the peculiarly shaped English hat, were finished at the back of the neck by their thin hair, coiled around to resemble sleeping adders.

And the old spinsters, still more lank, opening to the wind their national jaw, appeared to threaten space with their enormous yellow teeth. In passing near them one smells an odor of caoutchouc or some kind of dentifrice.

Sidonie repeated with an increasing anger:

"Nasty people! Why couldn't they be hindered from coming to France?"

I inquired laughingly: "Why, what do you care? As for me, I am perfectly indifferent to them."

He answered: "Yes, you are, indeed! But I—I married an Englishwoman. And there you have it!"

I stopped and laughed in his face. "The devil!" I said; "tell me about it. Has she made you so unhappy?"

He shrugged his shoulders as he replied: "No, not precisely."

"Then she—she has—deceived you?"

"Unfortunately, no. That would give me a cause for divorce, and I should be free."

"But I do not understand."

"You do not understand? That is not astonishing. Well, she simply learned the French language, nothing more! Listen:

"I had never had the least desire to marry when I went to pass the summer at Etretat two years ago. But there is nothing more dangerous than watering places. One cannot imagine to what an advantage young girls are seen there. Paris may be for women, but the country is for young girls.

"The idiotic promenades, the morning baths, lunches upon the grass, all are so many snares for marriage. And truly, there is nothing prettier than a girl of eighteen running across a field or picking flowers along the road.

"I made the acquaintance of an English family living at the same hotel as myself. The father resembled the men you see there, and the mother all other Englishwomen. They had two sons, boys all bones, who played at violent games with balls, sticks or rackets from morning until evening; then two girls, the elder a lean, well-preserved Englishwoman of maturity, the younger a wonder. She was a blonde, or rather a blondine, with a head that came from the skies. When they do undertake to be pretty, these wretches, they are divine. She had blue eyes, of the blue which seems to contain all the poetry, dreams, hopes and happiness of the world!

"What a horizon of infinite thought opens before you in the two eyes of a woman like that! How well she responds to the eternal, vague expectation of our hearts!

"It is only necessary to remember that Frenchmen always adore foreigners. As soon as we meet a Russian, an Italian, a Swede, a Spanish or an Englishwoman at all pretty, we fall in love with her immediately. Everything that comes from abroad fills us with enthusiasm, whether it be trouser cloth, hats, gloves, guns or—women. We are wrong, nevertheless.

"But I believe the most seductive thing about these exotics is their faulty pronunciation of our language. As soon as a woman speaks French badly she is charming. If she uses a wrong word she is exquisite, and if she jabbers in a manner quite unintelligible she becomes irresistible.

"You cannot imagine how pretty it is to hear a sweet, red mouth say: 'J'aime beaucoup la gigotte' (I like mutton so much)!

"My little English Kate spoke a most unlikely tongue. I could understand nothing of it in the first days; she invented so many unheard-of words. That was when I became absolutely in love with the comical, gay little monkey. All these crippled, strange, ridiculous terms took on a delicious charm upon her lips, and on the casino terrace in the evening, we had many long conversations, resembling spoken enigmas.

"I married her! I loved her foolishly, as one can love a dream. For the true lover adores nought but a dream which takes the shape of a woman. You recall Louis Bouilhet's admirable verse:

> *"You only were, in those rarest days,*
> *A common instrument under my art;*
> *Like the bow, on the* viol d'amour *it plays,*
> *I dreamed my dream o'er your empty heart.*

"Well, my dear, the greatest mistake I made was to give my wife a teacher of French. As long as she made a martyr of the dictionary and punished the grammar, I was fond of her. Our talks were very simple. She showed a surprising grace of mind, an incomparable elegance in her actions. She seemed to be a marvelous speaking jewel, a doll of flesh made to kiss, knowing how to make known or at least indicate the things she desired, uttering at times the strangest exclamations and expressing rather complicated sensations and emotions in a coquettish fashion, with a force as incomprehensible as it was unforeseen. She much resembled those pretty playthings which say 'papa' and 'mamma,' pronouncing them 'baba' and 'bamban.'

"Could I have believed that——

"She speaks now—she speaks—badly—very badly. She makes just as many mistakes, but I can understand her. Yes, I understand—I know—and I know her.

"I have opened my doll to see what was inside. I have seen. And one must talk, my dear!

"Ah! You don't know, you could never imagine the theories, the ideas, the opinions of a young Englishwoman, well brought up, in whom there is nothing to reproach, who repeats to me morning and evening all the phrases in the dictionary of conversation in use at the schools for young people.

"You have seen those favors for a cotillion, those pretty gilt-paper-covered execrable bonbons? I had one of them. I tore it open. I wished to taste what was inside and became so disgusted that now there is a rebellion in my feelings if I but see one of her compatriots.

"I have married a parakeet to whom an old-time instructress had taught French. Do you understand?"

The port of Trouville now showed its wooden piers covered with people. I said:
"Where is your wife?"
He answered: "I have just taken her back to Etretat."
"And where are you going?"
"I? I am going to try and divert myself at Trouville."
Then after a silence he added: "You cannot imagine how irksome a wife can become sometimes."

MADAME PARISSE

I WAS SEATED on the mole of the little port of Obernon, near the hamlet of La Salis, watching Antibes in the setting sun. I have never seen anything so wonderfully beautiful. The little town, inclosed within its heavy fortifications of masonry (constructed by M. de Vauban), was situated in the middle of the Gulf of Nice. The great waves rolled in from afar to throw themselves at its feet, surrounding it with a garland of foam, and above the ramparts the houses could be seen, climbing one above another up to the two towers pointing to the sky like two horns on an ancient helmet and standing out against the milky whiteness of the Alps—an enormous, illimitable wall of snow that appeared to shut off the entire horizon. Between the white foam at the foot of the walls and the white snow on the border of the sky, the little city, sparkling and upright on the blue background of the nearest mountain, shone in the rays of the setting sun, looking like a pyramid of red-roofed houses, the façades of which were white, yet of such different shades of white that they seemed to be of many hues.

The sky above the Alps was of a pale blue that was almost white, as if the snow had given to it some of its own whiteness. A few silvery clouds floated near the pale summit, and on the other side of the gulf Nice lay on the edge of the water like a white ribbon between the sea and the mountains. Two great lateen sails, forced onward by a strong breeze, appeared to run before the waves. I gazed at the scene, enchanted with its beauty. It was one of those sights so charming, so rare, so exquisite, which seem to take possession of you and become one of those moments never to be forgotten, like certain happy memories. We think, we enjoy, we suffer, we are moved, from various causes, but we love by seeing! He that can feel deep emotion through the power of sight experiences the same keen joy, refined and profound, felt by the man with a sensitive and nervous ear when listening to music that stirs the heart.

I said to my companion, M. Martini, a pure-blooded southerner, "That is certainly one of the rarest spectacles that it ever has been my good fortune to admire. I have seen Mont-Saint-Michel, that enormous jewel of granite, spring forth from the sands at sunrise. I have seen in the Sahara Lake Raianecherqui, fifty kilometers in length, shine under a moon as brilliant as our sun and exhale toward the clouds a vapor as white as milk. I have seen in the Lipari Islands the fantastic sulphur crater of Volcanello, a giant flower, the center of which is a volcano that smokes and burns with a limitless yellow flame that spreads out over the ocean. But I have seen nothing more impressive than Antibes, standing before the Alps in the setting sun. And I cannot tell why, at this moment, souvenirs of olden days haunt me. Verses of Homer come into my mind. It is a city of the old Orient, Antibes; it is a city of the *Odyssey*, it is a western Troy—even though Troy was far from the sea."

M. Martini drew from his pocket a Sarty guide and read:

"'The city was originally a colony founded by the Phoenicians of Marseilles about the year 340 B.C. It received from them the Greek name of Antipolis, that is to say, "city over against," "city in front of another," because, in reality, it was situated opposite Nice, another colony of Marseilles. After the conquest of the Gauls, the Romans made of Antibes a municipal city, and her inhabitants enjoyed the privileges of a Roman city.

"'We know,'" he continued, "'by an epigram of Martial, that in his time—'"

I interrupted him, saying: "I don't care what it was! I tell you I have before my eyes a city of the *Odyssey*. Coast of Asia or coast of Europe—they are alike, and there is nothing on the other shore of the Mediterranean that awakens in me the memory of heroic days as does this."

The sound of an approaching step caused me to turn my head; a tall, dark woman was passing along the road that follows the sea in the direction of the cape.

M. Martini murmured, emphasizing the last words: "It is Madame Parisse—you know!"

No, I did not know, but this name thrown out, the name of the shepherd of Troy, confirmed me in my dream.

I said, however, "Who is this Madame Parisse?"

He appeared surprised that I did not know her story. I reaffirmed that I did not know it, and I looked at the woman, who went on without seeing us, dreaming, walking with a slow, stately step, like the dames of antiquity, without doubt. She was about thirty-five years old and beautiful yet, very beautiful, though perhaps a trifle too plump.

After she had passed out of sight M. Martini told me this story.

"Madame Parisse, a Mademoiselle Combelombe, had married, a year before the war of 1870, Monsieur Parisse, an employee of the government. She was then a beautiful young girl, as slender and gay as she has since become stout and sad. She had accepted Monsieur Parisse reluctantly; he was one of those little red-tape men with short legs, who make a great fuss in a pint measure, which is yet too large for them.

"After the war Antibes was occupied by a single battalion of line commanded by Monsieur Jean de Carmelin, a young officer who had been decorated during the campaign and had only recently received the four stripes. As he was greatly bored with the life in that fortress, in that suffocating molehill shut in by enormous double walls, the commander went quite often for a walk on the cape, a sort of park or forest, where there was a fine, fresh breeze.

"There he met Madame Parisse, who used also to come on summer evenings to breathe the fresh air under the trees. How was it that they loved? Can one tell? They met; they looked at each other, and when they could not meet they thought of each other, without doubt. The image of the young woman with the brown eyes, black hair and pale face, the image of that fresh and beautiful southern girl, who showed her pretty white teeth in smiling, remained floating before the eyes of the officer, who would continue his promenade, lost in thought, biting his cigar instead of smoking it. And the image of the commander in his close-fitting coat and red trousers, covered with gold lace, whose blond mustache curled on his lip, must have remained before the eyes of Madame Parisse when her husband, unshaved, badly dressed, short of limb and with pursy stomach, returned home for supper.

"From meeting so often, they smiled at seeing each other, perhaps, and from that they came to think they knew each other. He bowed to her, certainly. She was surprised and inclined her head slightly, only just enough to escape being impolite. But at the end of two weeks she returned his salutations from afar before coming face to face.

"He talked to her! Of what? Of the setting sun, without any doubt! And they admired it together, looking deep into each other's eyes more often than at the horizon. And every day during two weeks there was some simple pretext for a little chat of several minutes. Then they dared to take a few steps together in talking of something or other, but their eyes spoke of a thousand things more intimate, of secret and charming things, the reflection of which in the softness and emotion of a look causes the heart to beat, because they reveal the soul better than words. Then he must have taken her hand and murmured those words which a woman divines without appearing to have heard them.

"It was admitted between them that they loved, without submitting their mutual knowledge to the proof of sensuality or passion. She would have been content to remain indefinitely at the stage of romantic tenderness, but not he —he wished to go further. And he pressed her, every day more ardently, to give herself entirely to him. She resisted, did not wish it and even seemed resolved never to yield.

"One evening, however, she said to him, as if by chance: 'My husband has just gone to Marseilles and is going to remain there four days.'

"Jean de Carmelin threw himself at her feet, begging her to open her door that very evening near eleven o'clock. But she would not listen to him and returned home as if angry. The commandant was in a bad humor all the evening, and the next day, beginning at daybreak, he walked on the ramparts in a rage, going from the drum school to the platoon school and meting out reprimands to officers and men like one throwing stones into a crowd. But on returning for breakfast, he found under his napkin a note containing these four words: 'This evening, ten o'clock.' And he gave five francs, without any apparent reason, to the boy who served him.

"The day seemed long. He passed a part of it in prinking and perfuming himself. At the moment when he placed himself at the table for dinner another envelope was handed to him. He found inside this telegram:

"*My darling, business terminated. I return this evening: train at nine.*
"Parisse.

"The commandant gave vent to an oath so violent that the boy let the soup tureen fall on the floor. What should he do? Certainly he wanted her, and that very night, too, let it cost what it might, and he would have her. He would have her by some means or another, if he had to arrest and imprison her husband. Suddenly an insane idea crossed his mind. He called for paper and wrote:

"Madame: *He will not return this evening. I swear it to you, and I will be at ten o'clock at the place you know. Fear nothing, I guarantee everything on my honor as an officer.*
"Jean de Carmelin.

"And, having sent this letter, he dined tranquilly. About eight o'clock he summoned Captain Gribois, who was next in command, and said to him, while rolling between his fingers the rumpled dispatch of Monsieur Parisse: 'Captain, I have received a telegram of a singular character, which it is impossible for me to communicate to you. You must go immediately and guard the gates of the city in such a way that no one—you understand, no one—either comes in or goes out before six o'clock tomorrow morning. You must place guards in the streets also and compel the inhabitants to go into their houses at nine o'clock. Anyone who is found outside after that hour will be conducted to his domicile *manu militari*. If your men meet me during the night they must retire at once with an air of not recognizing me. Do you understand me thoroughly?'

" 'Yes, Commandant.'
" 'I make you responsible for the execution of these orders, Captain.'
" 'Yes, Commandant.'
" 'Would you like a glass of chartreuse?'
" 'With pleasure, Commandant.'

"They touched glasses, drank the yellow liquor, and Captain Gribois departed.

"The train from Marseilles came into the station at exactly nine o'clock and left on the platform two travelers, then went on its way toward Nice.

"One of the travelers was tall and thin. He was a Monsieur Saribe, merchant in oils. The other passenger was short and stout—it was Monsieur Parisse. They started on their way together, their traveling bags in their hands, to reach the town, a kilometer distant. But on arriving at the gate the sentinels crossed their bayonets and ordered them off.

"Alarmed, amazed and filled with astonishment, they drew aside and deliberated; then, after taking counsel together, they returned with precaution to parley and to make known their names. But the soldiers must have received peremptory orders, for they threatened to shoot, and the two travelers, greatly frightened, took flight at the top of their speed, leaving behind them their bags which impeded their flight.

"The two unfortunate travelers made the circle of the ramparts and presented themselves at the Porte de Cannes. This also was closed and guarded as well by a menacing sentinel. Messieurs Saribe and Parisse, like prudent men, insisted no longer but returned to the station to find a shelter, for the road around the fortifications was not very safe after sunset.

"The employee at the station, surprised and sleepy, gave them permission to remain until daylight in the waiting room. They sat there without light, side by side on the green velvet-covered bench, too frightened to think of sleeping. The night was long for them.

"Toward half-past six they learned that the gates were open and that one could at last enter Antibes. They started for the town but did not find their bags along the way. When they had passed through the gates, still a little uneasy, the Commandant de Carmelin, with a sly look and his head in the air, came himself to meet and question them. He bowed to them politely and made excuses for having caused them to pass a bad night but said he had been obliged to execute orders.

"The people of Antibes were mystified. Some talked of a surprise meditated by the Italians, others of the landing of the imperial prince, and still others imagined an Orléanist plot. The truth was not guessed until later, when they learned that the battalion of the commandant had been sent far away and that Monsieur de Carmelin had been severely punished."

M. Martini ceased speaking, and soon after Mme Parisse reappeared, her walk being finished. She passed sedately near me, her eyes on the Alps, the summits of which were ruddy with the last rays of the setting sun.

I desired to salute her, that poor, saddened woman who must think always of that one night of love, now so far in the past, and of the bold man who had dared, for a kiss from her, to put a whole city in a state of siege and compromise his future. Today he has probably forgotten her, unless sometimes, after drinking, he relates that audacious farce, so comic and so tender.

Had she ever seen him again? Did she love him still? And I thought: "Here, indeed, is a trait of modern love, grotesque and yet heroic. The Homer who will sing of this Helen and of the adventures of her Menelaus must have the soul of a Merimée. And yet the captain, this lover of that deserted woman, was valiant, bold, beautiful, strong as Achilles and more cunning than Ulysses."

MAKING A CONVERT

When Sabot entered the Martinville Inn they all laughed in advance. This rascal of a Sabot, how farcical he was! See how he disliked curates, for example! Ah yes, yes! He was ready to eat them, this merry fellow.

Sabot (Théodule), master carpenter, represented the progressive party at Martinville. He was a tall, thin man, with gay, cunning eyes, hair glued to his temples, and thin lips. When he said: "Our holy father, the priest," in a certain fashion, everybody was convulsed. He made it a point to work on Sunday during Mass. Every year he would kill his pig on Monday of Holy Week in order to have blood pudding until Easter, and when he passed the curate he would always say in a way of a joke:

"Here's a man who finds his good God upon the roof."

The priest, a large man, very tall also, dreaded him because of his talk, which made partisans. Father Maritime was a politic man, a friend of ease. The struggle between them had gone on for ten years, a secret struggle, provoking and incessant. Sabot was municipal counselor. It was believed that he would be mayor, which would be decidedly bad for the church.

The elections were about to take place. The religious camp in Martinville trembled. Then one morning the curate set out for Rouen, announcing to his servant that he was going to see the archbishop.

Two days later he returned. He had a joyous, triumphant air. The next day everybody knew that the choir of the church was to be remodeled. A sum of six hundred francs had been given by Monsieur from his private cashbox.

All the old pine stalls were to be removed and be replaced by new ones of heart of oak. It was a considerable piece of carpenter work, and they were talking about it in every house that evening.

Théodule Sabot did not laugh. The next day when he went through the village his neighbors, friends and enemies said to him in a joking manner:

"Is it you who is to make over the choir of the church?"

He found nothing to answer, but he raged and raged silently. The rogues would add:

"It is a good job, not less than two or three hundred clear profit."

Two days later it was known that the repairs had been given to Célestin Chambrelan, the carpenter of Percheville. Then the news was contradicted; then it was said that all of the benches of the church were also to be renewed. This would be worth two thousand francs, as someone had found out from the administration. The excitement was great.

Théodule Sabot was not asleep. Never within the memory of man had a carpenter of the country executed a like piece of work. Then a rumor was heard that the curate was desolate at having to give this work to an out-of-town workman but that Sabot's opinions were so opposed to his that it was impossible to give it to him.

Sabot knew it. He betook himself to the priest's house at nightfall. The servant told him that the curate was in the church. He went there. Two Ladies of the Virgin, sourish old maids, were decorating the altar for the month of Mary under the direction of the priest. There he was, in the middle of the choir, swelling out his enormous front as he directed the work of the two women who, mounted on chairs, disposed of bouquets about the tabernacle.

Sabot felt under restraint in there, as if he were on the enemy's ground, but the desire of gain was ever pricking at his heart. He approached, cap in hand, without even noticing the Ladies of the Virgin, who remained standing, stupefied and immovable, upon the chairs. He stammered:

"Good evening, Monsieur Curate."

The priest responded without looking at him, all occupied with the altar: "Good evening, Monsieur Carpenter."

Sabot, out of his element, could say nothing further. After a silence he said, however, "You are going to make some repairs?"

Father Maritime answered: "Yes, we are approaching the month of Mary."

Sabot repeated: "That's it, that's it," and then he was silent.

He felt now like withdrawing without saying anything more, but a glance of the eye around the choir restrained him. He perceived that there were sixteen stalls to be made, six to the right and eight to the left, the door of the sacristy occupying two places more. Sixteen stalls in oak would be worth three hundred francs, and in round numbers there ought to be two hundred francs' profit on the work if it was managed well. Then he stammered:

"I–I've come for the work."

The curate appeared surprised. He asked:

"What work?"

"The work of the repairs," murmured Sabot desperately.

Then the priest turned toward him and, looking him straight in the eye, said: "And you speak to me of working on the choir stalls of my church!"

The tone of Father Maritime's voice caused a cold chill to run down the back of Théodule Sabot and gave him a furious desire to scamper away. Nevertheless, he responded with humility:

"Why, yes, Monsieur Curate."

Then the priest folded his arms across his ample front and, as if powerless from surprise, replied:

"You—you—you—Sabot, come to ask that from me! You—the only impious soul in my parish! Why, it would be a scandal, a public scandal. The archbishop would reprimand me and send me to another place, perhaps."

He breathed hard for some seconds, then in a calmer tone he continued:

"I understand that it would be hard for you to see a work of so much importance go to a carpenter in a neighboring parish. But I could not do otherwise, at least not unless—no—it is impossible. You would never consent—and without that—never."

Sabot regarded critically the line of benches that came almost up to the door of the sacristy. Christopher! If one might be able to make this alteration! And he asked: "What is it you consider necessary? Say it."

The priest, in a firm tone, replied: "It would be necessary for me to have a statement of your good will."

Sabot murmured: "I should say nothing. I should say nothing—that would be understood."

The curate declared: "It would be necessary to take public communion at High Mass next Sunday."

The carpenter grew pale and without answering asked:

"And the church benches, are they going to be replaced with new ones too?"

The priest responded with assurance: "Yes, but that will come later."

Sabot repeated: "I would say nothing; I say nothing. In fact, I feel nothing derogatory to religion, and I believe in it, certainly; what ruffles me is the practice of it, but in this case, I should not show myself contrary."

The Ladies of the Virgin, having got down from their chairs, concealed themselves behind the altar; they were listening, pale with emotion.

The curate, seeing himself victorious, suddenly became friendly and familiar: "Well and good! Well and good!" he said. "You have spoken wisely instead of being foolish, you understand. We shall see. We shall see."

Sabot smiled in a constrained way as he asked: "Isn't there some way of giving this communion the slip?"

The priest, with severe countenance, replied:

"At the moment that this work is given to you I wish to be certain of your conversion." Then he continued more gently: "You will come to confess tomorrow, for it will be necessary for me to examine you at least twice."

Sabot repeated: "At least twice?"

"Yes."

The priest smiled. "You understand that it will be necessary to have a general clearing out, a complete cleansing. I shall expect you then tomorrow."

The carpenter, much moved, asked: "Where do you do this?"

"Why, in the confessional."

"In—that box there—in the corner? That is—scarcely—big enough for me, your box."

"Why so?"

"Seeing that—seeing that I am not accustomed to it. And seeing that I'm a little hard of hearing."

The curate showed himself lenient. "Ah well, you can come to my house, in my dining room. There we shall be all alone, face to face. How will that suit you?"

"That's it. That suits me, but your box, no."

"Well, tomorrow then, after the day's work, at six o'clock."

"It is understood, all plain and agreed upon; till tomorrow then, Monsieur Curate, and the rack for him who retracts."

And he extended his great, rude hand into which the priest let fall his own heartily. The smack of this handshake ran along under the arches and died away back in the organ pipes.

Théodule Sabot was not tranquil while he was at work the next day. The apprehension he felt was something like what one feels when he is going to have a tooth pulled. Every moment this thought would come to him: "I must go to confession this evening." And his troubled soul, the soul of an atheist not wholly convinced, became excited from the confused and powerful fear of some divine mystery.

He directed his steps toward the rectory when he had finished his day's work. The curate was waiting for him in the garden, reading his breviary as he walked up and down a narrow path. He seemed radiant and said with a great laugh:

"Ah well, here you are! Come in, come in, Monsieur Sabot, nobody is going to eat you."

And Sabot passed in first. He stammered:

"If you are not too busy I should be pleased to finish up our little business right away."

The curate answered: "At your service. I will get my surplice. One minute and I will listen to you."

The carpenter, so disturbed that he no longer had two ideas, watched him cover himself with the white garment with its pressed folds. The priest made a sign to him.

"Put your knees on this cushion."

Sabot remained standing, ashamed to have to kneel. He muttered:

"What's the use?"

But the priest became majestic. "One can only approach the tribunal of penitence on the knees."

And Sabot kneeled.

The priest said: "Recite the Confiteor."

Sabot asked: "What's that?"

"The Confiteor. If you do not know it repeat one by one, after me, the words I pronounce."

And the curate articulated the sacred prayer in a deliberate voice, scanning the words for the carpenter to repeat; then he said:

"Now, confess."

But Sabot said nothing more, not knowing how to commence.

Then Father Maritime came to his aid.

"My child, I will ask you some questions until you become a little more familiar with the customs. We will take up, one by one, the commandments of God. Listen to me and be not troubled. Speak very frankly, and never fear to say too much.

"*One God alone you shall adore*
And you shall love him perfectly.

Have you ever loved someone or something more than God? Do you love Him with all your soul, with all your heart and all the energy of your love?"

Sabot was sweating from the effort of his thought. Finally he said: "No. Oh no, Monsieur Curate. I love the good God as much as I can. That is—yes—I love Him well. To say that I love Him better than my children, no, I cannot. To say that if it was necessary to choose between Him and my children I would choose the good God, that I could not. To say that I would be willing to lose a hundred francs for the love of the good God, no, I could not. But I love Him well, be sure; I love Him well, all the same."

The priest, very grave, declared: "It is necessary that you love Him before anything."

And Sabot, full of good will, answered: "I will do my best, Monsieur Curate."

Father Maritime continued: "God will not have you take His name in vain. Have you sometimes made use of an oath?"

"No. Oh no, indeed! I never swear. Sometimes in a moment of anger I speak the sacred name of God. That's all. I do not swear."

The priest cried: "But that is swearing." And then gravely: "Do it no more. I will continue. You will remember the Sabbath to keep it holy. What do you do on Sunday?"

This time Sabot scratched his ear. Finally he said: "I serve the good God in my own way, Monsieur Curate. I serve Him—at home. I work on Sunday."

The curate was magnanimous in interrupting him. "I know you will be more proper in the future. I pass the Commandments following, sure that you have not failed in the first two. Let us see the sixth and the ninth. I repeat: 'The goods of another thou shalt not take, nor retain them knowingly.' Have you turned to your own use by any means the goods belonging to another?"

Théodule Sabot answered indignantly: "No! Ah no! I am an honest man, Monsieur Curate. I swear to that. Not to say that I have not sometimes counted more hours of work than I have done—I have sometimes done that. And I could not say that I have not put a few more centimes on notes, only a few sometimes. But as for robbing, no, no, indeed, no!"

The curate answered severely: "Take not a single centime, for that is robbery. Do it no more. 'False witness shalt thou not bear, nor lie about anything.' Have you lied?"

"No, not that. I am no liar. I am not that kind. If you ask if I have not told some stories for the sake of talking, I could not deny it. And to say that I have not made people believe what was not so, when it was for my interest to do so, I could not. But as for lies, I tell no lies."

The priest simply said: "Be a little more careful." Then he pronounced: "'Things of the flesh thou shalt not desire, except in marriage alone.' Have you desired or possessed another woman than your own?"

Sabot exclaimed with sincerity: "Oh no! As for that, no, Monsieur Curate. Deceive my poor wife? No! no! Not as much as the end of your finger. Not in thought, say nothing of action! That's true."

He was very silent for some seconds, then, very low, as if some doubt had come over him, he said: "When I go to town, to say that I never go into a house, you know, one of the houses of license, for the sake of a bit of laughter and frolic and see another kind of skin, that I could not say—but I always pay, Monsieur Curate, I always pay, but I won't embarrass you with this that you have neither seen nor known."

The curate did not insist but gave the absolution.

Théodule Sabot executed the work of the choir stalls and received the sacrament in the months following.

A LITTLE WALK

WHEN FATHER LERAS, bookkeeper with Messrs Labuze and Company, went out of the store, he stood for some minutes, dazzled by the brilliancy of the setting sun.

He had toiled all day under the yellow light of the gas jet at the end of the rear shop, on the court which was as narrow and deep as a well. The little room in which for forty years he had spent his days was so dark that even in the middle of summer they could hardly dispense with the gas from eleven to three o'clock.

It was always cold and damp there, and the emanations from that sort of hole on which the window looked came into the gloomy room, filling it with an odor moldy and sewerlike.

M. Leras for forty years arrived at eight o'clock in the morning at this prison, and he remained till seven at night, bent over his books, writing with the faithfulness of a good employee.

He now earned three thousand francs per year, having begun with fifteen hundred francs. He had remained unmarried, his means not permitting him to take a wife. And never having enjoyed anything, he did not desire much. From time to time, nevertheless, weary of his monotonous and continuous work, he made a platonic vow:

"Cristi, if I had five thousand livres' income I would enjoy life!"

He had never enjoyed life, never having had more than his monthly salary.

His existence passed without events, without emotion and almost without hopes. The faculty of dreaming, which everyone has in him, had never developed in the mediocrity of his ambitions.

He had entered the employ of Messrs Labuze and Company at twenty-one years of age. And he had never left it.

In 1856 he had lost his father, then his mother in 1859. And since then he had experienced nothing but a removal, his landlord having wanted to raise his rent.

Every day his morning alarm, exactly at six o'clock, made him jump out of bed by its fearful racket.

Twice, however, this machine had run down, in 1866 and in 1874, without his ever knowing why.

He dressed, made his bed, swept his room, dusted his armchair and the top of his commode. All these duties required an hour and a half.

Then he went out, bought a roll at the Lahure bakery, which had had a dozen different proprietors without losing its name, and he set out for the office, eating the bread on the way.

His whole existence was thus accomplished in the narrow dark office which was adorned with the same wallpaper. He had entered the employ young, an assistant to M. Burment and with the desire of taking his place.

He had taken his place and expected nothing further.

All that harvest of memories which other men make during their lives, the unforeseen events, the sweet or tragic love affairs, the adventurous journeys, all the hazards of a free existence, had been strange to him.

The days, the weeks, the months, the seasons, the years, were all alike. At the same hour every day he rose, left the house, arrived at the office, took his luncheon, went away, dined and retired without ever having interrupted the monotony of the same acts, the same deeds and the same thoughts.

Formerly he looked at his blond mustache and curly hair in the little round glass left by his predecessor. He now looked every morning, before going out, at his white mustache and his bald head in the same glass. Forty years had flown, long and rapid, empty as a day of sorrow and like the long hours of a bad night—forty years, of which nothing remained, not even a memory, not even a misfortune, since the death of his parents, nothing.

That day M. Leras stood dazzled at the street door by the brilliancy of the setting sun, and instead of returning to his house he had the idea of taking a little walk before dinner, something which he did four or five times a year.

He reached the boulevard, where many people were passing under the budding trees. It was an evening in springtime, one of those first soft, warm evenings which stir the heart with the intoxication of life.

M. Leras walked along with his mincing old man's step, with a gaiety in his eye, happy with the unusual joy and the mildness of the air.

He reached the Champs Elysées and proceeded, reanimated by the odors of youth which filled the breeze.

The whole sky glowed, and the Triumphal Arch stood with its dark mass against the shining horizon, like a giant struggling in a conflagration. When he had nearly reached the stupendous monument the old bookkeeper felt hungry and went into a wineshop to dine.

They served him in front of the shop, on the sidewalk, a sheep's-foot stew, a salad and some asparagus, and M. Leras made the best dinner he had made in a long while. He washed down his Brie cheese with a small bottle of good Bordeaux; he drank a cup of coffee, which seldom occurred to him, and finally a tiny glass of brandy.

When he had paid he felt quite lively and brisk, even a little perturbed. He said: "I will continue my walk as far as the entrance to the Bois de Boulogne. It will do me good."

He started. An old air which one of his neighbors used to sing long ago came to his mind:

> *When the park grows green and gay*
> *Then doth my brave lover say,*
> *"Come with me, my sweet and fair,*
> *To get a breath of air."*

He hummed it continually, beginning it over again and again. Night had fallen upon Paris, a night without wind, a night of sweet calm. M. Leras followed the Avenue de Bois de Boulogne and watched the cabs pass. They came with their bright lamps, one after another, giving a fleeting glimpse of a couple embracing, the woman in light-colored dress and the man clad in black.

It was a long procession of lovers, driving under the starry and sultry sky. They kept arriving continually. They passed, reclining in the carriages, silent, pressed to one another, lost in the hallucination, the emotion of desire, in the excitement of the approaching culmination. The warm darkness seemed full of floating kisses. A sensation of tenderness made the air languishing and stifling. All these embracing people, all these persons intoxicated with the same intention, the same thought, caused a fever around them. All these carriages full of caresses diffused as they passed, as it were, a subtle and disturbing emanation.

M. Leras, a little wearied finally by walking, took a seat on a bench to watch these carriages loaded with love. And almost immediately a woman came near to him and took her place at his side.

"Good evening, my little man," she said.

He did not reply. She continued:

"Don't you want a sweetheart?"

"You are mistaken, madame."

And she took his arm.

"Come, don't be a fool; listen——"

He had risen and gone away, his heart oppressed.

A hundred steps farther on another woman approached him.

"Won't you sit down a moment with me, my fine boy?"

He said to her:

"Why do you lead such a life?"

"Name of God, it isn't always for my pleasure."

He continued in a soft voice:

"Then what compels you?"

She: "Must live, you know." And she went away, singing.

M. Leras stood, astonished. Other women passed near him, similarly accosting him. It seemed to him that something dark was setting upon his head, something heartbreaking. And he seated himself again upon a bench. The carriages kept hurrying by.

"Better not to have come here," he thought. "I am all unsettled."

He began to think on all this love, venal or passionate, on all these kisses, bought or free, which streamed before him.

Love, he hardly knew what it meant. He never had had more than two or three sweethearts in all his life, his means not permitting. And he thought of that life which he had led, so different from the life of all, his life so dark, so dull, so flat, so empty.

There are beings who truly never have any luck. And all at once, as if a thick veil had been lifted, he perceived the misery, the infinite, monotonous misery of his existence: the past misery, the present misery, the future misery, the last days like the first, with nothing before him, nothing behind him, nothing around him, nothing in his heart, nothing anywhere.

The carriages kept passing. He saw appearing and disappearing in the rapid flight of the open *fiacre* the two beings, silent and embracing. It seemed to him that the whole of humanity was filing before him, intoxicated with joy, with pleasure, with happiness. And he was alone looking on at it, all alone. He would be still alone tomorrow, alone always, alone as no one else is alone.

He rose, took a few steps, and suddenly fatigued, as if he had walked for many miles, he sat down on the next bench.

What was awaiting him? What did he hope for? Nothing. He thought how good it must be when a man is old to find, on getting home, little prattling children there. To grow old is sweet when a person is surrounded by those beings who owe him their life, who love him, who caress him, saying those charming, foolish words which warm the heart and console him for everything.

And thinking of his empty room, neat and sad, where never a person entered but himself, a feeling of distress overwhelmed his soul. It seemed to him that room was more lamentable even than his little office.

No one came to it; no one spoke in it. It was dead, silent, without the echo of a human voice. One would say that the walls had something of the people who lived within, something of their look, their face, their words.

The houses inhabited by happy families are more gay than the habitations of the wretched. His room was empty of memories, like his life, and the thought of going back into that room all alone, of sleeping in his bed, of doing over again all his actions and all his duties of evening terrified him. And as if to put himself farther away from this gloomy lodging and from the moment when he would have to return to it, he rose and, finding all at once the first pathway of the park, he entered a clump of woods to sit upon the grass.

He heard round about him, above him, everywhere, a confused sound, immense and continuous, made of innumerable different voices, near and far, a vague and enormous palpitation of life—the breath of Paris respiring like some colossal being.

The sun already high cast a flood of light upon the Bois de Boulogne. Some carriages began to circulate, and the horseback riders gaily arrived.

A couple were going at a walk through a lonely bridle path.

Suddenly the young woman, raising her eyes, perceived something brown among the branches; she raised her hand, astonished and disturbed.

"Look—what is that?"

Then uttering a scream, she let herself fall into the arms of her companion, who placed her on the ground.

The guards, quickly summoned, unfastened an old man hanging to a branch by his braces.

It was agreed that the deceased had hanged himself the evening before.

The papers found upon him disclosed the fact that he was the bookkeeper for Messrs Labuze and Company and that his name was Leras.

They attributed his death to suicide, for which the cause could not be determined. Perhaps a sudden attack of madness.

A WIFE'S CONFESSION

My friend, you have asked me to relate to you the liveliest recollections of my life. I am very old, without relatives, without children, so I am free to make a confession to you. Promise me one thing—never to reveal my name.

I have been much loved, as you know; I have often myself loved. I was very beautiful; I may say this today, when my beauty is gone. Love was for me the life of the soul, just as the air is the life of the body. I would have preferred to die rather than exist without affection, without having somebody always to care for me. Women often pretend to love only once with all the strength of their hearts; it has often happened to be so violent in one of my attachments that I thought it would be impossible for my transports ever to end. However, they always died out in a natural fashion, like a fire when it has no more fuel.

I will tell you today the first of my adventures, in which I was very innocent but which led to the others. The horrible vengeance of that dreadful chemist of Pecq recalls to me the shocking drama of which I was, in spite of myself, a spectator.

I had been a year married to a rich man, Comte Hervé de Ker—a Breton of ancient family, whom I did not love, you understand. True love needs, I believe, at any rate, freedom and impediments at the same time. The love which is imposed, sanctioned by law and blessed by the priest—can we really call that love? A legal kiss is never as good as a stolen kiss. My husband was tall in stature, elegant, and a really fine gentleman in his manners. But he lacked intelligence. He spoke in a downright fashion and uttered opinions that cut like the blade of a knife. He created the impression that his mind was full of ready-made views instilled into him by his father and mother, who had themselves got them from their ancestors. He never hesitated, but on every subject immediately made narrow-minded suggestions without showing any embarrassment and without realizing that there might be other ways of looking at things. One felt that his head was closed up, that no ideas circulated in it, none of those ideas which renew a man's mind and make it sound, like a breath of fresh air passing through an open window into a house.

A WIFE'S CONFESSION

The château in which we lived was situated in the midst of a desolate tract of country. It was a large, melancholy structure, surrounded by enormous trees, with tufts of moss on it, resembling old men's white beards. The park, a real forest, was inclosed in a deep trench called the ha-ha, and at its extremity, near the moorland, we had big ponds full of reeds and floating grass. Between the two, at the edge of a stream which connected them, my husband had got a little hut built for shooting wild ducks.

We had, in addition to our ordinary servants, a keeper, a sort of brute, devoted to my husband to the death, and a chambermaid, almost a friend, passionately attached to me. I had brought her back from Spain with me five years before. She was a deserted child. She might have been taken for a gypsy with her dusky skin, her dark eyes, her hair thick as a wood and always clustering around her forehead. She was at the time sixteen years old, but she looked twenty.

The autumn was beginning. We hunted much, sometimes on neighboring estates, sometimes on our own, and I noticed a young man, the Baron de C——, whose visits at the château became singularly frequent. Then he ceased to come; I thought no more about it, but I perceived that my husband changed in his demeanor toward me.

He seemed taciturn and preoccupied; he did not kiss me, and in spite of the fact that he did not come into my room, as I insisted on separate apartments in order to live a little alone, I often at night heard a furtive step drawing near my door and withdrawing a few minutes after.

As my window was on the ground floor, I thought I had also often heard someone prowling in the shadow around the château. I told my husband about it, and, having looked at me intensely for some seconds, he answered:

"It is nothing—it is the keeper."

. . . .

Now one evening, just after dinner, Hervé, who appeared to be extraordinarily gay, with a sly sort of gaiety, said to me:

"Would you like to spend three hours out with the guns, in order to shoot a fox who comes every evening to eat my hens?"

I was surprised. I hesitated, but as he kept staring at me with singular persistency, I ended by replying:

"Why, certainly, my friend." I must tell you that I hunted like a man the wolf and the wild boar. So it was quite natural that he should suggest this shooting expedition to me.

But my husband, all of a sudden, had a curiously nervous look, and all the evening he seemed agitated, rising up and sitting down feverishly.

About ten o'clock he suddenly said to me:

"Are you ready?"

I rose, and as he was bringing me my gun himself, I asked:

"Are we to load with bullets or with deer shot?"

He showed some astonishment; then he rejoined:

"Oh, only with deer shot; make your mind easy! That will be enough."

Then after some seconds he added in a peculiar tone:

"You may boast of having splendid coolness."

I burst out laughing.

"I? Why, pray? Coolness because I go to kill a fox? What are you thinking of, my friend?"

And we quietly made our way across the park. All the household slept. The full moon seemed to give a yellow tint to the old gloomy building, whose slate roof glittered brightly. The two turrets that flanked it had two plates of light on their summits, and no noise disturbed the silence of this clear, sad night, sweet and still, which seemed in a death trance. Not a breath of air, not a shriek from a toad, not a hoot from an owl; a melancholy numbness lay heavy on everything. When we were under the trees in the park a sense of freshness stole over me, together with the odor of fallen leaves. My husband said nothing, but he was listening; he was watching; he seemed to be smelling about in the shadows, possessed from head to foot by the passion for the chase.

We soon reached the edges of the ponds.

Their tufts of rushes remained motionless; not a breath of air caressed them, but movements which were scarcely perceptible ran through the water. Sometimes the surface was stirred by something, and light circles gathered around, like luminous wrinkles enlarging indefinitely.

When we reached the hut, where we were to lie in wait, my husband made me go in first; then he slowly loaded his gun, and the dry crackling of the powder produced a strange effect on me. He saw that I was shuddering and asked:

"Does this trial happen to be quite enough for you? If so, go back."

I was much surprised and I replied:

"Not at all. I did not come to go back without doing anything. You seem queer this evening."

He murmured:

"As you wish." And we remained there without moving.

At the end of about half an hour, as nothing broke the oppressive stillness of this bright autumn night, I said in a low tone:

"Are you quite sure he is passing this way?"

Hervé winced as if I had bitten him, and with his mouth close to my ear he said:

"Make no mistake about it! I am quite sure."

And once more there was silence.

I believe I was beginning to get drowsy when my husband pressed my arm, and his voice, changed to a hiss, said:

"Do you see him there under the trees?"

I looked in vain; I could distinguish nothing. And slowly Hervé now cocked his gun, all the time fixing his eyes on my face.

I was myself making ready to fire, and suddenly, thirty paces in front of us, appeared in the full light of the moon a man who was hurrying forward with rapid movements, his body bent, as if he were trying to escape.

I was so stupefied that I uttered a loud cry, but before I could turn round there was a flash before my eyes; I heard a deafening report, and I saw the man rolling on the ground, like a wolf hit by a bullet.

I burst into dreadful shrieks, terrified, almost going mad; then a furious hand—it was Hervé's—seized me by the throat. I was flung down on the ground then carried off by his strong arms. He ran, holding me up, till he reached the body lying on the grass, and he threw me on top of it violently, as if he wanted to break my head.

I thought I was lost; he was going to kill me, and he had just raised his heel up to my forehead when, in his turn, he was gripped, knocked down, before I could yet realize what had happened.

I rose up abruptly and I saw kneeling on top of him Porquita, my maid, clinging like a wildcat to him with desperate energy, tearing off his beard, his mustache and the skin of his face.

Then as if another idea had suddenly taken hold of her mind, she rose up and, flinging herself on the corpse, she threw her arms around the dead man, kissing his eyes and his mouth, opening the dead lips with her own lips, trying to find in them a breath and the long, long kiss of lovers.

My husband, picking himself up, gazed at me. He understood and, falling at my feet, said:

"Oh, forgive me, my darling. I suspected you, and I killed this girl's lover. It was my keeper that deceived me."

But I was watching the strange kisses of that dead man and that living woman, and her sobs and her writhings of sorrowing love, and at that moment I understood that I might be unfaithful to my husband.

A DEAD WOMAN'S SECRET

She had died painlessly, tranquilly, like a woman whose life was irreproachable, and she now lay on her back in bed, with closed eyes, calm features, her long white hair carefully arranged, as if she had again made her toilet ten minutes before her death. Her pale physiognomy was so composed now that she had passed away, so resigned, that one felt sure a sweet soul had dwelt in that body, that this serene grandmother had spent an untroubled existence, that this virtuous woman had ended her life without any shock, without any remorse.

On his knees beside the bed, her son, a magistrate of inflexible principles, and her daughter Marguerite—in religion, Sister Eulalie—were weeping distractedly. She had from the time of their infancy armed them with an inflexible code of morality, teaching them a religion without weakness and a sense of duty without any compromise. He, the son, had become a magistrate and, wielding the weapon of the law, struck down without pity the feeble and the erring. She, the daughter, quite penetrated with the virtue that had bathed her in this austere family, had become the spouse of God through disgust with men.

They had scarcely known their father; all they knew was that he had made their mother unhappy without learning any further details. The nun passionately kissed one hand of her dead mother, which hung down, a hand of ivory like that of Christ in the large crucifix which lay on the bed. At the opposite side of the prostrate body the other hand seemed still to grasp the rumpled sheet with that wondering movement which is called the fold of the dying, and the lines had retained little creases as a memento of those last motions which precede the eternal motionlessness. A few light taps at the door caused the two sobbing heads to look up, and the priest, who had just dined, entered the apartment. He was flushed, a little puffed from the effects of the process of digestion which had just commenced, for he had put a good dash of brandy into his coffee in order to counteract the fatigue caused by the last nights he had remained up and that which he anticipated from the night that was still in store for him. He had put on a look of sadness, that simulated sadness of the priest to whom death is a means of livelihood. He made the sign of the cross and, coming over to them with his professional gestures, said:

"Well, my poor children, I have come to help you to pass these mournful hours."

But Sister Eulalie suddenly rose up.

"Thanks, Father, but my brother and I would like to be left alone with her. These are the last moments that we now have for seeing her, so we want to feel ourselves once more, the three of us, just as we were years ago when we—we—we were only children and our poor—poor mother——" She was unable to finish with the flood of tears that gushed from her eyes and the sobs that were choking her.

But the priest bowed with a more serene look on his face, for he was thinking of his bed. "Just as you please, my children."

Then he kneeled down, again crossed himself, prayed, rose and softly stole away, murmuring as he went: "She was a saint."

They were left alone, the dead woman and her children. A hidden timepiece kept regularly ticking in its dark corner, and through the open window the soft odors of hay and of woods penetrated with faint gleams of moonlight. No sound in the fields outside, save the wandering croak of toads and now and then the humming of some nocturnal insect darting in like a ball and knocking itself against the wall.

An infinite peace, a divine melancholy, a silent serenity, surrounded this dead woman, seemed to emanate from her, to evaporate from her into the atmosphere outside and to calm Nature herself.

Then the magistrate, still on his knees, his head pressed against the bedclothes, in a far-off, heartbroken voice that pierced through the sheets and the coverlet, exclaimed:

"Mamma, Mamma, Mamma!" And the sister, sinking down on the floor, striking the wood with her forehead fanatically, twisting herself about and quivering like a person in an epileptic fit, groaned: "Jesus, Jesus—Mamma—Jesus!"

And both of them, shaken by a hurricane of grief, panted with a rattling in their throats.

Then the fit gradually subsided, and they now wept in a less violent fashion, like the rainy calm that follows a squall on a storm-beaten sea. Then after some time they rose and fixed their glances on the beloved corpse. And memories, those memories of the past, so sweet, so torturing today, came back to their minds with all those little forgotten details, those little details so intimate and familiar, which make the being who is no more live over again. They recalled circumstances, words, smiles, certain intonations of voice which belonged to one whom they should never hear speaking to them again. They saw her once more happy and calm, and phrases she used in ordinary conversation rose to their lips. They even remembered a little movement of the hand, peculiar to her, as if she were keeping time when she was saying something of importance.

And they loved her as they had never before loved her. And by the depth of their despair they realized how strongly they had been attached to her and how desolate they would find themselves now.

She had been their mainstay, their guide, the best part of their youth, of that happy portion of their lives which had vanished; she had been the bond that united them to existence, the mother, the mamma, the creative flesh, the tie that bound them to their ancestors. They would henceforth be solitary, isolated; they would have nothing on earth to look back upon.

The nun said to her brother:

"You know how Mamma used always to read over her old letters. They are all there in her desk. Suppose we read them in our turn and so revive all her life this night by her side. It would be like a kind of road of the cross, like making the acquaintance of her mother, of grandparents whom we never knew, whose letters are there and of whom she has so often talked to us; you remember?"

. . . .

And they drew forth from the drawer a dozen little packets of yellow paper, carefully tied up and placed close to one another. They flung these relics on the bed and, selecting one of them on which the word "Father" was written, they opened and read what was in it.

It consisted of those very old letters which are to be found in old family writing desks, those letters which have the flavor of another century. The first said, "My darling"; another, "My beautiful little girl"; then others, "My dear child"; and then again, "My dear daughter." And suddenly the nun began reading aloud, reading for the dead her own history, all her tender souvenirs. And the magistrate listened, while he leaned on the bed with his eyes on his mother's face. And the motionless corpse seemed happy.

Sister Eulalie, interrupting herself, said: "We ought to put them into the grave with her, to make a winding sheet of them and bury them with her."

And then she took up another packet on which the descriptive word did not appear.

And in a loud tone she began:

"My adored one, I love you to distraction. Since yesterday I have been suffering like a damned soul burned by the recollection of you. I feel your lips on mine, your eyes under my eyes, your flesh under my flesh. I love you! I love you! You have made me mad! My arms open! I pant with an immense desire to possess you again. My whole body calls out to you, wants you. I have kept in my mouth the taste of your kisses."

The magistrate rose up; the nun stopped reading. He snatched the letter from her and sought for the signature. There was none, save under the words, "He who adores you," the name "Henry." Their father's name was René. So then he was not the man.

Then the son, with rapid fingers, fumbled in the packet of letters, took another of them and read:

"I can do without your caresses no longer."

And standing up with the severity of a judge passing sentence, he gazed at the impassive face of the dead woman.

The nun, straight as a statue, with teardrops standing at each corner of her eyes, looked at her brother, waiting to see what he meant to do. Then he crossed the room, slowly reached the window and looked out thoughtfully into the night.

When he turned back Sister Eulalie, her eyes quite dry, still remained standing near the bed with a downcast look.

He went over to the drawer and flung in the letters which he had picked up from the floor. Then he drew the curtain round the bed.

And when the dawn made the candles on the table look pale the son rose from his armchair and, without even a parting glance at the mother whom he had separated from them and condemned, he said slowly:

"Now, my sister, let us leave the room."

LOVE'S AWAKENING

No one was surprised at the marriage of M. Simon Lebrument and Mlle Jeanne Cordier. M. Lebrument came to buy out the office of M. Papillon; he needed, it was understood, money with which to pay for it, and Mlle Jeanne Cordier had three hundred thousand francs clear in stocks and bonds.

M. Lebrument was a handsome bachelor, who had style, the style of a notary, a provincial style, but, after all, some style, which was a rare thing at Boutigny-le-Rebours.

Mlle Cordier had grace and freshness, grace a little awkward and freshness a little fixed up, but she was, nevertheless, a pretty girl, desirable and entertaining.

The wedding ceremonies turned Boutigny topsy-turvy. The married couple was much admired when they returned to the conjugal domicile to conceal their happiness, having resolved to make a little simple journey to Paris after they had spent a few days together.

It was charming, these few days together, as M. Lebrument knew how to manage his early relations with his wife with a delicacy, a directness, and sense of fitness, that was remarkable. He took for his motto: "Everything comes to him who waits." He knew how to be patient and energetic at the same time. His success was rapid and complete.

At the end of four days Mme Lebrument adored her husband. She could not bear to be a moment away from him. He must be near her all day long that she might caress his hands, his beard, his nose, etc. She would sit upon his knees and, taking him by the ears, would say: "Open your mouth and shut your eyes." He opened his mouth with confidence, shut his eyes halfway and then would receive a very long, sweet kiss that made great shivers in his back. And in his turn, he never had enough caresses, enough lips, enough hands, enough of anything with which to enjoy his wife from morning until evening and from evening until morning.

As soon as the first week had slipped away he said to his young companion: "If you wish, we might leave for Paris Tuesday of next week. We shall be like two lovers who are not married, go about to the theaters, the restaurants, the concert cafés and everywhere, everywhere."

She jumped for joy. "Oh yes, yes!" she replied. "Let us go as soon as possible."

"And as we must not forget anything, you might ask your father to have your dowry ready; I will take it with me and at the same time pay Monsieur Papillon."

She answered: "I will speak to him about it tomorrow morning."

Then he seized her in his arms and began again the little tendernesses she loved so much and had reveled in now for eight days.

The Tuesday following, the father-in-law and the mother-in-law accompanied their daughter and son-in-law to the station, whence they set out for the capital. The father-in-law remarked:

"I tell you it is imprudent to carry so much money in your pocketbook." And the young notary smiled.

"Do not be disturbed, Father-in-law," he answered. "I am accustomed to these things. You know that in my profession it often happens that I have nearly a million about me. By carrying it with me, we escape a lot of formalities and delays, to say the least. Do not give yourself any uneasiness."

Then the trainman cried out, "All aboard!" and they hurried into a compartment where they found themselves with two old ladies.

Lebrument murmured in his wife's ear: "How annoying! Now I cannot smoke."

She answered in a low tone: "I am sorry, too, but not on account of your cigar."

The engine puffed and started. The journey lasted an hour, during which they could not say anything of importance, because the two old ladies did not go to sleep.

When they were in the Saint-Lazare station in Paris M. Lebrument said to his wife:

"If you wish, my dear, we will first go and breakfast on the boulevard then return at our leisure to find our trunk and give it to the porter of some hotel."

She consented immediately. "Oh yes," she said, "let us breakfast in some restaurant. Is it far from here?"

"Yes, rather far, but we will take an omnibus."

She was astonished. "Why not a cab?" she asked.

He groaned as he said smilingly: "And you are economical! A cab for five minutes' ride at six sous per minute! You do not deprive yourself of anything!"

"That is true," she said, a little confused.

A large omnibus was passing, with three horses at a trot. Lebrument hailed it: "Conductor! Eh, conductor!"

The heavy carriage stopped. The young notary pushed his wife inside, saying hurriedly in a low voice:

"You get in while I climb up on the outside to smoke at least a cigarette before breakfast."

She had not time for any answer. The conductor, who had seized her by the arm to aid her in mounting the steps, pushed her into the bus, where she landed, half-frightened, upon a seat and in a sort of stupor watched the feet of her husband through the windows at the back as he climbed to the top of the imperial.

There she remained, immovable, between a large gentleman who smelled of a pipe and an old woman who smelled of a dog. All the other travelers, in two mute lines—a grocer's boy, a workman, a sergeant of infantry, a gentleman with gold-rimmed spectacles and a silk cap with enormous visors, like gutters, and two ladies with an important, mincing air, which seemed to say: "We are here, although we should be in a better place." Then there were two good sisters, a little girl in long hair and an undertaker. The assemblage had the appearance of a collection of caricatures in a freak museum, a series of expressions of the human countenance, like a row of grotesque puppets which one knocks down at a fair.

The jolts of the carriage made them toss their heads a little, and as they shook, the flesh of their cheeks trembled, and the disturbance of the rolling wheels gave them an idiotic or sleepy look.

The young woman remained inert. "Why did he not come with me?" she asked herself. A vague sadness oppressed her. He might, indeed, have deprived himself of his cigar!

The good sisters gave the signal to stop. They alighted, one after the other, leaving an odor of old and faded skirts.

Soon after they were gone another stopped the bus. A cook came in, red and out of breath. She sat down and placed her basket of provisions upon her knees. A strong odor of dishwater pervaded the omnibus.

"It is further than I thought," said the young woman to herself.

The undertaker got out and was replaced by a coachman who smelled of a stable. The girl in long hair was succeeded by an errand boy who exhaled the perfume of his walks.

The notary's wife perceived all these things, ill at ease and so disheartened that she was ready to weep without knowing why.

Some others got out; still others came in. The omnibus went on through the interminable streets, stopped at the station and began its route again.

"How far it is!" said Jeanne. "Especially when one has nothing for diversion and cannot sleep!" She had not been so much fatigued for many days.

Little by little all the travelers got out. She remained alone, all alone. The conductor shouted:

"Vaugirard!"

As she blushed he again repeated: "Vaugirard!"

She looked at him, not understanding that this must be addressed to her, as all her neighbors had gone. For the third time the man said: "Vaugirard!"

Then she asked: "Where are we?"

He answered in a gruff voice: "We are at Vaugirard, mademoiselle; I've told you twenty times already."

"Is it far from the boulevard?" she asked.

"What boulevard?"

"The Italian Boulevard."

"We passed that a long time ago."

"Ah! Will you be kind enough to tell my husband?"

"Your husband? Where is he?"

"On the outside."

"On the outside! It has been a long time since there was anybody there."

She made a terrified gesture. Then she said:

"How can it be? It is not possible. He got up there when I entered the omnibus. Look again; he must be there."

The conductor became rude. "Come, little one, this is talk enough. If there is one man lost there are ten to be found. Scamper out now! You will find another in the street."

The tears sprang to her eyes. She insisted: "But, sir, you are mistaken; I assure you that you are mistaken. He had a large pocketbook in his hand."

The employee began to laugh. "A large pocketbook? I remember. Yes, he got out at the Madeleine. That's right! He's left you behind! Ha! Ha!"

The carriage was standing still. She got down and looked up, in spite of herself, to the roof, with an instinctive movement of the eye. It was totally deserted.

Then she began to weep aloud, without thinking that anyone was looking at or listening to her. Finally she said:

"What is going to become of me?"

The inspector came up and inquired: "What's the matter?"

The conductor answered in a jocose fashion:

"This lady's husband has left her on the way."

The other replied: "Now, now, that is nothing. I am at your service." And he turned on his heels.

Then she began to walk ahead, too much frightened, too much excited to think even where she was going. Where was she going? What should she do? How could such an error have occurred? Such an act of carelessness, of disregard, of unheard-of distraction!

She had two francs in her pocket. To whom could she apply? Suddenly she remembered her cousin Barral, who was a clerk in the office of Naval Affairs.

She had just enough to hire a cab; she would go to him. And she met him just as he was starting for his office. Like Lebrument, he carried a large pocketbook under his arm.

She leaned out of the carriage and called: "Henry!"

He stopped, much surprised.

"Jeanne," he said, "here?—and alone? Where do you come from? What are you doing?"

She stammered, with her eyes full of tears: "My husband is lost somewhere."

"Lost? Where?"

"On the omnibus."

"On the omnibus! Oh!"

And she related to him the whole story, weeping much over the adventure. He listened reflectively and then asked:

"This morning? And was his head perfectly clear?"

"Oh yes! And he had my dowry."

"Your dowry? The whole of it?"

"Yes, the whole of it—in order to pay for his office."

"Well, my dear cousin, your husband, whoever he is, is probably watching the wheel—this minute."

She did not yet comprehend. She stammered: "My husband—you say——"

"I say that he has run off with your—your capital—and that's all about it."

She remained standing there, suffocated with grief, murmuring:

"Then he is—he is—a wretch!"

Then overcome with emotion, she fell on her cousin's shoulder, sobbing violently.

As people were stopping to look at them, he guided her gently into the entrance of his house, supporting her body. They mounted the steps, and as the maid came to open the door he ordered her:

"Sophie, run to the restaurant and bring breakfast for two persons. I shall not go to the office this morning."

BED NO. 29

When captain epivent passed in the street all the ladies turned to look at him. He was the true type of a handsome officer of hussars. He was always on parade, always strutted a little and seemed preoccupied and proud of his leg, his figure and his mustache. He had superb ones, it is true, a superb leg, figure and mustache. The last-named was blond, very heavy, falling martially from his lip in a beautiful sweep, the color of ripe wheat, carefully turned at the ends and falling over both sides of his mouth in two powerful sprigs of hair cut square across. His waist was thin, as if he wore a corset, while a vigorous masculine chest, bulged and arched, spread itself above his waist. His leg was admirable, a gymnastic leg, the leg of a dancer whose muscular flesh outlined each movement under the clinging cloth of the red pantaloon.

He walked with muscles taut, with feet and arms apart and with the slightly balanced step of the cavalier who knows how to make the most of his limbs and his carriage and who seems a conqueror in a uniform but looks commonplace in mufti.

Like many other officers, Captain Epivent carried a civil costume badly. He had no air of elegance as soon as he was clothed in the gray or black of the shop clerk. But in his proper setting he was a triumph. He had, besides, a handsome face, the nose thin and curved, blue eyes and a good forehead. He was bald, without ever being able to comprehend why his hair had fallen off. He consoled himself with thinking that with a heavy mustache, a head a little bald was not so bad.

He scorned everybody in general, with a difference in the degrees of his scorn.

In the first place, for him the middle class did not exist. He looked at them as he would look at animals, without according them more of his attention than he would give to sparrows or chickens. Officers alone counted in his world, but he did not have the same esteem for all officers. He only respected handsome men, an imposing presence, the true, military quality being first. A soldier was a merry fellow, a devil, created for love and war, a man of brawn, muscle and hair, nothing more. He classed the generals of the French army according to their figure, their bearing and the stern look of their faces. Bourbaki appeared to him the greatest warrior of modern times.

He often laughed at the officers of the line who were short and fat and puffed while marching. And he had a special scorn for the poor recruits from the polytechnic schools, those thin little men with spectacles, awkward and unskillful, who seemed as much made for a uniform as a wolf for saying Mass, as he often asserted. He was indignant that they should be tolerated in the army, those abortions with the lank limbs, who marched like crabs, did not drink, ate little and seemed to love equations better than pretty girls.

Captain Epivent himself had constant successes and triumphs with the fair sex.

Every time he took supper in company with a woman he thought himself certain of finishing the night with her upon the same mattress, and, if unsurmountable obstacles hindered that evening, his victory was sure at least the following day. His comrades did not like him to meet their mistresses, and the merchants in the shops, who had their pretty wives at the counter, knew him, feared him and hated him desperately. When he passed, the merchants' wives in spite of themselves exchanged a look with him through the glass of the front windows, one of those looks that avail more than tender words, which contain an appeal and a response, a desire and an avowal And the husbands, who turned away with a sort of instinct, returned brusquely, casting a furious look at the proud, arched silhouette of the officer. And when the captain had passed, smiling and content with his impression, the merchants, handling with nervous hands the objects spread out before them, declared:

"There's a great dandy. When shall we stop feeding all these good-for-nothings who go dragging their tinware through the streets? For my part, I would rather be a butcher than a soldier. Then if there's blood on my table it is the blood of beasts, at least. And he is useful, is the butcher, and the knife he carries has not killed men. I do not understand how these murderers are tolerated, walking on the public streets, carrying with them their instruments of death. It is necessary to have them, I suppose, but at least let them conceal themselves and not dress up in masquerade, with their red breeches and blue coats. The executioner doesn't dress himself up, does he?"

The woman, without answering, would shrug her shoulders, while the husband, divining the gesture without seeing it, would cry:

"Anybody must be stupid to watch those fellows parade up and down."

Nevertheless, Captain Epivent's reputation for conquests was well established in the whole French army.

Now, in 1868, his regiment, the One Hundred and Second Hussars, came into garrison at Rouen.

He was soon known in the town. He appeared every evening toward five o'clock upon the Boieldieu mall to take his absinthe and coffee at the Comedy, and before entering the establishment he would always take a turn upon the promenade to show his leg, his figure and his mustaches.

The merchants of Rouen who also promenaded there with their hands behind their backs, preoccupied with business affairs, speaking in high and low voices, would sometimes throw him a glance and murmur:

"Egad! That's a handsome fellow!"

But when they knew him they remarked:

"Look! Captain Epivent! But he's a rascal all the same!"

The women on meeting him had a very queer little movement of the head, a kind of shiver of modesty, as if they felt themselves grow weak or unclothed before him. They would lower their heads a little, with a smile upon their lips, as if they had a desire to be found charming and have a look from him. When he walked with a comrade the comrade never failed to murmur with jealous envy each time that he saw the sport:

"This rascal of an Epivent has the chances!"

Among the licensed girls of the town it was a struggle, a race, to see who would carry him off. They all came at five o'clock, the officers' hour, to the Boieldieu mall and dragged their skirts up and down the length of the walk, two by two, while the lieutenants, captains and commanders, two by two, dragged their swords along the ground before entering the café.

One evening the beautiful Irma, the mistress, it was said, of M. Templier-Papon, the rich manufacturer, stopped her carriage in front of the Comedy and, getting out, made a pretense of buying some paper or some visiting cards of M. Paulard, the engraver, in order to pass before the officers' tables and cast a look at Captain Epivent which seemed to say: "When you will," so clearly that Colonel Prune, who was drinking the green liquor with his lieutenant colonel, could not help muttering:

"Confound that fellow! He has the chances, that scamp!"

The remark of the colonel was repeated, and Captain Epivent, moved by this approbation of his superior, passed the next day and many times after that under the windows of the beauty in his most captivating attitude.

She saw him, showed herself and smiled.

That same evening he was her lover.

They attracted attention, made an exhibition of their attachment and mutually compromised themselves, both of them proud of their adventure.

Nothing was so much talked of in town as the beautiful Irma and the officer. M. Templier-Papon alone was ignorant of their relation.

Captain Epivent beamed with glory; every instant he would say:

"Irma happened to say to me," "Irma told me tonight," or, "Yesterday at dinner Irma said—"

For a whole year they walked with and displayed in Rouen this love like a flag taken from the enemy. He felt himself aggrandized by this conquest, envied, more sure of the future, surer of the decoration so much desired, for the eyes of all were upon him, and he was satisfied to find himself well in sight, instead of being forgotten.

But here war was declared, and the captain's regiment was one of the first to be sent to the front. The adieux were lamentable. They lasted the whole night long.

Sword, red breeches, cap and jacket were all overturned from the back of a chair upon the floor; robes, skirts, silk stockings, also fallen down, were spread around and mingled with the uniform in distress upon the carpet, the room upside down, as if there had been a battle; Irma, wild, her hair unbound, threw her despairing arms around the officer's neck, straining him to her, then, leaving him, rolled upon the floor, overturning the furniture, catching the fringes of the armchairs, biting their feet, while the captain, much moved but not skillful at consolation, repeated:

"Irma, my little Irma, do not cry so; it is necessary."

He occasionally wiped a tear from the corner of his eye with the end of his finger. They separated at daybreak. She followed her lover in her carriage as far as the first stopping place. Then she kissed him before the whole regiment at the moment of separation. They even found this very genteel, worthy and very romantic, and the comrades pressed the captain's hand and said to him:

"Confound you, rogue, she has a heart, all the same, the little one."

They seemed to see something patriotic in it.

The regiment was sorely proved during the campaign. The captain conducted himself heroically and finally received the Cross of Honor. Then the war ended; he returned to Rouen and the garrison.

Immediately upon his return he asked of news of Irma, but no one was able to give him anything exact. Some said she was married to a Prussian major. Others, that she had gone to her parents who were farmers in the suburbs of Yvetot.

He even sent his orderly to the mayor's office to consult the registry of deaths. The name of his mistress was not to be found.

He was very angry, which fact he paraded everywhere. He even took the enemy to task for his unhappiness, attributing to the Prussians, who had occupied Rouen, the disappearance of the young girl, declaring:

"In the next war they shall pay well for it, the beggars!"

Then one morning as he entered the messroom at the breakfast hour, an old porter, in a blouse and an oilcloth cap, gave him a letter, which he opened and read:

MY DEARIE: *I am in the hospital very ill, very ill. Will you not come and see me? It would give me so much pleasure!* IRMA.

The captain grew pale and, moved with pity, declared:

"It's too bad! The poor girl! I will go there as soon as I breakfast."

And during the whole time at the table he told the officers that Irma was in the hospital and that he was going to see her that blessed morning. It must be the fault of those unspeakable Prussians. She had doubtless found herself alone without a sou, broken down with misery, for they must certainly have stolen her furniture.

"Ah, the dirty whelps!"

Everybody listened with great excitement. Scarcely had he slipped his napkin in his wooden ring, when he rose and, taking his sword from the peg and swelling out his chest to make him thin, hooked his belt and set out with hurried step to the city hospital.

But entrance to the hospital building, where he expected to enter immediately, was sharply refused him, and he was obliged to find his colonel and explain his case to him in order to get a word from him to the director.

This man, after having kept the handsome captain waiting some time in his anteroom, gave him an authorized pass and a cold and disapproving greeting.

Inside the door he felt himself constrained in this asylum of misery and suffering and death. A boy in the service showed him the way. He walked upon tiptoe, that he might make no noise, through the long corridors, where floated a slight, moist odor of illness and medicines. A murmur of voices alone disturbed the silence of the hospital.

At times through an open door the captain perceived a dormitory, with its rows of beds whose clothes were raised by the forms of the bodies.

Some convalescents were seated in chairs at the foot of their couches, sewing and clothed in the uniform gray cloth dress with white cap.

His guide suddenly stopped before one of these corridors filled with patients. He read on the door in large letters: "Syphilis." The captain started, then he felt that he was blushing. An attendant was preparing a medicine at a little wooden table at the door.

"I will show you," she said; "it is bed 29."

And she walked ahead of the officer. She indicated a bed: "There it is."

There was nothing to be seen but a bundle of bedclothes. Even the head was concealed under the coverlet. Everywhere faces were to be seen on the couches, pale faces, astonished at the sight of a uniform, the faces of women, young women and old women, but all seemingly plain and common in the humble, regulation garb.

The captain, very much disturbed, supporting his sword in one hand and carrying his cap in the other, murmured:

"Irma."

There was a sudden motion in the bed, and the face of his mistress appeared, but so changed, so tired, so thin, that he would scarcely have known it.

She gasped, overcome by emotion, and then said:

"Albert! Albert! It is you! Oh! I am so glad—so glad." And the tears ran down her cheeks.

The attendant brought a chair. "Be seated, sir," she said.

He sat down and looked at the pale, wretched countenance, so little like that of the beautiful, fresh girl he had left. Finally he said:

"What seems to be the matter with you?"

She replied, weeping: "You know well enough; it is written on the door." And she hid her eyes under the edge of the bedclothes.

Dismayed and ashamed, he continued: "How have you caught it, my poor girl?"

She answered: "It was those beasts of Prussians. They took me almost by force and then poisoned me."

He found nothing to add. He looked at her and kept turning his cap around on his knees.

The other patients gazed at him, and he believed that he detected an odor of putrefaction, of contaminated flesh, in this corridor full of girls tainted with this ignoble, terrible malady.

She murmured: "I do not believe that I shall recover. The doctor says it is very serious."

Then she perceived the cross upon the officer's breast and cried:

"Oh, you have been honored; now I am content. How contented I am! If I could only embrace you!"

A shiver of fear and disgust ran along the captain's skin at the thought of this kiss. He had a desire to make his escape, to be in the clear air and never see this woman again. He remained, however, not knowing how to make the adieux, and finally stammered:

"You took no care of yourself then."

A flame flashed in Irma's eyes: "No, the desire to avenge myself came to me when I should have broken away from it. And I poisoned them, too, all, all that I could. As long as there were any of them in Rouen, I had no thought for myself."

He declared in a constrained tone in which there was a little note of gaiety: "So far you have done some good."

Getting animated, and her cheekbones getting red, she answered:

"Oh yes, there will more than one of them die from my fault. I tell you, I had my vengeance."

Again he said: "So much the better." Then, rising, he added: "Well, I must leave you now, because I have only time to meet my appointment with the colonel."

She showed much emotion, crying out: "Already! You leave me already! And when you have scarcely arrived!"

But he wished to go at any cost and said:

"But you see that I came immediately, and it is absolutely necessary that I be at the colonel's at an appointed time."

She asked: "Is it still Colonel Prune?"

"Still Colonel Prune. He was twice wounded."

She continued: "And your comrades? Have some of them been killed?"

"Yes. Saint-Timon, Savagnat, Poli, Saprival, Robert, De Courson, Pasafil, Santal, Caravan and Poivrin are dead. Sahel had an arm carried off and Courvoisin a leg amputated. Paquet lost his right eye."

She listened, much interested. Then suddenly she stammered:

"Will you kiss me, say, before you leave me? Madame Langlois is not there."

And in spite of the disgust which came to his lips, he placed them against the wan forehead, while she, throwing her arms around him, scattered random kisses over his blue jacket.

Then she said: "You will come again? Say that you will come again. Promise me that you will."

"Yes, I promise."

"When, now? Can you come Thursday?"

"Yes, Thursday."

"Thursday at two o'clock?"

"Yes, Thursday at two o'clock."

"You promise?"

"I promise."

"Adieu, my dearie."

"Adieu."

And he went away, confused by the staring glances of those in the dormitory, bending his tall form to make himself seem smaller. And when he was in the street he took a long breath.

That evening his comrades asked him: "Well, how is Irma?"

He answered in a constrained voice: "She has a trouble with the lungs; she is very ill."

But a little lieutenant, scenting something from his manner, went to headquarters, and the next day when the captain went into mess he was welcomed by a volley of laughter and jokes. They had found vengeance at last.

It was learned further that Irma had made a spite marriage with the staff major of the Prussians, that she had gone through the country on horseback with the colonel of the Blue Hussars and many others, and that in Rouen she was no longer called anything but the "wife of the Prussians."

For eight days the captain was the victim of his regiment. He received by post and by messenger notes from those who can reveal the past and the future, circulars of specialists, and medicines, the nature of which was inscribed on the package.

And the colonel, catching the drift of it, said in a severe tone:

"Well, the captain had a pretty acquaintance! I send him my compliments."

At the end of twelve days he was appealed to by another letter from Irma. He tore it up with rage and made no reply to it.

A week later she wrote him again that she was very ill and wished to see him to say farewell.

He did not answer.

After some days more he received a note from a chaplain of the hospital:

The girl Irma Pavolin is on her deathbed and begs you to come.

He dared not refuse to oblige the chaplain, but he entered the hospital with a heart swelling with wicked anger, with wounded vanity and humiliation.

He found her scarcely changed at all and thought that she had deceived him. "What do you wish of me?" he asked.

"I wish to say farewell. It appears that I am near the end."

He did not believe it.

"Listen," he said, "you have made me the laughingstock of the regiment, and I do not wish it to continue."

She asked: "What have I done?"

He was irritated at not knowing how to answer. But he said:

"Is it nothing that I return here to be joked by everybody on your account?"

She looked at him with languid eyes, where shone a pale light of anger, and answered:

"What can I have done? I have not been genteel with you, perhaps! Is it because I have sometimes asked for something? But for you, I would have remained with Monsieur Templier-Papon and would not have found myself here today. No, you see, if anyone has reproaches to make it is not you."

He answered in a clear tone: "I have not made reproaches, but I cannot continue to come to see you, because your conduct with the Prussians has been the shame of the town."

She sat up with a little shake in the bed as she replied:

"My conduct with the Prussians? But when I tell you that they took me, and when I tell you that if I took no thought of myself, it was because I wished to poison them! If I had wished to cure myself it would not have been so difficult, I can tell you! But I wished to kill them, and I have killed them, come now! I have killed them!"

He remained standing. "In any case," he said, "it was a shame."

She had a kind of suffocation and then replied:

"Why is it a shame for me to cause them to die and try to exterminate them, tell me? You did not talk that way when you used to come to my house in Jeanne-d'Arc Street. Ah! It is a shame! You have not done as much with your

Cross of Honor! I deserve more merit than you, do you understand? More than you, for I have killed more Prussians than you!"

He stood, stupefied, before her, trembling with indignation. He stammered: "Be still—you must—be still—because those things—I cannot allow—anyone to touch upon——"

But she was not listening. "What harm have you done the Prussians? Would it ever have happened if you had kept them from coming to Rouen? Tell me! It is you who should stop and listen. And I have done more harm than you, I, yes, more harm to them than you, and I am going to die for it, while you are singing songs and making yourself fine to inveigle women."

Upon each bed a head was raised, and all eyes looked at this man in uniform who stammered again:

"You must be still—more quiet—you know——"

But she would not be quiet. She cried out:

"Ah, yes, you are a pretty poser! I know you well. I know you. And I tell you that I have done them more harm than you—I—and that I have killed more than all your regiment together. Come now, you coward."

He went away; in fact, he fled, stretching his long legs as he passed between the two rows of beds where the syphilitic patients were becoming excited. And he heard the gasping, stifled voice of Irma pursuing him:

"More than you—yes—I have killed more than you."

He tumbled down the staircase four steps at a time and ran until he was shut fast in his room.

The next day he heard that she was dead.

MARROCA

You ask me, my dear friend, to send you my impressions of Africa and an account of my adventures, especially of my love affairs, in this seductive land. You laughed a great deal beforehand at my dusky sweethearts, as you called them, and declared that you could see me, returning to France, followed by a tall ebony-colored woman, with a yellow silk handkerchief round her head, and wearing voluminous bright-colored trousers.

No doubt the Moorish dames will have their turn, for I have seen several who made me feel very much inclined to fall in love with them. But by way of making a beginning, I came across something better and very original.

In your last letter to me you say: "When I know how people love in a country I know that country well enough to describe it, although I may never have seen it." Let me tell you then that here they love furiously. From the very first moment one feels a sort of trembling ardor, of constant desire, to the very tips of the fingers, which overexcites the powers and faculties of physical sensation, from the simple contact of the hands down to the requirement which makes us commit so many follies.

Do not misunderstand me. I do not know whether you call love of the heart a love of the soul, whether sentimental idealism, platonic love, in a word, can exist on this earth; I doubt it myself. But that other love, sensual love, which has something good, a great deal of good about it, is really terrible in this climate. The heat, the burning atmosphere which makes you feverish, the suffocating blasts of wind from the south, waves of fire from the desert which is so near us, that oppressive sirocco which is more destructive and withering than fire, a perpetual conflagration of an entire continent, burned even to its stones by a fierce and devouring sun, inflame the blood, excite the flesh and make brutes of us.

But to come to my story. I shall not dwell on the beginning of my stay in Africa. After visiting Bona, Constantine, Biskara and Steif, I went to Bougie through the defiles of Chabet, by an excellent road cut through a large forest, which follows the sea at a height of six hundred feet above it and leads to that wonderful bay of Bougie, which is as beautiful as that of Naples, of Ajaccio or of Douarnenez, which are the most lovely that I know of.

Far away in the distance, before one rounds the large inlet where the water is perfectly calm, one sees Bougie. It is built on the steep sides of a high hill covered with trees, and forms a white spot on that green slope; it might almost be taken for the foam of a cascade falling into the sea.

I had no sooner set foot in that small, delightful town, than I knew that I should stay for a long time. In all directions the eye rests on rugged, strangely shaped hilltops, so close together that you can hardly see the open sea, so that the gulf looks like a lake. The blue water is wonderfully transparent, and the azure sky, a deep azure, as if it had received two coats of color, expands its wonderful beauty above it. They seem to be looking at themselves in a glass, a veritable reflection of each other.

Bougie is a town of ruins, and on the quay is such magnificent ruin that you might imagine you were at the opera. It is the old Saracen Gate, overgrown with ivy, and there are ruins in all directions on the hills round the town, fragments of Roman walls, bits of Saracen monuments and remains of Arabic buildings.

I had taken a small Moorish house in the upper town. You know those dwellings, which have been described so often. They have no windows on the outside, but they are lighted from top to bottom by an inner court. On the first floor they have a large, cool room, in which one spends the days, and a terrace on the roof, on which one spends the nights.

I at once fell in with the custom of all hot countries, that is to say, of taking a siesta after lunch. That is the hottest time in Africa, the time when one can scarcely breathe, when the streets, the fields and the long, dazzling, white roads are deserted, when everyone is asleep or, at any rate, trying to sleep, attired as scantily as possible.

In my drawing room, which had columns of Arabic architecture, I had placed a large, soft couch, covered with a carpet from Djebel Amour. There, very nearly in the costume of Assan, I sought to rest, but I could not sleep, as I was tortured by continence. There are two forms of torture on this earth which I hope you will never know: the want of water and the want of women, and I do not know which is the worst. In the desert men would commit any infamy for the sake of a glass of clean, cold water, and what would one not do in some of the towns of the littoral for the companionship of a handsome woman? There is no lack of girls in Africa; on the contrary, they abound, but, to continue my comparison, they are as unwholesome as the muddy water in the pools of Sahara.

Well, one day when I was feeling more enervated than usual, I was trying in vain to close my eyes. My legs twitched as if they were being pricked, and I tossed about uneasily on my couch. At last, unable to bear it any longer, I got up and went out. It was a terribly hot day in the middle of July, and the pavement was hot enough to bake bread on. My shirt, which was soaked with perspiration, clung to my body; on the horizon there was a slight, white vapor, which seemed to be palpable heat.

I went down to the sea and, circling the port, walked along the shore of the pretty bay where the baths are. There was nobody about, and nothing was stirring; not a sound of bird or of beast was to be heard; the very waves did not lap, and the sea appeared to be asleep in the sun.

Suddenly, behind one of the rocks which were half covered by the silent water, I heard a slight movement. Turning round, I saw a tall, naked girl, sitting up to her bosom in the water, taking a bath; no doubt she reckoned on being alone at that hot period of the day. Her head was turned toward the sea, and she was moving gently up and down, without seeing me.

Nothing could be more surprising than that picture of a beautiful woman in the water, which was as clear as crystal, under a blaze of light. She was a statue. She turned round, uttered a cry and, half swimming, half walking, hid herself altogether behind her rock. I knew she must necessarily come out, so I sat down on the beach and waited. Presently she just showed her head, which was covered with thick black plaits of hair. She had a rather large mouth, with full lips, large, bold eyes, and her skin, which was tanned by the climate, looked like a piece of old, hard, polished ivory.

She called out to me: "Go away!" and her full voice, which corresponded to her strong build, had a guttural accent. As I did not move, she added: "It is not right of you to stop there, monsieur." I did not move, however, and her head disappeared. Ten minutes passed, and then her hair, then her forehead and then her eyes reappeared, but slowly and prudently, as if she were playing at hide-and-seek and were looking to see who was near. This time she was furious and called out: "You will make me catch a chill, for I shall not come out as long as you are there." Thereupon I got up and went away, but not without looking round several times. When she thought I was far enough off she came out of the water. Bending down and turning her back to me, she disappeared in a cavity of the rock behind a petticoat that was hanging up in front of it.

I went back the next day. She was bathing again, but she had a bathing costume and she began to laugh and showed her white teeth. A week later we were friends, and in another week we were eager lovers. Her name was Marroca, and she pronounced it as if there were a dozen *r*s in it. She was the daughter of Spanish colonists and had married a Frenchman, whose name was Pontabèze. He was in government employ, though I never exactly knew what his functions were. I found out that he was always very busy, and I did not care for anything else.

She then altered her time for having her bath and came to my house every day to take her siesta there. What a siesta! It could scarcely be called reposing! She was a splendid girl of a somewhat animal but superb type. Her eyes were always glowing with passion; her half-open mouth, her sharp teeth and even her smiles had something ferociously loving about them, and her curious long and conical breasts gave her whole body something of the animal, made her a sort of inferior yet magnificent being, a creature destined for unbridled love, and roused in me the idea of those ancient deities who gave expression to their tenderness on the grass and under the trees.

And then her mind was as simple as two and two are four, and a sonorous laugh served her instead of thought.

Instinctively proud of her beauty, she hated the slightest covering and ran and frisked about my house with daring and unconscious immodesty. When she was at last overcome and worn out by her cries and movements, she used to sleep soundly and peacefully, while the overwhelming heat brought out minute spots of perspiration on her brown skin.

Sometimes she returned in the evening, when her husband was on duty somewhere, and we used to lie on the terrace, scarcely covered by some fine, gauzy oriental fabric. When the full moon lit up the town and the gulf, with its surrounding frame of hills, we saw on all the other terraces a recumbent army of silent phantoms who would occasionally get up, change their places and lie down again in the languorous warmth of the starry night.

In spite of the brightness of African nights, Marroca would insist upon stripping herself almost naked in the clear rays of the moon; she did not trouble herself much about anybody who might see us, and often, in spite of my fears and entreaties, she uttered long, resounding cries, which made the dogs in the distance howl.

One night, when I was sleeping under the starry sky, she came and kneeled down on my carpet and, putting her lips, which curled slightly, close to my face, she said:

"You must come and stay at my house."

I did not understand her and asked:

"What do you mean?"

"Yes, when my husband has gone away you must come and be with me."

I could not help laughing and said: "Why, as you come here?"

And she went on, almost talking into my mouth, sending her hot breath into my throat and moistening my mustache with her lips:

"I want it as a remembrance."

Still I did not grasp her meaning. Then she put her arms around my neck and said: "When you are no longer here I shall think of it."

I was touched and amused at the same time and replied: "You must be mad. I would much rather stop here."

As a matter of fact, I have no liking for assignations under the conjugal roof; they are mousetraps in which the unwary are always caught. But she begged and prayed and even cried and at last said: "You shall see how I will love you there."

Her wish seemed so strange that I could not explain it to myself, but on thinking it over, I thought I could discern a profound hatred for her husband, the secret vengeance of a woman who takes a pleasure in deceiving him and who, moreover, wishes to deceive him in his own house.

"Is your husband very unkind to you?" I asked her. She looked vexed and said:

"Oh no, he is very kind."

"But you are not fond of him?"

She looked at me with astonishment in her large eyes. "Indeed, I am very fond of him, very, but not so fond as I am of you."

I could not understand it all, and while I was trying to get at her meaning she pressed one of those kisses, whose power she knew so well, onto my lips and whispered: "But you will come, will you not?"

I resisted, however, and so she got up immediately and went away; nor did she come back for a week. On the eighth day she came back, stopped gravely at the door of my abode and said: "Are you coming to my house tonight? If you refuse I shall go away."

Eight days is a very long time, my friend, and in Africa those eight days are as good as a month. "Yes," I said and opened my arms, and she threw herself into them.

At night she waited for me in a neighboring street and took me to their house, which was very small and near the harbor. I first of all went through the kitchen, where they had their meals, and then into a very tidy, whitewashed room with photographs on the walls and paper flowers under a glass case. Marroca seemed beside herself with pleasure, and she jumped about and said: "There, you are at home now." And I certainly acted as though I were, though I felt rather embarrassed and somewhat uneasy.

Suddenly a loud knocking at the door made us start, and a man's voice called out: "Marroca, it is I."

She started: "My husband! Here, hide under the bed, quickly."

I was distractedly looking for my coat, but she gave me a push and panted out: "Come along, come along."

I lay down flat on my stomach and crept under the bed without a word, while she went into the kitchen. I heard her open a cupboard and then shut it again, and she came back into the room carrying some object which I could not see but which she quickly put down. Then as her husband was getting impatient, she said calmly: "I cannot find the matches." Suddenly she added: "Oh, here they are: I will come and let you in."

The man came in, and I could see nothing of him but his feet, which were enormous. If the rest of him was in proportion he must have been a giant.

I heard kisses, a little pat on her naked flesh and a laugh, and he said in a strong Marseilles accent: "I forgot my purse, so I was obliged to come back; you were sound asleep, I suppose?"

He went to the cupboard and was a long time in finding what he wanted; and as Marroca had thrown herself onto the bed, as if she were tired out, he went up to her and no doubt tried to caress her, for she flung a volley of angry *r*s at him. His feet were so close to me that I felt a stupid, inexplicable longing to catch hold of them, but I restrained myself. When he saw that he could not succeed in his wish he got angry and said: "You are not at all nice tonight. Good-by."

I heard another kiss, then the big feet turned, and I saw the nails in his shoes as he went into the next room; the front door was shut, and I was saved!

I came slowly out of my retreat, feeling rather humiliated, and while Marroca danced a jig around me, shouting with laughter and clapping her hands, I threw myself heavily into a chair. But I jumped up with a bound, for I had sat down on something cold, and as I was no more dressed than my accomplice was, the contact made me start. I looked round. I had sat down on a small ax used for cutting wood and as sharp as a knife. How had it got there? I had certainly not seen it when I went in, but Marroca, seeing me jump up, nearly choked with laughter and coughed with both hands on her sides.

I thought her amusement rather out of place; we had risked our lives stupidly. I still felt a cold shiver down my back, and I was rather hurt at her foolish laughter.

"Supposing your husband had seen me?" I said.

"There was no danger of that," she replied.

"What do you mean? No danger? That is a good joke! If he had stooped down he must have seen me."

She did not laugh any more; she only looked at me with her large eyes, which were bright with merriment.

"He would not have stooped."

"Why?" I persisted. "Just suppose that he had let his hat fall, he would have been sure to pick it up, and then—I was well prepared to defend myself in this costume!"

She put her two strong, round arms about my neck and, lowering her voice, as she did when she said, "I *adorre* you," she whispered:

"Then he would *never* have got up again."

I did not understand her and said: "What do you mean?"

She gave me a cunning wink and put out her hand to the chair on which I had sat down, and her outstretched hands, her smile, her half-open lips, her white, sharp and ferocious teeth, all drew my attention to the little ax which was used for cutting wood, the sharp blade of which was glistening in the candlelight. While she put out her hand as if she were going to take it, she put her left arm round me and, drawing me to her and putting her lips against mine, with her right arm she made a motion as if she were cutting off the head of a kneeling man!

This, my friend, is the manner in which people here understand conjugal duties, love and hospitality!

A PHILOSOPHER

Blérot had been my most intimate friend from childhood; we had no secrets from each other and were united heart and soul by a brotherly intimacy and a boundless confidence in each other. I had been intrusted with the secret of all his love affairs, as he had been with mine.

When he told me that he was going to get married I was hurt, just as if he had been guilty of a treacherous act with regard to me. I felt that it must interfere with that cordial and absolute affection which had united us hitherto. His wife would come between us. The intimacy of the marriage bed establishes a kind of complicity, a mysterious alliance between two persons, even when they have ceased to love each other. Man and wife are like two discreet partners who will not let anyone else into their secrets. But that close bond which the conjugal kiss fastens is widely loosened on the day on which the woman takes a lover.

I remember Blérot's wedding as if it were but yesterday. I would not be present at the signing of the marriage contract, as I have no particular liking for such ceremonies. I only went to the civil wedding and to the church.

His wife, whom I had never seen before, was a tall, slight girl with pale hair, pale cheeks, pale hands and eyes to match. She walked with a slightly undulating motion, as if she were on board a ship, and seemed to advance with the succession of long, graceful courtesies.

Blérot seemed very much in love with her. He looked at her constantly, and I felt a shiver of an immoderate desire for her pass through my frame.

I went to see him in a few days, and he said to me:

"You do not know how happy I am; I am madly in love with her, but then she is—she is——" He did not finish his sentence, but he put the tips of his fingers to his lips with a gesture which signified "divine! delicious! perfect!" and a good deal more besides.

I asked, laughing, "What? All that?"

"Everything that you can imagine," was his answer.

He introduced me to her. She was very pleasant, on easy terms with me, as was natural, and begged me to look upon their house as my own. I felt that he, Blérot, did not belong to me any longer. Our intimacy was altogether checked, and we hardly found a word to say to each other.

I soon took my leave and shortly afterward went to the East, returning by way of Russia, Germany, Sweden and Holland after an absence of eighteen months from Paris.

The morning after my arrival, as I was walking along the boulevards to breathe the air once more, I saw a pale man with sunken cheeks coming toward me, who was as much like Blérot as it was possible for a physical, emaciated man to resemble a strong, ruddy, rather stout man. I looked at him in surprise and asked myself: "Can it possibly be he?" But he saw me and came toward me with outstretched arms, and we embraced in the middle of the boulevard.

After we had gone up and down once or twice from the Rue Drouot to the Vaudeville Theater, just as we were taking leave of each other—for he already seemed quite done up with walking—I said to him:

"You don't look at all well. Are you ill?"

"I do feel rather out of sorts," was all he said.

He looked like a man who was going to die, and I felt a flood of affection for my old friend, the only real one that I had ever had. I squeezed his hands.

"What is the matter with you? Are you in pain?"

"A little tired, but it is nothing."

"What does your doctor say?"

"He calls it anemia, and has ordered me to eat no white meat and to take tincture of iron."

A suspicion flashed across me.

"Are you happy?" I asked him.

"Yes, very happy; my wife is charming, and I love her more than ever."

But I noticed that he grew rather red and seemed embarrassed, as if he were afraid of any further questions, so I took him by the arm and pushed him into a café, which was nearly empty at that time of day. I forced him to sit down and, looking him straight in the face, I said:

"Look here, old fellow, just tell me the exact truth."

"I have nothing to tell you," he stammered.

"That is not true," I replied firmly. "You are ill, mentally, perhaps, and you dare not reveal your secret to anyone. Something or other is doing you harm, and I mean you to tell me what it is. Come, I am waiting for you to begin."

Again he got very red, stammered, and turning his head away, he said:

"It is very idiotic—but I—I am done for!"

As he did not go on, I said:

"Just tell me what it is."

"Well, I have got a wife who is killing me; that is all," he said abruptly, almost desperately.

I did not understand at first. "Does she make you unhappy? How? What is it?"

"No," he replied in a low voice, as if he were confessing some crime; "I love her too much; that is all."

I was thunderstruck at this singular avowal, and then I felt inclined to laugh, but at length I managed to reply:

"But surely, at least so it seems to me, you might manage to—to love her a little less."

He had got very pale again and at length made up his mind to speak to me openly, as he used to do formerly.

"No," he said, "that is impossible, and I am dying from it; I know; it is killing me, and I am really frightened. Some days, like today, I feel inclined to leave her, to go away altogether, to start for the other end of the world, so as to live for a long time; and then when the evening comes I return home in spite of myself, but slowly, and feeling uncomfortable. I go upstairs hesitatingly and ring, and when I go in I see her there, sitting in her easy chair, and she will say, 'How late you are.' I kiss her, and we sit down to dinner. During the meal I make this resolve: 'I will go directly it is over and take the train for somewhere, no matter where,' but when we get back to the drawing room I am so tired that I have not the courage to get up out of my chair, and so I remain and then—and then—and then—I succumb again."

I could not help smiling again. He saw it and said: "You may laugh, but I assure you it is very horrible."

"Why don't you tell your wife?" I asked him. "Unless she be a regular monster she would understand."

He shrugged his shoulders. "It is all very well for you to talk. I don't tell her because I know her nature. Have you ever heard it said of certain women, 'She has just married a third time?' Well, and that makes you laugh like you did just now, and yet it is true. What is to be done? It is neither her fault nor mine. She is so, because nature has made her so; I assure you, my dear old friend, she has the temperament of a Messalina. She does not know it, but I do; so much the worse for me. She is charming, gentle, tender, and thinks that our conjugal intercourse, which is wearing me out and killing me, is natural and quite moderate. She seems like an ignorant schoolgirl, and she really is ignorant, poor child.

"Every day I form energetic resolutions, for you must understand that I am dying. But one look of her eyes, one of those looks in which I can read the ardent desire of her lips, is enough for me, and I succumb at once, saying to myself: 'This is really the end; I will have no more of her death-giving kisses,' and then when I have yielded again, like I have today, I go out and walk and walk, thinking of death and saying to myself that I am lost, that all is over.

"I am mentally so ill that I went for a walk to Père Lachaise cemetery yesterday. I looked at all the graves, standing in a row like dominoes, and I thought to myself: 'I shall soon be there,' and then I returned home, quite determined to pretend to be ill and so escape, but I could not.

"Oh! You don't know what it is. Ask a smoker who is poisoning himself with nicotine whether he can give up his delicious and deadly habit. He will tell you that he has tried a hundred times without success, and he will, perhaps, add: 'So much the worse, but I would rather die than go without tobacco.' That is just the case with me. When once one is in the clutches of such a passion or such a habit, one must give oneself up to it entirely."

He got up and gave me his hand. I felt seized with a tumult of rage and with hatred for this woman, this careless, charming, terrible woman, and as he was buttoning up his coat to go out I said to him, brutally perhaps:

"But in God's name, why don't you let her have a lover, rather than kill yourself like that?"

He shrugged his shoulders without replying and went off.

For six months I did not see him. Every morning I expected a letter of invitation to his funeral, but I would not go to his house from a complicated feeling of contempt for him and for that woman, of anger, of indignation, of a thousand sensations.

One lovely spring morning I was in the Champs Elysées. It was one of those warm days which make our eyes bright and stir up in us a tumultuous feeling of happiness from the mere sense of existence. Someone tapped me on the shoulder and, turning round, I saw my old friend, looking well, stout and rosy.

He gave me both hands, beaming with pleasure, and exclaimed:
"Here you are, you erratic individual!"
I looked at him, utterly thunderstruck.
"Well, on my word—yes. By Jove! I congratulate you; you have indeed changed in the last six months!"
He flushed scarlet and said with an embarrassed laugh:
"One can but do one's best."
I looked at him so obstinately that he evidently felt uncomfortable, so I went on:
"So—now—you are—completely cured?"
He stammered hastily:
"Yes, perfectly, thank you." Then, changing his tone, "How lucky that I should have come across you, old fellow. I hope we shall often meet now."

But I would not give up my idea; I wanted to know how matters really stood, so I asked:
"Don't you remember what you told me six months ago? I suppose—I—eh—suppose you resist now?"
"Please don't talk any more about it," he replied uneasily; "forget that I mentioned it to you; leave me alone. But, you know, I have no intention of letting you go; you must come and dine at my house."

A sudden fancy took me to see for myself how matters stood, so that I might understand all about it, and I accepted.

His wife received me in a most charming manner, and she was, as a matter of fact, a most attractive woman. Her long hands, her neck and cheeks were beautifully white and delicate and marked her breeding, and her walk was undulating and delightful.

René gave her a brotherly kiss on the forehead and said:
"Has not Lucien come yet?"
"Not yet," she replied in a clear, soft voice; "you know he is almost always rather late."

At that moment the bell rang, and a tall man was shown in. He was dark, with a thick beard, and looked like a modern Hercules. We were introduced to each other; his name was Lucien Delabarre.

René and he shook hands in a most friendly manner, and then we went to dinner.

It was a most enjoyable meal, without the least constraint. My old friend spoke with me constantly in the old, familiar, cordial manner, just as he used to do. It was: "You know, old fellow!" "I say, old fellow!" "Just listen a moment, old fellow!" Suddenly he exclaimed:

"You don't know how glad I am to see you again; it takes me back to old times."

I looked at his wife and the other man. Their attitude was perfectly correct, though I fancied once or twice that they exchanged a rapid and furtive look.

As soon as dinner was over René turned to his wife and said:

"My dear, I have just met Pierre again, and I am going to carry him off for a walk and chat along the boulevards to remind us of old times. I am leaving you in very good company."

The young woman smiled and said to me as she shook hands with me:

"Don't keep him too long."

As we went along arm in arm I could not help saying to him, for I was determined to know how matters stood:

"What has happened? Do tell me!"

He, however, interrupted me roughly and answered like a man who has been disturbed without any reason.

"Just look here, old fellow; leave one alone with your questions."

Then he added, half aloud, as if talking to himself:

"After all, it would have been too stupid to have let oneself go to perdition like that."

I did not press him. We walked on quickly and began to talk. All of a sudden he whispered in my ear:

"I say, suppose we go and have a bottle of fizz with some girls! Eh?"

I could not prevent myself from laughing heartily.

"Just as you like; come along, let us go."

A MISTAKE

THAT DAY Boniface, the letter carrier, found in leaving the post office that his route would not be so long and therefore felt a lively delight.

He had charge of the country around Vireville and, when he returned in the evening, he often found he had covered over twenty miles in his long march.

Today the distribution would be easy; he could even stroll along a little and be home by three o'clock in the afternoon. What luck!

He went out along the Sennemare road and commenced his work. It was June, the month of verdure and flowers, the true month of the fields and meadows.

The man, in his blue blouse and black cap with red braid, crossed through bypaths, fields of millet, oats and wheat, buried to the shoulders in their depths; and his head, moving along above the feathery waves, seemed to float upon a calm and verdant sea, which a light breeze caused to undulate gently. He entered the farms through wooden gateways built on the slopes and shaded by two rows of beech trees, greeted the farmer by name: "Good morning, Monsieur Chicot," and passed him his newspaper, *The Little Norman*.

The farmer would wipe his hand on his trousers, receive the paper and slide it into his pocket to read at his ease after the midday meal. The dogs, asleep in barrels under the drooping apple trees, yapped with fury, pulling at their chains, but the carrier, without turning, proceeded at his military gait, stretching his long limbs, the left arm over his bag, the right manipulating his cane which marched like himself, in a continuous, hurried fashion.

He distributed his printed matter and his letters in the hamlet of Sennemare, then set out across the fields with a paper for the tax collector who lived in a little isolated house a quarter of a mile from the village.

He was a new collector, this M. Chapatis, arrived but the week before and lately married.

He took a Paris paper, and sometimes Carrier Boniface, when he had time, would take a look at it before delivering it at its destination.

Now he opened his bag, took out the paper, slipped it out of its wrapper, unfolded it and began to read while walking. The first page did not interest him; politics did not arouse him; the finance he always passed over, but the general facts of the day he read eagerly.

That day they were very exciting. He became so much interested in the story of a crime executed in a gamekeeper's lodge that he stopped in the middle of a clover field to read it more slowly. The details were frightful. A woodcutter, in passing the forester's house the morning after, had noticed a little blood upon the sill, as if someone had been bleeding from the nose. "The keeper must have killed a wolf last night," he thought, but coming nearer, he perceived that the door was left open and that the lock had been broken. Then, seized with fear, he ran to the village, notified the mayor, who took with him as a reinforcement the keeper of fields and the schoolmaster; these four men returned together. They found the forester with his throat cut before the chimney piece, his wife strangled on the bed and their little daughter, aged six years, stifled under two mattresses.

Carrier Boniface became so wrought up over the thought of this assassination whose horrible details had been revealed to him one by one that he felt a weakness in his limbs and said aloud:

"Christopher! But some of the people in this world are brutes!"

Then he replaced the journal in its wrapper and went on, his head full of visions of the crime. He arrived shortly at M. Chapatis's. He opened the gate of the little garden and approached the house. It was of low construction, containing only one story and a mansard roof. It was at least five hundred feet from its nearest neighbor.

The carrier mounted the two front steps, placed his hand upon the knob, trying to open the door, but found it locked. Then he perceived that the shutters had not been opened and that no one had come out that morning.

A feeling of alarm took possession of him, for M. Chapatis, since his arrival, had always been up rather early. It was then only ten minutes after seven, nearly an hour earlier than he usually got there. No matter. The tax collector ought to be up before that.

He made a tour around the house, walking with much precaution, as if he himself might be in some danger. He noticed nothing suspicious except a man's footprints on a strawberry bed.

But suddenly he remained motionless as he was passing a window, powerless from fright. A groan came from the house.

He approached nearer and, stepping over a border of thyme, glued his ear to the opening in order to hear better; assuredly someone was groaning. He could plainly hear long, dolorous sighs, a kind of rattle, a noise of struggle. Then the groans became louder and oft repeated, finally being accentuated and changing into cries.

Then Boniface, no longer doubtful that a crime was being committed, took to his legs, recrossed the little garden, flew across the field and the meadow, running until he was out of breath, his bag shaking and hitting against his hip, and arrived gasping and in dismay at the door of the police headquarters.

Brigadier Malautour was mending a broken chair by means of some brads and a hammer. Gendarme Rauter held the damaged piece of furniture between his knees and placed a nail at the edge of the crack; then the brigadier, chewing his mustache, his eyes round and moist with interest in his work, would pound—blows which fell on the fingers of his subordinate.

When the letter carrier perceived them he cried out:

"Come quick; someone is assassinating the tax collector. Quick! Quick!"

The two men ceased their work and raised their heads, the astonished heads of people surprised and perplexed.

Boniface, seeing more surprise than haste, repeated:

"Quick! Quick! The robbers are in the house. I heard the cries. There is no time to be lost."

The brigadier, placing his hammer on the ground, remarked: "How was it you found out about this?"

The carrier answered: "I went to carry the paper and two letters, when I noticed that the door was locked and that the collector had not been out. I walked around the house, trying to account for it, when suddenly I heard someone groan as if he were being strangled, as if his throat were being cut—and then I started as soon as I could to get you. There's no time to be lost."

"And you didn't try to help any?"

The carrier, much frightened, replied:

"I was afraid that one was too small a number."

Then the brigadier, convinced, said:

"Give me time to get into my uniform and I will follow you."

And he went into the building, followed by his subordinate who carried the chair. They reappeared almost immediately, and all three started in quick, trained step for the scene of the crime.

Arriving near the house, they slackened their pace through precaution, and the brigadier drew his revolver; then they went softly into the garden and approached the walls of the dwelling. There was nothing to indicate that the malefactors had gone away. The door remained locked, the windows closed.

"Let us wait for them," murmured the brigadier.

But Boniface, palpitating with emotion, made them pass around to the other side and showed them an opening. "It is there," he said.

The brigadier advanced alone and fixed his ear against the board. The two others waited, ready for anything, watching him closely.

He remained a long time, motionless, listening. The better to bring his head near the wooden shutter, he had removed his three-cornered hat and held it in his right hand.

What did he hear? His face revealed nothing for some time, then suddenly his mustache rose at the corners; his cheeks took on folds as in a silent laugh and, stepping over the border of thyme, he came toward the two men who were looking at him in a kind of stupor.

Walking along on the tips of his toes, he made the sign for them to follow, and when they came to the gate he advised Boniface to slip the paper and the letters under the door.

The amazed carrier obeyed with perfect docility.

"And now, back again," said the brigadier.

When they had gone a little way he turned to the letter carrier with a jocose air, his eyes upturned and shining with fun, and said in a bantering tone:

"Well, you are a rogue, you are!"

The old fellow asked: "Why? I heard something. I swear to you I heard something."

Then the brigadier, no longer able to restrain himself, laughed aloud. He laughed to suffocation, his two hands holding his sides, doubling himself up, his eyes full of tears, and making frightful grimaces about the nose. Both of them were frightened to look at him.

As he could neither speak nor cease laughing, nor make them understand, he made a gesture, a popular, meaning gesture. As they could not comprehend that either, he kept repeating it, motioning back always with his head.

Finally his subordinate caught the meaning suddenly and in his turn broke into formidable laughter. The old fellow remained stupefied between these two men who were twisting themselves into all shapes.

The brigadier finally became calm and, giving the old man a great tap on his waistcoat, like a jolly good fellow, he cried:

"What a farce! A holy farce! I shall record it as the Crime of Father Boniface!"

The carrier opened his enormous eyes and repeated:

"I swear to you that I heard something."

The brigadier began to laugh. His subordinate sat down on the grass beside the ditch and laughed at his ease.

"Ah! You heard something. And your wife, do you assassinate her that way, hey, you old joker?"

"My wife?"

And he stood reflecting a long time, then he continued:

"My wife. Yes, she bawls if I strike her—and bawls that are bawls, why? Was Monsieur Chapatis beating his wife?"

Then the brigadier, in a delirium of humor, turned him around by the shoulders as if he had been a puppet and whispered in his ear something that caused him to look besotted with astonishment.

Then the old man murmured pensively:

"No? Not that—not that. She said nothing—mine—I would never have believed—— Is it possible? One would swear that a murder——"

And confused, disconcerted and ashamed, he went on his way across the fields, while the two policemen, laughing continually and calling back to him from afar with barrack-room wit, watched his black cap as it disappeared in the tranquil sea of grain.

FLORENTINE

We were talking about girls, for what else is there to talk about among men? One of us said:

"Wait! A strange story occurs to me on this subject."

And he related it:

"One evening of last winter I was suddenly taken with one of those desolate lassitudes which are overwhelming in their attack upon soul and body from time to time. I was at home alone, and I knew well that if I remained there I should have a frightful fit of despondency, of the kind that leads to suicide when they return often.

"I put on my coat and went out without knowing at all what I was going to do. Having descended to the boulevard, I began to walk along past the cafés, nearly empty, for it was raining. One of those thin rains was falling that dampens the spirits as much as the clothes; not one of those good showers, striking one in a cascade and driving passers under the porte-cocheres, out of breath, but a rain that unceasingly deposits upon you imperceptible droplets and covers your clothing with a glistening, penetrating moisture.

"What should I do? I went up and returned, seeking some place to pass a couple of hours and discovering for the first time that there was not a place of diversion in all Paris in the evening. Finally I decided to enter the Folies-Bergères, that theater so amusing to street girls.

"There were very few in the great hall. The long, semicircular promenade contained but a few individuals, of a race usually known by their walk, their clothing, the cut of their hair and beard, their hats and their complexion. It is not often that one sees among them a man who seems clean, perfectly clean, and whose clothing has altogether the same air. As for the girls, they are always the same, as you know, plain, weary, drooping, walking with that quick step and that air of imbecile disdain which they assume, I know not why.

"I said to myself that truly not one of these flagging creatures, greasy rather than fat, either bloated or very thin, with the paunch of a prelate and their long legs bowed, was worth the louis that they obtained with much difficulty after having demanded five.

"But suddenly I perceived one of them, a little one that appeared genteel, not at all young, but fresh, droll and provoking. I stopped her and, in beastly fashion, without thinking, set my price for the night. I did not wish to return home alone, all alone; I preferred rather the company and embrace of this worthless woman.

"And so I followed her. She lived in a big, big house in Martyr Street. The gas was already extinguished on the staircase. I mounted slowly, constantly lighting taper matches, striking the steps with my feet, stumbling and ill at ease, following a petticoat, the rustle of which I heard before me.

"She stopped at the fourth story and, having shut again the inside door, she asked:

" 'And you wish to remain until tomorrow?'

" 'Yes. You know that was the agreement.'

" 'All right, my dear. I only wanted to know. Wait for me here a minute; I will return immediately.'

"And she left me in the darkness. I heard her close two doors, then it seemed to me she was speaking with somebody. I was surprised and disturbed. The idea of blackmail occurred to me. But I have fists and solid muscles. 'We shall see,' I thought.

"I listened with all attention, both of ear and mind. Someone was moving, walking about, but with great precaution. Then another door was opened, and it seemed to me that I still heard talking, but in a very low voice.

"She returned, bringing a lighted candle. 'You can enter now,' she said.

"She spoke familiarly, as a sign of possession. I entered, and after having crossed a dining room, where it was evident nobody ever dined, I entered a chamber like that of all these girls, a furnished room with rep curtains and eider-down silk quilt with suspicious poppy-red spots.

"She continued: 'Put yourself at ease, my dear.'

"I inspected the apartment with an eye of suspicion. There seemed nothing disquieting, however. She undressed herself so quickly that she was in bed before I had my overcoat off. Then she began to laugh:

" 'Well, what is the matter with you? Are you changed into a pillar of salt? Come! Make haste!'

"I imitated her and joined her. Five minutes later I had a foolish desire to dress again and go out. But the overwhelming lassitude which had seized me at my house returned to me, depriving me of all strength to move, and I remained, in spite of the disgust which I had for this public bed. The sensual charm which I believed I saw down there under the lights of the theater had disappeared in my arms, and I had with me, flesh to flesh, only a vulgar girl, like all the rest, whose indifferent and complaisant kiss had an aftertaste of garlic.

"I began to talk to her:

" 'Have you been here long?' I said.

" 'Six months the fifteenth of January.'

" 'Where were you before that?'

" 'I was in Clauzel Street. But the janitor made me so miserable that I left.'

"And she began to relate an interminable story of the *concierge* who had made some scandal about her.

"Suddenly I heard something moving near us. At first there was a sigh, then a light noise, but distinct, as if someone had fallen from a chair.

"I sat up quickly in bed and demanded: 'What was that noise?'

"She answered with assurance and composure: 'Don't disturb yourself, my dear; it is my neighbor. The partition is so thin that we hear all as if they were here. These are dirty boxes. They are made of pasteboard.'

"My indolence was so strong that I got down under the clothes again. We continued our talk. Incited by the curiosity which drives all men to question these creatures upon their first adventure, to wish to raise the veil from their first fault in order to find in them some far-off trace of innocence, that we may find something to love, perhaps, in the rapid recital evoked by their candor and the shame of long ago, I asked her about her first lover.

"I knew that she lied. What did it matter? Among all the lies I might discover, perhaps, some sincere or touching incident.

"'Come,' I said, 'tell me who he was.'

"'He was an oarsman.'

"'Ah! Tell me about it. Where were you?'

"'I was at Argenteuil.'

"'What were you doing there?'

"'I was maid in a restaurant.'

"'What restaurant?'

"'At the Freshwater Sailors; do you know it?'

"'Well, yes; Bonanfan's.'

"'Yes, that's the one.'

"'And how did he pay his court, this oarsman?'

"'While I was making his bed. He forced me.'

"But suddenly I recalled the theory of a doctor of my acquaintance, an observing, philosophic doctor who, in his practice in a great hospital, had daily examples of these girl mothers and public girls and knew all the shame and misery of women, the poor women who become the hideous prey of the wandering male with money in his pocket.

"'Invariably,' he told me, 'is a girl debauched by a man of her own class and station in life. I have made volumes of observations upon it. It is customary to accuse the rich of culling the flower of innocence from the children of the people. That is not true. The rich pay for the culled bouquet. They cull also, but at the second flowering; they never cut the first.'

"Then turning toward my companion, I began to laugh.

"'You may as well know that I know all about your story. The oarsman was not the first, as you well know.'

"'Oh yes, my dear, I swear it!'

"'You are lying.'

"'Oh no, I promise you I am not.'

"'You lie. Come, tell me the truth.'

"She seemed to hesitate, astonished. I continued:

"'I am a sorcerer, my good child, a hypnotist. If you do not tell me the truth I shall put you to sleep, and then I can find it out.'

"She was afraid, being stupid like her kind. She murmured:

"'How did you ever guess it?'

"I replied: 'Come, speak.'

"'Oh! The first time, that amounted to nothing. It was at a festival in the country. They called in a chef for the occasion, Monsieur Alexander. After he came he had it all his own way in the house. He ordered everybody, even to the master and mistress, as if he had been a king. He was a large, handsome man who would not stay in place before his stove. He was always crying out: "Here, some butter—some eggs—some Madeira!" And it was necessary to carry him everything on the run, or he would get angry and say things to you that would make you blush under the skirts.

"'When the day was finished he would smoke his pipe before the door. And as I passed him with a pile of plates he said to me this: "Come, little goose, come down to the edge of the lake and show me the country." As for me, I went, like a fool, and scarcely had we arrived at the bank when he forced me so quickly that I did not even know that it was done. And then he went away by the nine o'clock train, and I never saw him again after that.'

"I asked: 'Is that all?'

"She stammered: 'Oh! I believe Florentine belongs to him.'

"'Who is Florentine?'

"'He is my little boy.'

"'Ah! Very well. And you made the oarsman believe that he was the father, did you not?'

"'Yes.'

"'He had money, this oarsman?'

"'Yes, he left me an income of three hundred francs for Florentine's support.'

"I commenced to be amused. I continued:

"'Very well, my girl, very well. You are all less sensual than one would believe. And how old is Florentine now?'

"She answered: 'Twelve years old. He will take his first communion in the spring.'

"'That is good, and since that you have made a trade with your conscience.'

"She sighed resignedly: 'One must do what she can.'

"But a great noise in another part of the room made me leap out of bed with a bound; it was the noise of one falling, then rising and groping with his hands upon the wall. I had seized the candle and was looking about, frightened and furious. She got up also and tried to hold me back, saying:

"'It is nothing, my dear; I assure you it is nothing.'

"But I had discovered on which side of the wall this strange noise was. I went straight toward a concealed door at the head of the bed and opened it suddenly—and perceived there a poor little boy, trembling and staring at me with frightened eyes, a pale, thin little boy beside a large chair filled with straw, from which he had fallen.

"When he saw me he began to cry and, opening his arms to his mother:

"'It was not my fault, Mamma; it was not my fault. I was asleep and I fell. You mustn't scold me, for it was not my fault.'

"I turned toward the woman and said:

"'What does he mean?'

"She seemed confused and disheartened. But finally she said in a broken voice:

"'What can you expect? I do not earn enough to put the child in school! I must take care of him somehow, and I cannot afford to hire another room. He sleeps with me when I have no one. When someone comes for an hour or two he can stay in the closet very well and keep quiet; he knows how. But when one remains all night, as you have, his muscles are fatigued from sleeping on the chair—and it is not the child's fault. I would like to see you—you—sleep all night on a chair. You would sing another song.'

"She was angry, wrought up, and was crying.

"The child wept too. A poor child, pitiful and timid, a good child of the closet, of the cold, dark closet, a child who came from time to time to get a little warmth in the bed a moment empty.

"I, too, had a desire to weep.

"And I returned home to my own bed."

CONSIDERATION

SIMON BOMBARD often found life very bad! He was born with an unbelievable aptitude for doing nothing and with an immoderate desire to follow this vocation. All effort, whether moral or physical, each movement accomplished for a purpose, appeared to him beyond his strength. As soon as he heard anyone speak of anything serious he became confused, his mind being incapable of tension or even attention.

The son of a novelty merchant of Caen, he glided along smoothly, as they said in the family, until he was twenty-five years of age. But as his parents were always nearer bankruptcy than fortune, he suffered greatly for want of money.

He was a tall, large, pretty youth with red whiskers, worn Norman fashion, of florid complexion, blue eyes, sensual and gay, corpulence already apparent, and dressed with the swagger elegance of a provincial at a festival. He laughed, cried and gesticulated at the same time, displaying a storm of good nature with all the assurance of the seasoned traveler. He considered that life was made principally for joys and pleasures, and as soon as it became necessary to curb his noisy enjoyment he fell into a kind of chronic somnolence, being incapable of sadness.

His need for money harassed him until he formed the habit of repeating a phrase now celebrated in his circle of acquaintance: "For ten thousand francs a year I would become an executioner."

Now he went each year to Trouville to pass two weeks. He called this "spending the season." He would install himself at the house of his cousins who gave him the use of a room, and from the day of his arrival to that of his departure he would promenade along the boardwalk which extends along the great stretch of seashore.

He walked with an air of confidence, his hands in his pockets or crossed behind his back, always clothed in ample garments, with light waistcoats and showy cravats, his hat somewhat over his ear and a cheap cigar in one corner of his mouth.

He went along, brushing by the elegantly dressed women and eying contemptuously the merry men who were ready to make a disturbance for the sake of it, and seeking—seeking—what he was seeking.

He was after a wife, counting entirely upon his face and his physique. He said to himself: "Why the devil, in all the crowd that comes here, should I not be able to find my fate?" And he hunted with the scent of a dog in the chase, with the Norman scent, sure that he should recognize her, the woman who would make him rich, the moment he perceived her.

It was one Monday morning that he murmured: "Wait, wait, wait!" The weather was superb, one of those yellow-and-blue days of the month of July, when one might say that the sky wept from the heat. The vast shore covered with people, costumes, colors, had the air of a garden of women, and the fishing boats with their brown sails, almost immovable upon the blue water which reflected them upside down, seemed asleep under the great sun at ten o'clock in the morning. There they remained opposite the wooden pier, some near, some farther off, some still farther, as if overcome by a summer-day idleness, too indifferent to seek the high sea or even to return to port. And down there one could vaguely perceive in the mist the coast of Havre, showing two white points on its summit, the lighthouses of Sainte-Adresse.

He said to himself: "Wait, wait, wait!" For he had passed her now for the third time and perceived that she had noticed him, this mature woman, experienced and courageous, who was making a bid for his attention. He had noticed her before on the days preceding, because she seemed also in quest of someone. She was an Englishwoman, rather tall, a little thin, an audacious Englishwoman whom circumstances and much journeying had made a kind of man. Not bad, on the whole, walking along slowly with short steps, soberly and simply clothed, but wearing a queer sort of hat, as Englishwomen always do. She had rather pretty eyes, high cheekbones, a little red, teeth that were too long and always visible.

When he came to the pier he returned upon his steps to see if she would meet him again. He met her and she threw him a knowing glance, a glance which seemed to say: "Here I am!"

But how should he speak to her? He returned a fifth time, and when he was again face to face with her she dropped her umbrella. He threw himself forward, picked it up and presented it to her, saying:

"Permit me, madame."

She responded: "Oh, you are very kind!"

And then they looked at each other. They knew nothing more to say. But she blushed. Then, becoming courageous, he said:

"We are having beautiful weather here."

And she answered: "Oh, delicious!"

And then they remained opposite each other, embarrassed, neither thinking of going away. It was she who finally had the audacity to ask: "Have you been about here long?"

He answered, laughing: "Oh yes, about as long as I care about it." Then brusquely he proposed: "Would you like to go down to the pier? It is pretty there such days as this."

She simply said: "I should be much pleased."

And they walked along side by side, she with her harsh, direct allurement, he alluring her with his dandyism, which makes for rakishness later on.

Three months later the notables in the commercial world of Caen received one morning a square white card which said:

M. and Mme Prosper Bombard have the honor to announce the marriage of their son, M. Simon Bombard, to Mrs Kate Robertson.

and on the other side:

Mrs Kate Robertson has the honor of announcing her marriage to M. Simon Bombard.

They went to live in Paris. The fortune of the wife amounted to fifteen thousand francs a year income, free and clear. Simon wished to have four hundred francs a month for his personal expenses. He had to prove that his tenderness merited this amount; he did prove it easily and obtained what he asked for.

At first everything went well. Young Mme Bombard was no longer young, assuredly, and her freshness had undergone some wear, but she had a way of exacting things which made it impossible for anyone to refuse her. She would say with her grave, willful English accent: "Oh, Simon, now we must go to bed," which made Simon start toward the bed like a dog that had been ordered, "To your kennel." And she knew how to have her way by day and night in a manner there was no resisting.

She did not get angry; she made no scenes; she never cried; she never had the appearance of being irritated or hurt or even disturbed. She knew how to talk; that was all, and she spoke to the point and in a tone that admitted no contradiction.

More than once Simon was on the point of rebelling, but before the brief and imperious desires of this singular woman he found himself unable to stand out. Nevertheless, when the conjugal kisses began to be meager and monotonous and he had in his pocket what would bring him something greater, he paid for satiety, but with a thousand precautions.

Mme Bombard perceived all this without his surmising it, and one evening she announced to him that she had rented a house at Mantes where they would live in the future.

Then existence became harder. He tried various kinds of diversion which did not at all compensate for the conquests he had a taste for.

He fished with a line, learned how to tell the places which the gudgeon liked, which the roach and carp preferred, the favorite spots of the bream and the kinds of bait that divers fishes will take.

But in watching his bob as it trembled on the surface of the water, other visions haunted his mind. Then he became the friend of the chief of the office of the subprefect and the captain of the police, and they played whist of evenings at the Commerce Café, but his sorrowful eye would disrobe the queen of clubs or the lady of the diamonds, while the problem of the absent legs on these two-headed figures would bring up images suddenly that confused his thoughts.

Then he conceived a plan, a true Norman plan of deceit. He would have his wife take a maid who would be a convenience to him, not a beautiful girl, a coquette, adorned and showy, but a gawky woman, rough and strong-backed, who would not arouse suspicions and whom he would acquaint beforehand with his plans.

She was recommended to them by the director of the city farm, his accomplice and obliging friend, who guaranteed her under all relations and conditions. And Mme Bombard accepted with confidence the treasure they brought to her.

Simon was happy, happy with precaution, with fear and with unbelievable difficulties. He could never undress beyond the watchful eye of his wife, except for a few short moments from time to time, and then without tranquillity. He sought some plan, some stratagem, and he ended by finding one that suited him perfectly.

Mme Bombard, who had nothing to do, retired early, while Bombard, who played whist at the Commerce Café, returned each evening at half-past nine, exactly. He got Victorine to wait for him in the passageway of his house, under the vestibule steps in the darkness.

He only had five minutes or more, for he was always in fear of a surprise, but five minutes from time to time sufficed for his ardor, and he slid a louis into the servant's hand, for he was generous in his pleasures, and she would quickly remount to her garret.

And he laughed, he triumphed all alone and repeated aloud, like King Midas' barber fishing for the goldfish from the reeds on the riverbank: "The mistress is safe within."

And the happiness of having Mme Bombard safely fixed within made up for him in great part for the imperfection and incompleteness of his conquest.

One evening he found Victorine waiting for him, as was her custom, but she appeared to him more lively, more animated than usual, and he remained perhaps ten minutes in the rendezvous in the corridor.

When he entered the conjugal chamber Mme Bombard was not there. He felt a cold chill run down his back and sank into a chair, tortured with fear.

She appeared with a candlestick in her hand. He asked, trembling:

"You have been out?"

She answered quietly: "I went to the kitchen for a glass of water."

He forced himself to calm his suspicions of what she might have heard, but she seemed tranquil, happy, confident, and he was reassured.

When they entered the dining room for breakfast the next morning Victorine put the cutlets on the table. As she turned to go out Mme Bombard handed her a louis which she held up delicately between her two fingers and said to her with her calm, serious accent:

"Wait, my girl, here are twenty francs which I deprived you of last night. I wish to give them to you."

And the girl, amazed, took the piece of gold which she looked at with a stupid air, while Bombard, frightened, opened his eyes wide at his wife.

WOMAN'S WILES

"Women?"

"Well, what do you say about women?"

"Well, there are no conjurers more subtle in taking us in at every available opportunity with or without reason, often for the sole pleasure of playing tricks on us. And they play these tricks with incredible simplicity, astonishing audacity, unparalleled ingenuity. They play tricks from morning till night, and they all do it—the most virtuous, the most upright, the most sensible of them. You may add that sometimes they are to some extent driven to do these things. Man has always idiotic fits of obstinacy and tyrannical desires. A husband is continually giving ridiculous orders in his own house. He is full of caprices; his wife plays on them even while she makes use of them for the purpose of deception. She persuades him that a thing costs so much because he would kick up a row if its price were higher. And she always extricates herself from the difficulty cunningly by means so simple and so sly that we gape with amazement when by chance we discover them. We say to ourselves in a stupefied state of mind, 'How is it we did not see this till now?'"

. . . .

The man who uttered the words was an ex-minister of the Empire, the Comte de L——, thorough profligate, it was said, and a very accomplished gentleman. A group of young men were listening to him.

He went on:

"I was outwitted by an ordinary uneducated woman in a comic and thoroughgoing fashion. I will tell you about it for your instruction.

"I was at the time minister for foreign affairs, and I was in the habit of taking a long walk every morning in the Champs Elysées. It was the month of May; I walked along, sniffing in eagerly that sweet odor of budding leaves.

"Ere long I noticed that I used to meet every day a charming little woman, one of those marvelous, graceful creatures who bear the trade-mark of Paris.

Pretty? Well, yes and no. Well made? No, better than that: her waist was too slight, her shoulders too narrow, her breast too full, no doubt, but I prefer those exquisite human dolls to that great statuesque corpse, the Venus of Milo.

"And then this sort of woman trots along in an incomparable fashion, and the very rustle of her skirt fills the marrow of your bones with desire. She seemed to give me a side glance as she passed me. But these women give you all sorts of looks—you never can tell.

"One morning I saw her sitting on a bench with an open book between her hands. I came across and sat down beside her. Five minutes later we were friends. Then each day, after the smiling salutation: 'Good day, madame,' 'Good day, monsieur,' we begin to chat. She told me that she was the wife of a government clerk, that her life was a sad one, that in it pleasures were few and cares numerous, and a thousand other things.

"I told her who I was, partly through thoughtlessness and partly, perhaps, through vanity. She pretended to be much astonished.

"Next day she called at the Ministry to see me, and she came again there so often that the ushers, having their attention drawn to her appearance, used to whisper to one another as soon as they saw her the name with which they had christened her: 'Madame Léon'—that is, my Christian name.

"For three months I saw her every morning without growing tired of her for a second, so well was she able incessantly to give variety and piquancy to her physical attractiveness. But one day I saw that her eyes were bloodshot and glowing with suppressed tears, that she could scarcely speak, so much was she preoccupied with secret troubles.

"I begged of her, I implored of her, to tell me what was the cause of her agitation.

"She faltered out at length with a shudder: 'I am—I am *enceinte!*'

"And she burst out sobbing. Oh! I made a dreadful grimace, and I have no doubt I turned pale, as men generally do at hearing such a piece of news. You cannot conceive what an unpleasant stab you feel in your breast at the announcement of an unexpected paternity of this kind. But you are sure to know it sooner or later. So in my turn I gasped: 'But—but—you are married, are you not?'

"She answered: 'Yes, but my husband has been away in Italy for the last two months, and he will not be back for some time.'

"I was determined at any cost to get out of my responsibility.

"I said: 'You must go and join him immediately.'

"She reddened to her very temples and with downcast eyes murmured: 'Yes—but——' She either dared not or would not finish the sentence.

"I understood and I prudently inclosed in an envelope the expenses of her journey.

.   .   .   .

"Eight days later, she sent me a letter from Genoa. The following week I received one from Florence. Then letters reached me from Leghorn, Rome and Naples.

"She said to me:

"*I am in good health, my dear love, but I am looking frightful. I would not care to have you see me till it is all over; you would not love me. My husband suspects nothing. As his business in this country will require him to stay there much longer, I will not return to France until after my confinement.*

"And at the end of about eight months I received from Venice these few words:

"*It is a boy.*

"Some time after she suddenly entered my study one morning, fresher and prettier than ever, and flung herself into my arms. And our former connection was renewed.

"I left the Ministry, and she came to live in my house in the Rue de Grenelle. She often spoke to me about the child, but I scarcely listened to what she said about it; it did not concern me. Now and then I placed a rather large sum of money in her hand, saying: 'Put that by for him.'

"Two more years glided by, and she was more and more eager to tell me some news about the youngster—'about Léon.'

"Sometimes she would say in the midst of tears: 'You don't care about him; you don't even wish to see him. If you could know what grief you cause me!'

"At last I was so much harassed by her that I promised one day to go next morning to the Champs Elysées when she took the child there for an airing.

"But at the moment when I was leaving the house I was stopped by a sudden apprehension. Man is weak and foolish. What if I were to get fond of this tiny being of whom I was the father—my son?

"I had my hat on my head, my gloves in my hands. I flung down the gloves on my desk and my hat on a chair.

" 'No, decidedly I will not go; it is wiser not to go.'

"My door flew open. My brother entered the room. He handed me an anonymous letter he had received that morning:

"*Warn the Comte de L——, your brother, that the little woman of the Rue Casette is impudently laughing at him. Let him make some inquiries about her.*

"I had never told anybody about this intrigue, and I now told my brother the history of it from the beginning to the end. I added:

" 'For my part, I don't want to trouble myself any further about the matter, but will you, like a good fellow, go and find out what you can about her?'

"When my brother had left me I said to myself: 'In what way can she have deceived me? She has other lovers? What does it matter to me? She is young, fresh and pretty; I ask nothing more from her. She seems to love me, and as a matter of fact, she does not cost me much. Really, I don't understand this business.'

"My brother speedily returned. He had learned from the police all that was to be known about her husband: A clerk in the Home Department, of regular habits and good repute and, moreover, a thinking man, but married to a very pretty woman, whose expenses seemed somewhat extravagant for her modest position. That was all.

"Now my brother, having sought for her at her residence and finding that she was gone out, succeeded, with the assistance of a little gold, in making the doorkeeper chatter: 'Madame D——, a very worthy woman, and her husband a very worthy man, not proud, not rich, but generous.'

"My brother asked for the sake of saying something:

" 'How old is her little boy now?'

" 'Why, she has not got any little boy, monsieur.'

" 'What? Little Léon?'

" 'No, monsieur, you are making a mistake.'

" 'I mean the child she had while she was in Italy two years ago.'

" 'She has never been in Italy, monsieur; she has not quitted the house she is living in for the last five years.'

"My brother, in astonishment, questioned the doorkeeper anew, and then he pushed his investigation of the matter further. No child, no journey.

"I was prodigiously astonished but without clearly understanding the final meaning of this comedy.

" 'I want,' I said to him, 'to have my mind perfectly clear about the affair. I will ask her to come here tomorrow. You shall receive her instead of me. If she has deceived me you will hand her these ten thousand francs, and I will never see her again. In fact, I am beginning to find I have had enough of her.'

"Would you believe it? I had been grieved the night before because I had a child by this woman, and I was now irritated, ashamed, wounded at having no more of her. I found myself free, released from all responsibility, from all anxiety, and yet I felt myself raging at the position in which I was placed.

"Next morning my brother awaited her in my study. She came in as quickly as usual, rushing toward him with outstretched arms, but when she saw who it was she at once drew back.

"He bowed and excused himself.

" 'I beg your pardon, madame, for being here instead of my brother, but he has authorized me to ask you for some explanations which he would find it painful to seek from you himself.'

"Then fixing on her face a searching glance, he said abruptly:

" 'We know you have not a child by him.'

"After the first moment of stupor she regained her composure, took a seat and gazed with a smile at this man who was sitting in judgment on her.

"She answered simply:

" 'No; I have no child.'

" 'We know also that you have never been in Italy.'

"This time she burst out laughing in earnest.

" 'No; I have never been in Italy.'

"My brother, quite stunned, went on:

" 'The comte has requested me to give you this money and to tell you that it is broken off.'

"She became serious again, calmly putting the money into her pocket and, in an ingenuous tone, asked:

"'And I am not, then, to see the comte any more?'

"'No, madame.'

"She appeared to be annoyed, and in a passionless voice she said:

"'So much the worse; I was very fond of him.'

"Seeing that she had made up her mind on the subject so resolutely, my brother, smiling in his turn, said to her:

"'Look here now, tell me why you invented all this long, tricky yarn, complicating it by bringing in the sham journey to Italy and the child?'

"She gazed at my brother in amazement, as if he had asked her a stupid question, and replied:

"'Well, I declare! How spiteful you are! Do you believe a poor little woman of the people such as I am—nothing at all—could have for three years kept on my hands the Comte de L——, minister, a great personage, a man of fashion, wealthy and seductive, if she had not taken a little trouble about it? Now it is all over. So much the worse. It couldn't last forever. Nonetheless, I succeeded in doing it for three years. You will say many things to him on my behalf.'

"She rose up. My brother continued questioning her:

"'But—the child? You had one to show him?'

"'Certainly—my sister's child. She lent it to me. I'd bet it was she gave you the information.'

"'Good! And all those letters from Italy?'

"She sat down again so as to laugh at her ease.

"'Oh! Those letters—well, they were a bit of poetry. The comte was not a minister of foreign affairs for nothing.'

"'But—another thing?'

"'Oh! The other thing is my secret. I don't want to compromise anyone.'

"And, bowing to him with a rather mocking smile, she left the room without any emotion, an actress who had played her part to the end."

And the Comte de L—— added by way of moral:

"So take care about putting your trust in that sort of turtledove!"

MOONLIGHT

Mme Julie Roubère was awaiting her elder sister, Mme Henriette Letore, who had just returned after a trip to Switzerland.

The Letore household had left nearly five weeks ago. Mme Henriette had allowed her husband to return alone to their estate in Calvados, where some matters of business required his attention, and came to spend a few days in Paris with her sister. Night came on. In the quiet parlor darkened by twilight shadows Mme Roubère was reading in an absent-minded fashion, raising her eyes whenever she heard a sound.

At last she heard a ring at the door, and presently her sister appeared, wrapped in a traveling cloak. And immediately, without any formal greeting, they clasped each other ardently, only desisting for a moment to begin embracing each other over again. Then they talked, asking questions about each other's health, about their respective families, and a thousand other things, gossiping, jerking out hurried, broken sentences and rushing about while Mme Henriette was removing her hat and veil.

It was now quite dark. Mme Roubère rang for a lamp, and as soon as it was brought in she scanned her sister's face and was on the point of embracing her once more. But she held back, scared and astonished at the other's appearance. Around her temples Mme Letore had two long locks of white hair. All the rest of her hair was of a glossy, raven-black hue, but there alone, at each side of her head, ran, as it were, two silvery streams which were immediately lost in the black mass surrounding them. She was, nevertheless, only twenty-four years old, and this change had come on suddenly since her departure for Switzerland.

Without moving, Mme Roubère gazed at her in amazement, tears rising to her eyes, as she thought that some mysterious and terrible calamity must have fallen on her sister. She asked:

"What is the matter with you, Henriette?"

Smiling with a sad smile, the smile of one who is heartsick, the other replied: "Why, nothing, I assure you. Were you noticing my white hair?"

But Mme Roubère impetuously seized her by the shoulders and, with a searching glance at her, repeated:

"What is the matter with you? Tell me, what is the matter with you. And if you tell me a falsehood I'll soon find it out."

They remained face to face, and Mme Henriette, who became so pale that she was near fainting, had two pearly tears at each corner of her drooping eyes.

Her sister went on asking:

"What has happened to you? What is the matter with you? Answer me!"

Then in a subdued voice the other murmured:

"I have—I have a lover."

And, hiding her forehead on the shoulder of her younger sister, she sobbed.

Then when she had grown a little calmer, when the heaving of her breast had subsided, she commenced to unbosom herself, as if to cast forth this secret from herself, to empty this sorrow of hers into a sympathetic heart.

Thereupon, holding each other's hands tightly grasped, the two women went over to a sofa in a dark corner of the room into which they sank, and the younger sister, passing her arm over the elder one's neck and drawing her close to her heart, listened.

.   .   .   .

"Oh! I recognize that there was no excuse for one; I do not understand myself, and since that day I feel as if I were mad. Be careful, my child, about yourself—be careful! If you only knew how weak we are, how quickly we yield, a moment of tenderness, one of those sudden fits of melancholy which steal into your soul, one of those longings to open your arms, to love, to embrace, which we all have at certain moments.

"You know my husband, and you know how fond of him I am, but he is mature and sensible and cannot even comprehend the tender vibrations of a woman's heart. He is always, always the same, always good, always smiling, always kind, always perfect. Oh! How I sometimes have wished that he would roughly clasp me in his arms, that he would embrace me with those slow, sweet kisses which make two beings intermingle, which are like mute confidences! How I wished that he was self-abandoned and even weak, so that he should have need of me, of my caresses, of my tears!

"This all seems very silly, but we women are made like that. How can we help it?

"And yet the thought of deceiving never came near me. Today it has happened, without love, without reason, without anything, simply because the moon shone one night on the Lake of Lucerne.

"During the month when we were traveling together my husband, with his calm indifference, paralyzed my enthusiasm, extinguished my poetic ardor. When we were descending the mountain paths at sunrise, when as the four horses galloped along with the diligence, we saw, in the transparent morning haze, valleys, woods, streams and villages. I clasped my hands with delight and said to him: 'What a beautiful scene, darling! Kiss me now!' He only answered, with a smile of chilling kindliness, 'There is no reason why we should kiss each other because you like the landscape.'

"And his words froze me to the heart. It seems to me that when people love each other they ought to feel more moved by love than ever in the presence of beautiful scenes.

"Indeed, he prevented the effervescent poetry that bubbled up within me from gushing out. How can I express it? I was almost like a boiler filled with steam and hermetically sealed.

"One evening (we had been for four days staying in the Hotel de Fluelen), Robert, having got one of his sick headaches, went to bed immediately after dinner, and I went to take a walk all alone along the edge of the lake.

"It was a night such as one might read of in a fairy tale. The full moon showed itself in the middle of the sky; the tall mountains, with their snowy crests, seemed to wear silver crowns; the waters of the lake glittered with tiny rippling motions. The air was mild, with that kind of penetrating freshness which softens us till we seem to be swooning, to be deeply affected without any apparent cause. But how sensitive, how vibrating, the heart is at such moments! How quickly it leaps up, and how intense are its emotions!

"I sat down on the grass and gazed at that vast lake, so melancholy and so fascinating, and a strange thing passed into me. I became possessed with an insatiable need of love, a revolt against the gloomy dullness of my life. What! would it never be my fate to be clasped in the arms of a man whom I loved on a bank like this under the glowing moonlight? Was I never, then, to feel on my lips those kisses so deep, delicious and intoxicating which lovers exchange on nights that seem to have been made by God for passionate embraces? Was I never to know such ardent, feverish love in the moonlit shadows of a summer's night?

"And I burst out weeping like a woman who has lost her reason. I heard some person stirring behind me. A man was intently gazing at me. When I turned my head round he recognized me and, advancing, said:

"'You are weeping, madame?'

"It was a young barrister who was traveling with his mother and whom we had often met. His eyes had frequently followed me.

"I was so much confused that I did not know what answer to give or what to think of the situation. I told him I felt ill.

"He walked on by my side in a natural and respectful fashion and began talking to me about what we had seen during our trip. All that I had felt he translated into words; everything that made me thrill he understood perfectly, better even than I did myself. And all of a sudden he recited some verses of Alfred de Musset. I felt myself choking, seized with indescribable emotion. It seemed to me that the mountains themselves, the lake, the moonlight, were singing to me about things ineffably sweet.

"And it happened, I don't know how, I don't know why, in a sort of hallucination.

"As for him, I did not see him again till the morning of his departure.

"He gave me his card!"

. . . .

And, sinking into her sister's arms, Mme Letore broke into groans—almost into shrieks.

Then Mme Roubère, with a self-contained and serious air, said very gently:

"You see, Sister, very often it is not a man that we love, but love. And your real lover that night was the moonlight."

DOUBTFUL HAPPINESS

I CAN NEITHER TELL you the name of the country nor of the man. It was far, far from here, upon a hot, fertile coast. We followed, since morning, the shore and the wheat fields and the sea covered with the sun. Flowers grew down very near the waves, the light waves, so sweet and sleepy. It was very warm, but a gentle heat, perfumed with the fat, humid, fruitful earth; one could believe that he was breathing germs.

I had been told that this evening I would find hospitality in the house of a Frenchman who lived at the end of the promontory in a grove of orange trees. Who was he? I do not know yet. He had arrived one morning, ten years before this, bought the land, planted his vines and sown his seed; he had worked, had this man, with passion and fury. Month after month and year after year he had added to his domains, making the fertile, virgin soil yield without ceasing and amassing a fortune by his indefatigable labor.

It was said that he worked constantly. Up with the dawn, going through his fields until night, superintending everything without rest, he seemed harassed by a fixed idea, tortured by an insatiable desire for money which nothing could distract or appease.

Now he seemed to be very rich.

The sun was setting when I reached his dwelling. This dwelling was at the end of a point in the midst of orange trees. It was a large, square house, very simple, overlooking the sea.

As I approached, a large, bearded man appeared in the doorway. Having saluted him, I asked for shelter for the night. He extended his hand and said, smiling:

"Enter, sir, you are at home."

He led me to a room, gave some orders to a servant with the perfect ease and good grace of a man of the world, then he left me, saying:

"We will dine when you are ready to come down."

We dined, tête-à-tête, upon a terrace opposite the sea. At first I spoke of his country, so rich, so far away, so little known! He smiled, answering in an abstracted way:

"Yes, this is a pretty country. But no country pleases one much when it is far from those they love."

"You regret France?"

"I—I long for Paris."

"Why not return there?"

"Oh! I am going to return there."

And gradually we began to talk of the French world, of the boulevards and of the many features of Paris. He asked me about men he had known, cities, names, all of them familiar names upon the vaudeville stage.

"Who does one see at Tortoni's these days?"

"The same ones, except the dead."

I looked at him with marked interest, pursued by some vague remembrance. Certainly I had seen that head somewhere! But where? And when? He seemed fatigued, although vigorous, sad, though resolute. His great blond beard fell upon his breast, and sometimes he would take it near his chin and draw it through his closed hand, slipping it along to the very end. He was a little bald but had thick eyebrows and a heavy mustache which mingled with the hair of his beard.

Behind us the sun was disappearing in the sea, throwing upon the coast a cloud of fire. The orange trees, in flower, exhaled a powerful, delicious fragrance on the evening air. Seeing nothing but me and fixing his look upon me, he seemed to discover in my eyes, to see at the depth of my soul, the well-known, much loved image of the broad walk, so far away, that extends from the Madeleine to the Rue Drouot.

"Do you know Bourtelle?" he asked.
"Yes, certainly."
"Is he much changed?"
"Yes, he is all white."
"And the Ridamie?"
"Always the same."
"And the women? Tell me about the women. Let us see. Did you know Suzanne Verner?"
"Yes, very well, to the end."
"Ah! And Sophie Astier?"
"Dead!"
"Poor girl! Can it be— Did you know—"
He was suddenly silent. Then in a changed voice, his face growing pale, he continued:
"No, it is better not to speak of her; it disturbs me so."
Then as if to change the trend of his thought, he rose and said:
"Do you wish to go in?"
"I am willing to go." And I followed him into the house.
The rooms downstairs were enormous, bare, sad, and seemed abandoned. Some glass dishes were set upon the table by the tawny-skinned servants who constantly roamed around this dwelling. Two guns hung upon two nails on the wall, and in the corners were to be seen some spades, some fishlines, dried palm leaves and objects of every kind, placed there at random by those entering, that they might find them at hand should they chance to have need of them on going out.
My host smiled.
"This is a lodge, or rather the lodging place of an exile," he said, "but my chamber is more as it should be. Let us go in there."
I thought, on entering, that I was in a curiosity shop, so filled was the room with all kinds of things, things disconnected, strange and varied, that one felt to be souvenirs of something. Upon the walls were two pretty engravings of well-known paintings, some stuffs, some arms, swords, pistols; then, in the middle of the principal panel, a square of white satin in a gold frame.
Surprised, I approached to look at it, when I perceived a pin which held a hair in the middle of the shining silk.
My host placed his hand on my shoulder and said, smiling:
"That is the only thing that I see here and the only thing I have seen for ten years. Monsieur Prudhomme exclaims: 'This sword is the most beautiful day in my life.' But I say: 'This pin is all of my life.'"
I sought for a commonplace phrase and ended by saying:
"You have suffered through some woman?"
He replied brusquely: "You may say I have suffered miserably, but come out on my balcony. A name has suddenly come to my lips that I have not dared to pronounce, because if you had answered 'dead' as you did when I spoke of Sophie Astier, my brain would be on fire, even today."
We were upon a large balcony where we could see two gulfs, one on the

right and the other on the left, shut in by high, gray mountains. It was the hour of twilight, when the sun, entirely out of sight, no longer lights the earth, except by reflection from the sky.

He continued: "Do you know if Jeanne de Limours still lives?"

His eye, fixed on mine, was full of trembling anxiety. I smiled and answered: "Yes indeed, and prettier than ever."

"You know her?"

"Yes."

He hesitated. Then asked: "Completely?"

"No."

He took my hand. "Tell me about her," he said.

"I have nothing to tell; she is one of the most charming women, or rather girls, in Paris, and the most courted. She leads an agreeable, princesslike existence; that is all."

He murmured: "I love her," as if he had said: "I am going to die." Then, brusquely: "Ah! For three years that was a frightful but delicious existence of ours. I was very near killing her five or six times, and she tried to put out my eyes with that pin you were just looking at. Wait! Do you see the little white point under my left eye? That shows how we loved each other! How can I explain this passion? You could never comprehend it.

"There should be such a thing as a simple love, born of the force of two hearts and two souls, and assuredly there is such a thing as an atrocious love, cruelly torturing, born of the invincible rapture of two beings totally unlike, who detest while they adore each other.

"This girl ruined me in three years. I possessed four millions which she squandered in her calm way, tranquilly, and destroyed with a sweet smile which seemed to fall from her eyes upon her lips.

"You know her? Then you know that there is something irresistible about her! What is it? I do not know. Is it those gray eyes, whose look enters into you and remains there like the barb of an arrow? Or is it rather that sweet smile, indifferent and seductive, which stays on her face like a mask? Her slow manner penetrates little by little and takes hold of you like a perfume, as does her tall figure, which seems to balance itself as she passes, for she glides instead of walking, and her sweet voice, which drags a little and is so pretty that it seems to be the music of her smile; her gestures, too, her always moderate gestures, always right, which intoxicate the eye, so harmonious are they.

"For three years I saw only her upon the earth! How I suffered! Because she deceived me as well as everybody else. Why? For no reason, only for the sake of deceiving. And when I found it out and accused her of being a street girl, a bad woman, she said tranquilly: 'Well, we are not married, are we?'

"Since I have come here I have thought much about her and have succeeded in understanding her; that girl is Manon Lescaut over again. Manon could never love without deceiving, and for her love, pleasure and money were all."

He was silent. Then after some minutes he added:

"When I had squandered my last sou for her she simply said to me: 'You understand, my dear, that I cannot live on air and weather. I love you very much; I love you more than anyone, but I must live. Misery and I can never dwell in the same house.'

"And if I could only tell you what an atrocious life I led by her side! Whenever I looked at her I had as much desire to kill her as I had to embrace her. Whenever I looked at her there came to me a furious desire to open my arms, press her to me until I strangled her. There was something about her, behind her eyes, something perfidious and unseizable which made me furious against her, and perhaps it was for that very reason that I loved her so much. In her the Feminine, the odious, frightful Feminine, was more prominent than in any other woman. She was charged and surcharged with it, as with a venomous fluid. She was Woman, more than anyone else has ever been.

"And whenever I went out with her she would cast her eyes over all men in such a fashion that she seemed to give herself to each one with only a look. This exasperated me but attached me more strongly to her, nevertheless. This creature belonged to everybody from merely passing through the street, in spite of me, in spite of herself, from her very nature, although the allurement was most modest and sweet. Do you understand?

"And what torment! At the theater, in a restaurant, it seemed to me that everyone possessed her before my eyes. And whenever I left her alone others did, in fact, possess her.

"It is ten years now since I saw her, and I love her now more than ever."

Night had spread over the earth. A powerful perfume of orange flowers was in the air.

I said to him: "Will you try to see her again?"

He answered: "Surely! I have here now, in money and land, seven or eight hundred thousand francs. When the million is completed I shall sell all and set out. With that I can have one year with her, one good, entire year. And then—adieu; my life will be finished."

I asked: "And after that?"

"After that," he answered, "I don't know. It will be finished. Perhaps I shall ask her to take me as a *valet de chambre*."

HUMILIATION

THE TWO YOUNG WOMEN had the appearance of being buried in a bed of flowers. They were alone in an immense landau filled with bouquets like a giant basket. Upon the seat before them were two small hampers full of Nice violets, and upon the bearskin which covered their knees was a heap of roses, gillyflowers, marguerites, tuberoses and orange flowers, bound together with silk ribbons, which seemed to crush the two delicate bodies, only allowing to appear above the spread-out, perfumed bed the shoulders, arms and a little of their bodices, one of which was blue and the other lilac.

The coachman's whip bore a sheath of anemones; the horses' heads were decorated with wallflowers; the spokes of the wheels were clothed in mignonette, and in place of lanterns, there were two round, enormous bouquets, which seemed like the two eyes of this strange, rolling, flowery beast.

The landau went along Antibes Street at a brisk trot, preceded, followed and accompanied by a crowd of other garlanded carriages full of women concealed under a billow of violets. For it was the Flower Festival at Cannes.

They arrived at the Foncière Boulevard where the battle took place. The whole length of the immense avenue, a double line of bedecked equipages was going and coming, like a ribbon without end. They threw flowers from one to the other. Flowers passed in the air like balls, hit the fair faces, hovered and fell in the dust where an army of street urchins gathered them.

A compact crowd, clamorous but orderly, looked on, standing in rows upon the sidewalks and held in place by policemen on horseback who passed along, pushing back the curious brutally with their feet, in order that the villains might not mingle with the rich.

Now the people in the carriages recognized each other, called to each other and bombarded one another with roses. A chariot full of pretty young women, clothed in red like devils, attracted and held all eyes. One gentleman, who resembled the portraits of Henry IV, threw repeatedly, with joyous ardor, a huge bouquet retained by an elastic. At the threat of the blow the women lowered their heads and hid their eyes, but the gracious projectile only described a curve and again returned to its master, who immediately threw it again to a new face.

The two young women emptied their arsenal with full hands and received a shower of bouquets; then after an hour of battle, a little wearied at the last, they ordered the coachman to take the road to the Juan Gulf, which skirts the sea.

The sun disappeared behind the Esterel, outlining in black upon a background of fire the lacy silhouette of the stretched-out mountain. The calm sea was spread out blue and clear as far as the horizon, where it mingled with the sky and with the squadron anchored in the middle of the gulf, having the appearance of a troop of monstrous beasts, immovable upon the water, apocalyptic animals, humpbacked and clothed in coats of mail, capped with thin masts like plumes and with eyes that lighted up when night came on.

The young women, stretched out under the fur robe, looked upon it languidly. Finally one of them said:

"How delicious these evenings are! Everything seems good. Is it not so, Margot?"

The other replied: "Yes, it is good. But there is always something lacking."

"What is it? For my part, I am completely happy. I have need of nothing."

"Yes? You think so, perhaps. But whatever well-being surrounds our bodies, we always desire something more—for the heart."

Said the other, smiling: "A little love?"

"Yes."

They were silent, looking straight before them; then the one called Marguerite said: "Life does not seem supportable to me without that. I need to be loved, if only by a dog. And we are all so, whatever you may say, Simone."

"No, no, my dear. I prefer not to be loved at all than to be loved by no one of importance. Do you think, for example, that it would be agreeable to me to be loved by—by——"

She looked for someone by whom she could possibly be loved, casting her eyes over the neighboring country. Her eyes, after having made the tour of the whole horizon, fell upon the two metal buttons shining on the coachman's back, and she continued, laughing, "By my coachman?"

Mlle Marguerite scarcely smiled as she replied:

"I can assure you it is very amusing to be loved by a domestic. This has happened to me two or three times. They roll their eyes so queerly that one is dying to laugh. Naturally, the more one is loved, the more severe she becomes, since otherwise, one puts herself in the way of being made ridiculous for some very slight cause, if anyone happened to observe it."

Mlle Simone listened, her look fixed straight before her; then she declared:

"No, decidedly, the heart of my valet at my feet would not appear to me sufficient. But tell me how you perceived that you were loved."

"I perceived it in them as I do in other men; they become so stupid!"

"But others do not appear so stupid to me when they are in love."

"Idiots, my dear, incapable of chatting, of answering, of comprehending anything."

"And you? What effect did it have on you to be loved by a domestic? Were you moved—flattered?"

"Moved? No. Flattered? Yes, a little. One is always flattered by the love of a man, whoever he may be."

"Oh, now, Margot!"

"Yes, my dear. Wait! I will tell you a singular adventure that happened to me. You will see what curious things take place among us in such cases.

"It was four years ago in the autumn, when I found myself without a maid. I had tried five or six, one after the other, all of them incompetent, and almost despaired of finding one, when I read in the advertisements of a newspaper of a young girl knowing how to sew, embroider and dress hair, who was seeking a place and could furnish the best of references. She could also speak English.

"I wrote to the address given, and the next day the person in question presented herself. She was rather tall, thin, a little pale, with a very timid air. She had beautiful black eyes, a charming color, and she pleased me at once. I asked for her references; she gave me one written in English, because she had come, she said, from the house of Lady Ryswell, where she had been for ten years.

"The certificate attested that the girl was returning to France of her own will and that she had nothing to reproach her for during her long service with her, except a little of the *French coquettishness*.

"The modest turn of the English phrase made me smile a little, and I engaged the maid immediately. She came to my house the same day; she called herself Rose.

"At the end of a month I adored her. She was a treasure, a pearl, a phenomenon.

"She could dress my hair with exquisite taste; she could flute the lace of a cap better than the best of the professionals, and she could make frocks. I was amazed at her ability. Never had I been so well served.

"She dressed me rapidly with an astonishing lightness of hand. I never felt her fingers upon my skin, and nothing is more disagreeable to me than contact with a maid's hand. I immediately got into excessively idle habits, so pleasant was it to let her dress me from head to foot, from chemise to gloves—this tall, timid girl, always blushing a little and never speaking. After my bath she would rub me and massage me while I slept a little while on my divan; indeed, I came to look upon her more as a friend in poorer circumstances than a servant.

"One morning the *concierge*, with some show of mystery, said he wished to speak to me. I was surprised but let him enter. He was an old soldier, once orderly for my husband.

"He appeared to hesitate at what he was going to say. Finally he said stammeringly: 'Madame, the police captain for this district is downstairs.'

"I asked: 'What does he want?'

" 'He wants to search the house.'

"Certainly the police are necessary, but I do detest them. I never can make it seem a noble profession. And I answered, irritated as well as wounded:

" 'Why search here? For what purpose? There has been no burglary?'

"He answered:

" 'He thinks that a criminal is concealed somewhere here.'

"I began to be a little afraid and ordered the police captain to be brought that I might have some explanation. He was a man rather well brought up and decorated with the Legion of Honor. He excused himself, asked my pardon, then asserted that I had among my servants a convict!

"I was thunderstruck and answered that I could vouch for every one of them and that I would make a review of them for his satisfaction.

" 'There is Peter Courtin, an old soldier.'

"It was not he.

" 'The coachman, Francis Pingau, a peasant, son of my father's farmer.'

"It was not he.

" 'A stableboy, also from Champagne and also a son of peasants I had known, and no more except the footman, whom you have seen.'

"It was not any of them.

" 'Then, sir, you see that you have been deceived.'

" 'Pardon me, madame, but I am sure I am not deceived. As he has not at all the appearance of a criminal, will you have the goodness to have all your servants appear here before you and me, all of them?'

"I hesitated at first, then I yielded, summoning all my people, men and women.

"He looked at them all for an instant, then declared:

" 'This is not all.'

" 'Your pardon, sir,' I replied; 'this is all, except my own maid who could not possibly be confounded with a convict.'

"He asked: 'Could I see her too?'

" 'Certainly.'

"I rang and Rose appeared immediately. Scarcely had she entered when he gave a signal, and two men, whom I had not seen, concealed behind the door, threw themselves upon her, seized her hands and bound them with cords.

"I uttered a cry of fury and was going to try and defend her. The captain stopped me:

" 'This girl, madame, is a man who calls himself John Nicholas Lecapet, condemned to death in 1879 for assassination preceded by violation. His sentence was changed to life imprisonment. He escaped four months ago. We have been on the search for him ever since.'

"I was dismayed, struck dumb. I could not believe it. The policeman continued, laughing:

" 'I can only give you one proof. His right arm is tattooed.'

"His sleeve was rolled up. It was true. The policeman added, certainly in bad taste:

" 'Doubtless you will be satisfied without the other proofs.'

"And he led away my maid!

"Well, if you will believe it, the feeling which was uppermost in me was that of anger at having been played with in this way, deceived and made ridiculous; it was not shame at having been dressed, undressed, handled and touched by this man, but—a—profound humiliation—the humiliation of a woman. Do you understand?"

"No, not exactly."

"Let us see. Think a minute. He had been condemned—for violation, this young man—and that—that humiliated me—there! Now do you understand?"

And Mlle Simone did not reply. She looked straight before her, with her eyes singularly fixed upon the two shining buttons of the livery and with that sphinx's smile that women have sometimes.

THE WEDDING NIGHT

MY DEAR GENEVIEVE, you ask me to tell you about my wedding journey. How do you think I dare? Ah! Sly one, who had nothing to tell me, who even allowed me to guess at nothing—but there! Nothing from nothing!

Now you have been married eighteen months, yes, eighteen months, you, my best friend, who formerly said you could conceal nothing from me, and you had not the charity to warn me! If you had only given the hint! If you had only put me on my guard! If you had put one little simple suspicion in my soul, you might have hindered me from making the egregious blunder for which I still blush and which my husband will laugh at until his death. You alone are responsible for it! I have rendered myself frightfully ridiculous forever; I have committed one of those errors of which the memory is never effaced—and by your fault, wicked one! Oh! If I had known!

Wait! I take courage from writing and have decided to tell you all. But promise me not to laugh too much. And do not expect a comedy. It is a drama.

You recall my marriage. I was to start the same evening on my wedding journey. Certainly I did not at all resemble Paulette, whom Gyp tells us about in that droll account of her spiritual romance called *About Marriage*. And if my mother had said to me, as Mme d'Hautretan did to her daughter: "Your husband will take you in his arms—and——" I should certainly not have responded as Paulette did, laughing: "Go no farther, Mamma, I know all that as well as you."

As for me, I knew nothing at all, and Mamma, my poor mamma who is always frightened, dared not broach the delicate subject.

Well then, at five o'clock in the evening, after the collation, they told us that the carriage was waiting. The guests had gone; I was ready. I can still hear the noise of the trunks on the staircase and the blowing of Papa's nose, which seemed to indicate that he was weeping. In embracing me the poor man said: "Good courage!" as if I were going to have a tooth pulled. As for Mamma, she was a fountain. My husband urged me to hasten these painful adieux, and I was myself all in tears, although very happy. That is not easy to explain but is entirely true. All at once I felt something pulling at my dress. It was Bijou, wholly forgotten since morning. The poor beast was saying adieu to me after his fashion. This gave my heart a little blow, and I felt a great desire to embrace my dog. I seized him (you remember he is as large as a fist) and began to devour him with kisses. I love to caress animals. It gives me a sweet pleasure, causing a kind of delicious shiver.

As for him, he was like a mad creature; he waved his paws, licked me and nibbled, as he does when he is perfectly content. Suddenly he took my nose in his teeth, and I felt that he had really bitten me. I uttered a little cry and put the dog down. He had bitten, although only in play. Everybody was disturbed. They brought water, vinegar and some pieces of linen. My husband himself attended to it. It was nothing, after all, but three little holes which his teeth had made. At the end of five minutes the blood was stopped and we went away.

It had been decided that we should go on a journey through Normandy for about six weeks.

That evening we arrived at Dieppe. When I say evening, I mean midnight.

You know how I love the sea. I declared to my husband that I could not retire until I had seen it. He appeared very contrary. I asked him, laughing, if he was sleepy.

He answered: "No, my dear, but you must understand that I would like to be alone with you."

I was surprised. "Alone with me?" I replied. "But you have been alone with me all the way from Paris in the train."

He laughed. "Yes—but—in the train—that is not the same thing as being in our room."

I would not give up. "Oh well," I said, "we shall be alone on the beach, and that is all there is to it!"

Decidedly he was not pleased. He said: "Very well; as you wish."

The night was magnificent, one of those nights which brings grand, vague ideas to the soul—more sensations than thoughts, perhaps—that brings a desire to open the arms as if they were wings and embrace the heavens, but how can I express it? One always feels that these unknown things can be comprehended.

There was a dreaminess, a poesy in the air, a happiness of another kind than that of earth, a sort of infinite intoxication which comes from the stars, the moon, the silver, glistening water. These are the best moments of life. They are a glimpse of a different existence, an embellished, delicious existence; they are the revelation of what could be, of what will be, perhaps.

Nevertheless, my husband appeared impatient to return. I said to him: "Are you cold?"

"No."

"Then look at the little boat down there which seems asleep on the water. Could anything be better than this? I would willingly remain here until daybreak. Tell me, shall we wait and see aurora?"

He seemed to think that I was mocking him and very soon took me back to the hotel by force! If I had known! Oh, the poor creature!

When we were once alone I felt ashamed, constrained, without knowing why. I swear it. Finally I made him go into the bathroom while I got into bed.

Oh, my dear, how can I go further? Well, here it is! He took, without doubt, my extreme innocence for mischief, my extreme simplicity for profligacy, my confident, credulous abandon for some kind of tactics and paid no regard to the delicate management that is necessary in order to make a soul wholly unprepared comprehend and accept such mysteries.

All at once I believe he lost his head. Then fear seized me; I asked him if he wished to kill me. When terror invades, one does not reason or think further; one is mad. In one second I had imagined frightful things. I thought of various stories in the newspapers, of mysterious crimes, of all the whispered tales of young girls married to miserable men! I fought, repulsed him, was overcome with fright. I even pulled a wisp of hair from his mustache and, relieved by this effort, I arose, shouting: "Help! help!" I ran to the door, drew the bolts and hurried, nearly naked, downstairs.

Other doors opened. Men in night apparel appeared with lights in their hands. I fell into the arms of one of them, imploring his protection. He made an attack upon my husband.

I knew no more about it. They fought and they cried; then they laughed, but laughed in a way you could never imagine. The whole house laughed, from the cellar to the garret. I heard in the corridors and in the rooms about us explosions of gaiety. The kitchenmaids laughed under the roof, and the bellboy was in contortions on his bench in the vestibule.

Think of it! In a hotel!

Soon I found myself alone with my husband, who made me some summary explanations, as one explains a surgical operation before it is undertaken. He was not at all content. I wept until daylight, and we went away at the opening of the doors.

That is not all. The next day we arrived at Pourville, which is only an embryo station for baths. My husband overwhelmed me with little attentions and tender care. After a first misunderstanding he appeared enchanted. Ashamed and much cast down over my adventure of the evening before, I was also amiable as could be, and docile. But you cannot figure the horror, the disgust, almost the hatred that Henry inspired in me, when I knew the infamous secret that they conceal from young girls. I was in despair, as sad as death, mindful of everything and harassed by the need of being near my poor parents. The next day after we arrived at Étretat. All the bathers were in a flurry of excitement. A young woman had been bitten by a little dog and had just died of rabies. A great shiver ran down my back when I heard this story told at the hotel table. It seemed to me immediately that I was suffering in the nose, and I had strange feelings all along my limbs.

That night I could not sleep; I had completely forgotten my husband. What if I were going to die, too, from rabies? I asked for some details the next day from the proprietor of the hotel. He gave me some frightful ones. I passed the day in walking upon the shore. I thought I could no longer speak. Hydrophobia! What a horrible death!

Henry asked me: "What is the matter? You seem sad."

I answered: "Oh! Nothing! Nothing!"

My staring eyes were fixed upon the sea without seeing it, upon farms, upon the fields, without my ever being able to say what came under my gaze. For nothing in the world would I have confessed the thought that tortured me. Some pain, true pain was felt in my nose. I wished to return.

As soon as I was back in the hotel I shut myself up in order to examine the wound. There was nothing to be seen. Nevertheless, I could not doubt that it was working me great harm. I wrote immediately to my mother, a short letter which probably sounded strange. I asked an immediate reply to some insignificant questions. After having signed my name, I wrote: "Especially, do not forget to give me some news of Bijou."

The next day I could not eat, but I refused to see a physician. All day long I remained seated upon the beach, looking at the bathers in the water. They came, the thin and the stout, all hideous in their frightful costumes, but I never thought of laughing. I thought: "They are happy, these people! They have not been bitten! They are going to live! They have nothing to fear. They can amuse themselves at will because they are at peace!"

At that instant I carried my hand to my nose, touching it; was it not swollen? And soon I entered the hotel, shut myself in and looked at it in the glass. Oh, it had changed color. I should die now very soon.

That evening I felt all at once a sort of tenderness for my husband, a tenderness of despair. He appeared good to me; I leaned upon his arm. Twenty times I was on the point of telling him my distressing secret but ended in keeping silent.

He abused odiously my listlessness and the weakness of my soul. I had not the force to resist him, or even the will. I would bear all, suffer all!

The next day I received a letter from my mother. She replied to my questions but said not a word about Bijou. I immediately thought: "He is dead and they are concealing it from me." I wished to run to the telegraph office and send a dispatch. One thought stopped me: "If he really is dead they will not tell me." I then resigned myself to two more days of anguish. I wrote again. I asked them to send me the dog, for diversion, because I was a little lonesome.

A trembling fit took me in the afternoon. I could not raise a full glass without spilling half. The state of my soul was lamentable. I escaped from my husband at twilight and ran to the church. I prayed a long time. On returning I felt anew the pains in my nose and consulted a druggist whose shop was lighted. I spoke to him as if one of my friends had been bitten, asking his advice in the matter. He was an amiable man, very obliging. He advised me freely. But I forgot to notice what he said; my mind was so troubled. I only remember this: "Purging is often recommended." I bought many bottles of I know not what, under pretext of sending them to my friend.

The dogs that I met filled me with horror, creating in me a desire to flee at top of my speed. It seemed to me many times, also, that I had a desire to bite them. My night was horribly disturbed. My husband profited by it.

The next day I received a response from my mother. "Bijou," she said, "is very well, but it would expose him too much to send him alone on a railroad train." Then they would not send him to me. He was dead.

I could not yet sleep. As for Henry, he snored. He awoke many times. I was annihilated.

The next day I took a bath in the sea. I was almost overcome in entering the water; I was so frightfully cold. I was more than ever shocked by this frigid sensation. I trembled in every limb but felt no more pain in the nose.

By chance they presented me to the medical inspector of the baths, a charming man. I led up to my subject with extreme skill. I then said to him that my little dog had bitten me several days before and asked him what was necessary to be done if we discovered any inflammation. He laughed and answered: "In your situation, madame, I see only one remedy, which would be for you to make a new nose."

And as I did not comprehend, he added: "Your husband will see to that." And I was no better informed on leaving him than I was before.

Henry that evening seemed very gay, very happy. We went to the casino, but he did not wait for the end of the play before proposing to me to return. As there was nothing of interest to me, I followed him. But I could not remain in bed; all my nerves were unstrung and vibrating. Neither could he sleep. He embraced me, caressed me, became all sweetness and tenderness, as if he had finally guessed how much I was suffering. I accepted his caresses without even comprehending them or thinking about them.

But suddenly an extraordinary, fearful crisis seized me. I uttered a frightful cry, pushed back my husband who took hold of me, ran into my room and began to beat my head and face against the door. It was rage! Horrible rage! I was lost!

Henry raised me up, himself frightened and trying to understand the trouble. I kept silent. I was resigned now. I awaited death. I knew that after some hours of respite another crisis would seize me, even to the last which would be mortal.

I allowed them to put me in the bed. At the point of day the irritating obsessions of my husband caused a new paroxysm, which was longer than the first. I had a desire to tear and bite and howl; it was terrible and, nevertheless, not so painful as I had believed.

Toward eight o'clock in the morning I slept for the first time in four nights. At eleven o'clock a beloved voice awoke me. It was Mamma, whom my letters had frightened and who had hastened to see me. She had in her hand a great basket, from whence came some little barks. I seized it, foolish in hope. I opened it, and Bijou jumped upon the bed, embraced me, gamboled about, rolled himself upon my pillow, frenzied with joy.

Ah well, my dearie, you may believe me if you will; I did not comprehend all until the next day! Oh, the imagination, how it works! And to think that I believed—— Tell me, was it not too foolish?

I have never confessed to anyone, you will understand why, the tortures of those four days. Think, if my husband had known! He has teased enough already about my adventures at Pourville. For my part, I cannot be too angry at his jests.

I am done. We have to accustom ourselves to everything in life.

THE NONCOMMISSIONED OFFICER

Quartermaster varajou had obtained permission to pass eight days with his sister, Mme Padoie. Varajou, who was in garrison at Rennes and led a jolly life there, finding himself high and dry with his family, had written to his sister that he would devote his week of liberty to her. Not that he loved Mme Padoie so much, for she was a little moralist, devout and always irritating, but he was in need of money, in great need, and he remembered that of all his relatives, the Padoies were the only ones from whom he had never borrowed.

Father Varajou, an old horticulturist of Angers, now retired from business, had closed his purse to his rake of a son and had scarcely seen him for ten years. His daughter had married Padoie, a former employee of the Treasury, who had since become collector at Vannes.

Varajou, then, on getting out of the train, took himself to the house of his brother-in-law. He found him in his office, in process of discussion with some Breton peasants of the neighborhood. Padoie raised himself from his chair, extended his hand across the table, which was covered with papers, and said:

"Take a seat; I will be with you in a moment." Then he seated himself again and continued his discussion.

The peasants could not understand his explanations; the collector could not comprehend their reasoning; he spoke French; they spoke Breton, and the deputy who acted as interpreter seemed not to understand anyone.

It was long, very long. Varajou looked at his brother-in-law, thinking: "What an idiot!" Padoie must have been about fifty. He was tall, thin, bony, slow, hairy, with his eyebrows arching until they made spears of hair above his eyes. He wore on his head a velvet cap ornamented with gold braid, and his look had the tameness which his action showed. His words, his gestures, his thoughts, were all slow. Varajou kept repeating: "What an idiot!"

He was himself one of those noisy brawlers for whom life has no greater pleasures than those of the café and the public women. Outside these two poles of existence he understood nothing. Boasting, blustering, full of disdain for everybody, he despised the whole universe from the height of his ignorance. When he had said: "What a devil of a holiday!" he had expressed the highest degree of admiration of which his mind was capable.

Padoie, having finished with his peasants, turned to him and asked:
"You are well?"
"Not bad, as you see. And you?"
"Very well, thank you. It is amiable of you to think of coming to see us."
"Oh! I have thought of it for a long time, but you know in the military profession one doesn't have much liberty."
"Oh! I know, I know, and that is why it is very amiable of you."
"And Josephine is well?"
"Yes, yes, thank you; you shall see her very soon."
"Where is she?"
"She has gone to pay some visits; we have so many relatives here, and this is a very exacting, proper town."
"I have no doubt of it."

Then the door opened and Mme Padoie appeared. She went toward her brother without eagerness, held up her cheek and asked:
"Have you been here long?"
"No, scarcely half an hour."
"Ah! I thought the train would be late. If you are ready, come into the parlor."

They passed into a neighboring room, leaving Padoie to his accounts and his collections. When they were alone she said:
"I have heard of some of your fine actions."
"What, for instance?"
"It appears that you have been conducting yourself like a blackguard, that you get tipsy and have been getting into debt."

He appeared very much astonished. "I?" he said. "Never in my life."
"Oh, you needn't deny it; I know all about it."

He still tried to defend himself, but she closed his mouth with so violent a lecture that he was forced to silence.

Then she said: "We dine at six o'clock; you are free until dinner. I cannot ask your company because I, not unfortunately, have some things to do." Left alone, he hesitated between sleeping and taking a walk. He looked for a door leading to his room and found one to the street. He decided in favor of the street.

He began to wander around slowly, his sword hitting against his legs, through the sad Breton town, so sleepy, so calm, so dead, that on the border of its inner sea they call it "The Morbihan." He looked at the little gray houses, the few passers, the empty shops, and said to himself: "Not gay, surely, or amusing, is Vannes. A sad idea, coming here!"

He sought the port, so dreary, returned by a solitary, desolate boulevard and was back before five o'clock. Then he threw himself upon his bed to sleep until dinner.

The maid woke him by knocking on the door and saying: "Dinner is served, sir!"

He descended. In the humid dining room, where the paper was nearly all unglued by the sun, a supper was waiting upon a round table without a cloth, for which three melancholy plates were set.

M. and Mme Padoie entered at the same time as Varajou. They were seated, then the husband and wife made the sign of the cross upon the pit of their stomachs, after which Padoie served the soup, a thick soup. It was the day for potpie. After the soup came the beef, beef too much cooked, melted and fat, which had fallen apart in boiling. The noncommissioned officer masticated it slowly with disgust, with fatigue and rage.

Mme Padoie said to her husband: "Are you going to the president's house this evening?"

"Yes, my dear."

"Do not stay late. You are all worn out every time you go out. You are not made for the world, with your bad health."

Then she spoke of the society of Vannes, of the excellent society where the Padoies were received with consideration, thanks to their religious sentiments.

Then they served a purée of potatoes with a dish of pork, in honor of the new arrival. Then some cheese, and it was finished. Not even coffee.

When Varajou understood that he was to pass the evening face to face with his sister, forced to undergo her reproaches, listen to her sermons, without even a solacing glass to cool his throat or to aid the remonstrances in slipping down, he concluded that the punishment was more than he could bear and declared that he must go to the armory to execute some commission under his leave of absence.

And he escaped at seven o'clock.

Scarcely was he in the street when he began to shake himself, like a dog just out of the water. He murmured: "What a blankety-blank-blank life of drudgery!" And he began to search for a café, the best café in town. He found it over a room, behind two gas jets. Inside, five or six men, some semi-gentlemen, a little noisy, were seated around some little tables drinking and chatting, while two billiard players were walking around the green cloth on which the ivory balls were hitting each other. They were counting: "Eighteen—nineteen. No luck. Oh! good shot! Well played! Eleven. You must play on the red. Twenty. Froze! Froze! Twelve. There! Was I right?"

Varajou ordered a demitasse and a small glass of brandy, of the best. Then he sat down and waited its coming.

He was accustomed to pass his evenings at liberty with his comrades in the clatter of glasses and the smoke of pipes. This silence, this calm, exasperated him. He began to drink, first his coffee then his brandy, and then he gave a second order. Now he had a desire to laugh, then to cry, then to sing and then of fighting someone.

He said to himself: "Jove! How this sets me up! I must make a feast of it." And the idea came to him of finding some girls to amuse himself with.

He called one of the employees: "Hey, waiter!"

"Yes sir!"

"Say, waiter, where can one go here to have a merry time?"

The man looked stupid at this question. Finally he answered: "I don't know, sir. Only here!"

"Here! And what do you call a merry time, I should like to know!"

"Oh! I don't know, sir, drinking beer or some good wine."

"Go on, you oyster! And the girls, where are they?"

"The girls! Ha! ha! ha!"

"Yes, the girls, where are they to be found here?"

"Girls?"

"Yes, yes, girls!"

The waiter came nearer to him and said in a low voice: "You want to know where there is a house?"

"Yes, of course!"

"You take the second street to the left and then the first to the right. It is number fifteen."

"Thanks, old man. Here is something for you."

"Thanks, sir."

And Varajou went out, repeating: "Second to the left, first to the right, fifteen." At the end of a few seconds he thought: "Second to the left—yes. But in coming out of the café, do I turn to the left or to the right? Bah! It doesn't make any difference. I shall soon find out."

And he walked on, turning into the second street at the left, then into the first at the right, and looked for number fifteen. It was a house of very good appearance, where he saw the windows of the first story lighted behind the closed shutters. The vestibule door was half open, and a lamp was burning in there.

"This is the place," thought the noncommissioned officer.

Then he entered and, as no one came, he called: "Hey there! Hey!"

A little maid appeared and was struck dumb on seeing a soldier. He said to her: "Good evening, my child. The ladies are upstairs?"

"Yes sir."

"In the salon?"

"Yes sir."

"And I can go right up?"

"Yes sir."

"The first door I come to?"

"Yes sir."

He went up and perceived in a room well lighted with two large lamps, a luster and two candelabra containing wax candles, four ladies in evening gowns, who seemed to be waiting for someone.

Three of them, the younger, were seated, with a somewhat starched appearance, upon a garnet velvet sofa, while the fourth, a woman about forty-five years of age, was arranging flowers in a vase; she was very large and wore a green silk frock which seemed like the envelope of a monstrous flower, her enormous arms and neck being like a rice-powdered rose.

The noncommissioned officer saluted: "Good evening, ladies."

The eldest one turned, appeared surprised, but bowed: "Good evening, sir."

He sat down. But seeing that he did not seem to be welcomed with any enthusiasm, he thought that without doubt only officers were admitted there, and the idea troubled him. Then he said to himself: "Bah! If one of them comes we shall see." And then he said: "Well, everything goes well?"

The large lady, the mistress of the house, doubtless, answered:

"Very well, thank you."

He found nothing more to say, and everybody was silent. Finally he began to be ashamed of his timidity and, laughing with a constrained laugh, said: "Oh well, there is nothing very merry about this—I'll pay for a bottle of wine——"

He had not finished his sentence when the door opened and Padoie, in evening clothes, appeared.

Varajou uttered a howl of joy and, jumping up, rushed at his brother-in-law, seized him in his arms and made him dance all around the room, crying: "Well, if here isn't Padoie! It is Padoie! It's Padoie!"

Then releasing the collector, who was lost in surprise, he said mockingly in his face: "Ah! Ah! Ah! Joker! Joker! You do break away then sometimes. Ah, what a joker. And my sister! You let her loose too—say!"

Realizing all the benefits from this unlooked-for situation, so impressed was he with the full force of it, that he threw himself upon a sofa and began to laugh so loud that the very furniture seemed to crack.

The three young ladies arose with one accord and escaped, while the elderly one repaired toward the door, ready to flee if it became necessary.

Then two gentlemen appeared, both in evening clothes and decorated. Padoie rushed toward them, saying: "Oh, Mr President, he is mad—surely he is mad. They sent him to us to convalesce. You can see at once that he is mad."

Varajou seated himself, comprehending nothing about him but guessing that he had done something monstrously foolish. Finally he arose and, turning toward his brother-in-law, asked: "Where are we?"

And Padoie, seized suddenly with a foolish anger, stammered:

"Where are—where—where are we? Unfortunate—miserable—infamous fellow—where are we? In the house of the president—of the president of Mortemain—of Mortemain—of—of—of—Mortemain. Ah! Ah, you scamp—scamp—you scamp!"

IN THE COURTROOM

The hall of the justice of the peace of Gorgeville is full of peasants who, seated in rows along the walls, are awaiting the opening of the session.

There are tall and short, stout and thin, all with the trim appearance of a row of fruit trees. They have placed their baskets on the floor and remain silent, tranquil, preoccupied with their own affairs. They have brought with them the odor of the stable, of sweat, of sour milk and of the manure heap. Flies are buzzing under the white ceiling. Through the open door the crowing of cocks is heard.

Upon a sort of platform is a long table covered with green cloth. An old, wrinkled man sits there writing at the extreme left. A policeman, tipped back upon his chair, is gazing into the air at the extreme right. And upon the bare wall a great Christ in wood, twisted into a pitiable pose, seems to offer his eternal suffering for the cause of these brutes with the odor of beasts.

The justice of the peace enters finally. He is corpulent, high colored, and rustles his magistrate's black robe as he walks with the rapid step of a large man in a hurry; he seats himself, places his cap upon the table and looks at the assemblage with an air of profound scorn.

He is a scholarly provincial, a bright mind of the district, one of those who translate Horace, relish the little verses of Voltaire and know by heart Vert-Vert as well as the snuffy poetry of Parny.

He pronounces officially the words:

"Now, Monsieur Potel, call the cases." Then, smiling, he murmurs:

"Quidquid tentabam dicere versus erat."

Then the clerk of the court, in an unintelligible voice, jabbers:

"Madame Victoire Bascule versus Isidore Paturon."

An enormous woman comes forward, a lady of the country town of the canton, with a much beribboned hat, a watch chain festooned upon her breast, rings on her fingers and earrings shining like lighted candles.

The justice greets her with a look of recognition, which savors of jest, and says:

"Madame Bascule, state your troubles."

The opposing party stands on the other side. It is represented by three persons. Among them is a young peasant of twenty-five, as fat-cheeked as an apple and as red as a poppy. At his right is his wife, very young, thin, small, like a bantam chicken, with a narrow, flat head covered, as in Crete, with a pink bonnet. She has a round eye, astonished and angry, which looks sidewise, like that of poultry. At the left of the boy sits his father, an old, bent man, whose twisted body disappears in his starched blouse as if it were under a bell.

Mme Bascule explains:

"Mr Justice, for fifteen years I have treated this boy kindly. I brought him up and loved him like a mother; I have done everything for him; I have made a man of him. He promised me, he swore to me, that he would never leave me. He even took an oath, on account of which I gave him a little property, my land at Bec-de-Mortin, which is worth about six thousand. Then this little thing, little nothing, this brat——"

The Justice: Moderate your language, Madame Bascule.

Mme Bascule: A little—a little—I think I am understood—turns his head, does, I know not what, to him, neither do I know why, and he goes and marries her, this fool, this great beast, and gives her my property, my property at Bec-de-Mortin. Ah no; ah no. I have a paper—here it is—which gives me back my property now. We had a statement drawn up at the notary's for the property and a statement on paper for the sake of friendship. One is worth as much as the other. Each to his right, is it not so?

She holds toward the justice a stamped paper, wide open.

Isidore Paturon: It is not true.

The Justice: Keep silent. You shall speak in your turn. [*He reads.*]

"I, the undersigned, Isidore Paturon, do, by this present, promise Madame Bascule, my benefactress, never to leave her while I live, and to serve her with devotion.

Gorgeville, August 5, 1883."

There is a cross here for the signature. Do you not know how to write?

Isidore: No. I don't.

The Justice: And is it you who made this cross?

Isidore: No, it was not I.

The Justice: Who did make it then?

Isidore: She did.

The Justice: You are ready to swear that you did not make this cross?

Isidore [*earnestly*]: Upon the head of my mother and my father, my grandmother and grandfather, and of the good God who hears me, I swear that it was not I. [*He raises his hand and strikes it against his side to emphasize his oath.*]

The Justice [*laughing*]: What have been your relations with Madame Bascule, the lady here present?

Isidore: I have helped to amuse her. [*Grinning at the audience.*]

The Justice: Be careful of your expressions. Do you mean to say that your connections have not been as pure as she pretends?

Father Paturon [*taking up the narrative*]: He wasn't fifteen years old yet, not fifteen years old, Monsieur Judge, when she debauched——

The Justice: Do you mean debauched?

The Father: You understand me. He was not fifteen years old, I say. And

IN THE COURTROOM

for four years before that already, she had nursed him with the greatest care, feeding him like a chicken she was fattening, until he was ready to split, saving your respect. And then when the time had come that she thought was just right, then she depraved him.

THE JUSTICE: Depraved? And you allowed it?

THE FATHER: Her as well as another. It has to come.

THE JUSTICE: Then what have you to complain of?

THE FATHER: Nothing! Oh, I complain of nothing, of nothing, only that he cannot get free of her when he wants to. I ask the protection of the law.

MME BASCULE: These people weary me with their lies, Monsieur Judge. I made a man of him.

THE JUSTICE: I see!

MME BASCULE: And now he denies me, leaves me, robs me of my property.

ISIDORE: It is not true, Monsieur Judge. I wanted to leave her five years ago, seeing that she had fleshed up with excess, and that didn't suit me. It troubled me much. Why? I don't know. Then I told her I was going away. She wept like a gutter and promised me her property at Bec-de-Mortin to stay a few more years, if only four or five. As for me, I said yes, of course. And what would you have done? I stayed then five years day by day and hour by hour. I was free. Each to his own. I had paid well.

[*Isidore's wife, quiet up to this time, cries out with a piercing, parrotlike voice*]: Look at her, look at her, Monsieur Judge, the millstone, and see if it wasn't well paid for.

THE FATHER [*raising his head with a convinced air*]: Indeed, yes, well paid for. [*Madame Bascule sinks back upon her seat and begins to weep.*]

THE JUSTICE [*paternally*]: What can you expect, dear madame? I can do nothing. You have given your land at Bec-de-Mortin away in a perfectly regular manner. It is his; it belongs to him. He had the incontestable right to do what he has done and to give it as a marriage gift to his wife. I have not entered into the question of—of—delicacy. I can only lay bare the facts from the point of view of the law. There is nothing more for me to do.

THE FATHER [*in a fierce voice*]: Then I can go home again?

THE JUSTICE: Certainly. [*They go out under the sympathetic gaze of the peasants, as people do who win their case. Mme Bascule sits in her seat, sobbing.*]

THE JUSTICE [*smiling*]: Come, come, dear madame, go home now. And if I had any counsel to give you, I should say find another—another pupil.

MME BASCULE [*through her tears*]: I cannot—cannot find one.

THE JUSTICE: I regret not being able to point one out to you. [*She throws a despairing look toward Christ being tortured on the cross, then arises and walks away with little steps, hiccuping with chagrin and concealing her face in her handkerchief. The justice adds in a bantering voice*]: Calypso would not be consoled at the departure of Ulysses. [*Then in a grave tone, turning toward his clerk*]: Call the next case.

THE CLERK [*mumbling*]: Célestin Polyte Lecacheur versus Prosper Magloire Dieulafait.

A PECULIAR CASE

When Captain Hector Marie de Fontenne married Mlle Laurine d'Estelle the parents and friends feared it would be a bad match.

Mlle Laurine, pretty, thin, blonde and confident, had at twelve the assurance of a woman of thirty. She was one of those precocious little Parisians who seems born with a full knowledge of life and of feminine tricks, with that audacity of thought, with that profound astuteness and suppleness of mind which make certain beings seem destined by fate to play with and deceive others, as they do. All their actions seem premeditated, their manner calculated, their words weighed with care, their whole existence a role which they are playing with people like themselves.

She was very charming and lively, with the liveliness that cannot restrain itself or be calm when something seems amusing or queer. She would laugh in the face of people in an almost impudent fashion but with so much grace that they were never angered. Then she was rich, very rich.

A priest served as intermediary when she married Captain de Fontenne. Brought up in a religious house, in a most austere fashion, this officer brought to his regiment the morals of the cloister and very strict, intolerant principles. He was one of those men who invariably becomes either a saint or a nihilist, in whom ideas install themselves as absolute mistresses, whose beliefs are inflexible, whose resolutions are not to be shaken.

He was a large, dark, young man, serious, severe, ingenuous, of simple mind, curt and obstinate, one of those men who pass through life without comprehending anything beneath them in variety or subtlety, who divine nothing, suspect nothing and admit what they think, what they judge and what they believe only when someone differs from them.

Mlle Laurine saw him, understood him immediately and accepted him for her husband. They made an excellent pair. She was yielding, skillful and wise, knowing how to show herself to best advantage, always ready in good works and at festivals, assiduous at church and at the theater, at once worldly and religious, with a little air of irony and a twinkle in her eye when chatting gravely with her grave husband. She would relate to him all her charitable enterprises with all the priests of the parish and the vicinity, and she made use of these pious occupations in order to remain away from morning until night.

But sometimes, in the midst of the recital of some act of beneficence, a foolish laugh would seize her suddenly, a nervous laugh, impossible to check. The captain would look surprised, then disturbed, then a little shocked, as his wife would continue to laugh. When she became a little calm he would ask: "What is the matter, Laurine?" And she would answer: "Nothing. It is only the memory of such a funny thing that happened to me!" And she would relate some story.

Then during the summer of 1883 Captain Hector de Fontenne took part in the grand maneuvers of the thirty-second regiment of the army. One evening as they camped on the edge of a town, after ten days of tent and open field, ten days of fatigue and privation, the comrades of the captain resolved to have a good dinner.

At first Captain de Fontenne refused to accompany them; then as his refusal surprised them, he consented. His neighbor at table, the governor of Favré, talking continually of military operations, the only thing that interested the captain, turned to him to drink glass after glass with him. It had been very hot, a heavy, parching, thirst-inspiring heat, and the captain drank without thinking or perceiving that a new gaiety had entered into him, a certain lively, burning joy, a happiness of being, full of awakened desires, of unknown appetites and undefined hopes.

At the dessert he was tipsy. He talked and laughed and moved about, seized by a noisy drunkenness, the foolish drunkenness of a man ordinarily wise and tranquil.

Someone proposed to finish the evening at the theater. He accompanied his comrades. One of them recognized one of the actresses as someone he had formerly loved, and a supper was planned where a part of the feminine personnel of the troupe assisted.

The captain awoke the next day in an unknown room, in the arms of a pretty little blonde woman who said to him on seeing him open his eyes: "Good morning, sweetheart!"

He could not comprehend at first; then little by little his memory returned, somewhat cloudy, however. Then he got up without saying a word, dressed himself and emptied his purse on the chimney piece. A shame seized him when he found himself standing up in position, his sword at his side, in this furnished room, where the rumpled curtains and sofa, marbelized with spots, had a suspicious appearance, and he dared not go out, since in descending the staircase he might meet someone; nor dared he pass before the *concierge* or go out in the street in the eyes of neighbors and passers-by.

The woman kept saying: "What has come over you? Have you lost your tongue? You had it fast enough last evening! Oh, what a muzzle!"

He bowed to her ceremoniously and, deciding upon flight, reached his abode with great steps, persuaded that one could guess from his manner and his bearing and his countenance that he had come out of the house of some girl.

And then remorse tortured him, the harassing remorse of a rigid, scrupulous man. He confessed and went to communion, but he still was ill at ease, followed ever by the memory of his fall and by a feeling of debt, a sacred debt contracted against his wife.

He did not see her again until the end of the month, because she went to visit her parents during the encampment of the troops. She came back to him with open arms and a smile upon her lips. He received her with an embarrassed attitude, the attitude of a guilty man, and until evening he scarcely talked with her.

When they found themselves alone she asked him: "What is the matter with you, my dear? I find you very much changed."

He answered in a constrained tone: "Oh, nothing, my dear, absolutely nothing."

"Pardon me, but I know you so well, and I feel sure there is something, some care, some angry feeling, something, I know not what!"

"Oh well, yes, there is something."

"And what is it?"

"It is impossible for me to tell you."

"To tell me? Why so? You disturb me."

"I have no reasons to give you. It is impossible for me to tell you."

She was seated upon a divan, and he walked up and down before her with his hands behind his back, avoiding the look of his wife.

Then she said: "Let us see. It is necessary for me to make you confess; it is my duty that I exact from you the truth; it is also my right. You should no more have a secret from me than I should from you."

His back was turned to her, framed in the high window, as he said:

"My dear, there are some things which are better not told. That which vexes me is one of them."

She got up, crossed the room, took him by the arm and, having forced him to turn around, placed her two hands upon his shoulders, then, smiling and cajoling, raised her eyes as she said:

"You see, Marie [she called him Marie in moments of tenderness], you could never conceal anything from me. I should believe you had done something bad."

He answered: "I have done something very bad."

She said gaily: "Oh, is it so bad as that? I am very much astonished at you!"

He responded quickly: "I shall say nothing further. It is useless to insist."

But she drew him to an armchair, forced him to sit down in it, then seated herself on his right knee and began kissing him with light, rapid kisses which just brushed the curled end of his mustache. Then she said:

"If you don't tell me we shall always be angry."

Pierced by remorse and tortured by his anguish, he answered: "If I should tell you what I have done you would never pardon me."

"On the contrary, my friend, I would pardon you immediately."

"No, it is impossible."

"I promise you."

"I tell you, it is impossible!"

"I swear that I will pardon you."

"No, my dear Laurine, you never could."

"How simple you are, my friend; you cannot deny it! In refusing to tell me what you have done, you allow me to think you have done something abominable, and I shall think constantly about it, regretting your silence as much as your unknown crime. While if you speak frankly, I shall forget it all by tomorrow."

"It is because——"

"What?"

He blushed up to the ears and said: "I shall confess to you as I would to a priest, Laurine."

On her lips was the sudden smile that she had sometimes in listening, and with a little mocking tone she said: "I am all ears."

He began: "You know, my dear, that I am a sober man. I drink only red wine and never liquors, as you know."

"Yes, I know."

"Well, imagine how I allowed myself to drink a little one evening toward the end of our encampment, when I was very thirsty, very much worn out with fatigue, weary and——"

"And you got tipsy? Oh, how hideous!"

"Yes, I was intoxicated," he replied with a severe air.

"And now were you wholly intoxicated so that you couldn't walk?"

"Oh no, not so much as that. But I lost my reason if not my equilibrium. I talked and laughed and made a fool of myself."

As he kept silent, she asked: "Is that all?"

"No."

"Ah, and after that?"

"After that I committed an infamous deed."

She looked at him, disturbed and troubled as well as somewhat excited.

"What then, my friend?"

"We had supped with—with some actresses—and I do not know how it was done, but—I have deceived you, Laurine!"

He made the statement in a grave, solemn tone. She gave a little toss to her head, and her eye brightened with a sudden gaiety, a profound, irresistible gaiety. Then she said:

"You—you—you have——"

And a little dry, nervous laugh broke forth and glided between her teeth two or three times and prevented her from speaking. She tried to take him seriously, but each time she tried to pronounce a word the laugh trembled at the bottom of her throat, leaped forth, was quickly stopped, but constantly reappeared, like gas in a bottle of champagne, pushing for escape, until the froth can no longer be retained. She put her hands on her lips to calm herself, that she might restrain this unfortunate gaiety. But the laugh ran through her fingers, shaking her chest and bursting forth in spite of her. She stammered: "You—you—have deceived me! Ha! ha! ha! ha! ha! ha! ha!"

And then she looked at him with a singular air, so mocking in spite of herself that he was speechless, stupefied. And suddenly, as if able to contain herself no longer, she burst forth again, laughing with the kind of laugh that seemed like an attack of nerves. Little jerking cries issued from her mouth, coming, it seemed, from the depths of her lungs. His two hands supported her bosom, and she was almost suffocated with long whoops like the cough in whooping cough.

With each effort that she made to calm herself a new paroxysm would begin, and each word that she tried to utter was only a greater contortion.

"My—my—my—poor friend. Ha! ha! ha! ha! ha! ha!"

He got up, leaving her alone upon the armchair and, becoming suddenly very pale, he said: "Laurine, this is more than unbecoming."

She stammered in a delirium of laughter:

"What—do you want? I—I—I cannot— But—but you are so funny—ha! ha! ha! ha! ha!"

He became livid and looked at her now with fixed eye, a strange thought awakening within him. Suddenly he opened his mouth as if to say something but said nothing; then, turning on his heel, he went out and shut the door.

Laurine, doubled up, weak and fainting, still laughed with a dying laugh, which occasionally took on new life, like the flame of a candle almost ready to go out.

A PRACTICAL JOKE

The jokes that are played nowadays are somewhat dismal. They are not like the inoffensive, laughable jokes of our forefathers; still, there is nothing more amusing than to play a good joke on someone, to force them to laugh at their own foolishness and, if they get angry, to punish them by playing a new joke on them.

I have played many a joke in my lifetime and I have had some played on me; some very good ones too. I have played some very laughable ones and some terrible ones. One of my victims died of the consequences, but it was no loss to anyone. I will tell about it someday, but it will not be an easy task, as the joke was not at all a nice one. It happened in the suburbs of Paris, and those who witnessed it are laughing yet at the recollection of it, though the victim died of it. May he rest in peace!

I will narrate two today. One in which I was the victim and another in which I was the instigator. I will begin with the former, as I do not find it so amusing, being the victim myself.

I had been invited by some friends in Picardy to come and spend a few weeks. They were fond of a joke like myself (I would not have known them had they been otherwise).

They gave me a rousing reception on my arrival. They fired guns, they kissed me and made such a fuss over me that I became suspicious.

"Be careful, old fox," I said to myself, "there is something up."

During dinner they all laughed immoderately. I thought to myself, "They are certainly projecting some good joke and intend to play it on me, for they laugh at nothing, apparently." I was on my guard all evening and looked at everybody suspiciously, even at the servants.

When bedtime came everybody escorted me to my room and bid me good night. I wondered why, and after shutting my door I stood in the middle of the room with the candle in my hand. I could hear them outside in the hall, whispering and laughing; they were watching me no doubt. I looked at the walls, inspected the furniture, the ceiling, the floor, but I found nothing suspicious. I heard footsteps close to my door; surely they were looking through the keyhole. Then it struck me that perhaps my light would go out suddenly and I would be left in the dark, so I lighted all the candles and looked around once more, but I discovered nothing. After having inspected the windows and the shutters, I closed the latter with care; then I drew the curtains and placed a chair against them. If someone should try to come in that way I would be sure to hear them, I thought. Then I sat down cautiously. I thought the chair would give way beneath me, but it was solid enough. I did not dare to go to bed, but as it was getting late I realized that I was ridiculous. If they were watching me, as I supposed they were, they certainly must have laughed heartily at my uneasiness, so I resolved to go to bed. Having made up my mind, I approached the alcove. The bed looked particularly suspicious to me, and I drew the heavy curtains back, pulled on them, but they held fast. "Perhaps a bucket of water is hidden on the top, all ready to fall on me, or else the bed may fall apart as soon as I lie on it," I thought. I racked my brain to try and remember all the different jokes I had played on others, so as to guess what might be in store for me; I was not going to be caught, not I!

Suddenly an idea struck me which I thought capital. I gently pulled the mattress off the bed, and it came toward me, along with the sheets and blankets. I dragged them in the middle of the room near the door and made my bed up again the best way I could, put out all the lights and felt my way into bed. I lay awake at least another hour, starting at every little sound, but everything seemed quiet, so I at last went to sleep.

I must have slept profoundly for some time, when suddenly I woke up with a start. Something heavy had fallen on me, and at the same time a hot liquid streamed all over my neck and chest, which made me scream with pain. A terrible noise filled my ears, as if a whole sideboard full of dishes had fallen in them. I was suffocating under the weight, so I reached out my hand to feel the object, and I felt a face, a nose and whiskers. I gave that face a terrible blow with my fist, but instantaneously I received a shower of blows which drove me out of bed in a hurry and out into the hall.

To my amazement I found it was broad daylight and everybody coming up the stairs to find out the cause of the noise. What we found was the valet, sprawled out on the bed, struggling among the broken dishes and tray. He had brought me some breakfast and, having encountered my improvised couch, had very unwillingly dropped the breakfast as well as himself on my face!

The precautions I had taken to close the shutters and curtains and to sleep in the middle of the room had been my undoing. The very thing I had so carefully avoided had happened.

They certainly had a good laugh on me that day!

The other joke I speak of dates back to my boyhood days. I was spending my vacation at home, as usual, in the old castle in Picardy.

I had just finished my second term at college and had been particularly interested in chemistry and especially in a compound called *phosphure de calcium* which, when thrown in water, would catch fire, explode, followed by fumes of an offensive odor. I had brought a few handfuls of this compound with me, so as to have fun with it during my vacation.

An old lady named Mme Dufour often visited us. She was a cranky, vindictive, horrid old thing. I do not know why, but somehow she hated me. She misconstrued everything I did or said, and she never missed a chance to tattle about me, the old hag! She wore a wig of beautiful brown hair, although she was more than sixty, and the most ridiculous little caps adorned with pink ribbons. She was well thought of because she was rich, but I hated her to the bottom of my heart, and I resolved to revenge myself by playing a joke on her.

A cousin of mine, who was of the same age as I, was visiting us, and I communicated my plan to him, but my audacity frightened him.

One night when everybody was downstairs I sneaked into Mme Dufour's room, secured a receptacle into which I deposited a handful of the calcium phosphate, having assured myself beforehand that it was perfectly dry, and ran to the garret to await developments.

Pretty soon I heard everybody coming upstairs to bed. I waited until everything was still, then I came downstairs barefooted, holding my breath, until I came to Mme Dufour's door and looked at my enemy through the keyhole.

She was putting her things away and, having taken her dress off, she donned a white wrapper. She then filled a glass with water and, putting her whole hand in her mouth as if she were trying to tear her tongue out, she pulled out something pink and white which she deposited in the glass. I was horribly frightened but soon found it was only her false teeth she had taken out. She then took off her wig, and I perceived a few straggling white hairs on the top of her head. They looked so comical that I almost burst out laughing. She kneeled down to say her prayers, got up and approached my instrument of vengeance. I waited awhile, my heart beating with expectation.

Suddenly I heard a slight sound, then a series of explosions. I looked at Mme Dufour; her face was a study. She opened her eyes wide, then shut them, then opened them again and looked. The white substance was crackling, exploding at the same time, while a thick, white smoke curled up mysteriously toward the ceiling.

Perhaps the poor woman thought it was some satanic fireworks, or perhaps that she had been suddenly afflicted with some horrible disease; at all events, she stood there, speechless with fright, her gaze riveted on the supernatural phenomenon. Suddenly she screamed and fell swooning to the floor. I ran to my room, jumped into bed and closed my eyes, trying to convince myself that I had not left my room and had seen nothing.

"She is dead," I said to myself; "I have killed her," and I listened anxiously to the sound of footsteps. I heard voices and laughter, and the next thing I knew my father was soundly boxing my ears.

Mme Dufour was very pale when she came down the next day, and she drank glass after glass of water. Perhaps she was trying to extinguish the fire which she imagined was in her, although the doctor had assured her that there was no danger. Since then when anyone speaks of disease in front of her, she sighs and says:

"Oh, if you only knew! There are such strange diseases."

A STRANGE FANCY

It was at the end of the dinner opening the hunting season at the house of Marquis de Bertrans. Eleven hunters, eight young women and the doctor of the neighborhood were seated around the great illuminated table covered with fruits and flowers.

They came to speak of love, and a great discussion arose, the eternal discussion as to whether one could love truly but once or many times. They cited examples of people who had never had but one serious love; they also cited other examples of others who had loved often, violently. The men, generally, pretended that the passion, like a malady, could strike the same person many times and strike to kill if an obstacle appeared in his path. Although the point of view was not contestable, the women, whose opinion depended upon poesy more than on observation, affirmed that love, true love, the great love, could only fall once upon a mortal; that it was like a thunderbolt, this love, and that a heart touched by it remained ever after so vacant, ravaged and burned out that no other powerful sentiment, even a dream, could again take root.

The marquis, having loved much, combated this belief in lively fashion:
"I will tell you that one can love many times with all his strength and all his soul. You cite to me people who have killed themselves for love as proof of the impossibility of a second passion. I answer that if they had not been guilty of this foolishness of suicide, which removed them from all chance of another fall, they would have been healed, and they would have recommenced again and again, until their natural death. It is with lovers as it is with drunkards. He who has drunk will drink—he who has loved will love. It is simply a matter of temperament."

They chose the doctor as arbitrator, an old Paris physician, retired to the country, and begged him to give his opinion.

To be exact, he had none. "As the marquis had said, it is an affair of temperament."

"As for myself," he continued, "I have known of one passion which lasted fifty-five years without a day of respite and which was terminated only by death."

The marquis clapped his hands.

"This is beautiful," said a lady. "And what a dream to be so loved! What happiness to live fifty-five years enveloped in a deep, living affection! How happy and benign must be the life of one who is adored like that!"

The doctor laughed.

"In fact, madame," he said, "you are deceived on that point, because the one loved was a man. You know him; it is Monsieur Chouquet, the village pharmacist. And as for the woman, you knew her, too; it is the old woman who put cane seats in chairs and came every year to this house. But how can I make you comprehend the matter?"

The enthusiasm of the women fell. On their faces a look of disgust said: "Pooh!" as if love could only strike those fine and distinguished creatures who were worthy of the interest of fashionable people.

The doctor continued:

"I was called three months ago to the bedside of this old woman. She was dying. She had come here in the old carriage that served her for a house, drawn by the nag that you have often seen and accompanied by her two great black dogs, her friends and guard. The curate was already there. She made us the executors of her will, and in order to unveil the meaning of her testament, she related the story of her life. I have never heard anything more singular or more affecting.

"Her father made chair seats and so did her mother. She had never known a home in any one place upon the earth. As a little girl she went around ragged and dirty. They would stop beside the road at the entrance to towns, unharness the horse and let him browse; the dog would go to sleep with his nose in his paws; the little one would play in the grass while the father and mother, under the shade of the elms bordering the roadside, would reseat all the old chairs in the neighborhood.

"No one ever talked in this ambulance dwelling. After the necessary words to decide who should make the tour of the houses and who should call out the well-known 'Chairs to mend!' they would sit down to plait the straw, face to face or side by side.

"When the child went too far away or struck up an acquaintance with some urchin in the village the angry voice of the father would call her: 'You come back here, you brat!' And these were the only words of tenderness she ever heard.

"When she grew larger they sent her around to collect the worn-out chairs to be rebottomed. Then she made some acquaintances from place to place among the street children. Then it would be the parents of her new friends who would call brutally to their children: 'Will you come here, you scamp! Let me catch you talking to that barefoot again!'

"Often the boys would throw stones at her. Sometimes ladies would give her a few pennies and look at her closely.

"One day—she was then eleven years old—as they were passing through this place, she met the little Chouquet behind the cemetery, weeping because some comrade had stolen two sous from him. The tears of this little well-to-do citizen, one of those fortunate ones from whom in her queer noddle she had imagined herself cut off, one of those beings always content and joyous, quite upset her. She went up to him, and when she learned the cause of his trouble, she poured into his hands all her savings, seven sous, which he took quite naturally, drying his tears. Then, mad with joy, she had the audacity to embrace him. As he was counting the money attentively, he allowed her to do it. Seeing that she was not repulsed or beaten, she did the same thing again. She embraced him with arms and heart. Then she ran away.

"What could have taken place in her miserable head after that? Did she attach herself to this booby because she had sacrificed for him her vagabond fortune or because she had given to him her first tender kiss? The mystery is the same for the small as for the great.

"For months she dreamed of this corner of the cemetery and of this boy. In the hope of seeing him again, she robbed her parents, keeping back a sou here and there, either from a chair seat or upon the provisions which she was sent to buy.

"When she returned here she had two francs in her pocket, but she only saw the little druggist very properly behind the big colored bottle of his father's shop, between a red decanter and a tapeworm. She loved him there still more, charmed, aroused to ecstasy by this glory of colored water, this apotheosis of shining crystal.

"This picture became an ineffaceable memory, and when she saw him the following year playing marbles near the school with his comrades, she threw herself upon him, seized him in her arms and kissed him with such violence that he began to howl with fear. Then in order to appease him, she gave him all her money—seventy cents, a real treasure which he looked at with bulging eyes.

"He took it and let her caress him as much as she wished.

"During the next four years she turned into his hand all her surplus, which he pocketed with a clear conscience, in exchange for permitted kisses. There was sometimes fifteen cents, sometimes forty and once only five and one half —and she wept with pain and humiliation at this, but it had been a bad year. The last time there was a five-franc piece, a great round piece that made him laugh with content.

"She thought of nothing but him, and he waited her return with a certain impatience, running to meet her, which made the heart of the girl leap with joy.

"Then he disappeared. They sent him away to college. She found it out by skillful questioning. Then she used her diplomacy to change her parents' itinerary and make them pass through there in vacation. She succeeded but for one year; then for two years she did not see him; then she scarcely recognized him, so much was he changed; he was so large and handsome in his coat with the brass buttons and so imposing. He feigned not to see her and passed proudly by near her.

"She wept over it for two days, and after that she suffered without ceasing.

"Every year she returned here, passing him without daring to bow and without his deigning to raise his eyes to her. She loved him passionately. She said to me: 'Doctor, he is the only man I have seen on earth; I have not known that there are others existing.'

"Her parents died. She continued their trade but took with her two dogs instead of one, two terrible dogs that no one would dare encounter.

"One day in entering this village, where her heart still remained, she perceived a young woman coming out of the Chouquet shop on the arm of her well-beloved. It was his wife. He was married.

"That evening she threw herself into the pond on the mayor's estate. A drunken man got her out and took her to the pharmacy. Chouquet, the son, came down in his dressing gown to care for her and, without appearing to recognize her, loosed her clothing and rubbed her, then said in a hard voice: 'My, but you are foolish! It is not necessary to make a beast of yourself like this!'

"That was sufficient to cure her. He had spoken to her! She was happy for a long time.

"He wanted no remuneration for his services, but she insisted upon paying him well. And all her life was spent like this. She made chair seats and thought of Chouquet. Every year she saw him behind his large windows. She had the habit of buying from him all her medical needs. In this way she could see him near to and speak to him and still give him a little money.

"As I told you in the beginning, she died this spring. After having related her sad history, she begged me to give to him whom she had so patiently loved all the savings of her life, because she had worked only for him, she said, fasting, even, in order to put aside and to be sure that he would think of her at least once after she was dead.

"She then gave me two thousand three hundred and twenty-seven francs. I allowed the curate twenty-seven for burial and carried off the rest when she had drawn her last breath.

"The next day I took myself to the house of the Chouquets. They had just finished breakfast, sitting opposite each other, large and red, smelling of their pharmaceutical products, important and satisfied.

"They made me be seated; they offered me a *kirsch* which I accepted; then I commenced my discourse in an emotional voice, persuaded that they were going to weep.

"When they understood that he had been loved by this vagabond, this chair mender, this rover, Chouquet bounced with indignation, as if she had robbed him of his reputation, of the esteem of honest people, of his honor, of something of that delicacy that was dearer to him than life.

"His wife, also exasperated, kept repeating: 'The beggar! The beggar! The beggar!' without being able to find any other word.

"He got up and walked around the table with long strides, his Greek cap tipped over his ear. He muttered: 'Think of it, Doctor! This is a horrible thing to happen to a man! What is to be done? Oh, if I had known this while she was alive I would have had her arrested and shut up in prison. And she wouldn't have got out, I can tell you!'

"I was stupefied at the result of my pious proceedings. I neither knew what to say nor what to do. But I had to complete my mission. I said: 'She has charged me to give you all her savings, which amount to two thousand three hundred francs. As what I have told you seems to be so very disagreeable to you, perhaps it would be better to give this money to the poor.'

"They looked at me, the man and the woman, impotent from shock. I drew the money from my pocket, miserable money from all the country and of every mark, gold and sous mixed. Then I asked: 'What do you decide?'

"Madame Chouquet spoke first. She said: 'But since it was the last wish of this woman—it seems to me that it would be difficult to refuse it.'

"The husband, somewhat confused, answered: 'We could always buy with that money something for our children.'

"I remarked dryly: 'As you wish.'

He continued: 'Yes, give it to us, since she has put it in your charge. We can always find means of using it in some good work.'

"I laid down the money, bowed and went out.

"The next day Chouquet came to me and said brusquely: 'She must have left a wagon here, that—that woman. What are you going to do with this wagon?'

"'Nothing,' I said. 'Take it if you wish.'

"'Exactly. Just what I want. I will make a lean-to of it for my kitchen stove.'

"He was going, but I recalled him. 'She also left an old horse and her two dogs. Do you want them?'

"He stopped, surprised: 'Ah no,' he answered, 'what could I do with them? Dispose of them as you wish.'

"Then he laughed and extended his hand, which I took. What else could I do? In our country a medical man and a druggist should not be enemies.

"I have kept the dogs at my house. The curate, who has a large yard, took the horse. The wagon serves Chouquet as a cabin, and he has bought five railroad bonds with the money.

"This is the only profound love that I have met in my life."

The doctor was silent. Then the marquis, with tears in his eyes, sighed. "Decidedly, it is only women who know how to love."

AFTER DEATH

ALL VEZIERS-LE-RETHEL had assisted at the funeral and interment of M. Badon-Leremince, and the last words of the discourse of the delegate of the district remained in the memory of all:

"He was an honest man, at least."

Honest man he had been in all the appreciable acts of his life: in his words, in his example, in his attitude, in his bearing, in his step, in the cut of his beard and the form of his hats. He had never said a word that did not contain an example, never gave alms without accompanying it with advice, never held a hand without having the air of giving it a kind of benediction.

He left two children, a son and a daughter. His son was general counselor, and his daughter, having married a notary, M. Poirel de la Voulte, held a high place in Veziers.

They were inconsolable at the death of their father, for they loved him sincerely.

As soon as the ceremonies were over they returned to the house of death, and all three together, the son, the daughter and the son-in-law, opened the will, whose seal was to be broken by them alone, and that only after the coffin had been placed in the earth. A direction upon the envelope expressed this wish.

It was M. Poirel de la Voulte who opened the paper, being accustomed to these things in the capacity of notary and, having adjusted his eyeglasses over his eyes, he read in a dull voice, made for particularizing contracts:

"'My children, my dear children, I could not sleep tranquilly the eternal sleep if I did not make a confession to you from the other side of the tomb, the confession of a crime, remorse of which has rent my life. Yes, I have committed a crime, a frightful, abominable crime.

"'I was twenty-six years old, had just been called to the Bar in Paris and was living the life of young people from the provinces, stranded, without acquaintances, friends or parents in the city.

"'I took a mistress. There are people who are indignant at this word, "mistress," but there are also beings who cannot live alone. I am one of these. Solitude fills me with a horrible agony, especially solitude in a lodging, before the fire in the evening. It seems to me then that I am alone upon earth, frightfully alone, surrounded by vague dangers and terrible, unknown things, and the partition which separates me from my neighbor, from my neighbor whom I do not know, makes him as far removed as the stars that I see from my window. A sort of fever invades me, a fever of impatience and fear, and the silence of the walls overpowers me. It is so profound, so sad, this silence of a room where one lives alone! It is a silence about the soul, and when the furniture cracks or starts, the courage wanes, for one expects no sound in this mournful dwelling place.

"'How many times, unnerved, frightened by this mute immobility, have I begun to speak, to pronounce some words, without sequence, without reason, in order to make some noise. My voice then appeared to me so strange that I was afraid of that also. Is there anything more frightful than talking alone in an empty house? The voice seems like that of another, an unknown voice, speaking without cause to no one into the hollow air, with no ear to listen, for one knows, before the words are uttered into the space of the apartment, what the lips are about to say. And when they resound lugubriously in the silence they seem more like an echo, the echo of singular words pronounced low by the thoughts.

"'I took a mistress, a young girl like all those young girls who live in Paris at some trade insufficient to support them. She was sweet, good and simple. Her parents lived at Poissy. She went to stay a few days with them from time to time.

"'For a year I lived tranquilly enough with her, fully decided to leave her when I should see some young person with whom I was well enough pleased to want to marry. I would leave to this one a small income, since it is admitted in our society that the love of a woman ought to be paid for in money when she is poor, in jewels if she is rich.

"'But behold, there came a day when she announced to me that she was *enceinte*. I was struck down and perceived in an instant the ruin of my whole existence. The chain was apparent that I must drag to my dying day, in the near future, in my old age, always, the chain of a woman bound to my life by a child, the chain of a child whom it would be necessary to bring up, watch over and protect, always concealing myself from him and him from the world. My mind was overturned by this news, and a confused desire, which I did not formulate but which I felt in my heart, took to showing itself, like people concealed behind portieres, waiting until someone tells them to appear, a criminal desire that roamed around at the bottom of my thoughts: If some accident could happen! There are so many of these little beings who die before birth!

" 'Oh! I did not desire the death of my mistress. Poor girl, I loved her well! But I wished, perhaps, the death of the other before I had seen it.

"It was born. I had a household in my bachelor's quarters, a false household with a child—a horrible thing. It resembled all infants. I could scarcely love it. Fathers, you see, do not love until later. They have not the instinctive, surpassing love and tenderness of mothers; their affection is awakened little by little, as their mind is drawn toward their children each day in the bonds which unite living beings together.

" 'A year passed away. I now fled from my too-small dwelling, where linen and blankets and stockings, the size of a pair of gloves, were dragging around, and a thousand things of this kind were left upon the furniture, especially upon the arm of the easy chair. I fled particularly to escape from hearing him cry, for he cried at all times, when he was changed, when he was washed, when one touched him, when he was put to bed, when he was taken up, without ceasing.

" 'I had made some acquaintances and had met her who was to become your mother. I came to love her, and a desire to marry her was awakened in me. I paid her my court; I asked her in marriage; she accepted me.

" 'And now I found myself in this predicament: To marry, having a child, this young girl whom I adored—or to tell the truth and renounce her and happiness, the future, everything, for her parents, rigid and scrupulous people, would never give her to me if they knew.

" 'I passed one month of horrible anguish, of moral torture, a month where a thousand thoughts frightened and haunted me, and I felt growing in me a hate against my son, against this little piece of living, crying flesh who barred my way, ruined my life and condemned me to an existence without hope, those vague hopes so charming to youth.

" 'At this time the mother of my companion fell ill, and I remained alone with the infant. It was in December. It was terribly cold. What a night! My mistress had gone. I had dined in my narrow dining room and then entered softly into the chamber where the little one slept.

" 'I seated myself in an armchair before the fire. The wind sighed, making the glass crack, a wind dry with frost, and I saw out of the window the stars scintillating with that bright light which they have on frosty nights.

" 'Then the besetting thought which had haunted me for a month entered my head again. Whenever I remained still it descended upon me, entered into me and roamed about. It gnawed me as fixed ideas gnaw, as a cancer gnaws into the flesh. It was there, in my head, in my heart, in my entire body, it seemed to me, and it devoured me as if it had been a beast. I tried to drive it, push it away, to open my thoughts to other things, to new hopes, as one opens a window to the fresh air of morning to drive out the vitiated air of night, but I could not, even for a second, get it out of my brain. I know not how to express this torture. It gnawed at my soul, and I felt with a frightful grief, a physical and moral grief, each succeeding pang.

" 'My existence was ended! How could I ever get out of the situation? How draw away or how confess?

" 'And I loved her who was to become your mother with a mad passion which this insurmountable obstacle further exaggerated.

" 'A terrible anger grew in me which tightened my throat, an anger which approached madness—mania! Surely I was mad that night!

" 'The child slept. I arose and went and looked at him sleeping. There he was, this abortion, this larva, this nothing, who condemned me to a life of unhappiness without appeal.

" 'He slept, his mouth open, buried in the bedclothes in a cradle near my bed, where I could not sleep myself!

" 'How did I accomplish what I did? Do I know? What force drove me; what power of malice possessed me? Oh! The temptation of the crime came to me without announcing itself. I only recall that my heart was beating furiously. It beat so strongly that I heard it as one hears the blows of a hammer behind a partition wall. I only recall that! My heart beating! In my head there was a strange confusion, a tumult, a derangement of reason, of complete cold-bloodedness. I was in one of those frightful hours of hallucination when a man is no longer conscious of his acts, either in direction or will.

" 'I gently raised the covers which concealed the body of my child; I threw them upon the foot of the cradle and looked at him all bare. He did not wake. Then I went toward the window very gently and opened it.

" 'A breath of cold air came in like an assassin, so cold that I drew back before it. The two candles flickered. And I remained there near the window for a long time, not daring to turn and see what was behind me and feeling ever upon my forehead, my cheeks, my hands, the fatal air that was constantly gliding in. This lasted a long time.

" 'I did not reflect. I was thinking of nothing. Suddenly a little cough made a frightful shiver pass through me from head to foot, a shiver which I can feel at this moment at the roots of my hair. With a startled movement I closed brusquely the two sides of the window and, turning, hastened to the cradle.

" 'He still slept, his mouth open, all bare. I touched his limbs; they were icy, and I covered him again. My heart seemed suddenly to break and to be filled with pity and tenderness for this poor little innocent being whom I had wished to kill. I kissed him over and over again upon his fine hair. Then I returned and seated myself before the fire.

" 'I thought with horror of what I had done and asked myself whence came these tempests of the soul when man loses all notion of things, all control of himself, and moves in a sort of fearful drunkenness, without knowing what he does, without knowing where he goes, like a ship in a hurricane.

"'The child coughed once again, and I felt torn to the heart. If he should die! My God, my God! What would become of me?

"'I got up and went to look at him; and with a candle in my hand I bent over him. Seeing him breathe tranquilly, I was reassured, even when he coughed for the third time. But I felt such a shock and made such a movement to arrest it (as one does at the sight of some frightful thing) that I let the candle fall.

"'And, straightening myself after having picked it up, I perceived that my temples were moistened with sweat, with a sweat hot and cold at the same time, which produced an agony of the soul like that of some frightful, moral suffering or some unnamable torture, burning like fire and cold as ice, piercing the bones and the skin of my head.

"'I remained bending over my son until daybreak, calming myself when he was quiet and transfixed by an abominable grief when a feeble cough came from his mouth.

"'He awoke with red eyes, an inflamed throat and difficult breathing. When my mistress entered the house and saw him we sent immediately for a physician. He came in an hour and asked, after having examined him:

"'"Has he taken cold?"

"'I began to tremble, as very old people tremble, and stammered:

"'"No, I think not." Then I asked:

"'"What is the matter? Is it anything grave?"

"'He answered:

"'"I cannot say yet. I will return this evening."

"'He returned in the evening. My son had passed nearly the whole day in an invincible sleepiness, coughing from time to time. A congestion of the lungs now showed itself.

"'This lasted ten days. I cannot express what I suffered during those interminable hours which separate the morning from evening and the evening from the morning.

"'He died. . . .

"'And since—since that moment I have not passed an hour, no, not an hour, without that atrocious, cutting memory, a memory which gnaws, which tortures and rends the mind and stirs in me like a writhing beast chained up in the bottom of my soul.

"'Oh! If I could have become mad!'"

M. Poirel de la Voulte put up his glasses, a movement which was usual with him when he had finished reading a contract, and the three heirs of the dead man looked at each other without saying a word, pale and immovable. At the end of a minute the notary said:

"This must be destroyed."

The two others lowered their heads in sign of assent. He lighted a candle, separated carefully the pages which contained the dangerous confession from the pages which contained the disposition of the money, then he presented them to the flame and threw them into the fireplace.

And they watched the white leaves as they were consumed. Soon they were nothing more than a lot of little black heaps. And as they still perceived some letters which were legible on the paper, the daughter crushed it with the end of her foot, mixing it with the old ashes.

Then they all three remained quiet for some time, looking at it as if they feared that the charred secret might fly away up the chimney.

ON CATS

Cape of Antibes.

SEATED ON A BENCH the other day at my door in the full sunlight, with a cluster of anemones in flower before me, I read a book recently published, an honest book, something uncommon and charming, *The Cooper*, by George Duval. A large white cat that belonged to the gardener jumped upon my lap and by the shock closed the book, which I placed at my side in order to caress the animal.

The weather was warm; a faint, suggestive odor of new flowers was in the air, and at times came little cool breezes from the great white summits that I could see in the distance. But the sun was hot and sharp, and the day was one of those that stir the earth, make it alive, break open the seed in order to animate the sleeping germs and cleave the buds so that the young leaves may spring forth. The cat rolled itself on my knees, lying on its back, its paws in the air, with claws protruding, then receding. The little creature showed its pointed teeth beneath its lips, and its green eyes gleamed in the half-closed slit of its eyelids. I caressed and rubbed the soft, nervous animal, supple as a piece of silk, smooth, warm, delicious, dangerous. She purred with satisfaction, yet was quite ready to scratch, for a cat loves to scratch as well as to be petted. She held out her neck and rolled again, and when I took my hand from her she raised herself and pushed her head against my lifted hand.

I made her nervous, and she made me nervous also, for although I like cats in a certain way, I detest them at the same time—those animals so charming and so treacherous. It gives me pleasure to fondle them, to rub under my hand their silky fur that sometimes crackles, to feel their warmth through this fine and exquisite covering. Nothing is softer, nothing gives to the skin a sensation more delicate, more refined, more rare, than the warm, living coat of a cat. But this living coat also communicates to me, through the ends of my fingers, a strange and ferocious desire to strangle the animal I am caressing. I feel in her the desire she has to bite and scratch me. I feel it, that same desire, as if it were an electric current communicated from her to me. I run my fingers through the soft fur, and the current passes through my nerves from my finger tips to my heart, even to my brain; it tingles throughout my being and causes me to shut my teeth hard.

And if the animal begins to bite and scratch me, I seize her by the neck; I give her a turn and throw her far from me, as I would throw a stone from a sling, so quickly and so brutally that she never has time to revenge herself.

I remember that when I was a child I loved cats, yet I had even then that strange desire to strangle them with my little hands, and one day at the end of the garden, at the beginning of the wood, I perceived suddenly something gray rolling in the high grass. I went to see what it was and found a cat caught in a snare, strangling, suffocating, dying. It rolled, tore up the ground with its claws, bounded, fell inert, then began again, and its hoarse, rapid breathing made a noise like a pump, a frightful noise which I hear yet. I could have taken a spade and cut the snare; I could have gone to find the servant or tell my father. No, I did not move, and with beating heart I watched it die with a trembling and cruel joy. It was a cat! If it had been a dog I would rather have cut the copper wire with my teeth than let it suffer a second more. When the cat was quite dead, but yet warm, I went to feel of it and pull its tail!

These little creatures are delicious, notwithstanding, delicious above all, because in caressing them while they are rubbing against our skin, purring and rolling on us, looking at us with their yellow eyes which seem never to see us, we realize the insecurity of their tenderness, the perfidious selfishness of their pleasure.

Some women also give us that sensation—women who are charming, tender, with clear yet false eyes, who have chosen us entirely for their gratification. Near them, when they open their arms and offer their lips, when a man folds them to his heart with bounding pulses, when he tastes the joy of their delicate caress, he realizes well that he holds a perfidious, tricky cat, with claws and fangs, an enemy in love who will bite him when she is tired of kisses.

Many of the poets have loved cats. Baudelaire has sung to them divinely. I had one day the strange sensation of having inhabited the enchanted palace of the white cat, a magic castle where reigned one of those undulant, mysterious, troubling animals, the only one, perhaps, of all living creatures that one never hears walk.

This adventure occurred last year on this same shore of the Mediterranean. At Nice there was atrocious heat, and I asked myself as to whether there was not, somewhere in the mountains above us, a fresh valley where one might find a breath of fresh air.

Thorence was recommended to me, and I wished to see it immediately. To get there I had first to go to Grasse, the town of perfumes, concerning which I shall write someday and tell how the essences and quintessences of flowers are manufactured there, costing up to two thousand francs the liter. I passed the night in an old hotel of the town, a poor kind of inn, where the quality of the food was as doubtful as the cleanliness of the rooms. I went on my way in the morning.

The road went straight up into the mountains, following the deep ravines, which were overshadowed by sterile peaks, pointed and savage. I thought that my advisers had recommended to me a very extraordinary kind of summer excursion, and I was almost on the point of returning to Nice the same day, when I saw suddenly before me, on a mountain which appeared to close the entrance to the entire valley, an immense and picturesque ruined castle, showing towers and broken walls, of a strange architecture, in profile against the sky. It proved to be an ancient castle that had belonged to the Templars, who in bygone days had governed this country of Thorence.

I made a detour of this mountain and suddenly discovered a long, green valley, fresh and reposeful. Upon its level were meadows, running waters and willows, and on its sides grew tall pine trees. In front of the ruins, on the other side of the valley but standing lower, was an inhabited castle, called the Castle of the Four Towers, which was built about the year 1530. One could not see any trace of the Renaissance period, however. It was a strong and massive square structure, apparently possessing tremendous powers of resistance, and it was supported by four defensive towers, as its name would indicate.

I had a letter of introduction to the owner of this manor, who would not permit me to go to the hotel. The whole valley is one of the most charming spots in summer that one could dream of. I wandered about there until evening, and after dinner I went to the apartment that had been reserved for me. I first passed through a sort of sitting room, the walls of which were covered by old Cordova leather; then I went through another room, where by the light of my candle I noticed rapidly in passing several old portraits of ladies—those paintings of which Théophile Gautier has written.

I entered the room where my bed was and looked around me. The walls were hung with antique tapestries, where one saw rose-colored donjons in blue landscapes and great fantastic birds sitting under foliage of precious stones! My dressing room was in one of the towers. The windows, wide on the inside and narrowed to a mere slit on the outside, going through the entire thickness of the walls, were, in reality, nothing but loopholes through which one might kill an approaching enemy.

I shut my door, went to bed and slept. Presently I dreamed; usually one dreams a little of something that has passed during the day. I seemed to be traveling; I entered an inn, where I saw at a table before the fire a servant in complete livery and a mason—a strange association which did not astonish me. These people spoke of Victor Hugo, who had just died, and I took part in their conversation. At last I went to bed in a room, the door of which I could not shut, and suddenly I saw the servant and the mason, armed with sabers, coming softly toward my bed.

I awoke at once, and a few moments passed before I could recollect where I was. Then I recalled quickly my arrival of the day before at Thorence, the occurrences of the evening and my pleasant reception by the owner. I was just about to close my eyes when I saw distinctly in the darkness in the middle of my room, at about the height of a man's head, two fiery eyes watching me.

I seized a match, and while striking it I heard a noise, a light, soft noise, like the sound of a wet rag thrown on the floor, but after I had lighted the candle I saw nothing but a tall table in the middle of the room. I rose, went through both apartments, looked under the bed and into the closets and found nothing. I thought then that perhaps I had continued dreaming after I was awake, and so I went to sleep again but not without trouble.

I dreamed again. This time I traveled once more, but in the Orient, in the country that I love. I arrived at the house of a Turk, who lived in the middle of a desert. He was a superb Turk—not an Arab, but a Turk, fat, friendly and charming. He was dressed in Turkish attire, with a turban on his head and a whole shopful of silk on his back—a real Turk of the Théâtre Français, who made me compliments while offering me sweetmeats, sitting on a voluptuous divan.

Then a little black boy took me to a room—all my dreams ended in this fashion in those days! It was a perfumed room decorated in sky blue, with skins of wild beasts on the floor, and before the fire—the idea of fire pursued me even in the desert—on a low chair, was a woman, lightly clothed, who was waiting on me. She was of the purest oriental type, with stars tattooed on her cheeks and forehead and chin; she had immense eyes, a beautiful form and slightly brown skin, a warm and exciting skin.

She looked at me, and I thought: "This is what I understand to be the true meaning of the word hospitality. In our stupid and prudish northern countries, with their hateful mawkishness of ideas and silly notions of morality, a man would never receive a stranger in this fashion."

I went up to the woman and spoke to her, but she replied only by signs, not knowing a word of my language, which the Turk, her master, understood so well. All the happier that she would be silent, I took her by the hand and led her toward my couch, where I placed myself by her side. . . .

But one always awakens at those moments! So I opened my eyes and was not greatly surprised to feel beneath my hand something soft and warm, which I caressed lovingly. Then, my mind clearing, I recognized that it was a cat, a big cat rolled up against my cheek, sleeping there with confidence. I left it there and composed myself to sleep once more. When daylight appeared he was gone, and I really thought I had dreamed he had been with me, for I could not understand how he could have come in and gone out, as my door was locked.

When I related my dream and my adventure to my agreeable host (not the whole of it!) he began to laugh and said: "He came in through his own door," and, raising a curtain, he showed me a little round hole in the wall. I learned then that the old habitations of this country have long narrow runways through the walls, which go from the cellar to the garret, from the servants' rooms to the rooms of the *seigneur*, and these passages render the cat king and master of the interior of the house. He goes where it pleases him, visits his domain at his pleasure, sleeps in all the beds, sees all, hears all, knows all the secrets, all the habits, all the shames of the house. Everywhere he is at home, the animal that moves without noise, the silent prowler, the nocturnal rover of the hollowed walls. And I thought of Baudelaire.

ROOM NO. 11

"What! You do not know why President Amandon was removed?"

"No, not at all."

"As far as he is concerned, it would never have been known. But it is a story of the strangest sort."

"Relate it to me."

"You remember Madame Amandon, that pretty brunette, thin, and so distinguished and pretty that she was called Madame Marguerite in all Perthuis-le-Long?"

"Yes, perfectly."

"Very well, then. You recall also how much she was respected and considered and better loved than anyone in the town; she knew how to receive, how to organize a festival or a charity fair, how to find money for the poor and how to please the young people in a thousand ways.

"She was very elegant and very coquettish, nevertheless, but in a Platonic fashion, and with the charming elegance of the provinces, for she was a provincial, this pretty little woman, an exquisite provincial.

"The poets and writers who are all Parisian sing to us of the Parisian woman and of her charm because they know only her, but I declare here that the provincial is worth a hundred times more when she is of superior quality.

"The provincial has an attraction all her own; she is more discreet than the Parisian, more humble, promising nothing and giving much, while the Parisian, for the most part, promises much and gives nothing but deshabille.

"The Parisian is a triumph in the elegant effrontery of falseness; the provincial, an example of the modesty of truth.

"Yet the provincial, with her air of homely alertness, her deceitful, schoolgirl candor, her smile which means nothing and her good little passions, direct and tenacious, is capable of a thousand times more deceit, artifice and feminine invention than all the Parisians together for gratifying her own tastes or vices, and that without awakening suspicion or scandal or gossip in the little town which watches her with all its eyes from all its windows.

"Madame Amandon was a type of this rare race, but charming. Never had anyone suspected her; never had anyone thought that her life was not as limpid as her look, a sly look, transparent and warm, but seemingly so honest —you should have seen it!

"Then she had admirable tact, a marvelous ingenuity and power of invention and unbelievable simplicty.

"She picked all her lovers from the army and kept them three years, the time of their sojourn in the garrison. In short, she not only had love; she had sense.

"When some new regiment arrived at Perthuis-le-Long she carefully observed all the officers between thirty and forty years of age—for before thirty one is not discreet, and after forty one is often feeble.

"Oh! She knew the list of officers as well as the colonel. She knew all, all the habits, manners, instruction, education, physical qualities, the power of resistance to fatigue, the character, whether patient or violent, the fortune and the tendency to closeness or prodigality of each of them. Then she made her choice. She gave the preference to men of calm allurement, like herself, but they must be handsome. She also wished them to have had no previous entanglements, any passion having the power to leave traces, or that had made any trouble. Because the man whose loves are mentioned is never a very discreet man.

"After having decided upon the one she would love for the three years of his regulation sojourn, it only remained to throw down the gauntlet.

"While some women would find themselves embarrassed, would have taken ordinary means, following the way of others, having court paid them in marked-off stages of conquest and resistance, allowing her fingers to be kissed one day, her wrist the next, her cheek the following, then the lips, then the rest, she had a method more prompt, more discreet and more sure. She gave a ball.

"The chosen officer was invited to dance with the mistress of the house. Then in waltzing, led on by the rapid movement, bewildered by the intoxication of the dance, she would throw herself against him, as if giving herself, and hold his hand with a nervous, continued pressure.

"If he did not comprehend he was only a fool, and she passed on to the next, classed as number two, on the list of her desires.

"If he comprehended the thing was done, without fuss, without compromising gallantries, without numerous visits.

"What could be more simple or more practical?

"How women might make use of a process similar to this to make us understand their pleasure! How much it would suppress difficulties, hesitations and trouble from misunderstanding! How often we pass by, without knowing it, a possible happiness, without suspecting it, because we are unable to penetrate the mystery of thought, the secret abandon of the will, the mute appeal of the flesh, the unknown soul of a woman whose mouth preserves silence, whose eye is impenetrable and clear.

"When the chosen one comprehended he asked for a rendezvous. But she always made him wait a month or six weeks in order to watch and be sure that he had no dangerous faults.

"During this time he was racking his brain to think of some place where they could meet without peril and imagining combinations difficult and unsafe.

"Then at some official feast she would say to him in a low voice:

"'Come Tuesday evening at nine o'clock to the Golden Horse Hotel near the ramparts, on the Vouziers road, and ask for Mademoiselle Clarisse. I shall be waiting for you. And be sure to be in civil dress.'

"For eight years she had, in fact, rented this furnished room by the year in this obscure inn. It was an idea of her first lover which she found practical, and after the man departed she kept the nest.

"Oh, it was a mediocre nest: four walls covered with gray paper adorned with blue flowers, a pine bedstead under muslin curtains, an armchair bought at her order by the innkeeper's wife, two chairs and some necessary articles for the toilet—what more was needed?

"Upon the walls were three large photographs. Three colonels on horseback, the colonels of her lovers! Why not? It would not do to preserve the true likeness, the exact likeness, but she could perhaps keep some souvenirs by proxy.

"And she had never been recognized by anyone in all these visits to the Golden Horse, you ask?

"Never, by anyone!

"The means she employed were admirable and simple. She had thought out and organized some charity reunions and religious meetings, some of which she attended, others she did not. Her husband, knowing her good works, which cost him dear, lived without suspicions. Then when a rendezvous had been agreed upon, she would say at dinner before the servants:

"'I am going this evening to the association for making flannel bandages for old paralytics.'

"And she went out about eight o'clock, went straight to the association, came out again very soon, passed through divers streets and, finding herself alone in some little street, in some somber corner without a light, she would take off her hat, replace it by a maid's cap which she carried under her mantle, fold a kerchief after the same fashion and tie it over her shoulders, carrying her hat and the garment she had worn in a napkin; she would go trotting along, full of courage, the hips uncovered, like a good little maid that had been sent upon some errand, and sometimes she would even run, as if she were in a great hurry.

"Who could have recognized in this trim servant the lively wife of President Amandon?

"She would arrive at the Golden Horse, go up to her room, of which she had the key, and the big proprietor, Master Trouveau, seeing her pass his desk, would murmur:

"'There is Mademoiselle Clarisse coming to meet some lover.'

"He had indeed guessed something, the rogue, but did not try to learn more, and he would certainly have been much surprised to find that his client was Madame Amandon, or Madame Marguerite, as she was called in Perthuis-le-Long. And this is how the horrible discovery took place.

"Never had Mademoiselle Clarisse come to her meeting place two evenings in succession, never, being too nice and too prudent for that. And Master Trouveau knew this well, since not once in eight years had he seen her come the next day after a visit. Often, therefore, in days of need he had disposed of her room for a night.

"Now sometime last summer Monsieur Amandon, the trustful president, absented himself from home for a week. It was in July. Madame was ardently in love, and as there was no fear of being surprised, she asked her lover, the handsome Commander Varangelles, one Tuesday evening on leaving him if he wished her to return the next day.

"He replied: 'With all my heart!'

"And it was agreed that they should return at the usual hour on Wednesday. She said to him in a low tone:

"'If you arrive first, my dear, you can wait for me in bed.'

"Then they embraced and separated. The next day, as Master Trouveau sat reading the Perthuis *Tablet,* the Republican organ of the town, he cried out to his wife who was plucking a fowl in the courtyard:

"'Here! The cholera has broken out in the country. There was a man died yesterday of it in Vauvigny.' But he thought no more about it, his inn being full of people and business very good.

"Toward noon a traveler presented himself on foot, a kind of tourist, who ordered a good breakfast, after having drunk two absinthes. And as he was very warm, he absorbed a bottle of wine and two bottles of water at least. Then he took his coffee and his little glass, or rather three little glasses. And feeling a little heavy, he asked for a room where he might sleep for an hour or two. There was no longer a vacant room, and the proprietor, after consulting his wife, gave him Mademoiselle Clarisse's.

"The man went in there, and toward five o'clock, as he had not been seen to come out, the landlord went to wake him. What was his astonishment to find him dead!

"The innkeeper descended to find his wife: 'Say,' he whispered to her, 'the tourist I put in number 11, I believe is dead.'

"She raised her arms, crying: 'It's not possible! Lord God! It is the cholera!' Master Trouveau shook his head:

"'I should sooner believe that it was a cerebral congestion, seeing that he is as black as the dregs of wine.'

"But the mistress was frightened and kept repeating:

"'It is not necessary to say; it is not necessary to say that we think it is cholera. Go and make the report and say nothing. They will take him away in the night, and no one will know about it. What is neither seen nor heard perplexes nobody.'

"The man murmured: "Mademoiselle Clarisse was here yesterday; the room will be free this evening.'

"And he found the doctor who made out the certificate, 'From congestion after a copious repast.' Then he made an agreement with the commissioner of police to remove the dead body toward midnight, that there might be no suspicion about the hotel.

"It was scarcely nine o'clock when Madame Amandon went secretly up the staircase of the Golden Horse without being seen by anyone. She reached her room, opened the door and entered. A candle was burning upon the chimney piece. She turned toward the bed. The commander, she thought, was already there and had closed the curtains.

"She said to him: 'One minute, dearie, and I will be there.'

"And she disrobed with a feverish haste, throwing her boots upon the floor and her corset upon the armchair. Then, her black dress and skirts having fallen in a circle around her, she stood in her red silk chemise like a flower that is ready to blossom.

"As the commander said not a word, she asked:

"'Are you asleep, my big fellow?'

"He did not answer, and she began to laugh, murmuring:

"'Wait! He is asleep. It is too funny!'

"She kept on her black silk stockings and, running to the bed, glided in quickly, seizing him full in the arms and kissing him on the lips in order to wake him suddenly. It was the cold dead body of the traveler.

"For one second she remained immovable, too frightened to comprehend anything. But the cold of this inert flesh penetrated her own, giving her an atrocious fright before her mind had time to reflect.

"She made a bound out of the bed, trembling from head to foot; then running to the chimney piece, she seized the candle, returned, and looked! And she perceived a frightful visage that she had never before seen, black, swollen, with eyes closed and a horrible grimace of the jaw.

"She uttered a cry, one of those piercing, interminable cries which women utter in their fright, and, letting the candle fall, she opened the door and fled, unclothed, down the passage, continuing to scream in frightful fashion. A commercial traveler in his socks, who occupied room number 4, came out immediately and received her in his arms.

"He asked, much startled: 'What is the matter, pretty child?'

"She stammered out, terrified: 'Someone has been killed—in—my room!'

"Other guests appeared. The landlord himself ran out.

"And suddenly the commander showed his tall figure at the end of the corridor. When she saw him she threw herself toward him, crying:

"'Save me, save me, Gontran. Someone has been killed in our room.'

"Explanations were difficult. Master Trouveau, however, told the truth and demanded that they release Mademoiselle Clarisse, for whom he vouched with his own head. But the commercial traveler in socks, having examined the dead body, declared that a crime had been committed, and he convinced the other strangers that Mademoiselle Clarisse and her lover should not be allowed to depart.

"They were obliged to await the arrival of the police commissioner, who gave them their liberty, but was not discreet.

"The following month President Amandon received promotion with a new place of residence."

ONE PHASE OF LOVE

THE WALLS OF THE CELL were bare and whitewashed. A narrow, barred window, so high that it could not easily be reached, lighted this little room; the crazy man, seated on a straw chair, looked at us with a fixed eye, vague and haunting. He was thin, with wrinkled cheeks and almost white hair that one would think had grown white in a few months. His clothes seemed too large for his dried-up limbs, his shrunken chest and hollow body. One felt that this man had been ravaged by his thoughts, by a thought, as fruit is by a worm. His madness, his idea, was there in his head, obstinate, harassing, devouring. It was eating his body little by little. It, the Invisible, the Impalpable, the Unseizable, the Immaterial Idea, gnawed his flesh, drank his blood and extinguished his life.

What a mystery, that this man should be killed by a thought! He was an object of fear and pity, this madman! What strange dream, frightful and deadly, could dwell in his forehead to fold such profound and ever-changing wrinkles in it?

The doctor said to me: "He has terrible paroxysms of rage and is one of the most singularly demented people I have ever seen. His madness is of an amorous, erotic kind. He is a sort of necrophile. He has written a journal which shows as plainly as daylight the malady of his mind. His madness is visible, so to speak. If you are interested you may run through this document.

I followed the doctor into his office, and he gave me the journal of this miserable man.

"Read it," he said, "and give me your opinion about it."

Here is what the little book contained:

"Up to the age of thirty-two years I lived tranquilly without love. Life appeared to me very simple, very good and very easy. I was rich. I had a taste for some things but had never felt a passion for anything. It was good to live; I awoke happy each day to do things which it pleased me to do, and I went to bed, satisfied, with calm hope for the next day and a future without care.

"I had had some mistresses without ever having my heart torn by desire or my soul bruised by love after the possession. It is good so to live. It is better to love, but terrible. Still those who love, like everybody else, should find happiness, less than mine, perhaps, for love has come to me in an unbelievable manner.

"Being rich, I collected ancient furniture and antiques. Often I thought of the unknown hands which had touched these things, of the eyes that had admired them and the hearts that had loved them—for one does love such things! I often remained for hours and hours looking at a little watch of the last century. It was so dainty, so pretty with its enamel and gold embossing. And it still went, as on the day when some woman had bought it, delighted in the possession of so fine a jewel. It had not ceased to palpitate, to live its mechanical life, but had ever continued its regular ticktack, although a century had passed. Who then had first carried it upon her breast, in the warmth of the dress—the heart of the watch beating against the heart of the woman? What hand had held it at the ends of its warm fingers, then wiped the enameled shepherds, tarnished a little by the moisture of the skin? What eyes had looked upon this flowered dial, awaiting the hour, the dear hour, the divine hour?

"How I wished to see her, to know her, the woman who had chosen this rare and exquisite object. But she is dead! I am possessed by a desire for women of former times; I love all those who have loved long ago. The story of past tenderness fills my heart with regrets. Oh, beauty! The smiles, the caresses, of youth, the hopes! These things should be eternal!

"How I have wept during whole nights over the women of old, so beautiful, so tender, so sweet, whose lips have opened to the kiss and who are now dead! The kiss is immortal! It goes from lip to lip, from century to century, from age to age! Men take it and give it and die.

"The past attracts me; the present frightens me, because the future is death. I regret all that which is gone; I weep for those who have lived; I wish to stop the hour, to arrest time. But it goes, it goes; it passes away, and it takes me, from second to second, a little of me for the annihilation of tomorrow. And I shall never live again.

"Adieu, women of yesterday, I love you.

"And yet I have nothing to complain of. I have found her whom I awaited, and I have tasted through her of inconceivable pleasure.

"I was roaming around Paris on a sunny morning with joyous foot and happy soul, looking in the shops with the vague interest of a stroller. All at once I saw in a shop of antiquities an Italian piece of furniture of the seventeenth century. It was very beautiful, very rare. I attributed it to a Venetian artist named Vitelli, who belonged to that epoch. Then I passed along.

"Why did the remembrance of this piece of furniture follow me with so much force that I went back over my steps? I stopped again before the shop to look at it and felt that it tempted me.

"What a singular thing is temptation! One looks at an object, and little by little it seduces you, troubles you, takes possession of you like the face of a woman. Its charm enters into you, a strange charm which comes from its form, its color and its physiognomy. Already one loves it, wishes it, desires it. A need of possession takes you, a pleasant need at first, because timid, but increasing, becoming violent and irresistible. And the merchants seem to suspect, from the look in the eye, this secret, increasing desire. I bought that piece of furniture and had it carried to my house immediately. I placed it in my room.

"Oh! I pity those who do not know this sweet hobby of the collector with the trinket which he finally buys. He caresses it with his eye and hand as if it were flesh; he returns every moment to it, thinks of it continually, wherever he goes and whatever he may be doing. The thought of it follows him into the street, into the world, everywhere. And when he re-enters his house, before even removing his gloves or his hat, he goes to look at it with the tenderness of a lover.

"Truly, for eight days I adored that piece of furniture. I kept opening its doors and drawers; I handled it with delight and tasted all the intimate joys of possession.

"One evening, in feeling the thickness of a panel, I perceived that there might be a hiding place there. My heart began to beat, and I passed the night in searching out the secret, without being able to discover it.

"I came upon it the next day by forcing a piece of metal into a crevice in the paneling. A shelf slipped, and I saw, exposed upon a lining of black velvet, a marvelous head of hair that had belonged to some woman.

"Yes, a head of hair, an enormous twist of blonde hair, also red, which had been cut off near the skin and tied together with a golden cord.

"I stood there stupefied, trembling and disturbed! An almost insensible perfume, so old that it seemed like the soul of an odor, arose from this mysterious drawer and this most surprising relic.

"I took it gently, almost religiously, and lifted it from its resting place. Immediately it unwound, spreading out its golden billows upon the floor, where it fell, thick and light, supple and brilliant, like the fiery tail of a comet.

"A strange emotion seized me. To whom had this belonged? When? Under what circumstances? Why had it been shut up in this piece of furniture? What adventure, what drama, was connected with this souvenir? Who had cut it off? Some lover on a day of parting? Some husband on a day of vengeance? Or, perhaps, some woman herself, who bore on her brow the look of despair? Was it at the hour of entering the cloister that she had thrown there this fortune of love, as a token left to the world of the living? Was it the hour closing the tomb upon the young and beautiful dead that he who adored her took this diadem of her head, the only thing he could preserve of her, the only living part of her body that would not perish, the only thing that he could still love and caress and kiss in the transport of his grief?

"Was it not strange that this hair should remain there thus when there was no longer any vestige of the body with which she was born?

"It curled about my fingers and touched my skin with a singular caress, the caress of death. I felt myself affected, as if I were going to weep.

"I kept it a long time in my hands, then it seemed to me that it had some effect upon me, as if something of the soul still remained in it. And I laid it upon the velvet again, the velvet blemished by time, then pushed in the drawer, shut the doors of the closet and betook myself to the street to dream.

"I walked straight ahead, full of sadness and full of trouble, of the kind of trouble that remains in the heart after the kiss of love. It seemed to me I had lived in former times and that I had known this woman.

"And Villon's lines came to my lips, bringing with them a sob:

> "*Tell me in what far-off land*
> *The Roman beauty, Flora, lives;*
> *Hipparchia, Thais' cousin, and*
> *All the beauty nature gives;*
> *Echo speak, thy voice awake*
> *Over river, stream, and lake,*
> *Where are beauty's smiles and tears?*
> *And where the snows of other years?*

> "Blanche, as fair as lily's chalice,
>   Singing sweet, with voice serene,
> Bertha Broadfoot, Beatrice, Alice,
>   Ermengarde, Le Mayne's dear queen?
> Where is Joan, the good Lorraine,
> Whom th' English brought to death and fame?
> Where are all, O wisest seers,
> And where the snows of other years?

"When I returned to my house I had a strange desire to see my strange treasure again. I took it up and felt it, and in touching it a long shiver ran through my body.

"For some days, however, I remained in my ordinary state, although the thought of this hair never left me. Whenever I came in it was my first desire to look at it and handle it. I would turn the key of the secretary with the same trembling that one has in opening the door of his well-beloved, for I had in two hands and in my heart a confused, singular, continued, sensual need of burying my fingers in this charming rivulet of dead hair.

"Then when I had finished caressing it, when I had returned it to its resting place, I always felt that it was there, as if it were something alive, concealed, imprisoned; I felt it and I still desired it; again I had the imperious need of touching it, of feeling it, of enervating myself to the point of weariness from contact with this cold, glistening, irritating, exciting, delicious hair.

"I lived thus a month or two, I know not how long, with this thing possessing me, haunting me. I was happy and tortured, as in the expectation of love, as one is after the avowal which precedes the embrace.

"I would shut myself up alone with it in order to feel it upon my skin, to bury my lips in it, to kill it and bite it. I would roll it around my face, drink it in, drown my eyes in its golden waves and finally see the blonde life beyond it.

"I loved it! Yes, I loved it. I could no longer live away from it or be contented an hour without seeing it. I expected—I expected—what? I know not —her!

"One night I was suddenly awakened with a feeling that I was not alone in my room. I was alone, however. But I could not go to sleep again, and as I was tossing in the fever of insomnia, I rose and went to look at the twist of hair. It appeared to me sweeter than usual and more animated.

"Could the dead return? The kisses with which I had warmed it failed to give me happiness, and I carried it to my bed and lay down with it, pressing it to my lips, as one does a mistress he hopes to enjoy.

"The dead returned! She came! Yes, I saw her, touched her, possessed her as she was when alive in former times, large, blonde, plump, with cool breasts and with hips in form of a lyre. And I followed that divine, undulating line from the throat to the feet, in all the curves of the flesh, with my caresses.

"Yes, I possessed her every day and every night. She had returned, Death,

Death the Beautiful, the Adorable, the Mysterious, the Unknown, and returned every night.

"My happiness was so great that I could not conceal it. I found near her a superhuman delight, and in possessing this Unseizable, Invisible Death, knew a profound, inexplicable joy. No lover ever tasted joys more ardent or more terrible.

"I knew not how to conceal my happiness. I loved this possession so much that I could not bear to leave it. I carried it with me always, everywhere. I walked with it through the city, as if it were my wife, conducting it to the theater and to restaurants as one would a mistress. But they saw it and guessed —they took me and threw me into prison, like a malefactor. They took it away. Oh, misery!"

The manuscript stopped there. And suddenly, as I raised my wondering eyes to the doctor, a frightful cry, a howl of fury and exasperated desire, filled the asylum.

"Listen," said the doctor, "it is necessary to douse that obscene maniac with water five times a day. It is only Sergeant Bertrand, the man who fell in love with the dead."

I stammered, moved with astonishment, horror and pity: "But that hair— did it really exist?"

"The doctor got up, opened a closetful of vials and instruments and threw toward me, across his office, a long thick rope of blonde hair, which flew toward me like a bird of gold.

I trembled at feeling upon my hands its caressing, light touch. And I stood there, my heart beating with disgust and desire, the disgust we have in coming in contact with objects connected with crimes, and the desire like that which comes with the temptation to test some infamous and mysterious thing.

Shrugging his shoulders, the doctor added: "The mind of man is capable of anything."

GOOD REASONS

Solles Villa, July 30, 1883.

My dear Lucy:
There is nothing new. We still live in the parlor, looking out to see the rain fall. One can scarcely go out at all in this frightful weather. We can only play comedies. And how stupid they are, my dear, these pieces in a drawing-room repertoire. So forced, so heavy and gross! The jokes are like bullets from a cannon, always hitting someone. Nothing bright, nothing natural, good natured or elegant. These writers, truly, can know nothing of the world. They are entirely ignorant of how people think or speak among us. I could easily forgive them for scorning our customs or our manners, but I cannot forgive them for being ignorant of them. In order to be pointed they make a play

upon words that a barracks would do well to deride; in order to be gay they serve us the wit they have culled outside the boulevard, in the beer shops of so-called artists, where the same studied paradoxes have been repeated for fifty years.

Yes, we play a comedy. As there are only two women, my husband takes the part of a soubrette, shaving his face for it. You cannot imagine, my dear Lucy, how it changed him! I should not have known him—either by day or night. If he had not allowed his mustache to grow again immediately I believe that I should have become unfaithful, so much did I dislike it.

Truly, a man without a mustache is not a man. I do not care much for a beard; it always gives an appearance of neglect, but the mustache, oh, the mustache is indispensable to a manly physiognomy. No, one never could imagine how useful this little brush of hair upon the lip is to the eye and—to the relation of married people. There have come to me many reflections upon this subject, which I scarcely dare write to you. I could say them to you easily—in a low voice. But it is difficult to find words to express certain things, and some of these, which it would be hard to replace, cut a villainous figure upon paper, so that I can scarcely pen them. Then the subject is so delicate, so difficult, so awkward, that an infinite knowledge is necessary to approach it without danger.

Well, so much the worse if you do not understand. And now, my dear, try to read a little between the lines.

When my husband came to me shaved, I understood for the first time that I could never have a weakness for a strolling player or for a preacher, were he Father Didon himself, the most seductive of all! Then when I found myself alone with him (my husband), it was much worse.

Oh, my dear Lucy, never allow yourself to be embraced by a man without mustaches; his lips have no taste, none whatever! There is no longer that charm, that softness and that—pepper, yes, that pepper of the true kiss. The mustache is the spice of it.

Imagine a piece of dry or even humid parchment applied to your lips. That is the caress of the shaven man. One wants very few of them, assuredly.

But whence comes the seduction of the mustache, you ask me? How do I know? At first it tickles in delicious fashion. One feels it before the mouth, and it makes a charming shiver pass through the whole body, even to the tips of the toes. It is that which caresses, which makes the flesh tremble and start, which gives the nerves that exquisite vibration and causes the utterance of that little "ah!" as if one had received a sudden chill.

And upon the neck! Yes, have you never felt a mustache upon your neck? It intoxicates and makes you shiver, runs down your back and to the ends of your fingers. You turn, shake your shoulders, twist your head; you wish to go and to stay; it is adorable yet irritating! But it is good!

And then again—truly, do I dare say more? A husband who loves you, yes, entirely, knows how to find spots and little corners for concealing kisses, little corners one would scarcely dream of alone. Well, without a mustache these kisses lose much of their zest, without saying that they are unbecoming! Explain that as you will! For my part, here is the reason I find for it. A lip without mustaches is bare, like a body without clothes, and it is necessary to have clothes, very few if you wish, but still some!

The Creator (I dare not use any other word in speaking of these things), the Creator saw the need of veiling the nooks of our flesh where love is concealed. A shaven mouth appears to me to resemble a forest, cut down, which sheltered a fountain where one came to drink and sleep.

This recalls to me the saying of a political man, which has been in my head for three months now. My husband, who reads the newspapers, read a very singular thing to me one evening by our minister of agriculture, who was then called M. Meline. Is there another one by this time? I am sure I do not know.

I was not listening, but this name, Meline, struck me. It recalled, I know not why, *Scenes of Bohemian Life*. I believed at once that he lived with a *grisette*. Only certain scraps of this piece entered my head. But M. Meline made to the inhabitants of Amiens, I believe, this statement, the meaning of which I have sought until now: "There is no patriotism without agriculture!" Well, this means, I have found out recently and now declare to you in my turn, that there is no love without a mustache. If one should tell him that it would seem strange, would it not?

There is no love without a mustache!

"There is no patriotism without agriculture," asserts M. Meline; he is right, this minister; I know it now!

From another point of view the mustache is essential. It determines the physiognomy. It gives it a sweet, tender, violent, foolish, rakish or enterprising air! The bearded man, really bearded, he who carries all his hair (oh! villainous word) upon his cheeks, never has any delicacy of expression because his features are concealed. And the form of the jaw and the chin show many things to him who can see.

In a mustache, a man preserves at the same time his attraction and his finesse.

And of what varied appearance they are, these mustaches! Some are curved, curled and coquettish. These seem to love women above all things!

Some are pointed, sharp as a needle, wicked. These have a preference for wine, horses and fights.

Some are enormous, drooping, frightful. These great ones generally conceal an excellent character, a goodness that approaches weakness and a gentleness that borders on timidity.

And then, above all else, why I adore a mustache is because it is French. It has descended to us from our fathers, the Gauls, and has continued as a sign of our national character.

It is romantic, gallant and brave. It dips itself daintily in wine and knows how to laugh with elegance, while large, bearded jaws are heavy in all that they do.

Wait! I recall something which made me weep bitter tears and which also made me love a mustache upon a man's lip, as I now plainly see.

It was during the war, when I was at home in Papa's house. I was a young girl then. One day there was a battle near the house. Since morning I had heard cannons and guns and, in the evening, a German colonel entered our house and installed himself there. He went away the next day. They came to tell my father that there had been many deaths on the field. He went to find them and bring them home, in order to bury them together. They laid them all along the avenue of pines on both sides from the stretcher on which they brought them. And as they commenced to smell badly, they threw some earth on the bodies to await the digging of the great ditch. In this way only their heads were to be seen, which seemed to come up out of the soil, yellow as the soil itself, with their eyes closed.

I wished to see them, but when I perceived these two lines of frightful faces I thought it would make me ill. I began to examine them, however, one by one, seeking to find out to what nation they belonged. Their uniforms were buried, concealed by the earth, but immediately, yes, immediately, my dear, I recognized them as Frenchmen by their mustaches!

Some had been shaved the day of the battle, as if wishing to be attractive to the last moment! Their beard, nevertheless, had grown a little, for you know it grows a little even after death. Others seemed to have gone a week without shaving, but all wore the French mustache, distinctly the proud mustache which seemed to say: "Do not confound me with my bearded friend, little one, I am your brother."

And I wept. Oh, I wept more than if I had not thus recognized them, the poor dead men!

I did wrong to tell you this story. Here I am now, sad and incapable of chatting any more. Adieu, then, my dear Lucy; I embrace you with all my heart. Long live the mustache!

JEANNE.

Submitted to GUY DE MAUPASSANT.

A FAIR EXCHANGE

M. BONTRAM, the celebrated Parisian advocate who for the last ten years had obtained many separations between badly matched husbands and wives, opened the door of his office and stood back to allow a new client to enter.

He was a large red man, with close blond whiskers, a corpulent man, full-blooded and vigorous. He bowed.

"Take a seat," said the advocate.

The client was seated and, after some hemming, said:

"I came to ask you, sir, to plead a divorce case for me."

"Speak, sir," said the advocate. "I am listening."

"I am, sir, an old notary."

"Already!"

"Yes, already. I am thirty-seven years of age."

"Continue."

"Sir, I have made an unfortunate marriage, very unfortunate."

"You are not the only one."

"I know it, and I pity the others. But my case is entirely different, and my complaint against my wife is of a very particular nature. I will commence at the marriage rite. I was married in strange fashion. Do you believe in dangerous ideas?"

"What do you mean by that?"

"Do you believe that certain ideas are as dangerous for the mind as poison is to the body?"

"Well, yes, perhaps."

"It is certain. There are ideas which enter into us, corrode us, and kill us or render us mad if we do not know how to resist them. They are a sort of poison to the soul. If we have the misfortune to allow one of these thoughts to glide in upon us, if we do not perceive at the beginning that it is an invader, a mistress, a tyrant, then it will extend itself hour by hour and day by day, will keep returning and finally install itself, driving out all ordinary occupation of our minds, absorbing our attention, changing our views and our judgment until we are lost.

"That is what happened to me, sir. As I have told you, I am a notary at Rouen, not poor but in straitened circumstances, full of care, forced to a constant economy, obliged to limit my tastes, yes, in everything! And it is hard, at my age.

"As a notary, I read with great care the advertisements on four pages of the newspapers, the wants, offers, little correspondence, etc., etc., and I had been enabled sometimes by this means to make advantageous marriages for my clients.

"One day, I fell upon this:

"*'A pretty girl, fashionable, well brought up, would marry honorable gentleman and bring him two million five hundred thousand francs, clear. No agencies.'*

"On that very day I dined with two friends, one an attorney and the other the proprietor of a spinning mill. I don't know how the conversation turned to marriages, but I told them, laughing, about the pretty young lady with the two million five hundred thousand francs.

"The spinner said: 'What can these women be thinking of?'

"The attorney affirmed that he had several times seen excellent marriages made under these conditions and gave some details. Then he added, turning to me: 'Why the devil don't you look this up for yourself? Jove! That would drive away care, two million five hundred thousand francs.'

"We all three laughed over it and then spoke of other things. An hour later I returned home.

"It grew cold that night. Besides, I lived in an old house, one of those old houses of the provinces which resemble mushroom beds. In taking hold of the iron balustrade of the staircase a coldness penetrated my arm, and as I put out the other to find the wall, in coming in contact with it, a second shiver enveloped me, joining with the other in my lungs, filling me with pain, with sadness and weakness. And, seized by a sudden remembrance, I murmured: 'Gad! If I only had the two million five hundred thousand!'

"My room was dreary, the room of a bachelor in Rouen, which is taken care of by a maid who is also in charge of the kitchen. You know that kind of room! A great bed without curtains, a wardrobe, a commode and a dressing table, no fire. Some coats were on the chairs, papers on the floor. I began to sing to the air of a concert-hall tune that I frequently heard about that time:

> "*Two millions, two millions*
>   *Are fine,*
> *With five hundred thousand*
> *And woman divine.*

"In fact, I had not yet thought about the woman, but I thought of her then as I was sliding into my bed. I even thought of her so much that I was a long time getting to sleep.

"The next day, on opening my eyes, I remembered that I ought to be at Darnetal at eight o'clock on important business. To do this I must be up at six—and it was cold! Only think of two million five hundred thousand!

"I returned to my study about ten o'clock. In it was the odor of the red-hot stove, of old papers, with the papers of advance proceedings—nothing can equal these—and an odor of clerks—boots, overcoats, hair and skin, skin in winter, too little bathed, and all heated to seventy degrees.

"I breakfasted, as I do every day, on a cutlet and a piece of cheese. Then I put myself to work. For the first time I then began to think seriously of the pretty young lady with the two million five hundred thousand. Who was she? Why not write to her? Why not find out?

"Finally, sir, to abridge, for two weeks this idea haunted me, possessed me and tortured me. All my little cares and troubles, of which I had plenty but had thought little about before this time, began to sting me now like the sharp points of needles, and each of my sufferings made me think still more of the pretty young lady with the two millions.

"I ended by imagining all her history. When one desires a thing, sir, he is very apt to figure it as he hopes it to be. Certainly it was not natural that a young girl of good family, dowered in such a generous fashion, should be seeking a husband by means of the newspapers. Yet it might be that this girl was honorable but unhappy.

"Then at first this fortune of two million five hundred thousand had not struck me as anything fairylike. We are accustomed, we who read the offers of this nature, to propositions of marriage accompanied by six, eight, ten or even twelve millions. The figure of twelve millions is common enough. It pleases. I know well that we can scarcely believe the validity of these promises. They, however, make us enter into the spirit of fantastic numbers, render probable, up to a certain point in our listless credulity, the prodigious sums which they represent and dispose us to consider a dowry of two million five hundred thousand as very possible and right.

"Then a young girl, the natural child of a rich man and a chambermaid, having suddenly inherited from her father, could have learned at the same time of the stain upon her birth, and in order not to have to reveal it to some man whom she might have loved, she might make an appeal to the unknown by this means, which carries in itself a sort of avowal of defect.

"My supposition was stupid. I believed in it, nevertheless. We notaries ought never to read romances, but I read one in this, sir.

"Then I wrote, as a notary, in the name of a client, and I waited. Five days later, toward three o'clock in the afternoon, when I was hard at work in my office, the chief clerk announced:

" 'Mademoiselle Chantefrise.'

" 'Let her come in.'

"There appeared a woman about thirty, a little stout, dark and somewhat embarrassed.

" 'Be seated, mademoiselle.'

"She sat down and murmured: 'It is I, sir.'

" 'But I have not the honor of knowing you.'

" 'The person to whom you wrote.'

" 'About a marriage?'

" 'Yes sir.'

" 'Ah, very well!'

" 'I have come myself because I thought it better to attend to those things in person.'

" 'I am of your opinion, mademoiselle. And so you desire to marry?'

" 'Yes sir.'

" 'You have some family?'

"She hesitated, lowered her eyes and stammered: 'No sir. My mother and my father—are dead.'

"I started. Then I had guessed right—and a lively sympathy was suddenly awakened in my heart for this poor creature. I could not altogether spare her delicacy of feeling and I inquired:

" 'Your fortune is in your own right?'

"She responded this time without hesitating: 'Oh yes, sir!'

"I looked at her with close attention, and truly she did not displease me, only a little hard, harder than I would have liked. She was a beautiful person, a strong person, a masterly woman. And the idea came to me of playing with her a little comedy of sentiment, of becoming her lover, of supplanting my imaginary client, when I was once assured that the dowry was not illusory. I spoke to her of this client whom I depicted as a sad man, very honorable, but a little of an invalid.

"She said vivaciously: 'Oh, sir, I love people to be well.'

" 'But you will see him—only not for three or four days, because he left for England yesterday.'

" 'Oh, how annoying,' she replied.

" 'Well, yes and no. Are you in a hurry to return home?'

" 'Not at all.'

"'Then stay here, and I will attempt to make the time pass pleasantly for you.'

"'You are very amiable, sir.'

"'You are at some hotel?'

"She named the best hotel in Rouen.

"'Well then, Mademoiselle Chantefrise, will you permit your future—notary to offer to take you to dinner this evening?'

"She appeared to hesitate, seemed disturbed and undecided. Then she said: 'Yes sir.'

"'I will be at your hotel at seven o'clock.'

"'Yes sir.'

"'Then until this evening, mademoiselle?'

"'Yes sir.'

"And I conducted her as far as my door.

"At seven o'clock I was at her hotel. She had made a fresh toilet for me and received me in a very coquettish fashion. I took her to dine in a restaurant where I was known and ordered a troublesome menu. An hour later we were very friendly, and she had told me her story.

"She was the daughter of a great lady seduced by a gentleman, and she had been brought up among peasants. She was rich now, having inherited large sums from her father and from her mother, whose name she would never divulge, never. It was useless to ask it of her, useless to beg; she would never tell it. As I cared little to know these things, I asked about her fortune. She spoke about it like a practical woman, sure of herself, sure of her figures, of her titles, of her income, her interest and investments. Her understanding of these matters gave me great confidence in her, and I became gallant, with some reserve, nevertheless. But I showed her clearly that I had a liking for her.

"She affected an excessive refinement, not without grace. I offered her some champagne, and I drank some, which blurred my ideas. I then felt clearly that I was going to be entrapped, and I was afraid, afraid of myself and afraid of her, afraid that she was not moved and that she would not succumb. In order to calm myself I began again to speak to her of her fortune, saying that it would be necessary to precisely understand matters, since my client was a man of affairs.

"She answered with gaiety: 'Oh! I know. I have brought all the proofs.'

"'Here to Rouen?'

"'Yes, to Rouen.'

"'You have them at the hotel?'

"'Yes, I have them all there.'

"'Could you show them to me?'

"'Yes indeed.'

"'This evening?'

"'Yes indeed.'

"That pleased me in every way. I paid the score, and we went back to the hotel. She had, in fact, brought all her certificates. I could not doubt them, for I held them in my hands, felt them and read them. They put such a joy in my heart that I suddenly felt a violent desire to embrace her. I understood this as a chaste desire, the desire of a contented man. And I did embrace her, in fact, once, twice, ten times—so much that—with the aid of the champagne—I succumbed—or rather—no—she succumbed.

"Ah, sir, I had a head after that, and she! She wept like a fountain, begging me not to expose her or she should be lost. I promised all that she wished, and I myself got into a terrible state of mind.

"What was to be done? I had abused my client's confidence. That would not have been so bad if I had had a client for her, but I had none. I was the client, the simple client, the deceived client, and deceived by himself. What a situation! I could let her go, it is true. But the dowry, the handsome dowry, the good dowry, palpable and sure! And then, had I the right to let her go, the poor girl, after having thus surprised her? But what of the disquiet later on? How much security would one have with a woman who thus yielded?

"I passed a terrible night of indecision, tortured by remorse, ravaged by fears, buffeted by every scruple. But in the morning my reason cleared. I dressed myself with care and, as eleven o'clock struck, presented myself at the hotel where she was staying.

"On seeing me she blushed to the eyes. I said to her: 'Mademoiselle Chantefrise, there is only one thing to do to repair our wrong. I ask your hand in marriage.'

"She murmured: 'I give it to you.'

"I married her and all went well for six months. I had given up my office and lived as a stockholder, and truly I had not a reproach, not a single fault to find with my wife.

"Then I noticed that from time to time she made long visits. This happened on a certain day, one week Tuesday, the next week Wednesday. I began to believe myself deceived and I followed her. It was on a Tuesday. She went out on foot about one o'clock into Republic Street, turned to the right, by the street which follows the archiepiscopal palace, and took Great-Bridge Street to the Seine, followed the wharf up to Peter's bridge and crossed the water. From this moment she appeared disturbed, turning around often and looking sharply at all passers.

"As I was dressed like a coal driver, she did not know me. Finally she entered a dock on the left bank. I no longer doubted that her lover would arrive on the one forty-five train.

"I seated myself behind a dray and waited. A blow of the whistle—a crowd of passengers. She advanced, rushed forward, seized in her arms a little girl of three years, whom a large peasant accompanied, and embraced her with passion. Then she turned, perceived another child, younger, either girl or boy it might be, carried by another nurse, threw herself upon it, drew it to her with violence and went along escorted by the two monkeys and the two nurses toward the long, somber, deserted promenade of the Queen's Course.

"I returned home dismayed, distressed in mind, comprehending and still not comprehending, nor daring to guess. When she returned for dinner I threw these words at her:

" 'Whose children are those?'

" 'What children?' she asked.

" 'Those that you waited at the Saint-Sever train for.'

"She gave a great cry and fainted. When she returned to consciousness she confessed to me in a deluge of tears that she had four. Yes sir, two for Tuesday, two girls, and two for Wednesday, two boys.

"And this was—what shame! This was the origin of her fortune. The four fathers! She had amassed her dowry! Now, sir, what do you advise me to do?"

The advocate replied with gravity: "Recognize your children, sir."

THE TOBACCO SHOP

I WENT DOWN to Barviller alone because I saw in the guidebook (I do not remember which one): "A beautiful museum, two Rubens, one Tenier and a Ribera." I thought to myself: "I will see that. Then I will dine at the Hotel Europe, which the guidebook affirms excellent, and return tomorrow."

The museum was closed. They only opened it at the request of travelers. It was opened for my benefit, and I was able to look upon some daubs attributed by a whimsical collector to the first masters of painting.

After that I found myself alone with absolutely nothing to do. I was in a long street of a little unknown town, a kind of artery, through which I wandered, examining some of the poor little shops. I found it was only four o'clock, and I was suddenly seized with that feeling of discouragement which makes simpletons of the most energetic.

What could I do? Great heavens! What was there to do? I would have paid five hundred francs for some distracting idea. Finding myself barren of invention, I simply decided to smoke a good cigar and looked about for a tobacco shop. I soon recognized one by its red lantern and entered it. The saleswoman held out several boxes for me to choose from. Having looked carefully at the cigars, all of which appeared detestable, I turned by chance and glanced at the proprietress.

She was a woman of about forty-five, strong and gray-haired. She had a fat, respectable face, in which I seemed to see something familiar. Could I have known this woman somewhere? No, assuredly not. But it might be that I had seen her somewhere. Yes, that was possible. The face before me must be an acquaintance of my eyes, some old acquaintance lost to sight and, without doubt, changed by being enormously fattened.

I murmured: "Excuse me, madame, for looking at you so closely, but it seems to me that I have seen you before, long ago."

She responded, blushing a little: "It is strange—but I also——"

I exclaimed: "Ah, so it goes!"

She raised both hands in a comical despair, frightened by the sound of the old name. and stammered: "Oh, oh! If anyone should hear you——" Then suddenly she cried out in her turn: "Wait! It is you—George!" Then she looked around in terror to see if anyone were listening. But we were alone, all alone!

"So-it-Goes!" How had I ever recognized her! "So-it-Goes," the poor "So-it-Goes," the thin, the desolate "So-it-Goes," transformed into this fat, tranquil functionary of the government.

"So-it-Goes!" How many memories this name awakened in me: Bougival, "The Frog," Chatou, the Fournaise restaurant, long journeys in a yawl along the steep banks, in short, ten years of my life passed in that corner of the country, upon that delicious part of the river.

There was a band of a dozen of us inhabiting the Galopois house at Chatou, living a queer kind of life, half nude and half tipsy. The customs of canoeists have changed since then. Now these gentlemen wear monocles.

Our band was composed of twenty canoeists, regular and irregular. On certain Sundays there would only be four of them, on others, all. That is to say, some there were there to stay; others came when they had nothing better to do. Five or six of them lived together, after the fashion of men without wives, and among them dwelt "So-it-Goes."

She was a poor, thin girl who limped. This gave her some of the attractions of a grasshopper. She was timid, awkward and unskillful in all that she did. With fear she attached herself to the humblest, the most unnoticed of us, anyone who would keep her a day or a month, according to his means. How she ever came to be among us, nobody knew. Someone had met her one evening at poker dice at a riverside ball and had been led into one of those raffles for wives that were so much the fashion. We invited her to lunch, seeing her seated alone at a little table in the corner. No one could have asked her, but she made a part of our band.

We baptized her "So-it-Goes" (Ça Ira), because she was already complaining of her destiny, of her misfortune and her sorrows. Each Sunday morning they would say to her: "Well, 'So-it-Goes,' how goes it?" And she would always answer: "Not so bad, but we must always hope that it will be better someday."

How this poor, ungraceful, awkward being came to adopt the trade which demands the most grace, tact, cleverness and beauty was a mystery. However, Paris is full of girls of love that are ugly enough to disgust a policeman.

What did she do the other six days of the week? She told us many times that she worked. At what? We were as ignorant of it as we were indifferent to her existence.

After that I nearly lost sight of her. Our group had dispersed little by little, leaving its place to another generation, to whom we also left "Ça Ira." I heard of her in going to breakfast at the Fournaise from time to time.

Our successors, not knowing why we had christened her as we did, believed her name to be oriental and called her Zaïra; then they bestowed her, with all their canoes and some of the canoeists, to the following generation. (A generation of canoeists generally lives three years upon the water, then leaves the Seine to enter the law, medicine or politics.)

Zaïra had now become Zara, and later Zara was modified into Sarah. Then they thought she was an Israelite.

The last ones, those with the monocles, called her simply "the Jewess." Then she disappeared. And behold! I had found her in Barviller, selling tobacco.

I said to her: "Well, how goes it now?"

She answered: "A little better."

I had a curiosity to know the life of this woman. At any other time I would not have cared; today I felt interested, puzzled, attracted. I asked her: "How did you come to get this place?"

"I don't know," she said. "It came to me when I was expecting the least."

"Was it at Chatou that you came upon it?"

"Oh no!"

"Then where?"

"At Paris, in a hotel where I lived."

"Ah, then you had a place in Paris?"

"Yes, I was with Madame Ravelet."

"Who is she, this Madame Ravelet?"

"And you don't know who Madame Ravelet is? Well!"

"No, I do not."

"The dressmaker, the great dressmaker of Rivoli Street."

And then she told me a thousand things of her former life, a thousand things of the secret life of the Parisian woman, the interior workings of a great dressmaking establishment, the life of the young ladies there, their adventures, their ideas, the whole story of the heart of a working girl, that sparrow hawk of the sidewalk who haunts the streets—in the morning in going to the shop, at midday strolling along bareheaded after her luncheon, and in the evening when she comes out to show herself.

Happy to speak of other days, she said: "You don't know what a mob it is, or what raids they make. We used to tell each other about them every day. Truly one can make a fool of a man, you know.

"The first tale I have to tell is on the subject of an umbrella. I had an old alpaca one, an umbrella to be ashamed of. As I was closing it upon my arrival one day there was the tall Louise before me, saying:

"'What! You dare to go out with that?'

"'But I have no other, and at this moment funds are low.'

"They were always low, funds were.

"She said to me: 'Go and get one at the Madeleine.'

"I was astonished. She continued: 'That is where we all get ours; one can get all one wants there.' And then she explained the thing to me. It was very simple.

"I went with Irma to the Madeleine. We found the sexton and explained to him how we had forgotten an umbrella the week before. He asked us to describe the handle, and I gave him a description of a handle with an agate apple on it. He took us into a room where there were more than fifty lost umbrellas; we looked them all over, but I did not find mine; I had, however, chosen a beauty, a perfect beauty with a carved ivory handle. A few days after Louise went and reclaimed it. She described it before seeing it, and he gave it to her without a suspicion.

"In order to do that sort of thing one has to dress very stylish."

And she laughed, opening the cover of a large box of tobacco and letting it fall again upon its hinges. She continued:

"Oh, we each had our turn at it and we did have some queer experiences. There were five of us living in the studio, four ordinaries and one very pretty, Irma, the beautiful Irma. She was very distinguished, as she had a lover in the Cabinet Council, but that did not hinder her from making him support her prettily. And one winter she said to us: 'You don't know what a way I have thought of to make a good thing.' And she told us her idea.

"You know, Irma had such a face to trouble the heads of all men, and such a figure! And hips that would make the water come in your mouth. So she thought of a way for each of us to make a hundred francs to buy some rings with, and she arranged the thing like this:

"You must know that I was not rich at that moment, any more than the others, and we were scarcely making a hundred francs in a month at the shop, certainly not more. We wished to know her plan. We each had two or three lovers who gave a little, but not much, and it sometimes happened that in the noonday walk we nabbed a gentleman who would come the next day; we would keep him for two weeks and then give him up. Such men as that never give very much. Those at Chatou—that was for pleasure. Oh, if you only knew some of the sly things we did; truly you would die from laughter. So when Irma proposed to us to make a hundred francs we were all on fire. It is very bad, what I am going to tell you, but that makes no difference; you know what life is, and when one has stayed four years at Chatou——

"Well, she said to us: 'At the Opera Ball we are going to get hold of some of the best men in Paris, the most distinguished and the richest. I know who they are.'

"We did not believe it at first, because such men are not made for dressmakers; for Irma, yes, but not for us. Oh, she was so stylish, that Irma! Do you know, we had the habit at the studio of saying that if the emperor had seen her he would certainly have married her.

"She made us dress ourselves in our best and said to us: 'You, none of you, will enter the ballroom but will stay outside in cabs in the neighboring streets. A gentleman will come and get into your carriage. When he has entered you will embrace him as prettily as you can, and then you will utter a great cry to show that you have made a mistake and that you expected someone else. This will excite the pigeon to take the place of another, and he will try to remain by force; you will resist; you will give him a hundred blows to drive him away—and then—you will go to supper with him—and you ought to get good damages.'

"You do not quite understand it yet, do you? Well, here is what she did, the rogue!

"She made all four of us get into carriages, four carriages of the circle, that were just as they should be, then she placed us in streets near the opera. She went to the ball alone. As she knew by name the most conspicuous men in Paris, because our establishment catered to their wives, she chose them for her intrigue. She could talk with them about anything, for she had a mind also. When she saw that one was half drunk she threw off her mask, and he was taken as in a net. He wished to take her away immediately, but she preferred to make an appointment with him in half an hour in a carriage opposite number 20 Taitbout Street. It was I who was in that carriage! I was well wrapped up and my face veiled. Suddenly a gentleman put his head in the door and asked: 'Is it you?'

"And I answered in a low tone: 'Yes, it is I; get in quickly.'

"He did so, and I seized him in my arms and embraced him, until his breath was almost gone; then I said:

" 'Oh! I am so happy! I am so happy!'

"But suddenly I cried out: 'But it is not you! Oh dear! Oh dear!' And I began to weep.

"You can judge whether the man was embarrassed or not! He tried to console me; he excused himself and protested that he was also mistaken. As for me, I kept on weeping, but less and less, and I uttered great sighs. Then he said very sweet things to me.

"He was a man that was a man; and it pleased him to see me weeping less and less. To put a short thread in the needle, he proposed to take me to supper. I refused; I tried to leap from the carriage; he held me by taking me around the waist; then he embraced me, as I had him upon his entrance.

"And then—and then—we had supper—you understand—and he gave me—think of it—he gave me five hundred francs! Would you believe that there are such generous men?

"And the thing was a success for everybody. Louise, who received the least, got two hundred francs. But, you know, Louise—truly she was very thin!"

The woman of the tobacco shop went on thus, emptying her heart of all the memories amassed in the long time that she had been shut up with her official duties. The past, poor and queer though it was, moved her soul. She regretted this gallant, Bohemian life of the Parisian sidewalk, made up of privations and paid-for caresses, of laughter and misery and moments of stratagem and true love.

I said to her: "But how did you get into the tobacco business?"

She smiled, saying: "Oh! That is a story too. You must know that I had for a neighbor in my apartment, exactly opposite my door, a student—but one of those students who amounts to nothing. This one lived at the café from morning until evening; he loved billiards, as I have never seen anyone love the game.

"When I was alone we sometimes passed the evening together. It is by him that I had Roger."

"Who is Roger?"

"My son."

"Ah!"

"He—he gave me a little pension for the boy's education, but I did not think that man would ever amount to anything, as I had never seen a man so idle, never. At the end of ten years he was still in his first examinations. When his family saw that he would do nothing they called him home to the provinces, but we remained in correspondence on account of the child. And then, imagine, at the last elections, two years ago, I learned that he had been made a deputy in his county. And then he made some speeches in the Assembly. Truly, in a kingdom of blind men, as the saying is— But, to finish, I went to find him, and immediately he obtained this tobacco business for me, as the daughter of an exile. It is true my father was exiled, but I never thought of this fact serving me in any way.

"Briefly—wait! Here is Roger."

A tall young man entered, grave, correct and proper.

He kissed his mother on the brow and she said: "This, sir, is my son, head clerk at the mayor's office. You know, he may be a future subprefect."

I saluted this functionary in a worthy manner and went back to my hotel, after having pressed with gravity the extended hand of "So-it-Goes."

A POOR GIRL

YES, THE MEMORY of that evening can never be effaced. For half an hour I had the sinister sensation of invincible fatality; I had the same shivers that one has in descending the shaft of a mine. I touched the black depths of human misery; I seemed to comprehend fully how impossible an honest life is under some conditions.

It was just past midnight. I was going from the vaudeville to Drouot Street, following a crowd on the boulevard, all carrying umbrellas. A deluge of water poured rather than fell, veiling the gas jets and giving the street a sad appearance. The sidewalk glittered, more sticky than wet. The mass of people pressed on, seeing nothing.

Girls, with skirts raised, showed their ankles, allowing a white stocking to peep out in the dim nocturnal light, and waited in shadowed doorways. Some called to and some, bolder, jostled the passers, pronouncing in their ears two obscene, stupid words. They would follow a man some seconds and push against him, breathing in his face their putrid breath. Then, seeing their beguilements useless, they would leave him with an abrupt, discontented motion and start on again, swinging their hips.

I went along, spoken to by all, taken by the sleeve, harassed and moved with disgust. Suddenly I saw three of them running as if frightened, talking to each other in rapid fashion. Others also began to run, to flee, holding their robes with both hands in order to run more quickly. That day a blow had been given to the network of prostitution.

All at once I felt an arm under mine, while a terrified voice murmured in my ear: "Save me, sir, save me; do not leave me."

I looked at the girl. She was not twenty years old, yet faded already. I said to her: "Remain with me." And she murmured: "Oh, thank you!"

We arrived at the line of agents. She disclosed herself in order to let me pass. I met her farther on in Drouot Street.

My companion asked: "Will you come home with me?"

"No."

"Why not? You have rendered me a service that I shall not forget."

I answered, so not to embarrass her: "Because I am married."

"What difference does that make?"

"You see, my child, that is sufficient. I have helped you out of your difficulty, leave me quietly now."

The street was deserted and dark, truly unpleasant. And this woman, who held me by the arm, rendered more frightful still the sensation of sadness which enveloped me. She wished to embrace me. I recoiled with horror. And in a hard voice she said: "Once, for peace, won't you?"

And she made a movement of rage, then abruptly began to sob. I stood lost in wonder, not quite comprehending. Finally I said:

"Tell me, what is the matter with you?"

She murmured through her tears: "If you only knew it, it is not gay, this isn't."

"What is not gay?"

"This kind of life."

"Why have you chosen it then?"

"It was not my fault."

"Whose fault was it?"

"I know whose, I do."

A kind of interest in this abandoned creature took me and I said:

"Tell me your story."

And she told it to me.

"I was sixteen years old and in service at Yvetot at the house of Monsieur Lerable, a grain dealer. My parents were dead. I had no one. I saw, of course, that my master looked at me in a queer way and that he pinched my cheeks, and I had not long to ask myself what he meant. I knew things, certainly. In the country, one is sharpened. But Monsieur Lerable was old and devout, going to Mass every Sunday. I somehow never believed him capable! But the day came when he wished to take me in my kitchen. I resisted him, but it was done.

"There was opposite us a grocer, Monsieur Dunstan, who had a very pleasant boy in his shop, so much so that I allowed myself to be cajoled by him. That happens to everybody, does it not? I would leave the door open evenings that he might come in.

"But one night Monsieur Lerable heard some noise. He went up and found Antoine and tried to kill him. It was a battle with chairs, jugs of water and everything. As for me, I found my courage and fled into the street. That was how I started out.

"I was afraid, afraid of the world. But I dressed myself under a doorway and began to walk straight on. I believed of a truth that someone had been killed and that the policemen were after me already. I reached the highway to Rouen. I told myself that at Rouen I should be concealed well enough.

"It was so dark I could not see the ditches, and I heard the dogs barking on the farms. Do you know all the things one hears at night? There are birds that cry like a man being murdered, beasts that yap and beasts that whistle, and many other things that I do not understand. I was all goose flesh. Each step I made the sign of the cross. One cannot imagine how the heart can be helped by that. When the day appeared the idea of the policemen always took me by force, and I ran all that I could. Then I tried to calm myself.

"I felt hungry, all the same, in spite of my fear, but I had not anything, not one sou, for I had forgotten my money, all that I had on earth, which was eighteen francs. So I was obliged to walk with an empty stomach.

"It was hot. The sun burned. Midday was past, and I kept going on. Suddenly I heard some horses behind me. I turned to look. The mounted policemen! My blood gave a leap; I thought I should fall, but I went on. They would catch me. They were looking at me now. Then one of them, the elder, said:

" 'Good day, mademoiselle.'

" 'Good day, sir.'

" 'Where are you going to?'

" 'I am going to Rouen in service at a place that has been offered me.'

" 'Walking, like this?'

" 'Yes, walking.'

"My heart beat, sir, so that I could say no more. I kept thinking to myself: 'Now they will take me.' And I had such a desire to run that my legs danced. But they would have caught me immediately, you see.

"The old one began: 'We can journey together as far as Barantin, mademoiselle, since we are taking the same route.'

" 'With pleasure, sir,' I said.

"And we chatted a little. I made myself as pleasant as I could, you see, so much so that they believed what was not so. Then as we passed into a wood the old one said: 'Would you like to stop and rest a little on this moss?'

"And I, without thinking, said: 'As you wish, sir.'

"Then he dismounted and gave his horse to the other, and we two went away in the wood. There was nothing to be said. What could you have done in my place? He took what he wished and then said to me: 'It won't do to forget the comrade.'

"He returned to the horses, and the other rejoined me. I was so much ashamed that I could have wept, sir. But I dared not resist, you understand. Then we went on our way. I could speak no more; I had too much grief in my heart. And then I could no longer walk, I was so hungry. But in the village they gave me a glass of wine, which gave me new force for some time. And then they took to the trot so as not to go through Barantin in my company. And I seated myself by a ditch and wept until I had no more tears.

"I walked then for three hours more before reaching Rouen. It was seven o'clock in the evening when I arrived there. At first all the lights dazzled me. And then I did not know where I could sit down to rest. On the way there were the ditches and the grass where I could even lie down and sleep. But in the city, nothing.

"My limbs refused to hold my body, and I felt as if I were going to fall. And then it began to rain, a little fine rain, like this evening, which goes through you without your knowing it. I have no luck when it rains. I commenced to walk the streets. I looked at all the houses, saying to myself: 'There are beds and bread in there, but I cannot find as much as a crust or a bed of straw.'

"I went through some streets where women were speaking to men along the way. In such cases, sir, one must do what one can. I took my place with the others, inviting everybody. But no one answered me. I wished I was dead. This must have been near midnight. I no longer knew what I did. Finally a man listened to me. He asked me: 'Where do you live?' Some kind of ruse was necessary, and I answered: 'I cannot take you to my house for I live with Mamma. But are there not some houses where we could go?'

"He answered: 'It is not often that I spend twenty sous for a room.' Then he added: 'Come along. I know a quiet spot where we shall not be interrupted.'

"He made me pass over a bridge then led me to the end of the town, into a meadow near the river. I could do nothing but follow him. He made me sit down and then began to ask why we had come there. As he was long in his affair, I found myself so worn out with fatigue that I fell asleep. He went away without giving me anything. I could not see a single step. Since that day I have had troubles that I can never be cured of, because I slept all that night in the wet.

"I was awakened by two officers who took me to the station house and then to prison, where I stayed eight days, while they tried to find out who I was and where I had come from. I would not tell for fear of the consequences. They found out, however, and released me after a verdict of innocence.

"Then it was necessary for me to make my living. I tried to find a place, but I could not because I had come out of prison. Then I recalled the old judge who had a turn to his eye, while he was judging me, like that of Father Lerable of Yvetot. And I went to find him. I was not deceived. He gave me a hundred sous when I left him, saying: 'You shall have as much every time, but don't come too often, not more than twice a week.' I understood that well because of his age. But it gave me a reflection. I said to myself: 'Young people make merry and amuse themselves, but they are never fat, while with the old it is the other way.' And since then I can always tell them, these old apes with their eyes in a groove and a little ghost of a head.

"Do you know what I did, sir? I dressed up like a country girl who had come to market and I walked the streets for my living. Oh! I could pinch them at the first blow. I would say to myself: 'Here is one who will bite.' He would approach. And then commence:

"'Good day, mademoiselle.'

"'Good day, sir.'

"'Where are you going, like this?'

"'I am returning home to Master's.'

"'Do they live far, your people?'

"'Rather far, but not so very.'

"Then he would not know what to say, and I would make my step a little slower to allow him to explain. Then he would give me some compliments in a low voice and then ask me to go home with him. I would refuse at first, you understand, and then yield. I had two or three of that sort each morning, and all my afternoons free. That was the good time of my life. I was not made of spleen.

"But it seems one can never be quiet for a long time. It was my misfortune to make the acquaintance of a rich man of the world, an old president, who was all of seventy-five years old. One evening he took me to dine in a restaurant of the neighborhood. And then, you understand, he did not know how to be moderate. He was dead at the dessert.

"I had three months in prison, because I was not under superintendence. Then I came to Paris. And, oh, sir, it is hard here! Hard to live! One cannot expect to eat every day; there are too many. But that is only so much the worse. Each to his trouble, don't you say so?"

She was silent. I walked along by her side, my heart touched. Suddenly she began to be familiar with me, saying:

"So you will not go home with me, my dear?"

"No, I have told you so already."

"Oh well, good-by, and thanks all the same, without any hard feeling, but I assure you that you are wrong."

And she went away, plunging into the rain which was as fine as a veil. I watched her pass under a gas jet and then disappear in a shadow. Poor girl!

THE SUBSTITUTE

"Madame Bonderoi?"

"Yes, Madame Bonderoi."

"Impossible."

"I tell you it is."

"Madame Bonderoi, the old lady in a lace cap, the devout, the holy, the honorable Madame Bonderoi, whose little false curls look as if they were glued round her head?"

"That is the very woman."

"Oh, come, you must be mad."

"I swear to you that it is Madame Bonderoi."

"Then please give me the details."

"Here they are: During the life of Monsieur Bonderoi, the lawyer, people said that she utilized his clerks for her own particular service. She is one of these respectable middle-class women, with secret vices and inflexible principles, of whom there are so many. She liked good-looking young fellows, and I should like to know what is more natural than that? Do not we all like pretty girls?

"As soon as old Bonderoi was dead his widow began to live the peaceful and irreproachable life of a woman with a fair, fixed income. She went to church assiduously and spoke evil of her neighbors but gave no chance to anyone to speak ill of her, and when she grew old she became the little wizened, sour-faced, mischievous woman whom you know. Well, this adventure, which you would scarcely believe, happened last Friday.

"My friend, Jean d'Anglemare, is, as you know, a captain in a dragoon regiment which is quartered in the barracks in the Rue de la Rivette. When he got to his quarters the other morning he found that two men of his squadron had had a terrible quarrel. The duel took place between them. After the duel they became reconciled, and when their officer questioned them they told him what their quarrel had been about. They had fought on Madame Bonderoi's account."

"Oh!"

"Yes, my dear fellow, about Madame Bonderoi. But I will let Trooper Siballe speak":

" 'This is how it was, Captain. About a year and a half ago I was lounging about the barrack yard between six and seven o'clock in the evening, when a woman came up and spoke to me and said, just as if she had been asking her way: "Soldier, would you like to earn ten francs a week honestly?" Of course I told her that I should, and so she said: "Come and see me at twelve o'clock tomorrow morning. I am Madame Bonderoi, and my address is number 6, Rue de la Tranchée."

" ' "You may rely upon my being there, madame." And then she went away, looking very pleased, and added: "I am very much obliged to you, soldier."

" ' "I am obliged to you, madame," I replied. But I plagued my head about the matter until the time came, all the same.

" 'At twelve o'clock exactly I rang the bell, and she let me in herself. She had a lot of ribbons on her head.

" ' "We must make haste," she said, "as my servant might come in."

" ' "I am quite willing to make haste," I replied, "but what am I to do?"

" 'But she only laughed and replied: "Don't you understand, you great stupid?"

" 'I was no nearer her meaning, I give you my word of honor, Captain, but she came and sat down by me and said:

" ' "If you mention this to anyone I will have you put in prison, so swear that you will never open your lips about it."

THE SUBSTITUTE

" 'I swore whatever she liked, though I did not at all understand what she meant. My forehead was covered with perspiration, so I took my pocket handkerchief out of my helmet. She took it and wiped my brow with it; then she kissed me and whispered: "Then you will?"

" ' "I will do anything you like, madame," I replied, "as that is what I came for."

" 'Then she made herself clearly understood by her actions, and when I saw what it was, I put my helmet on a chair and showed her that in the dragoons a man never retires, Captain.

" 'Not that I cared much about it, for she was certainly not in her prime, but it is no good being too particular in such a matter, as francs are scarce, and then I have relations whom I like to help. I said to myself: "There will be five francs for my father, out of that."

" 'When I had finished my allotted task, Captain, I got ready to go, though she wanted me to stop longer, but I said to her:

" ' "To everyone their due, madame. A small glass of brandy costs two sous, and two glasses cost four."

" 'She understood my meaning and put a gold ten-franc piece into my hand. I do not like that coin. It is so small that if your pockets are not very well made and come at all unsewn one is apt to find it in one's boots or not to find it at all, and so, while I was looking at it, she was looking at me. She got red in the face, as she had misunderstood my looks, and said: "Is not that enough?"

" ' "I did not mean that, madame," I replied, "but if it is all the same to you, I would rather have two five-franc pieces." And she gave them to me, and I took my leave.

" 'This has been going on for a year and a half, Captain. I go every Tuesday evening, when you give me leave to go out of barracks; she perfers that, as her servant has gone to bed then, but last week I was not well and I had to go into the infirmary. When Tuesday came I could not get out, and I was very vexed because of the ten francs which I had been receiving every week, and I said to myself:

" ' "If anybody goes there I shall be done for, and she will be sure to take an artilleryman," and that made me angry. So I sent for Paumelle, who comes from my part of the country, and I told him how matters stood:

" ' "There will be five francs for you and five for me," I said. He agreed and went, as I had given him full instructions. She opened the door as soon as he knocked and let him in, and as she did not look at his face, she did not perceive that it was not I, for you know, Captain, one dragoon is very like another with a helmet on.

" 'Suddenly, however, she noticed the change and she asked angrily: "Who are you? What do you want? I do not know you."

" 'Then Paumelle explained matters; he told her that I was not well and that I had sent him as my substitute, so she looked at him, made him also swear to keep the matter secret, and then she accepted him, as you may suppose, for Paumelle is not a bad-looking fellow either. But when he came back, Captain, he would not give me my five francs. If they had been for myself I should not have said a word, but they were for my father, and on that score I would stand no nonsense and said to him:

"'"You are not particular in what you do, for a dragoon; you are a discredit to your uniform."

"'He raised his fist, Captain, saying that fatigue duty like that was worth double. Of course everybody has his own ideas, and he ought not to have accepted it. You know the rest.'

"Captain d'Anglemare laughed until he cried as he told me the story, but he also made me promise to keep the matter a secret, just as he had promised the two soldiers. So above all do not betray me, but promise me to keep it to yourself."

"Oh! You may be quite easy about that. But how was it all arranged in the end?"

"How? It is a joke in a thousand! Mother Bonderoi keeps her two dragoons and reserves his own particular day for each of them, and in that way everybody is satisfied."

"Oh! That is capital! Really capital!"

"And he can send his old father and mother the money as usual, and thus morality is satisfied."

A PASSION

THE SEA WAS BRILLIANT and unruffled, scarcely stirred, and on the pier the entire town of Havre watched the ships as they came on.

They could be seen at a distance in great numbers, some of them, the steamers, with plumes of smoke; the others, the sailing vessels, drawn by almost invisible tugs, lifting toward the sky their bare masts, like leafless trees.

They hurried from every end of the horizon toward the narrow mouth of the jetty which devoured these monsters, and they groaned, they shrieked, they hissed while they spat out puffs of steam like animals panting for breath.

Two young officers were walking on the landing stage, where a number of people were waiting, saluting or returning salutes and sometimes stopping to chat.

Suddenly one of them, the taller, Paul d'Henricol, pressed the arm of his comrade, Jean Renoldi, then, in a whisper, he said:

"Hallo, here's Madame Poincot; give a good look at her. I assure you that she's making eyes at you."

She was moving along on the arm of her husband. She was a woman of about forty, very handsome still, slightly stout, but, owing to her graceful fullness of figure, as fresh as she was at twenty. Among her friends she was known as the Goddess, on account of her proud gait, her large black eyes and the air of nobility attached to her person. She remained irreproachable; never had the least suspicion cast a breath on her life's purity. She was regarded as the very type of a virtuous, uncorrupted woman—so upright that no man had ever dared to think of her.

And yet for the last month Paul d'Henricol had been assuring his friend Renoldi that Mme Poincot was in love with him, and he maintained that there was no doubt of it.

"Be sure I don't deceive myself. I see it clearly. She loves you—she loves you passionately, like a chaste woman who had never loved. Forty years is a terrible age for virtuous women when they possess senses; they become foolish and commit utter follies. She is hit, my dear fellow; she is falling like a wounded bird and is ready to drop into your arms. I say—just look at her!"

The tall woman, preceded by her two daughters, aged twelve and fifteen years, suddenly turned pale on her approach as her eyes lighted on the officer's face. She gave him an ardent glance, concentrating her gaze upon him, and no longer seemed to have any eyes for her children, her husband or any other person around her. She returned the salutation of the two young men without lowering her eyes, glowing with such a flame that a doubt at last forced its way into Lieutenant Renoldi's mind.

His friend said in the same hushed voice: "I was sure of it. Did you not notice her this time? By Jove, she is a nice woman!"

. . . .

But Jean Renoldi had no desire for a society intrigue. Caring little for love, he longed, above all, for a quiet life and contented himself with occasional amours such as a young man can always have. All the sentimentality, the attentions and the tenderness which a well-bred woman exacts bored him. The chain, however slight it might be, which is always formed by an adventure of this sort, filled him with fear. He said: "At the end of a month I'll have had enough of it, and I'll be forced to wait patiently for six months through politeness."

Then a rupture would exasperate him, with the senses, the illusions, the clinging attachment, of the abandoned woman.

He avoided meeting Mme Poincot.

But one evening he found himself by her side at a dinner party, and he felt on his skin, in his eyes and even in his heart the burning glance of his fair neighbor. Their hands met and almost involuntarily were pressed together in a warm clasp. Already the intrigue was almost begun.

He saw her again, always in spite of himself. He realized that he was loved. He felt himself moved by a kind of pitying vanity when he saw what a violent passion for him swayed this woman's breast. So he allowed himself to be adored and merely displayed gallantry, hoping that the affair would be only sentimental.

But one day she made an appointment with him for the ostensible purpose of seeing him and talking freely to him. She fell, swooning, into his arms, and he had no alternative but to be her lover.

And this lasted six months. She loved him with an unbridled, panting love.

Absorbed in this frenzied passion, she no longer bestowed a thought on anything else. She surrendered herself to it utterly; her body, her soul, her reputation, her position, her happiness—she had cast all into that fire of her heart as one casts, as a sacrifice, every precious object into a funeral pyre.

He had for some time grown tired of her and deeply regretted his easy conquest as a fascinating officer, but he was bound, held prisoner. At every moment she said to him: "I have given you everything. What more would you have?" He felt a desire to answer:

"But I have asked nothing from you, and I beg of you to take back what you gave me."

Without caring about being seen, compromised, ruined, she came to see him every evening, her passion becoming more inflamed each time they met. She flung herself into his arms, strained him in a fierce embrace, fainted under the force of rapturous kisses which to him were now terribly wearisome.

He said in a lanquid tone: "Look here! Be reasonable!"

She replied:

"I love you," and sank on her knees, gazing at him for a long time in an attitude of admiration. At length, exasperated by her persistent gaze, he tried to make her rise.

"Sit down. Let us talk," he said.

She murmured: "No, leave me," and remained there, her soul in a state of ecstasy.

He said to his friend D'Henricol:

"You know, 'twill end by my beating her. I won't have any more of it! It must end, and that without further delay!" Then he went on: "What do you advise me to do?"

The other replied: "Break it off."

And Renoldi added, shrugging his shoulders:

"You speak indifferently about the matter; you believe that it is easy to break with a woman who tortures you with attention, who annoys you with kindness, who persecutes you with her affection, whose only care is to please you and whose only wrong is that she gave herself to you in spite of you."

But suddenly one morning the news came that the regiment was about to be removed from the garrison. Renoldi began to dance with joy. He was saved! Saved without scenes, without cries! Saved! All he had to do now was to wait patiently for two months more. Saved!

In the evening she came to him more excited than she had ever been before. She had heard the dreadful news, and without taking off her hat she caught his hands and pressed them nervously, with her eyes fixed on his and her voice vibrating and resolute.

"You are leaving," she said; "I know it. At first I felt heartbroken; then I understood what I had to do. I don't hesitate about doing it. I have come to give you the greatest proof of love that a woman can offer. I'll follow you. For you I am abandoning my husband, my children, my family. I am ruining myself, but I am happy. It seems to me that I am giving myself to you over again. It is the last and the greatest sacrifice. I am yours forever!"

He felt a cold sweat down his back and was seized with a dull and violent rage, the anger of weakness. However, he became calm and, in a disinterested tone, with a show of kindness, he refused to accept her sacrifice, tried to appease her, to bring her to reason, to make her see her own folly! She listened to him, staring at him with her great black eyes and with a smile of disdain on her lips, and said not a word in reply. He went on talking to her, and when at length he stopped, she said merely:

"Can you really be a coward? Can you be one of those who seduce a woman and then throw her over through sheer caprice?"

He became pale and renewed his arguments; he pointed out to her the inevitable consequences of such an action to both of them as long as they lived —how their lives would be shattered and how the world would shut its doors against them. She replied obstinately: "What does it matter when we love each other?" Then all of a sudden he burst out furiously:

"Well then, I will not. No—do you understand? I will not do it, and I forbid you to do it." Then, carried away by the rancorous feeling which had seethed within him so long, he relieved his heart:

"Ah, damn it all, you have now been sticking onto me for a long time in spite of myself, and the best thing for you now is to take yourself off. I'll be much obliged if you do so, upon my honor!"

She did not answer him, but her livid countenance began to look shriveled up, as if all her nerves and muscles had been twisted out of shape. And she went away without saying good-by.

The same night she poisoned herself.

For a week she was believed to be in a hopeless condition. And in the city people gossiped about the case and pitied her, excusing her sin on account of the violence of her passion, for overstrained emotions, becoming heroic through their intensity, always obtain forgiveness for whatever is blameworthy in them. A woman who kills herself is, so to speak, not an adulteress. And ere long there was a feeling of general reprobation against Lieutenant Renoldi for refusing to see her again—a unanimous sentiment of blame.

It was a matter of common talk that he had deserted her, betrayed her, ill treated her. The colonel, overcome by compassion, brought his officer to book in a quiet way. Paul d'Henricol called on his friend: "Deuce take it, Renoldi, it's a damnable shame to let a woman die; it's not the right thing, anyhow."

The other, enraged, told him to hold his tongue, whereupon D'Henricol made use of the word "infamy." The result was a duel; Renoldi was wounded, to the satisfaction of everybody, and was for some time confined to his bed.

She heard about it and only loved him the more for it, believing that it was on her account he had fought the duel, but, as she was too ill to move, she was unable to see him again before the departure of the regiment.

He had been three months in Lille when he received one morning a visit from the sister of his former mistress.

After long suffering and a feeling of dejection, which she could not conquer, Mme Poincot's life was now despaired of, and she merely asked to see him for a minute, only for a minute, before closing her eyes forever.

Absence and time had appeased the young man's satiety and anger; he was touched, moved to tears, and he started at once for Havre.

She seemed to be in the agonies of death. They were left alone together, and by the bedside of this woman whom he now believed to be dying and whom he blamed himself for killing, though it was not by his own hand, he was fairly crushed with grief. He burst out sobbing, embraced her with tender, passionate kisses, more lovingly than he had ever done in the past. He murmured in a broken voice:

"No, no, you shall not die! You shall get better! We shall love each other forever—forever!"

She said in faint tones:

"Then it is true. You do love me, after all?"

And he, in his sorrow for her misfortunes, swore, promised to wait till she had recovered and, full of loving pity, kissed again and again the emaciated hands of the poor woman whose heart was panting with feverish, irregular pulsations.

The next day he returned to the garrison.

Six weeks later she went to meet him, quite old looking, unrecognizable and more enamored than ever.

In his condition of mental prostration, he consented to live with her. Then when they remained together as if they had been legally united, the same colonel who had displayed indignation with him for abandoning her objected to this irregular connection as being incompatible with the good example officers ought to give in a regiment. He warned the lieutenant on the subject and then furiously denounced his conduct, so Renoldi retired from the army.

He went to live in a village on the shore of the Mediterranean, the classic sea of lovers.

And three years passed. Renoldi, bent under the yoke, was vanquished and became accustomed to the woman's unchanging devotion. His hair had now turned white.

He looked upon himself as a man done for, gone under. Henceforth, he had no hope, no ambition, no satisfaction in life, and he looked forward to no pleasure in existence.

But one morning a card was placed in his hand with the name "Joseph Poincot, Shipowner, Havre."

The husband! The husband, who had said nothing, realizing that there was no use in struggling against the desperate obstinacy of women. What did he want?

He was waiting in the garden, having refused to come into the house. He bowed politely but would not sit down, even on a bench in a gravel path, and he commenced talking clearly and slowly.

"Monsieur, I did not come here to address reproaches to you. I know too well how things happened. I have been the victim of—we have been the victims of—a kind of fatality. I would never have disturbed you in your retreat, if the situation had not changed. I have two daughters, monsieur. One of them, the elder, loves a young man and is loved by him. But the family of this young man is opposed to the marriage, basing their objection on the situation of—my daughter's mother. I have no feeling of either anger or spite, but I love my children, monsieur. I have, therefore, come to ask my wife to return home. I hope that today she will consent to go back to my house—to her own house. As for me, I will make a show of having forgotten, for—for the sake of my daughters."

Renoldi felt a wild movement in his heart, and he was inundated with a delirium of joy, like a condemned man who receives a pardon.

He stammered: "Why, yes—certainly, monsieur. I myself—— Be assured of it. No doubt—it is right; it is only quite right."

This time M. Poincot no longer declined to sit down.

Renoldi then rushed up the stairs and, pausing at the door of his mistress's room to collect his senses, entered gravely.

"There is somebody below waiting to see you," he said. " 'Tis to tell you something about your daughters."

She rose. "My daughters? What about them? They are not dead?"

He replied: "No, but a serious situation has arisen which you alone can settle."

She did not wait to hear more but rapidly descended the stairs.

Then he sank down on a chair, greatly moved, and waited.

He waited a long, long time. Then he heard angry voices belowstairs and made up his mind to go down.

Mme Poincot was standing up, exasperated, just on the point of going away, while her husband had seized hold of her dress, exclaiming: "But remember that you are destroying our daughters, your daughters, our children!"

She answered stubbornly:

"I will not go back to you!"

Renoldi understood everything, came over to them in a state of great agitation and gasped:

"What, does she refuse to go?"

She turned toward him and, with a kind of shamefacedness, addressing him without any familiarity of tone in the presence of her legitimate husband, said:

"Do you know what he asks me to do? He wants me to go back and live under one roof with him!"

And she tittered with a profound disdain for this man, who was appealing to her almost on his knees.

Then Renoldi, with the determination of a desperate man playing his last card, began talking to her in his turn and pleaded the cause of the poor girls, the cause of the husband, his own cause. And when he stopped, trying to find some fresh argument, M. Poincot, at his wit's end, murmured in the affectionate style in which he used to speak to her in days gone by:

"Look here, Delphine! Think of your daughters!"

Then she turned on both of them a glance of sovereign contempt, and after that, flying with a bound toward the staircase, she flung at them these scornful words:

"You are a pair of wretches!"

Left alone, they gazed at each other for a moment, both equally crestfallen, equally crushed. M. Poincot picked up his hat, which had fallen down near where he sat, dusted off his knees the signs of kneeling on the floor, then, raising both hands sorrowfully, while Renoldi was seeing him to the door, remarked with a parting bow:

"We are very unfortunate, monsieur."

Then he walked away from the house with a heavy step.